This book—*The Darkness Within*—represents a lifelong dream to write and complete a trilogy. That I have plans (and drafts) for several more novels, I wanted to take this moment to thank you for buying this book. It's thick, unwieldy, and could make an excellent doorstop.

I look at his book and cannot help but to think back upon where I was when I first discovered the character, when I felt the impulse to write about him, and several other key points in the journey to now.

While I don't know how often I will be able to come back an play in this world, please know that I fully plan to. There are several story arcs that I want to explore, but I must first turn my attention to a few other projects with looming deadlines.

If I don't start a new Benjamin Baxter trilogy next year, there will be several short stories that take place in this world available on my website. And, if you send me a picture of you with this collection, I will get the electronic version of the short stories to you at no cost.

Until next time,
E.J.

BENJAMIN BAXTER: THE DARKNESS WITHIN TRILOGY

Books One, Two, and Three

EZEKIEL JAMES BOSTON

ELSEWHERE
E
P
PUBLISHING

Adventures of Benjamin Baxter:
The Darkness Within trilogy

Published 2016 by Elsewhere Publishing
www.ElsewherePublishing.com

ISBN-13: 978-1-62538-055-5

Elsewhere Publishing
www.ElsewherePublishing.com

Dedicated to:

Family & Friends
Mentors & Minions
Kay McGarvey

EZEKIEL JAMES BOSTON

THE ADVENTURES OF
BENJAMIN
BAXTER
THE DARKNESS WITHIN

THE COMPLETE TRILOGY

BOOK 1: BIRTHDAY BEDLAM

Chapter One

BIRTHDAY BEDLAM

Unusually bright, an early October full moon hung in the Las Vegas sky cutting light through the darkness of Meadows Towing sprawling junkyard. Benjamin Baxter edged to an intersection and placed a careful hand on the jagged kinks of flattened cars stacked twenty high and hoped his car hadn't already met the same fate.

He peered around the corner.

A light desert breeze worked down the long row of vehicles squashed and stacked like large Legos. The dry air pressed against Ben's face, bringing the heavy smell of rust and neglected plastic. Bathed only in moonlight, the true colors of the cars turned into muted tones. Shadows did most of the coloring here.

Doing his best not to break the silence that lay over the scrapyard like a warm blanket. Ben hurried down the row.

Movement at the far edge of the row caught his eye. He sucked in a quick gulp of air and froze.

This boar, like the one before, had long tusks, stood waist-high and looked thoroughly pissed off as it crossed between rows of compacted cars thirty feet ahead. Ben eyed the spiked leather collar as it snorted and stalked.

He pulled out his new Anvilsmith tablet—a birthday gift from the Archon Primary Academy—and a spell card he'd crafted and programmed for a situation like this, and lined the SD card up with the slot on his device.

Ben kept the surprised gulp locked in his lungs. Like before, he hoped the boar would continue on.

According to the scry he had bought from Crystal, this was supposed to be a moonlit stroll through a vacant scrapyard to recover his stolen car. This guard animal, the second he had come across, signaled otherwise. Why'd they take his car in the first place? Better yet, what kind of lunatic would use ravished boars as guard animals.

He frowned. Worst sixteenth birthday ever.

If the operators of this lot were crafty enough to conceal the beasts from Crystal's divination, they were, at the least, starwise and, at the worst, well-practiced in the arts.

Ben let his breath ease out as the animal began to go around the corner.

His device gave a small tick. Ben's robotic companion—Tex—also searched Meadows Towing for his car and had just unsilenced his Anvilsmith. Unable to slide his finger to lower the volume and keep the spellcard ready, Ben pressed the tablet into his gut and prayed to muffled the speakers enough.

Loud and proud, Tex's synthesized voice blared, "Found it!"

The boar turned with a sharp snort and bristled.

Ben slid the spellcard the rest of the way in and pressed "activate."

The SD card shot from the Anvilsmith like a miniature black comet with a snapping green energy tail. It pulsed strongly with the same energy when it struck the ground.

His school tie and trench coat started to react to the pull from the sudden vacuum before the crackling energy shattered the card. It released a gust of wind, whipping Ben's coat and hair back when Orion, a large gorilla made of sparkling green energy, appeared from the destroyed spellcard. The magical glow faded as his conjured protector materialized.

Focused on Ben, its original target, the boar lowered its menacing tusks and charged. It tried to plow through the gorilla.

Orion dropped its center of gravity. Strong arms caught the boar and redirected on a tangent to slam into wall of smashed wrecks.

Ben was saved.

Orion fought on.

Ben felt the familiar tingling sensation at the center of his brain when the conjurer's link formed.

A rush of adrenaline surged through him as he piggybacked on Orion's awareness and the gorilla's senses became his own.

Together, they rolled with the force from the boar's charge. They had one of the beast's tusks in hand and beat at it with the other.

The boar got its feet beneath it and jerked its neck back to break free.

With a focused thought, Ben made Orion grab the other tusk. Before he could issue a follow-up command, the gorilla acted on instinct. A mighty yank ripped one tusk away from the creature's snout with a sickening crack.

Ben recoiled from the link and regained his own senses.

The boar's squeals of pain were cut short as Orion stabbed it repeatedly with its own tusk.

A chill ran up Ben's spine. His throat constricted.

Ben had summoned conjurations in the past to perform tasks around the Archon Private Academy. He had used this same gorilla to move Master Reynolds's heavy black cauldrons. There were joys in controlling creatures to do chores, but having conjured one who had killed filled him with disgust.

Orion thumped its chest in victory and sidled next to Ben, offering the bloody tusk to show it had completed the task set to it. Further, it tried to give Ben the mental reins to embody it again.

Ben shook his head at both the tusk and control. Appreciative of the gesture, he pet-patted the gorilla's massive hairy arm, but looked away in disgust. Between the rows of the compressed cars, his gaze went to the boar. He didn't want to see the dead creature, but his attention floated to the area.

Orion stood in the way, and Ben was glad his conjuration blocked the view.

"I said, *found it*." Tex reminded him, its light metallic voice carrying through the Anvilsmith. "It is..." A ping sounded as Tex plotted coordinates. "Right here." That and a couple of deep breaths of the steel-laden air helped remind Ben of why he had come.

Ben turned his back to the boar and thumbed the volume down to

25%. He rubbed his face with vigor and tried to rid his memory of the crack and last life-ending whine.

"Need I remind you of how Master Reynolds will respond to your loss of a birthday gift on the night of its gifting?" Tex imitated Master Reynolds's Southampton accent. *"Lose one of your sixteenth's gifts, Benjamin, and you lose them all."*

Ben clenched his fist against failure. It would be the same as when he had lost one of the three gifts he received for his thirteenth birthday.

Most annoyingly, his third gift—Tex, a small Golemcast robot—was right. If he lost his car—a sleek, APA red convertible Transcend— Master Reynolds would demand he forfeit Tex and the Anvilsmith tablet.

No one ever had to surrender a second set of gifts. He'd be the grand fool of the APA.

Ben's brow pulled into a decisive knot. If he couldn't recover his car, he wouldn't return to school.

The dead boar had slipped back into his mind. Focused on the task, Ben swallowed the lump of bile trying to escape his throat. He took a steadying breath. "Tex, why do you always override my silent setting?"

"You are asking the wrong question, Junior Apprentice."

"Am I?" Ben looked up to the moon in the clear night sky. This far from Las Vegas, the brighter stars pushed through the neon light pollution. His Master would say it was a good omen.

Tax answered, "Yes. You should be asking yourself, *Why is my silent setting so easily overridden?*" The robot paused in mock contemplation. "Perhaps you should have a word with your programmer..."

Even though no one would know, Ben pursed his lips to keep his amusement from showing.

Tex knew Ben programmed his own gear. The robot had taken a solid shot at him. The hallmark of the Golemcast models was to analyze the assigned student and use the best associated method to challenge them to greater heights. Apparently Tex had pegged him for humorous sarcasm.

Aware that it would only be around a short amount of time, the gorilla pushed Ben's shoulder.

Ben nodded. "Tex, come to where I am and salvage what you can. Then, make an intercepting path to meet up with me."

Tex replied, "Will do, Junior Apprentice, but this is a scrapyard. There is a lot to *salvage*."

Ben groaned at Tex's response and pressed his lips tight to keep his biting reply in check.

Unlike his past two companions, Tex registered when he was snide to it. Even though Ben couldn't find the subroutine in Tex's code to prove it, he would bet anything that the small robot spitefully performed worse until plugged back into the mainframe. "Salvage what you can *from the spellcard* and combat Orion had with a boar in this vicinity."

A chime sounded. Tex noting his location. "Will do, Junior Apprentice, and will continue in stealth mode."

Even though Orion's time dwindled, Ben pressed *Modes* on his Anvilsmith and scanned the list presented. It went from *Silent* to *Survival*, and he noted his silent setting was still no longer active. He tapped it with a sigh and grumbled as he earmarked his next few programming sessions to create a *Stealth* mode. "Maybe that'll keep him silent."

Clearing the screen, Ben checked Orion's remaining time—three minutes. He tapped the timer and set a vibration reminder for when thirty seconds remained.

He then pressed Modes and Map. The Anvilsmith went blank for half a second. A top-down view of Meadows Towing appeared. Ben had created it from various Internet maps and modified it with what Crystal had told him. A green dot lit where Tex marked his car's location. A red dot marked where the boar's body lay.

Ben took control of Orion. Through the gorilla's eyes, he looked into dazed far off look of his vacant body standing there in full school uniform like he was lost simply lost in thought and not inhabiting a conjuration.

Using Orion's strong arms, he scooped his physical body close, and continued moving through the desolate maze. Two turns and five lengths of crushed cars later, Ben came across another boar.

He released his body, relinquished control of the gorilla, and was back in his own body before hitting the ground.

Having recently dealt with a boar, Orion made short work of this one in the same fashion. This time, it did not offer Ben the detached tusk as proof of its good work.

The tablet vibrated the reminder.

Ben considered pumping more power into Orion, but the least amount of time was for another five minutes and would pull ten arcane watts from the Anvilsmith's remaining ninety-five.

Having engineered a few devices able to store *awatts* from scratch and without guidance, Ben had become quite familiar with the measurement of arcane energy. A seven capacity laptop proved to be his top end.

Now he held a hundred in a tablet. Astounding.

As a matter of habit, Ben moved forward to have his hand in position to catch the small obdurium-steel strip that held Orion's memory from this casting.

Ben patted Orion's dense chest twice with a regretful smile. It saved him and battled for him. If it wasn't so expensive to keep the conjuration around longer...

The gorilla disappeared.

With a practiced flick, Ben caught the strip and pressed the obdurium into the base of the Anvilsmith. Amazingly, it backed up the data in five seconds.

Ben beamed.

His first tablet, a refurbished Tsuku model he had modified five years ago, would have taken ten seconds for each real-life second that passed. This badass tablet copied a minute per second.

Ben nodded his approval. "Nice."

Chapter Two

MEADOWS TOWING

A TWO-STORY AUTO shop sat at the center of the scrapyard. Across the second floor, above the six dark windows, squat fat letters spelled out *Meadows Towing*. Shadows filled the yawning mouth of the five work bays. Strange music, heavy on window-rattling drums and the sound of metal striking metal, screamed from the bays.

Though he'd expected something more formidable, the desolate customer waiting area—no less the maze-like columns of wrecked cars —made Ben doubt anyone ever came here, even during the day.

Like a gentle tug on his ears, the slight pull from the Inscription spell he had cast on the front fender directed his eyes.

Convertible top retracted, they had his Transcend up on a lift with the doors open. Gone was the standard, scintillating, candy red Archon Private Academy paint job. Matte black paint now covered every inch of his car.

Only a span of a hundred feet—without cover—separated him from his favorite gift.

Crouched behind the column of junked cars closest to the building, Ben pressed *Spells*. All the spells he had programmed during his time at the APA lay within the seven main categories of spell-type icons. He pressed the asterisk for enchantments. He tapped glowing eye icon for *Soul Sight* and noted options his old tablet never offered.

The old, one hundred and twenty feet max range now sat toward the left of a slider as the default position. The bar had thirty feet on the low end and topped out at six hundred. A second slider, duration, defaulted to a low of one minute, but could go out to ten minutes.

A ghostly image flashed behind his screen.

Ben fumbled the tablet and caught it. He'd forgotten about his addition of the animated background, and grabbed his chest. He made a mental note to change it to something less startling. He then slid the markers to the top end of the distance and duration bars.

The *Cast* button—which he had been so proud of when he designed it—looked like a burnt out neon sign. *-50*, the cost of the spell, lit behind it. Not part of the spell, red text appeared across the bottom of his screen. *This will decrease current capacity by fifty arcane watts. You will have forty-five arcane watts left.*

He smiled broadly before setting the spell back to the defaults. The note went away and usage dropped to one *awatts*. He'd have ninety-four left.

Ben remembered the emphasis of Master Reynolds' annual commencement speech. "Never use more energy than you need."

He stood and hovered his finger over *Cast*. His pulse quickened. His stomach tightened. He tried to shake the nerves away, but like the memory of the tusk being torn from the boar's skull, his nervousness refused to leave.

Ben tapped the icon, and the Anvilsmith started shooting magical energy into his hand. Each mystic discharge resonated through his body, stronger and warmer than the last. The injections were at their quickest and strongest toward the end, and he realized he had forgotten to put his mouthpiece in only when his teeth chattered.

Ben preferred casting by SDs. The magic washed over and through him, but rebuilding the tiny spell cards was extremely time-consuming and quite expensive. Spells cast from tablets—as long as one doesn't mind having magic forced into them—were effectively free of material cost.

His eyes tingled as the power settled in his irises. There were no living creatures in the spell's range. He took another look at the windows for movement. None. He rushed across the opening.

In the garage, he felt the presence of three beings further in the building. If he could walk through walls, two were forty feet away and the other lay on the floor above him.

He looked toward the two on the ground level and focused his spell upon them.

Wall by wall, his vision penetrated the structure until he could see the shape of the two pale white outlines. Both were over six feet tall and built like professional football players. They had enlarged heads. He concentrated on their upward turned, pig-like snouts.

Involuntarily, Ben had held his breath. Since they wouldn't hear him over the blaring music, Ben dared to quietly exhale. "Orcs..."

Having read many stories about their greedy and violent natures, Ben searched for the control to lower his car so he could get out of there.

The main panel just inside the garage had several buttons and levers, but none of them looked to be what he needed. He moved over to the stall with his car and searched there.

The spell warned him of a presence, big and powerful, coming from along the outside edge of the building.

"Shit." Ben hustled up the lift ladder to his car and dove onto the backseat. "Shit. Shit."

Chapter Three

THE ORC MASTER

THE SPEAKERS BLARED the insane crashing music. Closer to where they rattled in their housing, Ben grimaced.

"Wha—" He lifted his hands away from the seat. The paint job didn't bother him so much, but if someone had ripped out his leather interior and replaced it with crappy vinyl. Unable to see in the darkness, he squeezed the cushion and didn't like what he felt or the plastic smell. "Someone's going to pay for this."

He shook his head. There'd be time to worry about that later.

Ben focused on the new presence closing in. It radiated power. A caster. Casters always registered stronger. His spell allowed his vision to penetrate the car door and the exterior wall to see a massive ten-foot body.

Its torso—longer and thicker than anatomically possible, even for orcs—connected to narrow hips. Its squat, powerful legs only made up a third of its height rather than half. The head sat thick on its shoulders like a short-snouted dog, and small horns rose just over its concaved ears.

Deep purple energy—Krotosian magic—emanated from the towering monstrosity.

The creature entered the work bays. It had to duck and turn sideways to squeeze into the building.

Ben caught a flash of light blue skin, a white t-shirt, and dark baggy jeans as it forced its way into the building. Voice deep and gruff, it barked.

The music shut off.

Its woofing continued.

Ben's ear picked out inflection and structure to the barking. Since his mother had refused to teach him her native tongue, he had approached Adept Yeffaux—the Archon Private Academy's Master Linguist—about learning Sylvan. Yeffaux's high eyebrows arched higher at the request, before snidely stating they don't teach *that kind* of language.

More than a hunch, Ben pressed *Options,* then *Translate,* and *To Text.* The Anvilsmith displayed Dwarven futhark. He knew Dwarven and this jumbled mess didn't read like it.

The Anvilsmith flashed *Orcish to English.* A number one appeared followed by a colon as the futhark morphed into English. "Why aren't you pigs out feeding the little pigs?"

A two followed by a colon blinked as a second deep, but not-as-gruff, voice answered, "They haven't been back in a bit. We figured they caught an intruder and are dining on fresh flesh."

"An intruder?" The massive teal creature asked, and the Anvilsmith italicized *amusement* in parenthesis. "You two better pray your pigs left remains or you'll be honor battling tonight!" A pop-up window hovered over *Honor Battle.*

Honor Battle (v.) A ritual called by overlords pitting failed minions against each other in a fight to the death. The idea behind this outdated practice is to weed out the failures and grant the victor another chance to prove their mettle.

Two more white figures, more orcs, came into Ben's spell range from deeper in the building.

The four orcs jogged into the garage. Two Colon pointed at each. "You, go north. You, south. You, east, and I'll take west. Blow on your horn twice when you find something."

The four orcs separated to their directions.

Giving them a little time to get far enough away, Ben laid on the backseat with the Anvilsmith on his chest. Dark streaks and splotches lay on the ceiling. How did they manage to get oil up there?

The being on the second floor stirred. He'd almost forgotten about it.

Ben focused his spell on it and felt power radiate. Great, another caster. This one smaller, human-sized—a girl—and framed with Argosian red energy.

His head shook in disbelief as his spell ended. He could have sworn the girl's lips moved as if to say, "Help me."

It wouldn't be long before the orcs came across one of the dead boars. A part of him wanted to hit the button to lower the lift and peel out, but his starwise self knew he couldn't leave an Argosian in the hands of a vile Krotosian.

Ben tapped the rust-colored GC icon on his home row and whispered orders for Tex into the Anvilsmith, "Get here, get the car down, and be ready to roll." He then pressed *Modes* and *Survival* before Tex could reply.

Hoping, he tapped to *Pop*. The screen showed the effective radius of the weak teleportation spell. He grimaced. Just enough distance to get stuck between floors. No thanks.

Ben cued *Soul Sight*, topped the range out at six hundred, and pressed *Cast*.

His wattage tracker dropped to eighty-nine.

Twenty-six other life forms headed away from the building. He examined the cursory information. Searching, he wondered aloud, "Where'd the Krotosian go?"

His nervousness dissipated as he set his mind to saving the Argosian.

Ben climbed down from his car and entered the building.

They had built a kitchen into the customer service lounge and promptly neglected it. Odors of rotten cheese and rancid meat assaulted his nose before his eyes took in the slimy dishes piled in a sink. With each step something sticky pulled at the bottom of his shoes. The silver handle of a battered refrigerator, where it hadn't been caked over by muck, shone.

In a hurry to leave the nasty kitchen, Ben turned and entered the den. The smell worsened.

A disgusting, gray slab of meat hung from a hook in front of a massive hundred-and-three-inch television. Part of it resembled a rib cage, but the rest didn't resemble any animal Ben had ever seen. A legion of maggots worked the surface. Liquor bottles in varying stages of wholeness to shattered remnants covered the floor like mosaic tiles. Smashed glass formed sparkling mounds down the backs of the five battered sofas.

Given their relative cleanliness, Ben would bet the TV and four large concert-stage speakers mounted in the corners must've been new.

Two sets of stairs on opposite sides of the room led up out of the mess. Faint crunches accompanied each step as he moved to the closer one.

Buried under layers of crud and discarded wrappers, the staircase reeked with a sour tang. The center of every step had a sure, foot-wide strip of ground-in grime—except for the last two at the top.

He stopped short of them and leaned.

A business-quality wooden door stood to the left of the landing, while the right seemed to open into a hallway.

Ben considered the dirty and untrammeled stairs a moment longer.

All of these creatures' strides were longer than his, but something felt really peculiar about those last two steps. Though he hadn't taken anything from the Traps course offered by the school, the number of classes almost equaled the array that had to do with spells.

Not willing to risk the stairs, Ben put his mouthpiece in and cued up *Pop*. Noting the -20 behind the *Cast* button made of bubbles, he focused on the landing above the stairs, and pressed cast.

The Anvilsmith gave a magical shock.

He bit hard.

Another shock, and another, and another. *Pop* took two seconds to cast and made all of his muscles tighten—almost seizing—eight times.

Facing the wall, Ben appeared where he intended. Sixty-nine *awatts* left.

The door to his left would lead to the room above the car bays, but his knees turned to rubber and bladder weakened upon looking right.

At the far end of the hall, in a room with dark shag carpet, the hulking, light-blue-skinned Krotosian monster faced him.

Chapter Four

THE KROTOSIAN & THE ARGOSIAN

THE AWFUL TANG from the stairs still filled Ben's nose. An acidic taste—fear—lit the back of his mouth when the creature's growl rumbled down the hall.

Ben faced it.

The creature dropped a turkey leg, snarled, showing jagged black teeth, and pulled a sword from over a shoulder as its pearl-white irises deepened to a hate-filled purple.

Focused on moving backward, Ben bit into his mouthpiece. His hand trembled. He tapped *Cast*.

Movement from the creature's non-sword hand called Ben's attention. Darkening wisps of lavender energy played around the creature's fingers.

Ben's Anvilsmith shocked magic into him.

Purple wisps floated around the monster's hand before it pointed and released a sinister blast of the woeful dark energy.

Ben flinched.

The hall disappeared. Darkness surrounded him. The air smelled of corn chips.

A smack hit the door, rattled the hinges, and pushed bright purple power through the cracks.

Forty-nine *awatts* left.

A horn warbled twice in the distance. Ben presumed one of the orcs must've found a dead boar.

Ben cranked up the brightness of the Anvilsmith screen and used it as a light source to navigate broken tables and furniture to get to the girl with the Argosian aura.

The door rattled violently behind him.

He reached out to the bag and his fingers lit on a shoulder through coarse material. Ben warned, "Be ready for a fall." He estimated the distance down through the floor. The backseat of his car would be right below them.

Ben bit into the mouthpiece and activated *Pop*.

The energy flowed through him and into the girl.

She shook from the seizing magic. Her teeth clacked eight times as power flowed through her and *Popped* her to the other side of the floor.

Twenty-nine *awatts* left.

A heavy lavender fog began to roll in from under the door.

Ben frowned at it and focused through the floor onto an area which should be above the driver seat.

The fog gathered and thickened.

Ben tilted in fascination. "Weird."

Two small, violet orbs—the eyes of the Krotosian monster—formed and glowered at him.

Ben activated *Pop* and bit into his mouthpiece as the Krotosian's top-heavy shape started to form in the fog.

Nine *awatts* left.

Ben dropped further than expected and banged his leg on the steering wheel.

Tex had lowered the vehicle.

"Thanks." Ben glanced to his little robot companion in the passenger seat, stole a quick glance to the still bagged, but rescued Argosian, and pointed to the ignition. "Jump it!"

Tex sprung over the center console. It slid its small hand into the keyhole. All the lights lit. The engine revved to life. "Done."

Ben slapped on his seatbelt and stomped on the gas. The tires squealed on the bay floor for a second before they caught traction. The Transcend shot out of the garage.

Shattering glass rang out behind them.

Ben checked his rearview mirror.

The Krotosian had plowed through the window and levitated in the air. Hovering, it scanned, found them, and flew to give chase.

Ben blew out a breath of air. He would have been in serious trouble if he was on foot, but the car easily began to put distance between them.

Energy began to form around the creature's hands as it gave pursuit.

The burlap bag spoke. "Undo my thumbscrews." Her voice didn't sound rough or monstrous. She actually sounded, normal. "I can help."

"No time!" Ben veered.

A purple blast kicked up dirt and rock.

Tex clunked into the door well.

Ben swerved again to avoid another attack.

The small robot slid under the seat.

They approached the edge of the scrapyard. Though he wouldn't admit it aloud, Ben yearned to see what kind of damage the Ram enchantment would do. "Alright, Tex. Get ready to hit the wall!"

His companion's voice came from the backseat. "My leg is stuck. I cannot get to the control interface."

Ben growled. This was exactly why he didn't think there should be a block between the driver and the car's systems.

The A. P. A. insisted that any student wanting to have their cars enchanted must have their Golemcast as an intermediary. If he'd had control, they would've been out of here already.

Closing on the perimeter, Ben eased his foot from the accelerator and checked the rearview mirror. The distant creature no longer fired.

Ben asked, "Can you reach her, Tex?"

"Yes."

He pumped the brakes, cranked the wheel, and drifted into a row which would lead to the front gate. Ben corrected the car. "Hey, bag-lady. Lower your hands to the floor."

She said, "My name is Penelope!"

"Okay." Ben shook his head at her demanding tone. "Penelope, put your hands toward the floorboard."

Penelope said, "They're there."

Ben could barely hear the fabric tearing as they raced through columns of bleak, destroyed vehicles. If she had this kind of attitude while being saved, what would she be like under normal circumstances?

Penelope said, "I'm not a bitch."

Ben wondered.

She answered, "Yes, I'm reading your thoughts."

He frowned. His knuckles whitened on the steering wheel. He wasn't remotely close to forming a true opinion of her and even further away from possibly voicing it.

Before he could voice his protest, she started casting. "Great sky spirits, lend us your ways." As though driving up a grade, the car rose into the air. "I'm controlling the elevation. You still control speed and direction."

Above the column of cars, color began to return to Ben's knuckles. He gave the steering wheel a slight turn. The Transcend reacted as though it gripped a road and eased left.

Moments later, they were higher than the wall and over.

He said, "We're clear. Whoa!" His body didn't press against the seatbelt, but Ben's guts and gonads felt like they'd stayed above the wall as gravity dropped the car toward the ground. The rapid descent slowed for the last few inches.

They landed like a feather set down by a soft wind.

Penelope climbed into the passenger seat. At near arms' length, she held Tex like a toddler with a messy diaper.

Tex had a long black strip of spiked leather—the salvaged boar's collar—wrapped thrice around its waist and shoulders.

Penelope wore the burlap like a dress. Her long, dark hair was matted with blood. Her legs, arms, and the parts of her face he could see sported wicked bruises and scabs from where her skin had been split open.

She sat and cut her blue eyes to him.

Ben put his attention back on the road.

"We need to make it to Pepperjacks," she offered without a verbal prompt. He knew she had read his thoughts again when she added, "No, I am not going clubbing. I know people there. They'll keep me safe until I can cross back."

"Will do," Ben replied and wondered what she meant by *cross back*.
She didn't offer and explaining.

He tried to mentally broadcast, *Stop reading my mind!*

Penelope turned away from him and pulled the mess of hair to shield the worst of her arms and obscure her face.

They were both silent on the drive back to the city. Expecting to be chased, Ben kept checking his mirrors for headlights in the dark. Surely there must be another working vehicle in Meadows Towing. Though the Krotosian proved too massive to fit any standard car, the orcs could drive.

Its voice less hollow at close range, Tex asked, "Are you going to disable the survival mode, or am I going to have to eventually override that, too?"

Ben lowered his Anvilsmith to the floorboard.

Tex hopped from Penelope to Ben, dropped to the floor. It checked the energy level. "Only nine arcane watts left?" The robot raised its face to Ben and shook its head in disapproval before looking back to the tablet. "Junior Apprentice, you should have conserved better than that."

Having not wasted a single *awatt*, Ben smiled before reminding his little companion, "And you said something about the survival mode?"

"Ah, yes." Focused on the Anvilsmith, Tex pressed *Modes* and *Normal*.

Normal. Ben considered the word. Tonight had been anything, but normal. He noticed his leg had started to bounce in anticipation. If Penelope truly knew people at Pepperjacks, he might be the first from the APA to enter the posh nightclub. He wouldn't mention a word about Meadows Towering to any of his schoolmate, but to actually make it into Pepperjacks... Would he be able to not share that?

Chapter Five

PEPPERJACKS

BEN STAYED hot on Penelope's heels.

So far, following her instructions had gotten his car valeted and him through Pepperjacks' stained glass front doors.

Something of a rite of passage, most underage casters tried to sneak into the private supper club, and his fellow Junior Apprentices often pointed out that he numbered amongst the few who didn't.

Ben noted each of those who had attempted as an untrustworthy slink. Why try to force your way into a place that actively tried to bar you?

Still, from their retelling of failed attempts, he'd already passed the first two hurdles that stymied most of his classmates. Self-conscious, Ben noticed his mouth watered in anticipation. Now, all he had to do—

Heady lavender incense snaked into his nose. It forced its way into his lungs and made his head spin.

The lobby he'd yet to observe went black.

All sound ceased.

He froze. First willingly, then he couldn't move.

A primal part of his mind flooded his body with adrenaline for a fight.

Forewarned by his classmates of what usually happened, Ben focused on keeping his wits. He swallowed the panic lumped in his throat. He'd thought Penelope could get him through. Apparently she didn't have as much juice as she thought. Well, unlike the slinks, at least he was invited. Penelope really didn't need him now anyway. She'd be safe.

He heaved a disappointed sigh. Having experienced it first hand, Ben understood how Pepperjacks kept their perfect record of keeping minors at bay.

Worry slid into his gut. What would happened next?

A tug on his sleeve guided him. Ben wanted to pull back and remain still, but found his legs in motion as he shambled behind the pull.

He'd heard stories of bouncers beating the crap out of people. Pepperjacks was supposed to be *the* place where magic could be openly discussed. They'd doubtlessly employ minotaurs, giants, or other physically powerful creatures for protection.

Given the light-blue skinned monster he'd encountered earlier, all of the things he grudgingly learned about at the APA—but hadn't ever seen—might actually be real.

A brick red curtain, trimmed with gold tassels, appeared in the darkness.

In front of him, a hand faded into existence pushing the heavy-looking curtain aside. A second hand, the other holding his sleeve, appeared. Then the rest of Penelope faded into existence. She said, "Welcome to Pepperjacks."

Ben had imagined the club would be full of mystical creatures, dressed for a night out, gyrating to insane beats by a celebrity DJ.

Reality proved more disturbing.

Having slid through the weighted curtains, Ben marveled at the three story interior. On the opposite side of the large empty dance floor, a long bar lined a curtain-drawn stage. The masking lavender scent disappeared revealing the Pepperjacks' true succulent steak-and-seafood aromas

Ben exhaled his disappointment.

Contrary to the rumors, Pepperjacks seemed to be more of a dinner venue than a nightclub. Worse, the place felt entirely devoid of magic. He nodded. Even at near-maximum occupancy, it proved to be nothing more than a large, upscale restaurant.

Penelope released his sleeve, turned, and speed-walked between the two rows of crushed red velvet booths just on the inside of the club curtain.

Ben frowned and followed.

He checked each opulent booth they hurried past. No elves. No dwarves. No Halflings. No gnomes. Nothing special at all. Only humans chatting and enjoying their meals. He shook his head. Without the slightest hint of being starwise, even the patrons proved to be a complete letdown.

Was this what he had to look forward to after completing his magical education? Heck, the simple foyer at the Archon Private Academy alone held more mystique.

"Baxter!" An arm shot out from a booth. The hand grabbed his sleeve and reeled him. "What are you doing here?"

Ben tried to pull away.

The hand twisted, tightening the coat like a vice on his wrist, and pulled harder.

Ben knew the move well from school. How dare this mundane grab him? He stared death at the Asian man. The harder he stared, the quicker the facade faded. The Asian business man—suit and all—vanished, leaving an Archon Private Academy trench coat, like his own, covering the arm and torso. A blond man's harsh features and green eyes verified what his subconscious told him about the arresting twist of his sleeve.

Ben's anger burst. His jaw worked as he searched for words. "Uh, Senior Adept Collins—"

Collins' hissed, "This establishment is off limits to all Apprentices, including *Juniors*."

Ben wanted to break the grip. As the Senior Adept slowly articulated his title, Ben felt as though Collins dragged him through filth that would forever stain his skin with an irremovable stench.

The rumor of Geotheon Mossburg's—the student who successfully pulled away from Collins some six years ago—cruel punishments kept Ben from resisting.

The Senior Adept pulled Ben closer and asked, "How'd you get in?" Searching for an aura concealer, he patted Ben's waist. Not finding anything, Collins dug into Ben's pockets for any of the other enchanted totems that could do the trick. Collins pulled him a bit closer.

Held so, he had to lean over the booth, Ben extended his arm for balance. His fingers sunk into the plush velveteen cushion. Used to being frisked, Ben relaxed. He knew better than to offer a reply before Collins addressed him by name. And he worked on a good response.

Ben's his gaze fell on the Senior Adept's tablet. An Anvilsmith? The corner of Ben's mouth curled into a smirk. It was the same basic model as his own. All students under sixteen would kill for one. Ben had been gifted his, but an Adept—a Senior Adept? No, they should be onto something better, or, at the very least, have the Triforce model.

Collins patted the small of Ben's back. His hand then slid up to Ben's shoulders to check for a shadow harness. Ben had heard a demand for answers come from those clenched white teeth in the past, but this was the first time the depths of the Senior Adept's throat released a dangerous growl. "I asked you a question, Baxter."

About to answer, Penelope whispered over his shoulder, "Let him go."

Collins' hand popped open.

Ben couldn't believe how fast Collins' had complied. Even Master Reynolds had to repeat an order a couple of times when the Senior Adept locked his jaw. He took a step away from Collins and Penelope filled the space by his side.

The Senior Adept's lips were still pulled tight. His face taut with rage.

"He's with me." Penelope tugged at Ben's coat. "Enjoy your meal, you two."

A smile started to spread across Ben's mouth at the Senior Adept being told what to do when he noticed the person sitting across from Collins. She hadn't been there a moment ago.

Her white skin, veined with silver, looked as though she were made of marble. Deep crimson spiral tattoos covered the back of her hands from wrists to fingertips.

Ben tried to look at her face, but her high pointed ears stole his attention. An elf?

Penelope pulled him further away.

He didn't resist, but wanted to see more.

The oddity of Collins' dinner date disappeared in a shimmer as he and Penelope moved further from the table. Ten feet away, the woman appeared to be an Asian woman in a business suit sitting across from an Asian man in a similar suit — though the illusion didn't mask the man's locked jaw.

As he followed Penelope, Ben wondered how many people were paying attention to her bare feet, wounds, burlap dress, and mess of hair.

Everyone *appeared* to be eating and talking, seemingly oblivious to anything outside their booth. But if Collins and the elf were masked, what was really going on in the booths. As Ben focused to see past the illusion masking the diners; they started to shimmer.

Penelope pulled at his sleeve to keep him moving when he started to slow.

Chapter Six

THE PAINTING

THEY RODE in two ultra-slow elevators. Since they exit through a second door at the back, Ben didn't think actually moved at all. Their footsteps echoed as Penelope walked him the length of another long, warm underground hallway. Unlike the first, extensive murals covered this one's grey stone walls. The smell of the restaurant's delicious food had yet to diminish.

All the way down the hall, Ben tried to spot what filled the hall with light, but couldn't find a source.

They closed on a large antechamber. A set of massive oaken double doors were built into the far wall, rising further than Ben could see in the hall. Set in each door were more doors. One at thirty feet, another twenty, and the last at ten.

Penelope stopped him shy of the room. "Stay put." She hurried through the smallest set of doors. Why had she brought him this far only to have him stop? He tried to guess, but couldn't figure out a reason she didn't take him with her, or even into the antechamber.

Ben decided not to defy her. If Collins obeyed in an instant, he'd stayed put.

Soon, the largest set of doors, some forty feet high, caught his attention. There were a handful of things Ben had learned about in Mythic Monsters class at the Academy which could have need for the larger doors—cyclopes, dragons—but he hadn't paid much attention as, before tonight, he thought only humans existed.

Ben chuckled at his former naiveté. The Meadows Towing monster would probably love to have a set of doors he didn't have to squeeze through.

Waiting and waiting, he clapped his hands in arcs around his body.

Clap in front.

Clap in back.

Clap in front.

Clap in back.

Ben heaved a slow sigh. "Lame."

Still clapping, he turned to the oil painting.

Though he'd traveled its ridiculous length, he still couldn't quite believe it stretched all the way back to the elevator.

A battle scene?

Ben examined further. All manner of creatures fought and cast spells in the mural. Keeping his feet planted, he stopped clapping and leaned closer. Conscious of slack loosening his jaw, he closed his mouth.

A female caster in ornate robes dedicated to an unfamiliar deity, hurled a fireball made of white power across the battlefield. Hisboian energy was supposed to be healing magic, but in this painting, she used the ivory energy to release one of the world's best-known offensive spells.

The battle looked to be white, orange, and red versus purple and black. He nodded to the two-sided battle. It only made sense that the good Hisbo, Vibros, and Argos casters would have banded together against vile users of Krotos and Nilos.

Doubt twisted his lips. He'd projected battle lines where he wanted to see them and uncertainty began to push against his assumption. Wanting to study more, he moved away from the antechamber. Halfway back down the hall, he switched to assessing a similar oil painting on the wall behind him.

He'd been wrong. He'd been really wrong.

Though this painting had many more fantastical creatures, both pieces of art showcased war.

War with no alliances.

War with no loyalty.

A whimper slid through his throat as the all-out-free-for-all-battle motif sunk in. He thought he'd only have to wait for his hue of magic to develop to be aligned with like-minded casters.

His skin crawled with disgust and he felt sick.

The dream—his dream—of being able to tell friend from foe upon observing a single spell cast to form an ideal allegiance with any caster of the same magic, burst.

Ben absentmindedly ran his fingers over the nine remaining SD cards along his left flank. They were his combat-related spells. Before, they'd given him a sense of security, now they felt woefully inadequate.

Having never heard of spells being cast with Nilosian black, Ben had just started to focus on the casters and their spell effects when Penelope's voice echoed in his head from all directions. *Run!*

Ben tensed, ready to spring, but didn't know which way to go.

He glanced to the elevator, but whipped his head around the other way to where doors slammed shut with muffled thuds behind Penelope. The antechamber's threshold rippled prismatic waves as Penelope crossed.

Ben began backpedaling toward the elevator. She'd changed into jeans and a red, long-sleeved shirt, and her hair flowed free behind her.

The doors swung open again.

A tall, gangly, burnt-red-scaled creature, clad in a suit of black chainmail, chased after her. Large, bat-like wings unfolded from its back. It flapped once, lifted from the ground, and smashed into an invisible force at the threshold. Dazed, like a dog running into a sliding glass door, it crumpled.

Ben paused, pointed, and laughed.

His laughter slowed when the gruesome form registered. It looked to be a hybrid between a dragon and some other horrible thing.

The creature jumped back to its feet.

Ben stood three-quarters of the way down the hall speculating at the hybrid's other part. According to his books, it had to be a near-giant race. The bipedal, wide-mouthed monster he pictured in his head had an insatiable hunger which was rumored only to be outstripped by a want for violence. He tilted his head and guessed. "Tuzvul?"

Penelope urged him again, "Run!"

About to ask why, Ben motioned to the glaring dragon-tuzvul unable to cross the threshold.

A gargantuan red fist, as tall as the dragon-tuzvul, and covered in similar burnt-red scales, pounded open the smallest of the double doors sending them crashing from their hinges. In the same powerful stroke, the clenched fist slammed into whatever force kept the dragon-tuzvul from giving chase.

Air shattered away from the threshold in prismatic shards. The lighting dimmed and the hallway reverberated with a deep resounding *bong*.

Ben ran.

A muffled booming voice hiss-gargled two strings of syllables from beyond the door.

It didn't sound like anything Ben had heard. He couldn't imagine the alphabet, but figured the command wouldn't translate into *Tickle them*.

Running to the elevator, Ben pulled an SD and—angling his device upwards—slipped it into his Anvilsmith. Like usual, the infused item shot from his tablet like a comet, but the crackling green energy trail had a faint sizzling to it.

Confused by the extra sound, Ben stole a glance over his shoulder.

The large bald eagle spell card had shattered against the wall. Green shimmering energy clung to a fierce black-feathered fiend, which vaguely resembled the majestic bird of his planned conjuration.

It flew toward Penelope with menace as the tuzvul gained ground behind her.

Chapter Seven

BETWEEN TWO MONSTERS

A GHASTLY SCREECH, half eagle, half something from beyond, filled the hall. The usual casting chill ran up Ben's spine and settled in his brain before fading away. Unlike his gorilla spells, his eagle never handed over control.

He planted his feet and his dress shoes slid to a stop. Ben spun and willed the creature's reins to his hands. Ephemeral leather crossed his palms. He closed his hands.

The abomination resisted.

"Whoa." The reins ripped from his hands. Ben checked for rope burns in the dim light. "Where's my conjuror's link?"

The fiend flapped toward Penelope.

The dragon-tuzvul closed in behind her.

Ben extended his hands. The leathery material lay at the ready. He only had to close his hands. He waited.

The conjuration dove at Penelope.

Ben balled his fists and yanked hard toward the ceiling.

Commanded, the creature belted a defiant screech as its body rose and it shirked his control. It stretched its talons at Penelope.

She ducked.

It dove harder. Its talons glanced Penelope's shoulders, nicking shirt and flesh instead of digging into muscle and bone.

Penelope ground her teeth and didn't lose a step.

Having missed its first target, the eagle-based, black-feathered demon aimed its attack at the tuzvul. It scored as the creature's red scaled hand reached to snatch Penelope's trailing hair.

The creatures battled it out in the air.

Ben held the doors open.

His monstrous conjuration possessed greater maneuverability than the dragon-tuzvul. The demon-eagle arced and turned. Each time, it made several long ferocious slashes in the dragon-tuzvul's wing membrane, ruining the large monster's ability to maintain lift.

Penelope made it to the elevator.

Ben looked away from the fight to the elevator's flat brass control panel. "No buttons."

Penelope turned and pressed her palm against the brass plate. The doors began to close.

A triumphant roar brought Ben's attention to the dragon-tuzvul.

In a move reminiscent of Orion defeating the boar, the dragon-tuzvul got both of its clawed hands on its foe and rent a wing from the fiend's body. Being magic, the eagle-abomination winked from existence.

The elevator doors closed.

Penelope focused on the wall.

Ben leaned to make eye contact. "What the Hell is going on?"

Her eyes dipped and glassed over on *Hell*.

Ben waved his hand in front of her face. Nothing. He pulled his other gorilla card and held it at the port of his Anvilsmith.

Given what had just happened to his eagle, he didn't want to conjure again. However, if the door opened to a dragon-tuzvul, his twisted conjuration would attack the closest living creature. He just had to make sure it wasn't them.

Nodding to his decision, Ben tapped his Anvilsmith settings and changed the *Conjuration Delay* from a tenth of a second, the lowest setting, to five seconds. Enough time to get distance from whatever unruly abomination came into being.

Ben pressed *Communicate* and *Companion*, then pressed *Modes* and *Map*. A faint ping signaled the tablet connecting. "We'll be coming out hot," he advised Tex. "Show me where the car is parked?"

A choppy robotic voice, not Tex, replied, "I do not know."

Though he knew the voice, Ben flipped the tablet over. The magical inscription he made by combining his initials with the school's gorilla mascot shone green on the device. It looked untouched. Ben asked, "Remy?"

"Yes." Rembrandt, Ben's companion before Tex, answered.

"Activate and ping the GPS Master Reynolds has installed in my vehicles."

Remy answered, "Will do."

One extremely active day with Tex, and Ben had forgotten how he had to spoon-feed commands to his former companion and how slow it talked. He added, "Add it to my map and contact back when done."

Remy answered, "Yes, sire."

Ben chewed on his lip and tapped *System*.

The elevator stopped, Penelope came back from her stupor and tugged on his coat.

He missed *Diagnostic* and hit *Restart*. The device pinged and began the shutdown sequence. For the first time, Ben felt the sting from always toggling *Never Ask to Verify* on his tablets. No verification made for faster casting—and, apparently, potentially dire accidents.

The doors started to slide open. She aimed for the narrow dark gap and tugged again. "Let's go."

Ben waited for the doors to open fully.

She gave an impatient sigh.

Another long corridor. This one without any illumination save a beacon of light at the very far end. Warmth poured an ozoney smell into the elevator. The elevator went dark.

"It's clear." She pulled him to walking, jogging, then running toward the light.

Ben couldn't help but wonder if there were paintings on the walls here, too. Fleeing a real monster, he shook the trivial thought away. "What the—" he paused to edit *Hell* out of the sentence in case it happened to be a trigger word for her. "What's going on?"

Penelope answered, "An assault on The Node!"

What the hell was a node? They never covered anything like that in school. He repeated, "The Node?"

"Yeah—" Penelope's tone held an *I know, right?* sound to it. "Nodes can be damaged physically and by magic. If destroyed, all spells in the region casted with the energy in The Key end. Worse, casters' magic would flag and possibly be—effectively—mystically neutered until they get close enough to an aligned Key." Her eyes widened as she took the explanation to grander scales. "It also dampens likewise energy around the world. Sometimes, effects can even ripple across dimensions."

She'd presumed he'd known what *The Node* was and thought he questioned how it could be attacked.

Region? World? Dimensions? While her explanation registered, Ben still wasn't sure what was going on or how The Key played into an attack on The Node.

About to ask the question another way, the true immensity of the attack occurred to him as they closed on the well-lit antechamber. Local casters of the type of magic in the key could be rendered entirely powerless. A bit selfishly, a small wave of relief chuckled from his throat. "So, this has nothing to do with my car then?"

The question stopped Penelope cold. She spun around with a gasp.

Ben pulled up short behind her. He hadn't caught her soapy smell in the elevator. His eyes went to the large inset oaken doors in the antechamber then back to Penelope.

Mouth agape, eyebrows raised, and eyes widened, she asked, "You're kidding me, right?"

Her offended tone turned his skin cold. He wished they were still in a darker part of the hallway. Back there, he couldn't have seen her reaction and she wouldn't see the guilt on his face. Defensive about what would go through his mind next, Ben said, "Don't read my thoughts."

She turned from him to walk into the well-lit antechamber and motioned for him to come with her. "No need. It's obvious."

Head bowed slightly to avoid the stunned look on her face, Ben followed.

Still taken aback, Penelope shook her head.

He'd just wanted to express the Transcends' importance since he had just earned it—and his driver's license—a little over twelve hours ago.

She asked, "What is your name?"

"Huh?" Ben looked up to see her hard expression had eased a bit.

Penelope said, "Your true first and family name. What are they?"

Ben's lips twisted. Who still said *family* for last name? "Name's Benjamin Baxter."

She studied his coat. "Of House Reynolds?"

Ben exhaled. "I've asked you not to read my mind."

"Relax." Penelope turned to the door, knocked, and backed up to stand next to him. "It's the stitching that gives you away. Besides," she said, throwing him a wry smile when he glanced at her. "You've only barred *reading* your thoughts. You didn't say anything about *controlling* them." She mocked an over-the-top evil laugh.

At least Ben hoped she mocked it.

Chapter Eight

KOGRAKKEN

PRECIOUS MINUTES PASSED. Distant shouts, so faint Ben thought he could be imagining them, came and went. The hall behind them remained dark and the nested oaken doors before them remained closed.

He alternated between trying not to think—so his thoughts couldn't be read—and not sneaking a glance at Penelope. Her *tsks* had let him know when he failed either. Blessedly, his Anvilsmith vibrated as it powered back on. Ben put his tablet through a diagnostic check and smelled smoke. To make sure it wasn't him, he sniffed his tablet. It wasn't.

"I smell it, too." Penelope twisted to examine the corridor behind them. Worry worked at the edges of her calm voice. "I think the building is on fire."

Between keeping his eyes from scanning her contorted body. Her near casual tone almost missed her voicing his growing concern.

The handle on the second inner set of doors rattled, then opened. A bald giant, in full plate armor with a helmet tucked under his arm, had to duck his head to get through the twenty-foot-tall door. The giant closed the door behind itself, slid its rear tree trunk leg back and considered them.

Ben's insides tightened and shook. Reflexively, he leaned back and had to fight the desperate urge to run. This was the first giant he'd ever seen, and he barely stood taller than its knees. Being this close made him feel quite small.

It heaved a ragged breath.

Though his nerves began to settle, Ben had to fight to keep the vision of being punted halfway down the hallway from dominating his thoughts.

A giggle from Penelope let him know he failed.

Ben ground his teeth and projected. *Stop that!*

She chuckled and projected back. *Stop thinking so loudly.*

Though upset with her, he found a smile on his face. Her infectious mirth had traveled a tenuous telepathic bond between them.

The giant's face turned sour. Larger than both of them, it changed the mood and set the tone. It nodded to Penelope. "You may pass."

Ben winced. His ears rang from the sheer volume of the giants booming voice.

It focused on Ben. "I do not recognize him."

Penelope said, "He is Benjamin Baxter of House Reynolds."

The giant nodded and lowered his voice. "The House is respected well enough, but this one is still stitched in Junior Apprentice robes."

Ben bristled at his title, but then calmed. The giant didn't judge him for being a Junior Apprentice, it merely stated what its large eyes observed. He decided to correct the giant just the same. "It's a trench coat."

It looked back to Penelope. "Sorry, Junior Miss. He must wait."

Ben rolled her title in his head. He knew all the ranking titles of local schools and covens. None of them tracked their practitioners' with *Miss*.

Penelope said, "Kograkken, The Node is under attack."

The giant's eyes went from them to down the hall. It pulled out a sword the length of a small car.

Ben took a tentative step back.

"Then he will prove his mettle with me in The Hall." Kograkken swung a couple of practice arcs and bent at the knees as though he braced to catch something. "Afterwards, The Painting will show if he is worthy. Then, and only then, will I let Baxter-Reynolds through."

The Node, The Key, The House, The Hall and now *The Painting*. Ben tried to keep his smile inwards as he wondered where *The Bathroom* could be.

Penelope gave Ben a brief disappointed gaze before pointing over his shoulder. "He's already there."

"I am?" Ben turned.

The giant's shadow fell over him as it followed her point.

There, in oil at the edge of the painting as though he belonged in the battle. With his Anvilsmith in hand, The Painting had him controlling the black-eagle fiend as it faced-off with the dragon-tuzvul.

Ben smiled at his likeness. Whoever did this absolutely captured the way conjurations always blew his hair and coat back. "Heh, look at that." He leaned a bit closer and frowned at the black magic reins between him and the demon-bird.

Kograkken must've seen it too. The giant roared. "Nilosian!" The giant whacked him.

"Oof!" Ben's air burst from his lungs and through his lips from the surprise blow.

Stunned, first by the giant's booming voice then by its backhand, Ben found himself laid out on the ground. An ache played on the left side of his body—where he'd been whacked—for a moment before quickly settling in his bones. A dull throbbing from the rough landing filled his right shoulder.

Ben tried to recover his breath.

Kograkken slipped the blade's thin tip under his chin. "What have you to say before you die?"

Still gasping for air, Ben looked to Penelope for help.

She moved to the painting to study it.

Ben scrambled backward on the stone floor.

Kograkken matched his retreat with steady platemail rattling strides while keeping the sword at Ben's throat.

Penelope's eyes shot wide. Absolutely transfixed by what she saw, she covered her mouth.

As his thoughts raced, Ben realized that the only time he had ever heard of Nilosian casters in the past were when they had been uncovered and—to his thinking then—rightfully slain. Ben blurted, "I'm colorless!"

Kograkken continued after him. "Lies."

Ben continued to shuffle back. "Someone must've swapped out my spell cards." The top of his head hit stone.

Kograkken kept the sword steady, pinning Ben against the wall with his stare as well as the tip of his blade. "Junior Miss?" The giant's head turned slightly, but those large eyes stayed on Ben. "Your orders?"

Why had his formerly pure green magic turned black? Ben's mind went back to when Senior Adept Collins had frisked him for an aura concealer. The jerk must've done something to him. Ben's brow furrowed at the betrayal. He never liked the Senior Adept, but this was some serious bullshit and now he might be killed.

Hand by his side, Ben snapped his fingers and his eyes widened. "Check my aura!" The regular disappointment his mother tried to keep secret when he had cast at home would be his saving grace. "Either of you." He failed to keep the desperation from his voice. "It'll show what I am."

Kograkken twisted his hilt. The sharp tip swiveled under Ben's chin. The metal began to take on a green hue. The giant pulled the blade away when the faint seafoam tinge darkened to a solid emerald.

That close to being killed, Ben used the smooth stone wall to stand, and rested against it. His whole body was shaking.

"Baxter-Reynolds." Kograkken towered over him and leaned further until it loomed close. "Those who use the darkest magic deserve the worst deaths."

Being found innocent of not being a Nilosian, and being allowed to live, Ben glared at the giant. Vindication gave him a bit of moxie. He straightened his trench coat, dusted the shoulders, and waited for an apology.

Kograkken sneered and repeated, "*The worst deaths.*"

A light ding, that of the elevator, traveled the hall. Penelope hustled to the doors. "Come on."

The giant put on its helmet.

Ben followed behind her and stopped at the door. "I'm colorless"

Kograkken's focus lay at the far end of the hallway. Faint frenzied screams and roars grew in strength. The giant gave his sword two more warm-up swings.

Leery of the giant taking another cheap shot, Ben walked backward through the door.

Before it closed, Kograkken whispered, "For now."

Chapter Nine

CASTING TROUBLE

As though timed with the warm golden sunlight coming through the chunky one-foot-square windows, the smell of delicious, freshly-baked bread grew in intensity. Savoring the scent, Ben took in another deep breath. His stomach growled. He'd have to find the bakery.

Shuffling feet behind him raised his hopes. Maybe Penelope had finally come back for him.

The wide hallways on this side of the door were equally as long as the ones on the other side, but red marble had replaced the dreary granite. The walls here arched in a ceiling some twenty feet overhead.

Instead of long murals, paintings of wizards in gold and crimson robes peppered the walls at ten foot intervals. As much as the magic battle royal bothered him, Ben would much rather study the spells being cast than try to guess the rank of the people in the portraits. Though they were stock still, it started to feel like they disapproved of him being there.

If only the hallways were shorter; there'd be less of them to make him feel like an interloper.

As with the few other folks he'd seen. The person coming from the corner also wore red robes. This one proved too tall to be Penelope.

When she left him, Penelope said he could explore, but there was only so many red-marbled halls filled with hundreds of portraits one could look at...

"*Just don't leave the building.*" Ben quietly mocked her voice. He heaved a sigh. "Like I could get out."

Not for the first time, the fatigue of being up all night began to press upon him. Ben yawned and tried to stretch his weariness away.

He approached another one of the thickly set clear windows centered between the portraits, but—as though it could tell his intent to look out and judge his proximity—the glass grew cloudy and opaque as he neared to gaze upon the outside world.

Ben shook his head. "Lame."

A portrait grabbed his attention.

Nearly all of the people in the other painting were much older than him, but the boy in this one looked to be no older than Ben was when he became an Initiate at the Archon Private Academy six years ago.

The kid's eyes were so bright and joyful that Ben felt his own spirits lifting.

"Five more years." Ben spoke to the portrait about what would bring joy to his own heart. "Then I won't need an escort. I'd be able to go anywhere. Paragon Casino. Geyser Palace. Pepperjacks..."

The robed person who passed Ben stopped, his light voice alive with interest. "*Pepperjacks*, you say?"

Ben turned to see a male version of Penelope about to pass him. He stood a good ways over six feet tall, much taller than Ben, and had his waist-length dark hair hanging in twin braids in front of his shoulders. He wore red robes similar to what Ben presumed were the lower-ranked people in the portraits. Ben nodded. "Yeah."

"You pronounce the name like all the others from your side do." The guy's smooth voice held regal intonations. "This leads me to wonder, does anyone over there actually read the sign in front of the building?"

Thinking back, Ben could readily recall the logo, but not the words underneath.

The man looked him over. "The proper name is, truly, *Pepper & Jack's.*" He leaned in a slight bow and extended his hand with his fingers spread wide apart. "And I should know, for I am Jack."

Hesitant to engage in conversation—she didn't say not to talk to anyone—with this guy, Ben's trench coat parted when he offered his own hand. "Name's Ben."

Jack's eyes dropped to the Anvilsmith and SD cardholder on Ben's waist. They widened. He smiled before reestablishing eye contact. "So, you are the one who rescued Pepper from the Ogre's camp?"

Figuring *Pepper* was a childhood nickname, Ben angled at a clarification. "If by Pepper, you mean Penelope..."

Jack's eyes darted to the right before nodding.

Ben nodded in return. "Then, yes."

Jack brought his hand back and extended it perpendicular to his body. He bent at the hip and swept it across his body at the shoulder. His hand barely missed the floor as he executed a *deep folding bow* with perfect form. "You have our family's deepest gratitude and, rest assured, you will be rewarded handsomely."

Jack's fluid moves triggered a bit of envy.

Adept Matton had given Ben an Unsatisfactory in Courtmanship V last eighth. The last prereq to the rest of the Spell Programming curriculum, Ben needed to retake it—and pass—next eighth to keep his record setting advancement.

Only if Matton allowed tutors for his classes, or gave pointers outside class hours. Ben would then only need pass Spell Programming IX and X to become a permanent part of APA history for being the fasted to advance through Programming. Anyone else could only tie him. Almost able to taste it, Ben licked his lips. As much as Jack's presence made him uneasy, he could learn a great deal by just being observant of the wizard's actions.

Jack, still bent low, commented. "I see you carry an Anvilsmith."

Ben placed his hand over his trench coat and protectively pressed the device against his body. "Just got it."

"For saving my sister," Jack said, still folded in half and speaking to his own knees, "I am certain my father will reward you with nothing less than a Sunforge."

Avid about tablets, Ben looked up and slowly shook his head. No such thing as a *Sunforge*. "I haven't heard of—"

Ben looked at Jack to see him still fully bent. He growled at his huge breach of etiquette. Matton would've had him stand with his nose in the corner—like a misbehaved child—and given him detention. Ben brought the heels of his dress shoes together.

Upon hearing the slight clack, Jack unbent. He barely drew breath.

Ben's envy turned into admiration. Bending that far always taxed him and he couldn't help but draw a deep refreshing drag of air after being granted permission to stand upright. Inwardly, he reaffirmed his vow of working on the move when alone.

Yeah, he could use all of Jack's fluid moves as a primer. Ben kept a keen eye out for the small moves Adept Matton drilled.

From Jack, they flowed naturally.

Ben shook his head and continued his earlier thought. "There is no such device."

"On your side." Jack gave a sly smile. A perfect flip of the wrist turned Jack's hand palm up and he brought it close to his body. "Over here, we have our own makers." With a sweep of his arm, Jack gave another flawless courtly gesture for Ben to walk with him.

Obligated by politeness, Ben did.

"Though it may not be as good as your Master's tablet—" Jack gave a subtle shrug as if to rhetorically ask *what could*. "—it far out strips all Anvilsmiths—even the touted *breakthrough* Triforce model from last year."

Though Jack wore robes of a traditionalist, he knew his stuff when it came to the tools of technocasting.

Hungry to have an even better tablet, and items that would further enhance his casting ability, Ben wondered what other gadgets he could get his hands on over here.

They talked and walked. Jack went to lead Ben down a series of red-marbled stairs. Glad to have company, Ben went, but kept Penelope's instructions in mind. He'd let Jack give him a tour, but would draw the line at leaving the building.

Chapter Ten

SIDEWAYS, NOT DOWN

BEN LICKED HIS LIPS. Not only were they getting closer to the bakery, but, very soon, the weight of a vastly superior tablet could grace his hip. When he got it, should he keep the device hidden or parade it around?

Both options had their pros and cons. Most students often showed off their new stuff and ridiculed others for not having the latest and the greatest.

He'd have something none of them could possess. Ben braced himself against becoming one of *them*.

Instead of letting his possessions define him, he'd do something of worth, something they—even if they could do it all over again—couldn't do. Completing all ten levels of Spell Programming with half a year to spare before first graduation would do the trick.

He'd keep the Sunforge strapped to the small of his back. Ben wanted to give a portrait a knowing nod, but there were none around.

Somewhere along the way, the hall color changed from red to gold and then to orange. Their footfalls, particularly his hard soles, made a bit more noise as though he were walking through the APA's marbled main entrance.

He began to feel a kinship with Jack. They both were fascinated with tablets.

Jack's eyes lit as he talked about the different devices.

Ben often felt he bored his fellow Junior Apprentices when he went on a streak comparing the various models. Jack was more than game.

In fact, there were times when Jack rattled continually about how *his side's* tablets matched up against *Ben's side*. From the sounds of it, besides a small handful of Gnomecraft models, the majority of stuff available here surpassed comparable tablets Ben had once fantasized about owning.

Ben smiled at the thought of Senior Adept Collins making him pull the superior tablet during Spell Mastery IX. The look on the blond jerk's face would be priceless.

When it came to remembering the various specs of the myriad of devices—for the first time—Ben felt he met his superior. Given access to the same information, he'd be able to catch up, but it was possible that Jack's passion for tablets just might outstrip his own.

About to ask about the *Ivory Chain* tablet Jack named as top of the line, Ben thought of Collins again. A different question came to mind. He rubbed his hands together. Knowing this would be the decisive point of how to rank his forthcoming Soulforge. "What do Senior Adepts use on this side?"

"Senior Adepts?" Jack gave the title some thought and motioned Ben through another archway with him. "We do not have Senior Adepts on our side. Like the various other comparisons we have been making, our titles are different."

Ben nodded. Made sense. He raised a finger into interject.

Jack continued, "A Senior Adept would be somewhat comparable to our High Magus."

Ben said, "Why—"

Refusing to be derailed, Jack continued, "They would absolutely refuse to touch anything less than a Triforce." A quick reflexive motion, almost mistakable for a twitch worked the corner of Jack's nostrils. Coupled with the flare, his nose lifted up to the ceiling ever so slightly. "If they touched an Anvilsmith at all."

Adept Matton's words came back to Ben. *"A master courtier never shows even the slightest distaste."* He nodded to the memory. Jack proved to be a good model, but gratefully he wasn't faultless. The pressure of having to become as perfect as Jack eased.

Still, Ben smiled greedily.

If Adept Matton found out how he came across the tablet, his teacher would be sorely disappointed with him for accepting a reward for doing a good deed, but—no doubt—the Soulforge would be impossible for him to turn down.

"All right." Ben took advantage of the lull in the conversation. "Quick non-related question—" He eased into a smile to keep his shameful greed from showing. "—why do you keep making distinctions between *sides*?"

Seemingly lost, Jack blinked at him.

Ben wanted to punch himself for asking such a stupidly basic question.

"Well," Jack seemed to recover. "Sides of the portal, as in the two sides of the dimensional door at *Pepper & Jack's* guarded by the giant."

Why didn't he refer to Kograkken by name as Penelope had?

Ben looked back the way they'd came. A mild fear took root knotting his stomach. Talk about being stupid. He'd followed Penelope, a girl he didn't really know, to a very unfamiliar place. Now, he'd wandered off with someone entirely new, with no idea as to how he would get back to where Penelope had left him.

The portrait-filled red marbled hallways had gone away a while ago. Ben tried to recall the color of the halls between them and the cold gray stone passageway where he and Jack now stood. Coming up short, he took inventory of his surroundings.

Wanting food, he'd been absent-mindedly following Jack toward the fresh bread smell. While it increased in potency, the hallway had cooled. He found his arms folded across his chest for warmth. Torches lit the icy stone hallway. Their light barely threw shadows to meet with the next sconce and the weak fires did nothing to dispel the chill sinking into his heart.

"Pepper... I mean," Jack's eyes darted to the right again. He corrected himself, "Penelope did not tell you?"

Uncertain of what he should've been told, Ben came to a stop and shook his head. "She didn't tell me much of anything, really."

Jack's smile held a *we both know that's not true* feel. "Surely she told you to stay in the building."

Ben nodded. He motioned to the way they'd came. "Are we still in the building?"

"Oh yes." Condescension filled Jack's snicker.

Ben kept his annoyed reaction in check.

Jack didn't seem aware of his own laugh. He sniggered a little longer then gave a palm-up *walk with me* motion again. This one wasn't so smooth; it would have only barely gotten a passing mark in Courtmanship I or II. Jack said, "The Suntouched Spire has a great deal of underground—"

Spires rose high into the air. They'd gone down for a long while. The more Ben thought about it, they'd stopped descending a while ago and had been walking these gray hallways for about an equal amount of time. Ben's nape hairs began to rise.

Another quick snicker slipped from Jack.

Ben whispered, "Kograkken."

"Of course." Jack replied, but looked lost.

Ben took a small step away. Laughter aside, he could no longer ignore Jack's worsening etiquette. That and the fact Jack didn't know the giant's name was too much. His eyes narrowed and he jutted a thumb over his shoulder. Ben asked, "Why haven't we seen anyone el—?"

Hands aimed at Ben's tablet and SD cardholder, Jack lunged.

Chapter Eleven

FALSE FRIEND

FOR SOME REASON, a line from Julius Caesar went through Ben's head. *Et tu, Brute?* They'd made serious study of the Shakespearian play during Ego Control III. Ben thought the ultimate lesson to be learned from the class was about not letting power corrupt. Now he understood Adept Mong's closing lecture about Brutus' loyalty and eventual betrayal.

The thought caused him to hesitate. By the time he'd recoiled, Jack's hands were already inside his coat, both on their intended targets.

Ben grabbed the slack of red robes around Jack's wrist. As Senior Adept Collins often did to him—and many other students—Ben twisted, turned, and rotated at the hips

Jack's hand popped open.

In flurry of red flapping robes, Ben sprawled Jack on the floor.

Jack's other hand still clutched Ben's SD cardholder.

One of his cards flew free when Jack smacked flat on his back. It skittered to a quick stop.

With a twist of his own wrist, Jack slipped from the robes revealing a myriad of tattoos all over his torso.

Ben lunged for his cards.

Jack pulled his prize in tight and called, "Up!"

The air around them rippled. Warm arcane energy brushed by Ben to close on Jack.

Jack flashed with purple Krotosian energy. He went from prone to standing.

Ben grabbed one of Jack's braids. He went to pull the thief down and was left holding a wig.

Jack laughed as he raced down the hall.

Ben scooped up the card left behind and gave chase. He warned, "They're cursed!"

"Ev'n cursed," Jack's well-paced tones were now broken into a barely understandable cant. "These'll fetch a Barron's trove."

A fast runner, Jack pulled a little further away.

Ben noticed a larger shape formed from the dozens of smaller tattoos on Jack's back—a hand with a hole in the palm.

Huffing after Jack, Ben thought about slipping the spellcard into his Anvilsmith, but decided against it. If the card turned out to be a conjuration, Jack had enough distance on him that—if the creature came out tainted—there'd be only a fifty-fifty chance it would go after the intended target. It was just as likely to attack him as it was to go after Jack.

Turns in the stone hallway came quicker. Ben made another turn only to find they were in a long straightaway heading toward a door.

Desperately wanting to use his tablet to activate *Usain*, a speed spell he had renamed after Usain Bolt, to catch Jack, Ben knew if he stopped to cast, Jack would be through the door before the spell would activate.

Counter to his earlier thoughts, Ben wished the halls were longer.

Without losing a step, Jack clapped his hands and flashed purple again. When the light faded this time, he wore a new long black-haired wig, a long-tailed, gold lame server's coat, and a red kilt.

Jack went through the door.

Ben hit the door a bit later.

He busted into a kitchen. The full smell of baking bread and fried bacon smacked him. For a moment he forgot about the chase.

A little girl stood on a table skinning deer. Cast iron pots and pans bubbled and popped on two old-fashioned wood-burning stoves. Three men worked between the stoves and several large cauldrons over flames against a nearby wall, chopping carrots, peeling potatoes, and shucking corn.

All stopped in mid-motion. They looked from a swinging door—the way Jack must have gone—to Ben, and then to the girl.

A tomato from her direction grazed Ben's temple. She ordered in a not-so childlike voice, "Get out of my kitchen!"

Continuing after Jack, Ben swung the door open and scanned.

There were more than thirty men and women in the sitting room. All were older, with long gray hair and wore red and gold traditional-looking wizardly robes. Large, comfortable chairs of varying width, height, and material filled the room. Each seat was unique, lavish, and high-backed with elaborate designs, arranged around old-fashioned, round wooden tables piled high with books, maps, and loose papers. Smaller personal round tables with food and drink flanked the chairs.

His eyes fell upon Jack.

On the opposite side of the room, the thief looked over his shoulder at Ben while moving around the last table toward another door.

Jack's outfit matched the server delivering a tray of drinks. The thief's throat tightened. He cried in a high, nasally voice—sounding exactly like a startled old woman, "Non-wizard. Non-wizard!"

No one looked to see where the voice came from.

They all focused on Ben.

Their eyes drank in his coat, short hair, and the peach fuzz threatening to sprout in uneven patches on his chin.

"Hold!" A woman two tables away commanded, her finger pointed at him.

Ben tried to move to call Jack out as a thief, but found himself frozen in place, unable to speak.

The man next to her stood and pointed. "Hold."

Three more *Hold* spells were cast on him in the following second.

Across the room, standing next to a mounted lion's head, Jack saluted with a snide smile. He exited through the opposite door which opened into a courtyard. The sound of horses trotting and an anvil being struck poured into the room.

"Bo!" The first woman called.

The door did not close after Jack went though.

A man, who had not pointed a finger, gotten up, or even looked away from the book in his lap smiled around the end of a pipe. His words came out in puffs of smoke. "If we caught him with a Hold spell, do you honestly believe we need Bo?" A soft laugh pressed more smoke out of his lungs as he turned the page and took another deep drag.

A hulking, furry minotaur ducked to clear his horns and twisted to squeeze his nine-foot tall, barrel-chested frame through the exterior door. Two sword hilts stuck out over a shoulder, extending as far beyond its body as its horns did. The door closed behind it.

Jack was gone.

The minotaur, Bo, headed at Ben in a single-minded fashion.

Ben wondered—if he hadn't been paralyzed—would he have ran away or messed his pants. The possibly of both wasn't out of the question.

After clearing a sword from its scabbard, the minotaur swung it back with both hands.

The blade looked longer than Ben was tall.

Fully torqued and ready to swing, Bo growled in a deep voice, "Whenever you're ready to release him."

Chapter Twelve

WHAT MAKES A WIZARD

THE AIR in Ben's nostrils weighed thick with fresh bread and bacon. Frozen by magic, he couldn't inhale or salivate. His stomach didn't grumble. The very real possibility of being cut in two by the massive minotaur didn't fill his body with fear or adrenaline.

He'd been reduced to nothing more than a cognizant statue.

They quarreled amongst themselves in a raspy, multisyllabic language that sounded like they'd taken Elven—a language he knew pretty well—and knocked the lofty way of speaking on its butt before dragging it for miles over glass and sandpaper.

When they looked at him, they didn't really seem to see him as a person. They'd look at his coat, his hair, his shoes, his pants, his tie, but never look him in the eyes.

Ben concentrated on being able to move.

The APA drilled on respecting elders, and if Master Reynolds were here, he'd probably be the youngest amongst this group. But they'd didn't acknowledge him, so why should he respect them?

He felt hunger begin to return. His stomach gurgled.

The only woman in all gold robes, the one who first hit him with a Hold spell, ears piqued. She turned from the people she talked to face him.

Warmth—power—chased hunger from his gut. Once his abdomen

filled, the energy spread out through his body to push the paralysis away. As though lifting a great weight, sweat broke from Ben's brow as he struggled—and gained—control of his body. He exclaimed, "I am a wizard!"

Bo twitched.

Ben focused on controlling his sphincter.

The minotaur didn't swing.

Ben pointed at the door. "That server—"

"Ha!" The man with the pipe laughed smoke. He pulled a piece of paper from the table between them. Without raising his head, he presented it for Ben to see.

The paper had four large ornate red symbols on it. Ben didn't recognize any of them.

The man set the paper back on the table. "And you fancy yourself a wizard, hmm?"

Feeling his mouth tighten, Ben fought against clenching his teeth as he glared at the old man. "I *am* a wizard."

"Refer to yourself as a wizard again, boy," Bo growled slowly, his gaze remained set on Ben's neck. "And we will no longer be exchanging words."

The woman in all gold took a step forward. Her robes were exactly the same style as the ones in all the portraits. Her loose gray hair curled up slightly at the end to keep from sweeping the floor as she closed behind Bo and put her hand on the small of his massive back.

The minotaur untwisted and lowered his weapon.

"We," she motioned to include everyone in the room, but Ben and Bo, "my young Trencher, are wizards."

Knowing Jack would be long gone by now, Ben committed to the conversation. "I cast spells."

The man with the pipe, whose eyes were still in the book, chuckled. He spoke loudly to no one. "Anyone can get food from a full platter!"

Almost everyone nodded, smiled, chuckled, or did a combination of the three. Calm returned to the room.

Ben fumed. How could they just write him off like that?

"Dear," said the woman as she moved in front of Bo.

The Minotaur put his sword away.

She smiled in a grandmotherly way. "You may be able to cast spells, but you are far from being a wizard."

His fist tightened. He'd been learning about, and using, magic for six years.

Her next words made it obvious that she'd been reading his thoughts. "Yes, you surely are a Magic-User, a Trencher to be precise, but you are not yet, and may never become, a true Wizard."

Ben wanted to shake his head, but kept it still. What did she know? He could cast spells and he knew damn well what he was.

To negate his inner-affirmations, she added, "Yes, you do cast spells, but you are not a wizard. There is a line and, no—" She'd paused to acknowledge the rest of his thought that she was splitting hairs. "—the line is not that fine. To help, think about the difference between a wyrmling and a dragon."

Ben narrowed his eyes at her and tried to project, *Stop reading my thoughts.*

The old man with the pipe used a finger to bookmark the large tome in his lap. He removed his pipe. As though he were blind, his eyes drifted to the woman's back as he spoke. "He has potential."

They both looked at him, deep into his eyes.

He did his best not to think of anything so they couldn't start answering before he asked.

"True potential," she added.

"Agreed," the man said and went back to his pipe and book.

Motioning for Ben to walk with her as she went into the kitchen her armed with such fluidity that any liquid short of water would be jealous. "Come with me, dear. I will explain."

Chapter Thirteen

ARGOSIAN FONT

BEN TOOK in another deep inhalation. While he didn't know the name of the faint flowers, his lungs registered the freshest air he'd ever took in. Breathing on top of the Suntouched Spire made him feel silly for having ever visited an oxygen bar and paying for canned *Ocean Air*. Clear-headed, he felt honored to stand next to the woman, Elder Komir.

Though the sun shone on them, she'd raised her hands into the sky, and spoke in the raspy, warped Elven. She'd cast some spell that started to push the sun down and roll back the night.

Holy crap! Did she just cast a spell to move backward in time? He realized *honored* didn't do justice to how he felt, but he couldn't come up with a word better than *lucky*—and that didn't really fit either.

Three lamp-lit roads left the Suntouched Stronghold, the fort-city which expanded from the Spire. Elder Komir explained, *The road into the northern rolling hills leads to wild lands, where barbarians roam. The east road goes to that distant speck of light, which is Wilshire, this area's capitol.* She pointed to the last. *That one goes into a forest and, beyond that, an ocean.*

He knew he smelled salt water.

For a moment, Ben wondered how high they were, he wanted to go look over the edge, but felt his city-boy guts tighten each time he considered it.

Though she focused on where the roads went, Ben's eyes kept turning south.

Small blips of light moved as people moved backwards. Shorn crops mended as scythes and sickles worked away from the earth in a fast rewind fashion.

She had turned back time.

Astonished. That was the best word to describe the profound reverence he'd felt for her and her magic.

Deep shadowed forest, which hooked outward from the southeast all the way to the northwest, rose up to blot out the horizon. The trees at the northwest tip were the largest. Against them, at regular intervals, outpost lit as sunlight waned.

With the Stronghold arranged around the Spire, what did those distant stations guard against?

Night time again, Ben looked to the sky.

Clear. Totally clear. No smog. No light pollution. He spotted the North Star, the dippers, and a few other constellations. He regretted not committing more to memory than what was necessary to pass Astrology I & II. Still the stars were nearly the same as when he had seen them at Meadows Towing.

Elder Komir moved to stand in front of him. She projected softly, *We will get to that. For now, extend your arms.*

He did as she instructed. "Use words please."

If you want me out... She slid a bracelet onto his left wrist, her thoughts became stern like he imagined her words would have been, *...you have to will me out.* She slid a second bracelet onto his right.

"How do I—" Ben stopped. Caught by a swell of energy, his head lulled back. Another wave traveled from his feet, through his torso, and down his arms to rhythmically pulse in his hands. It—magic— throbbed gentler than the hard whacking feeling from using a tablet. Instead of the energy being forced into his being, the magic came from within his chest.

He checked the seeping feeling around his hands. They radiated with Argosian red.

Ben steeled his thoughts to try and keep her out.

Good. She transmitted, *I can no longer read you, but I am still able to send.* She smiled. *Shielding is a step on the path to blocking, and infinitely more vital.*

Between casting the black-eagle fiend, The Painting, and Kograkken's ominous farewell, Ben didn't want her to sense his relief at seeing crimson energy surrounding his hands instead of black.

Elder Komir pointed to his hands. *This is magic, but not magic as you know it.* She pulled one of the lockets from around her neck. *For saving my great-granddaughter, you will know true magic.* She placed the thin necklace on him.

Another energy swell.

He nearly swooned.

The warmth of its vibration gathered and rolled in his chest.

This magic is not channeled by a device, as you are doubtlessly accustomed. She pressed a hand to his chest over the locket.

Like a clog had been removed, magic coursed through his heart, veins, and arteries. Every hair on his body felt like a lightning rod, diverting ambient energy from the air into him.

His blood began to feel like raw energy.

Letting it wash through him, wanting the euphoria to never end, his eyes rolled and closed. "Yes," escaped his lips.

She removed her hand, and the magic kept swimming through his veins. *This is close to what it feels like to be a wizard.*

Ben nodded. His body swayed with the rhythm pulsing through him. "How do I become a true wizard?"

Study and practice. And plenty of both. She showed him his remaining spellcard and placed it in his hand. *You do not know any proper spells yet, but until you do, the energy you feel can be channeled through these.*

"But it's cursed."

Pish-posh! She sent, and he felt the air around him react as she waved her hand in three quick, dismissive arcs. *When you are a wizard, the only curses that stick are those in which you believe.* She looked at his spellcard hand. *Focus the energy into your spell-square.*

Fearing the worst, he warned, "Be ready," Ben pushed a small amount of his energy into his SD card. A conjured swarm of red bees sprung from his hands. The swarm gathered above him and waited for commands. He didn't have to take the reins. The conjurer's link had formed automatically, and he was already in control.

Normally the spellcard would have been destroyed. He'd then have to catch the data strip, scavenge what he could from the remains, and return home to build a new circuit board and housing. Amazed, he held the card, which looked as though it hadn't even been used.

Cast again, she urged.

Ben summoned four more swarms before the energy, which had become a part of him, faded. The spellcard never broke apart.

The large, buzzing mass of five crimson swarms was indistinguishable to the eye. Yet, he could feel each individual casting. He used them to form *B E N* in red buzzing letters.

You have used all of the universal energy available to you before resting. Elder Komir beamed at him and took a step back. Obviously, she expected big things from him. *Now, tap into your personal energies and let the true magic happen.*

Ben focused on channeling his own energy into the spellcard. An extra energy swell rolled in the center of his mind.

The energy felt anxious to be released.

A freezing shiver ran through him. An ice-cold pang racked his brain. He dropped the card and turned away from Elder Komir to look at the black energy around his hands.

The magic from his brain tried to force its way out to get into the spellcard. *Use me.* The Nilosian energy surrounded his hands pulsed.

Stumbling away from her, he tried to will it back in.

Elder Komir screamed to him.

Ben couldn't make sense of her words. He felt dizzy. Scared. Exhausted. Angry.

A fog, with a fury of its own rolled in his head. *It* desperately wanted to be used.

A strange sensation—falling—filled him before he blacked out.

BEN WOKE. No idea where he was, he floated in blackness with no sense of direction. Did he face north? East? Down?

He wasn't alone.

A voice, sounding like his own, but malicious and all too close, whispered, "The first person we should kill is Collins."

Ben recalled the Senior Adept patting him down. As though outside his body, he could see the blond Adept switch his Anvilsmith with the one in the booth. Not wanting to, Ben couldn't help but agree, "It's his fault."

"Exactly." The voice. "He did this to us."

Ben could feel a small but potent rage at his core. He questioned it. "Us?"

The dark rage—the frenzied wrath—rushed to fill him. "Us!"

———

BEN SPRANG FROM THE BED. Blankets entangled his legs. He tripped and fell to the fur-covered floor.

Penelope, in long crimson robes, leapt onto the chair she'd been sitting on. Her hands were extended, ready to cast.

He lay on the fur rug, breathing hard, looking up at a red-marbled ceiling. The fall had awoken the many aches from Kograkken's backhand.

She asked, "*Us* what?"

"Huh?" Realizing he wasn't alone, Ben imagined his brain behind four layers of steel.

Penelope answered, "You screamed, '*Us*.'"

Ben rubbed his face as he tried to steady his breathing. He didn't want to answer that question. Heck, he didn't know *how* to answer. He shrugged and remembered his stolen spellcards. Guessing the likely answer, he asked anyway. "Where's Jack?"

She asked, "Who?"

Warm against him, Elder Komir's locket slid across his bare chest when Ben rolled onto his side to look at Penelope. Argosian energy softly pulsed in his chest. A different energy—the Nilosian energy—boiled in his mind. He couldn't focus on anything but Jack.

The dark magic wanted to be tapped, and lusted to inflict exacting vengeance upon the thief.

Worse yet, Ben did, too.

Chapter Fourteen

PRINCIPLE

EACH STAGE of their four course lunch had been orchestrated by a foppish servant in golden silk robes. A league of servants in red silken robes carted the old food away and brought new.

Not interested in food, Ben had barely managed to eat a handful of grapes and strawberries. Both Elder Komir and Penelope told him to put the theft of his spellcards out of his mind, but how could he? If it were only that easy.

A slight stinging, like a low-grade headache forming, seemed to taint Ben's thoughts.

While Elder Komir picked from platters overflowing with juicy meat and dozens of different cheeses, she had tried to comfort Ben by pointing out that the loss of his spellcards had ferreted out the spy within the Suntouched Spire. As a reward for his loss, besides an unspendable *thank you*, she'd also given him a thick—useless—dusty book with weird symbols in it to study until he could get back through Pepperjacks.

Unspendable? What kind of jerk-thought was that? It didn't feel like his own.

Ben had wanted to pinch himself. That wasn't his way of thinking at all. If Elder Komir offered the book, it must have value. Heck, even if it didn't, she'd given him the gift of being able to cast without technology. True magic. He had no idea how long it'd be before he was a real wizard, but now he at least felt his feet were on the path.

That stinging in his head painted Penelope, too. It was as though she had been no better than her great-grandmother when she had agreed and given him a small pouch of coins. She admitted her family owned Pepperjacks and promised management there would more than reimburse him for his stolen items. He'd only have to give the purse to any Pepperjacks employee.

While Ben had considered the stinging a word—*Us*—pulsed in his head. Remembering the darkness of the dream, Ben tried to lock the ingratitude and *Us* away in a steel box as the Komirs tried to console him... but the stinging had continued.

The old guy with the pipe came, had sat at the table with a book, and didn't said a word. He flipped a page, took a puff, and mumble into his beard.

Ben had spent half a school year crafting each one of those cards. Jack hadn't merely helped himself to seven easily replaced or forgotten SD spellcards, he had stolen three-and-a-half years of Ben's blood, sweat, and magic.

None of them understood, though. How could they? They weren't technomancers like—*Us*—him.

It was easy for them to tell him to just let it go. The massive meal, just for the four to them, had told the tale of them never having to skimp or scratch or claw to earn enough to buy supplies for school projects. They had tossed him a few token gifts and expected him to forget the theft.

He couldn't. He wouldn't.

The man with the pipe said Jack would've headed to the docks for a quick escape...

...And that was where Ben went after ditching the guard keeping tabs on him. He had hopped on a wagon heading to the docks and kept his eyes peeled for Jack.

Now, Ben sat at the docks. He'd been for half the day. The rolling sapphire water gently lapping against the bay threatened to steal his anger as he watched the ebb and flow of waves. Similarly, ships came in, did their business, and left.

"Are you lost, long hair?" A rough-talking man stood in front of Ben. A wide Captain's hat on his head, grizzled gray hair covered his chin. A telescope hung from one hip next to a rapier, and, on the opposite hip, a dagger. Faded brown leather leggings tucked into knee-high boots and his loose cloth shirt billowed from the eastward breeze.

Ben turned his gaze to the docks. Quietly comparing this guy's dress to the folks there. All of them appeared fresh from being extras on a *Pirates of the Caribbean* movie. Add eyeliner, a pistol, and a bottle of rum and this guy could be Captain Jack's father.

Best to ignore him.

Undaunted, the man continued, "If'n you're lookin' to get lost, I've got the best ship on the seas to do it with." The man motioned vaguely further down the docks to where three ships were being unloaded.

Unsure which one he should be appraising, Ben eyed each. They were large and sleek. He didn't know anything about boats, but they looked faster than the massive blocky ships he had seen earlier.

"Five Stags will get you clear to First Light." The Captain let a boisterous laugh loose to cover up checking over his shoulders. He then whispered, "And ten will keep it secret *if'n* you really want to go."

Ben shook his head and took a moment to fix his mind to imitate the pompous Komir accent like he'd heard in the Suntouched Spire. "No, I do not want to broker passage. I am looking for someone." Unrolling a length of cloth he had drawn the pattern of Jack's back tattoo on, Ben showed it to the sailor. "He has body markings in this shape."

Looking around the dock again, the man leaned in. "If'n I was you, I'd be careful with showin' that around." He folded the cloth over twice, his calloused hands closing Ben's own hand around it. "The Friendships don't much care for people who're lookin' for one of their members."

"Friendships?" Ben asked.

The man muttered, "Long hairs..." He looked around the docks again. He spoke in a loud, patronizing tone, "Where is your guard?"

A set of whistles sounded. Dockworkers. Being there for half the day, Ben already knew what the main whistles meant. Laborers from one ship exited the now-empty vessel and doubled up to work the next boat. Over his shoulder, Ben only found dockworkers and seamen, he had lost the knight who tried to trail him at a distance. "Don't have one."

Leaning away from Ben, the Captain looked him over, his eyes focusing on the long, red robes and the wig—pulled from Jack's scalp —on Ben's head. He stepped closer and rested his forearms on his raised knee. His voice lowered again. "You mean to tell me you left the Red Spike without swords at your call?"

Ben took a deep breath of the salty air and tightened his grip on his last SD card. He'd reprogrammed it from the swarm's specifications to Orion's and had included the scrapyard combat data. Deep in his palm, he prepped to channel magic into it. "Don't need them."

"You've got spirit, boy!" The Captain pulled away and let loose another boisterous laugh.

Not feeling it, Ben smiled with him.

The man added, "And a heapin' extra helping of dumb."

Ben's smile waned.

The Captain chuckled, "If'n your purse went to a cutthroat, it'd be a shame." He pointed to one of the many sea worn brick-walled taverns. "Buy me lunch, boy, and I'll tell you what I know for a Stag."

"My name is Ben."

The Captain smiled at him. "Quite demandin', aren't we?" He then continued without moving his lips. The rasp and broken words disappeared. "While I am saving your life, long hair, you are going to go by *Boy* and you will call me Captain. Got it?"

Ben blinked at the sudden change. Then nodded.

Chapter Fifteen

THE EVEN KEEL

THE STENCH OF ALCOHOL, sweat, and mildew hung in the Even Keel's air. Ben and Captain made their way through six long tables to one of the two booths in the back. Captain eased his way down, and Ben fell into the seat expecting it to offer resistance, but his teeth clacked. The cushion had long lost its spring.

Captain drummed his fingers on the table. "The Stag?"

Ben reached into the small bag—which he refused to call a purse—and pulled out a few of the steel pieces under the table. Comparing them, he separated a coin with a Stag's bust on both sides from similar Sun-embossed ones. Sliding the rest back in, Ben put his hand face down on the table, covering the coin, and prompted, "The Friendships?"

Captain smiled, he extended his hand to be next to Ben's. "The coin."

Ben's hand had barely left the coin.

Captain covered it and kept eye contact with Ben's while he pulled it back with a slight scrape. His eyes flicked to the coin cradled in his lap for a second. "It's open talk for The Guilds, or The Brotherhoods, or whatever else the collective thieves' dens deem fancy enough to refer to their *profession* as a whole."

A server came with a dented, oblong platter piled high with

different slices of meats and roasted red potatoes. She filled out all the curves of her stained, flowing light gray dress. Pressing her chest against Captain's back, she set the food in front of him with a peck on his grizzled cheek. "There you go, Cornelius."

Ben's eyes rose from her low-cut blouse.

With a wink, she turned her lustful smile on him.

Caught, Ben's cheeks burned.

She asked, "Anything for your new cabin boy?"

"He ain't—" Cornelius—Captain—popped a potato into his mouth, and steam puffed out between open-mouthed chomps. "—earned his salt just yet."

"Shame." She licked her lips and twirled away.

Ben's shin lit with pain and he bounced in his seat. Cornelius had kicked him. He stopped watching the server's swaying hips to frown at the man.

Cornelius spoke without moving his lips again. "She'd be the first to slit you." He speared a slice of meat with a knife, brought it to his mouth, and spoke before taking a bite. "With how anxious you are, Boy, you'd probably not even get your relief first."

Ben shook his head. He wondered if Cornelius knew the difference between taking *in* beauty and being taken *by* beauty. His mind flashed back to Penelope running in the hallway. Ben shook the memory away. "So, to which Friendship does the guy I'm looking for belong?"

"From the looks of it," Cornelius spoke through a disappearing mouthful of meat. "You've got yourself a Brother of the Bottomless Palm." He paused to add a quarter of potato to his mouth which helped to quiet the smacking. "Ask anyone who knows of them and they'll agree, The Palm are the greediest of the lot. Also, the most daring."

"Greed and daring." Ben recalled how Jack's eyes had focused on his Anvilsmith and spellcards before befriending him.

"Aye, deadly combo. No other guild would dare to infiltrate the Red Spike, but, if the money is right, The Palm will try anything." Cornelius speared a potato Ben had been eyeing and offered it.

Ben took it and bobbled it hand-to-hand to cool. "Where can I find them?"

"Keep flashing that drawing and you won't." Cornelius stopped and turned an ear.

Ben listened to the whistles with him.

Cornelius grinned. "The dockworkers have finished my boat."

Having heard the finishing sound a dozen times, Ben nodded.

Cornelius said, "Soon, they'll all be in here swallowing swill until the next boat comes." He pointed to Ben's robes and hair. "It will serve you well to lose the robes and hide the hair. They might show your status up at the Red Spike and Red Brick, but out here, they'll get you cut."

Ben repeated his question, "Where can I find them?"

"Are you listening to me, Boy?" Cornelius pointed the knife at him. "I'm saying like that..." He jabbed with the knife at the air pointing to Ben's robes and hair. "You won't. They'll find you, cut you, and walk away richer." He waved his knife around his face and hat. "You die seeing me last, and the Red Spike will have my head for sure."

Ben kept from balling his fists, but his frustration sounded in his wavering voice. "Then what do I do?"

Cornelius motioned to the server who, not having anyone else to serve, whirled back to the table. "I need some proper local color for my boy here. Those worked for smuggling him from Lomka, but now I need to get him up to the Ros'."

Her attention solely on Cornelius, she turned her back on Ben to face the Captain. "In exchange for those red silks, I'm sure I can find somethin' that'll keep the Dock Master from waking up."

"Good." Cornelius took a small bite of meat. "Keep him sleepin'."

Ben bit into the potato, looked away from their flirting, and out the window. Not jealous of the workers' labor, he eyed them as they teemed like ants on the remaining ship. The delicious mixture of garlic and other seasoning brought his attention back to the potato.

On the edge of his vision, Ben spied a note extended behind the server to him. He reached for it, but missed when Cornelius sent her away with a hearty smack on her rear.

Cornelius stood. "She's going to try and undress you. Don't let her." He then slid the platter, and what remained of the meal, across to Ben. "Once you're changed, and fit in with this lot, I'll send you the information."

About to leave, Ben grabbed the man's wrist.

Cornelius barely turned his head, looking down at Ben's hand on him. His voice, a sharp blade. "Boy?"

Ben snaked his hand back. He clasped it in his lap. "Why not just tell me now?"

"Because, seeing how thick you are, you'd probably go right away." He looked Ben up and down one more time. "And if you are truly from the Suntouched Stronghold, no less the Spire, your eyes need time to forget my face."

As the Captain walked away, Ben discovered a note under the plate.

Chapter Sixteen

LOOKING THE PART

THE SERVER HAD COME BACK with a bundle of clothes. She tried to make Ben give up the red robes first, but heeding Cornelius' warning, he demanded the clothes instead. He slipped behind the booth to change and found a note in the pocket, *Salt or not, for two silvers we can share the night. Cornelius need not be the wiser.*

Ben removed the wig.

A muffled sigh came from a dark hole in the dark wood. She must've been watching him from a secret area.

He turned his back to where he heard the sound come from. Ben pulled on the loose tan V-neck cotton top and brown cotton pants. It almost felt like wearing the old-fashioned pajamas his grandmother had given him.

Holding his tablet, he faked a trip and jammed his tablet between the booth and the wall.

As though nothing had happened, Ben then slipped the red cotton sash through the wide pant loops. There wasn't enough to go around twice. The excess hung from the knot he tied. Now, except for his haircut, he looked like he belonged amongst the pirate extras.

"Best to be rid of those fine shoes and into one of the pairs there." Her voice mostly carried over the booth, but also slipped from her viewing station.

Ben grimaced at the repulsive hodgepodge of worn leather boots, tattered cloth shoes, and frayed rope sandals. No telling who wore them last or what nastiness waited to spread.

From habit, Ben pulled the loose cloth together around his neck to fasten a top button that wasn't there. Suddenly worried about cleanliness, he sniffed at the collars. Only finding the salty scent of the sea, he let them fall open.

Keeping his red leather boots on, he stepped out.

Hip kicked out to the side, top a little wider exposing a bit more cleavage than before, she waited.

Trying to be polite, he handed over the robes, the wig, and cleared his throat before handing over the note with a soft. "No, thank you."

She accepted all the items, but the wig captured her attention as she turned and left.

Ben returned to the booth. He slipped the Captain's note out again —*codeword cheeks*—and put it away. What was that about?

Another set of whistles sounded the arrival of a fourth ship. Ben's last potato had gone cold before the third and fourth ships were both unloaded.

As Cornelius had predicted, workers brought in a fresh wave of sweat for the cushions, ordered, dropped copper and silvers coins, and drank ale by the pitchers.

A bartender had come in and help the server keep up with business.

Just as the crews worked on the ships, they worked in the building. Lively whoops, hoots, and hollers shook the structure when a three-piece band—two mandolins and a drummer—started rounds of bawdy drinking songs.

As though timed to an inaudible cue, the workers stopped their revelry. A few took bread, but other food and drink where left where they lay as the workers piled down to the docks.

Ben's eyebrows raised. When did the new ship pull in? How had they heard it?

After cleaning up most of the mugs and leaving platters with food, the server returned with a heel of bread for him.

Ben spun the empty platter, muttering Cornelius's *fit in* sentence. How in the heck was he supposed to do that?

She leaned in to take the platter. Though she got close, she avoided pressing her body against his. The small smile she showed him felt genuine. "If you want to fit in, learn the songs or—" Her elbow kicked out to the docks. "—go work with them."

Ben shook his head and tried to button the non-existent collar button again. "I don't know how to do that kind of labor."

"No one does the first time." She gave him a wink. "Just get out there. They'll show you the ropes."

Chapter Seventeen

ONE OF US

WHILE WORKING ON SHIPS, Ben slid away and hid whenever he spied men and women wearing red leather armor with golden studs walking by. On their torsos, they wore a badge he'd seen inside the Suntouched Stronghold. It had a red spire, outlined in yellow, which stood in front of a red sun, also outlined in the same yellow. It was the same armor as the guard who he had ditched.

They combed the docks, but didn't board.

He had reacted to seeing them the first time and bumped into a bald, tattooed man who reeked of cloves.

He nodded to Ben.

Ben nodded back.

A quick shrill whistle sounded twice each time the guards came around, and they came around often. Each time he'd drop out of sight and would see someone else hiding.

They'd nod to each other.

Soon, all the crates were emptied and new cargo loaded. Ben returned to the Even Keel with the dockworkers.

Oddly enough, the funky mildew scent had disappeared. All he smelled upon re-entering was seasoned meat and garlic potatoes. His arms, back, and legs ached, but the soreness amplified his want of the well-seasoned food.

The man who had repeatedly blown the warning whistle raised his drink. "Cups up."

Everyone grabbed one of the earlier abandoned mugs. Anyone empty handed raised a fist. Ben followed the latter group's their example.

The whistler raised his chin. "Those Redblades were hungry today, boys, but we all remained free!" He shook his flagon and liquid splashed over. Unrestrained cheers sounded through the room before the spilt drink hit the table. "Drinks down!"

Having drained his cup, the man wiped his mouth dry with the back of his arm and called, "Music!"

The trio got up and played.

Ben learned and yelled the lewd lyrics right along with the rest. As with the others who were younger, he'd been given a wooden cup of water in place of ale. The worker part of him wanted to try the brown drink, and he almost swiped a mug before he remembered why he had worked in the first place.

He'd been accepted as one of them.

Seeing some of the other younger workers trying to sneak a drink, Ben made a purposefully slow attempt at a mug.

"Na'uh." The bald, clovey tattooed man lifted it out of his reach with a knowing smile.

A boy no older than ten, the same age as Ben had been when he became an Initiate for his first eighth at the Archon Private Academy, tried as well. The kid managed to drain one before catching a heavy boot in the butt for it.

The whistler called, "Wood boys out!"

This ban on youth applied to everyone underage. Anyone drinking from a wooden cup—five, Ben included—had to leave.

On their way out, the whistler pushed an almost perfectly halved silver coin with a raised lion's head on both sides in each boy's hand.

The sun had gone down and cool air washed in from the sea.

They stood in the street. The five of them, each holding their wage.

The ten-year-old's words came out slurred. "Let's go to the Beakless Griffon." He pointed vaguely. "They'll let anyone with coin drink until they pass out there."

Ben cheered with the others. For a moment, he considered returning to the Even Keel and wait outside for Cornelius.

Just then, another boy, Ben's height, slung his arm around his shoulder and started singing.

Ben smiled and sang with him. The others joined in as they made their way down the wharf and, near the end, turned away from the witnesses on the docks.

Chapter Eighteen

THE BEAKLESS GRIFFIN

ALONE, as though sent away from the other taverns as punishment, a squat, two-story structure sunk into the earth. Its horribly cracked deep blue paint exposed a gray layer, and under where the gray peeled away, light blue. Even at a distance, music poured from inside. A piano played the loudest.

The song inside floated their way. *Boomerang Jane*. They'd sung it at the Even Keel. The song about a quiet dock master's daughter becoming a pirate captain struck a chord with Ben. If she knew what she'd develop into, would she still had made the same choices?

Ben led the group in changing tunes.

Walking down the slope to the front door, Ben noted the griffon-shaped wooden sign swaying in the wind. Indistinguishably faint divots, carved letter or symbols had long since faded and been painted over. Plain wood shone where the mythical animal's beak would have had been worn smooth with time.

When the first of his group opened the door, a roared greeting rolled out of the building. The smell of alcohol within overpowered the salty sea behind them. The muggy warmth from below collected on Ben's skin and a soft crosswind licked his dampening hair.

Halfway down the slope, Ben paused at the top of the short set of stairs.

For a reason he couldn't quite nail down, this felt like the point of no return that Boomerang Jane had faced. Ben nodded to set his resolve and descended into the growing heat and noise. Ready to take in the rowdy madness, he crossed the threshold.

"Coin!" A voice bellowed from his right.

Ben jumped.

A wide mouth of golden teeth barked laughter. The man who'd startled him hooted, slapped his knee, and pointed at Ben. "Got cha!"

Working a smile to his face, Ben handed the gold-toothed joker his half-silver.

The man turned the coin over in his hand, dipped it in an amber fluid, and watched in. His gold teeth flashed as he spoke, but the ruckus proved too much to overcome.

Not wanting to, Ben leaned toward the man. "What?"

The man gave a sly wink. "You want leaks, weeks, or beaks?"

About to yell a question about the difference, Ben remembered the Captain's note. "Cheeks."

Gold-teeth nodded as though he'd expected nothing less. He set the half-coin over a slit on a tiny wooden table. With the press of a button, a blade shot down, and cut the coin into two quarters. The man held one of the quarters toward Ben with that same sly wink. "Cheeks it is then, brother."

Ben accepted the sliver and returned the wink.

Gold-teeth swept three half coins and two quarters into a small wicker basket. He hung the basket on rusty hook connected to a length of rope. The bucket began to rise.

Scanning to where the bucket would go, a smiling, red-haired man with an air of authority looked down at Ben. Fat rubies lined the golden goblet in his hand. The guy looked familiar. From the docks? Having made eye contact, the man raised his cup in greeting and nodded.

Ben nodded back.

Next to the redhead, another man pulled the rope. With brown hair chopped short in a haphazard fashion, his face held a permanent scowl. Deeper on the left, scars ran up both cheeks. He didn't wear a patch to cover the wrecked and sunken eyelid over the shadowed socket.

With a shudder, Ben turned his eyes away. He found the beat with the seven-piece band and sang along, "No, Jane. You'll surely hang if you dare to cross your father again."

In three evenly-spaced rows from the stage, eighteen long tables divided the main floor. They were bolted down and, somehow, twice as packed as the full tables at the Even Keel. The boys he'd come in with had scattered through the building. Only the smallest, the one that had gotten them kicked out, could be found—and only by the narrow gap he made amongst the rambunctious patrons.

The tables nearly butted against four booths lined up on the back wall. All taken. In the booth furthest to the right, sat Cornelius, his hat pulled low to cover his face.

Seven shapely women in vibrant light blue dresses, nearly fluorescent from the many glass-contained light orbs bouncing in a fancy chandelier, made their way into the room. The vivacious women served, cleaned, danced, and sang.

Ben lost the words to Boomerang Jane...

He picked up the tune again. "No, Jane. You've got nothing to gain, why dare cross your father again?"

A second floor overlooked the first, and at least fifty men and women filled the visible areas of space, but there were no stairs or ropes leading up. Trying to piece it together, Ben wondered how one gets up there? Their faces were stern and set. Like gargoyles. The man with the goblet seemed to be the only one capable of smiling.

Some of them were focused on Ben.

He squeezed into a nearby table and looked for utensils. None. Everyone pulled portions with their dirty hands—some with gloves, most without—before plopping meat or cheese into their mouths.

The stares from the second floor felt like a weight on his shoulders. Now wasn't the time to be squeamish. Ben picked a strip of greasy warm meat with his bare hands. Under the slick feel, the meat felt tough. He put it in his mouth to pull a bite away. Tasty juice oozed into his mouth, but his teeth verified the lack of tenderizing. He placed the full piece in his mouth and worked at it.

Three styles of wooden cups to grab filled the spaces between platters. The drunk kid—a natural born lush—from the Even Keel grabbed the smallest style. *It must have the highest alcohol content.* Factoring that in, Ben took the tallest of the three types.

He brought it to his mouth and smelled cherries. A sip confirmed the strongest ingredient of the red drink along with a faint hint of roasted almonds which faded to a slightly bitter aftertaste.

The weight of stares began to lift.

Still not daring to inspect the second floor again, Ben noticed Cornelius' hat at a normal angle. He made eating motions with his hands.

Ben set the cup down and dove for the last heel of bread before one of the lovely servers danced away with the nearly empty platter.

She winked at him.

Not sure if the Captain would approve, he smiled secretly and bit into the deliciously buttered honey oat. This was the kind of bread his mother liked to make. The grain felt heartier than anything she'd made and Ben liked it. He wanted more. More of all of it.

Chapter Nineteen

DEN OF THIEVES

A GONG RANG from the second floor. The music stopped and the din started to die. The gong rang again. The red-haired man with the ruby encrusted gold goblet raised it over the edge. "Cups up, lads. Cups up."

Ben joined everyone in lifting a cup.

"Last night started what could be the end for the Red Spike, and word has come…" He flicked the chalice. It gave a dull thunk. "Even Leighlan Komir, the *Red Baron* himself, had to join in the fray."

Everyone cheered.

To blend, Ben cheered with them. He liked Elder Komir. He hadn't met Leighlan the Red Baron, but something about the way the redhead talked about him made Ben's neck hairs stiffen.

The man continued, "Granted, we make our money anywhere we can…" he paused, and everyone shared a dirty laugh. "We all know there is money in war, and of all the casters, the Argosians are notoriously cheap!"

A mixture of chiding laughs and hardy boos fill the room.

Ben added to both in turn.

"So," the man raised his goblet higher, his smile broadening as he swirled the cup. "This cups up is for whichever force takes down the Red—"

"Guild Master," the young boy slurred. His shrill voice cut through the room. Everyone looked at him. "What if Orange comes in, or worse, White?"

"Use your brain, Meacon." All eyes returned to the man and his broad smile. "Do you really think either of them wants to war with Red?" He shook his head. "No, as long as a deeper color doesn't control The Node, they're happy holdin' hands and singing songs!" He crossed his eyes and bobbled his head.

The band struck up a jaunty tune. Their piper punctuated the highs with happy pipe bursts. The rest of the band came to a sudden stop, but the piper kept chirping away. Copying the Guild Master, his eyes were crossed and he bobbled his head. When two of the other band members mock-stabbed the piper, cheers rang out. The piper's toots worsened and weakened with each fake stab in his fake death.

"Brother!" Cornelius called out. All heads looked to him as he tilted his hat back to see the second floor. "Do you foresee success?"

The man looked into his goblet. His smile died and a somber expression washed over his face. "One can never know for certain."

Ben noticed an oracular glint to the man's eyes. He seemed to be looking through the cup.

"If the Argosians are able to keep a grip on victory's hips, we'll serve them as well." He seemed to come back into himself and took a small sip. Losing the fight to keep the smile from his face as he spoke over the rim. "Though my glass wouldn't be as full!"

Cheers arose, and his grin flashed back to full force.

The man addressed Cornelius, "Worry not, my good Captain. From what I hear, your native land has the upper hand."

Cornelius raised his cup, one of the smaller ones, and bowed his head.

Breaking the dying cheer, Meacon spoke, his voice higher than before and his words slushier. "I heard they got the girl back!"

Everyone seemed annoyed with him. Ben wanted to help Meacon keep quiet, but there were too many bodies between them.

Searching the room, the Guild Master purposefully avoided eye contact with the servers in light blue as he pointed at Meacon. "Someone get that boy another drink!"

Soft laughter arose as someone near Meacon put one of the small cups in his small hands.

The man added, "True, Penelope is back, but she'll be of no help tonight and she doesn't have the key!"

This last statement lost the general populous.

Ben did not know how to react.

The servers, band members, and bartender clapped. Finally showing life, everyone on the second floor joined in.

Those at the tables searched one another with weak, wanting smiles.

The man raised his goblet to those on the second floor and spoke flatly to the main floor. "This is a good thing."

Everyone cheered again, and Ben joined.

"So, everyone. Cups up!" He paused, looking over everyone in the room. Making sure no one had want for a cup, he commanded with a sharp nod, "Drinks down!"

The only ones who really slammed their drinks back were the one with the smaller cups. Those with medium and large cups took a swig.

Ben raised the cup to his lips and his eyes went back to Cornelius for direction.

Suddenly the Captain jabbed an angry finger at him. "Boy!"

Ben froze. The drink wetting his upper lip.

Everyone stared at him.

He lowered his cup. "Yes, Captain?"

"Are my quarters clean?" Cornelius shot out of the booth, taking long thumping strides toward Ben.

Everyone shifted, pressing against others, to give Cornelius a clear path.

Not knowing how to answer. Ben tensed. "Yes."

Cornelius grabbed him by the scruff of the neck and shook hard. "I thought I saw you doing dock work today."

"True." A gruff voice called. "He was there, Cap."

Ben tried to look, but Cornelius had a tight grip on him.

A woman's voice rang out. "I saw him there too, Cap."

Ben opened his mouth to reply, but Cornelius dragged him toward the door and yelled over him, "You're saying you're fast enough to clean *and* do side work *and* drink?"

Doing his best to not fight the strong hand gripping him, Ben went with Cornelius.

Roars of laughter and insults followed them across the room and out the door. Most encouraged Cornelius to give him—the scrub—a solid beating. The scarred, eye-less man from the second floor growled. "Run sweet-meat across the deck 'til the edge is gone from those pretty red lady-boots."

"Tell me the order in which you cleaned, boy!" Up the stairs, the slope, and a few paces away from the building, Cornelius still held Ben in tight control. He began to speak in a low, angry voice.

Ben tried to follow the low words, but lost them when Cornelius sent a telepathic message. *My informant just relayed the news. The Palm's spy is returning to the Suntouched Spire to assure none loyal to Red can join in defending The Node.* He turned Ben around when they hit the sand. His mouth still moved with whispers.

Ben ignored the words and focused on the voice in his head.

Cornelius projected, *You have to warn Elder Komir.*

Ben's mouth opened to ask who was the spy and closed it to rephrase the question.

You know him. Cornelius had read his mind. *He probably still has your spellcards since they haven't hit the black market yet.*

Ben pressed his lips together and narrowed his eyes at the Captain in suspicion.

Cornelius' face morphed, changing to the knight who had trailed him for the first half of the day. The features shifted, and the guard's skin paled to match Elder Komir's wizard-friend, the one with the book and pipe. Then the features slacked, darkened, and contracted back to Cornelius's face. *Understand?*

Ben nodded.

Cornelius got loud again and gave Ben two more shakes before turning him back to the boats. The Captain slipped Ben's Anvilsmith down the front of his shirt.

About to ask how Cornelius got it, a swift kick lit on Ben's butt. He ran.

The Captain yelled after him, "The galley better be spotless! You hear me, boy? Spotless!"

Chapter Twenty

SUNTOUCHED SHOWDOWN

JUST AFTER SUNDOWN, Ben made it back to the Suntouched Stronghold from the docks. As much as he wanted to rush in, he took the time to help the elderly wagoner—who'd kindly gave him a free ride—stable the horses.

Ben had gotten used to the animals' smell on the road, but a stable full of them, their feed, and their waste, proved to be an aromatic nightmare.

Someone slowly whistled the filthy *Heave Your Load* song. A song that made Ben blush in the Even Keel once he understood the lyrics. The tune, when drawn-out in a lazy dawdle, almost sounded like a love song.

Ben bent to see the whistler from under the horse.

Coming from the long clearing to the red marbled spire, a man—about Jack's height, Jack's slender build—in red robes and with his hood pulled up, looked around casually as he strolled toward the stables.

Ben pulled his tablet and last spellcard from the wagon. At the doors of the stable, Ben called to the whistler. "Hey, Jack."

The person, who may not have been Jack, didn't even glance. He pivoted and sprinted back toward the spire.

Ben channeled Argosian energy into the spell card. "Jack!" The snapping energy flew into his fist. The distance at which he could cast Orion had grown. The faint red shadowy gorilla formed next to him before Orion's actual body materialized. Instead of taking control, Ben pointed at Jack. "Stop him!"

Orion thumped after the fleeing thief.

Ben leapt the chain barring wagons and followed. If Jack got into the spire, it'd be over.

Orion lunged.

Jack rolled to the side.

Ben's conjuration blew past, rolled, and turned.

A fully materialized gorilla, made of purple energy, sprang from Jack's hands.

Ben's mouth fell open. He blinked in disbelief. No one had ever summoned a creature with such rapidity.

On the ground, Jack flashed a defiant smile. "Don't know how you survived the room of wizards last night, but I hope you're ready?"

Their gorillas faced each other.

Jack's eyes became glassy—the look of someone inhabiting his conjuration.

Ben slid his consciousness into Orion as the gorillas charged and clashed.

On initial impact, Jack's gorilla pushed Orion back.

Orion caught the purple fists on the down stroke. Snagging the control reins, Ben gripped them, pushed Orion's hips into the gorilla, and twisted while pulling. The purple gorilla flipped over them from the hip throw. Ben released.

Orion leapt to rain his fists down on the fallen foe.

The purple gorilla caught Orion's wrists and pressed to get back to its feet.

Standing, Orion leaned his weight in, but Jack's gorilla managed to get a foot under and made slow progress in standing.

Ben backed into his own body. This shouldn't be happening. He had rarely activated the actual spellcard Jack used. His own SD had easily been through a hundred use cycles. Orion should've been dominating this contest.

Yet, the purple gorilla was somehow stronger and had gotten to its feet.

Ben pulled his Anvilsmith and cued up *Heracles*, his strength spell. Not meaning to, he gawked at the power meter. How was it full? It had been at nine last night and only gained an *awatt* per hour, as nearly all devices did. It should've been at thirty-three.

A frustrated grunt brought Ben's attention back.

Jack's gorilla not only had its feet beneath it, it towered over Orion, forcing him down to a knee.

Ben tapped *Cast*.

Though not visible against the evening sky, the sizzling of the black Nilosian energy could be heard in the volley of the emerald green crackling power as it plowed into Orion.

His conjuration bellowed when the spell hit it. The gorilla's muscles bulged to twice the size they should have been. Crimson fur turned green. Red nails turned black and grew into jagged claws.

Orion roared with might as it powered up and recovered.

The purple gorilla struggled hopelessly.

Wanting to taste the victory first hand, Ben extended his thoughts for the reins. The magical control lit in the center of his mind and slapped against his palm, but he didn't grab on. Jack gaze was still vacant.

Ben bolted to Jack's body and dove on it.

He searched for, and found, his nylon spellcard holder. The six remaining cards sat snug in their elastic pockets.

Using both hands, Ben pried Jack's fist open and snagged his last spellcard.

He glanced to see how the fight was going.

Orion had the other gorilla down. His mouth cranked open when its shoulders arced back displaying a mouthful of serrated black teeth. Nearly a flash, it struck. Those horrid teeth dug into the purple's jugular.

Jack's gorilla winked from existence.

Jack, back in his body, kicked.

Ben's side lit with pain.

As Jack started to run, the thief's hand went to where he'd carried the spellcards, and came out empty.

Ben smiled. He took control of Orion and began to give chase.

Jack turned, his fingers twisting like the ogre at Meadows Towing had. He belted two hiss-gargled words, and forked bolts of purple energy shot from Jack.

The thief had cast without a spellcard or device. How? Ben dove Orion's body in front of his own

The magic pelted into Orion's side. The gorilla winced, groaned, and checked the wound.

Three baseball-sized holes had been burnt into Orion's side. A shudder flashed through the gorilla's body. An angry hoot rolled in his throat.

Besides the pressure of the impact and a slight tingle, none of the pain reached Ben. It was almost like being in a first-person shooter.

Jack started to cast.

Orion launched at the thief.

Jack jammed his wrists together.

Chains rattled behind Orion.

Ben seized control and turned.

The stable chain, now an incandescent purple, had broken free and snaked halfway to them. Its far end stuck in midair, the rest lashed out with great clamor.

Orion ducked under it.

Ben took control and grabbed the chain.

The extra length in the center arced out.

As he had wound rope on the docks, Ben looped a length around an elbow. In no time, he had it tight and straining against the unseen anchor. Using every augmented muscle fiber in the gorilla's body, Ben yanked.

The last link cracked open. Instead of reverting to magical energy and dispersing, the chain changed natures. It went from striking viper to crushing constrictor. The loops Ben thought he had, turned out to have him.

He spun once, swung the remaining length over his head like a lariat, and let it go in Jack's direction.

The chain hooked out toward the thief.

Jack almost leapt over it.

He would've been clear it if the chain hadn't arched up and wrapped his legs.

Jack crumpled to the ground with a wholly satisfying crunching thud.

To free Orion's arm, Ben pulled at the loops.

The chain wanted both of them.

A swell of magic—what the heck was that—expanded within Orion. Jarred, Ben tried to analyze it. Did Jack have a way of stealing control of conjurations?

Another surge of Nilosian energy filled every inch of his conjuration. The control reins vanished and Ben found his consciousness flung back into his own body. How was that possible? Orion was his spell. He'd cast it.

Uncontrolled. Orion ignored the chains to rush Jack. It dropped both fists on Jack's ribs. Muffled cracks punctuated the air as furry fists pounded further into a body than whole bones would allow.

Jack jabbered nonsensical cries. The chain vanished.

Ben gave a practice blink to dismiss the gorilla.

The green and red energies obeyed. They stripped themselves away and dissipated into swirling motes, but the black...

The serrated teeth and jagged claws kept their shape. A faint shadow—translucent Nilosian energy—held a vaguely gorilla-ish silhouette that loomed over Jack. Sprung wide like a steel trap, the black teeth chomped down on Jack's casting arm.

The thief's screams rose higher. He writhed and tried to pull free. The struggle made the teeth sink further which spurred Jack to higher screeches and further hysterics.

Mouth perfectly dry, the heady tang of fresh blood—how'd he know the taste?—gushed into Ben's mouth.

Reeling from the conjurer's link, Ben snapped it shut and focused on dismissing the teeth and the claws.

They resisted. No. They fought back, struggling hard—*punish the betrayer, make the false friend pay*—to remain. To finish.

Ben rubbed his forehead to expel the dark thoughts. They weren't his. That's not how he felt. It couldn't have been.

The teeth...the claws...turned to ash, then smoke.

Both bones in Jack's forearm broken, his wrist and hand dangled by white sinew. The bones showed white for an instant before blood washed over. Mangled arm cradled, Jack wailed and shrank away.

Trying to clear his mouth of the ghastly coppery taste, Ben forced himself to salivate and spat repeatedly.

Two stronghold guards, decked in red leather shot past. They leapt on Jack, rolled him face down, and secured him in thumbscrews.

Chapter Twenty-One

ON BEING A MESSENGER

JACK CAPTURED, the Redblades—Ben would have to find out their real title instead of referring to the Komir guards by The Friendship's slang —brought Ben in to stand next to Elder Komir's throne-chair at the end of a series of grid-set, long oaken tables. The redblade missing his left pinky called it the dining room. From the head of the room, Ben figured this *dining room* could hold the entire Archon Private Academy's cafeteria with room to spare.

Zesty foreign spices hung in the air. Besides the light rattling of the man's chainmail as he left, the room seemed to eat noise.

Alone, Ben wondered how much trouble he'd gotten himself into. He had his stuff back. However, in having gone after Jack, he went against what Elder Komir had *suggested*—her way of *telling*—him to do.

Trying to distil everything he knew about the elder, his imagination geared up to play *Guess the Reprimand*.

Before round one began, Elder Komir bustled into the room. Her red, gold-trimmed robes whisked faint pink dust. "My young Baxter, I need to send you back to relay a message to your Master and only to him."

Ben frowned at having to tell Master Reynolds that he'd disobeyed someone of equivalent rank to his Master. "I'd rather take whatever punishment you have for me."

Elder Komir paused.

Dressed in similar robes, Penelope, who he hadn't seen enter behind the Elder, moved a step beyond her great-grandmother.

The Elder asked, "Punishment?"

Thrilled not to be in trouble, Ben smiled.

Penelope on her heels, Elder Komir hurried to close the distance. Her solemn expression remained fixed. She presented a golf ball sized metal orb. "The Node is under attack. We have discovered who is behind the offensive."

Ben's smiled waned. He gave a serious nod.

"It all started with the ogre kidnapping me." Penelope added, "The key is probably in the room where I was kept."

"No." Contradicting her, Elder Komir handed Ben the cool sphere. "Your Master will know what it looks like."

Her opinion dismissed, Penelope's brow furrowed.

"From what she explained of the monster—" Komir laid a soft, loving hand on Penelope's shoulder. "The Ogre Magi is probably wearing it like a charm." She removed the hand to palm the top half of the sphere. "He's fond of turning to gaseous form if the tide of the fight turns against him." Her wrinkled lips turned in disgust. "Once it goes gaseous, your Master will be able to capture the monster with this Encapsulating Orb."

"Okay." Ben nodded to both of them and found himself sinking into Penelope's blue eyes.

Breaking the eye contact, Elder Komir stepped between them. "Time is of the essence."

Ben nodded. His eyes flicked to Penelope when she moved around her great-grandmother. Did she like him, too?

Instead of regaining eye contact, Penelope's gaze went to the orb.

Ben took the small sphere with both hands. To be sure he recapped, "Tell Master Reynolds *The Node is under attack* and *the ogre at Meadows Towing is a part of it*. Give him this." He shook the orb. "To capture the monster when it turns into gas."

"Precisely." Elder Komir nodded. The lines on her serious brow twisted a bit. Concern? She said, "The door to Pepperjacks is not safe right now. To get you back, I'm going to have to Banish you."

Banish sounded like she said it with a capital B. Making it sound—capital B—Bad.

His eyes turned to Penelope. Ben's mental fortitude and resolve began to double. He nodded to Elder Komir. "Let's do it."

"I cannot put you at your school, but I can put you near your car."

A tentative fear fluttered into Ben's gut. Relenting to spells went again everything the Archon Private Academy taught. Yes, there were some good spells out there, but an instinctual resistance made his stomach tighten. Focusing through it, he nodded.

This, she projected to him, pushing her sleeves back to reveal liver-spotted arms. *Is going to hurt.*

Ben shot Penelope a confident, playful grin and dragged it to the Elder. "Hit me."

Faint golden energy played amongst the crimson as she began chanting in a hiss-gargling language. Her hands turned circles. Argosian energy trailed. Gold—unnamed, unknown energy—counter pointed from her index fingers. *Time is of the essence.*

Ben tried to ask about the new energy, but Elder Komir directed her spell at him.

A wave of yellow-traced red magic washed the Komirs, and the room, away.

Chapter Twenty-Two

BANISHED

THE BRILLIANT RED flash clamped Ben's eyes shut. Each muscle fiber in his being seared and went slack.

He fell on hard ground.

His noodley muscles came back to life with a tight constriction. Cramped and twitching, they seized in violent spasms.

Trying to find a way to flee, the Argosian energy in his veins—newly awoken by the Elder herself—expanded into needle-tip spikes. Wanting to seep from his ears, eyes, and nose, the vengeful energy in his head—the black stuff—had turned to fire, broiling his brain.

Ben tried to release them. To stop the pain, he'd let both go. Neither fled. Betraying him, his body held them in.

His legs kicked.

Teeth gnashed.

Back convulsed.

Ben's fingers tried to dig into the unyielding surface—concrete—beneath him.

The pain lessened enough for slight awareness to register. A coppery taste—blood—filled the right side of his mouth. He had chomped down on the inside of his cheek.

Elder Komir had mentioned the spell would *hurt*. Clearly their pain thresholds were vastly different. She should've said *writhing twinges* or *agonizing pain*.

The red light faded. The ground's coolness pressed through his coat. His legs occasionally twitched, and his arms had gone asleep.

Laying there, he opened his eyes.

Bright white filled his vision.

The light faded and tightened into florescent tubes locked behind protective grates. Beyond them, the concrete ceiling gently sloped away to hundreds of empty parking spots.

When he turned his head, he nearly came face to face with matte black metal. He lay next to the passenger side of his Transcend.

"Was that a new dance?" A synthesized voice—Tex—asked.

The back spasms ceased, but Ben's legs stayed as useless as his limp arms. Ben's gaze raked his companion, who wore one of the junkyard boar's spiked collar twisted to cover both shoulders like dual bandoleers. His companion stood on the dashboard and surveyed him with an expression of mild amusement.

"Once I heard you," Tex continued. "I started recording. You know, so you can watch it later... Maybe add music?"

Inhaling deeply, Ben noted something in the air. He stayed where he lay as the magic in his system eased its assault. Fuzzy ants-crawling-across-his-flesh feeling started coming back into his arms and legs. Sore and dry, his throat choked the question, "How long—"

"Twelve seconds." Tex gave an enthusiastic nod. "All the way from the mindless grunts through the incoherent babbling."

Ben redefined agony to *so much pain as to not be aware of time.*

He sniffed the warm air. It held a long-burning, high-heat smell that reminded him of when he had to work the kiln during Glass Works II all those years ago. Slicking his throat with saliva and blood, he asked, "Do you smell smoke?"

"When the wind blows this way." Tex tapped the flat space above its mouth-shaped speaker box to remind Ben it didn't have a nose and pointed beyond the windshield. "My air quality sensors detect higher than normal levels of carbon which has been steadily increasing for several hours."

Almost good to go, Ben arched to see. Laying on the ground, a low concrete wall blocked direct view of whatever his companion motioned at, but something lit the Las Vegas night sky.

Keeping his hand pointed, Tex glanced to Ben. "Something inside Pepperjacks is on fire."

Ben sprang to his feet. Complete recovery not yet arrived, his legs buckled and he leaned on his door. He looked beyond the front of the car. They were on a higher floor of the parking garage and had a mighty fine view of Pepperjacks.

Mundane fire trucks surrounded the property, but did not approach the building.

Ben couldn't see flames, but steady plumes of smoke rose from the building's top floor.

Remembering why Komir had blasted him with the—capital B— Banishment spell, Ben snapped his fingers. "Master Reynolds." He pulled his Anvilsmith from his hip and pressed *Call*. The screen with his programmed numbers came up, but the device flashed *no signal*.

Tex's optics twisted. "Where'd you get that?"

Feeling better, Ben stood and tested his balance. Yup. Good. He turned his focus to Tex. "What are you talking about?"

The small robot pointed down to the glove box. "Look inside."

Ben flicked it open to see another Anvilsmith.

"When you didn't respond to my ping, I bypassed your silent mode, sorry, and heard a conversation." Tex shrugged. "None of the voices were yours, and so I tracked down your tablet."

Ben pulled the device out.

"I snatched it and returned to the car." Tex shrugged. "Figured if I got all the gifts together, you'd eventually come to us."

Nodding, Ben compared both devices. They were the same, all the way down to his arcane mark on the back. He woke the screens. The device he had with him still showed ninety-nine arcane watts while the device Tex had in the glove box only had thirty-four. He eyed Tex. "Where did you find this again, exactly?"

His companion pointed to Pepperjacks. "Tucked into a booth eight in from the main entrance, against the wall. Two adults were, uh, *getting busy* in it."

Recalling when Collins had patted him down, Ben bit his lip to stifle the string of expletives he wanted to use. Feeling them about to fly free anyway, he bit harder.

If he ranted about the blond bastard, Tex would report him for slandering a higher-ranking caster. At least that's what the first page of the manual said would happen. Part helper. Part guide. Part tracker. If only he could find a way to make the robot one-hundred percent ally.

Pushing Collins further from his mind, for now, Ben pressed call. As with the other device, the screen showed his contacts, but flashed no signal.

On both, he tapped *System, Diagnostics*, and *Run*.

"Tex, ping out to the APA." Ben dropped the tablets into the passenger seat and went around his car and got in. "I need to get a message to Master Reynol— Shit!" Patting his pockets, Ben searched around.

Tex asked, "What are you doing?"

"An orb! I had an orb." Ben focused on his companion. "A metal sphere about the size of a golf ball. Did you see one?"

Tex pointed. "It rolled to the wall and stopped over there."

Ben followed the tiny finger to see the Encapsulating Orb propped against a beer bottle. He went to get it. "Ping out."

"I can't." Tex looked from Ben to the devices in the passenger seat. His optical lenses twisted. "My pings are relayed through the tablet. If it cannot get a connection, I can't connect either."

Ben retrieved the sphere. It felt colder. He put it in his pocket, went back to his car, and dropped into the driver's seat. From Pepperjacks, Meadows Towing was a twenty minutes out toward Pahrump. If he didn't hit traffic, the Archon Private Academy—out by Sam Boyd Stadium—would be a forty-minute drive in almost the opposite direction.

Pepperjacks continued to smoke.

Time is of the essence, Elder Komir's words rang back.

He leaned over and clipped the tablet Tex had stashed in the glove box into the center council. He left the other in the seat. "When the tablets come up, Tex, do a deep check on both of them."

"Will do." Tex unclipped the spiked collar, hooked the ends into grooves on the dashboard, and hung in front of the console.

Ben took a moment to admire the rig. While it wasn't a perfect fit, it was ingenious. He'd have to see if something like that was on the market, it not, he would make the harness himself. "Tell me where they vary and try to get a signal."

Tex nodded.

Ben clicked his seatbelt on, started the car, and peeled out toward the exit.

Chapter Twenty-Three

24-SEVEN

HAVING STOPPED at the last 24-Seven convenience store on the edge of town, Ben tried using a mundane payphone to call the school.

As the phone rang and rang, cars zoomed along the Las Vegas Strip going into, or coming from, the city's main attraction. The line picked up. "Thank you for calling—"

Ben pumped his fist and spoke quickly. "Yes, this is Benjamin Bax—"

With even tones, the voice continued, "The Archon Private Academy. No one is here—"

Ben slammed the scarred receiver home on the graffitied cradle. He had expected to reach the on-duty Councilor, but got a message machine. "What's the point of having a twenty-four-hour hotline that goes to voicemail?"

Still on task, Tex's voice came from the passenger seat, "Did you leave a message?"

Ben grabbed his hair and walked to the Transcend. "Elder Komir said, specifically, to deliver the message only to Master Reynolds."

"Hmp, a conundrum." Tex turned its attention from the tablets and reported, "Several subroutines should not have been running on the tablet you had on your person, but both Anvilsmiths are identical from serial numbers to lack of connectivity. I stopped the subroutines and cleared them out, but cannot do anything about getting signal."

A 24-Seven store attendant, in his orange and red bowling shirt uniform, shoved someone with offensive body odor from the store. "Get out of here, you bum!" In a huff, the attendant rushed back inside.

The bum stumbled, recovered, and jutted a middle finger over his shoulder. He pulled a frosty tall can of beer from a pocket, cracked it, and started to drink.

Ben leaned on his Transcend, crossed his arms, and reassessed.

Only if he could've coded a real teleportation spell instead of the curriculum-mandated *Pop*. He'd be able to flash to the school and, if unable to find Master Reynolds, flash to Meadows Towing.

All teleports—all the really dope spells—were explored at the Advanced Spell Programming level. More than ever, he looked forward completing regular Spell Programming X.

Ben rubbed his face. Only if the Councilor would've answered...

It might've taken some serious conversational acrobatics to prove an emergency without stating the exact situation, but Master Reynolds would've teleported to him for full disclosure. Ben would have had a chance to explain everything and, hopefully, be done with the whole entire mess.

But the Councilor didn't answer.

Having gone toward Meadows Towing, it'd be an even longer drive to the school now. Sunday. Ben heaved an angry sigh. The school, besides the on-duty Councilor—who wasn't worth a doodie right now —always stood vacant on Sundays.

The Node is under attack. We have discovered who is behind the offensive...wearing the key like a charm...time is of the essence.

Ben realized his leg had started to shake. He had to do something. Every bit of him knew it.

In watching the bum walk further away, still drinking his tall beer, Ben began to nod to himself. He didn't have to take down Meadows Towing or the Krotosian. He only had to get the key.

He spun and pointed to the tablet in the passenger seat. "Start channeling all the arcane wattage from that device—" He pointed to the one latched on the console. "Into this one."

"Transferring arcane wattage from—"

"I know," Ben interrupted. He slid into his car. Tex had started giving him the same spiel Rembrandt had given him a few years ago when Erik—his lab partner during Spell Programming IV—needed some extra energy to pass Applicable Magic II. He started the car. "I'd just use that one, but it's cursed."

Tex tilted its head, a move Ben believed it learned from him. "Still, transferring arcane wattage from device to device is not optimal usage. There will be a twenty-five percent loss, and the process will take nearly ten minutes."

Ben nodded to the timetable in his head. He'd be at Meadows Towing in fifteen. "Yes, that's fine. Please do it."

The little robot's hands folded back to reveal a microSD extension on each wrist. Tex stopped. "You do not have authority to approve such a waste."

Thankful the robot couldn't read thoughts, Ben pressed his lips together and paraphrased the second page of the manual—it was as far as he'd gotten before the day span out of control. "As a Junior Apprentice, I'm allowed one override, with which you have to comply. The override will be reviewed and either approved or disapproved by my Councilor." Ben focused on his companion. "Texas, buddy, I *really* don't want to override you."

The robot's head dropped for a half-second before it slid one of its wrist-jacks into an Anvilsmith.

Figuring the half-second pause must've been the equivalence of Tex's processors giving the thought thirty minutes of consideration, Ben smiled at the outcome.

Tex's shoulder disconnected. A cord extended from the socket as it leaned over to plug the other wrist into the second Anvilsmith in the car seat. "I would rather not be overridden."

Ben smiled. "Texas, you're the best companion anyone could hope for."

Tex nodded, shone green and began to slowly pulsate light. Arcane watts transferred from one tablet, to Tex, and then into the device.

Too late to change his mind or stop Tex, Ben wondered if the curse Collins installed on the tablet would transfer along with the energy.

Chapter Twenty-Four

SCRAPYARD REPRISE

BEN KILLED the headlights before he turned onto the unnamed dirt road which led to Meadows Towing. From here he could see the shadowy blot of its silhouette standing out against the distant hills on the dark desert floor. He killed the engine and coasted to a stop half a mile away from the scrapyard.

Sucking in a deep inhalation of clean desert air, Ben held it, tried not to think about what he planned on doing, and let it out. He spat his grape gum into its spent wrapper and tucked it into the ashtray.

Crickets started to chirp.

A click next to him—the glove box—gave the insects a moment pause as Tex pulled out something that scraped as it left the glove box.

Ben leaned in to see the thin thing by the faint green glow of Tex's eyes. A second spiked collar? "What am I to do with that?"

Tex lifted it toward him. "Wear it."

Ben took the leather strap and carefully turned the spiked collar over in his hands. "Why?"

Tex tapped its own spiked collar, wrapped around shoulders and waist. "If these blocked Chrystal from being able to see the boars in her divination, it stands to reason that it should keep anyone from seeing you." His companion pointed at the tablet on the left. "That one is full, the other should be put away."

Ben nodded and held the collar around his neck.

It snapped close and cinched.

He tugged at it.

It loosened at his pull and tightened again when he released it. The boars had massive necks. The collar should hang loose.

Ben pulled at it one last time.

It came back tight.

He sighed and relented. He'd heard that the Red Rock Witch had worn a foreign necklace—the fabled Nether-Choker—only once and when sunlight hit her, she transformed from whatever she was before the necklace turned her into the distant rotting hag she was rumored to be.

To be safe, he'd have this thing off well before sunrise.

Tex climbed to the top of the car door and leapt. Ben locked up, got out, and scooped up his Anvilsmith. He tapped *Maps* and noticed the path they were taking now was nearly the same as when they originally came to Meadows Towing. Hoping his bicycle would still be where he left it, he thoughtlessly gave the collar another pull. "Lead on."

It cinched tight.

Ben eyes started to adjust to the night as his companion led him across the dark desert floor before coming to a stop.

Tex said, "We're a hundred yards out." The green dot that represented where Ben had left his bike disappeared. "And consider your bike stolen."

Ben refused to mope. He had a car now.

The tall, rotating, star-shaped Meadows Towing sign, which had shed lavender-white light like a lighthouse the night before, stood as a silent sentry. All the lights were out. The moon barely lit the hardpan, and Ben recognized the maze more by the shadows cast by the towering wrecked cars.

Ben tried to recall the path he took a couple of nights ago...Too many turns. Too many dead ends. He shook his head. So much for the easy way.

Tex asked, "Did you mark the car?"

"Yes." To prove it to himself, he stole a glance at his tablet and nodded at the small red dot there.

"So," Tex looked from him into the scrapyard. "Are we going the way I went to the center building or the long meandering way you took?"

Meandering? Ben pointed. Exasperation filled his voice. "You ran across the top of the rows."

"Not my fault you'd make too much noise."

Ben pinched the screen. The overview he created before their first adventure into Meadows Towing came up. Two paths ran from where they were to the center. Tex must've tracked their movement.

About to bathe Tex with compliments, Ben bit his lip. A blue line, with *winner Tex* repeated along the length, took a near direct path to where the Transcend had been stored in the work bays. Ben's route, yellow—stamped *non-winner Ben*—showed the way he'd taken to the building.

Companions' personalities were supposed to become a caricature of the owner traits, but Ben never thought of himself as competitive. He'd be more mindful to notice that trait in the future so he could keep it in check.

He tapped the screen. A lime-green line lit under his fingertip and he traced his past path. He short-cutted the dead ends and skipped the loop he made to avoid a boar.

Before he could present the path to Tex, his companion nodded. "Got it."

Though his tablet and the robot were distinctly separate devices, Ben marveled at how well they synced.

Ben tapped *Spells*, the *Enchantments* icon, and then *Elf Sight*.

He had begrudged having to build it in Spell Programming VI and lamented the lost time he could've spent programming productive spells. Aside from proving that it worked during his final, Ben never imagined he would actually be casting the spell. Inwardly he had bet against it.

Ben resented the spell so much that he hadn't designed a background and used the default *Cast* button. A lone slider—*Duration*—lay under the glass. Ben slid it to the far right. An hour. Enough time to get in, try to sneak the key, and get out. The *Cast* button flashed a -5 below it. He'd have ninety-five arcane watts left.

Looking from his device to the sky, Ben slid his mouthpiece in and took a moment to note the constellations.

Even this far from the city, Las Vegas washed out many of the weaker stars, leaving the stronger celestial bodies alone in the night sky. A small part of him wanted to return to the Komir spire just to look up at the universe.

Ben shook the fantasy from his head. If he didn't act now, Pepperjacks would burn down and ruin any chance he had of ever getting back to the other side to see the stars—or Penelope—again.

He tapped the plain *Cast* icon.

The Anvilsmith vibrated weakly in his hands for a brief second. Then nothing.

"Don't give me that." He knew a dud when he felt one and shook the device. "I ran the program through a debugger..." For a moment, he wondered if he had accidentally loaded an earlier version of the spell. No. He'd remember that. Ben shook the tablet again. "There's nothing wrong with the coding—"

A hundred feet away, a beam of white light shot down from the sky.

Fearing an attack, Ben froze, and searched.

Tex moved to his side. "What?"

In the distance, another single beam of light came from the sky.

Ben pointed. "There."

Tex asked, "Where?"

Dual beams of light dropped down. Then seven. Then more and more.

Ben turned his face to the sky.

The washed out stars lit brilliantly in the night. It seemed like each distant heavenly body twinkled. The brighter ones leaked light which fell on the desert floor like ephemeral rain.

He held out his hand.

The light didn't have a feel to it, but bounced and splashed on his palm like water. *So fricking cool!* Ben cupped his hand, but the splatters of light evaporated before it could pool.

He'd only ever cast the spell in the clinically-lit classroom. His device had shocked magic into him, and Collins had sneered at having to give Ben an A.

Now, through the sheets of light, Meadows Towing—the ground, the wrecked cars, the sign above the scrapyard, even the prison-like bars spanning the thirty feet between concrete columns—glimmered as though they were wet.

Planning to enter the way he had before, Ben swiped back to his other enchantments and tapped the kangaroo icon. He had extra time in Courtmanship IV, so he rewrapped his jumping spell. "Hmm. Missed changing the main icon." He'd gone back and forth between a tarsier and a flea—since fleas could also jump ridiculously far for their size—but the small simian, with its bugged eyes, won out.

Ben puzzled at the grayed-out duration bar. The slider defaulted to the top, wanting to give him the full ten minutes for one arcane watt. "It should cost three."

"What?" Tex asked.

"Tarsier." Ben swiped from the spell. Investigating, he called up his speed spell. The background of the spell had *Usain Bolt* running through a finish line, arms raised in a vee, over it, a grayed-out duration bar with a highly italicized *Cast* with speed streaks trailing left. For ten minutes, a *-1* lit behind *Cast* instead of the normal *-3*. Maximum duration for an *awatt*. "And Usain is only one too."

He turned the Anvilsmith over. The magical sigil—his name arched in lightning around his studious version of the APA's gorilla mascot—flashed at him. He lowered the tablet to show it to Tex. "This is the one from Pepperjacks, right?"

Tex looked the tablet over for a moment. Probably way longer than it needed to. "Yes." It angled its pale green orbs up at Ben. "Why?"

"*Usain* and *Tarsier* say they only need one *awatt* to cast top-slide. Each is supposed to be three." Ben rubbed his chin and frowned at the device. "The spells are acting funny."

Was it possible that Tex had stolen Senior Adept Collins' tablet when he snuck in, instead of recovering the correct tablet? If Tex had, why would Collins have any arcane mark besides his own on his tablet?

Thinking of the duplicate inscription on the second Anvilsmith, Ben shook his head. The jerk already slipped him one, maybe he was planning to switch it out again.

Feeling a bit paranoid, Ben made a mental note to come up with a different way of marking his device since—despite what teachers and counselor said—the *Inscription* spell could obviously be faked.

Another task for another time.

Ben swiped out and tapped *Tarsier*. He activated the thick block cast button made to look like small simian's bugged eyes.

As before, the Anvilsmith merely vibrated in his hands, indicating the spell had failed. A moment later, a powerful infusion of magic washed over him and pulsed into his legs—sinking into his muscles.

The spell had cast, it didn't hurt, and only cost one *awatt*. Something was going on, but what?

Chapter Twenty-Five

DEADLY GROUND

"GRAB ON, TEX." Ben strode forward across the starlight-bathed desert hardpan to the thirty-foot column he had jumped up to before. Meadow's Towing steel-laden air filled his nose. In the distance, a coyote howled.

He eyed the protruding stone lip. Tex's weight registered on his coat. Ben squatted, aimed, and leapt.

Before, with all of his effort, his fingers barely hooked over the top. This time, he scraped his knee on the edge as he overshot the lip by ten feet and landed on the flat top.

Tex asked, "How'd you do that, Ben?"

He shrugged. "Has anything like this ever been reported before?"

"I still don't have connectivity, so I can't check, but we're programmed with thousands of situations that are likely to happen to young casters—" Tex looked to where Ben had leapt from. "And there's nothing like this in my memory stores."

Be asked, "Do you have to report that this happened?"

"No." Tex shook its head. "You have me in companion mode so I'm able to keep secrets. You'd just have to tag the occurrence as private."

"Good." Ben narrowed his eyes to carefully choose his wording. "For the record, Tex. Consider anything I do with magic, private."

"Nice!" Tex nodded. "Excellent blanket coverage."

Atop the thirty-foot concrete column, Ben scanned the starlight-bathed scrapyard. Thanks to his *Elf Sight* spell, the darkness of night had retreated to a soft, sunny day. When he gazed out into the desert, the brightness gave way at a certain point to a distant curtain of night. "So cool."

Noting his path through the general pattern of the main aisles among the dozens of rows of wrecked cars, Ben leapt down. He set Tex on the ground, and jogged to the first main aisle. Nearing the end of the row, Tex advised, "You should get a spell ready."

Not looking down, Ben flashed Tex a glimpse of the Orion SD card he had in his hand. "Got one."

"But your Anvilsmith is hanging on your hip." His companion pointed. "It should be in your hand."

"I'm good, Tex. Thanks." He spared his companion a wink and a confident smile. "Help me keep an eye out for the boars."

They hustled across to the rows on the other side.

Tex picked up his pace to get a lead. At the edge of the next row, it peeked around the corner. Its little robot arm went up.

Ben stopped. His grip tightened on the SD card. He eyed Tex's arm and listened.

A soft steady wind whistled through the wrecks and pushed the collected smell of neglected plastic and steel into his face. At last, a faint gruff voice barked foreign words.

Keeping Tex in his peripheral vision, Ben pulled his Anvilsmith. He tapped *Options*, *Translate*, and *To Text*. The screen went blank. It couldn't register the distant words. Splitting his attention between the Anvilsmith and Tex's arm, Ben crept down the row toward the corner.

The black screen now showed a small green sound wave dancing below the registration point. The voice had grown a little louder, but the mic on his device wasn't sensitive enough.

The robot's arm stayed raised.

Just shy of the corner, the device flashed *Orc to English*. Ben focused on the sentence as it appeared. "Say what you want, but this is bullshit."

The voice sounded close. Almost too close.

Ben looked from the screen. Tex had disappeared. No, the robot had crouched under the crushed front fender at the corner car. The little robotic arm shook like an air pressure needle, directing him back, back, back.

Ben back-pedaled.

Halfway down the row, Tex's hand turned sideways.

Ben stopped and tried to flatten his body against the wall of wreckage towering over him. Points of metal kept him from leaning too far back.

The sloped facial profile of an orc—with a Bluetooth device flashing in its ear—came into view and turned away to walk the perimeter.

Its broad shoulders were rounded forward and its head hung low. Barefoot, it wore a large sword strapped across its white t-shirt clad back, and a holstered gun bounced on its right jean-covered hip. It barked Orcish, but the orc's steps were sulking tromps seemed overly pouty.

Tex waved him forward and gave hand signs to come fully around the corner.

Doing as suggested, Ben stayed close to the wreckage, but not so close as to snag his coat on something, and slunk around the corner.

Tex moved out to scout the length of the next row.

About to read the orc's translated text, two groups of words both had a pop-up. *Might-Fist* and *Shame-Feast.*

Might-Fist (n.) A title used amongst goblinoids and wild races to denote the ruler of a vast region. One Might-Fist may have many lesser Fists who help control the area.

Ben didn't tap *Fists.* Context told him what it meant.

Shame-feast (v.) A ritual called by overlords after pitting failed minions against each other in an honor battle. When a Shame-feast is called, the victor of the honor battle must immediately do the following or be slain.

Ben recalled honor battle from before. He read the first of five bullet points.

The victor is to eat the feet of the fallen foe.

Ben envisioned the horrific act and grimaced. His stomach constricted. Without hesitation, he tapped the tiny *x* at the corner. *Shame-feast* highlighted as a hyperlink and the pop-up vanished.

The mental image of the grisly bullet point tried to force its way into his imagination. Ben shook his whole body to slip the vision in disgust.

Tex motioned him forward.

Ben moved up behind his tiny companion who—of course—had been right about the need to keep his Anvilsmith at the ready. While he'd be ready to cast if he needed a creature, he'd be a half-second behind being prepared if he needed another spell.

In Introduction to Dueling, Adept Love always went on and on about how a half-second could be the difference between life and death. Though Ben had dismissed the tired warning in class, he now understood why the Adept drilled it.

Best to prepare.

Pop, his short range teleportation spell, would be the quickest way to keep from being spotted. Ben swiped the transcription away, tapped *Spells*, and then the fat exclamation point icon to get to *Conjurations*.

He came to the corner just in time to come face-to-chest with a different orc turning onto his row.

Ben gazed up into its black irises and found no space for love there.

The orc took a quick half step back. Dressed like the other, its massive green hands went to the gun on its hip. It frowned. Then went for the sword.

Ben rolled backwards over his left shoulder to get some distance and channeled Argosian energy into the spell card.

His hand flashed red before he finished the roll.

A tiny clap of thunder sounded Orion's appearance, scarlet fur over ruby skin. The red gorilla caught the orc's arms on the downstroke.

Ben had never materialized a creature so fast.

The blade stopped just above his head.

Taller than his earlier casting, the crimson Orion stood eye-to-eye with the orc.

The orc dropped a hand from the hilt toward his hip.

Squatting, Ben took control of Orion. He caught hold of the orc's wrist just shy of the gun.

The orc grunted. It tried to force the sword hand down into Ben's comatose body while also trying to force its other hand toward the gun.

Recalling a lesson from Adept Love's *Surviving Brutes* combat class, Ben stopped pushing against the orc. Instead, he turned Orion's hips into the creature, pulled both arms down and tucked his toward his torso.

The orc flipped over. Slapped flat on its back, the orc's breath came out in a hard puff.

Ben tried to think what to do next and realized he'd accidently stalled Orion. He let Orion act on its own.

Raining blows, they dropped on the orc.

Tex called, "Your body!"

Ben turned Orion's head to glance.

The first, Bluetoothed orc had its sword out and angled back as it charged down the row at Ben's limp body.

Chapter Twenty-Six

DOUBLE THE TROUBLE

BEN EJECTED FROM ORION. The gorilla's adrenaline—through piggybacking on its senses—always felt dull and distant. In his own body, Ben's heart thumped and his muscles keyed for action.

His eyes tried to make sense of his surroundings. That's right, he had squatted.

Feet thumped behind him. Drawing closer.

He glanced beyond the orc coming behind him with its sword cocked back over its head. Popping to the other side of the junked cars would provide complete safety, but he'd lose precious line of sight of Orion and the gorilla would disappear.

He tapped *Pop*.

The Anvilsmith gave a worryingly weak vibration.

The sword came down.

Ben reappeared behind the Bluetoothed orc, who stabbed at the air around where Ben had been. The orc must've thought he had gone invisible.

No sooner had he thought about sending Argosian energy through the Orion spellcard still in his hand, did his hand flash red and—with a faint thunderclap—a second red gorilla appeared.

The Bluetoothed orc had just started to shift its weight from a missed attack at an invisible foe to look back when the second Orion slammed it into the wall of jagged points from compacted cars.

His gorilla gripped Bluetooth around the waist, lifted the orc—pulling it away from the compacted metal it tried to grasp onto—arced its simian back to heave the orc over its body and slam Bluetooth into the hard packed earth.

"A suplex?" Ben gaped at the wrestling move.

The gorilla then rolled over the limp orc, picked it up in a belly-to-belly bear hug and arched back to suplex-spike Bluetooth's head into the ground again.

A horrifying crunching crack made Ben shudder.

The back of the orc's head had, for a split-second, made full contact with its back.

Mouth agape, Ben found his head had tilted in wonder. He corrected his neck and shut his mouth.

The first Orion grabbed its orc's sword with its foot, tossed the sword toward its shoulder, transferred control of the orc's wrist from hand to foot, caught the hilt of the weapon in the air, and drove it down into the orc's chest.

Ben found his jaw unhinged again and let it be. Where had they learned that stuff?

The two gorillas rolled their dead orcs over and were grunting to each other. The Second Orion pulled the Bluetooth device from the broken necked orc's ear, sniffed it, and let out a small grunt before tossing it to the side.

As though responding, the First Orion echoed the grunt. It pulled a knife from the orc that Ben had not seen, then gave a hoot and a grunt.

The Second Orion went to the orc's hip to pull a knife from its scabbard. It grunted twice, and tossed that scabbard dagger to the first. Then, it pulled the sword free from the limp body and gave two quick hoots.

The First Orion stood up, knife in hand and swung it back and forth as it recovered the knife tossed its way.

His conjurations' actions gave Ben goose bumps. He inched toward them, recognizing what they were doing. "No. Flipping. Way."

Between the grunts and different weapon choices, Ben realized these gorillas were not two versions of Orion working in unison, but two entirely different beings, communicating about what could be worthwhile.

They were looting the bodies.

Ben closed his mouth. "Amazing." He motioned toward the two as they swapped bodies and continued their search. He asked Tex. "Has anything like this ever been documented before now?"

"No." Tex shook its head. It moved to Ben, arcing wide and away from the gorillas. "I don't have record of anyone being able to cast red creatures."

"What? No, I meant the looting?" Ben considered Tex's response. Besides his red gorillas and Jack's purple one, all summoned creatures were supposed to be green. What had changed? For a moment, Ben wondered how the tablets were able to tap into the emerald power.

Elder Komir had gifted him a reserve of the red magic. The Argosian font of power in his chest. That's what changed. A jubilant rumble filled his heart and lungs. He wanted to roar in happiness that he actually belonged to a color of magic.

The quiet and cold smell of steel pressing in around him tamped his enthusiasm. This was not the time to yell in celebration. Later. He'd celebrate later.

The gorilla with the knives sniffed at the gun on the dead orc's hip.

Its fingers looked too thick to fit all the way into the trigger guard, but the tip could pull the trigger. If it did, shots would sound and ruin Ben's plan for stealth.

Ben froze and prepared to dismiss both of the gorillas.

Seemingly aware of his thoughts, the gorilla looked at Ben. Something—Ben couldn't quite put his finger on what—exchanged between them. The Orion then batted the gun away with an uninterested grunt.

The second gave a similar grunt before doing the same.

Appreciation spread a smile across Ben's lips. "They just read my intentions."

Tex asked, "How do you know?"

"I felt the first one acknowledge my concern about the guns." Feeling as though someone watched him, Ben checked behind him. Nothing. His smiled broadened further when he figured out how. "He used the Conjurer's Link as a guide."

"Oh." Tex had a way of turning away that showed its total disinterest in the conversation. The robot did it now. It extended its eye sockets. "Since we're looting, their rings are magical."

Each gorilla lifted a hand and a sliver glint played on the thumb.

Ben asked, "You can detect magic?"

Tex's eye sockets twisted as they retracted. "Did you even touch the owner's manual?"

Each gorilla tossed a ring at Ben. He picked up the first one with a nod to the gorilla with the sword. "Thank you, Slash." Ben picked up the second ring and nodded to the knife-wielding gorilla. "Thank you, Slice."

They hooted softly at him.

Tex turned back to give Ben an apprising stare.

Ben defended his naming convention with a slight shrug. "What? They're obviously not Orion."

Tex gave a passing gesture toward them. "So you named them Slash and Slice?"

"They feel like verbs." Ben gave another a shrug. "How about Abe and Oscar?"

Tex went to the edge of the row to keep a look out. "Your conjurations. Your call."

Not sure how longsword-wielding Abe and knife-wielding Oscar would last, Ben started the group toward the main building.

Chapter Twenty-Seven

HOOTING AND LOOTING

THOUGH THEY HADN'T RUN into any further opposition, they maintained their system. Tex scouted, next—knives at the ready—Oscar walked in front of Ben, and Abe brought up the rear.

Hunkered down behind the final row of cars before the long gap of desert hardpan to Meadows Towing auto shop garages, Ben noted the silence and succulent smell of bacon before peeking at the building through gaps in the crushed cars.

The doors to the five car bays were closed. Darkness lay beyond the two large kitchen windows. *Elf Sight* functioned well under the stars, but would be useless inside the pitch-black building where the raining starlight couldn't splash.

Ben whispered, "The place seems too quiet."

Peering at the building, Tex matched the hushed down and agreed. "Yup, and no boars, either."

Guessing at the source of the delicious smell, Ben replied. "We probably won't see any."

Tex asked, "What makes you say that?"

Ben took in the scent again. "You don't smell the bacon?"

"I don't have a nose, Ben. Remember?" Tex gave an annoyed tap at the space between his eye sockets and mouth-shaped speaker box. As

Ben started to feel silly for asking, the corners of Tex's lips kicked up to a smile. "Still, this smells like a trap."

Keeping his eyes on the building, Ben's finger tapped on the screen from memory to cue *Soul Sight*. He glanced at the slider, moved the range to six hundred feet, and narrowed his eyes.

Two things were wrong with his Anvilsmith. First, it showed him having eighty-nine arcane watts. *Pop* usually cost twenty, now—like the others—it cost much less. Even the cued *Soul Sight* typically cost five, but the indicator under the aura-like *Cast* icon showed *-1*.

He still couldn't figure out why everything suddenly became cheaper and more powerful. Pressing *Cast*, Ben gave a dismissive grunt. He'd figure it out later.

The device gave the lame-duck vibration then magic gently pulsed into his eyes.

Contemplating making his entrance through the door leading into the customer service area, Ben focused his spell to get a hint of what waited for him inside.

The last row of wrecked cars faded from view, leaving a vague outline marking where they were. Like he had x-ray vision, Ben could see the building through the cars. Then, as he focused on each wall in the building, they faded to outlines as his spell penetrated further, and further.

Large and purple, the only soul in range—the Krotosian—paced the room on the second floor. Ben couldn't help but wonder if it had picked up the turkey leg or left it to rot.

Elder Komir had said Master Reynolds would know what to do, what the key looked like. She also said that the Krotosian would probably be wearing it. In thinking about what he, not Master Reynolds, had to do, Ben found he'd moved so his elbows were at his side and his forearms formed a tight protective x across his chest.

The memory of Penelope trying to cover the multitude of various bruises and wounds on her arms and face with her blood-matted hair came into his mind's eye. He recalled the multiple rings of rope burns around her wrists. She didn't say, but he knew they had bound her hands together, hung her from the hook in the TV room, and beat her. They had been willfully able to viciously harm her. Heck, they probably considered it entertainment.

If he were to fail, Ben figured that he'd somehow be subjected to even worse brutalities and no one would be coming for him.

Oscar pulled on Ben's shoulder. The knife-wielding gorilla gave him three soft hoots. Giving two similar hoots, Abe bumped him from behind.

Almost forgetting they were there—surprised they hadn't winked out—Ben nodded to them. He had to do this or The Node would be destroyed or—as they said in the Beakless Griffin—controlled by a darker magic.

Ben set his jaw and scanned the building one more time.

The Krotosian still paced alone, but when he turned… When he turned, a small red light—the Node Key, it had to be the Node Key—lay on his wrist.

"Once we get through the service door, Tex, I want you to go to the far stairs and see what is up there." Ben nodded to Oscar and Abe with a determined grin. "We'll take care of the ogre magi."

Tex and the gorillas nodded back.

Ben glanced up at the distant stars raining light. He drew a deep breath of the bacon-slathered air. Striving to ignore it, Ben focused past the smells of cooking and neglected metal to get at the underlying desert air, and made a mental note to—after tonight—stop and appreciate the simple things in life.

"On three." His nerves bundled up in his guts. Fear threatened to arrest his body. A small part of him wanted to slink away. This Node business—this crazy, *crazy* ogre-fighting Node business—should be handled by his Master. Not him.

Gathering his courage, Ben counted, "One… two…

Chapter Twenty-Eight

INTO THE FRAY

"THREE."

Oscar went around the corner.

Heart pounding, Ben pushed through his mounting terror. He rounded the edge of wrecked cars. The smell of bacon smacked him. The silence felt deeper. The building appeared taller. Darker. His legs full of lead as his feet slapped hard to cross the long open space to Meadows Towing.

A quarter of the way across the clearing, his body got on board with his mind and loosened up.

A third of the way across the clearing, the Krotosian stopped pacing and turned their direction.

Halfway across the clearing, the five bay doors shot up with a rattling bang as though their counterbalances had broken. Starlight splashed just inside the darkened entrances, showing an orc at the mouth of each bay. Braced against their hips, a submachine gun.

Ben's bowels liquefied. His cheeks clenched to keep his poop in. He froze.

Oscar stopped, shifted his body and shielded Ben.

Muzzles flashed as gunfire cracked in small, controlled bursts.

A tapping lit on Ben's leg like he'd been hit by low-speed

paintballs. Before his eyes, another tap pressed his slacks against his leg as a small, flattened, piece of metal fell from where he had been hit.

The locket around his neck warmed against his skin. More bullets—I should be Swiss cheese—squished flat against an invisible barrier before falling around his feet.

A mist—blood—came from Oscar's shoulders and sprinkled his face. Ben wiped and gawked at the crimson on his fingers.

Conjurations don't—weren't supposed to—bleed.

Ben's lips tightened. His nostrils flared. His brow knitted as he glared at the orcs. Argosian energy poured from him into the spell card. Gorilla after gorilla appeared next to the orcs in the bay.

Oscar had dropped to a knee after Ben had cast his second one.

The locket around his neck began to rise in temperature. A part of him equated it to how many more bullets pelted him.

Ben cast two more gorillas before feeling the dark energy in his brain start to press for release. The sinister energy abated when Oscar fell, but came right back banging at Ben's mental doors when he cast a fifth gorilla to engage the last orc.

The locket burned against his skin.

Ben yanked his tie loose, ripped the top of his shirt open, and stared at the Komir's talisman.

A purple flash lit around him, washing the world in an arcane glow.

The locket—fixed fire—lay one button lower, pressed against his skin. Trying to get at it, Ben stumbled.

A flash of purple lit behind him.

Ben spun.

Dirt filled the air as though something had shot at him from the roof of the building.

Remembering the Krotosian, Ben spun again.

A secondary effect from having both Soul Sight and Elf Sight going at the same time lit the ogre magi's form at the edge of the roof, making the creature a bright purple beacon against the raining starlight. Its body looked like an eldritch, stained-glass figure moving behind a thin waterfall.

As though in slow motion, Ben could see the magic happen.

Krotosian energy wavered in the center of the ogre's body,

undulating from its core. The knotted violet mass rolled as a part of it slid up to the ogre's left shoulder, pulsed there for a moment, then dropped down to its hand to pulse again. A third pulse lit the ogre's hand before the purple energy fluttered to full intensity. Finally—flashing bright enough to be seen by Ben's natural vision—the Krotosian caster's hand hooked forward as it hurled another magic blast at him.

Seeing it coming, Ben kept his eyes on the ogre and ran his fingers along his cardholder. He stopped on the fourth SD card. Instead of pulling his *Shield* spell to slap it into his Anvilsmith, Ben channeled Argosian energy into it.

Where his tablet would normally make a physical green shield appear on his arm, the standard minty smell filled his nose, but no shield appeared. Mercifully, the burning locket on his chest cooled. Though there hadn't been a physical manifestation of the *Shield* spell, two years of combat practice made Ben's arm go up to block the incoming blast.

The purple energy dissipated against his forearm.

No impact. Weird. The locket on his chest started to heat up—the talisman pulled energy from his Argosian font—before cooling again. Aware, Ben felt the gorillas pull power from him, too, using him as a source to stay active.

The strain of power flowing through him from his dwindling Argosian reserve made a vein on his forehead.

Not having to move his arm to block incoming blasts, Ben tapped *Spells, Evocation,* then *Missile.* He aimed, and pressed *Cast.*

The Anvilsmith vibrated, lit green, before giving a slight kick as the bolt of emerald energy flew from his tablet.

It struck the purple stained-glass ogre, and pushed it away from the edge.

The Krotosian came back, then toppled over the ledge.

Victorious, Ben pumped his fist. "Yes!" A part of him—*too easy*—marveled at the violet body wreathed—*way too easy*—in green energy. The angle of the fall seemed off. A trick of the light, or magic—

Ben's eyes widened.

Flying, the Krotosian barreled at him.

Ben dove.

The ogre blew past in a powerful rush of air.

Like the *Shield* spell, the locket gave him protection in a casting duel, but, also like *Shield* spell, would probably be useless against physical assault.

Ben wanted to cast another gorilla, but five proved to be his limit and they were still engaged with the orcs.

The dark energy in his mind brimmed, offering full access to its untapped stores.

Recalling the teeth and shadowy form looming over Jack—and even more so his inability completely control the magic—Ben shook his head against the Nilosian energy.

The ogre looped and barreled through the air at him again.

Faking left, Ben dove right.

The ogre blew past again. Closer this time making his coat flap.

Ben tapped *Cast* three times.

The spell was cued. The tablet vibrated.

Ready for the kick, Ben grinned at the Krotosian.

The ogre spun in mid-air, turned to face Ben, and swiped his hand through the air three times. The lump of purple energy traveled from its gut to its shoulder, then to its hand.

Each motion caused the Anvilsmith to emit an annoying buzz as the spell's energy fizzled.

Ben's breath caught in his throat.

Eyes aglow with violet energy, the ogre landed, sneering its black teeth at Ben.

Fear grabbed a hard hold of Ben's guts and gave them a cruel shake. Again, he thought of the sinister teeth that had bit Jack. Then, he recalled how Jack had screamed as though his soul had been rendered.

Ben took a step back.

The ogre's derisive grin widened.

The fear that had taken hold of Ben's stomach branched out into his limbs telling him to *run*. To *get to safety.*

He'd heard of nullifying another caster's spell by channeling energy into the same spell, and focusing on canceling the magic, but no one ever wasted power on counter-spelling. In tournaments, you were always better served casting your own spell than to sap the opponent's energy.

Ready to counter-spell again, the ogre's lips peeled back further and it chomped at the air. It gave another predator's grin as it stalked toward Ben, salivating as it carefully started to close the distance to its prey.

Hoping to be faster, Ben tapped *Cast* again.

Purple energy moved up through the ogre's body and sucked the green from his tablet.

Taking another step back, Ben gained a new understanding of counter-spelling. In tournaments, if both casters ran out of energy, the match would be declared a draw.

This wasn't a tourney.

Ben didn't have to reach far to guess the hulking monster's tactic was to run him out of energy, then beat him to a bloody pulp—like it had Penelope—with its massive fists.

A vision of himself, hands bound, hanging from the hook like a punching bag rolled through his head.

Ben shook the image away. He wasn't going to let that happen, but how to stop it?

The Nilosian energy swam frantic circles in his head. At the ready. Looping.

Ben tightened his grip on the Orion spellcard. The Nilosian energy knew the path from his brain, down his arm, and into the card, but waited. He just had to release it.

The Krotosian lifted from the ground. It must've sensed the coming change of spells. Charging, it growled.

Ben turned the energy loose.

It flashed down his arm and sizzled into the spell card. There, the Nilosian energy didn't flash black in his hand. No, more to the point, it absorbed raining starlight in the area around him and plunged Ben into darkness.

Chapter Twenty-Nine

WAKING THE BEAST

UNLIKE THE ARTIFICIAL, uninvolved feeling of casting through a tablet or having to tap into the Argosian energy in his chest, Ben found focusing Nilosian energy from his mind into the card felt graceful. No. *Natural*.

Roaring into being, Bastion, a pitch black, nine-foot-tall four-armed gorilla, materialized next to him. A sour smell—spoiled milk—filled Ben's nose

The raining starlight returned, lighting the desert earth around him. For an exhilarated moment, Ben thought they had teleported outside Meadows Towing to safety. Then the first row of stacked, decimated cars came into view.

His thoughts turned to the ogre a split-second before it rammed into him.

Pain shot through Ben's chest. His wind exploded from his mouth.

The ogre's massive teal arms grabbed him. Squeezed him.

Hairy black arms wrapped the teal set.

The pressure lessened. Then Ben fell and hit the ground.

Snarls of the two large monsters flew on.

Blurred into one, earth and sky flip-flopped positions. Ben tumbled. The spinning horizon slowed. He came to a stop. Dizzied, he got to his knees, rocking from the continual motion in his inner ear.

"Have to recover." Ben pulled his tablet and jabbed. His finger missed the enchantment icon by millimeters on one side, then again on the second poke.

The two writhing masses of muscle struggled against each other.

Ben found tenuous equilibrium in rocking with the sway. *Got it.* His enchantment icons spread out on the screen. He ran his finger along the edge as a guide and tapped Heracles.

Recovering, Ben got to his feet.

The world leaned hard.

He leaned with it and pulled back at the last second to keep from falling over.

Seemingly wise to his attempt to balance, the world lurched the opposite direction.

From the corner of his right eye, Ben kept trying to use the Meadows Towing sign as a needle to gauge when he neared level or reached a tipping point.

He'd never find balance that way. Ben closed his eyes.

The world gave a wild buck.

Ben lowered his shoulder and swung his head the opposite way. *Even.*

The following lurches were now manageable.

He kept his focus on Bastion, the dark body in the rapidly shifting black-and-teal yinyang-ish dog-fight.

The ogre planted a foot, twisted, and heaved.

Thrown, Bastion traveled in a high arc.

Ben pressed cast. The tablet vibrated. Green energy flashed past the ogre and lit Bastion. Bastion's hair and eyes turned green as it crashed into the ground.

The ogre uttered a grunting laugh.

Ben's eyes widened.

With a grenade launcher braced on his hip, the ogre grinned like a wickedly deranged clown.

He's going to shoot.

In the vague background beyond the ogre, the hulking darkness—Bastion—got to his feet.

Ben reached out for the conjurer's bond to control Bastion, to have him do anything to help, and found a deeper connection. Disturbingly, Ben felt a union with the bestial, four-armed gorilla.

Counter to everything Ben knew about having total control of conjurations, Bastion—in the form of a slight pull on the link between them—invited Ben into it.

Thunk! A grenade wound toward him.

Forgetting about ducking, Ben winced and rode the bond into Bastion.

From Bastion's tall point of view—a good four feet higher—Ben blinked their conjoined eyes in surprise at his vanished body. *Their eyes?*

Yes.

Though Bastion didn't speak, a rough understanding donned on Ben. They occupied the same body, the same mind, but had different souls. Either one of them could give control to the other—or steal it away.

Through Bastion's senses they could smell decaying bodies under the heady bacon smell. They could hear the orcs and gorilla shuffle, struggle, and fight. The hair all over their body registered the northwest wind whistling through the scrapyard.

His Anvilsmith thumped to the earth.

The grenade flew just over the collar of the trench coat where Ben's head had been. Its riotous impact ejected shrapnel from the end of a column of cars causing the length to screech and careen.

His coat dropped to the earth covering the rest of his school uniform.

Taking control of Bastion, Ben rushed the ogre.

Spinning, it's teal index flexed on the trigger. *Thunk!*

Ben rolled to the left.

The grenade whizzed by. A dull explosion sounded behind them.

Again, the ogre's finger pulled the trigger.

Bastion pressed their four arms down. Ben recruited their powerful legs. Together, they leapt the next shot.

The ogre raised the gun toward their chest.

They were on the Krotosian.

Controlling the lower set of arms, Ben gripped the launcher, turned it away, and yanked it from the monster's hands.

Thunk! Air from the shot puffed along their gut as the grenade whistled away.

The upper set of hands—controlled by Bastion—slipped under the thick chin to wrap around the Krotosian's muscular neck.

The ogre grabbed hold of the thumbs around its neck. Leapt to plant the feet on the end of its short legs onto their torso. It extended, pulled at the thumbs to peel their grip, and started to fly away.

No! Ben took control of the upper arms and leapt after it. He caught a hold of the ogre's ankle.

In charge of the lower arms, Bastion released the weapon.

Relief washed briefly over Ben when the beast released the launcher, fading at the realization that Bastion wanted to beat and eat the monster that lorded over Meadows Towing.

Bastion tried to climb the ogre's leg.

The ogre kicked them in the face.

The impact rocked their head back. No pain. Ben kept a grip on the Krotosian.

The ogre strained as they started to descend.

Must be too much weight.

The Krotosian's purple eyes glowered. Ready to kick again, it stared down its leg.

Bastions' toes, then whole feet, touched earth.

"By Demitria!" The ogre's deep voice rumbled. "You and your family are going to be bloodspots!"

As soon as Bastions full weight registered on the earth, Ben yanked. The ogre crashed at their feet.

It made eye contact. "You hear me in there, Ben?"

How'd it know his name?

Spittle flew from its mouth as its voice turned into a growling howl. "Bloodspots!"

Bastion leapt on it.

Trying to break its jaw, Ben swung their massive fist.

The scowling, black-toothed ogre's head turned to mist. Its violet eyes seemed to smile as the rest of its body followed suit.

Their fist wafted through. Ben relented full control to Bastion. He needed to think.

What would happen now? Was he stuck in this body? Would his just reappear when he tried to return?

Still trying to get at the ogre through its gaseous form, Bastion tromped and stomped. Unsuccessful at striking the fog, the large, four-armed gorilla switched to trying to disperse it.

Mostly undisturbed, the fog remained in the same relative loose form, as it crept across the scrapyard toward the building.

They neared his trench coat. The orb lay in the right pocket of Ben's coat, but Bastion's hands were too large to retrieve it.

With Bastion's lower arms, Ben lifted his coat.

Something akin to the initial understanding between them flashed. In it, Bastion acknowledged his plan and relented completely.

Bastion's body winked from existence.

Ben found his feet exactly where Bastion's had been. Komir's necklace, and the cool night air, pressed on his bare chest.

Sparse as always, the arm hairs on his mystically pumped arms were like thin emerald grass. The Heracles spell he had cast on Bastion remained active on him. The feeling of union... Where he and Bastion one in the same?

Ben scooped his coat, fished the Encapsulating Orb from his inner pocket, and pushed it into the fog.

Nothing happened.

He focused on the sphere to activate it. Nothing.

The fog kept rolling.

Rolling the orb in his hands, Ben lagged a step behind the Krotosian mist.

A gorilla hooted.

Ben surveyed the work bays. Two of his gorillas had managed to subdue their orcs while three stood over motionless bodies—heads either smashed or grotesquely askew.

He dismissed the idle gorillas.

As though it could tell Ben had power available to him, the Encapsulating Orb sucked at his hands.

Ben eased Argosian magic into it.

The metal sphere flashed red. Then shone a translucent silver with a liquid, mercury-like core.

Given the name Elder Komir called it, Ben figured it would only be a capturing device. Powered, the item imparted its true name—Imprisoning Orb—and abilities as a mystical prison. It wanted the user to know what the subject would go through.

Any creature tapped within would cease to age, but would be keenly aware of its surroundings. It would know the passing of time. Feel hunger. Crave drink. Slowly go mad from never-ending starvation, thirst, and loneliness.

The fog stopped and started to pool.

With full understanding of what the ogre would have to suffer through, Ben paused. Cruel and unusual punishment couldn't hold a candle to this.

Glowering violet eyes started to form in mist.

Recalling what the ogre had said. *You and your family are going to be bloodspots! You hear me in there, Ben? Bloodspots!* Ben targeted the Krotosain with the orb and willed it to act.

In a snap, like watching video of someone exhaling smoke in reverse, the sphere sucked in all the fog.

The quarter-sized sphere expanded to the size of a softball. Along with the growth in size, the hollow-feeling orb took on the mass of a solid, steel object and started to thump in his grip.

Could the ogre be throwing itself around inside?

"You might want to hold it with both hands." Tex came from the building to stand next to him. "Your Heracles spell is about to end."

Using both hands, Ben held the orb comfortably close to his body. With pulsing thwacks, like the high-speed automatic pitcher at batting cages, the sphere spat out various items

First out, in rapid succession, three throwing knives. The grenade launcher followed. Two solid silver rings. A baton. A thick leather belt with a thicker, star-embossed plate buckle.

It stopped. *Was it over?*

A pounding from within the orb nearly wrenched it free from his grip.

Ben struggled to hold it.

A flittering golden object wrapped in Argosian energy—*the Node Key, has to be*—arced to the ground.

Chapter Thirty

TEXAS & THE NODE KEY

THE NIGHT BREEZE against his back, a building desire in his gut for a BLT, Ben leaned to examine the last item ejected from the Imprisoning Orb.

Quite fittingly, the Node Key turned out to be a skeleton key, just like in the old movies. In the base of the golden handle, a faintly pink gem lent an aesthetic balance to the two, thick, v-shaped teeth on the opposite end.

Breath hitched in his chest, Ben hoped it would disappear from here to appear wherever it belonged.

It didn't.

He closed his eyes and tried to will it to happen.

No such luck.

He'd give it some time.

As he waited for it to vanish, a warm pulse pushed into the base of his skull. Feeling like he was being watched, Ben checked over his left shoulder. The two gorillas kept the orcs in check. Over his right, only row and rows of wrecks out into the distance.

The feeling—not so different than what he felt from his fellow students when he took his time to decide what he wanted for lunch at the APA—wanted him to do something. Anything.

The annoyed patience was coming from the key.

More of a sound than a word, "Huh," escaped Ben's lips.

To his side, Tex's optics whirled and clicked to full extension before retracting with a slap. A series of small pops sounded from Ben's companion.

Ben turned.

The tiny robot's sockets went dark and it fell over. Emerald smoke, the same green as the energy in his tablet, seeped from Tex's seams.

A sudden fear—*Master Reynolds is going to revoke my gifts*—widened Ben's eyes. In the hierarchy of worst things to happen to gifts in the first week, ruining them placed slightly lower than outright losing them. "Tex?"

Ben thought the car held top spot as his favorite of the trio of gifts, but seeing his companion laying there fried, dormant, and smoking, told him otherwise. More than losing a possession, Tex's burning out weighed on his heart.

Setting the Imprisoning Orb down, Ben reached to lift Tex.

As his arms went out, the crystal at the end of the Node Key shimmered with intense sparkles.

It stole his full attention.

Everything else in the world, Tex, the gorillas, the orcs, the scrapyard, and even the Imprisoning Orb with the murderous Krotosian captured within, faded from his mind.

Using both hands, Ben lifted the key from the ground with great care.

His left hand shone red, radiating Argosian energy, while his right lay within dark Nilosian magic, anti-shining with equaled strength.

The two energies in him cajoled, begged, and demanded to be released into the key.

What Ben *should* do conflicted with what he *wanted* to do. The key had belonged to the Argosians, but the black Nilosian energy had a natural ease and flow. The Komirs had lost the key to the ogre, and he had won it from the monster. An almost alien part of him supposed that if the Argosians were strong enough in the first place, they would've kept control of the key instead of letting it fall into the Krotosian's hands.

A soft smile spread Ben's lips as he recalled learning how to channel energy atop the Suntouched Spire with Elder Komir. As though smacked away, the smile died at the vivid memory of Kograkken's sudden backhand. The giant's damning accusation —*Nilosian!*—overpowered the fond, spire-top recollection.

Ben frowned. The giant being right was worse than him being a Nilosian. He looked to the full moon and asked, "Why'd it have to be black magic?"

Distant and indiscriminant, the moon shone on.

The struggle to do what he should instead of what he wanted lessened. He'd gotten the key from the Krotosian. If the Komirs wanted to change the magic once he returned the key, that was on them.

Ben tucked the Node Key into his right coat pocket and channeled the dark, natural feeling, energy into it.

Putting the coat on properly, he buttoned it, and stood barefoot—in what his mother called *nature-feet*—on the hard earth. Leaving the grenade launcher where it lay, he picked up the knives, rings, and baton and stashed them in his inner pockets.

Lifting the heavy belt, Ben admired the star—identical to the Meadows Towing sign—on the belt buckle. He flipped the belt over his shoulder and lifted the Imprisoning Orb.

Tex's optics twisted.

Ben turned.

Rocking slightly, his companion sat up. Focused on either the orb or the belt, Ben wasn't sure, Tex's optics whirled once then went back to their default length. "What is that?"

Ben's gaze went to the building, glancing over the five work bays to take in the overall size of the two-story building. With proper management, this place could really be something. He had heard of winning possessions during a duel, but no one had ever said stuff like this happened.

Since they'd already talked about the orb earlier, Ben patted the belt as he looked at the Meadows Towing sign with a smiling sense of ownership. "A trophy."

Tex climbed up his coat, grabbing both coat and flesh beneath to steady itself.

Ben winced as it ascended. The short must have damaged the robot's motor control or pressure setting.

Tex plopped down on his other shoulder. "I have been here before."

"Yes, Tex." Ben sighed his relief and patted his companion. "We have."

"Tex. I like that name. Is it mine?"

Holding his composure, Ben pressed his lips together to keep from showing disappointment. His companion had been reset all the way back to factory default. Would any of the old Tex, the one that had decided not to be overridden, still be in there? A ghost program maybe? Would the new Tex do the same? "It's short for Texas."

"I like Tex better."

Ben walked toward the gorillas and orcs in the work bays.

Tex asked, "What is your name, Master?"

Ben sighed at having to go through the imprinting process again. Memory of the former Tex brought a small, fond smile to his face. He'd make a concerted effort to not be sarcastic this time around. "I am Benjamin Baxter."

Chapter Thirty-One

(IN) THE END

BEN STOPPED short of entering the concrete work bays. Dark splotches crisscrossed the ground. Whether they were blood or marks from mechanic work, he didn't know. Either way, he made sure not step in any of it. The smell of old motor oil overtook the bacon aromas that had been stirring his hunger and barely covered the rotten smell from the kitchen.

Metal clinks, like wind chimes made of steel called his attention. At the feet of one of his red gorillas, wrapped from neck to ankles in chains, an orc fretted. Worry lines wrinkled its wide forehead and its wide-set eyes focused on the other conscious orc.

Curling his toes on the packed earth, Ben recalled a lesson from his mother in their garden. *Squeeze the earth, ease the tension.* It wasn't working. He turned his attention to the other orc.

Ben's other remaining gorilla held a bearded orc with its arms pinned up behind his head in a full-nelson. Both orcs wore white t-shirts and jeans. The bearded one had a Meadows Towing star ironed on over its heart.

The bearded orc bowed its head to avoid eye contact.

Still, Ben asked, "Do you speak English?"

The orc shifted its eyes to Ben's bare feet.

Ben eyed the other bound in chains. "Do you?"

It also trained its eyes on his feet.

When Ben would look at one, it would lower its eyes while the other would look at him and vice versa.

Even more annoying was not knowing if they were both male or only the one with the beard. Ben had heard some races were extremely androgynous. Could orcs be one of those races? His lips drew up and kinked with frustration. He pulled the Anvilsmith, pressed *Options* then *Translate*. Ben tapped English and scanned for a moment before finding *Orcish*. "Do you guys understand this?"

The tablet barked out a few harsh syllables.

The orcs looked to each other and back to him. Their eyes betrayed their surprise before they nodded.

The bearded one looked up a bit, but kept its eyes focused below Ben's knees. It barked a short response then let loose a string of rattling consonants.

His device had yet to start translating, but Ben picked out the words *Might-Fist* from the previous translation. "We do. If you spare our lives now, Might-Fist, we shall shed them at your whim. We will not fail you as we did Flayer Ur-Krurk."

"Ur-Krurk," Ben repeated. "The ogre?"

The bearded orc nodded.

In his head, the Nilosian energy—Bastion—looped rapid infinity symbols. It liked being called *Might-Fist* and, to a certain extent, Ben understood why. They had defeated the Krotosian, and now all of its possessions transferred to them. It only made sense the orcs would swear allegiance to the new Might-Fist.

Bastion's elated desire proved highly infectious.

Having henchmen, in addition to controlling Meadows Towing, brought a broad grin to Ben's face.

The chained orc mewed something, which, without being translated, sounded like a heavily accented, "Let us live."

A surge of disgust bled through from Bastion and filled Ben with a firmly set disdain for the creature begging for its life. Ben pointed his tablet at the bound orc while his other hand hovered over *Cast*.

Bastion urged Ben to channel its Nilosian power to obliterate the whiner.

Ben nodded to the empathetic union-link. Toneless words—part his, mostly Bastion's—poured from his mouth. "All weakness needs to be culled."

He let the Nilosian energy travel down his arm.

Darkness engulfed his hand on the tablet, waiting to be channeled into the device. Impatient, it sizzled and flickered, sucking light from the area with each quick pulse.

The orc mewed. "I did not want to fight."

Ben spoke. His words whistled through clenched teeth. "Oh, now you speak English."

The bearded orc spoke in even tones. "Kill us or draft us. Don't allow that goblin turd to beg." It spat on the other orc. "You're skin-shame!"

"Of course, you both speak English." Ben's Anvilsmith pinged, letting him know a translation of the term was available for him to read, but orc calling the other a *goblin turd* gave the gist of *skin-shame* without it.

"I'll take a blood-oath." The whiner stopped and started to nod. "I'm a shaman. Let me serve."

"Skin-shame! Twice more!" The bearded orc fought against the gorilla. Not prepared for the violent shift, the orc slipped free and a muted *thunk* sounded when its steel-toe cracked the other's jawbone.

Both gorillas tackled the bearded one to the concrete floor.

Pinned, the bearded orc rebuked the self-proclaimed shaman further, "Why not offer up your anus, Toad?"

The graphic insult jarred Ben's senses as a disgusted shudder rose up his spine. Whatever blasé haze that had a firm hold of him—driving him to kill the orc—vanished. Aware, he wondered how long had he been contemplating murder.

Though disgust still filled Bastion, the energy's disappointment at the lost opportunity ceased sizzling as the darkness crept back up his arm to return to its roost.

Ben made note to be extra mindful in distinguishing his feelings from Bastion's. Ben pointed to the three bodies. "Can you heal them, Toad?"

The shaman nodded emphatically. "If they're not dead."

Ben directed the gorilla to free the orc.

Toad went to the first body and pulled a knife.

Ben tensed.

Kneeling next to the fallen orc, it slid the blade across its own chest, cutting shirt and skin.

Not having a system to track the Argosian energy, Ben blinked as his two conjurations vied for what remained of the dwindling red energy. Ben suppressed a gasp as the chain-holding gorilla disappeared.

Toad threw his blade next to Ben's feet. It then removed a ring. The orc's pale outline appeared.

Ben had forgotten about his active spells.

Toad's ring sang along the concrete as it slid toward Ben. "I am bonded."

The second orc whispered, "I'll blood-oath."

Ben turned. He raised his eyebrows to the orc. "What about *your* anus?"

Its eyes dropped, searching its soul for what it would do to keep its life.

Chuckling, Ben extended his hands. "I kid. I kid."

The gorilla let go of one of the bearded orc's arms.

The orc drew the blade from its hip scabbard.

Ben's Argosian reserve ran dry. The last gorilla disappeared.

Glancing to where the gorilla had been, the bearded orc nodded once as though he and Ben had come to some kind of unspoken agreement. "You will not regret this." It put its blade away without doing the blood-oath. "I give my word as my bond."

Ben extended his hand further. "The ring?"

"It protects from divination." The orc removed the ring. Its pale aura appeared. "Might-Fist, if I flip the ring to up-end Ur-Krurk's symbol, may I still wear it?"

Remembering how Chrystal had not seen all what the scrapyard had for defense, Ben nodded to the tactical advantage the magic ring provided. He picked up the ring at his feet and noted the small crossed-axes insignia.

Ben turned to study the shaman's aura as it worked on the injured orc. It deepened to blue as it wiped its palms on the chest wound, coating its hands with blood. Except for the shaman's hands, the cobalt blue aura faded to gray. The bloody hands were aglow with the new blue energy—*how many colors of magic were there?* Ben wondered—when the shaman pressed his hands to the motionless orc. The energy poured into the body.

The orc groaned and sputtered shallow breaths.

Pointing to the last fallen orc, whose body lay chest down with its head facing up, Toad looked to Ben. "That one is beyond my magic."

THOUGH HIS HANDS still sort of ached from the boat work on the other side, Ben wanted to help bury the dead. He'd been responsible for taking their lives, he would take the blisters from working the shovel.

As they worked, the four living orcs grumbled their dissent, stating the dead's family would come for final rights. The orcs looked to one another, uncomfortable with meeting the shaman's eyes.

Toad shifted in place before stepping away to point at the belt slung over Ben's shoulder. "You act with honor, but have not donned the belt." The shaman rubbed its bloody chest.

Ben braced for a charge or a challenge. His Anvilsmith still had plenty of juice.

Toad continued, "My blood-oath is only to the rightful Might-Fist."

Ben took a few steps back, putting twenty feet—the minimal distance for a proper spell duel—between himself and the shaman. Though Bastion lay quiet, the Nilosian energy in his head began to boil. Ben's brow furrowed and his fingers ran across his SD cardholder. Two fingers came to rest on *Orion*, and one on *Shield*. "So you figure you can take it from me and claim the title for yourself?"

Extending both hands, palms out in a slow, non-threatening motion, Toad broke eye contact. The shaman focused his vision on the ground between them. "No. Not at all, but if you do not put the belt on, my blood-oath, and those bound by my blood, is null." Toad motioned to the two who he had healed. "If you refuse, we can leave when the sun rises."

Astonished Ben frown undid itself. "Why are you telling me this? You all could be free."

Toad kept his motions small and slow. "The Century of Shadows is coming, and serving a Nilosian is our only chance of surviving."

Ben bristled at indirectly being called a Nilosian. Though true enough, it didn't take away the socially programed inner-shame.

Toad continued, "You are the first human Nilosian we have seen."

Ben tightened at *Nilosian* again, but not quite as hard this time.

"You say we could be free, but life for an orc is never that simple." Toad motioned to the orcs and pointed to the belt again. "We serve the strongest. We have always served the strongest. You have proven to be the strongest here. You are human, and humans are rumored to reward loyalty." Again, the orcs nodded along with the shaman who bowed his head. "We want to be rewarded."

While Ben hadn't planned to put the belt on, he wondered how they could've not been rewarded before now. They must've been thanked before—even if in some weird ogre-ish custom. Then he recalled that there were four other bullet points under the Orcish words for shame-feast.

All four orcs looked at him with honest yearning.

Ben pulled the heavy belt from his shoulder. He ran his fingers over the large buckle, letting his fingertips explore the embossed grooves. He traced the star.

"I want to record this." Tex said, pinching him as it climbed down from his shoulder. "May I?"

"Yes, Tex." Ben held the buckle with both hands at shoulder height. The wide leather strap meant to go around him folded over its length on the ground. "Please do."

Tex backed up until he stood inline with the orcs. "Ready."

Ben wrapped the belt around his waist. Aside from it shrinking to fit him, nothing special happened. He shrugged at Toad. "It's on."

The relief amongst their faces was like finding out the hardest test of the school year was one of those trick quizzes where you only had to put your name on it.

Ben asked, "Better?"

Toad and the two he healed nodded. The bearded orc gave him a thumbs up.

ALMOST FOUR WEEKS had passed and the orcs had made serious

progress on cleaning the inside of the Meadows Towing building. Though the smell of rancid meat smothered in rotten cheese lingered, the sources had been mostly removed. Still, more years of crap had yet to be discarded. Clean as they might, nothing short of new carpet, tile, and paint would bring Meadows Towing's customer center back into acceptable standards.

Due to overwhelming homework, Ben chose late Saturday nights to visit. He'd have most of his weekend homework done and the orcs wouldn't be there to see him checking their paperwork.

Ben didn't want to sneak, but their arguments against his decision to shut down the chop shop arm of Meadows Towing made him suspicious. Their lives were easier when stolen cars were brought to them. Now they were busy doing legitimate tows.

He liked to think that without a place to unload, car theft across the Vegas Valley would drop.

Part of him wondered what the *Mystique* made the orcs look like as they serviced those who were not starwise. The same part of him wanted to take an orc to his parents' house to watch the mundane neighbors react.

Ben closed the filing cabinet, wrote the *Mystique* question at the bottom of his checklist, and continued his musings as he got back in his car.

Now, all he had to do was see if Pepperjacks had reopened so he could return the Node Key. Oddly, the supper club had been repaired, but remained closed with mystical barring like he'd never seen. Still, he'd drive by and check. Then he'd watch the recording on him becoming the first human Might-Fist of Meadows Towing before heading off to the Samhain festival.

Pleased as usual with his inspection, Ben started his car, and drove away with a smile. He began to plan the party for the orcs to reward their hard work and help them to celebrate Halloween...

...utterly unaware of the schemes being hatched behind his back to wrest control of Meadows Towing, steal the Node Key away, and end his life.

BOOK 2: SAMHAIN SHENANIGANS

Chapter One

SAMHAIN SHENANIGANS

BENJAMIN BAXTER TOOK A DEEP INHALATION. Even though the large starwise only parking lots were full, the distinct Samhain Festival buttered popcorn smell extended all the way out into starwise overflow parking amongst the mundanes—the magic-less.

He licked his lips, and flipped the switch to close his coverable top.

Thrilled cheers rose in the distance. A round of faint applause chased it across the parking lot. Wondering what trick had been performed, Ben turned his attention toward the lit entrance so far away beyond rows and rows of cars.

Hoping to catch some remnant of the prestige, his gaze crawled along the Ferris Wheel, the Thompson Twister, The Screaming Meemie, and the various tents that filled the span between the rides.

Nothing. He snapped his fingers at missing it. *Well, they'll be more performances. That's for sure.*

The simple red, white, and dark lights of the festival held his interest in a way that the millions of Las Vegas casino lights blinking for attention never could. Only the *click, click, click* of his closed convertible top gear over cranking pulled him from the momentary entrancement.

One of the largest gatherings for Samhain Shenanigans in the country, the festival pulled every student from the Vegas Valley and thousands of students from schools from nearby prefectures.

With all the practitioners here, I shouldn't be surprised that starwise parking is stuffed. Ben took a moment to center his red Archon Private Academy tie and got out of the car. He put on his tan A. P. A. trench coat to cover the huge star belt buckle of his Meadows Towing Might-Fist belt, and buttoned it closed.

He dusted one shoulder and then the other to activate a minor prestidigitation. A swift breeze whooshed down his body as the wrinkles in his clothes flattened out.

His mind went back to the popcorn. Every year, since he had the free first-year's serving, he wanted to get a bag, but had always opted for a hot pretzel, garlic cheese knots, or cotton candy.

Not this year.

This year he had a plan.

He'd do a few games to fill his pockets with prizes before grabbing a bag of the buttery good stuff and casually munch on it as he strolled through the festival. Then he'd return each of following nights through Halloween for more games and treats.

The keyword for this year's festival? Moderation. Slow and steady fun. Prolong the experience. Tonight would be great. Each night would be great so long as he stuck to his plan.

An odd tingling—*magic*—settled across his brow. A nearly overwhelming urge to take off his tie and leave it on his windshield washed over him and faded.

Ben scanned to find the source.

Two girls in Sunrise Mountain orange blazers, white blouses, and orange-and-white plaid skirts focused on him. One, dark haired, sported long pigtails. The other, a blonde, had her hair cut short like a pixie. Later than Ben to the first-night events, they'd had to park even further out in the mundane lot.

The brunette didn't have the thin orange tie to complete her school uniform. She locked eyes with him and moved to get closer.

Bastion—the monster locked away in Ben's head—roared and slammed into his temples. The beast tried to force its way through the bond that linked him and the monster together. It wanted to tear the girls apart.

Ben set his will against Bastion and wondered if he had been wearing one of the red, white, and black Samhain Shenanigans-logoed armbands to partake in the evening's school-pride scavenger hunt, would he still have been able to resist the girls' spell?

Bastion knocked around his head.

Denying the beast's horrible desire to materialize proved taxing. Ben gave a strained smile and frequent grimaces broke his grin. "Sorry, girls." He patted the part of his arm where the participation band would have been if he were in play. "But I'm not in on The Shenanigans."

The brunette gracefully slid to close on him.

Ben backed away.

She gave a momentary pout before flashing a flawless smile. "Can I have your tie anyway?"

He shrugged. "It wouldn't be worth any points."

Temptation dripped from her playful lips as her tongue ran between them. "Can't you imagine me with your tie on?"

The magical tingling on his brow came back strong before fading out again.

A vision of a girl wearing his school uniform came to mind, but not the temptress in front of him. In his vision, Penelope stood in Pepperjacks with his trench coat on. A sole lower button held it closed. Besides his tie, he didn't know what else she had on under the coat, but wanted to find out.

Bastion slammed his temples again.

Ben grimaced. He stopped nodding to his imagination and switched to shake his head. "No. No, sorry."

This time, her pout stuck and her blonde friend pulled her away. "Let's get to the big top." She gave Ben a playful sneer, the kind that causes those cute little nose wrinkles. "We're bound to find *friendly* casters there."

Even as she was being dragged away, the brunette steepened her hands and lipped, "Please."

Ben gave a regretful smile.

She turned and fell in stride with her friend. Their skirts swung in unison for a few seconds.

The tie and trench coat vision flashed again. It had been almost a month since his run-in with Penelope. Ever since then, the hot, raven-haired beauty from the other side had become a constant in his dreams. Except for this recent vision, the Dream-Penelope still wore burlap. The bruises and scabs were healed, but her cutting blue eyes kept their edge.

He hadn't even notice the color of the Sunrise girl's eyes.

Faintly, Ben registered people yelling. He almost turned, but continued to the fairgrounds. Penelope crawled back into his mind and he focused on the memory. What had she worn after changing out of the makeshift bag-dress at Pepperjacks?

Reimagining her running for her life, a scaled hand closing in on her long, dark, trailing hair. Again, her intense blue eyes stole his focus.

Bastion bounded around Ben's head. The beast whipped the black Nilosian energy there into a whirlpool which flash-flooded the vision away.

Annoyed, Ben snapped out loud at the creature in his head, "What?"

They didn't actually share a language. Bastion felt primal. It probably wasn't even capable of words. The only time they had any form of communication was during the combat with the ogre magi, when Bastion motioned to Ben before pulling him in.

Ben stiffened. Bastion only reacted to combat.

From a ways behind him, a vaguely familiar voice called, "Yeah, we're talking to you!"

Ahead, the girls dropped their playful walk and sprinted toward the carnival entrance.

Undaunted, Ben turned. He registered three bodies in hoodies —*Dunn-Blatt or Clark casters*—beyond three small, snapping green energy hooks shooting at him. Each hook trailed a wisp of emerald power back to one of the three hooded casters.

He dodged one.

The green hook flew past him. The faint line of energy dissipated.

Ben twisted. Too late.

The other hooks hit him in the center of his chest.

The faint lines of energy—challenge tethers—shone brilliantly as they twisted, strengthened, and locked Ben into a magic duel.

Chapter Two

HOOKED

AMBIENT DIMENSIONAL ENERGY flowed into the fetters binding Ben to the challengers. Not a valid target for the night's game, Ben didn't struggle for the dominant caster's advantage. Instead he focused on the subtle rush that came with being in a duel.

Just under his skin, the hook dissipated when the emerald strands solidified and thrummed as though some great entity strummed to test the sound. A heightened sense of awareness—the rush of air bringing intoxicating scents from the food court, distinct *clacks* of the Bull Dog speed coaster carts being tugged up toward the first summit, that vague knowledge that nearby, other wills were pitted against each other—came to him.

Ben rubbed the growing heat in his chest. The feeling spread into his hand. He stroked his neck and, like a topical cream, the warmth spread there, too.

Neither challenger noticed his lack of a participation band. The two hooded casters had turned toward one another and, in unison, said, "Let go."

Ben had watched Jameson Brown's exit interview when the World Dueling Federation forced him out for not having won any of his first twenty-five professional matches. When the interviewer had asked Brown why he kept competing instead of quitting from embarrassment, he bounced in place like a jacked-up aureole addict. "The better the competitor, the better the buzz."

As though plugged into the world, Ben finally understood. His eyes narrowed in suspicion. Bastion had relaxed. *Why?*

The shorter one pushed the other. His voice an angry squeak. "He's mine!"

The last thing to come to Ben through the tethers, the challengers' intent. Ben found himself become even more nonchalant about being hooked. These two were at war with each other. Being connected to both, Ben could feel the deep-seated disdain between them.

This play for perceived power further unfurled as the taller guy pushed the smaller one back. "Let go."

From the voice, the taller caster had been the one who called out to him. Ben shook his head. Both were so petty and desperate to scavenge for Samhain Shenanigan items.

The smaller guy pointed to the tether in his chest. It pulsed a pale, neon green. "My hook hit first!"

The taller one grabbed the other by the collar. "Let. Go." He shook the smaller boy hard in time with each word.

Ben had been hooked for the first time three years ago when he'd just turned thirteen and had to take Adept Love's *Intro to Dueling* class. Malcolm—a bully—whose birthday fell nine months earlier, had tethered him. The hook felt like a real fishhook forced into his skin. Though there wasn't any blood, the pain burrowed cruelly up his arm before tearing to the center of his chest. Ben had dropped to a knee and struggled to keep from tearing up. Nothing would've been more embarrassing than crying on his first day of Dueling.

Before Adept Love had made it over to them, Malcolm had towered over him, mumbling insults about Ben losing his birthday gifts from the school and calling him a baby for crying, even though he had successfully held back the tears.

The taller boy jammed his knee into the smaller one's crotch.

The smaller boy collapse, but clung to the tether.

If being hooked would always remind Ben of Malcolm, he'd have to do something extreme to change it. But what?

Ben had often wanted to get back at Malcolm, and had formed several plans, but the bully had been kicked out of the Archon Private

Academy. The faculty didn't say why, but since Malcolm often hooked sixth and seventh graders, it had to be for *conduct unbecoming of an enlightened individual.*

The tether from the small guy faded away.

Competition between them done, the intent of the guy with the remaining fetter came through clear. He wanted to do permanent damage and take as many scavenger hunt items as he could instead of obeying the mandatory limit of one per duel.

Though not a part of the multi-school event, Ben loathed bullies. He walked down the tether toward the hooded figure towering over the one on the ground. Closer, the purple and black of hooded zip-ups became apparent. *Dunn-Blatts.*

The victor flexed over the downed one and had been speaking softly. He spun to face Ben. "Give up four items, Ape, or I'll break you and take your car."

That snide tone. *No way.* Ben leaned to the side to see into the dark hood. Magical shadows kept the face in darkness. Ben's throat constricted with growing rage. "Malcolm?"

The tall boy pulled the hood back. "Baby Ben!" The magical darkness around the face vanished. Much taller and skinnier now, that same aggravatingly smug smile still haunted Malcolm's stupid face. "Do you still cry when hooked?" He chuckled and pointed. "Look, boys, I think I see tears starting."

Ben's fist balled. A primitive desire—*smash that hooked nose*—went through him. His muscles tightened. The direction of power through the fetter between them changed. Energy flowed in Ben's favor. To assure every iota of his anger would be felt, he projected his menace through the tether. "We've a score to settle."

That only add fuel to Malcolm's smugness. "Oh." Malcolm glanced to Ben's arm, where the Samhain Shenanigan's band should have been. "You aren't in the hunt?"

As the one challenged, it was up to Ben if he wanted to end the duel. Adept Love had chirped endlessly about that rule and, by Ben's count, he had three years of anger and two fonts of magic to unleash on the bully.

He held tight. "You're not getting off that easy!"

Malcolm blew him a kiss then extended his hands palms up. As if cued to the motion, two mystic whirlwinds appeared.

One next to him.

One next to Malcolm.

The swirling vortexes siphoned power from their tether. Wind flapped loose, dull gray robes, signaling the imminent arrival of Primaries.

No! Ben opened his Argosian font to try and blast Malcolm with pure power, but his energy drained off to the forth-coming Lesser Judges without so much of a flash of color. He closed his font.

Hoods drawn, both appeared in the thick official robes of the Las Vegas Magistrates. Each teleported into being with their two feet long battle rods—the true symbol of their power—at the ready.

The tips of their batons crackled with red energy as the two dour Argosian men scanned the area for greater trouble.

A third set of robes flapped. In an instant, the wearer materialized. She wore the same dull gray uniform, but her rod hummed with orange Vibrosian energy. Without taking time to appraise the situation, she demanded, "What is going on here?"

The third Dunn-Blatt—Ben had forgotten about him—helped the one Malcolm kneed to his feet. The three of them kept silent.

Ben struggled to keep a civil tongue and found himself at a lack of words. Anything he might say would be hash and pointed at Malcolm. His personal limit met, Ben kept his mouth shut. Actions could be explained away. Words could be quoted, and if he opened his mouth, he'd only regret it when the grey-robed Magistrates reported it to the head of his school.

The vibrant orange glow on the tip of the baton dimmed. She gripped it with her free hand and looked them over. "Junior Apprentice? Bravados?"

Malcolm tried to loosen the hook.

Holding it tight, Ben rocked with the small mystic tug in his chest.

Malcolm said, "A simple misunderstanding, Primaries." He shot Ben a *be cool* wink—as though things could ever be cool between them—and gave another tug. "I, along with my Junior Bravados, thought this A. P. A. student was in on The Shenanigans."

Ben shook his head slightly and held the tether.

Malcolm tugged again and narrowed his eyes. "It's become obvious. He isn't."

"You do not have an armband, Junior Apprentice." The Vibrosian Primary pointed her battle rod at Ben. "Release the Dunn-Blatt or risk censure."

Wishing the fetter would whip to slap Malcolm across the face, Ben relaxed his will and muscles. The hook came free. Without flair, the tether between them dissipated.

Malcolm's hand stashed something into his pocket. Probably his tether totem.

Ben's jaw tightened. Was the totem still the same rusty nail Malcolm had used to hook him years ago?

Smiling at Ben's building anger, Malcolm rubbed his hair opposite the Magistrates with his fingers crossed. He gave a small laugh. "Sorry about that, friend."

The energy faded from the Primaries' battle rods. The two Argosian Primaries spun a quick circle. Air sucked from where they were headed, their gray robes flapped a cotton candy smell before they teleported. Small pink and pale emerald dust devils swirled together in the lot where they once stood.

The Vibrosian Primary turned to Malcolm. "Be careful where you throw your hook, Bravado."

"Yeah." Ben did not want to say anything, but found his mouth echoing the Magistrate as he continued to stare at Malcolm. "*Be careful.*"

She pointed her rod at Ben as an unspoken warning. *Behave*, it said.

He continued to stare at Malcolm and a light thumping in his head —Bastion—urged him on.

The Magistrate angled her wrist back and directed it at Ben a second time. Another unspoken warning. *You are not behaving.* An orange glyph lit the tip. "Look elsewhere, Junior Apprentice."

Ben looked up into the night sky. The light pollution from the casinos stole the grandeur. He focused on the North Star, wishing he could call it down to slam Malcolm deep into the earth.

She said, "Now, to the fairgrounds, you three. Be vigilant. Have fun."

Holding his position, Ben felt them walk past.

The first one, the tallest—Malcolm—bumped his shoulder as he passed, whispering something too low for him to catch, but what Ben thought had been said—*lucky baby*—burned in his ears and sent Bastion tromping its rage through his head. Ben struggled to find his center.

As much as he wanted to go at Malcolm, he had to keep his cool lest the Primary ban him from this season's festival. Still, his rage continued to build...

Chapter Three

USELESS WORDS

A DISTANT ROAR of excitement rolled from the fairgrounds. Though curious, Ben ignored it and let his eyes wander from the North Star through the rest of the Little Dipper. Having birthmarks in a similar pattern on his face, spanning from one cheek to the other, Ben always thought of it has *his* constellation. The fading smell of cotton candy piqued his desire to get onto the fairgrounds again, but he had to wait for the—*high and mighty, power-tripping*—Magistrate to excuse him.

She finally snapped her fingers for his attention.

As he supposed, unless he wanted to be booted and be in trouble when the next school eighth began, Ben faced her and granted immediate eye contact.

Vibrosian energy flooded her eyes.

Ben looked into her orange orbs. He'd only seen one other caster—Ur-Krurk—do this when the ogre magi wanted to blast him to bits. Could this protector, one of Las Vegas's regulators, be thinking of doing the same to him?

The magic drained from her eyes revealing brown irises. She asked, nearly demanded, "What were you thinking, Junior Apprentice?"

Filling his mind with the void between stars, Ben blanked his thoughts to block having them read. Before learning about mind reading a month ago, he had always thought the reactions of others coinciding with his thoughts intriguing. Now—*like G. I. Joe would say*—knowing is half the battle.

She inched forward, paused, and looked deep into his eyes. Concern eased into her voice. "*Were* you thinking?"

She didn't insist on him answering the first question. Keeping his block in place, Ben nodded.

Her fists knuckled her hips. Indignant, she asked, "How did you think you would fare against three Dunn-Blatts, here, in the parking lot?"

Ben continued looking into her eyes. In a blink, he steeled his thoughts.

The Magistrate's lips parted, and she failed to fully suppress a startled gasp.

"No offence meant, Primary, but my personal trials and battles are mine alone." Bringing his Courtmanship studies into play, Ben bowed fifteen degrees. The perfect angle to ask for permission from any caster not directly over him. "By your leave, Ma'am."

With annoyed wrist flicks, she waved her baton under his face to dismiss him.

He turned and walked toward the festival.

Flapping cloth—her teleporting away—sounded behind him.

The long walk ahead of him, Ben's mind kept going back to her baton waving before his eyes.

Ben's parents forbade him from dueling. Heck, they had objected so strongly—to his great embarrassment—at the Arcane Private Academy, where he went to learn magic, that the school excused him from their minimum dueling requirements.

As such, he had only witnessed the baton—a widely accepted symbol of social standing, enforcement, and personal power—from a distance. This close to one, he became certain he'd seen a similar rod fairly recently, but it hadn't been in a Primary's possession...

A replay of the Magistrate's baton waved before his mind's eye. He stroked his chin, murmuring thoughtfully to himself. "Where've I seen one of those before?"

Chapter Four
MUNDANE PROBLEMS

His ABSENT GAZE only a few feet ahead of his black dress shoes, Ben made sure to keep them clean by avoiding the hastily lain chalk lines in the mundane overflow lot. His thoughts bounced between jerk-faced Malcolm, the hot Sunrise Mountain girls, and the misplaced memory of a Magistrate's battle baton.

The rough gravel lot gave way to smooth blacktop with uniformly spaced parking spots separated by paint instead of chalk. The swells of thrilled crowds grew steadily louder as he closed on the fairgrounds from the mundane overflow lot, to regular mundane parking, and now, closer still.

Absentmindedly, his hand played across the thick bundle of Magic Fair winnings in his pocket.

A proud smile formed on his face.

He gave the wad a conscious squeeze.

Placing in the Junior Apprentice/Apprentice group brought five times the reward as the Initiate level, and had netted him more tickets than his prior six years of prizes combined.

He had earned seventy-two tickets. Two for participating, twenty-five for Grand Prize in Efficient Construction, another twenty-five for Grand Prize in Circuitry, ten for second place in Spell Programming, and a bonus ten had been bestowed upon him for taking the fair's Outstanding Ingenuity award.

The judges had gawked over the circuit board in his spellcards. They couldn't seem to get over the overwhelming simplicity of him having moved the arcane resistors closer to the thin obdurium strip. Between that and working the path of his printed circuits from the obdurium he had made the card need less arcane wattage to activate.

About to envision what the large Junior Apprentice prize plaques would look like above his smaller Initiates awards, voices—*either unhappy or pissed*—rose from the joyous background buzz.

Ben lifted his gaze from where the white parking lines ended, and froze.

The *Shame on Sam Hain* protesters were back this year. He counted the twenty of them. Their numbers would swell over the next two days.

These people were why Ben came before Halloween. Anyone coming too late on the actual All Saints Day would find this group impossible to wade through. Worse yet, the mystique—the buffer that kept most of the mundanes from seeing magic and magical beings—would be stretched so thin that they'd be able to see any nearby caster.

Ben waited.

A few of them looked around, scanning over where he stood.

As long as he remained still, or only moved when they weren't looking his direction—*perhaps if I creep very slowly...*—he'd go undetected.

Most were in idle conversation. All of them held large signs usurping the glory of the spindly iron wrought Samhain Festival entry arch. They protested the festival with *Bring Back Orange And Black* and *This Halloween is Not What it Seems*. They also railed against its main organizer, Sam Hain, with *Shame on Hain* and *Hain is Insane*.

Three years ago, as the new President of Koffman's Clockworks, Hain took control of the festival. His change in theme colors from brown and orange to traditional red, white, and black—for blood, bone, and ash—brought more magic-users to what had become, arguably, the best Samhain festival in the country.

Ben looked back over the chocked-full parking lot. Cars whizzed down Sunset Drive. Several sets of headlights moved through the overflow lot to find a spot, but no one walked toward the entrance. *I really should've come earlier.* Ben pressed his lips together, took a deep breath of the popcorn-laced air, and mentally prepared to interact with the Mundanes.

Ready to trudge through, he took one step.

"Don't go in, son!" A rotund man in a loud, orange, Halloween-themed button-up shirt locked eyes on Ben, and waved a *Red, White & Black Is An Attack* sign at him. His voice deep and serious, the man continued, "The Koffman Corp is slowly turning this festival into Devil worship."

Ben entertained a whim about sharing the true origins of the Pagan holiday. *How much would this guy freak out if I went into the details covered in Adept Roman's two Hidden History courses?*

Neither of the classes had a lick of magic. Ben had wanted to skip them, but he fell into the three percent of students attending the Archon Private Academy who didn't come from Pagan families, which made taking both mandatory. Like *Spell Programming*, *Hidden History* had ten levels that spanned multiple school eighths, but he didn't know anyone going that route.

Ben nodded and arced to walk around.

The man pressed closer. He smelled like pastrami.

Ben began to arc wider.

Turning the sign around, the man waved a red, white and black *Hain Is Heinous* at him. "Don't you see?" The man's hot breath reeked of coffee. "Hain is trying to shape the holiday into something wicked."

Ben kept arcing to the edge of the entrance like a slow-motion soccer ball hooking toward the goal pole. *Hope I hit the net.* "Sorry sir, but I won tickets—"

"I'll buy them from you!" The closer they go to the white chalk line marking private property, the faster and louder the man spoke, "Just don't go in!" They reached the white chalk line marking the threshold to private property. "How much you want for them?"

Noticing his angle would be off from making it across at the entrance, Ben stopped.

The man did, too. He thumbed through a wad of mainly black and green ink on gray paper; mundane money.

Scanning the substantial number of—*they're called dollars? Yeah, dollars*—for the red on white *forge-strong notes* backed by the Anvilsmith Dwarves, or the orange on pink *monetary units* issued by the Sunrise Mountain Sisterhood, Ben saw none.

Having been raised as a Mundane until the age of ten, Ben had nearly forgotten just how much it would take to turn dollar bills into real currency. A term—*pennies on the dollar*—came to mind. *What were pennies again?* The exact meaning lay lost in his childhood memories, though he figured the exchange rate would be similar. Suddenly, he grasped that the man thought he would be purchasing regular ride tickets. Embarrassed at his own belated realization, Ben's cheeks began to warm and he grinned at how dim he felt. *Why would a mundane think of anything besides mundane attractions?*

Ben took a quick step to cross the thick line.

Trying to keep pace, the man moved, too. Some of his money threatened to come loose and the man paused to pinch the bills.

Just enough hesitation for Ben to take the final two steps across the line. "Sorry, sir." He turned and bowed a small courtly apology before walking backward. "But I really need to win some goldfish."

Chapter Five

CONJURER'S COURSE

CHEERS ROLLED from the opposite end of the midway games, near the entrance. The air positively brimmed with excitement. Ben had been hoping the attendant with Cody on his badge at the Conjurer's Course would share some of the fragrant spiced apple cider on a slow simmer in the booth, but he hadn't. Still trying to warm the guy up, Ben smiled with an appreciative nod at the Devils & Dragons midway worker as the employee deposited another four goldfish SD cards into his second bulging bag with an amazing lack of enthusiasm.

The attendant—*brain-dead on his feet*—only came alive when cheers rose in the distance and he searched for what had happened.

Ben wanted to think of the guy as more than just *The Attendant*, but Cody hadn't performed anything that could possibly pass for the customary introduction. He took out his last ticket. *Crap, I totally blew my plan to only play a little each day.*

If the usual attendant, Gary, had been here, Ben would've shared his plan with him and Gary would've made sure he stuck to it. The only game Ben ever played, he had gotten to know Gary over the years and—more so now than ever—truly appreciated the man's passion for the game.

Ben shrugged at the slightly older teen with long oily hair and a scant beard that looked like he suffered from mange. Gary had kept his red, white, and black harlequin vest clean and pressed. This guy, from the looks of various stains, seemed to mainly put his uniform on when he ate.

Wishing he'd stuck to his plan, Ben extended his last ticket. "I don't understand why more people don't play this game."

"Because this game sucks." The Attendant's voice came out in harsh wheezes. As though it were Ben's fault he had the crap-job, the Attendant snatched the ticket and gave it a vicious rip. The usual red, white, and black sparkles flew from the tear. He folded a ripped half and let the other go. Like flash paper, it disappeared into a falling cascade of lights. The Attendant leaned back against the wall and used the other half of the voided coupon to scoop dark gunk from under his nails. "You're the only guy dumb—" He bit off the rest of his wheeze and peered at Ben through his oily bangs with raised eyebrows.

Ben's eyes narrowed. They both knew what the rest of the sentence would've been. His neck craned back and Ben forced his lips into a grim line. "Dumb enough to play?"

"Look," The Attendant motioned down the row, trying to make his point. "This game is at the end of a long row of much better games."

Ben didn't turn to see. He didn't have to. He had to work his way through the throngs watching people at the seven Wrath of the Evoker booths—one more than last year—and the mass of people trying their luck at the Illusionist Shooting Galleys. Each booth on the way to the Conjurer's Course had a dwindling number of people waiting to play. With tickets in hand, a couple of younger kids had followed Ben this far only to turn back with dissatisfied groans that their curiosity hadn't paid off.

The Attendant unfolded his arm to full extension, leaned, and pointed with the ticket. "Win three times at Wrath and you get a Fireball." The Attendant spread his fingers wide. Released, the spent marker flashed away. "A flipping Fireball!" Alive for a moment, an unimpressed sneer twisted the Attendant's lips as he flopped against the wall again. "Compare that to this..." He used a limp wrist to roll his finger up the prize hierarchy in his booth. "One, goldfish. Three, cat. Nine, wolf. Twenty-seven, tuzvul. Eighty-one, treant."

As though pointing out lameness sapped his energy, the Attendant's arm went limp at his side. He motioned with his nose, barely raising his chin, as he continued. "Almost two-fifty for a minotaur and thrice that for a dragon." He then flicked Ben's first bags, brimming with goldfish spellcards. "You're good at this, man, but the best you can do is win a second treant."

Seeing the Attendant in a new light, Ben leaned away. He understood where he and the Attendant had a serious disconnect.

Since the guy worked the booth, Ben had thought they were alike. Now, he pegged this guy as exactly the type of caster he—because of Gary's annual *there's more to magic than flash-bang* lessons—despised. If he'd had this guy's narrow view of magic only being useful for combat, he wouldn't have survived his encounters at Meadows Towing.

Ben asked, "Mind telling me if you went to school around here?"

Fully materialized, the conjured frog croaked a *ribbit* to remind the player—him—that the game stood ready.

"Yeah." The Attendant leaned against the wall and watched the frog. "I did."

Ben extended his hands. Mystic reins to control the frog rose to his palms. Ben grabbed onto the invisible, leather-like strands, and he started the course. He directed the frog to make it hop only on the few yellow saucers polka dotted amongst a long field of large white plates. "Have you ever won three on Wrath?"

"Uh, yeah." The worker wheezed and chuckled as though Ben had made the understatement of the century. "More times than you could dream."

To advance, Ben released the controls when the frog landed on a small yellow plate, ending the first leg. The formerly invisible controls shimmered green when the frog vanished. Ben bent at the knees and caught the falling reins to stay in play.

A well-mannered spider monkey appeared on the left side of the game field. Ben directed the monkey to pick up darts, aim, and pitch them at a column of lavender balloons. One by one, they popped in succession up toward the violet one set at the top. Ben asked, "You ever cast a tuzvul?"

He caught a glimpse of the Attendant rolling his eyes. "More times than I care to remember."

Ben had a hard time believing that, but let it go. After all, the guy did work at a place that gave prizes away for every type of caster in the Las Vegas Valley. He could've come across one and stolen it.

With the two spare darts unused, the top balloon popped. The monkey vanished. Ben again leaned down to snatch the glimmering green controls which turned invisible in his hands.

A small air elemental pushed the pinned flaps of the top two balloons around.

Ben had the elemental form a tornado. He dipped the bottom it in the bowl of water to suck up some of the contents.

"And?" The attendant prompted.

Ben focused on the elemental. Like all conjurations, it excelled at repeating tasks. The trick? Showing it how to do it right the first time. Ben had it raise the water in the tornado, move to hover over an empty bowl and release. Guiding the tiny tornado back over to the bowl of water, he asked, "Ever cast a goldfish?"

A hard tilt bent the Attendant's neck. If his hair had been made of liquid, his bangs would have run down the side of his face. His upper lip rose and his jaw loosened, adding an exclamation point to his confusion. "Huh?"

Ben nodded at the elemental and released the reins. The controls flashed green until they hit the counter and faded. If he needed to make any changes to the commands, he'd be out of luck, but the tornado continued moving the water without further instruction.

Rummaging for the last of the red ones, Ben dug through the prize box of dusty goldfish spellcards and said, "No one ever casts goldfish."

Ben could feel the Attendant's bewilderment increase. Casters who think of magic the way the Attendant did could never see the use of casting a goldfish, and thus would never consider the container the conjuration came in as anything of value.

The first bowl had been drained and the second filled well over the top of the three red lines. Ben showed the topmost prize—four cards—to the Attendant. Sliding them into his pocket, Ben carefully lifted his prize bags.

"Duh!" The Attendant wheezed. He sneered as Ben as he began to walk away with his winnings. "Why would they?"

Ben could only shake his head at the ignorance. Recalling when Elder Komir had told him to put Jack's theft of his spellcards behind him, unresolved, he wanted to believe he would've acted differently. *If I had this many back then, I'd have done as she asked of me instead of going after the thief.* Though he seriously doubted that, he still wanted to believe it.

A man in a long Devils & Dragons red, white, and black harlequin robe walked their way from the main body of game players at the popular end of midway.

The Attendant's voice lost most of its former rasp and rose in pitch. He delivered a sing-song sentence packed with perky inflections. "Say, big winner, want to trade all those up to two treants and a cat?"

The sudden change gave Ben pause. This false, heavily-injected, excitement made him turn back. He offered the Attendant a weak smile. They both knew each other's feelings for the game. He replied with a flat, "No." Figuring the guy coming their way was probably the Attendant's supervisor, Ben wanted to wheeze out the rest. He didn't. "I like goldfish."

"So do I." The man, still beyond standard earshot, spoke out in a unique rapid cadence.

The corners of Ben's mouth shot up.

The man continued, "Their bowls, such lovely bowls, can hold such wondrous things. Things of much greater magnitude."

Ben turned. Sure enough, the robed man had a tightly cropped white beard, large ears, and a wide smile. Thin rings of varying color decorated each phalanx on both of the man's hands. Thrilled beyond measure, Ben dropped his prize bags and cheered, "Gary!"

Gary pointed to the attendant. "Please keep those in the booth for this winner, Cody." Without waiting for confirmation, Gary turned and waved for Ben to join him. "Walk with me, friend. Boy do I got a game to show you."

Chapter Six

ABOUT CASTING

AFTER SAYING 'EXCUSE ME' for the third time—without acknowledgement from the five tall Clark practitioners in their goldenrod and black lettermen's coats with hoods attached who blocked the spectator galley where Gary had told him to sit and wait— Ben lowered his shoulder and pressed through. Pushing between the last two, rapid-fire pops burst sweetened cinnamon into the air.

One of the Clark kids extended his arm. The large, coned paper cup in his hand held what remained of his order *Precious Puffs*. The bottom leaked the white icing-streaked delectable brown fluid released when a puff popped—usually in a mouth. The kid yipped, "Hey!" and lifted the bottom of the cone above his mouth and began to gulp the gooey trickle.

About to duck under the bar separating the line from the spectator gallery, a strong hand gripped Ben's shoulder. One of them hissed, "No cutsss."

Ben undid his button and with a practiced shrugged, slipped from his coat. He dipped under the bar, and stood in the empty, three-bleacher spectator stand. "Just trying to watch."

He turned. The Clark guy holding his coat wore those contact lenses in that made his eyes look like snakes. A quick scan found the others did, too. Having a cobra as a school mascot didn't explain why they were so obsessed with looking and acting reptilian. *No one at my school acts like a gorilla.* "My coat, please."

The Clark practitioner scanned the coat's arms for a Samhain Shenanigans band. Not finding one, he tossed the trench coat on the ground, stomped on it, and kicked it to Ben's feet. Sneering to show the fanged caps over his incisors, the guy leaned on the bar and hissed, "Watch yourself. I'm venomousssss."

Ben recoiled. "And your breath's horrid."

Those nearby in the winding line chuckled.

"I know cobras don't have toothbrushes—" Ben plugged his nose. "But, *come on.*"

Most of the chuckles turned into full laughter. Near spastic with mirth, one heavy guy in a Grisham green and white three-piece suit undid his vest buttons to make room so he could double over and laugh harder.

Ben scooped his coat from the ground, slung it on, and whipped the shoulders to activate the prestidigitation. The coat rippled. Dust and dirt flew away. Something close to audacity slipped through him. While he had regretted not participating in the Shenanigans, not being in on the games gave him a certain leeway.

He moved down the row of bleachers to be at the center for the first game at the mouth of the Devils and Dragon's midway and plopped down.

Having squeezed through the crowds earlier to get to his favorite game with the seemingly living-dead attendant, Cody, Ben had assumed this game was another *Wrath of the Evoker.* It had the same thirty-foot-glasssteel-cube-seperating-two-ten-foot-glasssteel-cubes   set up. Except where the competitor's cubes in Wrath were darkly-tented, both of these remained as clear as the large one separating them.

If I would've turned my head, instead of heading right to the Conjurer's Challenge, *I'd seen the ghostly six-feet tall* Challenge the Conjurer 500 *booth title forming from, and dissolving into, ambient emerald energy. I only had to glance.*

Gary stepped into the right-hand cube and raised his hands to the crowd.

Someone called, "He's back!"

A round of applause erupted from the casters in line.

Forgetting to hiss, the self-proclaimed venomous boy yelled, "You're going down, Gary. I'm going to become the new House Champion."

Ben counted eight people ahead of the Clark guy as Gary scanned the line.

"We'll find out in eight minutes, son." Gary gave his bearded cheek one long, slow stroke, and smiled. "With your schoolmates helping, you might have a chance."

Gary shot Ben a thumbs-up.

Ben returned it.

Gary rolled back his red, white, and black harlequin sleeves and nodded to a similarly dressed redhead orchestrating the ticket collection. Small jeweled earrings ran the curve of her large ears.

Figuring each jewel was a spell focus, and not knowing of a school that used earrings, Ben wondered under his breath, "Where'd she learned to cast?"

"Sssay," the venomous boy hissed, "Trencher?"

"What?" Ben answered, but didn't turn. His focus went from the ticket-taker's ear to the four large amethysts on her plump cheek. He couldn't quite tell if they were embedded or in piercings.

"You know that guy? The House Champ?"

Though it was a lie, Ben shook his head. If he spent time talking to the Clark Cobra, he'd miss out on watching Gary.

A voice, feminine and high-pitched, said, "I do. He's a ring-caster."

Ben tried to see the speaker, but from where he sat he could only see the people at the front of the winding line and legs.

"So is his daughter," she added.

Ben's gaze went back to the redhead. He studied her profile and could see Gary's pronounced brow in her features.

"He taught at Charon's Chantry in St. Louis years ago, before it shutdown. Heard he was three down from the School Master there."

Ben had spent a lot of time with Gary through the various Samhain Festivals. While the woman had been mostly right, Gary had been the school's Master Conjurer—*only two down from the Master*—before the school closed six years ago. Tempted to correct the woman, Ben kept his mouth shut.

Since learning of conjuration and meeting Gary during his first

Samhain Festival, Ben had checked around and found none of the schools in the Las Vegas Valley taught the conjuration. When he had asked, Gary attributed the decline to the top-tier competitors of the Spell Dueling Sport League opting for the crowd-pleasing flash-bang of Evocation.

As if on cue, there was a series of *pops* and astonished *oohs* from behind him. Ben didn't take his focus from Gary's booth.

The first competitor—a Dunn-Blatt with his hood up—stepped in and his cube darkened. A glowing red counter, set at twenty-five, appeared on both Gary's cube and the challenger's. The shifting *Challenge the Conjuror 500*, title became *501*.

Ben's jaw unhinged. The 'five hundred' he'd thought was part of the game title turned out to be the growing pool for beating Gary. Recalling the mundane wanting to buy his seventy-two tickets, Ben equated the prize to more than his mystically aware—but mundane— father, a dealer at a prestigious casino, made in a year. He whispered, "Well, that explains the line." Not sure he could beat Gary, the reward still made him want to try. "Good thing I don't have any more tickets," he murmured.

A bolt of violet energy flew from the dark square, across the center, and crashed against the wall before Gary. The twenty-five on Gary's cube dropped to twenty-four.

Though a phantom fight, Ben's pulse lurched and he fought the urge to cast at the challenger to help Gary.

Gary twisted a ring on his thumb. A vibrant orange German Shepherd appeared in the center of the cube and charged.

Another violet bolt from the Dunn-Blatt's cube dropped Gary's meter another point.

The energy faded from the dog as it became as deadly as any real dog for the spell's duration. Gary twisted a ring on his other hand and a teal hummingbird fluttered close to him in the center cube.

The dog attacked the Dunn-Blatt's glass.

The challenger's meter dropped by a point.

Another violet bolt flew from the challenger's cube.

The hummingbird, still glowing with greenish-blue magic, intercepted the blast and dispersed it. Dimmer—but still present—the teal bird hovered in place.

Gary twisted his dog ring again. Another dog, a Doberman Pinscher this time, appeared next to the German Shepherd.

The challenger's counter ticked down by two.

Gary remained focused on whatever he saw in the dark cube, but didn't cast again. Occasionally, he shot the hummingbird forward to deflect a different evocation, but the man Ben had learned conjuration from seemed as relaxed as though he were the conductor of a train moving down the rails to a foregone final stop to let this guy off and hurry the next rider on.

Under a minute later, the Dunn-Blatt caster burst from the dark cube. The darkened glass returned to being completely clear again. Ben stood to watch the hooded caster. Eagerly, he rushed to the end of the line.

The ticket taker extended her hand to an adult in yellow robes who handed over two tickets. She slid one into a slot next to the cube; the clear door opened. The man in yellow slid his sleeves back as he stepped in and the cube darkened again.

This time, Ben saw Gary's daughter put the second ticket into a different slot. The prize counter ticked up.

Even though the guy in yellow solely threw fireballs, the match pretty much went the same way, except for Gary using lions and an eagle instead of dogs and a hummingbird.

The count kept building as player after player entered, played, and lost. The game line kept growing.

No one could beat Gary.

Enthralled Ben almost lost track of time. Though his main objective for coming to the festival had been to win as many obdurium enhanced goldfish SD cards, so he could overwrite them with other spells, Crystal—a girl he considered to be his own personal seer—would kick his butt if he didn't see the diviner she idolized. *Diviners' Row will be the first part of the festival to close, but the education from watching Gary dominate is too much of a gift to turn away from.* Though Crystal had said she had to ask Papa Mojo for a personal favor to give Ben a reading, Ben chose to stay, and focus on trying to understand the 'why' behind when Gary would change tactics.

The dark cube became transparent again and the man in the yellow robes, who had lost early and had made the line again, beamed a tenacious grin and asked in an anxious squeak, "Right, so?"

Ben frowned. *Right, so what? You lost, buddy. You get back in line, again. That's what.*

Speaking in his fast patter, Gary gave his cropped beard that slow —*class is in session*—stroke Ben loved to see. "You've ramped up to a more powerful spell, but fared no better than your first two goes." Gary spread his fingers, tapped the index, the middle, and gripped his ring finger. "Think. Other than using conjuration, evocation, or more powerful evocation, you've done the same thing each time." Gary let go of his hand and motioned at the man in yellow as though he were trying to pull and answer from his reluctant mouth.

"I—" The guy paused and slapped his forehead. "I'm only casting one spell."

Gary clapped once, hard, and pointed at the man as though driving a nail home with one hammer-blow.

A jealous twinge cramped Ben's stomach and then rolled through. For a moment, he felt betrayed that Gary wasn't exclusively sharing his knowledge with only him. Then, he came to his senses. Gary had the kind of knowledge that shouldn't be kept locked away. *If only Senior Adept Collins was here to learn this higher lesson.*

Upon thinking the Senior Adept's name, a sneer turned Ben's lips. He wanted to spit. *Why'd that blonde bastard pop into my head?* To clear the building contempt for, arguably, the APA's most despised instructor, Ben wiped his forehead and flicked his hand as though he were throwing off sweat. *I'm not going to let the simple thought of Collins ruin the evening.*

Re-focused, he returned to watching Gary kick butt. Class was in session.

Chapter Seven

ABOUT DUELS

THE VENDOR CARTS of the Fae Fort Food Court were in full swing. Ben's eyes kept darting to Southern Sweets with their oversized red, white, and blue-striped umbrella. With a burning desire, he tortured his stomach by watching the workers spin cotton candy, inflate Precious Puffs, and load the soon-to-be aromatic festival popcorn kernels into a second deep kettle popper.

Gary had offered to get him something, but—to keep from feeling like a mooch—Ben had declined.

If he'd stuck with this plan—if he hadn't gotten caught up trying to show Cody, the oily-haired-undead-attendant how cool the game he worked was—Ben could've used a ticket—*just one*—to get a dine-all-night wristband and, as Gary dug into his gooey, chopped bacon-laden cheese shells, Ben could've been munching on the popcorn he'd been fiending for.

At Gary's request, Ben rattled on about his school year and his dislike for Senior Adept Collins strictly academic. As he recapped the year, Gary, the six hundred-streak strong and still undefeated House Champ of *Challenge the Conjurer*, shoveled food during his break.

Someone in an Archon Private Academy trench coat sauntered through the food court. More from the hell-with-all swagger than the spikey blonde flat-top, Ben recognized Collins. He slumped in his chair to use Gary, who sat across the table from him, as a shield to keep Collins from seeing him. "Man, how does he do it?"

Between spoonfuls, Gary glanced over his shoulder, returned to eating, and asked, "Who do what?"

"Collins." Ben pointed. "The A. P. A. guy."

Gary didn't turn. "What'd he do?"

"Nothing." Struggling to put his finger on exactly what it was, Ben shrugged. "I mean, I don't know. It just seems as though whenever I think about him, he appears."

Mid-route to his mouth, Gary's hand stopped. Tiny bacon chunks dangled in the strings of cheese between fork and plate like flies in a spider web.

Moving toward the chain-link fence between the food court and the employees only area, Collins' demeanor changed slightly to being watchful.

Ben could feel Gary's appraising stare, but kept his eyes on Collins as he walked to the fence and began to look around. Ben sunk down further.

Gary asked, "Is this normal?"

"Me hiding?" Squinting, Ben considered it.

Collins eyes landed on someone and he gave a courtly acknowledgement nod.

Ben didn't check to see who. "Well—" There had to be a reason why Collins was acting suspiciously, and Ben wasn't going to let the Senior Adept out of his sight. "He doesn't like me and has made trouble for me." About to spill his adventure with Penelope, Ben made a quick conversational turn back to school. "If my spells are one line of code longer than they're supposed to be, he gives me a zero."

"That's not what I mean." Gary's fork thudded on the paper plate.

Ben adjusted to the right. Instead of being a shield, Gary seemed to be leaning into Ben's line of sight. Almost like a weird, slow dance, Ben kept leaning further than Gary, and Gary leaned to make eye contact.

Without eye contact, Gary asked, "Is it normal for you to think of people and then they show?"

"No." Ben shifted directions to peek around Gary's other side. Dominic, Collins' favorite student, who couldn't get even a simple cantrip programmed in less than a thousand lines, walked up to the

Senior Adept. Collins went rigid at being approached. He gave a thin smile and shook Dominic's hand. Ben answered, "It started happening about a month ago."

Gary said, "Ben." And waited for his attention.

Ben remained focused on Collins. The Senior Adept seemed to be struggling to get Dominic to go away. Seeing the blond jerk put out by a coddled student brought a pleased smile to Ben's mouth. *Almost serves him right.* The area around Collins and Dominic dimmed slightly before, woodenly, Dominic turned and walked away.

Gary raised a finger in front of Ben's face. "Attention."

Ben shook his head and sat up in his chair to peer over Gary's white hair as Dominic—*Dom's legs are lightning rod stiff*—walked away. "Hold on. I think Collins is up to something."

A handclap preceded a glowing green stone wall, eight feet tall and wide, materialized behind Gary. No amount of leaning would allow Ben to see Collins. After a moment, the glow faded leaving a gray, freestanding wall.

About to get up, Ben turned to admonish Gary with an annoyed glance, but his eyes went to a rocking stopwatch Gary had out. Ben's eyes locked onto the timepiece as it moved side to side in graceful, captivating arcs.

More than he desired festival food, Ben desperately wanted to observe Collins, but he couldn't pull his attention away from the steady *tick* of the thin steel second hand which became the center of his existence. In five seconds Ben felt his consciousness swinging side to side with the watch, like the phantom pull of waves after being in the ocean all day, as he became dislodged from the present and forced into the timepiece.

The continuous hum of the fairgrounds dimmed, replaced by the constant, reliable *ticks* and perfect seconds of silence. The thick aromas faded and were overtaken with a sterile, metallic tang. A white fog filled his eyes, washing the bustle of the food court away into the pure white of the stopwatch's face, with black frets at fixed points in his peripheral vision.

The second hand stopped, yet the timepiece's ticking—steady, constant, precise—continued.

Gary's voice, amplified and inescapable, boomed, "I apologize for this inconvenience, my friend, but I need your complete attention for just a minute. Heed me, Ben. Underground duels are extremely dangerous. You may have won, and could continue winning, but only the worst sort of people go there to wager on the outcome. Win too often, and the people who lost too much betting on you to lose will come after you. Lose too often, and those who bet too much on you to win will try to kill you. While you may gain abilities, like this third-eye of yours, the risk is not worth it. Heed me, Ben. Wait until you're eighteen and can legally join the dueling circuits. Heed me, Ben, and I will help you."

In an instant, the second hand swung around. The stopwatch face —which had been lain over everything and had become everything— burst like a water balloon.

The glorious spectacle of the Samhain Festival washed back over Ben. Momentarily aware of his heightened sense of things, reality inundated Ben's fading amplified cognizance and brought him to safe rest at a table across from Gary where he could see lights strung between tents, hear the bark of street performers, smell the perfume of festival popcorn, and feel the growing hunger in his gut.

Ben found his head rotating. Unconsciously, he tried to keep up with the stopwatch as Gary spun it on a chain around his index finger.

His head wound tightening circles until Gary caught the timepiece.

As though waking up, Ben blinked. He dug his pinkies into his ears to clear what remained of the focused silence. *Had a minute passed?* If so, his memory of it began to fade... Until he focused.

Something he hadn't known about, hadn't been aware of, kept the unreal pocket watch—*time bubble*—reality intact. "Underground duels?" Vaguely remembering that he was trying to observe something or someone, Ben stood because it felt like what he had been wanting to do. He walked to the wall. "Didn't know they existed." He peeked around the edge and spied Collins scowling after a retreating A. P. A. student. Ben wondered who, but had recaptured his razor-sharp focus on the suspicious Senior Adept. A strong grip landed on Ben's shoulder and spun him.

With surprising strength, Gary had physically turned him to get— and got—that probing eye contact everyone over twenty seemed to possess. "You have battled someone, have you not?"

Ben had learned how to keep secrets when pinned by the stare. He hadn't expected it from Gary which made him slow in clamping his eyes shut and—before he could lock them away—Ben failed at not recalling the sense of betrayal as Jack ran away with his spellcards, and the near-choking fear he felt as the Krotosian ogre hurled blasts at him.

Gary gripped harder and shook. "That's not how this works."

Ben turned his face away, closed his eyes tighter, and consciously placed the two thoughts in a thick, solid-steel mental cube.

Gary's voice took on an anxious tone as he stated, "You *have* battled." Gary grabbed Ben's other shoulder and tried to regain eye contact. "Don't hide this from me, Ben. I'm trying to help."

This is Gary, Ben. Drawing a deep breath, Ben exhaled, opened his eyes, and slowly lowered his defenses to the one adult he considered to be a friend.

"This lesser oracular ability," Gary started, "You won it from someone named—" Ben's memory of the build up to duel at the Suntouched Stronghold's stables opened for Gary to analyze. That moment when Jack turned to face Ben to battle froze. Though Ben had been focused on Jack's face, Gary worked at the edges of the moment. The master conjurer's arms went limp. His eyes flew wide, and his voice dropped low in astonishment. "You've been to the other side..."

Gary began to roll the memory forward.

Ben blinked hard and shut Gary out. He had to, otherwise his mentor would see him activating a Nilosian-tainted Heracles enchantment. *If Gary has a chance to see that, he'll doubtlessly lock onto it.*

The urge to run overtook Ben. To keep his Nilosian secret, he had to get away.

Gary's arms went to grab his shoulders.

Ben dodged, pivoted, and sprung away.

Gary whispered after him, "Let me finish."

Chapter Eight

SENIOR ADEPT COLLINS

BEN WENT around the edge of Gary's wall and hurried to get in line at Southern Sweets. He still didn't have a way to pay, but being in line got him away from Gary and, more importantly, to a place where he could see Collins more clearly.

To not stand out as an APA student, he took off his coat, folded it, and held it over his belt buckle. The fresh batch of popcorn started to pop and flow over the edge of the kettle. For a moment, he looked away from Collins to longingly eye the bin pooling with the hot, butter-laced goodness. *If I only had a bag to dive into.* A slight gust, meant to fan the smells through the fairground blew through the line. He wasn't alone in inhaling the smorgasbord of treats, nor was his stomach alone in growling.

Unable to take the torturous scents any longer, Ben hustled to the middle ring of the food court to post up near the series of large manila spiced cider tents.

Collins' hands worked the air. The Senior Adept didn't touch the tablet on his hip and he didn't have a spellcard in hand. Collins' hands simply moved in circles before an Argosian-red bubble surrounded him.

Not seeing any of the other methods of casting around Collins, Ben wondered, "How is he casting?" He'd only seen people cast empty-handed on the other side, when he met Elder Komir. She—and the others—made the point that he wasn't a wizard awfully clear. A nearly undetectable disdain clung to their words, and Bo, the bouncer, had threatened him for clinging to the idea of being a wizard.

The magic bubble around Collins burst, coating the Senior Adept with red mystic mist, giving his blond hair an orange glow. Recognizing part of the effect, Ben identified the spell. "Non-Detection." His shoulder rose in a non-impressed half shrug. While not common, most wouldn't care to learn it since all the spell did was ensure that the caster would not be preternaturally observed casting other spells, Non-Detection lay just beyond Ben's own casting ability— he would be learning it the next couple of years, when he became a full Apprentice. "Not bad."

Refusing to believe Collins capable of being a real wizard, Ben scrutinized the Senior Adept to find the alternate method of casting. From the corner of his eye, he noticed Gary come around the wall, looking for him.

Collins faced the fence.

Ben changed location again, trying to mask his hurry with a careful speed-walk as he weaved through the dense crowds strolling amid full dining tables at the center of the food court.

He glanced back to see if anyone had started to take notice of him, and discovered Gary, still standing near the wall he'd made, motioning for Ben to return.

No way. Ben shook his head.

Gary sighed and, heading back toward the direction of the *Challenge the Conjurer* booth, walked away.

Ben neared the other spiced cider tents closer to Collins and focused on the man again.

Again, the Senior Adept pulled another spell from the air around him.

Ben frowned. He had missed what conjuring tool Collins had used and there wasn't anything obvious about the somatic aspect of the spell he had cast.

Collins hunkered down into a squat and then leapt. He cleared the twenty-foot chain-link fence and landed on the other side. There, Collins waved his hand over his face and stood photograph still.

In a whirl of gray robes, four Primaries appeared on the Employees Only side of the fence around Collins. The tip of their battle rods lit. Seemingly ready, red energy pulsed along their length, obscuring their hands in Argosian magic. Scowling, each scanned the area totally oblivious to Collins, standing right in their midst.

A Vibrosian Magistrate—the one from the parking lot—appeared in a whirl of robes. She glanced around.

The Argosians shook their heads at her.

She lifted her weapon into the air and squeezed it. The baton pulsed orange and sent a rippling wave of energy out in a thirty-foot radius. Some clinging to the air where Collins had leapt from the food court, most of it faded.

Bopping their batons first, all five Magistrates twirled their robes and were gone. Three swirls flashed on the food court side of the fence. The Vibrosian and two Argosians appeared next to the Vibrosian glow highlight where Collins had been moments before. The other two Argosian Magistrates did not reappear.

Directly behind the Primaries, Collins began to walk backward and then turned away, to jog further into the employee area.

A devious smile crooked the corners of Ben's mouth as he realized the amazing spell he grossly misidentified as Non-Detection proved to be a much stronger one. In spite of extreme dislike for the Senior Adept, Ben couldn't keep the awe from his voice. "He knows Obfuscation."

Watching Collins move further away from the Magistrates, Ben wished he knew if the spell was a seven, eight, or nine-stone spell. Whatever level, the Archon Private Academy—or any school he knew of—didn't teach anything from those lofty tiers. While no one would say as much, there seemed to be a general rule against it.

The Vibrosian and an Argosian Magistrates whirled their robes and disappeared. The other Argosian, a short squat man, strode into the food court, scooped a bratwurst, then twirled his robes and disappeared as well.

Collins faded into the darkness obscuring the festival's employee area.

"Damn it!" Ben rushed through the crowd. A long string of

apologies spilled from his mouth as he bumped the rest of his way through the busier parts of the Fae Fort Food Court.

Finally next to the gate, Ben checked behind him. There were a few people who had waited for him to look their way so they could shoot him dirty looks, but no one stayed focused on him.

Ben pulled the large, silver, anti-divination ring he had earned at Meadows Towing. Like the belt around his waist that had also been sized for an ogre, and shrunk to fit him, Ben poked his thumb into the wide band. Keeping the same ratios, the ring shrank to a snug fit. A wave of warm magic flowed through his core. *Wonder if I just flashed with magic.*

An orc's gruff voice—*no lilted vowels, so it's not Toad*—came from the ring: "Might-Fist, return to Meadows Towing." *All the other orcs pretty much all sound the same.*

Ben extended his arm and considered the ring to see if he could see the message on it. *No.* Being the Might-Fist, Ben felt obligated to return if they needed help. *But they didn't actually call for help. Last time they wanted me, they wanted me to pick out which color t-shirts they were going to get the Meadows Towing logo silkscreened on.*

Collins momentarily came back from the darkness, turning to go a different direction in the fenced area.

Ben pulled out his Anvilsmith. If the matter with the orcs proved to be really important, they'd leave a better message. *Or, maybe, actually use the landline I had installed at Meadows Towing to actually call my tablet.*

He eyed the top of the fence to consider how much power to put into his leap. Thinking on what he planned on doing, his head shook in disbelief. Employees Only at the Samhain Festival meant *employees only.* Unlike trying to sneak into Pepperjacks, he'd just seen Primaries show up in force.

Ben didn't know the penalty for crossing into the employee area, but Collins was up to something and he had to give chase. If he were caught and had a chance to point or speak, he would try his best to implicate Collins.

From casting hundreds of spells through the years, Ben's fingers slid over his Anvilsmith tablet without him needing to look. Lighting first on *Spells*, his finger tapped where the asterisk for his *Enchantment* spells would populate, and he tapped the spot where the icon for *Leap* would be.

Still waking, the screen flashed twice and the tarsier leaping from a branch background populated along with the *Cast* button made to look like a tarsier's bugged eyes. He tapped *Cast*.

Since earlier in the month, he had gotten used to the slight vibration from his device flowing magic into him instead of forcing it. Ben had even got used to faking being shocked when forced to cast at school. However, *Leap* only costing one arcane watt which still seemed weird.

Aiming for where Collins had landed, Ben crouched, leapt over the chain-link fence, and landed exactly where Collins had on the employee's side.

Fear tightened his muscles. Not visible from the other side of the fence, he had jumped into the middle of five—four red, one orange—rotating scrying sensors. All bobbed in the air above weird symbols like the ones he had seen in the Arcane Alehouse.

Worse yet, his gaze fell directly into the sensor left by the Vibrosian.

He clamped his eyes shut and he braced for impact.

Chapter Nine

TRESPASSING

BEN HAD HEARD rumors of the Magistrates being brutal, but he hadn't believed it until he saw the way the four Argosians teleported in ready to throw down. He had been outclassed—*mystically dwarfed, really*—at the Arcane Alehouse. Unlike like then, it might take the Primaries a bit to realize he wasn't fighting back.

A sudden coolness—*wind? A spell?*—on his flesh set Ben's pulse racing. Blood thumped in his empty stomach and sang in his ears. As prepared for a beating as he could be, Ben pointed in the direction Collins had gone.

What would Master Reynolds think?

A small burst of air escaped him. Then he laughed more fully before stifling it.

It struck him funny that he cared more about what Master Reynolds' reaction would be than that of his parents, but it made sense. Being brought before anyone for wrongdoing by the Magistrates meant receiving the worst allowable punishment. While his parents could ground him—indefinitely—Master Reynolds would expel him. With no other technomancy schools in southern Nevada, it would effectively end Ben's mystical education.

Though his magical career options would be extremely limited, a sudden wistfulness overtook him. *Maybe when I turn twenty-five—and, perhaps, no longer grounded—I could work the Conjuration Course. The booth doesn't need a caster near Gary's skill level, but it deserves someone a great deal better than Cody.*

Ready to explain, he opened his eyes.

The five eyeball sensors still scanned the area. Undisturbed, the symbols under each gracefully bobbed up and down. The mark under the orange one looked identical to the glowing glyph on the tip of the Vibrosian Primary's baton. It also looked like one of the symbols from the book Elder Komir had given him.

The darkness, which had obscured the employee area on the other side of the fence, began to blow away like someone had turned on a high-powered fan and the shadows were simply dense smoke leaving the area brightly lit by lights atop the scores of industrial shipping containers and double, or triple-hauled semi-trailers. Long corridors formed between the two mass shipping options.

Ben released his breath. Breathing a bit easier, the aroma of Bugsy's Brats swam around him and, now, he understood why the short Primary had grabbed one.

In case gestures were important, Ben repeated what Collins' had done. He bent down, twisted to avoid the sensors, walked backwards, then turned to jog the way Collins had gone.

Since the Senior Adept was neither directly ahead nor in sight at the first intersection, Ben occasionally squatted to scan as far as he could see under the truck trailers. Even though he knew both the starwise and mundane parts of the festival were in full swing, the absence of anyone in the employees' area bothered him. When he ducked down, he kept excepting to come eye-to-eye with a guard dog or an attack boar, but—thankfully—never did.

Starting to huff from the squats, Ben spied movement a few rows up and several columns over; where the long trailers and shipping containers gave way to smaller trucks, cars, and crates. He stayed low long enough to distinguish the swish of a trench coat before sprinting down the corridor.

He put his coat back on and peered around the corner.

Collins entered a dark, old-fashioned, old-west type stagecoach wagon. Leaving the windows open, thin pink hands, with slim fingers, closed the shades inside on which shadows, cast by candlelight, danced.

Not certain if the ring masked his sounds, Ben kept his suspicion unspoken. *Bet it's the woman with the elfy-ears that Collins had dinner with last month.*

Staying vigilant for employees, Ben crept closer to the antique wagon to eavesdrop. Even at two in the morning, the carnival still went on strong and no one else walked amongst the wagons. This would change in an hour or so when the mundanes petered away.

Strong sizzling—*black magic?*—sounds rose as he neared the wagon. *What kind of Nilosian spells are they silently casting in there?* Then the scent of sausage and peppers came through the window.

"Well, my love—" Speaking Elven, the woman's light voice carried the majestic, airy intonations better than Adept Yeffaux, the Archon Private Academy's Master Linguist. "How did it go?"

"Better than could be expected," Collins gruff voice replied in Elven. The Senior Adept often claimed he did not know the language, but obviously—by his proper inflection of the vowels—that was a complete lie. "Better than could be expected." Glass clinked. Silence filled the next few seconds. Collins continued, "He took Grand in two categories and got an Ad Hoc bonus."

"Amazing," She cooed.

Collins agreed, "I know."

Ben's jaw dropped and his mouth began to dry. He was the only magic faire entrant awarded a bonus this year. Why were they talking about him? Motion in the distance caught his attention. Keeping his ears perked, Ben turned to evaluate the movement.

Along the length of the distant fence separating the employees only area from the starwise parking, ran two girls in white shirts.

Ben strained to see what color their skirts were, but it was too dark and too far to be sure.

The woman asked, "Think I can approach him early?"

"No," Collins barked. "The path has been set..."

Three wisps of green energy—*tethers*—shot at the girls. The lines missed and the girls turned away from the fence to run into the packed parking lot.

Hooded figures—*Clark? Dunn-Blatt?*—gave chase.

"You..." Collins continued.

The woman giggled.

Collins continued, "Must be patient and walk it."

The emerald lines of energy flashed repeatedly from the aggressors toward the white-shirted girls. One of the lines went tight. A long, terrified scream full of desperate fright rocketed their way.

The scream gave Ben goose bumps

Even from so far away, the shriek had been belted fiercely enough to be heard halfway through the employee lot, but the cry would be battled back and swallowed by the mirth from the fairground.

The wagon shook a little. The woman asked, "Should you go check on that, my love?"

Beyond, near the girls, a bright flash of orange blossomed as a tall woman—*no, a centaur, the Sunrise Mountain Sisterhood summon centaurs*—materialized. The first row of distant cars blocked the legs, but most of the horse-like body stood taller than the hoods. Green flashed next to the orange, and another centaur formed.

Collins' sniggered. It held a *you should know better* sound. "That was a girl."

Near the aggressors, emerald flashes flanked the violet glow of Krotosian energy.

Another scream rolled across the lot.

Collins gave another dirty chuckle, and added, "I work at an all-boys school, remember?"

Ben couldn't see what the deep purple energy formed, but the two greens each summoned dangerous dusk buffaloes; the four thick prehensile tendrils on each beasts' back were reared up. Dunn-Blatts. Since discovering Malcolm had become a Dunn-Blatt after being booted from the APA, an instant dislike of the school—and its attendees—had taken root in Ben.

An elastic band snapped against flesh. The woman gave a slight yelp. Collins chuckled. "So, it's no one I'm responsible for."

A second snap sounded. The woman gave off something close to a whimper. "What if one of your boys caused it?"

Collins's constantly annoyed tone fell away and the Senior Adept's voice took on a never-heard-before warmth. "If it's my boys, let them have their fun. After all, it's Samhain."

Low and throaty, the woman replied, "Mmm-hmm."

Not a single Samhain Festival had gone by without reports of horrible things happening. What seemed to be taking place out in the starwise lot could be one of those dreadful rumors. Ben knew it. Collins knew it. In fact, the Senior Adept had implied one of the worst acts, and had no qualms about letting it happen.

Wishing he had a way to set part of the wagon on fire, Ben stood, scowled at it, and started toward the parking lot.

Chapter Ten

PART OF THE SOLUTION

NOT FOR THE FIRST TIME, Ben thought about programming spells directly to his Anvilsmith tablet's quick-launch bar. When he had tried in the past, the tablet wouldn't let the spells be assigned to the bottom row. Other Archon Private Academy students had unlocked their devices to install some cool cosmetic hacks, but he'd seen nothing substantial from a functionality point of view.

Unable to afford a replacement if he happened to brick his device, Ben had been afraid to hack his. The potential ridicule for showing up to *Spell Programming IIX* with his brightly painted, five-year-old Rainbow tablet proved enough to keep him from trying, but—Seeing Senior Adept and the lady together again—brought to mind the spare Anvilsmith tablet, deep in his closet. With the device came an old unanswered question. *Why had Collins switch a cursed device for my perfectly good one?*

Ben put the question out of his mind. He hadn't figured it out before, and thinking about it now only made him angry again. Instead, as his fingertips worked the cool glass on his tablet to enter his passcode, he focused on helping the girls. *Well, at least evening the odds.*

He tapped the fat exclamation point and, for the first time, noticed the slight wait for the icons of his seven *Conjurations* spells to populate. There had always been a lag. However, compared to the near-instant speed of casting from spellcards, these multiple one-second-between taps could add up to that *difference between life and death* Adept Love continually spouted during the *Dueling* classes.

Ben came to a stop. Instead of waiting for the various screens to populate, he mentally placed the locations he needed to tap in his head. After his tap of the lightning bolt icon for *Usain*, his speed spell, he sped through the rest of his taps.

He tapped where *Cast* would populate, swiped back up to *Conjurations*, tapped where the kangaroo icon would be for his *Tarsier Leap* spell, and tapped where the *Cast* button would be.

The splash screen showing Usain Bolt running through a finished line ribbon, arms raised in a 'vee,' appeared. The highly italicized *Cast* button lit. Energy vibrated into him and his mouth filled with the taste of oranges. The *Usain* spell screen swiped away. The kangaroo icon lit, and the Tarsier in a tree background shown.

Not waiting for the *Cast* button to depress, Ben smiled at his ingenuity and started running toward the parking lot. The wagons and trailers he ran past turned into flashes, the wind whipped at his hair and flapped his trench coat. The Anvilsmith vibrated again and magic thrummed in his legs.

His strides lengthened.

His speed increased further.

Coming up fast on the chain-link fence, Ben leapt to keep from ramming into it.

He cleared the fence, the confrontation, and eight rows of parked cars.

As he sailed over, a burst of green magic flashed as a centaur, having been ravaged by two dusk buffaloes, winked from existence. The triumphant beasts became indistinguishable from the dark lot, but their growls surrounded the two girls on the lone centaur's back. The three Dunn-Blatt boys were toying with them, savoring the pending victory.

Ben landed between aisles and slid into a pickup truck. The pause ended the speed spell, stealing the delicious orange taste from his rapidly drying mouth.

He wanted to channel Argosian into his Orion spell card to handle the dusk buffaloes, and Dunn-Blatts, but remembered all-too-well Oscar and Abe slaying half the orcs.

Bastion has awakened at the promise of combat, and offered the Nilosian energy.

Ben refused to use it. More worrisome than the disgusting cracks that had sounded from Jack's arm breaking between jagged Nilosian teeth, was the energy's way of not doing what he willed of it.

Hoping to be in time, Ben began to sneak between cars back toward the confrontation.

Keeping an eye on the girls—*they're the same Sunrise Mountain girls from when I arrived tonight*—and their centaur, he ran his fingers along his spellcard holder until he felt the three grooves indicating his fingertip had lit on Orion. Anvilsmith in the other hand, Ben focused on feeling for the energy inside his device.

One of the boys spoke to the girls in a factual, articulated way. "Did you know that three casters die each night of the Shenanigans? It's true, look it up."

Was that true? Ben had kept track of the various facts that he'd learned about the Shenanigans through the years, and though he had seen injuries, he hadn't heard about any fatalities.

The arcane wattage within his device answered his call. A smile spread across Ben's lips as the warm, green power thrummed from this device, through him, and into the Orion spellcard. Peeking through car windows, Ben summoned an emerald gorilla to each of the five points of a star behind cars around the boys. To not steal the girls' fight, he only planned on using one at a time, but—since the boys were talking about death—Ben had the other four at the ready.

"They won't be able to," voice husky from laughing, another boy added. "But at least there will only be one other death tonight."

"Didn't your teachers tell you to stay on the fairgrounds?" Ben searched out who said that. The three boys kept their mystic shadows obscuring their faces in their hoods, but he'd know that voice anywhere. It was Malcolm. "So, what are you girls willing to give up to keep living?"

The same height as the other tall Dunn-Blatt, Ben spied Malcolm by the cocky way he stood. Refusing to let the jerk have the upper hand one second longer, Ben had his gorillas hop from their hiding spots and attack the dusk buffaloes.

"Apes!" the first boy called.

Two gorillas landed on each of the green dusk buffaloes. One charged forward to challenge Malcolm's purple conjuration and—programmed to fight intelligently—paused when the wild beast spun and roared.

"Hook them!" Trying to locate the casters, Malcolm scanned the parking lot. "Commit them to a challenge!"

"There's five of them!" The husky-voiced one turned and ran as one of the dusk buffaloes fell beneath two gorillas. "Run!"

Given how easily his gorillas passed the green beasts' tendrils, the monsters couldn't have been *true* dusk buffaloes. The *Mythic Monster I* course had explained how deadly the creatures were. *The greens must just be regular buffaloes designed to look the part.*

The other boy gave a fist pump when his conjuration gored the throat away from one of the gorillas, but he released his hook and ran when another gorilla broke his beast's neck.

Malcolm stood alone, turning, and searching to find the gorillas' casters. His, probably real, purpled-eyed beast stared hard at the centaur, though it backed toward its caster when the gorillas began to encircle it.

The girls climbed from the orange centaur's back. The long haired, tie-less one produced a stone arrow tip from her coat pocket, and flicked her wrist at Malcolm. An emerald tether shot out and hooked into Malcolm's eye. Unfortunately, unable to do physical damage, the hook shifted to his chest.

"Come out of hiding, cowards!" Malcolm threw his head back and bellowed, "Line up, apes! I'll take each of you on!"

Ben stood from where he crouched and walked out into the lane. "Fight her first." He ground his fist into his palm. "Then we'll know if we have to turn you into a statistic."

Malcolm sneered. "I should have known that you, and your chicken-shit friends, couldn't face me like a men."

Don't be goaded into something stupid. Ben rubbed his chin. He tried to muster a lazy grin to mimic Malcolm's earlier smug smile. "We're just using the tactics you and your boys taught us."

Out of nowhere—*no, from my ring*—an orc's gruff voice called, "Please return to Meadows Towing."

Ben stiffened.

Neither Malcolm nor the girls reacted.

They didn't hear the orc's loud and clear request. Interesting.

With a pissed flick of his wrist, Malcolm dismissed his dusk buffalo. He pulled his hood and the shadow magic that had obscured his face splashed away. Defiant in relenting, he looked at the girl who had hooked him. "What do you want?"

She said, "Your tie." Her icy stare said, *your life.*

Sneering, Malcolm removed it and dropped it on the ground. The girl released her hook, and he turned to leave.

"Not so fast." Ben dismissed one of the gorillas and had the remaining three crouch to be ready to attack. As much as he wanted to turn them loose to beat down the Dunn-Blatt, it wouldn't have been right and Malcolm—being Malcolm—probably wouldn't learn anything from it. *No, I gotta do something that would bother, but not harm, him.*

The Dunn-Blatt turned back to face him.

Locking eye contact, Ben walked to Malcolm, his hand extended between them. "I'll take your hook."

Chapter Eleven

A CASUAL INSULT

STILL AMAZED that Malcolm had the tool that had been used to rip him into the horrible reality of dueling in his hand, Ben rubbed the rusty nail which had served as Malcolm's focus. Besides the rough surface, there was nothing special about it. However, on this cool autumn night, heavy with the sounds and fragrances of the festival, the nail—now, through cultural tradition, Ben's possession—meant more in victory than his wins at the Magic Faire.

One of the girls cleared her throat.

Ben turned.

They gave their courtly introductions and names with curtsies. The tieless brunette. "Sarah Coleman."

The pixie-cut blonde. "Clarissa Twinstar."

Though Ben wanted to break free and return to the dark wagon where Collins and the woman talked about him, re-entering the employees only area with anyone watching was out of the question. Ben bowed deeply, introduced himself. "Benjamin Baxter. And we should get moving before the Dunn-Blatts return with most of their school in tow."

They started speed-walking.

Clarissa tugged at the purple Dunn-Blatt tie dangling from Sarah's wrist. Clarissa said, "Was it not weird? Primaries should have appeared to bear witness to the Shenanigan Challenge?"

Sullen, Sarah shook her head. "You weren't hooked, Clarissa." A shiver ran through her. "You don't know what they were planning to do."

"What?" The blonde's hair touched her shoulder when she tilted her head with the question.

Sarah looked down to the tie. "I should have demanded his keys and hood."

Walking between rows of cars, Ben shifted his eyes from the girls to the dark wagon in the distance. The faint candle light within made the moving shadows on the curtains dance in odd ways. Tying back into the conversation, he said, "Those guys are perfect examples of why Dunn-Blatt's practitioners have the bad reputation." He looked to Clarissa. "They were out to do harm."

His peripheral vision registered Sarah nodding to support his statement.

An air of innocence and naiveté clung to Clarissa, and if her friend wasn't going to explain to her that the Primaries didn't show because the boys were issuing challenges far more sinister then the Samhain Shenanigan, Ben decided he wasn't going to either.

Clarissa didn't grasp the situation and her brown eyes begged for a solid answer.

Trying to clue her in, Ben changed his mind. *Maybe she'll get it if I lay a sugar-coated trail for her to follow.* "They probably, *probably*, would have stolen your tablets."

"That's just silly." Clarissa's eyes rolled as she quickly rambled, "Why would they steal our schoolwork? Our school's enchantment focus is nearly the opposite of theirs. Heck, we don't even have comparable classes. Further, why would they think I would bring it to the Samhain Celebration? That's just—" Her face tightened up as though the word forming in her mouth tasted sour. She blinked hard as though she had to fight to get the word out. "—stupid."

Sarah tapped Clarissa's arm and spoke in a gentle manner. "He means our bracers, dear."

Clarissa faced changed to shocked fear. She pulled her right arm into her chest and covered it tightly with her left. "Why would they do that?"

Sarah didn't respond.

"So you won't have them." Ben said, as he took a last look at the wagon. It became obscured by other wagons and trailers. "Well, that and to reap what they can from the spell memory."

Clarissa dropped her arms. "Huh?"

"He means, echo-cast." Sarah translated as her eyes went to Ben's Anvilsmith for a moment before returning to the tie. "We don't cast the way Apes do."

Apes? Even after I helped them out of a bind. The last thing he expected to hear from them was the horrible slur. Ben stopped. *Don't be rude in return.* He told himself again. *Ben, don't be rude in return.* He fought hard to squash the urge. Trying to squeeze the sudden anger away, he jammed his hands in his coat pocket and made tight fists.

Sarah glanced back, stopped, and turned. Realizing what she had said, her eyes widened and she sucked her bottom lip between her teeth, making her apology come out slushy. "Shit, shorry."

"Perhaps you girls should go on without me." Ben shrugged. *Keep cool.* He tried to seem aloof while his fists were clenching and unclenching. He wanted to prove the superiority of his style of casting, but flaunting skill stood against the Archon Private Academy's Charter, which he never understood since dueling—the ultimate form of casters showing off their skill—had brought techno-casting from zero to its current stature.

When the method was being pioneered in 1984, the entire Tradition mocked using technology to cast spells. At first, it had been slow and the spells were weak. *Traditional casters* collectively declared, "It was so easy, that a monkey could do it." Which gave rise to anti-tech posters of monkeys at computers, and *the slur.*

In 1992, *The Shroud,* a caster wrapped mummy-like, with thick hooded robes, took to The Circuit with a mundane laptop modified by Gnomecraft Artificers—later upgraded to tablets—and held The Circuit Crown until 2002. When The Shroud finally removed his coverings and revealed himself as Master Reynolds. The starwise world was infuriated. He had been the first in centuries to break vows to the Queen-Mother's Monastery. Cast out as a pariah, he had risen to be a champion and opened his own school, the first Archon Primary Academy.

Ben's hands stopped working. "Maybe one day, we *Apes* will be allowed to participate in the Junior Circuit. Then we'll see what we'll see."

As she had in the parking lot, Sarah took a step toward him. This time, she extended her hands, palms up, a foot from her hips. She wanted to take his hand to lower her forehead to it in apology.

Recognizing the courtly gesture, Ben stepped back to deny her. Logically, he felt like he had dismissed the anger the slur brought, but the Nilosian energy in his head burned the word in his brain as though she had branded him. Bastion wouldn't let him get over it. Ben pointed. "The opening to the fairgrounds is right up there."

She pouted and made a second attempt.

A sneer turned Ben's lips as he shifted further away. *If you think you're looks could make me forgive the egregious insult, you've got another thing coming.* He shook his head. "No, we're done." As an afterthought, he cursed Bastion.

Because of the beast reinforcing the insult, Ben knew he was being a complete ass, but couldn't stop.

He'd been so focused on keeping Sarah at bay that he didn't notice Clarissa bound forward until she slid her arms around his sides. Inside his coat, she had him wrapped in a hug, and planted a quick kiss on his cheek before going back to hugging him. She spoke into his chest. "Thank you, Benjamin Baxter."

Furious at Sarah, Ben was about to shove Clarissa away when the purity of her gratitude shook Bastion's manipulation and shrank Ben's anger to a manageable proportion. Ben closed his arms around her and returned the embrace. "You're welcome, Clarissa."

Sarah started to move forward to turn the moment into group affection.

No. He extended his hand, palm out.

Sarah stopped. Her eyes turned a careless roll. "Come on, Clarissa."

The blonde dragged her arms against Ben's sides as she released him to catch up with her friend.

Before they'd gotten too far from him, Ben remembered Jack's treachery. He verified the Anvilsmith still hung from his hip and ran a finger across his spellcard holder. Nothing had been taken.

The girls entered the fairground.

Ben turned back to the parking lot to look over the few remaining cars of the starwise who had to park in the mundane lot. Near three A.M., the mundane part of the carnival had closed. Though he could not see from the outside, a large number of duels—the festival's main draw—were taking place just on the other side of the entrance. These two weeks of light-hearted contests were the only ones in which the Archon Private Academy could partake; the normal stigmas forgotten in the spirit of Samhain.

The gruff voice came from his ring again. "Return to Meadows Towing."

"I will. I will." Ben removed the ring and put it in a pocket. He didn't know what the orcs needed, but his parents only allowed him to come to the festival this one night. If he'd stuck to his plan of only playing a few round of the Conjuror's Course and gone home with tickets, his dad probably would've talked his mom into letting him come back... Now, empty handed, he'd have to sneak to come back; which he loathed to do.

Ben stopped playing the *if* game. He had one night—tonight—to have fun and he'd yet to see Crystal's idol, Papa Mojo, for the free reading she had arranged. To soothe his mind for not immediately responding to the ring summons, Ben spoke to himself. "If it's of dire importance, they'll call."

Walking to the entrance, Ben raised his right arm to show he did not have a Shenanigans armband and moved onto the fairgrounds.

Though the APA sanctioned these bouts, his parents consistently refused to sign the disclosure, waiver, and consent forms... Which sucked. Ben tried to find the bright side of not participating in the games. "At least there won't be a line for the Seer." Failing at minimizing his desire to duel, he added, "If he's still open."

A hook landed just below his ribs and traveled to his sternum. His hand shot to his spellcards before he felt the jovial spirit of the person who had hooked him. Turning sideways, he looked down the taught emerald tether to see Clarissa. Color filled her dimpled cheeks and her small smile spread ever so slightly wider when her intent to duel him for a kiss registered.

His own cheeks beginning to warm, Ben smiled back.

Whirling gray robes appeared next to her. The Vibrosian Primary appeared. The Magistrate's gaze traveled down the tether to him with his hand held high in unquestionable non-participation. She pointed her baton at Clarissa.

Clarissa tried to unhook him.

Ben wanted to hold on to flirt with her, but he'd already been given a censure warning. Another strike might get him booted from the festival for the night.

He let his intent of wanting to hold on be known through the tether and let the hook go.

The Magistrate waved at Ben to move on to the safe zone in the starwise section of the fair.

He started walking.

Though he couldn't hear what she was saying, the Vibrosian Primary took to scolding Clarissa. Something about the excessive finger waggling made the Magistrate look like she moved beyond acting in official capacity. He'd never heard of this kind of thing happening. Was a Sunrise Mountain girl liking a technocaster that offensive? Ben couldn't help wondering aloud, "What's up with that?"

Chapter Twelve

UNDER SURVEILLANCE

BEN'S PLAN of returning to the dark wagon vanished when he viewed the anemic crowds inside the starwise area. Being generous with his guess, Ben figured only a tenth of the former crowd had been non-teens and these adults, and children, were the only ones still wondering around. Seemingly, without exception, everyone able to participate in the Shenanigans—the uncountable mass of teens—were. The thinned out crowd meant fewer games in operation, which, in turn, meant the released workers would be in the employee only area.

The Adults milling around, most with children too young to participate in the duels, eyed him—*the last teen on Earth, a pimple on an otherwise flawless face*—suspiciously.

"Ben," Gary called out. *Challenge the Conjurer* proved to be one of the few games that still had a decent line. He held up the bags of Ben's SD cards.

Even against the odds, a part of Ben wanted to try to make it back to where Collins and the woman talked about him. If he took the bags, they would slow him down or give him away if he had to leave them behind. Ben shook his head. "Can you hold onto them?"

"Sure." Gary set the bags down and began to make his way back up to his booth. "Have fun and keep an eye out for the dragon's assault."

"Will do," Ben replied as his mind started working on what the parting term could have meant. *Dragon's assault. Doubtlessly code for something...* Ben snapped his fingers. *Got it!*

Though he never went for it, Ben had asked Gary about the top spell at the *Conjuror's Course.* Wearing the attendant uniform instead of his current harlequin worker's robs, Gary had poo-pooed the prize, stating a dragon conjuration was no good if the caster didn't also know dragon tactics. Most didn't know how to fight dragon-style and always tried to start their attack from behind their target and over cover.

When Ben turned to scan the building and tent tops behind him, a bright orange scrying sensor dropped below the edge.

So far, he'd only seen the one Vibrosian Primary. *Is she keeping tabs on me?* He had to make sure he wasn't just being paranoid. Ben made his way through the midway and into the Fae Fort Food Court. *Holy...* Most of the booths were closed, but Southern Sweets had a sign out front. *We want to be in on the Shenanigans, too. If you want to play, but can't, come get a free Cotton Cloud.* Then in smaller print. *Offer only valid for school-aged practitioners.*

Feeling a bit foolish standing in lines with pre-teens, Ben waited his turn and ordered his favorite, a Kamikaze. The pie-faced lady smiled widely at him and spun him the largest serving of cotton candy Ben had seen. Before accepting, he bowed deeply and thank her. Made with all thirty available base flavors, his confection had a random pattern like a crazy, tie-dyed t-shirt with colors that ranged from white to deep brown. Strolling between the midway and Fae Fort Food Court, and back again, he tilted his head to eat the delicious sugar cloud. By the time he finished the massive thing, he had secretly spied the sensor a dozen times more. *Why is the Primary keeping tabs on me?*

Under direct surveillance, Ben had no chance of returning to the dark wagon without giving her a reason to fixate on him further.

He had only been an Initiate at the time, but he clearly remembered the three, bright red scry sensors that followed a near-graduating APA student everywhere. Later, when he had asked Adept Matton why, the Adept said the student was Geotheon Mossburge—as though the name alone would be answer enough. It had been Ben's first time seeing sensors and, as such, he figured they always came in threes.

Time proved otherwise. Three Magistrates kept tabs on Geotheon at all times. *What had Geotheon done?*

Heck, what did I do?

Even if he managed to fish his ring from his pocket on the sly, he'd probably suddenly vanish from her extrasensory field of vision.

Though not illegal, hiding from a Primary's scry would be akin to waving an *I'm up to no good* flag, as the mystical sensors were the Magistrates' main form of patrolling the city. He had heard that you were presumed innocent until they could prove you guilty, but if you tried to evade the Lesser Judges, the presumption switched.

Having seen how they responded to Collins' spell, he knew the latter half to be true.

Ben gave up on spying on the Senior Adept, and hoped Papa Mojo's had stayed open. *Perhaps the seer can tell me why the Primary has taken such an interest in me.*

Chapter Thirteen

PAPA MOJO

DIM LIGHTS LIT THE LONG, French Quarter-esqe, Diviner's Row. Various wagons of different designs were all packed tightly together to make the most of their limited section of the Samhain Festival. This late, all of the wagons were closed and the merchandise had been cleared away from most of the stands.

Figuring he wasn't far from the truth, Ben identified the ones he thought were the best at divination by their racks still having wares on display. Those rare few wagons might as well have had a sign posted that said *go ahead and steal, you'll be caught!* Some even had Everbloom flowering plants out front, battling for scent superiority. Roses versus sunflowers versus honey suckle. Nature's battle royal.

Ben stopped before the wagon he found to be the most colorful.

Its bright yellow base had grass and long green stems painted up the side, blossoming into clouds. The white-trim gutter of the roof above the front door rained hundreds of tiny bubbles. Four pinwheels set to the four directions squeaked softly as they all rotated clockwise. Instead of a trinket stand, there were rows and rows of wrapped candy with a real sign, reading *Have one.*

He smiled, picked a small, root beer barrel hard candy, and made a mental note to return here next year. With the chaotic taste of the delicious Kamikaze cotton candy still swimming in his mouth, he tucked the barrel away and hustled past the remaining wagons to the very end, where Crystal said Papa Mojo's cart would be.

Its glow more obvious in the darkened row, the Primary's orange sensor stayed behind the wagons, but kept pace.

To Ben's mild surprise, the row ended in a chain-link fence. He had expected a wagon.

Ben compared the two wagons which were pressed up against the fence, bowing it slightly. Both were dirty, had their lights out, and were made of dark, weathered wood. Neither had trinket stands or any other form of attention-getters out front. The only difference between them lay in the layer of dirt packed in every imperfection on the left-hand wagon. Both were aged, but the left one suffered from willful neglect.

As he turned toward it, a rope dropped before the chain-link fence. A deep, gravelly voice with a New Orleans drawl drifted down. "Benjamin. Crystal has told me about you."

Ben studied the rope. The bottom hung just above the ground and the top appeared to be suspended in midair. Grabbing hold, he gave it a shake. The bottom flopped freely, but the top point remained anchored to something he couldn't quite perceive. The hair on the back of his neck began to rise. Ben asked, "Do I climb up?"

"Depends," the voice answered, then asked, "Do you want a reading?"

What has Crystal signed me up for? Putting one hand above the other, Ben pulled on the rope to jump and heave his body up, and was about to wrap his legs around it when the area changed.

He still held the rope, but the top had loosened from its anchor point, and went limp in his hands.

Ben stood inside a darkened room. The lack of lighting made the area into an optical illusion as though he stood in infinite darkness. He put his hand in front of his face and couldn't see it. A part of him felt that if he were to extend his arms, he would probably be able to touch both walls. About to do so, an odor—a cross of mildew and acrid mothballs—crept into his nose.

Once idle in the font of Nilosian energy concentrated in Ben's head, Bastion roused.

The beast's apprehension translated through Ben as he lowered into a defensive stance. His hand went to the spellcard holder placing his index finger on Shield, his middle on Blast, and his thumb on Orion. Turning a slow circle, a faintly glowing sphere suspended in air at the far end of the room, caught his attention.

Something dark and slim settled on the other side of the sphere. The lighting from the orb barely lit a two-inch radius around it. A face, only visible from just under the nose, leaned forward, throwing shadows across the cheeks and higher. The pools of shadows in the eye sockets parted to a deeper darkness. Eyes opened, the face appeared to be a porcelain mask suspended just behind the orb of light.

The mouth moved and the same deep slow voice from the top of the rope rolled to him. "Come forward, Benjamin. I won't bite."

Instead of doing as beckoned, Ben paid attention to Bastion. The beast—Ben started to think of as his Nilosian personification—seemed leery, but had not become fully active.

Ben kept his fingers on his spellcards, sliding his pinky to Feather's Grace in case he fell into a pit or a trap door opened beneath him as he inched through the dark room. The floor gave slight resistance as though he walked on deep, plush carpet. He looked down again, but the darkness obscured everything not lit by the orb.

As he moved closer to the light source, the shape of the crystal ball on a squat black base registered. It lit the center of a checkered purple and black wooden table with chess pieces around it. The mildewed mothball smell grew stronger.

Ben couldn't recall the crystal ball that Crystal used ever glowing, but, then again, she never had all of the lights out in her apartment.

Proximity revealed precious little more of the face. The mouth—*not a mask, then. Ivory skin?*—moved with the words. "I am Papa Mojo. My visions are faultless. What I see cannot be questioned and cannot be denied." As though feeling Ben scrutinizing him, the face withdrew into the shadows to fade from view. "For what I see will always come to be."

Shielding his mind as Elder Komir taught him, Ben imagined his thoughts and memories secured in a thick iron box. He did this mostly for protection, but his inner skeptic began searching for faults. *Can I trust someone who obscures themselves in shadows?*

"Sit across the table from me." Papa Mojo bayed and the shape of a folding chair moved in the darkness. "Let my crystal ball see you so that we may divine what your future holds."

Ready to react to an attack or sinister laugh, Ben sat on the shadow chair.

Chapter Fourteen

FUTURE TELLING

BEN HAD SEEN a classic horror movie which ended when a teenage caster sought out a mad witch to divine the outcome of—what he thought would be his worst decision—leaving the starwise world to join the mundane. When the caster looked into the witch's crystal ball, he saw himself looking in on himself, looking in on himself, and when he looked up, he only saw the witch's face—monstrously huge, concaved, and laughing—looking down at him trapped inside her orb. The credits rolled.

Though the darkness in Papa Mojo's dank wagon kept the exact dimensions from being known, something about the darkness seemed to press in tight around the glowing crystal ball. The weight of shadows triggered a concern in Ben that could easily blossom into a full claustrophobic fear.

The mask—*white face paint slathered thick on his forehead, cheekbones, and chin*—drew a bit closer to the orb where Ben could make out the darker areas of the eyes. Doing his best to make light of the steadily increasing thump of his heart flooding his system with adrenaline, Ben spoke in the same airy cadence as Papa Mojo. "What do you see, for me?"

Dark irises, recessed further back in the painted face than Ben had thought, flicked from the orb, to him, and then returned to fixate on the crystal ball.

Ready to defend himself—*if you try to capture my soul...*—Ben pressed his lips together and swallowed.

The face floated back and away from the crystal ball as long, skeletal fingers—*four joints? Five?*—closed in on the light which never lit Papa Mojo's palms.

Almost subconsciously, Ben nodded a confessional agreement to his imagination that the worst nightmare it could conjure for him tonight would involve those impossibly long, disembodied fingers threatening to close tight around his neck when he closed his eyes to sleep.

Papa Mojo's voice rumbled across the table, "She likes you, but you and Crystal are not destined."

What the heck is he talking about? Ben felt his features tightened. *Not destined for what?*

Papa Mojo's floating face eased toward the light a little. The darkness made his white face paint look like something created from dingy gray papier-mâché. "Nor are you to be with Sarah."

My love life? Really? Ben's mouth curled into a smirk. Relationships were the first place unskilled diviners went to try and wow the customer with their ability to say—*not an ability to see the future*—what the customer wanted to hear. Nothing less than the world would have to be at stake for him to date the Sunrise Mountain elitist. Anything less could burn. Ben sighed. *How could Crystal see so much in this guy? He starts with a near slam dunk topic while not getting close to anything that I really want to know?*

Leaning in to interrupt and ask about the Vibrosian's sensor, Ben's tongue froze to the roof of his mouth when the mystic's fingers stopped moving and pulled away from the light. "Nor Clarissa."

Closer, floating inside Papa Mojo's scrying device, a fluid scene of the hug Clarissa had sprung on him replayed from a floating point of view which showed Sarah off to the side. Clarissa's eyes were closed as she pressed the side of her face again his chest. They remained closed as she lifted her face to peck-kiss his check before returning to the hug. From this angle, Ben could see her slip something into his pocket as they separated.

He slipped his hand into his coat and felt a small rectangle of stiff paper. Suddenly, a subtle fear of looking up and seeing Papa Mojo's masked face monstrously huge, concaved, and laughing—*just like in the movie*—settled on his shoulders like a freezing yoke.

The image wafted away as Mojo's fingers returned to working the orb.

Ben stole a glance up at the mask and, upon seeing the white paint turned dingy in the dark, breathed a bit easier.

Miniscule glints lit in Mojo's eyes as the orb brightened. "This is who you want to be with."

Cursing himself while he did so—*I might fall in*—Ben leaned in closer to the orb. A fond smile filled his face as a Penelope montage played inside the magical orb—Tex cutting open the burlap bag she had been stuffed in and removing her thumbscrews. Penelope standing in the back of his car while casting the spell which made the Transcend fly. Penelope walking through Pepperjacks. Penelope being chased by the dragon-tuzvul. Penelope covering her mouth at what she saw in the huge war scene painting. The meal they shared with Elder Komir. Penelope hiding in the stable and watching him fight Jack, and then—flash—Penelope in her gold and crimson robes at a desk looking into a crystal ball of her own.

"This didn't happen," Ben said. At least he didn't think it had. Trying to see what she was doing with her own crystal ball, Ben leaned over the table, even closer to Papa Mojo's orb. "What's she doing there?"

Mojo's fingers worked around the orb, at times millimeters in front of Ben's face, tracing symbols in the air. "I cannot tell." His deep voice sounded strained. "The wards in the room she's in are too strong."

Penelope turned in her chair to look up at them.

Instead of washing away like the others visions, this image flickered out to black. Then the crystal ball slowly lit again.

Ben's flushed with heat. He sat bolt upright and gripped the edge of the table. "Will I see her again?"

Papa Mojo's face faded back into darkness as the hands closed in on the sphere. Those long fingers nearly encircled the crystal ball, the diviner's palms were coated in the same white paint and came a hair's breadth from making contact. A hiss filled the area as Mojo's hands shook. Swirling red and black smoke whirled inside the orb. It rolled, undulated, and switched directions. Mojo's painted face shot toward the crystal ball. He blew on the glass.

Thick and voluminous, Ben could smell the contents. Smoldering *ashes*. It brought back the month-old memory of Pepperjacks burning. Then, that tangy sweet smell of freshly sawed and varnished wood.

The ball cleared.

Ben saw himself—the same—and Penelope—dark, curly hair flowing down from a golden, ruby encrusted, circlet set high on her head. They stood, together, outside Pepperjacks' front doors, newly remade front crimson stained glass. *The future.* She stepped forward. Ben licked his lips for a kiss. She reached out and shook his hand.

A quick surge of air puffed from Ben's lips. His dreamy hope of seeing her again, a reoccurring fantasy, burst. He sighed. "A flippin' handshake? That's all?"

Papa Mojo's fingers worked in quick motions and pulled back into darkness. The handshake grew to fill the crystal ball.

Ben's shoulders slumped at the sight of her red leather-clad hand in his. "She's even wearing gloves."

Papa Mojo's deep voice rumbled, "She knows what you are and the type of magic you were born to use."

What'd he just say? Ben's guts turned to ice. They churned in fear. Shook in anger. *Shouldn't have let my guard down.* Using black magic would make one an outcast, but being a true Nilosian—which he had discovered he was and could not undo, *so unfair*—would get you killed, and he'd been discovered.

A quick mental inventory found his protection still in place. *I didn't let my guard down. Wait, he said 'she knows.' Mojo may not.* Ready to fight for his life, Ben lifted his gaze from the crystal ball to the diviner.

Still white-faced, thin snake-like slits slashed through dull yellow orbs set in the dark hollows of Papa Mojo's eye sockets. Mojo rumbled, "It is my magic, too, Benjamin." His thin digits went to the light from the crystal ball. Black magic oozed from the fingertips like ink squirted into water before being sucked back in. "I show you now, for you will find out before you see me again. We are now joined in darkness, Brother." Papa Mojo bridged his fingers over the crystal ball, forefingers stippled between the reptilian eyes. "I cannot expose *you*, for you would reveal *me*."

Ben breathed a little easier for a moment. He tensed. *I'm in an accord with him.*

Leaning back, a dark cavernous maw, highlighted by the white face paint on the dark diviner's chin, grew when the man smiled. "Even the handshake may not happen if you do not last through tonight and save Clarissa tomorrow."

"What's happening tonight?" Ben's mind shifted from concern about his safety to worry for Clarissa's survival. *She's probably the only truly innocent person I know.* "What's happening tomorrow?"

"Purple on a car..." Papa Mojo's fingers dropped back to working the crystal ball. Malcolm, in a deep violet, hardtop Transcend—*he has the same car as me*—with a charging buffalo painted along the length. Mojo hummed before waving his hands. Malcolm, and his car, flew away in wafts of smoke. "Not that one." Another vehicle appeared, a trembling white Legerity muscle car with a dark magenta trunk and bumper.

Ben scanned the car vibrating from the stock, oversized engine crammed in and cranked up. *There's no identifiers on the car. Beyond the paint there, there was nothing to make it look different than any other Legerity.*

Mojo rolled his fingers around the ball. Inside, a flash of Ben, in his black Transcend, following the Legerity. "Chase this car." A flash of red taillights disappearing around an impossibly tight corner. "It will lose you in an industrial complex where Clarissa is being packed and shipped." Another flash. Ben smiled at seeing himself laying a body wrapped in burlap—*why do they use burlap*—in his backseat. His small robotic companion, Tex, was there and had to move quickly to get out of the way.

Papa Mojo waved at the vision. The Legerity came back for a moment before it puffed away into slow-moving white and purple smoke. His eyes dimmed to a darkened burnt yellow. "You won't have time to free her then. Whether you see them or not, her abductors will pursue until you get back here. Get her to the starwise entrance and she'll be safe."

Ben arced an eyebrow. "How will that make her safe?"

"We will be one day closer to Samhain." Papa Mojo answered, "There will be even more Magistrates on duty and one will see you race onto the fairgrounds. Then, after that one shows, they will all come."

"Okay." Ben nodded. He'd seen the Primaries at work a couple of times and they did run in packs. "So, what about tonight?"

As though he no longer needed the divining device, Papa Mojo moved his hands away from the crystal ball. The slightest remaining hint of his yellow eyes faded and shadows filled the seer's sockets. "The orcs are in trouble, but you'll have to weigh helping them versus exposing Collins for what he truly is."

Senior Adept Collins? Ben sat up straight. His mouth wetted. He swallowed. "What is he?"

"Expose him…" The face and fingers withdrew from the light. Papa Mojo drew a shallow breath and let it out with a wheeze. "…and find out. This session," The seer drew in a much deeper breath and exhaled, "is over."

The crystal ball went dark, so did the room.

A door creaked behind Ben. Bright illumination spilled in throwing his shadow across the table, blotting out the crystal ball, Papa Mojo, and his long creepy fingers. A cheery voice, as sweet as jelly beans, called over the brilliant P. A. system. "Attention, Benjamin Baxter."

Ben glanced over his shoulder.

With an otherworldly *pop*—which rang on Ben's ears—the darkness of Mojo's wagon burst like a balloon.

He stood right where the rope had dropped down in front of him between the weathered wagons at the end of Diviner's Row. The announcer continued, "Please report to Red Lot Five. Your tow is here."

Ben had many more questions before Mojo went *completely spent* on him.

Why do seer end sessions like that? This wasn't the first time a diviner had called a session done on Ben before he was ready. *Wonder if it's an act to keep the customer from asking for too much, or if spending arcane energy to glimpse the future is truly that taxing.*

The perky voice repeated the call for him to respond for his tow.

Doing as directed, Ben began to make his way over to starwise parking. *But I'm not parked in Red Lot Five, and I don't need a tow...*

Chapter Fifteen

CROSSING LINES

THRILLED to have fresh festival air—*I still want popcorn*—instead of the heavy, manure smell of his shortcut through the Mystic Menagerie, Ben took in a deep breath. *The animals may be magical, but their poop still stinks.* Ben took another deep breath to clear his lungs. His gazed settled across the long paved spans. He could see each of the five entrances from the Red, White, and Black starwise lots.

Before midnight, this area would be full of Samhain entertainers aiming to excite incoming festival goers and a person would be lucky to see fifty feet ahead of themselves. This late, the bare area almost felt sad. For the first time, Ben noticed the shape of large wild cats—*there's a whole lot of lions*—in the lengths of beautifully crafted, wrought iron fences separating the entrances. Beyond the fences, several Koffman Lanterns floated out in the dark parking lot, floating twenty-five feet above casters leaving the festival and illuminating the area around them.

Furthest away, under two ornate lion paws supporting a large glowing red "Five," Ben could make out the Vibrosian Primary, Collins, and Jek waiting for him. The Magistrate stood so straight, Ben would've guessed her baton was up her butt if she didn't have it pointed at him. Next to her, Collins. The Senior Adept tried to emulate the Primary's commanding presence, but failed to rise higher than simply being demanding. Quite a bit taller than both casters, Jek stood hunched in the white Meadows Towing t-shirt and blue jeans. The bearded orc had his neck bent and his thick, orcish brow cast foreboding shadows over his eyes.

A series of yells, students raising their voices to call out their school's name, in attempts to drown out all the other pulsed from further in the grounds. About to yell out himself, Ben stopped. No one was around that would appreciate him calling out *A. P. A.*, nor compete against him by voicing their own school. Not inside or taking part in creating the din, their rhythmic voices sounded like a cacophony of the insane.

Ben paused. It occurred to him that Jek was the only orc—*heck, the only non-human*—he had ever seen at the Samhain Festival. Broadening his scope, the reality of the entire city not having one non-human, besides Collin's elf, smacked him.

How could that be, when there was a towing company with only orcs as employees, and a giant inside of Pepperjacks?

Ben pulled his Anvilsmith and made a note to ask Councilor Eastly about this phenomenon at their monthly review. Sliding his tablet back on his hip, Ben felt no pressure to rush to the casters, but he had a feeling time was of the essence for his orcs.

Tone lofty and demanding, the Primary spoke first. She said, "Have you seen either of the Sunrise Mountain girls you followed into the fairgrounds recently?"

"You should know," Ben snapped. "You've been watching me since."

Her eyebrows lowered to draw a *you're-testing-my-patience* line between them.

Unabashed, Ben held her gaze.

Her lips pursed into a tight seal. They split to let out a single, strained, word. "Tone."

Ben tightened his throat to bar his sarcastic replies. He'd rushed headlong into a social faux pas. Years of following the rules, pressing his heels together in acknowledgment. *What would happen if I refused to bow?* Only a fleeting thought. Ben bowed at the waist until he bent at thirty degrees. He noted dust and dirt clinging to the hem of her outermost gray robe. *What have you been up to, Magistrate?* Softening his voice to a respectful tone, Ben said, "My apologies, Lesser Judge."

Her voice remained stressed. "A representative from your school is here, and I am certain he will make sure your *Courtmanship* Adept is made aware of this folly."

She didn't acknowledge my apology. Ben held his position. Though she had stopped speaking, he was to hold the position until she gave him permission to stand. She was testing his adherence to tradition and, probably because of his small act of defiance, waited in silence to impress her status upon him.

Inwardly, Ben frowned. *She's not worthy of the office. Oh, crap.* He focused to steel his thoughts, which were protected behind thick layers. Thankfully, he had shielded them out of habit.

Bastion stirred from his slumber in Ben's head and began a round of rebellious hoots.

Unfamiliar with the social rigors of magic-using society, and not knowing to be still until the highest ranking person gave permission to move, Jek shifted from foot to foot. A sound like two pieces of sandpaper rubbing together came from the orc.

Ben didn't shift his eyes—that would put him in deeper water—but from his peripheral vision, he could see the orc wringing his thick hands.

The Magistrate must have given Collins a nod, as the Senior Adept's brown cowboy boots sauntered into view. "Care to make another attempt, *Junior* Adept?" Collins' normally condescending tone felt heavier, but oddly not as personal.

Attempt at what? Apologizing? Ben blinked, making sure he didn't keep his eyes closed for too long or the power-tripping jerks would rightfully suspect him of entertaining unpleasant thoughts about them.

Bastion bounded around his head urging Ben to act on those thoughts. With Jek present, they could easy beat down the two mages and scram.

And go where? They'll hunt us. Ben said, "I decline."

"Noted." Collins' boots moved away before he prompted, "Then answer the Lesser Judge."

"I have not—" Ben managed to keep his voice even and his tone respectful. Further he kept his jaw loose to not show how much having to say these honorific words pissed him off. "My Lady."

She waved the baton under his nose, granting him permission to stand straight, and whirled her robes. In a suck of air, nature filling a vacuum, she teleported away.

"That was bullshit." Ben had not meant for the words to come out, but they did as he straightened and gained eye contact with Collins.

Free to return to his bitter demeanor, the Senior Adept said, "What did you say *Junior*—"

"What she did." Fuming, Ben extended a hand to where the Primary had been, and cut in. "I didn't do anything wrong." Wanting to leave, he took a step toward Jek. "Complete and utter bullshit, and didn't serve a purpose."

Collins hissed, "It was much-needed, to remind you of your place." His boot scrapped on the pavement. "Hey, Baxter, I didn't dismiss—"

Jek shuffled.

Collins *oofed* a surprised puff of air.

He turned to see the Senior Adept several feet away, sitting on the ground. Still, next to Ben, Jek brought his arms back from full extension. Ben's neck swiveled as he looked between the two, piecing together the scenario. Collins must have advanced on him to grab his arm like they were at the Archon Private Academy, but Jek had interceded, shoving the Senior Adept to the ground.

Staring death at Jek, Collins jumped back to his feet. Hot and dangerous, his voice came from deep in his throat. "How dare you, cur?" Abnormal bumps moved behind the flesh around Collins' mouth as though he had grown fangs. They showed when Collins thundered, "You will learn your place!"

Having seen Collins blast students not allowed to defend against the attack at school, Ben slipped his hand to the SD card on his hip. He stepped in front of Jek and channeled Argosian into it. "He's no student of yours."

Instead of a mystic bolt blasting from the Senior Adept's hand, neutered fizzing crimson smoke puffed from his fingertips and faded. Collins' jaw clenched tight. The pupil in his right eye cracked. Inky black flooded the blue iris.

The Senior Adept's face changed in an instant. His absolute rage became abject horror as his hand slapped over his eye socket.

Though quick, Ben didn't doubt what he saw.

"Loyalty, from an orc..." Muttering the rest, Collins turned away to flee.

"Don't use that word, Collins." Ben called as the Senior Adept's boots carried him away. Having waited for an opportunity to address Collins slipping him a cursed tablet, Ben chided, "I'm sure it burns your mouth."

Collins stopped. Lips still moving as he talked to himself, the Senior Adept looked back at Ben with his inky eye covered. Boots clicking, Collins continued to hurry away.

Ben wanted to chase Collins down. To flag anyone they came across to expose the Senior Adept's inky eye, doubtlessly full of Nilosian energy.

Papa Mojo's prediction came back to him. *The orcs are in trouble, but you'll have to weigh helping them versus exposing Collins for what he truly is.*

Knowing he had to choose between the two didn't make the decision any easier, but it did enable Ben to make his choice quicker. He pulled his tablet, typed a command to Tex, and motioned for Jek to take the lead. "Where's your truck?"

Chapter Sixteen

A TOUGH CONCEPT

WINDOW ROLLED DOWN, Ben had his arm hanging on the passenger side window of Jek's tow truck. The cool night air whipped his sleeve back, and every time they hit a bump too hard, he reeled his arm in to check the side mirror and made sure his Transcend was still hooked on the back.

Ben didn't share the orcs confidence in the tow chains. Even with both windows down, the cab still held the slight, persistent smell of freshly-sliced salami. Getting a tenuous grip on the situation, Ben peered into the darkness just beyond Jek's high beams.

Driving in silence, the orc kept both of his hands on the rocking, sheepskin-covered steering wheel. Waiting for the next question, he occasionally glanced at Ben.

For his part, Ben understood the basic tenants of orcs being either slaves or wild. Jek had done his best to give the short version of the reason why all the goblinoid races—weebos, goblins, orcs, hobgoblins, ubbos—all embraced *slave or wild* as a way of life. It had been the main reason his orcs decided to stay and *serve* rather than accepting their freedom when Ben had offered it to them.

Jek made a quick right turn.

After making sure his car hadn't broken free, Ben caught a visual of the Meadows Towing rotating, bright neon purple, star sign. He gave up wrestling with the concept to cut to summation. "So, this guy wants to challenge me for the scrapyard."

"No, Ben." Jek uttered a soft groan. "Just the title."

Almost feeling like a part of the *Who's on First* comic routine, Ben confirmed, "Might-Fist?"

"Yes." Jek nodded. "Exactly." The orc's nod looked tired, as though Jek had grown weary from trying to repeatedly explain something so simple.

Ben said, "All right." Pressing a finger on the sheepskin-covered dashboard with each fact, Ben gave understanding another shot. "Okay, the title gains him the belt. The belt gives him dominion over Meadows Towing." Jek opened his mouth to interject, but Ben rushed on. "Which makes *him* the Might-Fist. Once he's Might-Fist, he can turn ownership of the scrapyard to whomever he chooses by giving them the belt, but he'd still retain the title."

Jek gave a strong nod. "By Krilliloas, you got it!"

Ben tried to think of a way this could be handled peacefully. Nothing tangible came. *If an accord is struck, and I relent, there's no way to assure the deal would be upheld.* Defensive of how long it took him to get it, Ben explained, "I was likening it to human battle-sports, where the title and belt are inseparable."

Jek cut his eyes away. "This isn't a sport, Ben."

"Oh, trust me, I know." *Boy do I know.* Ben looked at the remaining eighty-five arcane watts on his tablet. "So, if I take this guy out—"

"When!" Jek corrected and slapped the steering wheel as though he squashed a bug. "*When* you do, his warriors stop fighting." The orc clenched his fist in victory. "And all of his possessions become yours."

Ben looked to the rotating purple star. "So, those are the rules."

"More like magical traditions." Jek stressed, "But only for the title."

Feeling a bit slow, Ben said, "Got it."

Within range, the orc pressed the gate opener strapped with rubber bands to his tattered sun visor. "You'd have to dominate his men into service." A casual single-shoulder shrug lulled Jek's head to the side. "Kill a few of the more defiant ones. That'll bring the rest quickly under heel."

As they drove onto the property, Ben's heart dropped. His neck tightened and his voice became small. "Thing is, I don't want to kill anyone."

In contrast, since hearing of the challenge, Bastion had swirled into a mass of pent-up rage in Ben's head, begging to be released.

Ben cleared his throat to loosen his tightening vocal chords. "So, they can't just murder me on sight, right?"

Another passive shrug. Jek's lack of concern started to become worrisome. Jek said, "He could, but then the title wouldn't transfer."

Afraid to ask, Ben did, "What would happen then?"

Jek answered, "Then, whoever defeats him, and pries it from his hands *and* defends the belt ten times, becomes the rightful Might-Fist of the area."

Hearing how bloody the process could be, Ben tried—for a moment—to imagine how many creatures had died on this ground for either the stupid belt or lofty title. In his mind's eye, the thought turned the numerous columns of countless wrecked cars into mounds of dead bodies. A shudder ran through him. "Why'd he even come?" Ben's budding paranoia—*thanks Collins*—searched for a reason. "I mean, why tonight?"

Jek dug in his left ear. "Last he heard, his father was the Might-Fist." The orc looked at the ear wax in his pinky nail for a moment before rubbing it into his seat. "As all good vassals will do, he came to pay tribute and discovered that his dad is dead—"

"Imprisoned," Ben cut in. "Not dead." He parted some of the sheepskin on the dashboard to indicate the subtle difference and defend himself. As much as he could, he had been humane to the captured ogre magi. "Ur-Krurk's getting food and water."

Either not seeing the difference, or not caring, Jek's shoulders raised and lowered.

Ben wished the orc would stop shrugging.

"He wants the title." Jek knocked on the large belt buckle hidden under Ben's coat, covering his abdomen.

What if I don't have the belt? Ben thought about asking, but decided against it.

Jek went hand over hand on the steering wheel to take the last turn to put them onto the final approach to the main building. Jek said, "You will have a minute to reach an accord of some sort."

The violet neon glow of the Meadows Towing sign bathed the front of the building where distant movement stirred, visible mostly by the shadows they cast. Ben sat up to pay more attention.

"Don't get your hopes up," Jek continued. "If an agreement is not made—which it won't be—he has to present half his forces and then..." The orc shot him a sideways glance. "... it's on."

Ben's Anvilsmith chimed. Though his device's communication had been shut down since they left the festival, they had moved into Tex's range. The robot's chat window popped up. "Here's how things look." A tight overlay of the front building filled the screen. "Blue blip is the Ogre Magi who is challenging you." The screen zoomed out to include the building where green dots lit up in the garage. "Green blips are your blood-oathed orcs." The map zoomed way out to show twenty red dots near the front of the building with another twenty peppered throughout the first dozen rows of compacted and stacked cars. They flashed. "These are his guys." The latter twenty flashed. "These guys might have moved from where I've plotted them."

Estimating forty opponents, Ben angled his screen toward Jek and waved his finger around the mass of red dots. "Are these all of his fighters?"

"No!" Jek's head could not have shaken faster if he were a freshly knocked bobble-head. "That's just his traveling guard. He has hundreds, if not a thousand, warriors under his homeland banner. If he had known he was coming to battle, he would have brought all of them." Jek looked at Ben. "There's a general presumption about your kind. So, he'd rather fight now than go home and return with his full army."

"Huh?" The mention of race got Ben's notice.

Jek returned his attention forward.

Ben asked, "Why use forty instead of a thousand?"

Jek's lips twisted in consideration before explaining. "If he gave you time, you'd probably play the human-card."

Ben arced an eyebrow at the orc.

"You know." Jek switched to guiding the steering wheel with his knees. "Call on your kind to," Jek's voice rose in pitch and wavered in fake fear as he flailed his arms. *Repel the monstrous invasion.*

The imitation made Ben chuckle a bit. He asked, "Is that what we sound like to you?"

Jek grinned with a hint of guilt clinging to his shrug. "Are you saying it's not true?"

"Only if..." Ben exhaled his regret and slumped into the chair. The springs pressed back against him through the thin cushion. "I wish." He had wanted to contact the school, but his Anvilsmith's communication relay had gone on the fritz shortly after he reached Tex. *Just like on the night of Pepperjacks' burning.* Ben's fist balled when he thought about Collins shutting down his ability to contact the outside world. It had to be Collins. *Can't just be a coincidence that it would happen again, tonight, after his Nilosian-ink-eye thing happened.*

The ogre's teal skin could be made out in the distance. Ben asked, "Do I have to uphold any traditions?"

"Nope." Jek remained still. "Just show that you have the belt."

Though the orc had already verified the trophy lay under his coat, Ben decided to try for a loophole. "And what if I don't have it?" Ben had gotten used to Bastion's swirling when it shifted directions and made his head dip. *Stop it!*

A confused frown wrinkled Jek's brow. "But you do have it."

"Let me try putting it a different way." Feeling that he could taste victory just on the other side of his question, Ben licked his lips. "What if I didn't have it when I meet with the ogre?"

"Ohhh..." Catching on, Jek nodded with something close to pride at Ben's being sneaky.

Ben started to nod with him and let a sly smile spread his lips. "Now you're getting it."

"Well, in that case..." Going along with the scenario Jek continued his conspiring nod for a second before shrugging. "Then they'll murder you, your orcs, and ransack the place searching for the belt."

Stunned at the reversal, Ben mouth's popped open, and worked silently before he managed to squeak, "What?"

"Yeah." Jek returned to nodding. "Didn't think you'd think of that, but the ogre could get the title that way, too."

Chapter Seventeen

CORNERMAN

As Jek drove the truck toward the clearing in front of the main building, the blue and red dots on Ben's display scattered. His gaze went from the three green blips on his device to where his orcs would be in real space. All alive in their white Meadows Towing tees, blue jeans, and the black steel-toe Tore Vex boots he got them for Samhain. Their dark green faces framed in relief, they got to their feet and pounded their chest at him

Ben pounded his back. Their thorough elation at seeing him put a nagging suspicion into words. Ben narrowed his eyes and asked, "Jek, why didn't you say, *kill us*?"

"I'm not blood bound, and I fetched you." Jek gave a lopsided grin as he drove them around back. "As long as I stay out of the way, I live."

Betrayal flashed through him. Ben wanted to hit the orc to use their way of showing how angry he'd become. Instead, he hammer-fisted the dashboard. It rattled. The glove box popped open and slapped his knees. Ben slammed it shut. "You son of a bitch!"

"Hey! I want you to win. That party you threw us was great and my brood liked the extra day you gave us for home-time." Jek drove past the other four tow trucks and pulled into a spot. "Trust me when I say that I've had enough of ogre overlords, but..." A helplessness clung to his shrug. "I have to watch out for my hide."

If Ben had done anything like the dashboard punch in the company of schoolmates, Adept Matton would hunt him down to drag him to detention. Ben exhaled hard to get himself under control again. *You slimy snake.* "And to think, I was starting to like you." Ben kept his eyes on Jek through the windows as they got out. The back of the building always smelled from the barrels of used motor oil. *I should punish him ogre-style and make him drink one.* "Unhook my car."

Jek didn't. Instead he took five long strides to get in front of Ben and started whispering as they walked.

Planning to use the car to get away, Ben stopped and pointed at his Transcend raised up onto its rear tires. Some of the orc's words registered.

"... which is why your best tactic is to show how powerful you are at the end of the accord phase." Jek opened the door and entered.

Ben followed. Because of the oil barrels, his mind went back to how a rancid meat and rotted cheese smell used to dominate the building. Now it smelled of Twilight Spring air fresheners.

Jek continued, "Though he won't be phased, it would give some of his forces pause because they know that the first ones in are bound to fall to your might, and—when not defending home-land—no orc wants to die that way."

My might? A deprecating laugh waved up from Ben's stomach as they passed the big-screen TV. *It took me and Bastion together to beat his dad alone.* With his car still hooked, Ben's plan to give his orcs a minute's head start on getting out of here remained the same. For him, though, he'd have to cast *Usain* to escape. A good alternative plan, he nodded. *As long as I don't stop, I should be able to make it to the gate before the Komir amulet runs out of shielding.* Concerned about his companion, his mental checklist spilled through his lips, "No, we're good. I already had Tex sneak out."

Jek stopped and faced him.

Regret snapped Ben's lips together. He pressed them tight.

Bastion's hurricane swirling picked up speed filling Ben's ears with an ever-so-slight whooshing sound.

Jek's eyes narrowed in calculation. From that one sentence, the orc pieced enough together to ask, "You're going to run?"

Ben hated the hopeless shrug that rocked his shoulders. "I don't see this going my way."

Jek tensed, bore his teeth, and balled his fist.

Ben stepped back. He slipped a finger onto his *Orion* spellcard.

Words weighted with anger or disappointment—perhaps both— spilled through the tiny gaps around the tusks in the large pointy ivory bear trap the orc had for teeth. "Put your ring on. Show him that you took out his flesh-father."

Ben retrieved the ring from the bottom of his coat pocket and slid the band warmed by his body heat onto his thumb. *Perhaps I could bluff my way out of this. Play the, look-what-I-did-to-your-dad card.*

Jek reached behind the television and pulled out a baton. The orc pounded its chest in pride before extending it. "How about now, Might-Fist?"

Ben jumped back. "That's a— Where'd you get—" His mind's eye recalled the baton flipping end over end from the Imprisoning Orb as it spat out Ur-Krurk's possessions. "That's... it can't be... that's a Primary's Battle Baton."

Jek stepped closer. "And it's yours."

"Ut-uh." Ben shook his head and slid further back than Jek had advanced. "It belongs to its rightful owner."

Extending it behind him, Jek twisted and hocked it right at Ben's face.

Ben had already ducked. Yet, the ring raised his hand. The rod slapped into his palm and his fingers closed around it.

"You killed the rightful owner." Jek tucked his shirt in. "So ownership transferred."

Ben opened his mouth to correct Jek, again, about Ur-Krurk not being dead, but imprisoned, when a mystic bonding—*it is mine*— relayed the magic stored within the weapon. As though he were holding programmed spellcards, the baton enabled him to cast Magic Volley, Fireball, Righteousness, and Degenerative Aura. *No one passes Spell P III without being able to code Magic Volley and everyone knows about Fireball, but what in the heck are the last two?*

The rod would appear in his hand, when he willed it, and it

enabled him to substitute acid for any element he cast, transmuting the stored Fireballs into Acidballs. Amazed, Ben's voice took on a husky waver as he spoke through his inhale, "Wow."

"Yes. And it's yours. Use it." Jek turned and to walk back out. "If a loss is inevitable, I'll have your car loose."

How could an Ogre Magi be a Primary? Studying the dull steel rod—*it's weightless*—Ben waved it back and forth as the Vibrosian Magistrate had at the festival. Where the tip of hers had turned orange, his turned black. *No, it's absorbing light. Wait, it's not light, it's ambient arcane power.*

With the influx of Nilosian energy through the baton, Bastion's swirling intensified. The pressured building within played with Ben's inner ears and made him rock slightly.

Ben stopped waving the baton and tucked it into his belt against the small of his back. Remembering an off-hand comment Adept Love had made about battling regenerators in the few days of *Dueling* class he'd attended before his parents pulled him out, the baton probably didn't belong to the Krotosian. *The weapon couldn't have belonged to Ur-Krurk. The acidic focus means it's supposed to combat regenerators like Ogre Magi. If someone disarmed him, they'd be able use his baton against him with devastating results.* Ben exhaled. *Then who did it belong to?*

Ben pushed the thought from his head as he went to the kitchen. Filling the air better than a freshener, a large pot of barbeque sauce had boiled over and splattered on the stovetop. He turned off the burner and looked out the window to see the Ogre Magi's forces.

Orcs wearing a style of studded, black leather armor he had only seen on the other side, had come out of hiding and now were bumping into one another, hyping-up for the coming battle.

The Nilosian energy in his head stilled. Bastion began soaking it up like one of those flat sponges that grows in size as it takes in moisture.

The beast really wanted out to go at the ogre and, for a moment, Ben considered giving in to let it loose. He mumbled to the window, "Where's the ogre?" He pulled his Anvilsmith and flipped the switch to make it voice-activated. "Ping. Set mode to silent. Ping. Record." He holstered it back on his hip and took a deep breath. "Ping. Vibrate after one minute."

Ben stepped into the work bays. Still considering a hasty retreat, he whispered as loud as he dared to his orcs, "Guys. Go."

They nodded. Toad was first into the kitchen. The other two followed. About to go back in himself, a deep, growling voice yelled, "I challenge for Might-Fist!"

The belt buckle against Ben's abdomen thrummed, pulling Ben's recollection of Ur-Krurk's defeat. *I did beat his father.* The idea of fleeing switched to the back burner as a desire to keep the belt—if not the title —took the spotlight. *Let's see how this goes.*

Gassed up, Ben turned to face the ogre.

Chapter Eighteen

TITLE FIGHT

A STEADY CALM filled Ben where fear and dread had been building during the drive to Meadows Towing. The rubber-oil smell of mechanic work filled the five work bays and, looking out the bays at the score of hunter-green orcs—*pure warrior breed*—in black, studded armor, Ben realized just how ridiculous he must have looked a month ago when he came to reclaim the Node Key with only two conjured gorillas. He, Abe, and Oscar had run from the last row of stacked cars a hundred feet away and got caught in the open. Right where the orcs stood.

A barking laugh came from above them and the ogre clad only in a loincloth—*he's a deeper teal than his father, wonder what that means*—floated down to stand before the orcs. Like his father, Ur-Krurk's son possessed a massive upper body set on a long torso that made up two-thirds of the monster's height. Unlike his father, the stunted legs were powerfully built. Totally discounting Ben, the ogre magi turned and spoke in a rumbling growl to his men.

Ben had been practicing the Giant tongue with Jek, but the ogre's words were too swift for his rudimentary grasp of the language.

The ogre stopped mid-sentence to laugh harder. His wide, powerful shoulders rocked up and down beneath a large bauble of top-knotted black hair.

The mirth jumped to the orcs who howled along with their master.

Waving at Ben with a massive, clawed hand, the ogre uttered another rapid string of sentences.

Before they could rekindle their spat of laughing at him again, Ben raised his chin. "Dare to say that in English?"

The orcs stopped laughing.

The ogre's shoulders stilled as he turned. His glowering violet irises fixed on Ben from the pitch-black orbs. English, vowels too short, consonants too hard, slopped out, "I say, 'You aren't ev'n a full-grow.'" It snarled, showing a mouthful of sharp tar-black teeth. The ogre continued, "I also say, 'Had I know my flesh-fath'r had grow so weak, I would've dethron'd him months ago."

Bastion threw itself at Ben's sinuses.

It stung. *What's it doing?* Ben eyes watered a bit. He rubbed them. "Leave my property now, and you get to live."

The ogre laughed again. In a near fit, he leaned his head back, and struggled to speak Giant while pointing at Ben. When he finished, his orcs joined in.

Hooting, they mirrored their master and kicked their heads back in laughter.

Ben's Anvilsmith started to vibrate down the last few remaining seconds of the minute timer. Remembering the small gap of time between when he set the timer, spoke to his orcs, and then faced the ogre, Ben slid his hand to his hip. Touching his *Orion* spellcard, he channeled as much energy into it as he could. Five reds bursts flashed before him as his gorillas materialized. Three of them were empty-handed, one—*Abe*—had two knives and—*Oscar*—held a greatsword.

The ogre's laughs eased as he spoke Giant. This time, Ben recognized the last word and translated in his head. *Argosian.*

"I'm not an Argosian!" Ben threw his coat open.

The ogre's gaze fell upon the belt and darted to the Primary Rod as Ben waved it in a low, rising arc.

A tenebrous sigil at the tip of his baton drew light in and formed a symbol similar to the ones Ben had seen in the book Elder Komir gave him.

All laughter stopped. The ogre paled to a powder blue. The closer of his warriors took a step back. Two dog-headed monster-men stepped out of their hiding place behind the first row and began to slink away.

In his head, Bastion roared.

A slight growl rolled from the base of Ben's throat. He focused on the ogre. "Yeah, this is what you face." Ben waved the rod again. The tip absorbed enough surrounding light to obscure the symbols and noticeably dim the area for fifty feet around him. "This is Meadows Towing and I—"

Before he could finish declaring himself the Might-Fist, Bastion threw itself at his eyes again.

Ow! Ben bit his lip as the blow made him lean forward.

The ogre flinched and the front row of orcs took a stepped back.

If they had been on the playground of Ben's elementary, prior to the Arcane Primary Academy, he would have given each of them two punches on the arm for punking. His Anvilsmith stopped vibrating. The minute had expired.

None of the ogre's forces advanced.

Bastion whipped the Nilosian energy in his head into a roaring whirlpool.

Ben almost swooned. His head rolled around his neck.

Bastion doubled in strength. The beast inside pounded at Ben's skull to get out at the ogre.

What are you doing? I can't fight you and him! Ben struggled to complete his earlier sentence.

One of the ogre's orcs took a tentative step toward him.

Ben's conjurations inched toward the enemies and pulled at the far range of their bounds. He only had to let them go and it would be on, but there was still a chance he could bluff the ogre and end this without any bloodshed.

Bastion roared again.

Instead of words, another growl came from Ben's throat. *What the—*

Bastion hammered harder.

Ben found his arm waving the baton of its own accord. Nilosian energy jumped from the tip, unbidden, to the five crimson gorillas. They grew four feet taller, their skin turned back and their hair darkened a ruddy brown. Their torso elongated and sprouted a secondary set of arms.

They've become whatever Bastion is.

More dog-men came from hiding at the rear of the ogre's wide-eyed forces and slid away.

Only the black-clad orcs stood their ground with the ogre. From deeper in the scrapyard, two large, gangly forms stalked through the shadows, drawing closer to the pending combat. They paused for a moment at the corner when they saw the five, nine-foot-tall, four-armed gorillas, then continued—with wide, blood-thirsty grins—into the violet light cast by the Meadow's Towing sign. Two nasty green tuzvuls, arms, nose, and ears stretched to nearly twice normal length —*just like in my books*—moved to the ogre's side. Fearless and ready for combat, they flanked the ogre.

Ben tried to direct the Nilosian energy into the Degenerative Aura spell.

As the energy swelled to his command, Bastion lunged again and again. The baton throbbed hard with each blow from the beast against his skull.

Stop! Ben stumbled forward. *It!*

The ogre flashed a jagged, ferocious grin to match his tuzvuls. Between the tuzvuls coming forward and Ben's erratic movements from refusing to let Bastion out, the orcs' fear abated.

Ben opened his mouth to tell them to stop.

Instead of words, a furious growl ripped up his throat.

Ben's vision through his own eyes—*what's going on?*—became disjointed. Distant. Limited. It was as though his awareness had been yanked backward in his own mind.

Bastion flung his consciousness aside and seized control of his body.

Dislodged in his own head, Ben splashed down in the swirling, ice cold Nilosian energy. *Ah! Freezing!* The dark power rolled his awareness around his skull like a leaf in a flash flood of black ink.

A distant familiarity—*Bastion's talking?*—worked his throat and vocal chords. The words that came were in perfect Giant. "I am Bastion!"

From inside his head, Ben could understand, perfectly, what was being said. Though he never spoke with Bastion, his suspicion about the beast had just been confirmed. *I knew he could understand me!* An icy undercurrent pulled Ben under again. He stroked hard against it to get back above the surface.

Bastion continued to work his throat. "I am your Might-Fist!"

As though disconnected, or coming out from under anesthesia, Ben's arm moved as Bastion waved the baton back and forth. The subzero black power in his skull around him began to rise higher.

The undercurrent yanked again.

Uh! No! Ben's strength waned.

Like looking through the wrong end of a telescope, Ben saw his hand through his own eyes. *Still human. He didn't transform.* Arcing the ebony rod in a slow, all-encompassing arc, his skull neared capacity.

"Now." Bastion said, "It's just a matter of how many die before the rest of you realize it." The beast in his body channeled Nilosian energy into the baton.

Ben's consciousness swam away.

Chapter Nineteen

VEGAS AFTER DARK

A SOFT LIGHT worked at the darkness. Though groggy—*I'm alive*—Ben's brain dumped a sense of euphoria into his sleepy bloodstream, putting his dim awareness on a faster track to recovery. After Bastion's betrayal, he wasn't about to take his return to consciousness for granted. The smell of sautéing onions filled the room.

Thank goodness. It was a nightmare. Ben exhaled and relief spread through him. *Mmm, wonder what mom's making. Hopefully omelets.* He rolled his head back into the pillow, took a deep breath of the intoxicating scent, and let it out.

Wait a minute.

Between the lack of sound from any of his family's televisions and the feeling of furs beneath him, a chilling reality—a reality he couldn't escape—settled upon him. *I'm not at home. I'm...*

Hoping against hope he would be wrong, Ben opened his eyes.

An eight foot by six-foot Crystal Waterfall Scrycell viewing glass covered most of the opposite wall. Gazing upon the inactive mystic viewing device—the largest he had ever seen anywhere—Ben heard his worried gulp. His gaze went to the spot on the beige shag carpet where he had first gotten a good look at Ur-Krurk standing with a turkey leg in one hand and a sword in the other. Besides the carpet and the room being clean, nothing had changed since Ben had stolen Penelope away from here.

Shit.

Ben had offered the room to the orcs, but each insisted that he, the Might-Fist of Meadows Towing, should keep the room. *Shame I never stayed here overnight.* His gaze went to the rungs he had installed above the headboard to get to the roof access latch in the Plexiglas ceiling. The support beams were also Plexiglas. *Talk about a gorgeous view of the sky.* The part of his brain that registered his situation tried—and failed —to derail his appreciation of the moment. *Waking up here's not bad. No alarm clocks and no knocks at the door to get me up for chores. Just an easygoing rouse by natural lighting.*

Like a bashful cat, the rising sun peaked over the wall spilling direct sunlight on him. Ben closed his eyes, sighed, and went to rub the weariness from his face. A length of chain rattled as his arm stopped six inches from the bed. The halt came from something wrapped around his wrist. When he pulled a bit harder, a similar bind on his other wrist pulled his arm into the mattress. "What the—"

He opened his eyes and tried to lift his head. A band pulled on his forehead. The further he lifted his head from the pillow, the greater the resistance became. Except for his coat—*the belt's gone too*—he still wore his school uniform dress shirt, red tie, and slacks. *Better than being naked.* He exhaled and tried not to think what being stripped would have meant. *Much better.*

Ben strained to hold his head up a bit longer to see his wrists. Each had one of those tanned, stiff leather, hospital-grade restraining cuffs. He lifted a leg—*where are my shoes? Where are my socks?*—to see a similar cuff on his ankle that pulled his other leg into the bed if he lifted it too high. *Oh shit, shit.*

His neck gave from the strain.

Ben's head fell back into the pillow. He opened his mouth to call out to his orcs and stopped. *From the setup, Bastion obviously lost. If I call out, my captors would know I'm awake and, doubtlessly, start a long series of torture sessions.*

Too clearly he recalled Penelope covering up the horribly split bruises on her face with the mess of her blood-matted hair.

Ben closed his eyes. He tried not to think of the ogre flaying his skin, strip by strip, to flash-fry his flesh before eating each slowly as though enjoying a rare delicacy. *Uhh.* Ben rolled the words over in his mind. *Rare. Delicacy.* His stomach took a tumble as the month old memory of the ghastly, maggot-infested gray meat that hung from a hook in the living room came to mind. Since taking over, he had the meat trashed and a heavy bag suspended from the hook, but the bag could easily be taken down to hang him like that last living thing that had graced the hook.

A section of the gray decaying meat on a nearly unidentifiable ribcage flash before his mind's eye. Countless wriggling maggots were going to town.

His throat constricted and his stomach burbled a queasy rumble.

Shaking his head against the images, Ben's imagination started to spiral into the different tortures that he would be subjected to. His thoughts froze. *What if Jek told them about Ur-Krurk not being dead, but captured in the Imprisoning Orb.* Ben gulped again. *He'll probably free his father and put me in. If I'm lucky, in the short run, they'll see what starvation and loneliness does to me.*

Soft padding, like a dog, sounded on the stairs.

Trying to appear like he was still unconscious, Ben closed his eyes lightly. He focused his will on being non-responsive to whatever stimuli they tried.

Two high voices whispered to one another as they entered the room. The language they were speaking had rolling vowel sounds with a guttural, Orcish edge to the consonants. Dragging sounds came from the wall to tap against the footboard of the bed.

Steady breaths, Ben. Keep 'em steady.

Like when his youngest brother would walk on his bed, pressure sank into the mattress near his right leg. Another mattress dip joined the first. They walked along his body and stopped at his torso. Whispering in the unknown language, one of them poked a narrow finger with a ragged fingernail into his stomach.

Ben didn't react.

His belly gurgled and churned. A strong oniony burp rolled up his throat and puffed through his lips. *Uhh, what the heck is that nasty taste?* Something horrid—barely masked by the strong onion flavor—bubbled his guts. *What in Hell did Bastion eat?* He wanted to suck the rank tang from his mouth and spit. *Whatever it was, it must've been, rubbed with onions, stuffed with onions, served with onions, and he must've had a nice oniony soda to wash it down.* Another burp passed through him. *How repugnant.*

They exchanged a volley of whispers before a narrow finger, without a notable nail poked into his other side. His gut gurgled again. The creatures brought a strong antiseptic smell with them.

They probably want to make sure I don't die from infection or bed rot before I could be thoroughly tortured.

The two started whispering again as they walked down toward his feet.

Please don't poke my feet.

Pressure on the mattress left from his left side, followed by the other. A short dragging sound started before a smack slapped from beyond the foot of the bed. A word, sharper and louder than any prior, whipped out like an aftershock. The short dragging ended with another tap on the footboard.

Crap, they're coming back.

Padding sounds shuffled through the shag carpet toward the door.

Ben dared to sneak a peek. About three feet tall, he noted their long thick-peaked ears, baldheads and gnarled skin. *Goblins...* His breath hitched in his chest. In the chapbook—*Grotesque Goblinoids*—handed out in the first week of *Mythic Monsters I* for home study, Goblins were supposedly the second smallest of the goblinoids, the most plentiful, and the most insidious of crafters. His former concern for what the ogre's brutish wrath may hold paled to the unknown torment the goblins could manufacture... Especially in a scrapyard.

The lead goblin's mottled, yellow-green skin had patches of deep green, like lush sprigs in a field of dying grass. The other was a calico of browns, tans, and black. Both wore yellow dish gloves and black rubber aprons which didn't fully wrap around their bodies, leaving their bottoms bare like hospital gowns. The calico smacked the back of the other's head, muttered, and closed the door as they left the room.

Ben waited five seconds to give the goblins time to get down the stairs. Then, taking the size their ears into consideration, he gave them another five. Taxing his neck muscles again, Ben lifted his head to scan for a means of escape.

Ur-Krurk's greatsword, a massive claymore with a human-sized metal skull where the blade went into the hilt and tiny skulls on the pommel and cross-guard—which Ben had stashed away in the basement—sat, tip down, behind the door. His coat hung from the right skull. The closet lay open. The spare set of clothes he had put there a month ago were still neatly folded on his Zephyr board on the top shelf. A tiny mechanical frog, Kermit—his first companion—sat idle next to the Zephyr's upturned rear.

Ben had been saving his allowance to buy the module which would make Kermit voice-activated, but he had forgotten the plan shortly after getting Remy. He sighed. The sigh weighed with all of his disappointment at how quickly he'd tossed aside the plan when a better companion had come along, and then again when he got Tex.

His neck muscles began to ache.

No companion. No tablet. Ben eyed the slight gap between Kermit and the Zephyr board where the formerly cursed Anvilsmith tablet used to sit. *If only I hadn't moved it to my budding basement laboratory...*

Though stuck for a solution, Ben refused to give up. *Gotta unscrew yourself. Clear your mind. You're missing something simple.* He eased his head back to the pillow and thought, and thought, and thought.

Chapter Twenty

COMPANION TROUBLE

As the sun rose higher in the sky, the slat of sunlight that had rested on Ben's face traveled down his body to just above his waist. If he were not held captive, he would have enjoyed basking in the warm rays. *There's just something about being bound against your will that saps the joy from things.* Though he couldn't bask in the humor, he allowed himself a quick, wry smile. His gaze went to the thick Plexiglas crossbeam under the Plexiglas roof. The smile faded. *When the sun hits it, will it cook me like an ant under a magnifying glass?*

The sustained quiet also weighed on his mind. It was as though he'd gone camping and had woke up before everyone else in the campground. The more he thought about it, the more certain he became that he had read about goblinoids having a tendency to be nocturnal. Then again, how much that certainty came through overthinking it? True, everything remained quiet, but how long would that last?

Only his steady heartbeat thumped softly in his ears. The silence lay complete and undisturbed over Meadows Towing.

In the silence—

Ben's hand gripped tight. His subconscious held on to the word for dear life. *Silence...* Consciously, he latched onto the word. *There's something there...* He turned the word over in his mind. Nothing. He went to the root. *Silent...* Ben clenched his fist tighter. *Yes!* He had set his tablet to be silent and voice activated. *I didn't use it to cast spells so they may not have taken it.*

Swallowing his spit to wet his throat, Ben called in a low whisper, "Ping." In his predicament, in the silence, his whisper felt like a jungle call. He pressed his lips together and strained his ears. No padding. No goblins. He continued, "Set volume to one."

No sound come up the stairs, but what came was coming up made him salivate. He swallowed again. Seasoning had been added to the onions to caramelize. Normally one of his favorite toppings on a burger, Ben's appetite died and goose bumps rose. *They're probably going to use me as the burger meat. I hope my orcs refuse to eat me.* He frowned at the silliness of the thought and sighed. The Orcish language had specific terms for types of cannibalism. *If they'd eat each other—and they do—they'd eat me.*

Ben lifted his head and turned his face to the coat. Neck outstretched against the restraint band, he hoped the victors didn't know the importance of his tech. "Ping."

A soft ping sounded from his coat. *Thank goodness!* Excitement ripped through him at the sweetest sound he'd heard since Adept Matton had rang the tiny bell to signal Ben passing *Courtmanship IV.*

He rolled his head to the side, a less taxing activity, and spoke toward his coat. "Ping Tex." A faint green light came from the inner folds. Ben smiled at it and relaxed his neck. *Only a matter of time before I hear that sweet synthesized voice. Well, not so sweet. Since the reset, Texas had lost all sense of intonation, but—still—one step closer to sweet freedom.*

Tex said, "Yes, Ben?"

The metallic echo had never been more welcomed. Ben eased out a calming breath. *Stay cool. There's a way out of this mess.* He formed a command stack. "Tex, return to the scrapyard, bring something sharp enough to cut hard leather—"

"Cannot," Tex interrupted.

Forgetting his belabored neck, Ben lifted his head momentarily, looking at the light in his coat as though he were looking directly at Tex and the companion could see his incredulous expression. The resistance on the band pulled his head back to the pillow. "Um, Tex, why not?"

"You gave me specific orders to go home, plug in, and wait for your return."

A quiver—fear, fear of his setting Tex on robot-mode after the pain of losing his companion, fear of the robot-mode's logic being bound to a strict adherence to linear commands—worked into Ben's voice. "Tex, I'm giving you new orders."

"Copy," Tex said. "I am listening."

"Okay." An old superstition ingrained by his father made Ben cross his fingers with hope. "Unplug and return to the scrapyard. Make sure you bring a tool to cut hard leather that is both quiet and something you can use as I cannot move my arms." Ben paused.

"Noted." Tex replied and added, "New commands acknowledged and placed on the stack of tasks for processing after you return. Is there anything else you would like to add?"

Ben's teeth ground. He constricted his throat to keep from bellowing his frustration and resisted the horrible desire to slam his fist into the bed. *That would make the chains rattle and that would call the goblins.* "Fine!" Ben nearly spat out the word. He bit his lip and took a moment to listen for anything on the stairs. *Nothing.* He continued, "Resume the earlier plug in and power back down orders."

"Copy. See you when you get here." As ironic as it seemed, Ben missed the life the old Tex breathed into the words. The old Tex would have sounded sleepy, excited, or sardonic—not monotone.

Ben waited ten seconds. Tex's power-down cycle took much less, but he wanted to make sure he didn't speak too soon. He turned his head to the coat again. The folds were dark. *How much battery life is left?* That momentary thought made him wonder if this was only the following morning or if he'd been out longer. *All in due time.* He put the caboose of the train of thought in its proper order of concern. "Ping." The inside of his coat lit green again. "Remy."

Rembrandt's choppy robotic voice replied. "Yes, sire?"

Ben drew a breath to even his tone and moved his lips precisely, enunciating each syllable. "Remy, go to the mainframe. Once there, back up Tex's data files."

"Yes, sire."

Ben said, "Ping me back when you are done."

"Yes, sire."

Ben waited. Remy was one of the first Golemcasts and even though he had upgraded its skeleton to the 1.21 model, its mobility still remained quite limited. A small smile turned the corner of Ben's mouth as he recalled Remy losing the race he had set up between it and Kermit. *Robotics is growing by leaps and bounds. Wonder what's—*

Metal screeched and groaned in the distance, mangling the former silence.

Startled, Ben shook. Someone had started the compactors. *What are they destroying?* His budding hope took a twisting dip. *Probably my car. None of them can really fit in it.* The full crushing cycle took two minutes. Right behind it, a second compactor, this one to the east and closer cried into life.

A rumbling came from Ben's stomach. This time, nothing had spurred it. The caramelizing onions had become a constant background aroma, he hadn't moved, and his stomach hadn't been poked. *It's almost like something's in there...* As much as he wanted to dismiss the thought as pure fantasy, he did have some kind of alter-ego-beast roosting in his head.

The thought brought his focus to his Nilosian font. He tried to detect Bastion only to find a halfway restored reserve of power.

Remy's monotone voice called, "Texas 2.0 is backed up."

"Okay." Ben licked his lips. "Overwrite the current programming with an install of the last version of Tex 1.0."

Remy did not reply.

Blood pounded in Ben's forehead. *Crap. Is this against some kind of weird companion Prime Directive? Change not thy mechanical kin for that is the realm of Engineers and Programmers?*

"Verifying," Remy said. "The last version of Texas 1.0 is 1.0000021. The current version is 2.0003015. Sire, are you sure you want to revert this Golemcast Robo-Zen 3.14 v2 with thirty cycles to version one?"

Yes. Wait. Recalling how literal Remy had proven to be, Ben considered the question to make sure the robot was going to do exactly what he wanted. *I haven't updated the chassis. Tex would be running the old firmware...* Everything seemed right. "First, Remy, switch the lever between Tex's shoulder blades from robot mode to companion mode.

"Done. The switch has sunk in and a sleeve covers the area. Do you still want to install Texas version 1.0000021?"

That switch going away had flipped Ben out the first time, which was what made the decision to take the deactivated Tex back to the Robo-Zen outlet to have the switch reset that much harder. Having lost the sarcastic, and somewhat scarily independent, companion to fried circuits hurt just like when his parents had their ailing Mr. Whiskers put to sleep. Ben didn't want to go through that again, but he needed help. The kind of help only the first version of Tex seemed capable of giving. Taking a deep inhalation for one last moment of consideration, He closed his eyes and said. "Yes."

"Doing so now, Sire."

"Thank you, Remy." Ben let the deep breath out. "Power Tex up and have him ping when operational."

"Understood, Sire."

More twisting metal—*they're using the southwest compactor? Are they going to try all five?*—cried in the distance while he waited... and waited....

Chapter Twenty-One

GETTING GONE

"Ben." Tex's synthesized voice came through his device. Sort of hollow and flat at first, his companion's voice came alive with a confused flavor. "Why does my clock read thirty days since I was last active?"

"Blessed be." Ben's fist balled, grasping victory. Having never used his mother's term for expressing good fortune, Ben relaxed his hand and steadied his thoughts. *I'm not out yet.* He looked to the inner folds of his coat as though he were looking at his companion. "Tex, I need you to come to Meadows Towing and bring something that you can use to quietly cut through hard leather—"

Tex interrupted, "I'm not finding any places by that name."

Good old, Tex. A fond smile spread Ben's lips. *Not even waiting for the complete order.*

Tex said, "And would you please answer my question?"

Ben said, "Ping my device and—"

His device sounded a soft ding.

Ben figured he didn't have to say the rest, but finished his sentence anyway. "Plot it on your map."

"Done and done. Now, my question?"

"It's a long story, buddy." Ben allowed relief to creep into his voice as hope began to make a slow return. "I will explain everything—and I mean *everything*—just get here as fast and as stealthily as possible."

Considering how the two commands might be at odds with each other, Ben clarified. "In fact, if you have to choose, pick stealth over speed."

Tex replied, "Yeah, yeah, got it." In the momentary silence Ben figured Tex had started on the task set before it. The volume on his tablet raised a bit. "Ben, why am I getting readings that there are two Anvilsmiths registered to you?"

Ben uttered a shushing sound. "Tex, I really need us to be as stealthy as possible."

"Got it." Tex had lowered the volume of its voice. "On my way."

The coat went dark.

The sun traveled across the room. The five compactors had each run five times. The goblins—still reeking of antiseptic, still poking him with rubber gloves—had checked on him twice more. Each time, Ben expected them to cut on him or try to smack him awake, but they hadn't.

Dusk began to dim the bright blue sky.

Tex's head poked up from the foot of the bed.

Startled, Ben shook on the furs then frowned into the emerald energy-lit two-inch diameter lenses set in the robot's orbital sockets.

Tex whispered, "Present." Not for the first time, Ben admired the Golemcast builder's work. Except for the lack of any form of artificial flesh, they had crafted the Robo-Zen cover plates to allow the chassis to move just like a person—albeit knee-high. Tex had an Anvilsmith strapped across its back.

Ben hadn't heard any ruffling by his coat. To confirm his suspicion, he whispered, "Is this the one from my lab?"

"Yeah." Tex whispered back. "Sorry it took so long, but I couldn't find anything quiet that could cut leather. I'd need some sort of tiny chainsaw since I probably couldn't summon the force to work proper sheers. Then, as I was coming up the secret passage—"

Secret passage?—

"From the basement, I thought, surely Ben couldn't be overlooking the simplicity of using his *Silence* spell to mute blasting off the restraints." Tex's lens closures wound quickly as the robot closed his iris and opened to simulate a blink at Ben. He then turned around and sat near Ben's hand so he could work the tablet. "I mean, surely not."

Ben echoed "Surely not." As though coming from behind a cloud, the thrill at having his companion back rose from the area where the month-old sting of loss had taken root.

As Tex sometimes would, it continued digging. "Then I thought, oh, the tablets are probably out of power…"

The extended good-humored mockery brought a grateful smile to Ben lips. If pushed by his companion, he would never admit to enjoying Tex's teasing, yet, a certainty—*the robot must know*—made Ben's smile blossom into a grin.

Ben tapped the blue *Spellbook* icon, the slim question mark for *Illusions*, and then the flat-lined EKG icon—the only *Illusory* spell he'd learned at the APA. *Wonder why they don't teach us to program any of the other illusion-based spells?* Having only created and cast the *Silentball* in *Spell Programming V*, Ben hadn't taken the time to customize the background or cast buttons. *I have to dress this one up some.*

Tex continued, "Then I thought, no, not Ben. He's too thrifty with his arcane watts. Surely the center of my universe would never be so brash as to expend all of the awatts at his disposal. No, the wise shepherd to which, I, only a lamb stumbling through life, look to for direction, protection, and guidance. Surely not…"

Yup, that's the old Tex—he'll keep on until I tell him to be quiet or silence him with the spell. Ben focused the spell on his companion and tapped the generic two-inch wide by one-inch-tall *Cast* icon. Ten of the hundred arcane watts drained away.

Tex raised his hands over his head and clapped. No sound.

Good. Ben tried to whistle. Nothing. *Good. Gotta make the most of these few minutes.*

Ben swiped back to spell types, tapped the dollar sign icon for his conjurations, and tapped the bullet icon for his *Blast* spell. Having cast from his spellcard so often recently, Ben tried to remember why he'd made the background a hammer driving nails into wood. *Later, figure it out later.* Four blasts, a slip of the headband, and a shove from the bed; he stood free.

He collected his coat. Also dangling on the claymore's hilt were his tablet holster and spellcard band. He strapped them on, collected his Zephyr board and Kermit, and slipped on his spare pair of loafers.

Tex motioned him toward the entrance in the bathroom.

I do have to go, but not here. Ben shook his head and pointed to the rungs at the head of the bed—built for him since Ur-Krurk could fly—that would lead to the roof. A more likely reason for Tex signaling him to the bathroom—*the secret passage is probably in there*—occurred to him, but he hoped there would be one more item to collect.

Tex clamped onto his coat.

Ben climbed up to the roof. Once through the door, the neglected metal, rubber, and plastic smell of the scrapyard filled his nose. Just the same—*freedom*—Ben took a deep inhalation of the crisp night air. *So nice.*

Checking for movement on the grounds, Ben peaked over the front. Several groups of three orcs in black armor did rounds on the grounds.

Trying to plot and time their paths, Ben watched.

When he had visited Meadows Towing on the weekends, Ben would retrieve the Imprisoning Orb from the first "O" in the Meadows Towing sign, and set it in front of the television as he pushed a week's worth of food and water into it. His orcs were almost always out on service calls, so getting it, and putting it back so Ur-Krurk could overlook the scrapyard without the orcs knowing where he was imprisoned, had never been a problem.

If he hadn't known what the mystical prison would do to the captive, Ben would've just buried it out in the desert, but the Orb had imprinted him with the knowledge of what would happen, and he couldn't be that cruel; even to a monster that threatened to make bloodspots of him and his family.

When the break in rotations came, Ben summoned Oscar, had the gorilla retrieve the Orb and come back up. With Tex still on his coat, the three of them made their way across the roof to the back of the building.

Ben peak ever the edge.

His Transcend sat unguarded where it had been towed and released.

Thank goodness. Ben climbed onto Oscar's back. The gorilla climbed them down.

Still under the magical silenced, Ben opened the card door, dropped into his seat and closed the door.

Tex already had his hand in the ignition. The robot turned his arm.

The car vibrated a bit, but made no sound.

Ben dismissed Oscar and, to keep from spitting rocks out behind him, eased away from the building. Once a row away, he jumped on the gas and zoomed toward a side exit.

Two dog-headed men posted there turned around when the gate started to open. They leapt from Ben's path as he escaped into the night.

Chapter Twenty-Two

MESSING WITH TEXAS

AFTER STASHING the Imprisoning Orb in his *Courtmanship* locker and retrieving the Nod Key, Ben scanned the long, narrow Archon Private Academy's student parking lot. His Transcend remained parked in the choice spot closest to the school doors, where the one-way U-turn doubled back to the second row and final row. The rest of the lot, empty.

Ben hustled to his car, searched all the way around it to make sure it hadn't been tampered with, and—checking for a tail—turned his gaze to the seemingly endless flow of headlights streaking by as cars whooshed down Tropicana Boulevard. *I wonder what the Mundanes see when they look this way? An abandoned school? An unused business complex? An empty dirt lot?*

Tex knocked on the glass.

Nerves strung tight enough to be strummed, Ben jumped away from the sound. Ready to cast, his fingers lay on his spellcards.

Tex waved.

Ben had grown used to the way the robot-mode Tex stayed right where he left it. He relaxed, opened the car door and plopped into the seat. "I take it the transfer of 2.0's data is complete?"

"Yes. Rooted, and indexed." Dismayed, Tex shook his tiny metal head. "Still can't believe you had me in robot mode for a full eighth of school."

"Look on the bright side." Ben carefully nudged his companion. "You're irreplaceable."

Tex looked toward the opposite car door as through talking to a camera. "And then he tried to flatter me…"

Ben slid his hand into his coat pocket. The old fashioned skeleton-key-shaped Node Key warmed his hand. *I should try to start my car with it.* The thought brought a mostly silly, partly wicked smirk to his mouth. "Tex. Face me, turn off your optics and open your chest compartment."

"Okay." The robot turned. The emerald light left his orbital sockets revealing the semi-reflective surface behind the thick lenses. "Just so you know, I'm hacking my programming to never forgive you if you stick a boiled egg in me."

Ben chuckled. "Wouldn't dream of it."

"Good." A quick series of clicks sounded before the chest cover slid down to Tex's knees.

I was looking all over for these. Ben took out his spare set of house and car keys. *Totally forgot I put them here.* He took the key ring, tossed it in a cup holder and placed the Node Key inside. Ben slid the cover back into place. Clicks locked it in.

Ben said, "Tex, set up a background process with the following specific parameters." He took a moment to organize his thoughts. *Can't believe I'm setting up a contingency plan for if I get killed or snatched up.* "If I go missing, without any form of communication with you for a month and a day, turn the contents stored in your chest over to Master Reynolds."

"Programming now." Tex nodded. "While we wait, could you fill me in on what happened between my backup and…, uh…, me popping my top?"

Ben snapped on his seatbelt, started the car, and flipped the convertible switch to start the slow process of putting the top down. "Okay, let's see… While you were out, we saved an Argosian from a Krotosian. I helped her get home, came back, captured the Krotosian, and recovered the Node Key." While Ben spoke, a wide smile had formed. He'd missed having someone to confide in, and realized just how delighted he was to have the original Tex back. He admired his companion standing there on the center console. *Best part.* Ben stared into the reflective metal behind the lenses. *He won't see this silly-ass smile.* Bringing the smile under modest control, Ben said, "Optics on."

The green energy flicked back on.

Remembering one last thing, Ben jutted a thumb toward the school. "Oh, and the usual drudgery that comes with an eighth of schoolwork."

Tex faced the Archon Private Academy. "So, *Courtmanship V* next eighth, right?"

"Yup." Ben jingled his keys.

Tex turned, slid down the side of the steering wheel, and placed his tiny hand in the ignition before Ben could place the key. The car revved and headlights flashed to life. "Remember, you have to pass to stay on track for the record."

I know, Tex. No pressure, right? Ben nodded.

The robot dropped onto his knee, hopped to the center armrest, and stepped into his safety harness, which resembled the swings at parks for toddlers. Tex hooked the first bungee-strap around his waist to the left. "The registrar codex shows Master Reynolds teaches *Spell P*. Ten and higher." He secured the second bungee strap around his waist to the right, and kicked off to dangle in front of the Transcend's control console. "This means only six more eighths of the draconian Senior Adept."

Ben's eyes widened. His smile broke. The integral part of their relationship—a shared understanding of Collins' trickery—had been lost. He dropped his face to his hands. His forehead tapped the horn.

Tex's tiny hand rested on his leg. "What's wrong?"

Removing his hands, Ben leaned back in his seat. With the top down, he looked at the dark blue sky. Dusk had settled across the Vegas Valley, and only a few stars shone through the city's strong ambient light. For a brief moment, he longed for the view from atop the Suntouched Spire. *Things were simpler over there. No Collins. No Bastion. No ogres and orcs wanting to end your life...*

Tex gave Ben's coat a gentle tug. "Ben?"

Can't tell him straight out. That'd be slandering an Adept and he'd have to report me. Ben rubbed his face. He tried to think of a way to explain what Tex would see as an impossible scenario. "Well." Ben thought a bit longer before he snapped his fingers. *Got it. First the defining difference between him and v2.*

Ben faced his companion. "Okay, so there was a moment when I was going to go after the Krotosian when I wanted you to channel the awatts from one Anvilsmith to the other…"

Tex had already started to shake his head. "Why would you ask that, Ben? You don't have the authority to approve such a waste."

Crap. He won't let me set the premise. With Tex shutting down his hopeful line of recovery, Ben set his mind to finding an alternative, and half-heartedly continued the conversation as he backed out of the parking spot. "I know." He shifted to drive. "However, when I spoke about not wanting to override you, you decided to do it on your own."

"I did?" The slight synthesized reverb in Tex's voice became a bona fide echo and rang for a full second.

Registering the phenomenon, Ben stared at the small robot. While looking at Tex, he missed slowing for a speed bump. The Transcend rocked hard.

"Okay." Tex fell from the armrest and dangled from the bungee cords. The echo gone, his companion asked in his standard, synthesized voice, "Where did I back myself up?"

Ben hit the brakes. "What do you mean?"

Tex swung. "Channeling awatts could have caused me to completely freeze." Tex turned in his harness, put his back to the console, and kicked his legs to continue swinging. "That level of back up is not a part of my standard programming, which is why it takes higher authorization to happen."

Ben shook his head and shifted his foot from the brake to the accelerator. "There was nowhere to back you up. It was just, me, you, the car, and the tablets."

Tex's hand flipped back and he stuck his USB port into the spare Anvilsmith. "There is an archive volume here for Tex 1.0000075, but I don't have rights to it."

Ben slammed on the brakes at the lot exit. "Root the file, and index it. Then reinstall."

Tex bumped against the console. "You do not have the authority to approve said task." The small robot's faceplates shifted away from the center, pulling the bumps he had for cheeks up and back. This turned the small, square speaker to an upward-turned half-moon slit.

Though the joints and plates had always been there, Ben's jaw hinged open with amazement. *He can make expressions? Cool! How many times have I wondered at that deadpan face?*

Tex continued. "You'd have to override."

Chuckling, Ben gave an enthusiastic nod. "Do it."

Tex mirrored the nod. "With pleasure."

Chapter Twenty-Three

PRYING THE THIRD EYE

BEN WAITED in the parking lot for a few minutes for Tex to reboot before he started to drive around Vegas.

When stopped at a light, with the top down, people looked at Ben as though he were crazy, but the cool October night air, and the wide night sky above, kept his freedom fresh in his mind. The magical knack in his coat—the same as all the other trench coat wearing APA students —would protect him from extreme temperatures. Last Yule, one of the coldest on record, he'd seen other casters' teeth rattle while he barely got goose bumps.

He'd only lost part of one night and day. Ben kept his eyes peeled for the Legerity with the purple rear-end that he'd seen in Papa Mojo's crystal ball. Just as he'd been taken captive, Mojo said Clarissa would be as well. After suffering through the thoughts of what could have happened to himself, Ben would do his best to keep real horrors from being visited upon another…

The light turned green. Ben didn't move his foot to the accelerator.

Car horns blared from behind him. The sound thinned away to nothing as a vision flashed—their Transcends parked on a long, paved road splitting the hardpan, he and Malcolm flinging spells at each other in the desert. They were being watched—and then it faded.

My thinking of people and then they show up… Gary called this a 'third-

eye.' Does it mean I have to battle Malcolm to save Clarissa? If so, why wasn't Clarissa in the vision? Was she one of the ones watching us?

Pressing his lips together, Ben muttered, "I have to learn to control this."

Tex stirred. "Control what?"

"Welcome back, buddy!" Ben checked the car clock. *Wow, ten already.* Tex had been idle for nearly three hours. "How'd it go?"

The small robot's face plates shifted to show the slit smile. "I'm back and feeling better than ever!"

Enthusiasm bent Ben's neck. If his stomach hadn't started to gnaw at him, he would have put his hand out to high-five. "So glad to hear it. The other you was..."

Tex's green lenses, and the world around him dimmed.

Another vision—him sitting at an intersection with 24-Seven convenience stores on opposite corners. Malcolm—

A pinch on Ben's pinky snatched him back to reality. He pulled his hand away from Tex and rubbed it. "Ouch!"

"Your eyes went glassy and you're driving." Though the robot could not see the road, Tex pointed forward.

Ben focused forward on the road and dipped his hand into the ashtray for one of the open packs of antacids he'd taken to keeping there. He ripped the pack a bit further, popped two of the chalky discs into his mouth, and began to chew. The hint of almost, but not-quite-there, cherry flavor signaled he'd grabbed the *Acid Aide* package. Chomping the antacids into granules, he placed the pack back in the ashtray.

Tex rummaged through them to read the names, and asked, "What's with these?"

Ben glanced.

Like a trained drug-detecting hound, Tex patiently scanned the back of the antacid packs in the ashtray.

Stopping for a red light, Ben's brow furrowed, he bit his lip, and cradled his abdomen. "My stomach is killing me."

"Well." Tex lifted a package to read the lower bits. "You can take too many—"

An air horn blared from the car next to him.

Ben's insides quivered. The grumbling in his gut almost seemed to bite him before another nasty, oniony burp rolled up his esophagus. His earlier question, while flanked by goblins and bounded to the bed, echoed back. *What in Hell did Bastion eat?*

"How in the Hell did you rate a Transcend, Baby Ben?"

Malcolm. Ben turned to see the Dunn-Blatt with his two cronies from last night. Though the purple paint job and black buffalo detailing made their cars look quite different, they both were the same make and model. *Of course!* Malcolm had little knobs added so, from head-on, he car would look like a low profile approaching buffalo.

Malcolm revved his engine. "Wanna race?"

Though his stomach churned again and he detested the Dunn-Blatt bully, Ben could not help but feel bad for Malcolm. *He really thinks he's hot shit and popular, but the guy in the backseat looks like he wants to bash his head in. Wonder where his drastic need to compete comes from?* Ben shook his head. "Sort of pointless, isn't it?" Ben added, "Since, you know, we have the same car and all."

"It's not about the car, Benny-Boy, it's about the driver!" Malcolm revved again. "Five golds against my hook says I beat you to The Strip!"

Ben felt bile crawling up his throat and forced it back down. "You disgust me."

Malcolm sneered. "What?"

"You're not getting your hook back so easily." Ben paused to burp, and grimace. Just beneath the strong onion mask, he detected the slightest taste of foul meat. "Hooks are only a gold." *Only a gold, it'd take me a year to earn that.* "Just go buy a new one."

"I need that particular one back." Malcolm revved his engine again. "A platinum, then. That's ten to one. Or are you chicken?"

A souped-up engine thundered from beyond the 24-Seven to the right. Ben's eyes sought the noise and spotted the white Legerity with a purple rear-end in the Pinball Hall of Fame's parking lot.

The light turned green. Ben jumped on the accelerator.

Chapter Twenty-Four

CHASING LIGHTS

TIRES PEELED BEHIND HIM. Malcolm zoomed past leaving a wake of noxious white clouds.

Ben held his breath, applied his breaks, and turned into the brightly lit 24-Seven lot.

Tex had pulled his release to shoot from the passenger seat and dangle in front of the control console. "What are you doing, Ben? We had him off the line! We could've won!"

"This isn't about him, Tex." To keep mundanes from having a reason to take further notice him, Ben backed into a parking spot as far away from the gas pumps and entrance to the convenience store. Once folks look away—and he didn't do anything to draw attention to himself—the Mystique would veil him and keep him concealed.

Ben had once gone near a mundane car as it sat at one of the gasoline dispensers. His curiosity about what the liquid did for cars had grown too great. When he got close, the fumes made him feel tipsy and dissuaded him from trying to steal a quick taste. When he had mentioned the experience to Blythe, the Junior Adept told him that mundane vehicles needed gas to run. *How ridiculous*, Ben had said, *What if you're running late for school and the gasoline runs out, or, worse, you wake up to find that it evaporated away while you were sleeping?* Blythe had twisted his lips up tight in shared confusion. There were just some things about mundanes no one could explain.

Two Tanaka Stingers rolled into the Pinball Hall of Fame parking lot. The lowered Japanese imports looked more like rolling lime-and-violet flashlights than cars. *It should be illegal to have that much aftermarket neon.* The two cars each had the same number of lights, but where one had light green, the other had light purple and vice versa. They pulled up to flank the Legerity in the parking lot.

Ben pointed. "It's all about the white one, Tex."

The drivers of the imports got out. *Whoa, they're grown men.* He didn't know thirty-year-olds—or close to—drove those kinds of cars. *They must miss high school.* One of them stuck their hands into the Legerity to shake hands with the unseen driver. *Can't see in. Must be some kind of cloaking magic.* Each of the thirty-year-olds pulled out a wad of mundane money from their jean jackets, folded thick, and passed it in through the Legerity's window. They then rushed back to their cars as thin slits for reverse lights lit up on the Legerity's purple trunk. Rocking with power from each rev of the engine, mufflers gurgling, the American-Steel muscle car slow-rolled—almost strutting with confidence—to the exit and into the center lane on Tropicana.

The two flash-light Tanaka Stingers zipped out to flank the Legerity, the three of them forming a ten-mile-an-hour rolling roadblock. Other cars that were cut off laid on their horns, their drivers cursing and jutting middle fingers out their windows.

Ben also exited the parking lot and wound up stuck in a lane behind three cars with angry drivers. He swerved to the fast lane which only had two.

He gripped the steering wheel and glanced at Tex. "I'm only concerned about keeping up with the white car."

The small robot's facial plates shifted again, this time two plates dropped from the top of his lenses while two rose from the bottom, making the round orbital socket seem to narrow in concentration. "Gotcha."

Don't think I've ever seen a Golemcast do that. Ben's throat pulsed an appreciative, "Hmph."

Abruptly, the three cars burned rubber and sped away. They raced up to Maryland Parkway and made sharp lefts.

Drawing honks and middle fingers of his own, Ben dipped and dodged through the small spaces that opened up when the slower traffic started to pick up speed. He paused at the red light at Maryland for a gap in cross-traffic before making the turn.

Far ahead, the three cars zoomed out to the newer part of McCarran airport.

Lowering his pedal to the floorboard, Ben's needle rotated over one hundred as he kept them in sight. He lost them for a moment on the Russell Road curve, but the light from bright Japanese imports signaled they were racing down Eastern to get on the Beltway heading out to Green Valley.

Thinking about Clarissa, Ben edged his car a little faster to make up some ground before also getting on the expressway. "Give me one of the boosts, Tex." Out of the corner of his eye, Ben noticed Tex punch a code into the console. *If I can learn the codes, I can be the master of my own vehicle.*

"Ready, steady," Tex warned. "Go!"

The boost didn't register on the speedometer.

Ben held the wheel tight and made small moves as Adept Dugan had instructed, keeping control while slaloming through traffic at high speed. The Stingers lights and the Legerity's slits, further down the highway steadily grew larger as he closed on them.

The Legerity led the three vehicles as they banked right into darkness.

Without looking down, Ben tapped *Spells, Enchantments, Elfsight,* and *Cast* on his Anvilsmith. He killed his headlights. As though called down from the sky, ephemeral magical starlight rained on the highway and surrounding area casting a sheen on the dry pavement.

There were knocked over cones at the entrance to the closed Pepcon Obdurium quarry off-ramp. *Crap! There going down into Old Hendo.*

Only recently finding out things like orcs and ogres were real, Ben didn't want to go down there to find out if the horror stories he'd heard about Old Henderson were also true. Almost too late, an image of Clarissa with her pixie-cut blonde hair flashed in his mind's eye.

Ben made the turn.

The dark industrial sprawl that had boomed after the Pepcon

discovery rose up to meet the freeway's height as the off-ramp went down, down, down.

Most of the buildings in Old Henderson were at least three stories tall, and all of them had been built with cinder blocks. Age showed in their peeling paint. A hundred feet above street level hovered a thin, smoggy haze. The distance Ben could see with his Elfsight spell dwindled to half.

He slowed down.

The Legerity's rumbles and the Stingers whines were quite audible.

Ben tried to sense the way they went. *Not possible. Too many echoes.* He admitted, "I lost them."

Tex popped above the dashboard and pointed. "Turn right up there."

Ben did. In the dark, his spell turned the neon-lit cars way down the street into beacons of amazing light. "Give me another speed surge, Tex." Not going over a hundred miles an hour this time, Ben tried to spy the code. *Six. One. Something. Nine. Something. Zero.*

Tex pressed the power button on the radio. In five seconds, the Transcend rocketed forward to the same speed as on the freeway. "Only one of those left," Tex said.

"Noted." Ben's knuckles went white on the steering wheel when the two neon cars split up to go in different directions. A glimpse of brake lights signaled the Legerity had turned left. Ben applied the brakes, ending the spell, and swerved to avoid a huge pothole—and an impossibly large postal mailbox on the sidewalk—as he turned onto Dove Boulevard.

The Legerity's taillights were in front of him.

Jumping back on the accelerator, Ben recalled a school field trip a few years ago to the Anvilsmith Industrial Complex at the far end of the ten-lane street. Even at night, the squat dome covering the Pepcon Obdurium deposit stood alone, like a spider in a web of buildings, protecting a meal.

When Ben had closed to fifteen lengths behind the Legerity, it took a sudden right—as though on rails—without tapping the breaks.

Ben slammed on his; almost standing on them. His car didn't stop in time for the turn. He backed up, and looked down the narrow service alley. A wall stood at the end. "How'd it make the turn?"

"Magic." Tex undid his harness.

Recalling what happened at Meadows Towing when Tex started detecting magic too often, Ben placed his companion on the dashboard and warned. "Be careful. You popped doing that."

"Will do," Tex replied. "It turned right before the wall."

Minding his speed at the end, Ben drove down the alley and turned right. "How do you know?"

"I'm able to track the magical trail it's leaving."

Ben nodded and followed Tex's direction.

The robot navigated him through a maze of buildings. A huge perk to getting a Robo-Zen model lay in the fact that it could detect magic. However, track it? *Great, between that and the face plates shifting, now I absolutely* have *to read Tex's manual from cover to cover.*

The Legerity went through the same areas several times, doubling and tripling back, until Tex finally said, "Sorry, Ben. I lost it."

Ben applied the brakes. "What?"

Tex gave an apologetic bow. "The car is no longer using magic and, as such, I can no longer track it."

"Okay." Ben glanced around the wide back ally with dozens of rolling metal doors leading into rows of conjoined buildings. *If only Papa Mojo had used his crystal ball to show me the actual building.*

Casing off the it-would've-been-nice thought, Ben said, "Then we're right where we're supposed to be." He hoped one of the rolling doors would stand out from the others. None did. He added, "We're here."

Chapter Twenty-Five

ON BEING A BAGMAN

TEX STOOD onto the dashboard and looked around. "*Here* where?"

Ben said, "Hold on." To hide his car, he backed around a corner and into the closes alcove he had seen.

Five large, forest-green industrial-sized dumpsters lined the length of two walls. Centered against the back wall, a cardboard compactor, just a little under half-full. To its left, a pile of compacted cardboard boxes, strapped tight. To its right, pallets. Surprisingly enough, the garbage area only had the faintest whiff of wood and rot. *Guess they don't dump food here often. Well, no food means no rats or pigeons.* In the open air area, Ben looked to the night sky and found the layer of smog still halved the distance of the *Elfsight* spell's raining starlight.

"Okay." Ben looked to Tex. "A diviner said 'when the car lost me,' I would be where I need to be to save Clarissa." He got out, pulled his Anvilsmith, and recast *Elfsight* to extend the duration of the spell, then put the tablet back on his hip.

"Who is Clariss—" Tex hopped onto the driver's seat and crossed his arms. "Why don't you have your tablet *in hand*?"

Tapping the SD cardholder on his side, Ben beamed. "I can cast without it."

A FedPS delivery truck gunned past the alcove.

Ben froze.

The engine droned away, idled, and sputtered out. A rolling metal door clattered open.

Tex leapt out of the car.

Ben quietly closed his door and turned. Tex was out of the alcove. By the time Ben stepped from the recess, Tex had already made it to the corner, his little arm waved for Ben to advance.

Ben hurried over and peeked around the corner.

A pale green orc in navy blue work pants and a blue, white, and green FedPS Delivery polo hefted a burlap bag from the back of the cargo truck onto his shoulder. He adjusted the weight and walked into a warehouse.

Having seen a body in a bag before, Ben knew what—*who*—made up the contents.

Two more orcs, the same light green and in similar FedPS Delivery uniforms, came from the cab to unload a few boxes from the back. The first orc came out with a dolly, slipped it under a stack of three two-foot-cubed crates, and wheeled them up a ramp and into the building. The other two did the same. They emptied the back of the truck, which had been full of the two-foot cubed crates.

Ben lost track of which orc had been the one to move Clarissa. Finally, two of the orcs climbed into the cab, the third clattered the rolling door closed, locked it, and got in the passenger side of the cab. The truck's engine started and they drove away.

After they were gone, Ben asked, "Any magic active over there?"

Tex answered, "We are too far away."

Ben nodded. He scanned the walls for camera mounts and scry sensors. None. He jogged to the large rolling door and looked at Tex expectantly.

The small robot shrugged at him.

Ben pulled his tablet and typed *Any magic auras (possible traps) here?*

Tex sockets twisted for a few seconds and he shook his head. *'No'* appeared after Ben's question mark.

Running his finger along his spellcards to *Orion*, Ben channeled Argosian energy. The red energy flowed through him and flashed into the card. A crimson gorilla materialized.

Bastion's been awfully quiet. Ben reached out to the wellspring of Nilosian energy still at his disposal and found only magic. Bastion, the creature he secretly feared he might be turning into, felt completely absent. Bastion wanted to use Nilosian energy exclusively, and Ben had grown accustomed to the constant struggle to not do so. For once, both of the energies within him were equally at his disposal.

Relief, like a prisoner with a life sentence receiving an instant pardon, relaxed his shoulders. *Free of the beast.* Then his growing smiled faltered and the tension eased back into his back and shoulders. *If Bastion's not here, where is he?*

The ape hooted softly and bumped him.

Ben took a small step back to check out the lock on the door between him and the burlap-sacked Clarissa. Cueing up *Heracles*, he turned to the gorilla. His eyes danced across the many small scars and then to the knives it held. He smiled. *Is this Oscar?*

Returning the recognition, Oscar bobbed his head and made several quick, quiet hoots.

Cool! I'm able to call the same gorillas. Ben aimed at Oscar and pressed *Cast*. The ape's red hair turned green, and its muscles bulged.

Turning to the door, Oscar sniffed the lock before taking hold of it and twisting.

The metal gave a sharp cry.

Ben glanced around for witnesses and found none. When he looked back to his gorilla, he chuckled.

Oscar held the perfectly intact lock. The metal slider the lock had been looped through, hung twisted away from the latch.

Well, at least the lock was worth the money. Ben lifted the door and held it so that it would not spring all the way up. Before he could point, Oscar had scooped up the burlap bag and cradled Clarissa in his arms. *Forgot these apes act before I can really form my orders into thoughts. So much better than Orion.* For a moment Ben felt bad for mentally slandering the conjuration that he used for most of his school chores, but only for a moment.

The Anvilsmith vibrated on his hip.

Ben pulled it and read the message from Tex. *Either the crates themselves are magical or they each contain something magical within.*

Ben's eyebrows tightened as he tried to admonish Tex with a scowl. He closed the door and led Oscar back to his car. In a hurry, Ben leapt over the car door into his seat.

To be as expedient, Oscar went to leap in, too.

Ben dismissed the conjuration before it landed. *That probably would've wrecked my suspension.* The burlap bag flopped down into the backseat.

A soft, drowsy groan. Then soft snoring.

Ben bit his lip. He hadn't thought to have Oscar lay the bag in the back. The inevitable chase Papa Mojo warned about would be starting soon. Ben set Tex in his harness. "Map a way out."

The robot's hand flipped back and he plugged in to the console. An overview map of Old Henderson populated. A white line showed the most direct route through the alleys to Dove Boulevard. To keep the car quiet, Ben drove at a crawl for the first two turns and applied more power as he hit a few straight paths. He opened the rest of the way up when they turned onto Dove.

While they were going up the onramp to the freeway, Tex asked, "What was that look you gave me at the door for?"

Ben checked his rearview mirror. *A dozen headlights, at least.* Minding them for any signs of erratic driving, he scanned the onramp they just came up for more headlights and, in case his expected pursuers didn't have them turned on, for moving shadows. He glanced to Tex. "We are not thieves."

"Oh." Tex looked down for a moment and then motioned his head to the bag in the back seat.

In case some were ahead, Ben returned his eyes to the road. *How can I explain why taking Clarissa—a person Tex doesn't know, from an area neither of us are familiar with—doesn't constitute a theft.* Ben kept his grin locked away. *Ah, Tex, old buddy, this isn't theft. It's kidnapping. Big difference, you know.*

"For the record," Tex swiveled in his harness. "I did not see it as *stealing*. I saw it as taking full advantage of an opportunity."

Though it sounds nicer, that's the same as theft. Ben turned to scold Tex, but the robot's face plates were shifted to pull a single cheek up in a half-smile. Mirroring the smirk, Ben checked his rearview mirror again. No one—as far as he could tell—followed. "Um, we were supposed to be chased."

Tex said, "And you're disappointed because we're not?"

Ben pulled Tex from his harness and set him on the dashboard.

The robot struck a pose to look like an adornment.

"Keep track of the cars behind us, Tex, and let me know if any light with magic or take this exit." Ben took the next off-ramp to Green Valley. This late at night, the street leading to the suburbs had zero traffic. Ben drove past the first two housing communities and asked, "Well?"

Tex looked at him. "I hate to burst your bubble, but we're clear."

Ben drove to a vacant business lot, brought the Transcend to a stop, and—*just in case*—left the engine running. "Well, if we're not being chased, I don't see why I have to speed back to the festival." Grabbing Tex, he held the small robot over the head side of the bag. "Give me a starter snip."

Tex pulled on the burlap with one hand. A slight snick preceded the thin sheet of metal that rotated from his other forearm to extend partway over his fist. With care, the robot drove the tip in while pulling to make the puncture into a small tear. "There you go."

"Thanks." Ben placed Tex on the dashboard and found his tongue wetting his lips in case Clarissa wanted to kiss her appreciation. Though he held onto the hope, he chastised himself. *You've seen too many movies, Ben.* Ripping the bag open, Ben leapt backward to the dashboard and heard Tex slide into the windshield.

Tex chided, "Watch it!"

"That's not Clarissa!" Unabashed, Ben scrambled from the car, slammed the door behind him, and focused on his door handle. His fingers landed on his *Blast*, *Shield*, and *Orion* spellcards. "Is that what I think it is?"

"Hold on." Tex unwedged himself from between the windshield and the dashboard. The robot moved to the edge and hopped down out of view. A moment later, his synthesized voice called out, "Hey, Ben."

Heeding his call, Argosian energy ran down Ben arm and pulsed at his fingertips. "Yeah?"

"What's brownish, has six sets of eyes, and is unconscious in your backseat?"

Just wanting verification that he hadn't lost his grip on reality, Ben didn't appreciate the riddle.

Chapter Twenty-Six

TEX'S RIDDLE

HEARING LIGHT BASS THUMPING, Ben checked over shoulder to make sure a car—particularly the Legerity—hadn't taken the exit. Headlights and taillights flowed on the distant expressway like leaves on a river. A light southbound breeze brought the smell of a fire pit and meat being grilled. A rumbling rocked his gut. Ready for the following bite-back from within his stomach, Ben tightened his abdomen. Nothing. Whatever he'd eaten wasn't getting back at him. Blessedly, he simply had a hunger pang.

Being careful to avoid the parking curb he'd been lucky to miss while scrambling away, Ben eased back to the car to gawk into the backseat. Metallic bronze scales cover its—*her*—skin. The proportions of her face were fairly close to a human's. *Slightly flatter nose, thin lips, a much wider mouth, higher cheekbones...* He studied where the hairline would normally have been and noted the scales became thinner and the flesh bulged to form the base of three fore-snakes. Behind the base of first row of serpents, many more. His eyes tracked one of the snake bodies of the medusa's hair through the rip to see that it ended in a snakehead two knuckles wide.

She whispered, "Don't be startled."

Opposite to the suggestion, Ben reeled back from the car. His finger slapped onto his spellcards and he was as ready as he'd ever been to avoid eye contact. He fixed his eyes on the door handle again. "I don't want to fight you."

Ben tensed at a short tear of burlap. "Good to know because I am at a dis—" Another rip. "Tinct—" The bag tore again. "Disadvantage." Several more short rips came before she gave an exasperated sigh. "Wow, who knew burlap would be so hard to tear?"

A corner of his mouth curled. Not noticing at first, Ben realized he stood a little easier. Remembering how offended Penelope had sounded when he called her *bag-lady*, he remained ready, and asked, "What's your name?"

Another rip. "Alice." And another. "Oh, come on!" Several rapid tears sounded before movement registered in his peripherals as she sat upright.

His eyes rose to see rows of snake bodies lying limp against her back.

She seemed to have more success with quick short tears instead of longer ones. Several more sounded before she turned sideways.

Ben dropped his gaze to the door handle again.

"Seriously," she said. "What is this? Triple stitched?"

Fearing a trick, Ben kept his mirth at her comical intonations from forming a chuckle, but the other corner of his mouth curled, forming a reluctant smile. *Her articulation is amazing. She can't be wild.* Ben asked, "Alice, is there someone you can call for a ride back into town?"

"Why would I do that?" He focused on a snakehead as it rolled forward over her shoulder. "I'm already in a running vehicle."

His index pressed on *Blast*. "It's my car."

"And it's a good one." In the pause, her shoulders shifted and turned. "I've never seen a Transcend in black." She stood in the backseat and his eyes lowered to the handle when he realized she wasn't wearing anything. "Sorry about that, hon." Movement above the door line. "Better?"

Against his better judgment, Ben's gaze rose to see she had the burlap wrapped around her waist. She stepped over the armrest and dropped into the passenger seat with a jiggle.

He lowered his eyes and his cheeks started to heat up. "You're still topless."

Alice laughed. "Well, I have to keep you from accidentally looking into my eyes somehow, don't I?"

Her musical, disarming, and infectious laughter removed his last bit of doubt. Ben found that earlier chuckle rolling from his mouth. His posture had completely relaxed and his fingers were nowhere near his spellcards.

"Seriously, though, this material makes for a lousy dress." Messing with something in her lap, her shoulders moved a few more times. "Perhaps if I'd ripped it better…" She turned toward him and he lowered his eyes. "Hon, listen, I know I owe you for saving me from whomever bagged me and knocked me out. I'm not going to turn you to stone."

Ben scratched his temple. "So, I just avoid eye contact and don't worry about your snake-hair biting me as I drive?"

"Ug!" Alice slapped her hand as though she were smacking sense into him. The muffled sound paled in comparison to a crisp flesh-slap. "I swear, whoever made those damned *Clash of the Titans* movies should have to live in a medusa's body for one year just to see how horribly awkward they've made our lives." A loud thud sounded in his car.

Ben eyes lifted to see she had pounded her fist on the dashboard. "Hey!"

"Sorry. Sorry." She flattened her hand and patted where her fist had struck. "This senseless shit seems so absurdly silly." Her wide, thin lips twisted several times. Part of the turn appeared to be dismay while another part showed pure exasperation. "Sometimes, it really gets to me."

Ben had delayed taking *Mythic Monsters II* and didn't know anything more than what had been presented in the only movie—and its remake—that he'd ever seen with a medusa. Feeling guilty about generalizing based on mundane media, he inched toward the car. "How about you clear up the stereotypes and debunk the myths for me?"

"Love to." Her voice rose with enthusiasm. His eyes went to her hands as she ticked facts on her fingers. "We can totally control the whole flesh-to-stone thing. The serpents are neither hair nor independent. I'm part of a naturally hairless race which, through a curse older and more obscure than vampirism, happens to have a slew of snakes on our heads. We aren't serpent chimerics, like, say, centaurs or satyrs, and, as I am sure you have noticed by how many words I've spoken without a single hiss, we are not sibilant."

She motioned to her mouth with all five fingers, exaggerating her 'esses' to make hissing sounds as she spoke. "Though sssometimesss we ssspeak this way on purpossse." She winked at him as she continued, "Sssince sssome guys love accentsss."

Having accidently made eye contact, Ben started to close the distance. *They're the same bright yellow as Papa Mojo's.* He leaned over the car door and looked closer. A faint filmy texture covered them. "You can see through your eyelids?"

"One, yes." She dropped the accent. "We have two sets." A tight roll of scales above her eyes unrolled. This set of eyelids were a myriad of miniscule yellow scales with a slit of black down the center. Besides the thickness of the pupil, the scales made it look as though she hadn't closed her eyes at all.

Ben waved his hand in front of her face and then leaned back. "So, how long were you awake?"

She raised the outer set.

He flinched, but didn't recoil.

Alice said, "Since you told your car that you guys aren't thieves."

Ben scanned the length of the Transcend. "My car?"

"Yes, very *Knight Rider*. I like it." Alice looked around, motioning to the air, and the completely vacant lot around them. "I mean, who else could you've been talking to?"

"Me." Tex waved. He rolled backward, pivoted, and leapt into the driver's seat to get out of range of the striking snakes.

Alice grabbed a hold of the serpents, which instantly went limp at her touch. "Sorry about that." The scales on her cheeks darkened to a coppery bronze. She looked at Ben with a bashful turn of her head. "It startled me."

Chapter Twenty-Seven

A NEW KIND OF TROUBLE

BETWEEN HAVING OVERBEARING parents and going to an all-boys school, Ben hadn't ever really had a completely casual conversation with a girl. At times he thought his parents had conspired to make sure he didn't have a social life where he could meet the opposite gender. After giving it some thought, that absence almost guaranteed him crushing on Penelope or any other girl he got to spend time around. He didn't feel that way about Alice. At least he didn't think he did.

Where the conversation with Penelope had been full of moody, awkward silences—*be fair, Ben. She had just been held prisoner*—the conversation with Alice flowed. Well, it did until he merged into the stream of lights from the whizzing traffic on the expressway taking them away from Old Henderson.

With the top down, the cool night air made a gust in the car and she was leaning forward toward the heater. They had to speak loudly to be able hear one another, but now she yelled, "Look, Ben. I know you think you saved me, but you're wrong!"

Ben arched an eyebrow at her. *So, you typically secure yourself in burlap bags and have orcs render you unconscious before taking you to unknown warehouses?* But sarcasm would get him nowhere. Instead, to try and get her to town faster so he could get back and get Clarissa, he returned his eyes to the road, accelerated, and switched into the fast lane.

"Canyon folk have been going missing since the beginning of the month." She pointed back to the dark industrial sprawl of Old Henderson. "This was the closest I came to seeing where the abductors are taking them."

Sitting on the dashboard, Tex nodded sagely, and added, "What she's saying does make some sense."

Ben shot Tex a look. It said *I've got more than enough dealing with her, so please shut your trap.* Though he had gone through hours of facial expressions so Tex could map them and distinguish under tones, Ben figured he would—eventually—have to actually tell Tex to be quiet.

A plate shifted from the small robot's chin to close its speaker.

Whoa! What the— Ben blinked hard. *He shouldn't—*

Alice wailed, "I smelled one of my sisters there!"

Why didn't she say that earlier? Ben's thoughts bounced back Tex who wasn't supposed to have a chin plate. *All Golemcast have a fixed chuck of metal there. How in the heck did he do that?*

The click of Alice's seatbelt being undone barely registered. Ben glanced over when she stood. The high speeds were making the snakeheads flop. She threatened, "Don't make me jump from this car!"

A bit over-the-top. Not sure how correct he was, Ben said, "Alice, sit down. Your scales aren't armor."

She yelled, "Well, it's either this or turn you to stone!" Fizzles— rainbow light—created an aura around Alice.

Ben frowned at the array of colors and tried to figure out which bands of magic were her primary casting sources. *Can't believe she has that much magic at her disposal...*

Tires screeched. The closer cars behind him swerved away.

Wow, that's not magic. Ben put it together. *It's the Mystique!*

While the Mystique would work to keep her race obscured, It— apparently—could not cover someone standing up in a speeding convertible.

Alice raised a foot to the door.

Does she even know about causing a breach? Wait, does she even know about the Mystique? Knuckles white with frustration, Ben squeezed the steering. "You're going to crack the Mystique!"

Not knowing or not caring, Alice looked out into the night.

Man! Time is shrinking to save Clarissa and now I gotta deal with her? Being known as one of the more obstinate APA students, Ben wasn't used to dealing with someone as strong-willed as himself. "Okay!" He blurted. *Obviously, she doesn't realize the effect she's causing.* Then, in a calm voice. "Okay. Please sit."

As though set to a microphone, the fizzling from the rainbow aura increased in volume and snapped to throw multi-colored sparks. Worse, the air around her scales began to bulge the aura out forming undulating prismatic tentacles which swished in a meandering fashion toward nearby drivers.

Her passive, I'm-not-playing-chicken, slitted yellow eyes flashed gold when lit by cars on the other side of the expressway.

A rainbow strand curled and whipped at a driver.

The car jammed on its breaks. Skidding and throwing up smoke, its hood dipped.

Holy! Ben slowed, crossed three lanes and took the next off ramp. The further he got from other traffic, the more purposeful the tentacles became. *We're going to flippin' breach!* "Sit! Alice! Please sit!" Fear—fear of breaking all that was sacred to magic-users, fear of being stripped of magic, fear of being forced to live as a mundane knowing a magical world lay just beyond reach—turned his voice into a shrill cry. "Sit! Sit! Sit!"

Jostled and eyes wide, Alice clung to the windshield. She pushed herself down into the seat.

Ben took a sharp right from the ramp onto—*I have no idea what street this is*—whatever and noticed the long wisps of rainbow light around Alice stopped growing. About to exhale his relief—*horror of horrors!*—small, matte gray tendrils extended from the cars that were close to them. Those dull grays reached over the edge of the freeway—*Goodness, what happens if they connect? A breach, that's what. Yeah, but what then?*—from the zooming cars. Ben could swear the occupants up there were looking his way. The Mystique had reached out to them and they were curiously trying to keep an eye on whatever a near-breach made them see.

The colorful and dreary vines came close, but—*blessedly*—did not touch.

Soon, the cars with gray were well on their way further down the freeway and the furthest reaches of Alice's Mystique-enhanced aura began to dissolve into quickly dispersed butterflies, bubbles, and glitter in the Transcend's wake.

A click—*her seatbelt*—came from the passenger seat. Finally able to breathe, Ben drew a deep one, held it, licked his lips, and let it ease out. He pulled over to take another one, and then, a third.

Tetchy, arms crossed over her chest, Alice said, "I'm not getting out."

Chapter Twenty-Eight

ALICE

My heart's thundering. Ben pulled his coat away by the collars to check his chest. The white dress shirt popped away from his body with each beat. *What was it that I read about visible heartbeats?* He tried to recall, but everything not connected to the Mystique, or consequences of a breach of it, flowed through his brain like water through a sock. The thought would hold long enough to register, then be gone when another notion flowed through.

The budding communities of Royal Ridge and Sonoma Springs flanked the road they idled on. From deep in one of them, a group of small dogs started yipping—high points playing against the pounding in his chest and the distant whoosh of traffic. Ben's stomach gurgled unreceptively. From recent habit, Ben popped one of the cherry antacids and chewed the chalky disk. "I said 'okay,' and I stand by my word."

"Great!" Alice's arms unfolded and she turned to face him. "If my sister's not there now, she has been in the last day or so." Almost a separate thought, she sucked a quick, excited breath. "Maybe we can find an office that has an inventory sheet or a manifest."

Ben dragged in one last long, deep breath. Though laced lightly with run-off exhaust from the expressway, it felt like truly fresh air when compared against the haze over Old Henderson. *Amazing how the smog settles over Old Hendo.* Finally, a thought stuck. He took it a step further as his heart stopped its insane mad rapping on his chest. *Almost like the hole the Anvilsmith Dwarves blew into the earth wanted to make amends by sucking away all of the valley's impurities.*

"Alright." *Ready and steady.* Ben started, "So, this might sound personal, but—" He glanced over. Her snakes were still entangled. He gained momentary eye contact before his eyes wavered in their sockets. Losing the fight against the natural urge to see what the serpents—*vipers, definitely some type of vipers*—had been covering, Ben turned his back toward her and tried to make out the graffiti under the white tile on tan stucco Royal Ridge façade.

"Humans." Alice gave an exasperated sigh. "Better?"

That was quick. Too quick. He turned. Her hands covered her breasts. "No." Ben said, "That's not what I meant."

Comfortable, she removed her hands.

A part of him—*are the scales of her areola darker? Does she have nipples?*—worked hard at getting his irises to drop below level. Ben brought lessons learned in Adept Matton's *How to Remain Composed Amongst Vixens and Succubi* section of *courtmanship III* into play. His vision stayed above the horizon. Matton's raspy voice—the Adept had a horrible cold that week—came back to him. "Just think there's no more to them below the chin."

But there is more Alice. Lots of Alice. More Alice than the one set of eyes could take in with a casual glance. Struggling—*get a hold of yourself, Ben*—he asked. "Well, maybe…, could you?"

Alice's yellow eyes kicked up high and rolled away as she sighed and concealed her chest again.

"All right." He could think. He could talk. *A different kind of petrification.* Ben didn't want to smile at the thought, but—since he had kept from perving-out—pride parted his lips to show a sheepish grin. "So, what I was going to ask you is, what color of magic do you use?"

"Magic?" Alice's head pushed back into the seat and the corners of her mouth moved further toward her ears when she pressed her lips together. "Psss, I wish."

Ben started the car. "Being naked—" He cleared his throat and kept his eyes from dropping to the burlap as he made a U-turn and started back toward the onramp that would take them to Old Henderson. "—

as you were, how were you going to fight whoever, or whatever, is inside?"

Alice turned in the seat to face him. The slits rose in her yellow eyes, again, and rolled away, again. "Honey, I can turn living creatures to stone."

Waiting for more, hoping for more, Ben checked for traffic at the bottom of the onramp. None. Given how late, and far out they were from the city, he wasn't surprised to only see infrequent streetlights dotting the darkness. Still, he came to a complete stop at the stop sign. His brow furrowed. *So, this is a one-trick pony.* Adept Love had used the term to explain why Jameson Brown never won a top-tier dueling match. The term had bothered Ben because he didn't see that quality in Brown's matches, but Love did.

Finally, he understood what the small Adept meant when he said all of Brown's opponents could see what was coming. *Any thinking person fighting Alice would avoid eye contact, negating her primary strength. Slow down. Maybe she's got some other things going for her. There's more to combat than magic.* Ben meant to ask casually, but the question came out barbed. "So, you're telling me you don't know magic, *and* you don't have any weapons?"

Alice shifted in her seat to face forward. Most of her front snakes slid over her shoulders to cover her.

An involuntary shudder—the thought of a single snake slithering on his skin, from behind his ear and down his neck—shook him.

Serpents coiled in place, Alice dropped her arms. "I didn't say that."

Making a left, Ben drove up the onramp. Taking her back to the warehouse now seemed like just that much more of a bad idea. *Tactics. Talk tactics.* Without a slanderous undertone, he honestly asked, "Then what happens when your stare doesn't work, or, if it works all the time, what about when people are out of range or refuse eye contact?"

She didn't answer.

Has she not given it any thought? Her body's mature. I wonder how old she is.

Before he could ask, she offered, "Part of my training is being familiar with all sorts of weapons. Weapons I get from opponents."

Ben merged in with the sparse traffic. "Yet you start with none?"

Tex raised a finger like he wanted to say something.

Sorry, buddy, Ben shook his head. *No sniping.*

Jabbing its small metal finger toward Ben's spellcards, Tex lowered his hand.

Ben made a mental note. *Ask Tex about that later.*

"Ugh," Frustration poured from her groan, yet his curiosity had increased with each of her exasperated sighs. Alice said, "Let's just say I'm highly trained for this, okay?"

"*Highly trained*? Like, ready for war?" His eyebrows knitted. Instead of shooting a barbed *I doubt it,* he asked, "How old are you?"

Alice fixed her serpentine eyes upon him. "I'm old enough not to dignify the question with an answer."

His mom had told him never to ask a woman's weight or age. His father had warned if he was ever asked what he thought, he was supposed to always under-guess by ten or twenty percent. It had been one of the few things in his rearing that his parents had been on the same page about.

After a moment, Alice settled into her seat and crossed her arms with no small degree of superiority. She shifted in her seat and flicked his shoulder. "How old are *you*?"

Instead of answering directly, Ben played to his abilities and experience. "I am a caster. I can throw from two types of magic and have over forty spells readily available. Further, I've been training for six years and have been in life-or-death combat." Something close to arrogance building, Ben looked over at her.

Her thin lips were pressed together and rippled with an unmistakably smug smile.

Ben asked, "What? You've fought for your life before?"

She nodded. "Oh yes, a couple of times." Alice pointed to her face. "This is not me doubting your experience." She flicked her index finger away to point back at her expression, "This is me gloating about being older than you."

What a zing and I can't fire back without playing into it. Ben gripped the steering wheel, leaned near it, and ground his teeth. "You know, Alice, I'm really starting to regret not letting you jump."

Alice guffawed, making a sharp sound akin to a snort. Embarrassed at the noise, she covered her bronzing cheeks and continued to laugh.

Ben laughed with her.

Chapter Twenty-Nine

SCOUTING IT OUT

BACKING into the same trash alcove, Ben angled his car in a pool of shadows cast by a sign on top of the warehouse blocking the main floodlight. *That light wasn't on before.* He kept a wary eye out for security guards. An excuse he could tell the guy, if the guard was a guy —*just trying to get lucky*—jumped to his mind and fled—balls to the wall, screaming—at the thought of her snakes reaching out to caress him. Ben could already hear the guard's response if he wasn't human. *Kid, you can't get lucky with a girl you can't look in the eye.*

To test his nerve, Ben wanted to look into Alice's eyes, but—*chicken* —ended up offering, "Tex is great at point."

His companion stood tall. Back ridged, the little golemcast basked in the compliment.

A generator kicked on. The hum honed Ben's attention back on the alcove. *The lack of a powerful odor. That's what's wrong.* For some reason, he had a hard time accepting the garbage area really only possessed a faint rotten smell. If he had time, he'd try to find out why. *The smell should really be stronger.* He put his train of thought back on track. "So, he goes first." Ben motioned to the Anvilsmith. "He relays the layout through my tablet."

Alice extended her hand to touch the Anvilsmith. "Cool! Is this the new—"

Ben smacked her fingertips.

A few of her snakes hissed as, scowling, she brought her hand back.

"It may look like it," Ben explained, "but it's better than any device you've ever seen."

Alice's lips turned in an *oh yeah?* smirk. "Does it have *Kings, Clergy, and Coffers?*"

Ben bit his lip. *That game!* He avoided students at the Academy who played KCC. Most played for real money and he couldn't afford even the smallest of stakes. An alternative iteration *Dragons, Mages, and Magic—same game, really, just rewrapped* proved very popular amongst younger casters. Both versions—all versions—of the game had been forbidden during school hours. There were rumors that the game had even been ported through the Mystique so mundanes could play it on their devices. Only the heavens knew what they call it.

He began to doubt her age again.

"Anyhow!" Ben tapped the dimmed device, tapped *Maps* and *Local*. The Anvilsmith lit showing an overview of the city-sized maze that was Old Henderson. A white line ran from the freeway and ended at a section of a building in the warehouse complex highlighted in red. "You were deposited here." Tapping a spot on the Anvilsmith, it zoomed into an interior view of the garbage alcove they were in with its wrought iron gates wide open like they were now. "We're here."

Alice looked up, then back at the tablet. "Heh, duh."

"Yeah, duh." Ben didn't want to lose momentum. He pressed *Local* again and the map changed to top-down. Ben spread his fingers and the map zoomed out to encompass only a few hundred feet around the warehouse. "We'll avoid as much opposition as possible, snatch your sister, grab the person I came for, and get out."

"Gotcha." Alice nodded. "Anybody in burlap?"

"No, a particular someone." Ben hadn't thought about coming across other abductees. *Crap!* "Well, I say if they are bagged, we free them."

"I concur." Alice gave a strong nod and the short serpents hanging down over her forehead like bangs seemed to agree as they bobbed with the movement.

A memory—Clarissa springing the hug on him—brought a knowing smile to Ben's face. Gary had called his thinking of someone and then that person showing a 'third-eye.' As when he thought of Collins and out of nowhere, the jerk would appear, now, he'd just thought about Clarissa. Ben snapped his fingers and winked at Tex. "We're going to get her this time."

Tex stood on the dashboard. "How can you be sure? What if there are dozens of bags in there?"

"One of them will be her. I'm sure of it." As soon as the words left his mouth, a sense of dread—*hopefully alive*—stole over Ben and faded. He switched his attention to Alice as he got out. "We'll get you armed as soon as possible. If you get to your bagged sister before we get to my bag, get her out and back to the car." Ben extended a fist to Tex. "He and I can sneak the rest of the way."

Exuding confidence, Tex nodded solemnly and gave Ben a fist bump.

Alice rolled her eyes.

Tex leapt onto the paved concrete with a small *tink*.

Ben turned his companion loose. "Scout it out, buddy."

Tex saluted, hustled to the gates, slowed to peer both directions, then ran around the corner.

Closing the car door quietly behind him, Ben pulled the Anvilsmith to show the populating map on his screen to Alice. He glanced over his shoulder. Instead of getting out on her side and coming around, she walked across his seat and—*she doesn't have a belly button*—stepped over the driver door to stand next to him.

Almost dismissively, she said, "Uh, it reeks in here."

On the screen, Tex, represented by a green dot, moved along the white path to the red area of the building. As they moved to the entrance to the trash alcove, Ben thought about showing her the live feed through the pinhole camera between Tex's lenses. He struck the thought down. Last thing he wanted was for her to start thinking of his companion as a way to get a low angle up at... Well, up at whatever she might think.

Perhaps he'd gone to Meadows Towing too often, but parking his car next to a large machine meant for crushing made Ben look back to make sure the cardboard compactor hadn't reached out to snag his Transcend.

His car was gone.

"Where—" His heart flew into his throat. He felt the familiar sickening roll in his gut when he had come out of *Card Crafters* on his birthday to find that his car had been stolen. Preparing to properly yell and freak out, he swallowed to clear his throat.

Alice looked back at him. "What?"

In the brief moment it took him to find his voice, he spied the faint outline of his front fender, then his hood, the side panel, and the rest of the car. *It's virtually invisible in the shadows.* His head tilted. *Is it magic? The paint?* A faint chime came from his device.

Ben said, "Nothing." He looked back to the tablet. The green dot was still at the front of the building, but next to it, *+30*. Though excellent scouting work, Ben made a note to ask Tex later why he'd climbed to the roof.

"Two on the roof," Alice whispered. "Looks like it's time for me to get my weapons." She ran, leapt high onto the wall, and stuck. Stuck like gum, like glue, like Spider-Man. He'd seen her make contact, but hadn't heard even the lightest slap. Still, somehow, she stuck. Body close to the wall, she climbed to the top and slipped over a rain gutter to the rooftop.

Ben hustled to the corner.

External piping that ran up to dim lights affixed on the wall of every fourth building. Under the third one, where the orcs had deposited Alice, Tex descended from the roof.

Good thing he checked. I didn't even think about checking up there.

His companion dropped to the ground, lay on his belly in front of the rolling door, and shimmied sideways into the building.

Ben checked his map to see Tex's relay of the inside of the building. The main area, fifty-feet wide had crates stacked forty-feet high at the far end, shortening the hundred-foot depth to eighty. Ben activated the camera feed and relegated the map to a corner of the screen. A catwalk ran along the right wall, above the crates, with an interior ladder just inside of the rolling door and another extending to the ground halfway through the warehouse. Three columns of boxes shone blue against the back wall. A legend popped up on the left of the tiny map in the corner, *blue = magic/magical*. Two more stacks lit on the screen, and then one of the Hawg motorcycles with high handlebars and equally high, long tailpipes.

What if Tex pops? Now would be the worst time for him to fry out and shut down. Ben whispered into the device, "Don't detect magic on items inside the warehouse. We're not going to capitalize on any of these, uh, *opportunities.*"

Tex's words scrolled. "Are you sure? There is a magical motorcycle."

Though amused, Ben put on his game face. "Positive. Don't want to go all sunny-side up."

"Right." Tex flashed a frying egg on the screen. "Good thinking."

Ben laid a finger on his *Orion* spellcard and smiled at how easily he managed to channel Argosian energy into it. *Really nice to not have to fight Bastion to not use Nilosian magic to power my spells.* Like a property thrown boomerang, a nagging concern—*where's Bastion?*—pinged in his head.

Red flashes of light lit at Ben's sides. Two glowing gorillas, Abe and Oscar materialized. The light from them faded. Both had their weapons from a prior conjuring in hand. *Orion never did that.* Ben eyed Abe's greatsword and Oscar's daggers with an appreciative nod. Ben smiled at each of them. "I've got to outfit you guys better."

The gorillas hooted their agreement.

A chime. Ben glanced at his tablet. His eyes were drawn to a red dot on the map of the catwalk. Tex's text popped up. "One just came in—hot!"

Ben jumped onto Abe's back. "Go."

Chapter Thirty

GO TIME

ORION, the green gorilla Ben would conjure from inserting his spellcard into his tablet, never had a smell. He couldn't remember any of his conjurations having a scent.

Abe did. The coarse, red hair pricking Ben's hands and neck—expecting the teddy bear softness of Orion, Ben had almost let go—carried the bouquet of an exotic old growth forest. On Abe's crimson skin, the musky exertion of swinging tree to tree. In the pores, the grimy odor of a normal, completely wild life. Riding on Orion had been an exercise in luxury, perfect-suspension comfort when compared to this jostling Argosian creature. *I hope he doesn't have fleas. Please don't have fleas.*

Not burdened with extra weight, Oscar made it to the rolling door first. Pinning a knife in his red palm with his thumb, Oscar yanked the rolling metal door up with one arm. Before the door banged up, the gorilla had thrown his other knife into the warehouse.

A soft clatter followed the door smacking home in its sleeve. Oscar hurried in.

Ben let go of Abe as they turned into the warehouse. His loafers offered no traction and he slid a foot on the smooth concrete floor. *Two more seconds without line of site, Oscar, and you would've poofed away.*

Oscar grunted his understanding as he leapt up the crates toward where a limp body in blue jeans and a black biker coat lay on the catwalk. A short width of dark green skin—a couple of shades darker than hunter green, that Ben had started to call *warrior orc green*—showed between the coat collar and a full-face motorcycle helmet. In that small section of skin, the hilt of Oscar's knife. Not an inch of blade remained outside the orc.

Abe also vaulted up the crates to inspect the body.

Ben had forgotten how smooth the conjuror's bond between him and the gorillas felt both in combat and post combat. *It almost felt like we three are one.* As they could feel his thrill once he realized what they were doing, he could sense the intense focus on looting the body.

I don't have to get them better gear. Smiling a pleased smile, Ben shook his head against his earlier thought, and hustled to the ladder in the middle of the room. *They know what they want and where to get it.* Thinking about his fingerprints—*I need to get a pair of good gloves*—Ben hesitated for a moment. *Oh well.* He gripped onto a rung. The chill in the metal brought home the coolness of the night that the magic of his coat protected him again. *Yup gloves.* He started up and his loafer slid to the heel. *And better shoes. Maybe a set of the black boots—*

"Ben!" Alice yelled from behind him. Danger colored her voice. "Watch out!"

Five feet up, he turned to look at her.

At his new eye level, his gaze met a large set of bloodshot eyes, then flicked out to the massive brownish-green hand lashing out at him.

A tuzvul! Where the Hell—

It grabbed him by the ankle.

Ladder must've had a spell-trigger. Ben jammed his hand into his coat.

The strong hand closed hard around his ankle, squeezed with a vice-like grip, and yanked.

Pain shot through Ben's shoulder as the tuzvul yanked him free from the ladder. His hand missed his spellcards. His bone gave to the pressure. Agony—*it broke my ankle!*—raced up his leg and burst out through his lips in a jagged moan.

The tuzvul's other hand closed around his arm, the one going for his spellcards, and squeezed with remarkable strength.

He's going to break my arm, too.

It didn't break his arm.

The room spun as the monster hoisted him above its head.

Alice screamed, "Ben!"

Ben looked to Alice. The thin membrane over her eyes peeled back, revealing vibrant, glowing golden irises with tiny brown flecks. *Gorgeous.* A tightening, worse than any stomach cramp Ben had ever had, constricted his guts and rapidly spread outwards. His eyes went wide at the tightening in his chest and he could feel his consciousness weaken. *Check out time.*

Ben thought he'd be unconscious, but—*on reflex?*—he'd shifted his consciousness to Oscar and rode behind the gorilla's eyes as it left the dead orc on the catwalk and leapt over the railing.

From Oscar's point of view Ben saw his body, hoisted above the tuzvul's head, turn to gray stone. More than his body, his coat, his clothes, he could even glimpse the—now also stone—Anvilsmith tablet.

The tuzvul's lanky arms tensed and flexed.

Remembering how easily the dragon-tuzvul had torn a wing from his creature when the massive monster had gotten both hands on it, Ben cheered Alice's quick thinking. *I need to get out of here. I can only piggyback for an hour.* His thoughts went to his body. *I need to find Master Reynolds. He can turn me back.*

The tuzvul tensed once again, glanced up at the turned-to-stone body, and tossed it aside to swipe at Alice.

She ducked, jumped to the side, and rolled away.

The monster's other massive hand swooped.

She dodged again. The snakes down her back reared up, struck the tuzvul's wrist, and released as the arm arced over.

Oscar hit the floor. The Gorilla threw a knife. It sank into the tuzvul's chest where the heart would be. *Blades not long enough.*

The tuzvul's mouth opened and its throat worked as to bellow, but no sound came. It drove a fist down at Alice.

Alice planted a foot and rolled backward.

Abe soared from the catwalk and plunged his greatsword deep into the tuzvul's back.

The monster reared, its mouth open again to belt a muted roar.

It's silenced? That's why I didn't hear it. Ben took control of Oscar. He rushed forward to wrap the tuzvul's knee in a bear hug. *Time to return the favor.* He twisted. A pop from the monster's leg resonated through the ligament and vibrated against Oscar's chest. *Got you!*

The tuzvul's weight shifted to its other leg, and it swatted Oscar away with a massive backhand.

The blow cracked Oscar's ribs—*glad I can't feel that*—and sent him reeling. They scrambled for purchase as they slid through the warehouse and out into the alley, but found none. They slammed into a rolling metal door across the way.

Ben tried to rush Oscar back to his feet, mewing, the gorilla rose.

Inside, the tuzvul peeled Abe from its back and crashed the gorilla into the concrete. The smack opened Abe's hand and the greatsword clattered away.

Just about to transfer into his other conjuration still in combat, Ben hesitated when the tuzvul grabbed his gorilla with both hands, hoisted it into the air above its head, and wrenched to twist the shrieking gorilla apart.

"Hey!" Alice called to the tuzvul. It looked at her as the general glow around her eyes focused into golden beams which struck the tuzvul's eyes.

Flesh turning gray, the tuzvul kicked out at her with its bad leg.

Alice jumped back.

Turning more and more gray, the tuzvul returned its attention to ripping Abe apart. One last action before—

It became a statue.

Abe, painfully contorted in its frozen clutch, beat fruitlessly at the stone fist with his free hand. Only a jackhammer could get him free. Abe tried the stone fingers to no greater effect.

Come on, Oscar. Ben urged. *Time is against me.*

Cradling his cracked ribs, Oscar got back to his feet and beat out a hurried, lopsided shuffle to get back into the warehouse. Ben made him stop just inside the threshold.

Alice had gone to his turned-to-stone body.

What's she doing?

She leaned in close. Her serpents dangled onto his stone coat and around the stone head of his statue-self. She hovered her face close to his and—

No way.

Kissed him.

Chapter Thirty-One

FIRST KISS

STANDING in one of his conjuration's bodies, forty feet away from his own—which had been turned to gray stone—Ben gawked as he was kissed. Stunned, he didn't think about her being a medusa, he didn't think about having no real friends at his all-boys school to tell about this moment, and he momentarily forgot about the series of events that brought him here. The whole of his existence centered on feeling somewhat cheated.

Slowly, his sculpture-self turned back into flesh. Her serpents went back to form a bra as she warmed up a smile.

His body went limp in her arms. *It's reversible. Thanks goodness. That would've been hard to explain.*

Her soft smile faded quickly. "Ben?" Her eyes widened as she shook his body. "Ben?"

Ben went to answer, but wound up uttering a hoot. *Oh! I'm still in my conjuration...*Using Oscar's good arm, he smacked his forehead, then released control and landed back in his body.

Alice leaned in and kissed him again.

Though dry and thin, her lips possessed a gentle suppleness and malleability he hadn't expected. Between her having been in a bag and driving with the top down, he hadn't noticed her faint lilac scent. One of her hands cradled his head. The other lay on the side of his neck feeling for a pulse.

All right! With his lips, Ben pressed back.

She dropped him and wiped at her mouth as she reeled away sputtering. "You jerk!"

The back of his head smacked on the concrete. *Crap! My head! My leg!* Expecting blinding agony to shoot through him, Ben clamped his eyes shut and grimaced. *Ready.* But only a dull throbbing pulsed in his ankle. *Huh?* He opened his eyes and looked at his foot. *It's aligned with my leg and the pain isn't as intense as when the tuzvul broke it.* Gauging the pain, he equated it to a severe sprain. He extended his hand.

Oscar hooked his massive arm under Ben's armpit, grunted, and hoisted him up.

Standing on his good foot, Ben gingerly set his toe on the concrete.

From above them, Abe belted a helpless cry.

Ben glance up to his other conjuration and—*I've got you, buddy*—dispelled Abe. He did the same to Oscar, then touched the *Orion* spellcard and channeled Argosian energy into it to re-summon both gorillas.

As their red flashes lit next to him, Ben put more pressure and lifted his foot. *Now it just feels like I twisted it.*

Alice kept her distance. Sounding equally astonished, she muttered, "Impossible. I heard it snap."

"I *felt* it snap," Ben said, his eyebrows lifted and mouth wide in excitement. He didn't try to mask his amazement as he tried again and his leg supported his weight without any pain. Standing on it, he lifted his other foot.

"Humans don't regenerate." Alice's voice lowered. She took another step back. "What are you, Ben, really?"

She's right. Trying to find the source of the healing, Ben focused on the Komir necklace under his shirt. *Dormant.* His mind went for another possibility and came back empty. Though he had heard that only Hisboian casters could cast curative spells, he focused on his energy sources to see if magic flowed into his leg from either of them. *No, but...* His eyes shot wide. He grasped at his gut and stumbled.

"What?" Alice twitched as she started toward him, but decided to keep her distance.

Oscar and Abe both had their arms out to catch him if he fell.

Ben flailed his arms out and steadied himself. "I'm okay." He returned his hands to his abdomen. A warm, arcane resonance pulsed from the rumble within. *Is that another chakra opening?* He squeezed his stomach and power trickled as his gut gave a gurgle. *Yes! That is another power source, but it's not what's healing me.*

Alice asked, "Then what's wrong with you?"

Applying pressure to his stomach was like squeezing a sponge inside his gut. *Force equals magic.*

Alice said, "Ben."

Trying to focus on the amazing warmth within, he waved an annoyed hand at her.

She made a short disgusted noise and crossed her arms. "Really?"

Ben raised his arms.

Abe slid behind him and, as though about to give the Heimlich Maneuver, gripped Ben firmly. Slowly, Abe applied pressure.

Ben's stomach began to gurgle uncontrollably and series of oniony burps rolled up through him. He leaned his head back, teeth clenched against the tightening pain as the new magic source gushed more power into him. "I'm okay." He gazed into Alice's yellow eyes. *Her inner eye lids are down.* He tried to notice the brown flecks he saw in the amazing gold around the slitted pupil. Almost giddy, he blurted. "I have another font of arcane power."

Alice returned to mumbling. "...at what cost?"

Ben patted Abe over his shoulder.

The gorilla released him and retrieved his greatsword.

What does she mean, 'at what cost?'

Worse than her question, her face. The corners of her mouth dropped down and a concerned frown cast soft shadows over her eyes.

She's not talking about my magic... It's about the kiss. When Ben applied the context to her face—which probably couldn't have contorted any further into disgust—it sapped his joy at having a new energy source. "Oh, come on." Ben flipped his hands out and let them drop to slap against his sides. "It was an accidental kiss." *Not a hundred percent true, but she did kiss me first.* "If I'd thought about it, I would've told you that I can leave my body to piggyback, or control, my conjurations..." He trailed off. *Is it my breath?*

Alice had placed a hand over her nose and turned away.

Ben, you idiot. It's not about the magic or the kiss, or even your breath. It's about her sister. He walked toward Alice and—*in case it is my breath*—tried to empathize from a distance. "Is your sister's scent gone?"

She kept her back toward him and whispered, "I smell death..."

Oh shit. His Anvilsmith vibrated. Ben flipped his coat open to see the small map Tex had continued to update. A long hallway stretched out behind the door on the catwalk and seven red blips were rushing their way.

Oscar and Abe were already on their way across the warehouse floor.

Ben warned Alice. "Incoming!"

Chapter Thirty-Two

THE GAUNTLET

THE GORILLAS THUMPED up the crates, climbing to get into position on the catwalk. Ben considered casting his other three gorillas, but decided against it. *There's only so many that can fit at the door.*

Alice climbed the tuzvul statue and stood on its upturned face. She seemed focused on the door.

Ben couldn't ignore the feeling that she climbed up to escape being in his immediate presence. *She said she smelled death. I only smell the closed-in, recycled air.* Standing sideways, he used the tuzvul's leg as cover and slid his hand onto his spellcards.

The door flew open with a bang as an orc in jeans, a biker coat, and full helmet came through.

Oscar slit the first orc's wrists, making it drop its gun. Leaping over Oscar, Abe swung his greatsword in a mighty chop. The gorilla cleaved the first orc in two and dropped the one behind it with a deep gash down its front. Blood rained through the catwalk onto the crates.

The two gorillas jumped from the catwalk as the remaining orcs crushed in. They leveled their guns and shot at the retreating red apes.

Alice called, "Hey!"

An orc looked across the room at her.

Golden rays flashed from her to it

The orc turned to stone.

Ben pressed his index finger against his *Blast* card and maxed his flow into it. Three bursts of Argosian magic crackled as it rocketed from him to the line of orcs. The first two slammed into an orc, caving in its chest. The third blast passed through the one falling and smacked into the chest of the orc behind it with muffled cracks.

Oscar threw a knife.

The indented orc dodged. The blade took another half a spin. The hilt rang off the biker helmet of the one behind hit.

Another set of golden rays flashed from Alice before she jumped from the tuzvul, swinging around its neck to get behind it.

Three orcs—one graying to stone—had their guns trained on her.

Ben leapt in front of her.

The rapid crack of gunfire rang through the warehouse.

His Komir necklace pulsed a mad drumbeat against his chest as each bullet crushed against the magical force field it provided. The necklace quickly heated on his skin signaling that its limited battery would soon fail.

The bit of eyes Ben could see through the orcs faceplates became rounded. One spat a curse.

To keep the necklace from burning out—and burning him—Ben slid his pinky back to his *Shield* spellcard, dedicated one of his magic channels to it, and let his Argosian energy flow.

The necklace took the current of magic.

Ben shunted the rest of his max into his *Blast* spellcard. The two missiles slammed into an orc, knocking it from the catwalk onto the crates just beneath it.

His pendant cooled, drawing its power from his Argosian energy.

The last orc moved to retreat.

Oscar's other knife sunk into the back of the orc's knee.

The orc wailed in pain.

Abe tackled the biker from the catwalk, riding the creature to the ground. The orc crunched against the concrete floor.

Abe tumbled away.

Ben winced at the sound. He'd heard helmet and shoulder pad collide before—*the horrible wet snapping sounds*—he shuddered. *They were doing worse... Even when I try to justify it, it's still ending a life.*

A faint shuffling sound moved away from him. Ready for whatever, Ben turned.

It was Alice, as she put more distance between them.

What is your deal? You turn people to stone! The guilt he had started to feel for stealing a kiss had been put into quick perspective when weighted against killing. *She's changed so much. There must be something drastic that I'm missing. Use your words. Communicate.* Ben steadied his voice and asked his question without hostility. "What is it, Alice? What's wrong?"

She looked ready to bolt. "It's just that—I've never known a caster who would do anything like what you've done."

The gloom over ending lives began to lift as her words struck a rarely strummed and unpretentious chord in him. *I wonder how many casters she knows.* His gaze dropped to his shoes and he shook his head against the reflexive mitigating thought. *Don't sully the compliment, Ben. She's saying you're special. Accept it.* Not knowing what to say, truly at a loss for words, a humble smiled spread his lips. Ben looked back to her face. *Her expression… The brow knotted, upper lip curled back, the corners of her mouth slightly downturned. That's not a look of amazement. She's horrified. Terrified. Why? Is being self-sacrificing a crime to her kind?*

His loss for words turned into a lack of concern. *I tried to understand. If medusas expect others to stand around and do nothing while they die, then let her be outraged.* He went to the ladder and, checking over his shoulder for another tuzvul, began to climb. His earlier thought flitted through. *Boots. Boots and gloves.* He marked both items on a mental 'to buy' checklist.

Every few rungs, he checked back. A tuzvul hadn't materialized to attack them and Alice remained rooted to the spot. "Time's ticking," he said. He glanced at his loafers as they made attention calling *clacks* on the catwalk. *These shoes aren't made for stealth.*

Abe hustled up the crates as Ben stepped over bodies, mentally apologizing to each for ending their lives as Oscar stripped them of the traditional daggers all orcs seemed to wear.

Ben kicked off his black dress shoes to stand in his school uniform dress socks, which were the same earthy brown as his school issued slacks. He shoved each shoe into the inner pockets of his coat, at the knees. *Better to have them tapping against me than waking up any sleeping guards.*

The Anvilsmith vibrated.

Ben checked it.

Tex had updated the map with a green arrow flashing down in the hallway beyond the door, the legend noting a possible magical trap. Tex had covered serious ground while they were still in the main warehouse. Again, Ben checked on Alice.

She'd backed out to the rolling door.

"Fine by me, Alice." He waved a dismissive hand at her. "If I find your sister, I'll free her and, if she'll ride with me, I'll drop her off at the Red Rocks."

Letting Abe lead, and avoiding the blood-wet parts of the catwalk, Ben followed Oscar through the door.

Chapter Thirty-Three

THE TRAP

THE WARM CORRIDOR began to darken. Ben's nose curled from the unfortunately familiar smell of orc body funk. *They should shower more often.* He had his gorillas pause. *Pretty soon it'll be too dark to see.* The brief hilarity he felt at the thought of orcs stumbling around and bumping into each other in the darkness got slapped serious. *You can't see in the dark, but they can!* Ben's eyes adjusted as much as humanly possible to the pitch black. Further in, barely distinguishable from the dark, he picked out areas with very dim glows.

The faint luminosity making him hopeful, Ben pulled his Anvilsmith, tapped *Spells, Enchantments, Elfsight,* and *Cast.* His Arcane Wattage counter ticked down by one to ninety-seven driving a point he'd missed—*I've mainly been using my own power*—as magic vibrated from his tablet into his fingers, making his eyes twitch. He grinned at the thought of being one step closer to being a true wizard. *Now, if only I could cast without anything in hand.* Where starlight would rain down outside, the hallway remained dark. Slowly, the few dim glows further down the hall seemed to intensify to offer pockets of light bright enough to see gray tiled floor between long sections of dark shadows.

Oh well. That'll have to be good enough. A light *thunk* sounded behind him. He spun.

A submachine gun in hand, Alice had pulled a clip from one of the fallen orcs closest to the door and its arm had flopped to the floor. Their eyes met for a brief moment.

Ben flinched and—remembering what she had said about the life of a medusa—fought the urge to look away. *That would be disrespectful.*

Alice, on the other hand, averted her eyes altogether as though he were the one in possession of a gaze attack.

She's making me feel like I'm the monster. Deep down he recognized that neither of them were monsters, but his offense at how her demeanor had changed made his thoughts superficial. He shook off wanting to yell—*just tell me what's wrong!*—at her. He shook it off again, presented the map on his tablet to her, and said, "The green arrow means a magical trap ahead. Do what I do."

She glanced at the map then angled her face away and mumbled something.

He stared at her, but she still wouldn't meet his gaze. *Don't let her attitude-change phase you Ben. Game face.* He had his gorillas start forward. *Game face.*

Abe and Oscar rushed down the hall and leapt through the area marked as a trap. Gauging it, Ben ran and leapt the same area. Nothing triggered. He had cleared the trap. Walking backward to give her room to jump, Ben waited to see if Alice would clear it, too.

A set of claws raked across his lower back.

He bellowed and dropped to his knees.

Alice raised her gun—

Oh shit!

She fired over him.

Rubble—*bullets*—rained on his back.

To get away from whatever had struck him, Ben tried to lunge forward to clear the trap. He got only a few inches away. It had hold of his coat.

Claws raked down his back, bumping down his rib cage like a mallet down a xylophone.

Incapable of expressing the pain, even in screams, yips, or cries, his mouth hung frozen open. He struggled against the coat for a moment before he twisted. His shoulders and arms slipped free. He flopped on the tile.

Ben rolled over to see his assailant. *Ahh!* His carved up back radiate pain. He arced up on his feet and shoulders from the agony of lying flat on his back.

More gunfire.

Grimacing, Ben rolled over on one shoulder toward Alice. He saw it. Them.

A stone demon, standing in front of a second stone demon, tossed his coat to the side.

Ben bellowed, "Gargoyles!"

"I know," Alice yelled back.

Claws outstretched, the closest one lunged at him.

Ben scrambled backward on the tile. He escaped the swipe only to hear a hollow *click* as he stumbled into the trap.

Powerful orbs pelted into him. Each broke open to blast a high-pitched sonic assault battering both his body and his ears.

He didn't know whether to shield his ears or try to guard against the brutal impacts.

A hand grabbed his collar and pulled him back.

Stone claws cut across his chest.

His abused ears alternated between piercing whines and deep ringing. The trapped area looked full of rippling bright blue water. He glanced back.

Alice had dropped the gun. Her mouth worked as she held her arm against her body.

"Back," he said, but couldn't hear his voice. He bumped her backward and fell on his butt. Pain rolled up his back flaring where he'd be sliced open.

The blue rippling kept the relentless statues at bay.

Beyond the trap, Ben could feel Oscar—*destroyed*—dissipate. "No!" He placed a finger on his *Blast* spellcard. Pointing at the first gargoyle, Ben channeled Argosian energy into his spellcard. Three bolts of energy flew from his hand, cracking it.

The gargoyle staggered, then recovered and lunged forward. Trying to fight through the bright blue air to get at Ben.

The trap beat the stone demon into gravely bits.

Ben sent another three blasts at the back of the other gargoyle.

It turned and charged at him, pulling up short just before the rippling air.

Abe slammed into the stone demon from behind and tackled it into the trap.

"Yes!" Ben pumped his fist. He quickly dispelled Abe before the trap beat him to bits.

The magical field battered the stone monster for a while before whatever powered the trap emptied and the rippling blue field winked out.

Badly cracked, the gargoyle pulled itself shakily to its feet.

Ben slapped his spellcard and finished the creature with three more blasts.

Breathing a sigh of relief, Ben stood. *So, the Komir necklace protects against magic and ranged weapons, but doesn't do crap for hand to hand.* The deep gashes on his back sang a choir of fresh pain as the movement had caused the closed wounds to reopen. *Duly noted.* He grunted and stood straight so they could close again. Curious, he pulled his shirt away from his chest to check the lighter slashes that streaked his chest. The cuts were closed with blood congealing over them.

Alice's words—*Humans don't regenerate*—came back to mind. He had been confused when she had asked, *What are you, Ben, really?*

Not being distracted by the joy of another magical font, Ben realized that her concern—coupled with Bastion having been in his head—was one hundred percent legit. *I wonder what the real answer to her question might be.* Ready to spring away, Ben inched onto the area where the trap had been.

The tiles *clicked*.

He leapt backward.

Nothing happened.

Still ready to leap, Ben rushed through the area to where his coat had been thrown. Carefully, he bent and picked it up. He examined the five vertical slashes across his lower back which formed an inverted "tee" with the horizontal gashes. He eased it on over his shoulders. *Neither of us would have gotten past this by ourselves.* Trying to get the words together to express his gratitude, he glanced back at Alice.

Cradling an arm to her stomach, she picked up the gun again. And, as though eye-contact with him contact would damage her soul, still refused to look at him.

Ben opened his mouth to say thanks, but clammed up. *Forget it.*

She's probably right. The ringing in his ears eased. The pain from his back began to fade, and the cuts on his chest were now only scab and memory. He placed a finger on his *Orion* spellcard and channeled Argosian energy to summon Oscar and Abe. Of the two flashes of red energy, one materialized into Abe. But instead of Oscar, the second gorilla appeared empty handed.

It hooted at him.

Thinking hard for a moment, Ben recalled this gorilla from Meadows Towing last month as the one who had wrapped Toad up in chains. Unable to think of a human name for the conjuration on the fly, Ben smiled warmly and patted the gorilla once on its powerful chest. "Welcome back, Chainer." He pointed forward.

Abe led the way. Chainer followed. Ben fell in line.

He didn't turn his head to advise Alice. Her not looking at him would make him bring the topic to the table and—*she'd probably be closer to the truth I'd be comfortable with right now*—he sort of feared what she would say. "We're moving on."

The complex grew uncomfortably warm as they moved down several long hallways, covering ground Tex had already mapped. Ben hoped to catch up to his companion.

Before they did, two brown dots appeared in a room with a red dot in each of the far corners. The legend updated, with a line stating brown indicated the presence of burlap bags.

Not attempting to look at Alice, Ben followed his gorillas and said, "We're getting close."

She didn't reply.

Ben held the device close to his mouth and whispered, "Good job, Tex. Go ahead and return to the car."

Tex's text window popped up. Entire sentences scrolled by faster than Ben could finish reading the first sentence. "Copy that, Ben. I'll be sure to send updates of the terrain on the way out and will send a warning if there's an ambush waiting at the car."

The small robot came around a corner at the end of the hallway.

Ben lowered his hand.

Tex raised his small metal hand, slapped him five, and kept with the plan.

Ben had his gorillas stop at the corner. He did, too. Glancing over his shoulder to catch a glimpse of Alice on his heels, he explained, "Okay. The gorillas go in first to draw fire. I go in next. If I call out 'caster,' you come in and try to get eye contact."

She didn't say anything.

In Adept Love's Dueling Hall, there was a saying painted on the back wall in foot-tall letters. *Through joint adversity, common bonds are formed. Let us grow hale and strong together.* Ben had only the one day in *Dueling* before his parents yanked him from the class. But he still remembered that saying and actually saw proof around the APA where the friendships built through the *Dueling* classes carried on while ones built in other disciplines faded at the end of the course. *This was my one chance to build a real battle-buddy*—the childish school term from three years ago felt ludicrous when applied in the real world—*and, somehow, I screwed it up.* Ben glanced back. "Could you at least nod that you understand the plan."

Still avoiding eye contact, Alice nodded.

He sighed. Without enthusiasm, Ben thought, *go time.*

Chapter Thirty-Four

TRUST, BUT VERIFY

WITH THE INCREASED heat in the deeper halls furthest from the warehouse entrance, the orc funk felt more pervasive. Almost like it could work into his skin to become Ben's own, constant stink.

Always smelling like an orc. The thought made him frown. He shook it off and considered the thirty-foot by thirty-foot layout of the room and the forty-foot hallway. *She should be okay.* He thought about the angles the two orcs could have on the hall if they simply moved to the middle instead of staying in the corners. *It would be horrible for her to make it this far to get gunned down here.* "Change of plans. Stay here around the corner."

He climbed onto Chainer's back and at first sniff decided he preferred to smell like the gorillas rather than the orcs. *Though neither would be preferable.* He sent Abe charging ahead to bash down the door. Chainer followed at the same breakneck speed.

Abe crashed through the door, knocking it from its hinges. Automatic gunfire cracked the air. The gorilla stumbled a few feet into the room—*he's being shot from behind*—before being dispersed into crimson smoke.

Just short of the door, Ben let go of Chainer. Hand on his *Blast* card, he landed on his feet and slid.

The gorilla charged in, determined to take one of the orcs down before being dispatched, but only made it to the middle of the room before twitching away in red motes of fading energy.

Sliding just inside the door. Ben channeled the last of his Argosian energy into the spellcard. Four bolts flew from him, two sizzling toward each of his targets in the far corners. He turned to blast the orc to his right. *I'm out.* His Argosian font had run empty. *I didn't even feel it wane.*

The blasts hit the orcs in the corners. They dropped.

About to switch to cast with whatever magic swam in his belly chakra, Ben realized the one he pointed at had fainted. The other had his hands up with a dark spot—*not by design*—around his crotch and puddling on the floor.

Pointing at the still-conscious orc, Ben spoke in the Giant tongue that he had been learning from the orcs at Meadows Towing. With hard consonants meant to be barked with force, the language sounded broken and weak coming out of his mouth. "Down to the ground."

The orc dropped to his knees and then laid belly down in his urine.

Ben slid his finger back to *Orion* and thought about summoning gorillas with his new energy. *What if they're as uncontrollable as the one from the stable? This guy surrendered. The last thing I want is for one of my conjurations to beat him to death.* Ben cleared his throat and tried to lower his voice when he spoke Giant this time. "Stay still and live." *Did I say that right?*

The orc froze in place.

Guess so.

Gun at the ready, Alice charged in the room with her petrification membrane peeled back. Golden light bathed each orc as she looked and aimed at each. She focused on the one remaining still.

Bathed in gold, the orc remained face down.

"Please don't kill him or turn him to stone." Unable to stop either if she decided to do so anyway, Ben went to the orc who'd fainted. He kicked the gun away and pulled the dagger. "I told him he could live if he stays still and, since he's laying in his own urine, I'm quite sure he wants to live."

The light from her eyes dimmed as the inner eyelid dropped. Seemingly stunned, she dropped the gun and tentatively stepped to the first bag. She sniffed it. Moved past it, and sniffed the other. Alice hissed at the bag.

Hissing returned from within the bag.

Alice hissed a longer string, her forked tongue showing for a couple syllables.

Ben pulled his tablet and tapped *Translate* and *To Text* as they exchanged several rounds. The right box, the box meant to be translated into, flashed *English*. The left box, the box to be translated from, repeatedly flashed a small italicized sentences. *Waiting for input.*

Alice ran her hands along the woven-shut bag.

Good luck. Ben had found two people in similar bags and neither had a way of opening them without cutting the bag.

Alice looked to him, her eyes not rising above his torso. "I need a knife."

Ben slid here the orc's blade hilt first.

She caught it and tried to cut at the top.

Ben went to the other bag and asked, "Hello?"

No response.

Alice asked, "Could you please help?"

"One moment." Being a jerk back to her didn't even occur to him as a viable option. Ben pulled his tablet, swiped back from *Elfsight*, tapped *Heracles*, and cast. His arcane wattage ticked down to ninety-six as the tablet pulsed magic into him. As though filled with water, Ben's muscles expanded in his shirt and pants. He put his hand out for the knife.

Still hissing with the other hisser in the bag, Alice handed it to him.

Ben pulled at a corner of the bag, drove the knife through, and ripped the top of the bag open. *That is some tough stuff. Even enhanced it's hard to rip.* For a moment, he wondered about Penelope's strength. She had been able to rip the bag she was in without much trouble. *It was probably a cheaper quality of burlap.*

Done with Alice's, he turned back to his.

Ben thought about the person in Alice's bag. *Her sister will probably be naked, too.* Ben slid his hand where the rips in his coat to feel for the slight vibration of the comfort knack. Nothing. *Ruined. Well, at least it could still cover her.* He transferred Malcolm's rusty nail and Clarissa's card to his pants pocket, pulled his shoes out, and handed his coat to

Alice without eye contact. Ben said, "In case she wants something to wear."

About to hoist the other bag and carry it out, Ben cut into the corner to see strands of blonde hair and an orange coat. To be sure, he ripped the bag open and peered in. *Clarissa.* He beamed with pride. *I've done it! Now to get you back to the fairgrounds.*

Grateful that Clarissa was dressed, it occurred to him that he should've made sure before offering his coat for a woman who probably didn't mind being nude.

Alice's voice sounded a bit husky as she called from the door. "Thank you."

She doesn't seem like the emotional type; her voice is probably that way from not speaking. Ben looked to the door. Alice stood there. Beyond her —hissing up a storm—a second medusa, wearing his coat, ran out the way they came. Glad to at least have Alice back on speaking terms, Ben nodded to her. "You're welcome."

Alice made eye contact. The inner eyelids had been drawn back and the bright, golden serpentine eyes bathed him in light.

She's trying to turn me to stone! Ben averted his eyes. His hand went to his spellcard holder. He pulsed sizzling Nilosian toward his Orion card and waited for the tightening feeling of being petrified. While not what he wanted, he made his plan. *Cast the ape. Enter the ape. Beat her down.*

Nothing. He still felt normal.

The light extinguished. "Idiot-boy!"

Idiot-boy? Ben's teeth clenched behind his lips. When he glanced up to lock his gaze at waist height, she had already turned and left. *The snakes are longer than Alice's. Wait, was that the one we just saved who tried to turn me to stone? You filthy ingrate!*

Sizzling magic played at his fingertips. In the mass of snakes, he spied a red choker with orange trim. *Filthy, filthy ingrate!* With vibrating Nilosian energy around his hand, Ben barely managed to keep from casting gorillas to chase her. Instead, he opted for a threat. *No, a warning.* "You better hope we don't meet again!"

He didn't mean it. While he didn't expect a reward, a simple sincere 'thank you' would've been nice, but her attempting to turn him to stone made the words fly.

Ben slid his shoes on, hoisted Clarissa onto his shoulder and made his way back to the catwalk. He hustled down the crates and, huffing for the last two hundred feet, made it back to the car. Carefully, he lay the bag in the backseat.

At that moment everything, even Tex moving out from under the body, unfolded exactly like the vision he had seen in Papa Mojo's crystal ball.

A whining alarm kicked up in the night.

Ben leapt into the Transcend, put his key in the ignition, and—*why am I waiting for them when Alice's friend tried to turn me to stone*—waited for Alice and her sister to show. *Because, if they're on foot, they're screwed.*

A motorcycle roared past the opening, too fast for him to tell who rode it. Ben glanced to Tex. "Was that them?"

"Alice and another medusa?" His companion nodded. "Yes."

"Then we're out of here!" Ben pulled out of the trash alcove and sped along the white line path presented on his Anvilsmith.

Out of the maze, he cranked the wheel to drift onto Dove Boulevard.

"Holy! What the heck is *that*?" He sucked in air and fully jammed on the brakes to stop. He gawked at what approached them from the opposite direction. "What is that?"

Chapter Thirty-Five

SO NOT STREET LEGAL

THOUGH BEN HAD NEVER UNDERSTOOD the purpose of most mundane vehicles, there had always been an implied logic to them. Alone, and need a cheap mode of transportation to get across town? Get a moped. Have more than one friend and the same goal? Get an econo-car. Want that ride in comfort? Get a luxury vehicle. Need to move big stuff across town? Get a truck. It all made sense, until now.

Five blocks ahead, a massive, matte grey vehicle—as tall as a semi-truck, wide enough to take up three of Dove's five lanes—rolled forward on some sort of treads instead of wheels.

With things like that rolling around, no wonder the streets are in such poor condition. As though also holding its breath against the rattling advance of the humongous car, the night had become still. The smog still hovered five stories up, placing a false, toxic, ceiling down the length of Dove Boulevard until the brown sky met with the blacktop sandwiched vertically between industrial sprawl.

Tex's own shock or disbelief at what he saw made his synthesized voice came out flat. "That's a tank, Ben."

A tank? Coming his way, the treads slowed as though the massive thing wanted to change directions, but physics demanded it follow the same rules as any other vehicle without specific enchantments to tell nature that the rules don't apply right now. *I wonder what's it for. It's huge! You probably could fit a dozen people inside.* Though it didn't look like a comfortable ride, Ben tried to equate it to things he knew. *Perhaps it's what mundanes use when they have particularly heavy stuff to move.*

The tank came to a stop. The loud, unmistakable gurgling pipes of a distant Hawg motorcycle momentarily stole Ben's attention.

Down Dove, shifting lanes, the motorcycle carrying Alice—*and her ungrateful sister*—zoomed away.

"Ben," Tex's voice had taken on a sense of gravity. "That's a tank."

Ben replied, "I heard you the first time, buddy." Still marveling, he thought, *I wonder what it's for?*

A faint, almost dainty, *thunk*, like striking an air conditioning vent with a small hammer, sounded. Somehow the sound made the massive tank rock back and a gleaming white chunk of light—*too slow to be real light*—sped away from the tank. That nearly oblong hurtling object arched gracefully before beginning to descend...

Right. At. The motorcycle. Ben's eyes went round with realization. He tried to will them to see what he saw; to know what he knew. He projected his thoughts, **Watch out!**

Before the light got to them, the Hawg motorcycle, and the riders on it, disappeared. No evasive maneuvers taken, they were—*How? Where?*—just gone.

The white blast landed just to the left of where the motorcycle had been heading. A pure, snowy hemisphere of light, taller than the surrounding buildings, filled all ten lanes and expanded into the neighboring alleys. Dirt kicked up from the street around the white dome as a shockwave blasted around it.

Tex had raised its volume with dire intonations. "Ben, that's a *tank*!"

The distant rolling force came.

Estimating he'd be unable to get all the way back into the alley in time, Ben backed the Transcend up so the tank lay between them and the coming wave.

As though the tank was nothing more than an open window on a gusty day, the rolling wind disturbing the dust and debris on Dove washed over and through Ben, Tex, and the car.

A tiny percentage of his remaining energy snuck away—ebbed if you will—by the wind which had pushed through them and continued to roll. *Why does my Argosian chakra itch?*

Bastion, the four-armed gorilla Ben had hoped was gone, glanced around in his Nilosian font for a moment before rolling over to utter a slightly annoyed, but mostly contented, grunt.

His—*ours?*—Nilosian energy sucked the beast down into the chakra. *It's still in me?* A sudden hopelessness stole over him. *How do I get rid of it?*

"Go, go, go." Tex's volume maxed out. "Go!"

Ben stomped on the accelerator. The Transcend shot into the alley across Dove. "What the heck *is* that?"

Tex answered, "It's a *tank*!"

"Yeah, Tex. I got that!" Ben made a left to run parallel with Dove. "What's it for?"

"Killing, you fool."

Fool?

Machinegun fire cracked into the night. Echoed through the desolate alleys.

Tex spun in his harness. "Good call on the turn."

Ben glanced back through his rearview mirror. White energy streaks became smaller as they flew across the corridor

Tex faced the console. "We'd be Swiss cheese if you had kept going straight."

Ben acknowledged, "Thanks. Find us a path back to the freeway."

"Will do."

As though they were driving on any two-lane street, the alley provided clear going. *Can't imagine what this would be like without the alcoves for trash.* Ben's gaze went to the rearview mirror to where the Anvilsmith Dome loomed, completely blotting out the horizon. Ben slowed.

"What is it?" Tex asked, "What's wrong?"

Something's not right. Ben stopped and turned back to focus on the buildings the light shot through and voiced the oddity, "There's no damage from the bullets. Bricks should be being torn away, and glass should be shattering."

The robot turned again and whirling—Tex's ocular sockets twisting —sounded. "Those are *magical* bullets, Ben."

Ben faced forward. He jammed the accelerator. "Get us out of here, and away from the tank."

His companion touched the screen and a path of five turns, starting with a short run and two diagonals, showed the way back to Main Street and the on-ramp.

Ben broke, turned, and floored it again.

The Transcend revved hard from the surge, accelerated to sixty miles per hour before something clunked under his hood and his car started losing power. "Oh, crap!" He glanced to Tex. His gazed jumped to check the Anvilsmith. They neared the turn. "We must've been hit."

"No." Tex tapped the tablet and a '55' popped up at the intersection.

Ben whipped around the corner at precisely fifty-five miles an hour, and then they were on a long straightaway.

Tex continued, "I set a program to not exceed the max turning speeds and—"

A buzzing in the sky caught their attention. Above them, a metallic hummingbird kept pace with the car as Ben accelerated to eighty miles per hour.

As though it had to be voiced, Tex said, "Not good."

Holding the wheel steady with a hand and a knee, Ben ran a finger along the card holder to his bald eagle spellcard. With more reason now to not trust the Nilosian energy than ever before, he channeled from his new font. Deep violet energy—*Krotosian magic!*—flashed his bald eagle into existence.

The purple conjuration appeared and snatched at the metal tracker with its talons. *Tinks* sounded it scoring twice, but the tiny machination moved too fast for the conjuration to keep hold.

Flying as quickly as it could to keep up, his eagle continued to lose ground.

Trailing them, streaks of white light came from about where the tank had been on Dove Boulevard.

The bird's a tracker! Gotta drop it. Unable to point at it without significantly increasing the chance of wrecking, Ben recalled Tex's ability to transfer energy between Anvilsmiths and yelled, "Point at it!"

Tex swiveled in his harness and pointed.

"Become a conduit." To keep his speed, Ben hit cruise control and braced his knees against the steering wheel. He touched his *Blast* spellcard and—*hope he don't pop*—channeled the Krotosian spell through his companion.

A violet blast flew from the small robot's hand.

Tex swung its fist through the air. "Count it!"

In Ben's mirror, the mechanical hummingbird dropped to the blacktop behind them and skidded like a shuttlecock.

The white streaks still closed on them.

Ben jammed on the brakes, took a left on a street that put them on a diagonal back to Dove.

The white streaks behind them stopped.

Ben slowed and made another turn that looked like it would do the trick. To be sure, he said, "Reroute us to the freeway again, Tex, and keep an eye out for those flipping birds."

Tex tapped the Anvilsmith again. Shades of gray showed the various ways back. All of them took them a long way around either west or north to avoid a large, walled industrial complex. "Nothing for it, Ben." His companion shook his tiny head. "We need to double back."

"No." Ben ran his finger up the screen. The least dingy gray line, indicating the best route, kept dancing around buildings trying to correct for him not following any of the alternate routes suggested as his finger ran up the street. With each adjustment by the map, the device flashed 'Turn around.' The line they were on darkened to being the worst route as he pushed his fingertip closer to the wall. If not for outlining one-half of an expansive corporate lot, the line would've been straight. *And, once on the other side, we'd be only one slanted street away from getting onto the freeway.* Ben asked, "Do you know what I want you to do?"

"The thing you've been wanting to do since you read about it in the owner's manual," Tex replied, punching a code—*one, eight, one, one, three. Got it!*—into the console. "It's meant for mundane walls, Ben. If this wall has any sort of magical reinforcement…" Tex didn't finish. He let the rest hang in the air.

He's right. Ben sighed. He wanted to ram through the wall. *This is the wrong time to needlessly toy around. Better double back and—*

A humming closed in on them.

Tex called out, "Bird!"

Heading directly at the barrier, the car began to slow. Ben ordered, "Remove the limiter." Tex complied before he finished the sentence. The engine revved to life and they rocketed toward the wall. Speedometer rolling past a hundred, The Transcend moved faster than the hummingbird could fly.

It dropped down to drift behind them, which—somehow—allowed it to keep pace.

"Aim at the bird." Ben didn't dare to let go of the wheel. Not yet.

"It's gone," Tex said. "Up and away."

Like a space shuttle reentering the atmosphere, the front of the Transcend had developed a faint green force filed.

The towering, tan, cinder-block wall drew closer.

The force filed grew darker.

Ben's knuckles when white on the wheel.

Closer.

He clenched his teeth.

Closest.

His body tightened. *Bye Tex.*

Crash!

Chapter Thirty-Six

BACK TO THE BIG TOP

THOOM!

Boom!

The world went dark as they rammed through brick, sand bags, and another layer of brick. *The world's shortest tunnel.* Shattered chunks and debris flew far and wide. They pulled sand in their wake which trailed away from the punched-open wall like a comet's tail. The mess danced behind the Transcend and settled in the empty parking lot.

They were back in the open air. The smoggy ceiling still hung over them and denied the moon's proper glow to shine through. The wide, dark building in the center of the lot didn't have any lights on. Keeping an eye out for any change, Ben passed it. *No parking lanes, no curbs, no front gates...* "Tex, what is this building?"

His companion tapped on the Anvilsmith.

They shot through the lot and exited through the parking lot's proper front entrance.

Tex answered, "Don't know. It's not listed."

On the final straightaway, Ben eased his foot a little further down and the speedometer steadily rotated to the right with their increasing speed. A glint of steel—*the bird*—showed in the rearview. It grew smaller…

And smaller…

Gone.

Ben slowed for the onramp, then sped back up to eighty miles per hour. "Tex, mind the traffic behind us—"

"To see if we're being followed." Tex cut in. "On it."

Cutting through the thin traffic, Ben's gaze occasionally bopped from the freeway ahead and to his mirrors to check the traffic behind them.

Tex advised, "No one is following us."

We're supposed to be followed... Ben shook his head as he slowed to fifty-five. Ben glanced at Tex and hoped. "Are you sure?"

His companion touched the Anvilsmith where they had gotten on the beltway from Old Henderson. "No headlights pulled on after us." The robot ran his hand up the freeway. "We have been doing nothing but overtaking cars, none of which have been acting erratically as if to keep up with us." He added, "From what I've seen, every car we passed reacted to our speed, then returned to normal driving." Tex clapped his small metal hands with a *tink* to indicate *case closed*. "Either we're in the clear and the Mystique is making the mundanes act as though nothing happened—or we're just in the clear."

Where's the pursuit? Clarissa's in the bag... Unless—I should've swept the whole complex for bags—unless, maybe, she has a sister, too, and that's who I have. Ben slapped his leg and steered toward the exit for Eastern. "Damn it, we should've swept the entire complex."

Ben hadn't used magic since getting on the freeway. There hadn't been a need. Every Adept at the APA harped on how using too much around mundanes would 'break the Mystique,' which would be bad for all mystics. He had heard about the Mystique all his school life, but no one ever explained what *It* was. He had gotten a look at It—at least he thought he had—in the psychedelic aura around Alice. *If the Mystique keeps mundanes from registering arcane effects, can it be strengthened? How much can the Mystique cover?*

He went down the off-ramp and stopped at a light.

Ben drew a breath, relaxed his mind, and let the air out. They'd slowly circle back. *Hopefully the alarm would be called off by then.*

Starting to feel a little hungry, he scanned the mundane fast-food places his mother loathed: Jill in the Cube, *line's too long*, Caliente Chicken, *closed*, and Pizza Kings. *Sure could go for a slice.*

Not certain if his stomach could handle the grease, Ben picked up the antacids, popped a cherry disc in his mouth, and checked the rearview mirror again. *Nothing.* He eyed the two cars that had been waiting for a left turn to Eastern. *Neither are of mystic make.* "I know you're always sure, Tex. Sorry for asking."

The robot leaned back in his harness. "Forgiven." His small shoulders lifted and fell as though heaving a sigh, too. "After what we just went through, double—even triple—checking is entirely understandable." He motioned to the back seat and flipped his puncturing sliver. "Are we going to pull over and let her out?"

The light turned green. Ben eased on the accelerator. "I guess." He pressed his lips together. *We're supposed to be followed...* "I really don't want to say this, buddy, but we might actually have to go back to Old Hendo again."

"What!" Tex sat up in his harness. "Why?"

He took in a deep breath to explain. "Well—"

A rapid howl closed on him. Pain rocked his shoulder forward as the world flashed purple.

Krotosian magic. The blast broke his budding melancholy. *On the city streets?* "Find the source." Ben gave the Mystique half a thought, *worse comes to worse, I'll breach.* He stomped on the accelerator.

A purple bolt of magic cast its light over him and his car as it missed.

Behind us and to the right. He began to swerve to make for a harder target.

"There!" Tex called. Two blips pinged into position on the Anvilsmith beyond the Eastern off-ramp.

Ben glanced over his shoulder. In the dark, under the freeway overpass, two Stingers—*the same ones from before*—lit up light green and purple.

They started after him.

A part of him admired their casting ability. *Wow, that's some distance to hurl a blast.*

The headlights of both cars dimmed to a deep violet for a moment. Krotosian magic bolts flew from their fenders toward him.

Whoa! That explains the distance. Ben cut across two lanes to dodge. "Their cars have weapons!"

"Illegal," Tex *tsked* inflecting sarcasm into his voice. "Where's a Magistrate when you need one?"

Speeding, Ben started to catch up to a small patch of traffic. "I know where." He planned his maneuvers.

A horn blared as he hooked around and nearly sideswiped a mundane car as he passed it.

His pursuers didn't fire.

They care about the Mystique. Good

Five long streetlights from the Samhain Festival, Ben sped away from the mundanes as the Stingers began to close some of the distance. *If I blast out a tire from each mundane car, there will be a pile up and the Stingers won't be able to get through.* While a solid strategy and, possibly, the correct tactic, Ben didn't act on the passing thought. *There are still alternatives.*

Where Ben had cut rudely through traffic, the Stingers seemed to purposefully make bad moves to allow the mundane traffic to block them.

Are they even trying to catch me? A crazy thought—*I should stop* —flew through his head when he spied the first entrance to the Samhain starwise parking.

All the lights on both Stingers flashed and they rocketed down Eastern.

Whoa! Ben cranked the wheel and jammed on the brakes to power slide into a drift. He jumped back on the accelerator and his Transcend banged sideways into Red Lot Five's wrought iron entrance fence. With his foot still down, the tires spun and shot him forward.

The Stingers' speed-boosting spell, unlike his, didn't end when, as though on rails—*just like the Legerity*—they peeled into the lot a few precious seconds later.

Ben shook his head as the lit cars grew closer in his mirror. "I don't like this, Tex."

"Neither do I," Tex started to punch a code into the console.

A muffle arose from the burlap bag.

Ben yelled over his shoulder, "You're almost safe Clarissa!" He made one more turn which put him in line with the entrance to the fairgrounds proper. Lowering his voice, he spoke to Tex. "No, I mean, there's magic going on in the parking lot." He spared a glance at his companion. "Papa Mojo said the Primaries would show."

"Did he?" the robot asked, then proposed, "Maybe Mojo lied?"

Racing down the row of cars, Ben shook his head in disagreement and opened his mouth to say so, but he couldn't think of an alternate possibility. *The diviner duped me into being a delivery boy.* A desperate desire to punch Mojo's floating face, rose, then faded. *This is not the time for frivolous anger. Focus. Get her safe.* He pointed to the Anvilsmith. "Give me turn velocities again, Tex."

With one tap, the turns into each lane came up with numbers indicating the speed he should not exceed.

The lights on the Stingers dimmed and their amazing speed faded. *They can corner, but their speed spell doesn't last nearly as long as mine.* While good to know, they had closed enough distance that he couldn't stop and let Clarissa out at the concrete pillars between the wrought iron lions.

Another string of muffles came from the bag.

"Tex." Ben pointed at the pillars. "Are those columns magically reinforced?"

Tex popped above the dashboard. Its optics whirred. "Yes."

"Knew it." Ben eyed the speed on the final turn. *Forty-five and I'm going sixty.* Not ready to hit his brakes as they sped down the rows of cars, Ben touched his *Orion* spellcard and channeled energy from his gut. Violet magic flashed and howled as his immature reserve emptied. A purple gorilla appeared in the backseat. The suspension creaked at the sudden increase in weight.

Unlike the insta-bond he felt when he cast Abe and Oscar, or the automatic bond when he would cast plain old Orion, Ben had to establish the link between him and Krotosian-based gorilla.

Mentally giving his order—*lift the bag and protect it, when I turn, as you leap onto the fairground*—Ben slammed on the breaks. Leaving a line of smoke behind them, the Transcend's tires belted out a whine as they skidded across the blacktop.

As directed, the gorilla lifted the burlap wrapped Clarissa and leapt hard—*too early!*—when Ben cranked the wheel to hit the turn— skidding—at forty-four miles per hour.

Cradling the bag, the gorilla landed and rolled onto the

fairgrounds. *Go further in.* Ben glanced at the gorilla through his side mirror and ordered. *Further. Further.*

The gorilla jogged further, and further, and stopped.

Keep going in until you dispel. That should do the trick. Though he meant to check on his gorilla, Ben's gaze locked on Malcolm coming out from between cars. The bully pulled up his pants as the two lit Stingers made the turn behind him. *Pooping in the parking lot, Malcolm? A quick laugh burst from Ben's mouth. Really?*

Ben eyed the last bend that would put him en route to the exit onto Sunset Drive. *Everyone who's starwise is here, but there's no way I can make it onto the fairground without either wrecking my car or having them catch me.*

Tex tapped the Anvilsmith. The map zoomed out to a wider, top-down view of the area. "Where to now?"

Ben tried to think of a safe place—the safest place—to go, and came up empty. Almost in protest to what he considered next, his gut gurgled. *Two birds with one stone? If not, perhaps one bird will kill the other...* He took another antacid, narrowed his eyes and said, "Chart the best path to Meadows Towing."

Chapter Thirty-Seven

NO SAFE PLACE

THOUGH BEN WOULD'VE PREFERRED GOING BACK down Eastern to the freeway, the Stingers had hit their speed boost spell as they pulled onto Sunset Road behind him. In reaction, he had Tex use their last one. They rocketed up the backside of McCarran Airport. While the Stingers' enchantment gave them better control, the Transcend's boost going well past Grier Drive. As though he were trying to drag-race the roaring plane taking off on the jetway on the other side of the chain-link fence.

The speed doubled, if not tripled, the night's chill and he longed for his slashed-up school coat. Even with the comfort enchantment destroyed, the physical coat would've offered some protection.

As Ben's nose filled with the pervasive plane fumes, he grinned at the thought of his pursuers' nostrils filling with his proverbial dust...

However, they continued to chase. Onto The Strip, past Town Square, onto the 215, and out toward Pahrump. *They're waiting for me to make a mistake.* The Stingers kept on giving chase. *Why are they fixed on me?*

Ben took the off-ramp where the freeway curved away from civilization and turned at the bottom to the long, straight-shot to Meadows Towing. Not slowing, Ben checked his mirrors in snatches.

The two glowing imports came down the exit, then made two quick turns to take the on-ramp heading back to the city.

Finally! Ben applied his brakes to slow and stop.

Even at a distance, he could spot their neon lights driving away. "Well." He took a deep breath of the clean desert air, and exhaled, "I guess that's that."

"Stingers away," Tex remained focused on the Anvilsmith on the center arm rest. "Only one more."

Ben tilted his head. "One more?"

"Yes." Undoing his harness straps, Tex motioned to the tablet with his head. "Take a look."

Ben picked up his Anvilsmith. *The Legerity?* Two red blips, the Stingers, moved away while a yellow blip closed in.

Tex continued. "In tracking the two Krotosian cars, I noticed a distant set of headlights speeding through traffic to catch up."

Ben scanned the dark land around the long road he had stopped on. The bright purple neon star sign above Meadows Towing shone alone, like a clasp holding the night's smothering cloak closed over the surrounding desert. Back the way he came, the freeway streetlights and car headlights came just so far from civilization before arcing back away from what the orcs called the Might-Lands.

He quick tapped through the menus to switch from *Heracles* to *Elfsight* and cast it. The Anvilsmith vibrated in his hand as the awatt meter ticked down to ninety-five. The stars' light began to rain through the darkness as the magic settled into his eyes. Still taken with the effect, Ben sighed at the beauty. *Doubtlessly, first place would've been mine if I entered this as my Spell Programming project in the Magic Fair, but then everyone would make knock-offs of it... And that would cheapen this.* He put his hand out. Light pooled briefly in his palm, evaporating nearly as quickly as it formed.

A pair of headlights came down the exit. Since a majority of students in the Las Vegas Valley drove the exact same model as his, Ben knew the shape of headlights well.

A Transcend... Ben holstered his Anvilsmith and got out of the car. *I'd bet both my tablets that it's Malcolm.*

Tex asked, "What are you doing, Junior Apprentice?"

"I think I know who this is." Ben answered, then realized what Tex had called him. Prior to the Node Key popping the robot's settings, his companion had always identified him by his title since that was how he'd introduced himself to his, then, new companion. He glanced at Tex who appeared to busy himself with work on the car console when none was needed. "Why'd you call me Junior Apprentice?"

Tex lowered his head, processed the question and did not look up when he answered, "This is not a wise course of action. As such, it triggered a permission subroutine. While your title slipped out, I was able to stop the subroutine before it made me ask you to contact an Adept to advise you." Tex's optics moved to look into Ben's eyes, the metal plates on the robot's brow layered to imitate a furrow. "I was hoping you hadn't noticed. Hope I didn't offend you."

"Meh." Ben waved a hand to dismiss the issue. With *Elfsight* active, the set of headlights coming from the freeway shone like a pair of searchlights moving in tandem. He shielded his eyes and made out the physical shape of the Transcend. *And there's those silly buffalo horn-nobs Malcolm had added.* "Mind the off-ramp, Tex. Let me know if any other cars start coming our way."

Tex climbed to the dashboard. "What are you doing now, Jun—" The robot cut his sentence. "Ben?"

This must seem like a really bad idea if it triggered another subroutine. Ben started to fold back the right sleeve of his dress shirt. A small part of him—the part that didn't want to possibly taint the school's name with his decision to duel outside of the night's Shenanigans—thought to remove his red school tie. *Even though it'll just be me and him.* Ben whipped his tie off and tossed it in the backseat. He answered, "Waiting for Malcolm."

Tex's optics whirled fast and its voice took on a faint echo. "Confirmed, the car has the same profile, after market add-ons, and color scheme."

Folding his left sleeve back, the odd sound made Ben eye his companion. The robot's optics completed quick turns, so at least it didn't look like he was going to shut down again. *Not hardware, then. Something must be going on with his programming.*

Ben asked, "Still with me, buddy?"

Tex took no notice of the question. "Confirmed. The license plate is the same as before."

Ben leaned in to look at Tex's optics from the side to make sure they weren't silently going haywire. The small binocular sockets inside the lenses made quick, controlled turns.

"Confirmed. The driver's face fits sonar concave mapping belonging to Malcolm."

"Tex?" Ben reached out his for the robot and stopped short to bite his lip. *I really hope he doesn't kick off a shock.*

The robot's optics shifted slightly to the left twice. "Concave mapping does not recognize the passengers."

"Passengers?" Ben turned.

The car zoomed closer.

He shielded his eyes as *Elfsight* lit three auras—*casters*—inside the car. Ben focused on them to discern what type of magic they used.

The high beams flicked.

"Ah!" He covered his eyes and leapt into his backseat.

A rush of air sucked at his slacks and his car rocked as Malcolm zoomed past. *That was close!*

"Verified." Tex continued, "Passengers are unknown."

Tires squealed.

Ben sat up and tried to rub the bright spots in his vision away.

Tire smoke rose up and away as people got out from both sides of the car. A Krotosian—*Malcolm*—got out from the left. Two Nilosians—*who are they?*—dashed from the right and out into the desert.

Malcolm yelled, "I've come to get my hook back!"

Ben hopped from the backseat onto the street. "Tex, stay vigilant of the unknowns and advise if they close in."

"Confirmed. Orders received."

Ben scanned. His spell helped him spot the Nilosians, who ran a good distance away, stopped, and turned to watch, seemingly. His pinky found his *Usain* spellcard. *I'll go head's up against Malcolm any day, but if they join in...* Ben struggled with his ego, which tried to convince him that he could take all three. He kept his pinky in position. *Just in case I have to split.*

Stepping away from his car, Ben focused on Malcolm.

The Dunn-Blatt moved purposefully to be at fifty-feet away for a mid-range duel, stopped, and pointed. "Give me back my nail, Ben, and I won't break you."

The onion taste started to rise in Ben's throat as the font in his gut swelled, oozing a small amount of Krotosian energy. He swallowed. "In consideration of the great many A. P. A. students you hooked before they were ready, I'm going to say no."

Elfsight showed purple power pulse from Malcolm's center. It shot up to his shoulder in the same manner Ur-Krurk's energy had when the ogre had hurled a magic blast at him.

If I have the wrong spell—don't think about it. Ben channeled the thrumming green energy from the Anvilsmith, through him, and to his *Blast* card to negate the Dunn-Blatt's spell with his own.

The magic moving within Malcolm faded as his mouth dropped open in astonishment.

Oh, what I wouldn't give to have a picture of that face! Talk about priceless.

"So, you can counter-spell?" Malcolm recouped and gave Ben a small nod. "Not bad, Baby Ben. Not bad at all. And here I thought this would be a brutal, one-sided fight that would only end with you licking my shoes, but I want that ability—so now, I will have to kill you, *if* you don't return what is mine so I can steal what's yours."

What the hell is he babbling about? Ben stole a glace to the Nilosians. *There's still at a distance, but what do they want?* He turned his attention back to Malcolm.

Malcolm began to dance in place as if he were Bruce Lee and his deep violet Dunn-Blatt school-issued jump suit leant an eerie validation. "This is your last chance to give up my hook or shit gets real."

Ben opened his mouth to reply...

Chapter Thirty-Eight

ON A DARK ROAD

...AND PAUSED. He dug his hand into his pocket and rubbed the coarse, rust-covered nail that Malcolm truly seemed ready to kill for. *I've wanted to duel him for years, but in a civilized way. With my Argosian font drained and my Krotosian chakra too immature, I'd have to resort to Nilosian if my tablet runs out, and may stir*—he didn't want to even think Bastion's name for fear of waking it—*The Beast.* Ben stole another glance to the two Nilosians standing off in the distance, watching. Somehow, they—*Collins and Papa Mojo?*—factored into this.

Malcolm has more dueling experience... The night's chill started to seep into his bones. Ben shivered and fended off a sneeze. *Am I willing to die in the cold, on a dark desert road over*—he rubbed the nail again—*something so trivial as a tether?*

"Ben." Malcolm called. "I can serve up this whoopin' however you want it." The Dunn-Blatt stroked his nose twice with his thumb before going back to his Bruce Lee stance. "Do you want this over hard, or over easy?"

Ben narrowed his eyes at Malcolm. Between thinking it over and Malcolm's boasting, he found his reason to lay it all on the line tonight. *It's the principle. If I let him bully me, yet again, when will I ever take a stand?* He thought about the duel he'd had with Jack who must've had dozens of duels under his belt. Though he had not beaten Ur-Krurk through dueling, the ogre's tactic would be the difference. He released the nail to let it fall in his pocket.

Instead of answering, Ben executed the courtly fifteen degree bow duelist were supposed to exchange.

A bow that Malcolm didn't return.

Sneering The Dunn-Blatt's body shuddered and shook as he dragged both of his hands across his abdomen and raised them high into the air. The energy at Malcolm's center undulated and rolled. He yelled, "This ends now!" A shot of Krotosian flew to Malcolm's shoulder while a second zoomed toward his throat.

Ben slapped his spellcard holder, channeled power into his *Blast*— the magic at Malcolm's shoulder poofed away—and *Orion* cards. The summoning spell sped up Ben's spine toward his throat. Instead of calling a green gorilla, Ben gambled and turned the magic to counter Malcolm's other spell.

The cone of violet light exiting Malcolm's mouth started to form his conjuration before winking away. "You can dual-cast, too?" Malcolm ground his teeth. "Duly noted." His face twisted into an offended scowl. "You can only counter with the exact same spell. So, which Dunn-Blatt taught you how to throw a dusk buffalo?"

Ben shook his head. "I don't owe you anything. Especially not answers."

"Fine! I'll beat it from you!" The purple in Malcolm's gut blossomed before diminishing by half as two glowering orbs began traveling up his torso.

What spell is that? Ben slid his fingers on his spellcard holder to channel energy into *Usain, Leap,* and *Shield.* The tablet vibrated. His legs became inhuman springs as the orange tang of Usain filled his mouth. Used to hooking his Shield spell into the burnt-out Komir necklace, he'd forgotten about the minty smell of the air hardening around him from *Shield.*

Gotta change that.

Malcolm pointed at him.

Keeping the Dunn-Blatt in his field of vision, Ben ran away from his car out into the desert

The pulsing tennis-ball-sized spheres, hallmarks of the most well-known evocation spell, whistled into being.

Cody would cream his pants.

The howling from the Krotosian magic's increased as the orbs flew closer and exploded into massive fireballs.

Ben leapt hard.

He out-legged the first's blast radius, but not the second. The fire burned against his shield as he flew through the air. The protective force began to crack. Heat poured through while blazes licked around the barrier. The protection faltered. The mint scent ceased. Shoes smoking, Ben landed and rolled just outside the second ball's radius. He ground his loafers into the dirt to smother the flames and disperse the heat.

A sense—*I'm going too far*—tugged at his spatial awareness. *Must be near ten times the starting dueling distance. Any further and I forfeit.* He stepped backward which violated the tenants of the Usain spell. The orange taste and spell benefits vanished.

Malcolm's remaining energy drained away as two more glowering purple orbs traveled up to his shoulders.

Glowing spheres appeared in Malcolm's outstretched hands.

If only I knew Fireball. I'd love to counter those.

The Dunn-Blatt waved his hands in small circles. "Last chance, Baby Ben!"

Darting back toward Malcolm, Ben placed his fingers on the same spellcards and let the energy flow through him.

Malcolm let the howling balls fly.

The orangey-mint combo barely registered Ben his mouth and nose before he leapt.

The violet globes broke open, blossoming into rolling conflagrations of purple doom.

Ben thumbed *Pop* and channeled into it. In a flurry of tiny bubbles, Ben's low-level teleportation spell raised him higher, allowing him to slide across the top of the flames that continued under him as though he were surfing the fire.

Ben landed before the balls completely dissipated behind him. "Do you bend?" He pointed at Malcolm, slid his finger to *Blast*, and warned. "I still have plenty of power."

Malcolm's stomach remained devoid of Krotosian magic. Still he raised his chin in defiance.

None of his other chakras are open. He's totally out of magic. Ben checked his Anvilsmith. *Sixty-seven awatts left. Good.* Ben stopped jogging. His *Usain* spell ended. *I can't fire on a defenseless caster.*

Ben lowered his arm.

Malcolm's lips arced up and parted in the single smile Ben disliked the most in the world.

It was the same one Ben had looked up to see after being hooked for the first time in Adept Love's class on the Monday following his loss of his thirteenth birthday school gifts. Embarrassed at having to return the two gifts he didn't lose, Ben had been trying to avoid the other students when something cold and green cut into his forearm. He had seen lines drawn between casters in practice, but never knew— never would've guessed—that there was a hook on the end. That tiny hook had landed clean. There hadn't been any blood where it landed, but the pain of his mystic self being pierced forced an almost helpless yelp.

Ben had become still and hoped the pain would, too. Adept Love would be over to him in a moment and—it ripped up his arm. He had belted a ragged cry as the hook tore through him, rounding his shoulder to slide down his chest, and pulse against his sternum. Ben hadn't recalled hitting the gym floor, but when his senses returned, he'd been on his knees and doubled over. Malcolm—*that lousy smile*— had stood over him, chiding, "Welcome to the real world. Man up. Quit crying, baby."

Recalling—and seeing—the same smug mug, green energy flashed through Ben as his emotions flared. A soccer-ball-sized blast of green energy—containing his full arcane flow—flew from his hand. It rocketed across the desert, crackling as the dirt and rocks beneath were highlighted with emerald menace.

Malcolm's smile faded and his eyes widened. He tried to dodge.

Too late.

The energy crashed into him and launched him backward. Holding his chest, Malcolm got to a knee and struggled to his feet. He lifted his chin again.

Ben bellowed and let another crackling blast fly.

This time, Malcolm pushed his chest toward the spell—and was thrown further.

Malcolm rose to a knee. Blood coated his trembling lips as they worked up to smile.

No, you don't get to smile! Ben let loose again. *Not now!*

The green power lit Malcolm's body as he fell back and slid across the dirt. Weakly, he said. "I bend."

The Anvilsmith pinged, Tex's voice echoed through. "Confirmed. He relented."

Don't care! Ben sneered.

Lost.

Enraged.

Nilosian energy flashed through Ben. Five sizzling spheres rocked and curved at Malcolm; their wake sucked little light there was from the night.

Malcolm's head started to lift.

Lips pressed tight, Ben struggled. A part of him didn't want to dismiss the spell, but—*he relented*—he came to his senses and dismissed the black energy.

The phantom wisps formed a hand and lurched to grab at Malcolm's throat—

A memory—defiant Nilosian teeth biting and breaking Jack's bloody arm. The thief's bellow—flashed. Ben grabbed his forehead. Fear of murder—*murderer!*—turned the breath in his chest to ice. *Oh shit, what have I done?*

The hand gripped Malcolm's throat.

Malcolm gasped and grabbed at his neck.

No!

The hand dissipated.

Ben exhaled hard. He placed his shaking hands on his weak knees and tried to steady himself. *Almost killed him.* He took a trembling inhalation. *Breathe, Ben.* The air, as though afraid of what lay inside him, stuttered through his throat and into his lungs. *Just breathe. In. Out. Just like that. In, and out.* Breath started to come easier.

Malcolm groaned and flopped over.

Concern—*how bad did I hurt him?*—framed Ben's features as he hustled over to where the Dunn-Blatt writhed ever so slowly. *Well, he's able to move…*

Malcolm's voice warbled and faded as he said, "Copy any ability you want from me, take spells, but," Malcolm drew a wet breath. His air flow strengthened to plead, "Please give me my hook back. It's a family heirloom."

Enchanted sight still keen, Ben scanned the desert for the Nilosians. They were gone. He asked, "Who rode here with you?"

"Huh?" Malcolm looked bewildered.

"Your car." Ben went to point at the passenger door that had been left open to find it closed. "Who else came with you?"

"What are you talking about?" The Dunn-Blatt rolled over onto his stomach. Scrunching up to his hands and knees, he croaked, "I—" He sighed. "I am alone."

"Very well." Ben examined the desert again, slower this time and still could not find them. *Too bad Tex couldn't verify either of them.* "Get up." Ben went and sat in his car. As he waited for Malcolm to collect himself, he put the top up, and turned on the heater.

Malcolm got back to his feet. "My hook?"

I need time to think and being on the road to Meadows Towing isn't the place for it. Ben started his Transcend. "Follow me to the festival. I'll have an answer for you there."

Chapter Thirty-Nine

GOODBYE MR. NICE GUY

WELL AFTER 4 A.M., the mundane parking lot had emptied out. Ben and Malcolm walked to the entrance—dark from the outside—in silence. All the while, Ben held the nail in his palm alternating between squeezing it and holding it loose. The closer to the entrance they got, the tighter he had to grip it as guilt—*it's not yours*—kept pressuring him to turn it loose.

The early morning air remained still and cold. Ben found his elbows tight against his sides, trying to retain some of his body heat. Like a punch, the fragrant Samhain Festival popcorn—*it'd be hot, buttery goodness in my stomach*—assaulted his nose making his mouth water and empty gut rumble. *You're purposefully not thinking about the Dunn-Blatt's family heirloom.* Ben nodded to the realization. His guilt wrestled with getting vindication for everyone who'd fell prey to the *former* bully.

He and Malcolm came to a stop just outside the fairgrounds. At the threshold, muffled shouts and laughs from dozens of spell duels bled through the silencing enchantment. *How much Mystique*—Ben's wondering thought got derailed—*Wow, Malcolm's bowing his head…*

Everyone inside would see the acknowledgment of being bettered and rumors would fly about what had transpired to make a notoriously unabashed—even by Dunn-Blatt standards—student publicly admit to being bested by another in front of everyone participating in the Samhain Shenanigans. *They're going to wonder who I am and how I bested him. Luckily, all APA students have been segregated to only duel near the smelly Mystic Menagerie and I'm not wearing my school uniform. Only me and Malcolm—and those two Nilosians—know the whole story.*

"My tether?" Malcolm kept his neck bent and swallowed hard. "Please?"

The faint shouts from within the fairgrounds had grown silent. *They've stopped their duels to watch this? Goodness.* Shocked at being at the center of attention, and Malcolm asking in front of everyone, Ben almost pulled the nail form his pocket. He let go and his hand came out empty. "No."

The Dunn-Blatt pulled up his hood and touched the center dangling over his forehead. A magical darkness filled the space, shrouding Malcolm's face.

Oh, man. Ben dove his hand back into his pocket. *Am I being fair?* He gripped the hook, and let it fall again. "If you keep my identity and my abilities to yourself, I will return it to you in a year and a day." *Anyone would call that fair.*

Malcolm nodded. Grateful in not getting his way, his voice came out meek and wet. "Thank you."

He seems really sorry. Ben tensed his neck to keep unbidden word— words of instant forgiveness—from passing through. *If I say them, I'll hand it over.* To get his hand away from the nail, Ben undid his top button and rubbed his throat to ease the building discomfort. *Stick with your decision.* Ben patted Malcolm on the back. "Until then, Malcolm, practice without tethers. It will make you a better caster."

The Dunn-Blatt nodded as he entered the fairgrounds.

Near starving, Ben got in his car and, for the last time that night, left the festival.

Chapter Forty

(IN) THE END

A FEW HOURS LATER, as Ben was about to fall asleep, Toad called on his Anvilsmith wanting to meet at Meadows Towing to talk business before sunrise that morning. Not exactly sure what they could possibly have to discuss, and reluctant to ever go out to Meadows Towing again, Ben insisted they meet in the city, at noon.

Now, with the Las Vegas sun high above and mundane traffic humming past, blissfully ignorant of the school of magic, Ben stood in the Archon Private Academy parking lot.

Though they had originally set a meeting spot near the Samhain Festival, Ben had made a last-minute location change to have the orcs —Toad and Jek only—come here so he would be able to see an ambush or assault being staged before it unfolded. Relieved that the Komir necklace had awakened with the rising sun, Ben rubbed it to activate the totem's shielding charm as a lone Meadows Towing truck clattered into the lot. He anchored the necklace to draw from his mostly recovered Argosian reserve.

Ben raised a hand to have the tow truck stop before the first speed bump. He wanted them far away from him and his car. Also, Ben didn't want to give away Tex's position when he whispered, "Remember the plan."

His companion's voice and syntax had returned to its synthesized norm shortly after the duel and the robot replied from where he had clamped himself onto the car's front fender. Tex said, "Barring an EMP, I am unable to forget."

Ben walked toward the tow truck. Jek sat behind the wheel with Toad in the passenger seat. Both wore thick sunglasses as though they were recovering from a late night of partying.

Toad, the shaman, got out. Though Ben wouldn't have been surprised if they both had been wearing black armor, the light green orc wore the standard Meadow's Towing t-shirt, blue jeans, and black boots. Also walking across the lot, Toad raised his thick hand to the top edge of his sunglasses to further shade his eyes from the midday sun. The orc raised his chin and uttered hearty grunts, speaking in the Giant's tongue. Toad asked, "Everything all right, Bastion?"

Ben didn't answer until he moved to stand fifty-feet—*a good dueling range*—away. "My name is Ben."

Toad lowered his eyes to a point between the two of them and extended his palms in a slow, supplicating fashion. He didn't want to fight. Toad switched to English. "Twice apologize, Might-Fist. Just following your last orders."

Why is he calling me Might-Fist? Ben walked forward and asked, "I told you to call me Bastion?"

"Yes." Toad's eyes adjusted to remain focused on a near-precise center between them as Ben moved forward. "And to speak Giant."

Ben stopped twenty-feet away. Any closer and he couldn't lock the orc into a duel. "When did I do this?"

"During the Ur-Krurkson feast. Two nights ago." Toad raised his eyes to meet Ben's but kept his arms wide and palms up to the sky. "After you defeated Ur-Krurk's son and took mastership over his forces."

Ben's brow furrowed. "So, you're saying I won?"

Toad nodded.

Ben asked, "Then why was I strapped to the bed?"

"None of us understood it, but—" Toad lowered his eyes to the center point between them. "Again, Might-Fist, only by your exact orders."

Ben asked, "Why were there goblins in the building?"

"They are yours." Toad paused to deepen his bow as far as he could and still retain the ability to make eye contact. "We bought the first one to clean around Meadows Towing. The second was property of Ur-Krurkson and, thus, part of your spoils."

Ben touched his *Orion* spellcard and channeled Argosian energy. Abe and Oscar appeared in red flashes. Both had their, now signature, weapons. Ben motioned Toad to stand. "One last question. If I won, why was the would-be victory meal be called the *Ur-Krurkson feast*?"

"Because, Might-Fist—" A proud, satisfied grin spread the orc's mouth as it straightened. That smile was the first Ben had seen from any of them. Toad enthusiastically rubbed his belly with both hands. "We feasted on Ur-Krurk's son."

Recalling his upset stomach and the haunting onion taste, Ben's facial features slacked. "I ate—" Blood retreated from his extremities, his gorge began to rise, and his stomach lurched. "I ate someone?"

Toad's delighted nod held too much enjoyment.

Ben's stomach heaved again. He turned away to throw up, but managed to hold his breakfast in.

Toad continued, "Don't worry, Might-Fist…"

Something very much like horror of what he would hear next filled Ben. He dared to look at the thrilled orc. Concerned, Toad had extended his arms as if to lend strength from a distance. *At least it feels like he's trying to help.*

Trying to console him, Toad earnestly swore, "You only had the best parts."

The information bowled Ben over. His stomach gave a mighty kick and he couldn't hold his sic back. Once he recovered, Ben thanked Toad for coming, then sent the orcs away so he could wonder—with true horror—at what Bastion had done while in control of his body.

Back in his car, Ben pulled his Anvilsmith and sat it on his. With his camera app open, he stopped to put his nerves in check and let his gaze search the light blue sky for any daytime stars. There were none. Ben took a deep breath. *Whatever I see is not my doing.* His attention on the device, his finger hovered over play. *It may be my body, but these are not* my *deeds.* He nodded to reaffirm the mental avowal and pressed play.

THE VIDEO mostly showed the inside of his coat, but the audio was complete. He whispered "go" to his orcs. He and Ur-Krurk's son exchanged words as his own voice growled and struggled before Bastion took control and gave his declaration.

Then the time for words was over. There were a few flashes of combat when his coat flapped open, but Ben found both his hands clenched tight against the sounds of the fevered pitch of battle. There had been some gunfire at the beginning, but everything soon devolved into clangs, grunts, screams, and curses.

Somehow worse than the sounds of killing and dying, hearing his voice uttering constant strings of sentences in a language he didn't know. It sounded similar to the hiss-gargles he had heard in Pepperjacks when the big red fist had knocked the doors from its hinges. The voice, then, had been thunderous. The words coming from his own mouth, commandeered by Bastion, failed to match that trumpeting volume, but they were being spat with unequaled venom.

Then.

Silence.

The profound quiet didn't last. Groans warbled up and someone gibbered softly.

Footsteps—his footsteps—as Bastion walked around repeatedly asking in Giant, "Will you blood-oath?" Eight had said no and, after each negative answer, his voice whispered in the hiss-gargle language. Then, fierce bellowing shrieks screamed out and became silent. From the ninth on, every voice answered yes to the question.

His voice called for a fire pit.

He gave a speech about how the mighty had fallen…about how he would enact a ritual that would make the victors become mightier by consuming their fallen foes…about reaping hidden powers from flesh and soul.

Bastion then changed back to the hiss-gargle language. He rattled on for a good ten minutes before calling, in the Giant's tongue, to start to the Ur-Krurkson feast.

Those remaining exploded into cheers. There were chopping sounds. Ripping sounds. Chomping sounds.

"I choose you to be my trusted ally here," Bastion said quietly. "As such, consume this heart and this mind, and reap with me."

Also in Giant, a voice, deeper than any orc's—*probably one of the tuzvuls*—replied, "My honor is yours."

Cheer rose. The disgusting sounds continued as orcs called which body parts they wanted until the video stopped.

BEN LOWERED HIS HEAD.

My Krotosian magic and regeneration... A numbing revulsion washed over him. *Bastion enacted a mystic ritual, and consumed Ur-Krurk's son. That's—* Wanting to hide from his revelation, Ben covered his face with his hands. *That's why I have these abilities.* He recalled his excitement at his ankle healing and shame struck. *I had been so excited. Then Alice—* "Alice." Her disgusted expression and her sudden aversion rang back. *When she said she smelled death, her olfactory glands must've picked up the ogre's demise on my breath, but only once we were face-to-face without the wind whipping the odor away...*

Ben thought about deleting the video, but—until the sun went down—he simply sat there. Stunned.

WHEN HE HAD RETURNED HOME, his dad had looked him over, gave him an approving, conspiratorial wink and suggested he get some sleep. Figuring his father made up a story to appease his mom—who had always been the disciplinarian. When he woke, Ben didn't question his parents' suggestion that he return to the Samhain Festival to observe the closing celebration. In the past, he had been only allowed one night and, last year, they had even allowed him to pick an evening other than the last night. Though his last year's trench coat was tight across the shoulders, Ben wore it to be in school colors.

Late—*again*—he had to park way out in the mundane lot—*again.* An orchestra played as a fireworks array pierced the fairgrounds sky.

Mundanes *oohed* and *ahhed.*

Ben turned his eyes skyward and found a relatively bland display.

He refused to slow at the line of *Shame on Sam Hain* protestors and ran with such abandon, that they hurried to get out of his way. Nearly reckless, he occasionally bumped into people in his rush through the mundane part of the fairgrounds to get to the open starwise viewing grounds.

Panting, Ben held his sides as he jogged to the edge of the open field, then had to watch where he moved as thousands of casters had gathered to take in the show. They covered the grass—almost all the way to the entrance—with a multitude of colored blankets, as families *ohhed* and *ahhed*.

Appreciative, he smiled, nodded, and bowed his apologies as he squeezed his way along the perimeter.

Here the mystic pyrotechnics seemed to split the sky open in vibrant colors which blossomed riotously in the night sky.

He leaned against the exterior chain-link fence and clapped with everyone else when three great rockets shot into the sky and opened with a cacophony to release three dragons made of fireworks. Circling high, the red, white, and black dragons in the festival colors also embodied the three most powerful colors of magic.

Readying for a grand mock battle where the red would doubtlessly win, again—*as it always dose*—the dragons began to vie for position.

Other latecomers trickled in, brushing by him to fill the remaining area.

Keeping one hand on his spellcard holder and the other on his Anvilsmith, Ben ignored them as the red dragon and white dragon teamed up to attack the black dragon.

Though the black is bigger this year, that's hardly fair. Still, he cheered with everyone else at the spectacular aerial display.

A set of arms slid along his flanks inside his coat. A soft body pressed into him. Hands climbed up his in a familiar fashion.

About to shove the person away, Ben recognized the owner of brown eyes and blonde hair. He flushed. His pulse quickened.

"I've been looking for you." Clarissa tiptoed and kissed him.

Mmm, cotton candy.

She said, "I'm glad you finally came back."

Ben had questions. Foremost of which was how she came to be sealed in a burlap bag in Old Henderson. But instead of asking the series of questions he had planned and prepared for, he wrapped his arms around her, and they went back to kissing.

The three energy sources in his body heated and swelled, along with his blood, making this wonderful moment sort of uncomfortable. The Nilosian whirlpool in his head rocked the worst. Thunderous booms—*too loud*—from the sky thumped against the blood in his ears. Timed with the explosions above, his three energy sources became still and he focused on enjoying Clarissa's cotton-candied lips.

They took a break.

He looked at her as she smiled looked up at the show. Amazingly, her brown eyes changed to a light violet and her blonde hair took on a silvery glow.

What had been cheers turned to horrified shrieks.

Why are they freaking out? Ben pulled Clarissa closer as people scattered, stealing fearful glances over their shoulders at the sky.

He turned his eyes skyward.

The red dragon had its head bowed. Next to it, the white dragon's body—*the white dragon never dies*—snapped and fizzled to nothing. *Whoa! That's why.* Many used the battle as an indicator of the year to come. *It's just a show.*

Triumphant, and spewing red pyrotechnic flame toward the field, the firework black dragon's eye sockets had formed rolling dark-purple orbs with menacing green irises, which scanned the field. As though honing in, the gaze racked over him and Clarissa a few times. To stand his ground, Ben told himself again, *It's just a show.*

Amidst the unending booms—booms so hard they registered on his skin—Ben noticed a suck of wind on his coat.

Swirling gray robes appeared before the Vibrosian Primary materialized. She grabbed Clarissa, pulled her away from his grip, and —before Ben could reach out to grab Clarissa back—spun her robes to disappear with Clarissa in tow.

One of the few not running for cover, Ben watched the two remaining dragons explode into thousands of roman candles.

Walking to his car, Ben tucked his hands into his pockets and, basked in the afterglow of cotton-candied lips. *Best night yet.*

BEN SAT on the back of his car, looking at Pepperjacks. Though the mundane papers said there had been a devastating fire here, mystic artisans had obviously been at work.

Tinted glass had been put in place on the front doors and would keep sunlight from flowing through. The valet awning had been rebuilt, with new ivory columns standing where the old ones had been. Even the deep red paint, which gave the building a brick-like appearance from a distance, had been reapplied.

He put his tablet away.

Clarissa hadn't responded to his texts and he'd even tried calling her number, again, and it rang to voicemail, again. For the week following the Samhain Festival, Ben had tried to connect with her daily, but had been unable to reach her. After the first week, he tried every Friday after school let out. Still nothing. He never got to ask her how she came to be in the burlap bag in the first place or why the Primary took her away.

His eyes flew open and he grabbed his jaw in sudden realization. *Has she been recaptured? If so—* Relenting to his lack of information or leads, Ben heaved a sigh. *If so, there's nothing I can do about it. Heck, if she is missing, I don't even know anyone to ask. And if I did, they'd probably suspect me!*

Though Papa Mojo said they weren't going to get together, Ben felt Clarissa—like Jek—was one of the few people true to themselves. Then again, the diviner could've lied about that too.

With Winter break here, Ben had been hoping to spend some time with her. He still had no idea what a proper Yule gift would be, but enjoyed the thought of exchanging seasonal gifts with her. Due to her lack of any kind of reply, Ben really wanted to forget her, but his dreams often centered on kissing her. When the dreams turned to nightmares, they would end with him touching Penelope's hand. And Alice... Well, he just tried not to think about her, as his thoughts would jump to—and focus on—how she reacted to him after the battle and what her sister tried to do to him. Their hissing to each other rang back. *Wonder what she said about me?*

Trying to put it all out of his head—for now—Ben read the new marquee under the Pepperjacks' sign. *Open next October.* "It looks to be ready now."

Even though he'd probably only get a handshake for his efforts

—*better than trying to turn me to stone*—Ben really wanted to return the Node Key. It had been a nagging concern when he believed he had lost to Ur-Krurk's son and, if he had, the ogre would have gained much more than Meadows Towing.

Ben heaved a sigh and climbed over the bags of winnings from his Conjurer's Course to drop into the driver's seat. Earlier in the week— as they would every year—Samhain Festival employees had delivered all items lost during the Shenanigans as well as delivering unclaimed prizes.

Wary of his SD cards, Ben took them to Crystal, the only diviner he knew who would give a straight answer, to see if—possibly courtesy of Collins—they were cursed. She said they were clean, so he had picked them up before driving to Pepperjacks.

Looking forward to a long week of joyful tinkering in his Meadows Towing basement lab, Ben drove away with a small smile...

...utterly unaware someone had riffled through his winnings and removed the hidden warning from Papa Mojo about both of their impending deaths.

BOOK 3: YULETIDE YIELD

Chapter One

YULETIDE'S YIELD

HAVING five seconds before the next attack, Benjamin Baxter scanned the throng of starwise patrons around him at Bauman's Bazaar. *Five.* The sea of brightly colored robes, cloaks, and wraps of the shoppers receded, clearing a forty-foot radius around him.

Four. A handful of shoppers and hawkers—who had stopped lending their voices to the constant chorus of sale barking—watched his plight.

Three. None had the intense gaze it took to control the ongoing spell and none were willing to help—and, worse, he didn't see a hint of tan trench coats anywhere. *Where are the guys?*

Two. Ben spun.

The bright metal of the whirling scimitar—a blade he had only seen in use by bodyguards from the middle east—reflected the corridor of lights vendors had set up to highlight their tents, tables, and wares in the largest outdoor night market in Las Vegas.

One.

Centered on him, for some reason, the tumbling blade stopped as the pommel seemed to press against its range thirty-feet away near an abandoned pewter mug at an abandoned table. The steel morphed into a rapier—*or is that a cutlass? Which one is it that pirates use again?*—pointed at his chest.

Now.

It shot at him.

Ben twisted sideways and bent.

The blade swooshed by. In its wake, the scent of delicious spiced cider.

Keeping his gaze on the blade, Ben jammed his hands into his coat and came out with his Anvilsmith tablet and mouthpiece.

Five. Though he didn't need it anymore, Ben jammed the mouth guard in as, by muscle memory, his fingers worked his tablet to press *Spells, Enchantments, Achilleus,* and *Cast.* The welcomed scent of fresh-cut pineapples pillowed in his nose as the spell flowed into him, winding his fast-twitch muscle up for action.

Four. To keep up appearances of what people were used to seeing technocaster do, Ben quivered his arms and worked his chin as though the magic had to be forced into his body.

Three.

"Daddy!" A small girl in a long, absurdly pink, full-length fur coat screamed and pointed at him.

The man in red furs next to her grabbed the child's upper arm, scooped her into a defensive hug, and bellowed, "Ape casting!"

Two.

A fierce-faced woman—*the mother*—leapt in front of the man and began to work the air to build a mystic barrier. She wasn't alone. Eyes wide in surprise, fear, or wonder, over a hundred casters' hands worked the air to throw up protective power to shield themselves, and loved ones, against his magic. More people had been keeping an eye on him than he had thought.

One. Ben hadn't seen this many spells thrown at once since the Arcane Alehouse wizards had stacked dozens of Hold spells on him. *They have no idea what spell I cast.* This knowledge made him smile around his mouthpiece. He sucked at the pineapple that had worked into his saliva, and turned back to the sword. It had already switched back to a scimitar. Ben stood sideways to present a smaller target. *Now.*

It whirled at him.

He waited.

It closed.

Leaning, Ben slid back.

The sword whooshed pass his chest.

He snatched at the hilt as it rotated—*got it!*—and found something small in his hand as the bright blade dispersed into red whirling mist.

The ghost of the spell flew on and faded.

Having cheered and applauded with crowds in the past when someone used flair to end a spell not of their casting, Ben spun to take in the crowd with hungry eyes and ears.

"Tradition's blight."

Instead of appreciation, insults where thrown as the crowds—which had formed a communal protective magic circle around him—began to move away. Tinted the same colors as their various robes, their translucent mystic barriers popped like a rainbow bubble and sparkled away.

"Lack wit."

The circle around him stretched into an oval as other bazaar buyers began to move through.

His eyes found the face of the little girl in the pink fur coat scrunched up in a tiny scowl as she stared at him over her father's shoulder. "Nobody likes you." Innocent disdain clung to her words. "Go home, ape."

That slur! Reflexively, Ben's fist balled.

The Nilosian font, the energy Ben regarded as belonging to Bastion —the monster in his head—flashed hot. Boiling, his vision dimmed momentarily as The Beast raised its head.

Ben tensed at Bastion waking and tried to relax. *I can't blame her for her parent's bias.*

Committing her face to their memory, Bastion sneered at the girl.

Ben's brow furrowed and he sneered.

No! Having expressed Bastion's reciprocal disdain, Ben covered his face. *Diffuse your emotions, Ben. Cool down.* He closed his eyes and lowered his head. *There's no way to change their prejudice. To them, their casting method will forever be pure and superior while 'techno-wizardry' will forever be an affront to 'true magic-users' everywhere.* His jaw and fist began to loosen.

Recalling the hard lesson he had learned from the Arcane Alehouse, Ben wanted to yell, *None of us are real wizards.* Instead, he took a deep, calming breath. *She's not a threat, Bastion.* He took another breath and insisted. *She's not.*

Unconvinced, Bastion snorted. Wary, it went back to rest.

That was close. Focused on his shoes—month old Tore Vex boots he got through Meadows Towing—the seams remained slack. His feet weren't growing to bastion-size. He exhaled his relief.

Adept Love had, in his nasal whine, warned against coming to Bauman's Bazaar which had set up in Vegas for a week before moving to Los Angeles next month. "It's a den of derision," he'd said. Love had been filling in for Senior Adept Collins, who went absent after the Samhain Festival. "You may be attacked, openly, and no one will come to your aid." The small man's face took on a shrewd smile. Everyone knew Bauman's Bazaar was the only place where an Archon Private Academy student could get the spells the Academy wouldn't—or couldn't—teach. "Which is why I'm breaking you all into groups of four. You will be responsible for each other."

Ben's throat rocked at the memory. "Hmph." *Responsible for each other, ri-i-ight.* Having been attacked, he temporarily forgot that he, Neil, Kevin, and LeRoy had agreed to split up to find vendors who sold technomancy spells. Remembering, Ben shrugged. *Guess Love knew what he was talking about.*

Curious about what he held, Ben opened his hand to see a miniature duplicate of the scimitar in his palm.

"Hey, showman," a high-pitched feminine voice called before he could really analyze what he had in his hand. "Give you a gold for that."

Chapter Two

RISKY BUSINESS

BEN SUCKED one last time at the pineapple flavor in his mouthguard before he pulled it out. The effect of his Achilleus spell persisted and he found it hard to keep his amped-up, thrumming body still. He closed his hand and looked to where the voice had risen above the clamor of vendors selling and shoppers haggling. He picked up on something he hadn't noticed earlier. *Everyone's dealing in one ounce units of precious metals...*

No vendor offered or accepted local, regional or global currency. Currency was backed by an institute or agency which would go after a seller if you got a really bum deal. No one backed ordinary gold or platinum. *Wow, guess all sells are final.*

"Right here." A tall, bald, slender woman—*that's a really long neck*—raised a hand. She stood in a light green sleeveless dress before a ten-foot wide emerald canvas tent. One of the flaps had been pinned inward showing a bare hint of what lay within the tightly packed rows. Something about her—*the large eyes?*—made her quite comely. Her neck scarcely bent, giving him the slightest degree of a courtly greeting.

Ben made sure to return the gesture. *That probably looked fast-forwarded.* He focused and gave a proper—*so slow*—bend of his neck.

She nodded in return. "You did well in defending yourself,

trencher, so why not profit from the momentary inconvenience?"

Trencher. Elder Komir had call him that, too. Hearing it again made Ben smile. *Heck, why not?*

"I'll give you two gold." Another woman, almost alike in every way except her dress had full sleeves and she stood in front of a red silk gazebo. "One and a half for the spell focus and the extra for the wonderful show."

"Two and two silver." The lady in green counter-offered. "My first offer was low just to get your attention."

"Two and five." Confidence accompanied the second's bid as she motioned to the opening to her gazebo. "That's the highest price it will fetch."

Ben gently squeezed the small blade in hand. *If that's the most it'll fetch here, what's it really worth? Better yet, do I even want to sell it?* While he wouldn't dare take the tiny thing home where his family could find it, it would look rather nice in his basement lab at Meadows Towing. *I'll hang it next to the soldering iron.*

The first woman, who Ben—lost in thought—had turned to face extended her hand to the red tent as well. "She is correct."

"Lies!" A squat rotund man called from across the way. He stood before a crimson-and-violet stripped pavilion made of hard, opaque plastic. His dense, parted mustachio wound two wide loops on each cheek. "I have a cousin who collects such items. If you look closely, ape, you'll see two tiny gemstones on the pommel. It points to its origin and true value." The man hooked his thumbs on his thick black belt. "The info is free and I'll give you the truest offer. Three gold." He raised his chin. "Neither gazelle will top it."

Though Ben had made his mind up on keeping it, the man calling him ape made him want to prove a point. He looked back to the women. *Long necks. Large eyes. I can see why he called them that.*

The woman in green bent her neck slightly, again, but both signaled open palms to the man, conceding to his bid.

Though the passing crowd, Ben examined the man. *There's something about him... besides him calling me ape...* Ben couldn't figure out what about the man bother him, but there was something there.

The mustachioed man raised his head a bit higher and a slight smile spread his face open in pride of winning Ben's business. Figuring

Ben would follow, the man turned and walked to the door of his store. "This agreement is beyond far, but the focus will thrill my collector cousin to no end."

Ben turned and bowed to the woman in front of the green canvas tent before approaching her. *She was the only one who extended any courtesy.* He made a point of speaking loudly, hoping the man would hear him. "Though your offer was the lowest, I would like to see what you can offer in trade."

Her neck bent again and, this time, her body folded slightly, too. "I will be honored."

"Three and two!" The man called. "A full ounce of gold more."

Ben did not look back as he moved to her tent.

"Three and five! No, four full!"

Ben crossed the threshold. The din of the bazaar faded, then fell silent. Soft music, like a string quartet playing from beyond the door behind him, took the place of the hustle and bustle of the marketplace. Sandalwood incense filled his nose as he took in the twenty-foot depth of tightly packed rows of similar cherry wood shelves covered with various traditional knickknacks, brick-a-brac, foci, totems, and spell components. Dangling from the center of the tent, a brass brazier caught his eyes.

"*Rawk.* Right this way." A green parrot with a hooked yellow and red beak whistled, and repeated, "Right this way." Its perch appeared to be the handle of a strong box in the far left corner.

Guess she's not worried about being robbed.

Next to the bird, the woman pushed on the canvas back wall. With a pop, it parted to reveal to a secret room.

Okay, that's cool. Making sure to go to the opposite skirt, along the edge of the tent opposite the parrot with the wicked beak, Ben carefully hustled along the narrow walkway to get into the back room. *She's got spells!* He spied the SD cards on a shelf in a glass display. Of his schoolmates, he'd been the first to find one of the rare merchants who had items to sell to technomancers. A bit less carefully, Ben picked up his pace and pressed the Anvilsmith's volume button down twice to signal the rest of his group.

The fact that he might be walking right into a trap didn't occur to him... until *after* he crossed the threshold.

Chapter Three

RELAX... RELAX

A SOFT LAVENDER SCENT—*ALMOST the exact scent mom keeps at home*—filled the seven-foot by seven-foot room. To the immediate left, a small round folding table with a pale green checked table cloth. Floating inches above the table, a manila ceramic teapot with cherry blossom trees—*they're moving*—painted on the side. *The falling petals look so graceful.* As the tiny pink flowers rocked to the base, a sense of serenity eased into him.

While he'd thought about raising his guard as he stepped in, as soon as he entered the room, all semblance of worry slipped from him.

Cool. A cherry blossom had spiraled away from the teapot to land on the side of one of the two thin-lipped manila tea cups set upon similar ceramic saucers. More drifted from the pot to the cup, which filled from the bottom up releasing a fragrant—*oolong?*—brew.

Voice softer in the quiet room, she said, "Feel free to take your coat off."

Ben didn't much feel like taking off his trench coat. Due to the magical enchantments placed upon it, he never felt discomforted from it and it regulated extreme temperatures to nothing more than either a slight chill or a subtle warmth. *Still, it sounds like a good idea.*

Checking to see if Bastion, who had a supernatural sense of when things were about to go wrong, had cause to be wary, Ben found the beast soundly asleep.

Well, why am I not surprised? A faint, pleasantly warm fog filled his mind. *With how peaceful this place is...* He slipped off his coat and looked for a place to hang it.

"There." She extended her long arm to point a long finger at a single-peg coat rack in the opposite corner. It stood at the foot of a long, narrow emerald green canvas camping cot—*heh, it and the blankets match the walls*—which, coat-rack notwithstanding, ran the full length of the right wall.

Something about the bed—*no, it's a cot, cots aren't comfortable*—felt inviting. His nerves jumped.

"Don't think about the bed." She gave his shoulders a slight rub before giving a mild directing push. "Just hang your coat on the peg."

Ben did. A price tag—*two hundred and fifty... 'Two hundred and fifty' what? Is that the number of days that I've worn it?*—flipped from the tip.

"Don't forget your tie."

"Oh yeah." *Did I want to take off my tie?* With the wonderful warm fog filling his head, Ben found it hard to tell. *Why'd I come back here in the first place?* In answer to this thought, his shoulders gave a lop-sided, drugged shrug. *Well, I took off my coat.* He slipped the red silk tie off and looped it over his coat collar. The rack sucked the tag back in and flipped another from the tip. *Two hundred and seventy-five. Weird. What does that mean?*

"If it chafes..." She began.

Ben faced her.

Nothing remained of what he thought the woman out front looked like. Instead—*the dress is the same*—a young lady, very similar to both Penelope and Alice—*if the medusa didn't have scales*—stood. The two semblances seemed to struggle against one another as though uncertain which visage it should take.

She took a step toward him. A soft lilac smell—*Alice's scent*—washed over him and all traces of Penelope faded. Voice tentative and hopeful, a human version of Alice suggested, "You can hang your tablet harnessss too."

What's with the hiss on harness? Ben recalled Alice ticking off common misconceptions of her cursed race. *She isn't sibilant.* The warmth in his head cooled a bit. He patted the holster that kept his Anvilsmith at easy reach over his leg. "No, I'm good."

"Sure, understandable." She said. All hint of hisses vanished. She lifted the two ceramic cups with cherry blossoms settled on the base, sat on the edge of the bed—*it's a cot*—and extended a cup to him. "How about we sit and have some tea?"

Without thought, his arm extended to accept. Ben pulled back just short of taking the cup. *Wait, Alice can't stand me!* The fog vanished.

Kevin, who always talked as though he were in a competition to get the most words out in a minute, chattered. "Come out from wherever you are, Ben. We got your location ping."

Tone confident and sharp, LeRoy called. "You know you're not going to scare us."

Ben glanced to the canvas wall separating him from the main store. A light from the other side projected Kevin and LeRoy's shadows on it. When he shifted his gaze back to where Alice had sat on the bed—*cot* —the tall, bald, lanky woman from early sat there, sipping tea... And had been there the entire time. *Well, I think she's been there...*

"Oh good. More customers." From her expression, the tea—*or something*—put a bad taste in her mouth and made her words sound bitter. "Perfect timing."

Something weird was going on. Ben tried to recall exactly what, but could only recall cherry blossom, oolong tea, and the smell of Alice's skin. *Why am I thinking of Alice? Better yet, why'd I take off my coat and tie?* He snatched both from the peg, gave the woman a dirty look. *Trickstress.*

She shot him a tight smile.

The glass rack of spellcards, which has been there all the time, seemed to sneak up on him.

Ben jumped away. *Whoa, that's right. Spellcards.* He called out, "In here, guys. Check this out."

Chapter Four

SOMETHING LIKE FRIENDS

Though LeRoy, Kevin, and Neil had done a great deal of haggling and some buying in the green canvas tent, Ben had remained a few steps behind. First, mentally, as his schoolmates worked hard for the best deal, then, physically, as the three of them left the tent and had to come back for him to pull him along.

In fact, the four of them had walked well out into the expansive dirt parking lot and located their cars amidst the thousands—*if not tens of thousands*—of hastily parked vehicles before, still smelling lavender, Ben finally started to come back into his own frame of mind—*they're like scattered cherry blossoms*—puzzling out the, mostly horrid parking situations much further away from the bazaar.

If the Bauman people laid down chalk parking lines, everyone would follow suit.

Late-comers were often the third, or fourth car blocking in people who had come early. Others parked to the side of a horizontal row meant for two cars to pass, narrowing the lane to one, in which—if two cars came toward each other with too many cars behind them—the lane would become yet another row of parking, locking in even more cars.

And thus his earlier plan to have at least have one direction to get out by parking side-by-side—Kevin's luminescent orange flame-tipped next to Ben's matte black—backed-in behind Neil, and LeRoy's A.P.A. approved, stock, bright reds had been foiled.

Both sides—*as far as the eye can see*—had been blocked in. *If this were my event, I'd have lines drawn and offer valet.* Ben found his head shaking. "This is atrocious."

"Oh, he's back." Kevin rattled, "Welcome back, Ben." He raised a powder blue spellcard with a large white energy bolt painted on the flat which branched out to seven strikes high near his crazy brown swath of windblown hair. "Check it. Chain Lightning."

Trying to focus on the spellcard, the mental image of raining cherry blossoms and phantom smells of the woman's back room finally faded to the buzzy ozone smell of too many arcane-powered vehicles in close proximity. Each of schoolmates, in their school uniform of white dress shirts, red ties, brown slacks, and tan trench coats, leaned on the corner of their cars facing the space between them.

Not remember anything after having parked, Ben tried to quickly piece the night back together. *We came right after Spell Programming, split up. Someone attacked me with a sword. No...* He opened his hand and rediscovered the small masterfully crafted light, high-quality silver, three-inch sword whose hilt alternated between strips of cooper and steel. *The ruby chips... The husky vendor had the highest bid, but I... I went to the lady in green...*

"Hey, wizzes." A guy in a dark trench coat and long oily hair called to them from the end of the row." For five hundred Strong or seven hundred M.U.s, I can get your car out. Then a second ride for half as much."

Wizzes. Ben used to toss the friendly, casual slang for unknown casters quite a bit. Now—*we're all sort of delusional*—now it just felt false. *No, it's pretentious.*

"Nah, wiz." LeRoy called back. "We're good for now. Please hit us up later though."

"You got it." The guy waved and walked on.

Ben asked, "How can he get our cars out."

Offhandedly, LeRoy answered, "He's a porter specialist." As though that explained everything, he turned his attention back to Kevin. "Nice buy." LeRoy shuffled several cards and presented a silver one at his hip near his red leather belt held closed by his Top Junior

Caster belt buckle. The low angle helped the lighting from the Koffman floating lights to highlight an embossed sword. "But not nearly as hot as my sweet Mage Sword."

Ben wanted to pry into porters, but his thoughts were still preoccupied. *She— She bewitched me and tried to rob me.* He balled his fist on the blade. It bit into his palm. *Ow.* He relaxed his hand and kept his fist closed so the cut could heal before being noticed by the others.

Kevin laughed a challenge. "You can't cast seven stones."

LeRoy shrugged. "You cannot cast Chain Lighting."

Kevin and LeRoy are jaw-jacking again, and Neil's off—as usual—in his own little world. None of them probably wouldn't have noticed if he held his hand opened and showed how the small cut on his bloody palm was healing shut.

LeRoy flipped the SD card over his knuckles, making it dance on top of his hand. "Perhaps you should master Lighting Bolt first?"

Ben winced. *Low blow!* While, between the four of them, he could out program and engineer the others put together, Ben wouldn't have dared to brag about it. LeRoy, on the other hand, had made direct reference to the spell he used to finish Kevin, twice back-to-back, to become the school's Top Junior Caster for last school eighth.

Kevin stopped laughing.

LeRoy drove the point. "I mean, it should come naturally, now, since you know what it tastes like."

"Want to go right here?" Kevin pointed to the ultra-narrow, walk-side-ways-only lane between the cars that had them blocked in. "Go ahead. Step out."

This spiraled fast.

Nonplussed, LeRoy rocked his head on his shoulders. "The duel was supposed to be a best of three match... You didn't even take one."

Oh, no! Ben extended his arm to stop Kevin from moving to the row to call LeRoy out to duel.

"Move, Ben." With contact being frowned upon, Kevin stopped short of Ben's arm. "All I need is one."

LeRoy flipped the card over his knuckles again before putting it into his pocket. "Easy, Kevin. Do you think the Magistrates want to be pulled from the Bazaar?" He crossed his arms and pressed more of his weight on his car. "This is like their vacation time."

Kevin's spoke slow dread through clenched teeth. "It would only take a minute."

Strength left Ben's arm. *The hawkish nose, flat cheeks, pronounced brow. Kevin looks just like Collins when the jerk threatens us...*

"Less, actually." LeRoy slid his hands into his pocket. "What's up with you, Ben?"

Ben studied Kevin's face a bit longer. *Could the number-two caster and the Senior Adept be related?*

Kevin stole a glance at Ben.

"Uh." Ben shifted his eyes to LeRoy, and lied, "Nothing."

Finally moving, Neil pushed a few strands of his white hair behind a pigmentless ear, and held up two of his four cards. One had a clear case to show off the circuitry within while the other was black with a faint gray line. Voice soft and steady, he said, "I don't know which I am more proud of..." He presented the clear one. "Wind Wall." Then the black one. "Or Enervation."

Ben eyed the black card. *What's Enervation?*

"Neil the Techno-Necro-mancer, you gotta know it's the Enervation," LeRoy answered with a sneer as though the question lay leagues beyond stupid.

Kevin's chin relaxed a bit as he raised a leg to his car and, in his normal fast patter, agreed, "Hands down."

Clever. A slight admiration kindled in Ben for Neil; the smallest, and softest spoken of the them. *He changed the topic and neither of them seem the wiser.*

"Yes, it is necromancy, which I adore." Neil slid the black card into the pocket of his heavily starched shirt, presenting the clear one. "And yes, it is more useful in combat, but this one completes my collection of standard three-stone spells."

What? Ben's ears rose, and his focus shot to Neil who still eyed the card. *I know he comes from a wealthy family, but if he has all three-stones...* Not sure if his question strayed into an area considered too personal, Ben asked, "So, you have all single and double stones too?"

Neil nodded absently as he bent over the card, putting his pigmentless face closer to it for inspection instead of raising the card before his powder pink eyes. "Interesting. There's a faint brick wall in fine white paint."

"Wait." Kevin stood again. "You mean to tell me you wasted coin on Erase?"

Neil bobbed his head again. He ran a finger on the flat. "Talk about craftsmanship. The paint is in miniscule grooves."

Kevin waved a hand. "Man, that's the most useless spell in the world."

Having programmed it for extra credit, and used it to keep Collins from seeing a letter of complaint he had composed against the Senior Adept during Spell Programming III, Ben ventured to disagree, "It has its uses."

"How?" LeRoy shook his head. "Okay Ben, there you are, standing across from me at dueling length. How would you use it?"

Ben opened his mouth to try and back out of LeRoy's hypothetical before it could accidentally spiral into a real challenge. Another flash from earlier in the night came to him. *Crap. I had a vision of dueling him, but we were between tents. Man, I really don't want to—*

Neil interjected, "Ben doesn't duel."

"In this example, he does." LeRoy looked from Neil, who hadn't stopped marveling at the card, to Ben. "So, there we are, hooks in and ready to throw." He stood and, in an instant, drew his hand from his pocket as though he held his tablet. "Somehow, in this fictional world, you gain the dominant caster's advantage." Staring into Ben's eyes, LeRoy took an aggressive step forward into Ben's personal space.

What are you doing LeRoy? The manner of approach meant 'go time.' *What's this about? You don't like someone disagreeing with you?*

Bastion—the Nilosian monster that could steal control of Ben's body—remained fast asleep. In its slumber, the beast uttered an annoyed grumble at the challenge.

LeRoy stared intensely.

Tension seized Ben's shoulders, back, and brought his brow into a tight knot. *Man, I really don't want to duel you LeRoy...* Ben stood up straight. *I really don't.*

Chapter Five

QUIET CONFIDENCE

LeRoy's breath smelled of bacon.

You want to start something from nothing? Ben took a small step forward, tightening the narrow space between them and a faint, invisible static, as though they were Tesla rods attracting dimensional energy, built between them. *I may not win, but I'm not going to slink away.*

"Shit." Kevin leapt forward to get his arm between them before they bumped chests.

Counter to the seriousness of the moment, a group of people—*they're enjoying themselves, why can't we be like them*—laughed. Staring into LeRoy's African brown eyes, Ben found an intense pinprick of cobalt blue at the center of the black pupils.

"You have first bang, Ben." LeRoy gave a dangerous grin. He lowered his voice to a threat. "I dare you, piss it away on Erase."

"First, I don't start fights." As he said the words, Ben tamped down the desire to cast Erase on LeRoy just to see if the Top Junior Caster would have attacked him. "More importantly, tactically, it'd be a waste again you."

LeRoy nodded a, *I didn't think you would* nod. "Exactly."

Ben added, "However—"

Breath hitched, Kevin bristled.

LeRoy's eyes narrowed.

Neil looked up to them.

Ben continued, "—since we're talking fictional events." He gave a dismissing wave to negate LeRoy's scenario and took half a step back. "Say you and a traditional caster are battling for real. Life or death. No minimum distance. You both have just enough juice for a single low-level spell." He slipped his hands into his coat pockets and dropped the miniature sword as he turned a small circle.

Paying them no mind, Koffman Lanterns floated above patrons moving to and from the bazaar.

Ben stepped back, bumping into Kevin's arm which bumped into LeRoy. "So, there you two are. Eye to eye. Nose to nose." He yanked his hand from his pocket. "He pulls a scroll!"

Expertly, LeRoy said, "I blast him."

"Yeah," Kevin agreed.

"Really?" Ben's brow eased. *He didn't even think to try and rip the scroll away.* His eyebrows raised. "It's not enough to take him down. He's mystically shielded."

LeRoy blurted, "I punch him!"

"Ah." Ben stepped backward and raised a finger. "Your spell hits, but he's made of sterner stuff. The strike lands, a solid shot, but we're not martial masters so it doesn't knock him out." Ben took another step back and leaned on his car.

LeRoy's eyes bounced around his sockets as he searched for another answer.

Ben added, "In fact, this trad-caster is well practiced at concentrating through such damage and activates the scroll."

Rapt in the scenario, knowing that LeRoy would have to eat whatever came, Kevin found the breath to ask, "What spell is it?"

LeRoy raised his chin and tightened as though he were preparing to take a punch. "Yeah, what spell?"

Ben hadn't thought the scenario that far. *Not important really. You're already cooked.* He shrugged at the two constant contenders for Top Junior Caster. "It could be anything, but to be sure, it's offensive and, remember, traditional mages can fit up to four spells on one of those scrolls. So, after the first, another would come, and another, and—most likely—another. Then, he still has juice for a personal spell."

Stunned by the reality of being totally screwed by his choices in the scenario, LeRoy stepped back from Kevin's arm.

Dumbfounded, Kevin still stood there with his arm out like a crossing guard at an empty street.

"Tactics, LeRoy." Ben peeked in his Transcend to check on Tex. The other guys' knee-high Golemcasts where there, but not his. *Darn it, Tex.* If the others check their robots, they'd see his missing, and then the awkward questions would come. Hoping none of the guys would, Ben returned his focus to LeRoy. "The main difference between you and me —in this scenario—is that I would make a play at grabbing the scroll and using my last arcane watt to erase the magic."

LeRoy frowned slightly. "But you'd still be at an impasse and he'd have a tick up on you."

"Yeah." Kevin lowered his arm and moved back to let his car support his weight. "What then?"

Ben gave another shrug and chastised himself. *I'm starting to act like Jek.* He looked away to the Bazaar, taking in the glorious spectacle of so many Koffman Lanterns hovering—*they're like stalking butlers*—to light people's way out into the parking lot. "Well, being civilized, we could call it a day and go our separate ways."

Kevin shook his head hard. "No. You said it was life or death."

"So, I did." Ben lifted his gaze to the night sky. He found the North Star. *Just one arcane watt...*

The horrified expressions on the Old Henderson orcs' faces when blasted their life from them came to his mind's eye and took roost. Expression left his face. The justifications—*they had Clarissa. They would have killed me*—still didn't ease the guilt.

Tonelessly, Ben said, "Then it's 'may the most determined man win.'"

"You mean the best man." LeRoy correct.

In an internal quagmire, Ben shook his head. "Winning doesn't make you the best."

"Wow." LeRoy cast his gaze to the sky as he fell back on his car. "That's deep."

"Yeah." Kevin nodded and did as LeRoy had. The two of them had a long time rivalry. While one might be the best for several school eighths, the other could pull out a win to take the Top Junior Castor belt buckle. No matter which one held the title, they tended to mirror each other.

Since looking up, Ben had felt Neil keeping a steady eye on him. Scrutinizing.

"Why are going this deep anyway." Ben tried to shake off his sense of woe. *Plenty of time for that later.* He cleared his throat. "Bauman's Bazaar is right there guys. There's bound to be more sellers. Plus, I haven't had one mug of spiced cider yet."

"Me too." Kevin sat up. "And I still got money."

LeRoy echoed, "Me, too."

"Then back into the den of derision we go." Neil tucked his clear spellcard away and stood. "Until cider come from your noses and moths from my pockets."

Ben laughed and clapped with LeRoy and Kevin, but wondered. *What does he mean by that?*

Chapter Six

NEIL

SEARCHING for other vendors with technomancy wares, the four of them crossed back into the heart of the bazaar and split up again... Or at least they were supposed to. Ben kept catching glimpses of Academy-trench coat tan when he least expected it. *One of them is following me.* Still, Ben wondered aimlessly through the bazaar, rarely pausing.

Ben came to a full stop. In the valleys of the hawkers calling out, he heard and—*mmm*—smelled bacon frying. He was standing at the corner of a pale orange and blue striped pavilion. He feigned interested by passing a curious glance over the wares in the rows and rows of glass cases with tiny glass boxes of powders, herbs, and fluids of various transparency before fixing his gaze on the deep fried bacon balls on sticks, freshly rolled in maple.

The vendor, an elderly Asian with a huge, mean-looking, twelve-legged spider tattooed on his face, eyed Ben and muttered in a Far-Eastern language.

That doesn't sound pleasant or welcoming. Hopeful, Ben approached the man.

"For paying customers only." The man waved him away. "Go feast your eyes somewhere else."

At least he didn't call me ape. Ben turned away. When he did, he got his best look at the flash of tan following him at it ducked behind two large whiskey barrels stacked atop each other. *Must be Neil. Too short to be either LeRoy or Kev.* He had a clear view of both sides of the barrels. Whoever it was, couldn't slip away around a corner like before. Ben headed back to the hiding spot. *I have to know why.*

He had made it most of the way there when a large, burley man in a long-sleeved golden shirt and red overalls stepped from a crimson dome tent with yellow and orange paisleys. The man seized something near the barrels, lifted it, and flung Neil like a sack of potatoes into the main thoroughfare.

The crowd of colored robes scattered away from Neil like frightened cats.

Can't believe how quiet everything got. Nearby hawkers fell silent. The immediate din quelled. Sales from rows over spilled in. Having just been on the inside of such a circle for the first time a short while ago, Ben scanned the crowd to note what kind of view the others had.

"We don't serve your kind!" The man barked and pulled a narrow —*is that bone?*—wand as he closed to only ten feet from Neil.

The shoppers formed a moving circle a few steps further out.

"My kind?" Neil stayed down on the packed earth and locked eyes with the man. He motioned to his pigment-free cheek and then to his trench coat, and asked, "Do you mean *albinos* or *apes*?"

The man didn't answer.

Not at the center of attention—*they want blood*—Ben could feel the unhealthy lust from the crowd like a coming storm. They pretended to mill about when they were entirely focused on what was about to happen in the dirty duel circle.

Blending into their movements, Ben angled and joined the second rank of people moving in slow circles. Like them, he tried to give off the appearance of minding his own business.

Still on the ground, Neil had one hand tucked inside his coat—the side where he kept his tablet—as he extended his other hand toward the man. "I did not mean to offend, good sir." The pigment-free hand motioned to the stand. "I could not help but notice your small, yet impressive, dragon fruit tree."

The merchant pointed the wand at Neil and laughed heartily. "I'm not looking away, ape." He shook his head and pointed a gaudy pinky ring of his other hand at Neil. A tangerine line of energy—*I haven't seen an orange tether before*—shot out and struck Neil's leg. The line slid to the center of each of their chests, binding them for the duel. "But, if you stand, and perform a proper folding bow in apology, I'll keep the charge in my pointer."

Moving behind the man, Ben couldn't see Neil when he spoke. "In fairness, good sir, I must let you know…"

Ben passed directly behind the merchant's broad back, he almost felt tethered himself as ambient dimensional energy flowed into the bond. A wealth of scents, chief being spiced cider and honey-mead—both staples at Bauman's—came to him and his hearing perked to hear bets—all favoring the merchant—being softly whispered.

Then he passed from behind the man and could see Neil's powder pink eyes fixed on the man. The feeling faded. No one's mouths moved. *How are they whispering?*

Neil had pulled his Triforce. "When I stand—and I will stand—I will not bend."

"Then die on the ground!" The merchant flicked his wrist. A cackling pale blue skull formed at the tip and shot at Neil.

Neil lifted his tablet.

The skull rebounded from Neil's device and zipped back at the man, striking him square in the chest. The skull squealed joyously as it disintegrated. The man crumpled.

Neil got to his feet and dusted himself off. The tan coat didn't appear dirty, but each strike knocked away small puffs. He stopped, gripped his device with both hands and jutted it out.

Dressed similarly to the fallen merchant, three guards, all more muscle-bound than their employer—*more muscle-bound than orcs*—leapt into the circle with their hands on their hilts over their shoulders. Strapped across their backs were wide, four-foot long, scabbards

Ben reached into his trench, put one hand flat on his tablet, and fingered his Shield and Orion spellcards with his other hand.

The mirror on the back of Neil's protective cover shone green as arcane watts slowly empowered the redirection enchantment. *It'll be ready to reflect again in a minute, but won't do a spit of good against those swords if they pull them.*

In unison, the guards called, "Life for life!"

Chapter Seven

RESPONSIBLE FOR EACH OTHER

TRYING to ignore the strong eucalyptus smell coming from a string of six young casters in ankle-length, greyish-purple robes and their similarly dressed chaperone who wore a flat, wide-brimmed hat like only old priests used to wear, Ben eyed a narrow gap between them and their escort. None of the six were older than twelve—*they don't want to miss a thing*—and they moved a bit slower than the rest of the inner circle.

About to perform a major breach of courtmanship by making contact with a caster he was neither familiar with or indebted to, Ben reflexively scanned around for Adept Matton, and then for anyone in a tan trench coat.

The kid in the lead, a boy by the voice, leaned back and whispered to the one behind him, "I hope the ape's head comes clean off."

"Me too," the second, a girl, replied.

They've more bloodlust in them than the adults. Ben lowered his shoulder and shoved his way into the circle, which instantly adjusted to form two feet behind him.

"It touched me!" The boy.

"Another ape!" The girl.

I'm a little too close to the guards. Ben began to walk just inside the circle toward Neil.

On the opposite side, some of the those in the second rank of the shoppers rotating around them as though they hadn't noticed a fight happening, squeezed in closer. *With all these colors moving around so slowly, it almost feels like the start of a Screaming Meemie ride.*

"Friar Zane." The boy Ben had bumped pawed at the chaperone. "That ape touched me!"

Ben ignored the true accusation, kept his hands in his coat and focused on the three guards. "If things get ugly..." Halfway to Neil, Ben backed slowly toward the toward the bloodthirsty watchers, forcing them to make the circle wider and wider. He kept going until he, the guards, and Neil formed an equilateral triangle. "They're going to get real ugly."

Mimicking expression Bastion made him make at the girl in pink, Ben furrowed his brow, sneered, and boasted, "We've already got you in a pinch and you have no idea how powerful A'Neilios, the White Dragon, Understudy of Master Reynolds who, as The Shroud, held the World Dueling Federation title for eight years, truly is."

Seemingly undaunted, the guards nocked elbows amongst themselves to indicate which one of them—Ben or Neil—they were going to attack. One began to eye him while the other two focused on Neil.

They're not buying my bluff. Ben's heart began to thump in his chest. As though concerned for those around them, Ben tried to keep his voice calm and spoke from the side of his mouth, "A'Neilios, please, I beseech you. Hook these three. You needn't close down Bauman's Bazaar as you closed the Samhain Festival."

Neil remained quiet.

The circle behind the guards began to break apart. *Some of them are buying it, but they're not the customers that I want.* Virtually everyone in the Vegas Valley, even if they weren't actually there, had claimed to be present when the pyrotechnic dragons shook free of their control and battled of their own accord. Nearly fifty people had died that night. Though all the deaths were from having been trampled, every death had been blamed on the dragons and the pyrotechnic company was still paying blood money to make amends. No one, not even Ben, knew the cause, but he did his best to make Neil seem responsible.

Regretful the guards hadn't cowered, Ben gripped his Anvilsmith and opened his mouth to call 'go time.'

"He fell from his own spell." A man in layered rubicund robes stepped from the front rank into the circle. He pulled his hood to show butchered short, brown hair.

The broken circle which had turned into a rocking horseshoe thickest behind Neil, grew accordingly.

The man started to close his hand on air. A Primary Baton appeared in his palm shining bright with Argosian red energy.

Relieved, Ben exhaled. *Thank goodness. A Magistrate.*

Neil cut his eyes to Ben.

What? Ben shrugged. *What?*

Neil turned his attention to the Magistrate. Ben did the same.

"As a Lesser Judge of Chief Magistrate Lars Lightningpalm, acting on the best interest of this event, I declare your claim of life for life to be invalid." He waved his baton at two of the guards and pointed at the merchant. "Collect your benefactor."

The lead guard kept his hand on his hilt, but the two did as they were directed.

"Hold," the Magistrate commanded, and the muscle-bound men heeded. He still had the tip of his baton aimed at the merchant. "He draws shallow breath. Stand him tall."

The guards hefted the unconscious man to their standing height.

The Lesser Judge pointed his rod at Neil. "Pick your prize, A'Neilios."

A weak orange flash shone and faded around both Neil and the merchant.

What the heck was that? Ben rubbed his eyes in disbelief. *I didn't imagine it.*

The Lesser Judge raised his rod to the crowd. "Now, go."

Instead of the circle going oblong and compacting in, everyone walked as directly away from the Primary as possible. Hawkers tried to call their attention with, supposedly, unbeatable deals, but the would-be buyers moved past the vendors and through open-sided shops.

Neil bowed formally to the out-of-uniform Magistrate. "Thank you, Lesser Judge."

The man opened his hand and the symbol of his office flashed away. No longer in his official capacity, he sneered contempt at Neil. "It was not for you, ape. It was for the good of all near." He pulled his hood to obscure his face. "One point your school, and Master, seem to constantly miss is this—" he walked after the north-moving crowd, and called back, "Tradition is Tradition!"

Most of the crowd around echoed, "Tradition is Tradition!" It came a second time with more people joining in. "Tradition is Tradition!" The pulse grew exponentially in strength and it felt like the entire bazaar boomed it on the third iteration. "Tradition is Tradition!"

Something about the calls 'life for life' and 'tradition is tradition' sounded quite familiar. Ben snapped his fingers. *Those are calls from the Kings, Clergy, and Coffers game?* Unable to afford the ante, Ben had never played. He made a mental note to verify with Dominic, a KCC junkie, and hurried to Neil to ask the question burning in his mind. Ben lowered his voice to a soft whisper, and asked, "Hey, what was that orange flash?"

Chapter Eight

PARTNERS

CALM, as though he hadn't had three large guards about to cut him down, Neil put a hushing finger to his lips. "If you want to trade questions, we should not do so aloud."

Appreciating the local silence—even with hawkers calling from a few rows over—Ben focused on bringing his heartbeat back down normal. *Is he talking about telepathy?* Considering letting a secret slip, he narrowed his eyes. *Should I let on that I know how to mindspeak?*

Neil projected his thoughts at Ben, *While telepathy would be quicker, I meant texting.*

Ben thumped his own forehead and smiled. The scent of the kid's eucalyptus clung to his arm. He frowned and put his arm down. "That's how you knew when I was going to look your way and bust you following me."

Neil's expression didn't change, but he nodded and projected, *Precisely.*

More as an afterthought, Ben shielded himself from other mind readers.

A small, brief smile flickered and died on Neil's lips. *Better. However, it still is not safe since others can pick up on waves between you and me.* Neil began to type on his device.

That green lady really did a number on me to slice through my defenses like that. Ben checked his sleeve. *How long is that eucalyptus going to cling to me?* He sniffed it and shook his head against the strength. *Lesson learned, never rub up against—* He paused. While he knew the school uniforms of the Las Vegas Valley and neighboring prefectures, the cut and length of their robes proved a conundrum.

Movement caught his attention. A young girl—*she can't be older than ten and she's shivering*—in jeans and a heavy, cream-colored winter coat came from between shops toward where the confrontation had been. *She must be freezing.* For the first time in a long while, Ben sent a thankful thought out to the universe for the comfort enchantment on his school coat. *Guess she didn't hear the Primary tell everyone to go.* Something about the fact that she didn't have her elbows tucked tight to her sides, or the way her eyes shifted side to side to take in the area, put Ben on guard. *What does this kid want?*

One of the large guards came from the shop. Anger—*perhaps disgust*—dug deep lines across his forehead and knotted his brow. Staring blades at Neil—who had his attention firmly fixed on his tablet—the man squatted near the fallen spellcaster's wand.

The preteen sprang around the guard, scooped up the white wand, and dashed between the shops on the opposite side.

The guard cried, "Stop! Thief!"

Vendors and their guards reached out for the girl.

She proved too nimble and, grabbing one of the maple bacon balls Ben had eyed earlier, disappeared into the crowd the next lane over.

Not looking up from his device, Neil said to the guard, "If you were not trying to intimidate me, you would have possession of your master's wand."

Ready for an attack, Ben turned to the guard.

His furrowed brow, cheeks, and neck had flushed with blood. Instead of coming at them, or going on a fruitless hunt for the girl, he stomped back into the merchant's shop.

I would've never pegged Neil as one to salt another's wounds. Ben's tablet chimed as a deep grey text made to look like fine calligraphy in a white bubble appeared holding Neil's message. "Was what you said about Master Reynolds being The Shroud true?"

Ben hadn't gotten around to formatting what his text balloons would look like on others' tablets, so his words appeared in the

Anvilsmith's stock emerald green stencil on steel. "Yes. What about the orange flash?"

Neil texted, "I'll prepare a document for you." He then motioned down the lane. "Come on. Let us continue our search for Technomancy vendors."

Ben said, "Okay. Follow me."

Neil followed Ben as he took the path the girl had taken. He kept from whimpering as they passed the maple bacon balls on a stick. Stepping through to the next lane, he walked side-by-side with his schoolmate.

Surprisingly, the various starwise patrons moved away to let them into the flow.

The parting wasn't only to let them in. The mostly bright robes around them—age, gender, and affiliation notwithstanding—afforded them an additional five feet of space... Even if they walked down the center of the lane. *So, when I walk alone, I'm—more or less—accepted by the crowd, but walk next to another Academy student and they give us air.* Though he thought it wrong to enjoy the feeling of power, Ben couldn't readily find shame in it.

From the general din of the bazaar, his ears began to pick up on a constant murmur of "Apes" which both preceded and followed them. While being called one grated his nerves, the word proved a small price to pay for commanding an area. Soon, the slur lost its impact and began to feel like a warning to everyone else to get out of their path. Though Ben knew the space granted them came from a place of fear seated in the souls of those around him, this proved to be the first time he had been afforded something that might be mistaken as respect. *And, most amazingly, it's actually for attending the Academy.*

His device chimed. Neil's text bubble had two document plus signs along the top. "I have sent you my notes from Dueling I and II. This should settle both your stepping in to back me and the information deficit created by your sharing the information about The Shroud."

"Thanks!" *Wow, notes from Dueling! Fantastic.* Ben's thoughts shifted. *Can't believe he didn't know about Reynolds being The Shroud.* Though he recalled getting the information from his mom, he figured if she—as a pacifist plant-based caster—knew, then everyone must've known.

Information deficit. Ben rolled the words around in his head as he spied an eight-foot tall man in a black shroud step from one tent to duck into another. *Given Neil's lineage, he must know lots of stuff I don't. Wonder if he'll be open to exchanging more.* Not wanting to share anything too heavy—*like Node Keys, what I know of the Mystique or the existence of the pocket realm where the Komirs reside*—Ben scanned the around for any sign of tan coats. Not seen Kevin, LeRoy, or any other A.P.A. folks, Ben whispered about technomancy. "Did you know that you can copy spells from one spellcard to another?"

Neil cleared his throat to warm up his voice again. "Of course you can move from one to another."

"I didn't say move." Ben corrected. "I said copy."

Neil stopped cold.

When Ben turned, the albino's index finger slid in mad dashes along his screen. *Wow, never seen him this passionate before.* Ben smiled inwardly. *Guess he didn't know that.* He looked to his device for Neil's message.

Neil presented his screen. Unlike his message, everything on Neil's Triforce was white with faint silver highlights which made anything but his message a strain to read. Ben read, *Copy, as in, not losing the original SD card?*

Ben nodded.

Neil double tapped the text and hit delete.

Ben frowned a bit. *Wonder why he doesn't want record of the message?*

Calmer, Neil's finger started a graceful slide over the keyboard.

Ben leaned in to read.

Each time Neil's finger stopped or turned on a letter, it appeared in the box. As the fingertip moved to the next letter, the tablet guessed—rather accurately—what the next letter would be. At times, full words would spring up in Neil's fancy text script after only a couple of letters. When correct, Neil lifted his finger and the word appeared in the text box.

More interesting than his classmate's typing was the symbol above the shift key where the caps lock should have been. *It's the same eye-shaped mark that accompanies stock Scry sigils. Wonder if the Triforce can be used as a divination focus?*

Neil tapped his unsent bubble. "How many copies can you make from one SD card, and is there a maximum spell level you can do?"

Ben checked over his shoulders again. *No one.* He mused, *feels like we're forming a cabal.* More in respect for how Neil acted than any real feeling that he should show discretion, Ben lowered his voice and whispered, "I've copied from my original Blast eight times." Ben cleared his throat. While him being the most disadvantaged student at the A.P.A. wasn't a secret, due to the subtle classism obvious in his non-school issued possessions and him being admitted under the Matton Grant funded by the one Adept whose classes Ben could never pass on the first attempt, having to admit it proved to be another matter altogether. Still, he had made enough room to swallow his pride. "I don't know about max level; I've never been able to buy spells."

Neil's finger went back to its keyboard ballet.

Nearby, a vendor tossed a freshly-turned-over-to-her coin purse to a guard.

The thump and jingle reminded Ben of the reward bag he'd been given for his lost spells. Ben typed a message to Tex. "Remind me to count the Komir coins when we return to the scrapyard."

Tex's reply was instant. "Remind me to never let you leave me in the car."

Guiltily, Ben sighed. *Tex would love this place. The tents. The wares. The various people and their diverse manner of dress...* "Sorry, buddy. They made a good point for leaving you guys behind."

"Look at these bots idle." The text popped up a split second before a snapshot of the other three Golemcasts in the backseat, their eyes dark and wound close. "They're Olympic class idlers, Ben." Another three full rows of text popped up. "This wouldn't be as bad if these guys played games like poker. Heck, I'd kill for Memory, Go Fish, or even Eye Spy right now. Ah! I've been slain. My assassin's name... Boredom."

Ben chuckled.

Neil looked up, finger still moving. "What?"

Ben angled his screen away. "Funny picture."

Neil frowned at the turned-away device, but returned his focus to his Triforce.

Ben typed, "Tell you what, Tex. Climb through the backseat to the trunk and pull the spare Anvilsmith. You have my permission to download any free play game."

Tex replied, "Bless you, Ben."

Ben imagined his companion army-crawling his metal body across the desert when an oil oasis appeared. Ben rolled his eyes and smiled at his imaginary Tex pinching his fixed nose while he cannonballed into the center. He added. "Nothing with a cost." Then clarified. "I mean no spending."

"Got'cha."

Almost fittingly, Ben had to take a turn at being idle as Neil worked his device. Though he liked tablets, Neil was mainly typing and pulling different documents together. *Non-cool, mundane, things any tablet could do.*

A whiff of sizzling bratwurst came to him. Casting his eyes around the nearby tents to find the food vender, Ben spied another solid green —*is that burlap?*—tent. Recalling the woman from earlier, he groaned. *Even if I see a green tent next year, it would be too soon.*

In front of the building, atop a huge, eight-foot tall, dark oak barrel set on end and tapped midway with a spigot, a little person with dense red mutton chops and wearing a seaweed-green monk habit considered them.

Accidently, Ben made eye contact. *Crap!*

Before he could bounce his eyes away, the merchant raised his squat, round mug to him with a true respectful bend of the neck.

Huh. Don't normally get both courtly, and courteous in the same gesture. Begrudgingly, Ben gave a short, almost dismissive bow in return. *Adept Matton would cut my tie and give me eternal detention if he caught wind of this.* He chided himself. *Do the right thing, Ben.* When he would've normally straightened, Ben involved his back and stopped deeper to give the man twice as much respect as was given to him.

The man struggled to mirror Ben's bow, but managed. Better still, he tilted at the waist to extend the cup in his hand in hospitable good will.

Free cider? Too good to be true! His earlier adventure into the green tent not forgotten, Ben fixed his attention on the merchant and tried to remain cool as anticipation to take the offer for a free spiced cider overcame his staunch reluctance to ever approach another vender in green. *This time, I have back-up.* He took a couple of steps toward the vendor and urged Neil, "Come on."

"Almost done." Neil replied.

I'm not going to wait. Ben moved toward the shop and spoke to his device, "Wake. Ping Neil. I'll be at the green tent five down on the left." A soft *ting*—*Neil's text tone sounds dull*—came from behind him.

Neil gave a dark mumble.

"Welcome." The man called in a tinny voice as he labored down a set of stairs built on the side of the barrel. "Welcome to both of you." Midway, he paused, took a gulp from the cup, and continued down. "Come in, my friends. Please, come in."

Chapter Nine

CIDER'S SIREN SONG

THOUGH THE SCENT of spiced cider and honey-mead intensified as Ben drew closer, he tried to keep his field of vision broad as paused at the wide, rolled-up entrance. *The dispensers smell like they're just inside, to the right.* His stomach rolled and gave an anxious groan. *Scope the place out first, then draw a drink.*

The little monk's habit rocked as he hobbled toward the back. Many of the tables within were the standard six-foot long folding kind. *The same style used at the Magic Faire to display projects.* To the left, past a large stuffed animal, were some lowered and narrowed tables for people of the owner's stature. A silver bell with gold leafed letters —*ring for service*—floated over each table just above eye level. *Smart. Don't distract from the wares.* To the right—*ah, glorious*—tapped, and raised up on their sides, were three quarter-kegs made of the same dark oak as the large one out front. *Whew, I can feel their heat.* Like birds on a wire, they sat next to each other, waiting and whistling softly.

The merchant, in his tiny voice, offered, "Something for that watering mouth of yours before I truly amaze you?"

Ben had to peel his eyes away from the barrel that read Goodspice's Old Fashioned Spiced Cider to look the shopkeeper in his eyes, bow respectfully, and respond to the gracious offer. An anticipatory grin spread his lips. "Only by your urging, of course."

"Of course! Of course." The monk laughed and waved Ben on to the kegs. He raised a warning finger. "But only spiced for you, my young friend."

"Wouldn't want otherwise." Ben crossed the threshold. Littered with wooden drinking cups of various widths and depths, a folding table appeared in front of the kegs. One last fleeting defensive thought seated by his experience in the tall, bald woman's shop flickered through his mind—*I can still hear what's going on outside which means they can hear what's going on inside*—before he relaxed.

The smallest goblets were nothing more than hollowed-out barrel plugs while the larger cups were like lidless, thirty-ounce timber steins. *I am feeling a powerful thirst.* Ben smiled at the greedy thought. Something about the merchant's mannerisms encouraged excess. He took the second-largest mug.

A light snort came from behind him.

Ben turned.

What he had dismissed as a stuffed animal on the inside left proved to be a living, breathing, minotaur. His—*wait, there're udders*—her thick, wooly brown coat made Ben want to reach out and stroke her. However, the array of hilts on her waist and over her back and shoulders kept his curiosity in check.

He gave her a tentative nod.

She nodded back.

If she wanted to cut me down, she would have. Ben faced the quarter kegs and—*it's so nice that Bastion's out for the count*—smiled. The beast probably would've been pounding at his temples for turning his back to a being as armed as she. He held the cup beneath the rightmost spigot. Aromatic, deep brown cider sloshed in, building a mountain of tan bubbles. Ben licked his lips, relished the mug warming in his hands, and kept it under the spout until it petered out. The fully-developed head threatening to spill over the lip.

Wish I could dive in! Ben dipped his nose into the fragrant foam and stole a slow sip of the hot beverage. The mixture of cinnamon and nutmeg—*so good!*—complemented the robust apple flavor as the intense beverage washed his mouth. Through tight lips, he mumbled, "Quite good!" He then swallowed and paused. A subtle flavor

—*walnut?*—washed his palate and poofed away. He smiled fondly at the disarming aftertaste. "Neil, you gotta try this!"

"No, thank you." Neil replied. "I am not thirsty."

Ben turned.

Still engrossed in his tablet, his finger still doing its mad ballet, his schoolmate had stepped just inside the entrance and propped himself, leaning against the minotaur. Not really out of his own thoughts, Neil nodded. "It does smell delicious, though."

"Old family recipe." The merchant gave his paunch a proud pat. "And now, without dinner..." He hobbled to the olive green back wall. "...time for dessert."

Ben followed.

A section as wide as the front opening rolled up and hung there. The merchant lowered his hand. To the left, at a table set for four, a dice game was in progress—*wow, they're playing KKC with real dice*—three guards in brown studded leather, each with a set of wooden and live-steel short swords on their hips, settled into their seats. The little man swept his lowered hand in a gameshow assistant's arc around the room.

Ben's hungry gaze skipped past the gaming table and bopped across multiple oak bookshelves stacked deep with display cases chockfull of spellcards. To the right, seven tablets were presented face-out. His jaw unhinged. He snapped his mouth shut and it eased open again. Ben blurted, "Paydirt!"

In his amazement, Ben had let his drink tip. Searing liquid spilled onto his fingers. *Ah! No!* More splattered and spilt with each rapidly worsening corrective tilt that he made. *No, no, no! Please don't let me drop it!*

The mug lifted from his hand and steadied, hovering in mid-air.

Thank goodness.

Holding it by the handle, a fourth guard—previously invisible—appeared. "Thanks." He winked, took a sip, then sat at the formerly vacant fourth spot at the gaming table, and set the cup next to his dice.

Beyond caring about his lost drink, Ben turned back to Neil, windmilling his hand in small, excited circles. "Neil. Neil!"

"What?" His schoolmate didn't even look up.

All right. Guess I'll shock you into moving. "Get off that minotaur and come in here."

Neil frowned at Ben, and stumbled away from the door guard when he realized he had been resting against a living being.

The minotaur's mouth moved, speaking in the Servant-Giant tongue. "Now I wonder not why the small, oblivious caster could resist the power-aroma of master-class cider, mead, and spirits."

Working his device in spell-prepping taps, Neil took a few worried steps, inching toward Ben.

Seeing where Neil's pale fingers moved, the upper right of his tablet—*he's readying a spell*—Ben decided to offer, "That wasn't a threat."

Neil's power pink eyes flitted to Ben's empty hands before returning to the minotaur. "You speak its language?" Coming next to him, Neil whispered, "What did it say?"

Ben hooked an arm around Neil's shoulder, guiding his schoolmate to the back room. "*She* said, 'nice tablet. Want some cider?'"

Neil continued to whisper. "Tell her, 'thank you, but no thank you.'"

Continuing to direct Neil, Ben glanced back at the door guard and, not thinking about how hard he hit the consonants, replied in the dialect of Giant reserved for leaders and rulers. "He said, 'you're huge and guard well.'"

The minotaur gave her chest a proud thump and snorted.

"By Smitton's Forge," Neil breathed, speaking under his breath signaling his equal astonishment with what the merchant had for sale. "Paydirt, indeed."

Ben removed his arm. He pressed his volume down twice to call Kevin and LeRoy. "Just pinged the guys."

Neil turned to face him. His free hand raised as though to grab Ben's lapel and lowered. He showed Ben his screen. "Is a contract." Neil hit send. "Until you read it, can I get a tentative, verbal response, battle-buddy?"

Battle-buddy. I hadn't even thought of that when I stepped up. "Sure." Ben said, "Pending a thorough read, you have a yes."

"Great." Neil slung his Triforce into its holster. He clapped his hands, hard, once, and turned to the merchant. "Impressive selection of spellcards you have, my good man. How much for one of each?"

Chapter Ten

CONTRACTUAL OBLIGATIONS

WITHOUT BUYING POWER, Ben began to feel sorely out of place. Deciding to put his time to use, he pulled a more manageable cup, filled it with the hot, fragrant cider, and—figuring the minotaur to be the best indicator if trouble broke out—moved a chair to sit on her left.

Not only had Kevin and LeRoy joined Neil in buying stuff, Neil told him later, but nearly every Junior Apprentice, Apprentice, and Senior Apprentice who attended the A.P.A. had come through in an unbelievable precession, haggled, bought, and left before he finished his own in-depth deal.

Engrossed with the contract, Ben hadn't noticed.

Twice he filled up his cup and saw different schoolmates. Each time, the clamor of the bazaar had dropped until by the time Neil had finished and they left the tent only a handful of vendors still called in casual volumes to the meandering patrons which had thinned to the point that the full lengths of several of shopping rows were visible under the soon-to-be dawning sun.

Ben had paused his reading while they returned to their cars in the mostly empty lot. He bid Neil a good night, directed Tex to plot a path to Meadows Towing, and read as his companion directed the car. He didn't notice when they stopped, or even when the sun rose just enough to affect the brightness of his screen.

A freezing chill rushing across the scrapyard got his attention. "Whoa!" Ben sat up straight and scanned the area. A four-foot tall, high-speed frost wave flashed away toward the city. From the wide arc trailing into the distance, the spell must've originated miles further out in the Might-Lands. Still, Ben gave a casual search for incoming casters. None.

The windows on the first floor of Meadows Towing were iced-over. Rows and rows of wrecked cars—*wow, it started off ten feet high*—sported frost, and he could see the power of the spell diminish toward the front gate in the receding level of frost on the row ends. *Well, it's not an attack.* He rubbed his face and tried to stretch away the weariness that had settled into his bones. "Tex, someone's casting *big* magic out there."

Holding the spare Anvilsmith tablet with an iced-over screen, his companioned faced him with an equal film of ice over his lenses. "You don't say."

Ben chucked and pulled the thin sheets away from the round sockets. He didn't know the name of that spell, but had seen the effect before. That wave of frost would continue until it coated enough obstacles to absorb the frost. "We call him Neil the Necromancer, but we should call him Neil the Negotiator."

"Huh?" Tex had remained still like a trained dog being groomed. "I don't think I was a part of whatever conversation you're continuing."

"You should have seen him haggle, Tex." Ben slid his tablet away, lifted his companion—which clung to the extra Anvilsmith—and stood. "Before I went to read, he had already talked the guy down twenty percent; and, from what I'm reading on the forum thread about the bazaar, he got everyone an amazing deal."

Ben stepped over his car door. The top layer of desert hardpan crunched under his boots as he stretch-strolled to the front door. "And then, from what he laid out in this contract... not only could we make some serious coin, we could make almost every spell available for every technomancer to buy."

"Ben," Tex motioned Meadows Towing sign. "The scrapyard makes coin."

"Yeah." Ben gave a non-committal shrug as he entered the spotless kitchen. He set Tex down and went to the refrigerator that had once had been the nastiest appliance he had had ever laid eyes upon. The handle had been so caked-over with crud that only the dull tips of chrome were visible. Now, two months later, he could clearly see his reflection in the handle he would've once only touched with a gloved hand. *The goblins really whipped the place into shape.* "But whatever this place makes belongs those who operate it on a day-to-day basis."

"I don't know..." Tex trailed off. It seemed that he had more to say on the matter, but switched topics. "Mind if I take a look at the contract?"

"Please do. Go ahead and pull it." Ben took an icy cold water bottle. *This should wake me up.* The heater kicked on. *Man, the place sure is quiet...* At home, his family always kept two mundane televisions going, each tuned to a different news channel. He often went to the roof so he could study in relative peace. *...And boy is it nice.*

His device dinged at Tex pulling the document.

Ben cracked the seal, popped open the sports top, and took a swig. *Ah, refreshing.* His eyes went wide. *Ah crap!* He set the bottle down and sent a text to his parents. "Going to be out of the house this weekend. Please reach out if I'm needed for anything."

Apparently waiting for communication, his mother texted back. "Okay."

Ben nodded at the reply. Ever since the Samhain festival, they've been giving him an unbelievable amount of latitude. He stifled a yawn. They no longer batted an eye when he went out or said he was staying out. *Also nice.* His mind switched back to the offer from Neil to go into business together. *Can't believe I have a chance to make real money and help others get spells.*

He scooped his bottle, made his way into the dining room and— might as well get working now—made a left to go down into his basement laboratory.

No sooner had he made it down the last carpeted step, though, then his eyes landed on the spare twin bed he kept near his desk. *Didn't realize how tired I am.* Soft breathing came from the hammock the goblins had fashioned by stitching together scraps of leather upholstery and hung by car door springs. Next to each other, Nuk and Uk'so's combined weight barely weighed the sling down. *Oh yeah, nearly forgot that they're communal sleepers. I better get to my bed upstairs or I'll wake and find them crowding me again.*

I'll just set my coat on the chair... He took off his coat, and did. *Kick my shoes off...* Ben tried, but unlike his school loafers, the mid-calf boots refused to be discarded so easily. *Man...* He sat down on the bed. Under the mounting weight of sleep, unlacing his boots became an arduous task. *I need magic laces or something...* When he finally got one undone, he laid back to kick it off. *Time to struggle with the other...*

BEN REGAINED consciousness hearing soft tapping sounds. *Must be sprinkling.* Diagonally across him, a small warm body weighted on his torso. *Jake must've had nightmares.* He put an arm over his youngest brother and, expecting the soft somewhat wooly feel of the various Disney themed onesies Jake slept in, frowned. *Rawhide?* Almost negligible at first, the tangy smell of—*ug, what is that?*—antiseptic registered when he yawned. *Oh, no. Not again.*

Ben opened his eyes.

Instead of Jake's mess of black hair under his arm, he found the bald brown, tan, and black calico head of Nuk, the bossy goblin. *The warmth against my side, just below Nuk's head must be Uk'so.* Though the second goblin had finally become the solid deep forest green that the orcs often admired in their own kind, Ben's mind conjured the mottled whitish-yellow-green skin that had covered Uk'so's body for the first few weeks. He fought the desperate urge to shove the quiet goblin away. *Easy, Ben. Whatever that was has been remedied.* With how hard Uk'so worked, and how often the others ignored him, Ben felt a bit of kinship with the scrapyard's least valued member.

The soft tapping sounds continued.

Feeling at ease with the goblins, Ben scanned for a window to watch the rain. All around, except for the cement-slabbed ceiling supported by wide square cement columns on cement flooring, the twelve-foot tall walls of the fifty-foot by fifty-foot space were bare, dull gray cinder block. *Wait, I'm in the basement. I shouldn't be able to hear rain.* His gaze went to where his ears estimated the source of the tapping.

Reclining against the springs, Tex sat on the top edge of the hammock, where the Frankensteined leather had been stitched around metal. The robot's lenses held a faint blue light, making its orbital sockets look like dull flashlights, about to wink out.

Ben eyed the one long pointed calico goblin ear he could see. *This'll probably wake them.* He whispered, "How long have I been asleep?"

The goblin's ear twitched.

Tex's lenses rotated to him. Matching the volume perfectly, the robot's synthesized voice answered, "Only two hours. You were up for over thirty so you've got at least six more coming. Go back to sleep."

"No." Practiced at moving Jake without waking him, Ben tried to apply the same gentle tactic to Nuk. "I got work to do."

His gruff, high-pitched voice at the ready, Nuk rolled away from Ben's grasp and elbowed the other goblin. "Up, Uk'so Tuk." Dressed in a Meadows Towing t-shirt and red jeans, Nuk shook his body in two sharp twist. Cracks and pops, clacked. "We got the work to do, too."

So glad I made them start wearing real clothes.

Groggy, the deep green goblin muttered and rolled out of the bed, clad only in blue jeans. His two twists were slow and labored.

Man, now I feel guilty. Ben offered, "Uk'so, if you want to sleep longer, you can."

The hunter green ears, a bit more pointy than that calico's perked up. Uk'so stroked his lengthy, angled chin with his three-fingered hands as though he actually considered taking Ben up on an offer— *that's a first.*

Ben had finally gotten Nuk to keep from dragging Uk'so around. This moment built hope in Ben's chest. *Do it. Just jump back on the bed and I'll back your play.*

Nuk rasped something that sounded like a heavily accented, "Saturday."

Uk'so nodded, scooped up his Meadows Towing tee, and headed toward the stairs.

Nuk followed.

Ben listened as they padded up the carpeted stairs. Nuk had a habit of smacking Uk'so when things weren't done to his exacting standard, and the slow rouse probably qualified. *You better not slap him, Nuk.* Though he gave orders, Ben figured the calico would find a way to circumvent them. A few second passed. He didn't hear a slap. Instead, a vacuum whirled to life.

Keeping an ear out for Nuk's petty physical dominance, Ben sat on the metal folding chair and made a dissatisfied face as he scooted into the shallow hollow under the four-legged wooden desk. *I need to get a real chair and a real desk. In fact, that's the first thing I'll do with my proceeds.*

Ben reached into his pocket, pulled one of the spellcards—*hmm, burnt orange case with royal blue spirals. Wonder what spell is in this inside* —and opened the shallow drawer. He took out a thin flat-head screwdriver, and pried at the fine line on the edge of the casing holding the two halves shut. *Only one way to find out.*

Chapter Eleven

PLAYING WITH POWER

THE SPELLCARD OPENED WITH A SNAP. *Crap, did I break it?* Ben checked the thin slats on the top card. All four were fine. *No matter how many times I do this, I always feel like I've broken it.* He sniffed at the rubber cement that had kept the two halves bound together, trying to get a hint at the card's origin. *Kiwi? Hmph, none of the major distributors use Kwik's kiwi scented sealant*—he paused feeling a bit honored—*maybe this card is from Australia.* He smiled at the possibility of working on a card that had traveled around the world.

Ben, set both halves on the desk, and pulled out his headband with a magnifying glass attached to it from the drawer. *Crap, the Liquid Forge Neil bought is still in the car.* Ben slipped the headband on and glanced back at Tex.

Tapping on the tablet, his companion still sat poised on the top hammock springs with one leg crossed over the other.

Ben folded a cuff back and continued to roll his sleeve up to his forearm. "Hey, Tex. What'cha up to?"

Tex didn't look up. "Playing Dragon, Deities, and Divinity."

Ben chuckled, shook his head, and worked on his other sleeve. "Hate to tell you this, but that's just a re-wrap of Kings, Clergy, and Coffers."

"Well..." Tex rocked his head to the side. "Yes and no. There are different calls to learn and more dice to unlock. In fact, I've collected all of the sets in K.C.C., including Ob, and the forums say TripD unlocks gems with an ultra-rare Ast set."

Jeeze, he sounds just like the addicts at school. All I really heard was him justifying the amount of time he's pouring into it. "Well, could you take a quick break and do me a favor?"

"Sure." Tex dropped the tablet into the hammock and started down. "What is it?"

"Please retrieve the small brown paper bag Neil left in the backseat." Ben turned back to the desk. "There should be a four ounce squeeze bottle in it."

Tex's metal feet *tinked* on the cement floor as he hustled to the stairs. "Will do."

"Thanks, buddy." Ben flipped his magnifying glass down and focused on the bottom half of the card. *Now, what do we have here?* He pointed with the flattop screwdriver as he gave the card's innards a thorough once over. *Standard Anvilsmith circuit board layout. They've got the obdurium strip at the back...* He rolled his eyes and sighed. *It's like since they found what works, no one tries to innovate any more. Wait, hold on a second, why'd they use a three on two diode config instead of three on one?* He followed the tiny wires to the memory core interface and found two single thin obdurium steel strips fused together to accept power and trigger the memory. "Ohhhh." He grabbed his forehead. "That's why! My cards need another strip to provide enough power to trigger second tier spells."

"Ohhhh." Mocking him, Tex's voice preceded him coming down the stairs. "You do know you're speaking gobbly-gook."

Ben flipped up his magnifying glass and smirked. "Listen here, Mr. Ob, Trip D, and Ast. I don't want to hear anything about not making sense from you." Holding the chair to his bottom, Ben hiked up, turned to face the stairs, and set himself and the chair back down with a clunk. *I really need to get a swivel chair.* "By the way, just figured out why I could transfer my mid-tier spells to the SD cards, but they wouldn't fire."

Water sports bottle strapped to its chest with a thick rubber band, Tex came down without the bag. In one hand he held a glass saucer and in the other, the clear plastic bottle with four ounces of pearly white. On the front, in large, molten-steel orange text, it read *Liquid Forge*. "Ben." His companion's synthesized voice hit a rare serious tone. "This stuff is dangerous. Especially when applied to obdurium."

Ben took the saucer and the Liquid Forge. He scanned the back and found the warning. *Use extreme caution when working with precious metals. Only to be used with obdurium by licensed, bonded, and insured professional smelters.* The last line gave him a moment's pause. "Just how dangerous is it?"

Tex flipped his puncture point forward and cut the rubber band. "Oh, how about Pepcon dangerous?"

Pepcon. Ben rolled the word around in his head as he took the cold bottle of water. *It's not just a word. It's a name...* He couldn't remember. "Pepcon? Why is that name both familiar and forgettable?"

Tex asked, "How about putting it in conjunction with May fourth, 1988?"

"Nope." Ben popped the water bottle top and took a sip. *Mmm.* He read the label. *Lemon infused.* "If I have to guess, I'm going to need another clue."

Tex stroked his chin. "Old Henderson?"

"Well, besides that being from before I was born..." Ben tried to place the name again. It solidified for a split-second before fading. *Nope. Still don't know.* He shook his head.

"Wow." Tex whistled. "Before you open the Liquid Forge, let me show you something on your tablet."

Ben flipped up the cover from the holster and watched Tex's tiny fingers navigate to the HistTube video archives. *History Tube? It's not fair to have school flashbacks while on Yuletide break.* Ben's eyelids already started to feel heavy. "Not this site, Tex. Anywhere but this site."

"Sorry, they have the best info." Tex made his way back to the hammock and pulled himself in.

Ben marveled at the goblins' ingenuity. *Wow, the springs didn't make a sound.*

"Besides." Text continued, "That's just a short, two-minute clip. There's a butt-load more information there if you want it."

"Nah, two minutes should do." Ben lifted his tablet, leaned back in his seat, and hit play. The video opened with a view from a hill showing the expansive desert brown earth around two manufacturing plants in the valley below. *Hard to believe the sprawling industrial city of Old Hendo had once been nothing, but a bunch of sagebrush. No one at school would believe it.* The video fast-forwarded to show a fire at one of the plants with white smoke pluming up to the sky.

The spare Anvilsmith strapped to his back, Tex lifted the two prize bags full of spellcards Ben had won at the Conjurers Course during the Samhain festival.

"Hey." Ben asked, "Where are you going with those?"

Tex continued toward the stairs. "Just keep watching."

Ben turned his attention back to the screen. The small fire ballooned into a massive explosion. Dirt shot up into the sky obliterating the early white plumes. A dust-filled shockwave rolled across the desert hardpan. The sight made his guts quiver. About to speak to Tex, his Anvilsmith speakers blew air into his hands when the thunderous boom of the rolling repercussion hit.

Holy! He dropped his device and scooped it out of the air before it completed a swing in his holster.

Before his eyes, a second blast—*that's more powerful than the first one*—blew black smoke up through the massive dirt cloud still in the air. He thumbed down his volume before the blast hit and it still rocked his speakers.

Stunned, Ben watched as the camera zoomed out to take in the massive black and brown smoke-haze clouds which also underscored just how powerful the explosions had been and just how unpopulated Henderson had been.

Tex came back down the stairs with Uk'so who now wore the long black apron and thick yellow kitchen gloves, which—before Ben laid down rules—had been the only items close to clothing that the goblins wore. Presenting two of the prize cards, Tex asked, "So, you see?"

"Yeah. Oh, yeah." Ben unstrapped his spellcard holder, holster—device and all—to hand them to Tex. He folded his trench coat, laid it over Uk'so's arms, and pulled his school tie off to go with the coat. Ben grabbed the Komir necklace and considered the gold castle inlayed in ruby surrounded by gold. He rubbed the small etched disc behind the highest tower. *Even the sun's not too high for them.* About to take it off, he triggered the protective charm and tethered its power need to his Argosian font. "Just in case."

Tex nodded. "Well, it couldn't hurt."

Ben patted himself down and felt a small prick. *Right, the little sword.* He took the token snatched from the magic weapon that had attacked him and handed it over. "Oh." Ben snapped the open card on this desk shut, and handed it off. "That's everything."

"Except for the Liquid Forge." Tex reminded. "I brought the saucer so you could dole some out for use."

"Yup." Following the instructions, Ben held the bottle upside down by its base and tapped the tip directly on the glass. The tip starred open and two droplets escaped before he could right-side the bottle which closed itself. He handed it off. "Here you go."

"Be careful." Tex took it and motioned for Uk'so to go with him. The goblin followed.

Ben rubbed his hands together and turned to the desk. He cracked open both SD cards, checked the slats—*both still good*—and, quite practiced at the process from changing spellcard casings, made short work of removing the obdurium strips with the flathead screwdriver and a pair of tweezers.

Okay. He removed the headband, put it away and reached for a toothpick. His mouth went dry. *Time to start making money.* He laid one of the thin obdurium ribbons on the saucer. Dipped the toothpick on the Liquid Forge and—*easy, easy does it*—applied it to most of the strip, leaving the tip dry so the excess had a place to go. *Alright, step one down. We got the bread, the spread.* He wiped his lips with the back of his hand and picked up the other obdurium strip with the tweezers. *One more slice and this sandwich is done.*

As he moved the tweezed ribbon toward the first, the one on the plate slid away slightly.

Huh? "Okay..." *Must be a matter of angle of approach.* He twisted his wrist and came at the Liquid Forge slick strip from the side. *It jumped again.*

Ben sighed. He pulled double-sided tape from the drawer that he typically used to affix his own custom labels to his spellcards. He put a piece on the saucer. *Then tap you into position with the screwdriver and press you down so you don't go nowhere this time...* Again, he picked up the dry obdurium ribbon with the tweezers and moved it toward the stuck strip.

As he moved them closer, the sheen on the stuck strip dried up. *Huh. Did it evaporate?* He bent to judge the reaction when the obdurium slivers were an inch from each other and felt slight resistance.

The ribbon he controlled curved away from the desk. A fine lather began to bubble on the stuck strip giving off tiny white flashes. *Crap!* He yanked his arm away. The flashes intensified to strobe light his action. *Horribly concerting!* A white arc spanned from the obdurium on the saucer to the strip in his hand, and he stumbled back out of his chair to get away from the one on the table.

A scorching flashed washed over him.

Then another.

"Holy shi—

One more.

BOOM!

Chapter Twelve

AGONY

*...Darkness...every bit of me...hurts...bad...*Cool water sprinkled on the back of Ben's neck and trickled down to his lower back before is spread outwards from whatever he sat against. *...Is it raining? ... Where... Where am I?...*The front of his body, his arms, his face, his ears, his head, his lower legs. All of it pounded with each pulse of blood through his system. A relentless two-tone warbled ringing filled his head. *...What's that...that noise?* He tried to lift his head to see. Searing pain washed the world white. Then unconsciousness... And again…

A faint stream of hot, thick air worked through a nostril...*Am I no longer in my lab? What...what's that horrible stench?...Maybe if I—* Ben tried to open his eyes and it felt like someone shoved coals against them. He tried to jerk away. Agony flooded his system. He went out...

...If I could look up... Out again.

Next time he came to, the steady patter of rain around him, running cool down his back relaxed his mind for a moment. The rain also landed on his upper legs. *...Why's it raining on my back and legs...I'm— I'm sitting up—propped up. Can't open my eyes. Can't... Can't move at all. Stuck. How...how damaged am I?* Each beat of his heart pumped blood. Everywhere the blood went reported pain. *My stomach hurts the most... The ringing.*

He listened.

The horrible high-pitch whines inside his head had ceased and a horrible—*at least it's external*—alarm rung rapid—*ear piercing, skull-splitting*—bells. The rings would break for a gruff voice yelling in a harsh language full of hard consonants. Then the alarm would continue.

Slowly, open your eyes. Ben tried. *They feel fused shut, but the rest of the pain.* He considered his overall condition like a burning wood smell piggybacked on the faint air already pregnant with other horrible smells. *It's not so bad, except—* His throat tightened. He swallowed. The air passageway through his sinuses nose grew a bit wider. *Why does my stomach still blaze?* The yelling between bells repeated. *It's the same message, and in Giant. Is that Ur-Krurk?* Ben tensed. The world behind his eyes flashed white. He desperately clung to consciousness. *Impossible. He's imprisoned.*

"Put out the fire or I'll roast all of you alive!"

It is Ur-Krurk. It must be a recording the ogre made, which means that I am still at Meadow's Towing; but, then, why is it raining? A bit of sound reasoning began to return. *Try something else.*

Ben tried to move his arm. *Arm feels fine. Is something holding me down?* He forced his arm to bend and something on top of his skin cracked sending light, stinging sensations into the crook so his elbow and shoulder. *Good. I can move. Now, what's over my face?* The pressure from his hand registered on his rigidly stiff fingers and forehead, but—*something's between them*—dulled his ability to feel.

Focusing, Ben forced his fingers to bend a segment at a time. Light stings registered there, too, before feeling returned and he had a handful of the nullifier. *What is this bumpy stuff? Sort of feels like—uh!—they feel like scabs.*

His thoughts went back to the obdurium and the bubbling Liquid Forge. The Pepcon explosion—*that horrible earth-shaking might*—played in his mind's eye. *I should have moved my hand away instead of leaning closer.* The strobe effect which had made him feel as though he moved in slow motion came back clear. *Wait. No, I did move away.*

The alarm stopped and, besides infrequent drips, so did the rain. A stampeding rush of footsteps clomped down the stairs.

I am in my lab.

Orcs rarely smiled and were almost never surprised which made the collective, astonished gasps that much more disconcerting.

I must be a flippin' mess.

A deep voice—*Toad*—wavered as it whispered in Giant. "Might-Fist?" The orc cleared his throat and switched to English. "Ben?"

Ben lifted his hand to acknowledge hearing his name. He then raised a finger. *Just give me a minute guys.* He motioned to the constant pain in his stomach. *Just need a bit longer to heal.*

A lone set of footsteps sloshed to him. Something pressed against his torso, cracking the slab of scab like a bug, just above the pain. The stabbing torment returned to his stomach as something long and thick was pulled out of him. A *thunk* sounded off the wall across room and a light splash followed.

Better. It did hurt, but almost like—Ben struggled to equate the feeling of the object leaving his body to anything else and grimaced inwardly at the only comparison that came to mind—*like being constipated passing.* He went to shake his head against the visual. His scabbed eyes denied the move. *How about it's just better.* He gave a thumbs up.

As though pulled by a magnet, Ben's hand went to where the intrusion had been. His fingers dropped into a moist, gooey hole. *Ugh! I just touched my guts!* His lips moved in his scabbed mask and he rocked back hard enough to crack the remaining casing that held his torso still and smack the back of his head against the wall, which didn't compare. *I just touched my guts!* He gave his hand rapid shakes to get the sticky gunk to fly from his hand. *I'm in water.* He splashed his hand down and waved it in the water.

When the frantic disgust finally passed, Ben heard Counselor Eastly's husky whisper from lessons long since passed. "We make mistakes to learn. Each mistake is a gift. It's called experience. If you think one day you may not remember, you should keep a token to keep you true. Make mistakes. Learn. And repeat. And repeat."

This'll be a horribly grisly reminder, but I definitely don't want to make this mistake again. Ben began to scrunch his features and gingerly lift the edge of the thick scab mask. He took extra care around the sticking points at the corners of his mouth. Able to, he drew a deep inhalation of disgusting air. *Tastes like smoke from a funeral pyre.* The corners around his nose—*easy, Ben. Easy*—also proved a bit tricky. Worst of the three, his eyes as he pulled off—*Ow! Ow! Ow!*—the scant few eyelashes on the inner corner of his right eye hadn't been burnt away.

Bright at first, the room darkened rapidly with each fluttering blink Ben took, as his eyes adjusted to the dim, single row of emergency lights down the center of the room. An orc stood over him. *Toad?* Lit from behind, Ben only had the shape of the body to work from. *No, too broad. Jek? How peculiar. I would've bet that Toad would've been the first to help me. Yup, there's that salami smell.* He held his disappointed sigh. *Crap. It is Jek.* Though he didn't harbor an active dislike for the orc, it would be a long time coming before Ben could forgive the orc who had retrieved him from the Samhain festival and then sat on the sidelines as he, and the other Meadow Towing orcs, fought for their lives.

A glint of steel, close to Ben's body, caught his eye.

The large orc, with grim business in his pale green eyes, leaned close. In his massive green hand, his blood-dagger.

It's angled to cut my throat.

Chapter Thirteen

A TROPHY LIKE NO OTHER

I DON'T KNOW *how either ogre shot bolts of raw magic without actually casting, but answer wrong Jek, and you're getting my full reserve.* Ben amped up his Argosian font, narrowed his eyes at Jek and, in a low, suspicious tone, asked, "What are you doing?"

"Looks like you're trying to keep it whole. "Jek's gaze shifted to Ben's forehead and then bounced around from his temples to his ears. "Which means cutting where the scab meets hair that didn't burn."

"Oh." Keeping a wary eye on the blade, Ben breathed a bit easier. "Thanks. And you're right. I do want this."

"Let me." Jek placed his large hand on top of Ben's head and moved the knife behind Ben's ear.

Be cool. If he really wanted me dead, he would've shot me when I was in his truck. To show his patience, and ready to pull back if he didn't like the feel—*the pain's nearly gone*—Ben folded his hands on his stomach, which was still covered with crusty remnants. *Is it healed?* He couldn't bring himself to let his fingers wander where the hole in his gut had been. *It could just be numb.*

Jek's nearness pressed the salami smell which began to overpower the nasty order.

What, does he use the meat as cologne?

The orc slid the cold metal blade across his cowlick and met little resistance.

Whoa! My hairline's way back there?

Jek's thick fingers landed on his ears and pulled gently. "I don't think there's a way to keep this intact with the ears."

"That's fine." *Can't believe I'm really going to keep this.* "Just as much as possible."

Jek's feet sloshed in the water as the orc moved around him to get the best angles to slide his dagger along the scabbed hairline across his crown. The tip moved expertly behind his ears in a way Ben had only experienced at barber shops. *I wonder.* "Jek, do you cut hair?"

"No." Driving the blade home into the scabbard clipped inside his jeans, Jek shook his head. "This was like demasking, and after a few hundred, you sort of gain a knack for it."

What's demasking? Opening his mouth to ask, Ben drew a quick breath—*not sure I really want to know*—and closed it. *At least, not right now.*

"Work the back, Ben," Jek said, sloshing a few feet away. "If you're careful, you'll have the thing whole."

Ben closed his eyes. Gathering a bit of courage, he did as suggested —*can't believe I'm doing this*—and lifted from the back. Like pulling off a helmet—*a bit snug against the temples*—he removed the fragile trophy from his face.

Raucous cheers and hoots erupted from the stairs. Feet splashed into the water and trudged toward him.

Open your eyes. Ben turned the scabbed shell-face around to face his own. *Open. Your. Eyes.*

He did.

Chapter Fourteen

CONTROLLING INTEREST

PULLING the cotton Meadow's Towing extra-large—*hard to believe this is the smallest size they have*—white t-shirt down over his head, Ben gathered the excess, tucked it into his blue jeans, and cinched his belt tight to keep it in place. As he came down the carpet-blasted-away, bare, blackened stairs, a gust of wind—*can barely smell that I blew everything up*—worked his loose sleeves and neckline to billow the shirt around him. He chuckled at himself. *Except for the purple star logo on my chest, I look like the Stay Puff Marshmallow Man.* With a *galoosh*, each of his backup pair of black books splashed down into the debris-strewn, mid-shin deep, sooty water.

He eyed the extension cords, some yellow, some red, duct taped to scrubbed clean spots on the blackened ceiling. Like bizarre Christmas lights, a series of car headlights ran the length of the room, creating make-shift rows of ceiling lights. *Wow, those goblins can jury-rig anything.*

His mind's eye went back to the bubbly-swoll of the scab mask made from his burnt flesh fused with whatever chemical reaction the liquid forge and obdurium made. His fingers recalled, all too clearly, the hard bumpy texture of the light-weight reminder to be ultra-careful. Ben shook them to try and lose the feeling.

The ashen water rippled from the force of an industrial, five-foot diameter fans in each of the three other corners. *While they push the air out, they also force the lighter junk toward the stairs.* Mindful of wreckage, floating buckets, and dark green Rubbermaid garbage cans, Ben trudged against the wind, Anvilsmith swinging against his leg, to the lone, four-foot tall, dark brown metal barrel set in the middle of the long wall opposite the stairs.

Hoisting himself onto the barrel. Ben worked his Orion spellcard from his jeans pocket and marveled at how black the formerly gray cinder-block walls were. *How much worse would that have been if Tex hadn't shown me that Pepcon video?* He found his head shaking. *Instead of still kicking, I might have kicked the bucket.* "Well." He exhaled hard to push the morbid wonder out of his mind. "Time to help with clean up."

Ben called the emerald energy from his Anvilsmith to go into his spellcard. Instead of just enough power to summon five gorillas snapping across his skin, in a flash, the Anvilsmith's full reserve flushed into him, looped around his chakras—*I have an eighth one?*—and poured into the card. The excess energy, a majority of what had flowed into him, dumped back into the tablet.

The Argosian energy in his chest crackled. The Krotostian energy in his gut howled. The Nilosian font in his head sizzled.

Bastion stirred. Ben found his lips moving to voice Bastion's question. "What are you up to, Host?"

Holy! Ben slap-covered his mouth. *He's using my mouth to talk.*

Muffled by his own hands, Bastion answered Ben's thought with his mouth. "Yes and you should use it to answer me."

Ben tried to steel his thoughts so they couldn't be read.

"*I am* your mind." Bastion's sinister, rumbling laugh filled his head. "You can't possibly shut me out." "Nor—" Bastion began to scour Ben's recent memories. "—can you keep secrets from me."

A cold numbing sense of betrayal filled Ben as Bastion rooted through his mind. The cold gave way to a building heat.

"Oh, you don't like this?" Not finding anything for the night, Bastion began to sift through Ben's last day at school before the Yuletide break. "You should be honored to by my host."

Anger formed a knot between his eyes. Ben thought his reply, *I'm not.*

"Well." Bastion stopped Its rooting around Ben's private thoughts. "In that case, if you really want me out, just tell me to get out."

Get out.

"No." Bastion's deriding laughter salted Ben's rubbed raw betrayal. "Tell me with your own words. I want the world to hear you tell me to leave."

Ben went to open his mouth. *What the Hell?* All feeling in his mouth —his sense of taste, his awareness of saliva—fled. Suddenly, he could move his lips, but had zero use of this throat. *He's toying with me.* Then, Bastion released use of his throat, but held all air locked in his lungs. *Asshole.*

Bastion took full control of Ben's body to punch himself in the eye. Hard. "You're my meat-puppet and only have freedom so long as I choose to give it to you." As though pulling covers over itself, Bastion rolled over in the Nilosian font.

"Once I'm done, I'll leave you to your pitiful life," the Beast said. Ben's fist plowed into his other eye. "Don't try to undo my plans." Ben's hands untucked his shirt, worked under the white cotton for a moment before ripping the coffee cup-wide, three-inch thick scab away. Bastion dropped it in the water.

Control and feeling came back to his body. His eyes hurt, but his gut lit with pain from the deeply seated scab being yanked out. Ben had to work to keep from falling off of the barrel.

Inside his head, Bastion's savage voice stung Ben's brain as it continued inside his head. *Or you'll be sorrier than you could ever imagine.*

His five conjured green gorillas, which had remained idle while Bastion seized control, rubbed each other's head as they usually did. After hundreds of cycles devoted to cleaning up during detention— mostly given by Senior Adept Collins—they got to work on the task at hand.

Ben's ability to regenerate made short work of the pulsing aches radiating from his eyes. He pulled his shirt up so the bloodied cotton would get fused to his stomach as the wound started the scabbing process, again.

However, the insult—*Bastion has dominion over my body. How'd that happen?*—continued to fester.

Chapter Fifteen

THE ART OF NOT BLOWING UP

BEN STOOD at the corner of the basement where the blackened metal and glass had been piled. Without working the soot away from the surface, he had to use shapes to tell what was what. *Springs from the goblins hammock... The steel toe parts of my Tore Vex steel-toed boots... Is that the saucer?*

He scooped up the pitch black, tiny plate that had held the Liquid Forge and turned the grungy dish over in his hands. *Curious. I don't know how this survived whatever kind of energy created by that explosion, but I would've thought it would have at least broken when it hit the ground.*

His gazed shifted to a thin, cylindrical piece of metal that used to be the screwdriver pinched on the end to work tiny screws lying on the ground beyond the saucer. *Ah, there is it.* He set the black coated glass down and picked up the handleless, tiny metal shaft. *So, this is what's left?* He sniffed it. *Hmph, smells like, uh...* He searched for a comparison and came up short of a single option. *Sort of smells like a mix of coal and ozone.*

A quick grin spread his lips. *Man, Adept Floyd would flip his lid if I brought this into the Electronics Lab.*

Ben's smile widened at the thought of the Adept's pinched-up face turning a furious red over a double violation of his Lab Commandments. The Adept called them rules, but everyone made a grandiose mockery over the trivialities that would make Floyd go red – which was great fun, until he handed out detention. Without a handle, the shaft of Ben's screwdriver would break Grand Commandment #25 - *Thy tools must have thine name on it* and Grand Commandment #1 - *Thine tools shall be in perfect working order.*

Recalling the bright white flash before the explosion, Ben's amusement drained away.

Now I know why he's such a stickler. Ben nodded, a plan forming in his head. *I'm going to copy his rules, word for word, and post them down here as a reminder.* Ben eyed a section of wall just inside the basement where they would be most visible. *Well, not number twenty-five. That one's a bit much.*

He returned to scanning the pile.

Looks like only glass and metal survived the blast. Scanning for any exceptions, Ben nodded in understanding at a nearly forgotten question as to why everything in the circuitry portion of the Academy's Electronics Lab—*including the very uncomfortable chairs that make your butt fall asleep halfway through class*—had been composed of metal parts. *So, I need to get a metal chair, and a cushion.*

Not needing anything else from the charred pile, Ben wiped his hands on his jeans. *Well, if at first you don't succeed...*

He quickly went about the building gathering another saucer, another drop of Liquid Forge, and two more spellcards that he had won at the Samhain festival. When he returned to the basement, he stood at the metal drum that he'd been sitting on earlier. *It's as good a workstation as I have right now; and, if I have to suddenly get clear of the flashpoint again, I won't have a chair in the way.*

Stifling a yawn, Ben worked the thin flathead into the grooves of one spellcard and then the next. Each opened with a snap. Tweezers! Ben went back to the jumbled mass of blackened objects, and searched the for tiny tool. *I must be getting tired. I didn't even check to see if I broke them.*

He returned to the drum and gave each half of spellcard a cursory check. *No broken slats. Good.*

Returning to the pile of debris, he searched through the smaller items for a bit before—*ah ha!*—pulling the tweezers from the blackened junk, then shuffled back to the drum and tweezed the obdurium strip from both cards.

He shook his head at the standard circuit board in each and stuffed the four halves of the powerless SD spellcard into his pocket. *Alright.* About to scoop into Liquid Forge, he paused, and rubbed his jaw. *Now to use just enough to wet one strip.*

He cautiously dabbed the flathead screwdriver shaft in the clear liquid and gave one of the strips a dainty coat.

Okay.

His mouth dried out.

"Okay."

As he reached his tweezers to the dry, thin rectangle of obdurium, a nervous flutter filled his gut and his heart started to thump like an orcish war drum. Worse, his hand shook a little.

Get it together. Focused on steadying himself, Ben drew a deep breath in through his nose, concentrated on fully expanding his lungs, and let it out slow. *Fear is an excuse not to try.* His thumping heart eased. He took in another deep inhalation. *You know what will happen. It might hurt like a son of a bear, but you'll survive.* His hand became sure. A conceited quote from Senior Adept Collins that everyone else at the school seemed incapable of not repeating—a viral earworm—pinged in his head. *Fear is for lesser folk.*

Ben shook his head to clear the arrogant infection and spoke his original thought. "Fear is an excuse not to try."

Hand perfectly steady, he reached out and picked the dry strip of metal up with his tweezers. Focusing on the reaction of the wet strip, Ben started with his hand extended his full arm's length behind him. It was as far from the other as he could make it. Taking his time, he eased the dry strip in little by little.

His hand just past his ear, a white flash popped in his peripheral vision.

A jolt of energy shot clamped down on his fingers, pinching them on the tweezers before reporting down his arm.

Oh shi—

The room flashed white. His wrist twisted. Hard.

Ah!

As though he were arm wrestling with a force much greater than he could begin to resist, his forearm spasmed and his bicep cramped. His shoulder tightened bitterly.

I'm not going to cry out in pain. Not going to call others to be blown— Ben screwed his face up as the energy ran painfully along his collar bone to his other shoulder and up his neck—*here we go again. Agonytown. Population me.*

The vision of the double Pepcon blast rang back.

And then…

…then…

…nothing?

Then his neck relaxed and the tightness in his shoulders eased. As did his bicep and his forearm. *Not out of trouble yet.* He rubbed his wrist and tried to get his fingers to release the black tweezers. *Can't let go. Almost feels like I dipped them in Colossal Glue.*

Wait, get back!

Scanning for the Liquid Forge-wetted strip that had been there—*it's gone*—Ben scooted away from the barrel.

No flashing lights. Almost afraid to think it, the thought—*I just might be in the clear*—went through his head when he backed into the opposite wall and began to breathe again. *At least there wasn't an earth shattering boom.*

Trying to let go again, Ben tried to get his fingers to part and—*ow, ow, ow!*—ripped scab away from his index finger. Blood welled in the gash and dried into another scab.

The tweezers remained embedded in the meat of his thumb.

Then, like watching a lit, slow-motion, carbon-snake firework turns from a small chunk of black material into a long stem of spent ash, a morbid fascination kept his gaze locked on tweezers as—encased in a thick, growing scab—they pushed themselves out of this thumb. He held his other hand open beneath to catch them, as the scab fell away with the tweezers. His fingerprints grew out from of the bald, flat flesh.

"Wow." *That was sort of cool.*

Instead of the lone obdurium steel strip being held by the tweezers tips, he found the second strip hugging the first around one of the tweezer's open prongs. *Oh, that's where it went.*

He began to ease the strips off. *They almost feel like strong magnets pulling on each other.*

The strips came off the end with a snap of white light and gust of electrified wind.

Ben shuddered and froze.

Black smoke rose as the two steel strips ground on each other. They became flush, still, and stopped smoking.

Ben remained still, waiting for anything else to happen. He asked, "Are you guys done?" Feeling as though he was tempting fate, he quickly added, "If not, don't blow up. Just take your time. I'm not in a hurry."

Stuffing the tweezers into his pocket, Ben took one of the dozen abandoned Rubbermaid bins to a corner of the room, sat it open end down, and placed the bonded—*or bonding*—obdurium on it.

Meticulously picking the process apart in his head, he went up to his room, retrieved two more cards and came back down. "Okay, so the flash happened when I had them about three feet apart."

Ben grabbed two more of the bins and sat them, open end down, six feet away from each other. Then he cracked opened two more cars, checked the slots—all good—and removed the obdurium from each to place one strip on each bin. After applying a light dusting of Liquid Forge, he pushed one bin toward the other.

Four feet apart, the two small pieces of metal flew together, snapping light, wind, and smoke as they fell to the cement floor. Like before, black smoke rose from for a few seconds, then stopped.

He picked them up, put them on a bin and—*no need to see what the flash is like if two pairs come together*—minded the other pair in the opposite corner.

Thinking about getting another couple pairs going, the goblins gave out heart wrenching screams.

Oh no, another attack! Ben sprinted across the room and, taking two at a time, bounded up the stairs.

Chapter Sixteen

RUNNING ON FUMES

M<small>EATY SMACKS</small>—*COMBAT!*—<small>CAME</small> from upstairs. *Someone beating the goblins with their fists.*

Adrenaline flooded his body. Ben lunged harder up the stairs.

From playback of the battle that took place on this very ground last month, Ben had learned the video game clanks of weapons striking bodies paled when compared to the true flesh-cleaving *thumps*, bone splitting *thunks*, and true cries of pain.

Pine scent growing. No fire. Reflexively raising his arm to guard against an incoming attack, Ben leapt up the last three steps, then stopped, staring in amazement. The goblins were smacking *their own bodies* while screeching at the screen.

Nuk ended an angry-sounding string of syllables with *wemic*. Uk'so spun to present his rhinestone-clad posterior to the television and smacked his butt at the man/lion graciously explaining the "unique and astounding power of angel feathers" to them.

Just as animated, Uk'so opted for the more common obscene gestures, alternating between one middle finger, then the other middle finger, and finally both middle fingers at once.

Laughter rolled in Ben's chest. He covered his mouth—*hold it together!*—rounded the banister to rush up to the second floor, and leapt the trapped stair just one down from the landing. Having made it up to the hallway outside his room, Ben couldn't hold back anymore and soft chuckles began to escape him.

Don't want them to think I got a bit of perverse joy in them experiencing the same frustration I felt after the bonus stage. Ben snapped his fingers at the lost opportunity. *Man, that would have made an epic Dragon Sage 3, Wemic Reaction video.*

Chuckling freely, Ben stepped into his room. *Hmm, it's a bit chilly.*

Like a Roman emperor perched on a mountain of pillows on top of the brown fur blanket covering the California king beg, Tex looked up from a tablet with an expectant look.

Ben waved a hand to discount his mirth. "Can't put it into words, buddy. But, if you want a good chuckle, watch the goblins react to the Great Sphinx bonus level in a couple of hours." A full belly laugh rolled through him at the thought. "In fact, please do take the time to watch it." He shook with excitement. "Oh! And record it. I'm not going to show it to anyone, but I'd like to see it, too."

"Will do." Tex nodded, then pointed to the sun through the Plexiglas ceiling. "Not including the explosion, you've been at it for more than twenty-four hours." The robot patted the bed. "You probably should lie down before you fall down.

Ben gave a discounting wave, pulled the eight spellcard halves from his pocket, and plopped down into his cushy high-backed desk chair to work at the backup—*now, only*—soldering station that he had set up on the large oak desk. "Bring the tablet, please."

Tex thumped onto the floor.

"And I will. I will." Ben plucked two board-halves from the pile in his hand and let the remaining six halves clatter unheeded onto the desk. *Alright, I'll set my soon-to-be scrap board here, and...* He leaned his elbows on the desktop, and pinched the medium binding clip to place the edge of the card under the clamp. "I just want to get one of these done so I'm just a strip insertion away from having a completed card when I wake."

Tex tapped his leg.

Ben reached down and, instead of just taking the tablet, lifted his companion holding the tablet up to sit on the edge of the desk. He took the Anvilsmith. "Thanks, Tex." *Though I built the schematic and ran it through the om-testers, I want to save the first build of my improved spellcard board.* "Hey, do me a favor. Record this process."

"Okay." Tex stood. His optics wound a little. "Alright. I have a good angle. Say 'go' when you're ready to record, and when making some of the tight printing, remember that I'm on your right."

"Understood." Tapping, *School Work*, *Electronics*, and *Circuitry* on his tablet, Ben scrolled to the middle of the thirty icons and tapped the folder entitled *Circuitry III: Final Project.* He refamiliarized himself with his blueprint, picked up his tools and said, "Go."

Adjusting his pendant-mount desk lamp for better lighting, he swiveled the magnifying glass over and carefully removed circuits from his scrap board to meticulously solder them onto what would become his masterboard. Fighting against the adrenaline dump and surmounting the weariness of the day, Ben kept his hand steady as he relocated diodes, one by one, onto the new master card. He yawned. *Just a few more.*

His hand dipped and he yanked his arm back to keep from burning the board. *Nope. I'm zonked.*

Running on a sort of last-ditch autopilot, Ben rolled the chair from the desk to his bed, crawled on, and put on his sleeping mask to block out the sun.

Tex asked, "Hey, Ben. Do you mind if I…

Chapter Seventeen

A SENSE OF OWNERSHIP

BEN DREW A DEEP, waking breath. *Bacon. How do the goblins know when I'm going to wake?* On the dense furs, he stretched and twisted. His back sent a series of crisp, relieving pops into the complete silence. *No TVs droning on. No siblings arguing. Just me, and my thoughts. Now, this is how to wake up.*

A soft, rhythmic tapping came from up in his closet.

What's that? Exhaling, Ben removed his sleep mask. In the closet, up on the shelf above his clothes, the glow of his Anvilsmith lit Tex lounging on a couple of hand towels. His companion had set up a cushy little throne for himself next to Kermit—Ben's first companion. The small robot had the tablet propped against the wall with Dragon, Deities, and Divinity on the screen. *Junkie.*

Ben rolled onto his back to gaze out beyond the Plexiglas ceiling into a sky darkening from a deep plum to a midnight blue. As usual, only a few stars shone through. Several clouds ranged high and full of the deep oranges and reds, holding onto the last bit of distant sunlight like delicate candle-boats on a dark lake.

The tapping had stopped then started back up again.

Ben rolled onto his side, to study the green orbital sockets in the Tex's metal face. He said, "I figure you would've gotten enough of the game already."

"Nope." Tex kept his focus on the screen. "I have two more unlocks before dusting this one."

Unlocks. Dusting. More nonsensical game chatter. Ben stretched again and let one leg dangle over the edge of the bed—*whoa, cold*—and snapped his foot back from the cold wood floor. "Where are my boots?"

"You kicked them off the foot of the bed." Without looking from the screen, Tex pointed to where Ben could doubtlessly find his shoes if he could see in the dark. Tex asked, "Want me to raise the lights?"

Expression training to the rescue. "Yes, please."

Tex paused the game and swiped away to a foreign screen with several knobs and sliders. The robot worked them and warm track lights lit and blossomed along the baseboards revealing his boots lying haphazardly on the clean floor. The bathroom lit and the showered started.

Ben pulled the cover up to his neck and whispered, "Is there someone in there?"

"No," Tex shook his head and pointed to the Anvilsmith. "This place is wired up tighter than a smart-house. Everything can be run from the tablet." The robot hadn't move much, but still shifted as though he was settling back into a comfortable spot. "Mind the water, Ben. And let me know when you have it at the temperature you like so I can program it into the system."

This is the life! Ben stretched one more time, hitched his breath, and jogged across the cold hardwood to the cold, beige bathroom tiles. *The cinnamon air freshener is a nice touch in here.* He disrobed, stood on his jeans, tested the water cascading in the center from the three double-showerheads, and hopped in. "Water's perfect!"

A soft ding came from the showerheads, and a yellow flight flashed at the top of the cold and hot knobs.

Given how large Ur-Krurk was, Ben looked around the knobs, and then the showerheads. *There must be some kind of level to expand the area. This stall is wide enough for four, but he was too tall to fit in here.*

Soon lost in the fleeting deep thoughts that only come during showers, Ben washed up, cut the water off, and dried his feet thoroughly. *It's going to be another sprint across icy tile and cold wood flooring to the closet for socks.*

To get a taste of what he was in for, Ben touched a foot out then raised it up in surprise. *The floor's warm?* He set his foot down again and relished the warmth coming up through the tiles. *Very nice.* He stepped out and walked a circle in front of the toilet, each step found toasty new ground. "Hey, the floor is heated!"

"I was going to tell you it could do that, but you shot from the bed like a demon." Tex's synthesized voice came from a group of tiny holes near the commode that Ben thought were a fan to suck smell away. "Normally, you take longer to rouse."

Finding heating vents at the base of the sink, Ben stopped before the wide mirror, wiggled his toes, and grinned indulgently as the warm air rolled in.

As the smell of bacon frying began to permeate the room. Ben drew a deep, appreciative breath. "Tex, my friend, I gotta admit…" admitting it aloud, Ben nodded in full agreement with his summation of the Meadow's Towing master bedroom. "…this place is five notches above nice."

"I know," Tex replied. "We should move here."

Dumbfounded by the thought, Ben's command of language fled with his ability to keep his mouth shut. Shocked numb by the prospect, he watched his jaw unhinge in the mirror. *At sixteen, can I do that?*

Chapter Eighteen

WORLD AWARE

MOUTH AGAPE, Ben leaned out from the bathroom to read Tex's body language. *Surely, he must be joking.*

Having added a couple of towels from the top shelf, Tex lazed like a Bronze Age emperor on a pillowed dais consulting a large glowing Tablet of the Gods which read: *You have our favor. Now, and forever.*

Ben's jaw quivered. His mouth popped closed as words nearly came, then left him speechless.

"What? You said *this is nice*…" Tex pointed to the ceiling. "The view is great." He waved his small arm in a wide graceful arc. "The room is fantastic." He gave the Anvilsmith a couple of taps, and nodded when the slow opening baseline of *Me and the Moon* by The Dryads thumped. Tex stood and reenacted the late night walker's steps from the video.

Ben's mind went to the last line. *Ain't nothin' gonna stop me this time, because the moon is high, and the night is mine.* The bacon smell made him think of breakfast which brought thoughts of his mother to mind. He founds words. "But I can't. My parents—"

"Can't stop you," Tex cut in. "You're sixteen. It's called being 'World Aware'. And if you want to move with your life, on your own terms, they cannot stop you."

Grateful to have regained conscious control over his jaw, Ben kept his mouth shut as he cast his eyes down to his toes at the threshold between the warm bathroom tile and the hardwood floor. Uncertainty had him frozen as he recalled asking his parents if he could return to the Samhain Festival to observe the closing ceremony. He had posed the question during dinner, and his parent had exchanged expressions back and forth without speaking. His father had seemed for it.

With the idea of being World Aware fresh in his mind, Ben realized that what he had taken as a shrug of *'why not?'* from his mom was a signal of powerlessness. Though he knew her doubting look all-too-well, Ben read the shrug as a new level of 'bad idea'—until something beyond doubt tugged at the corner of her mouth and she said, "We cannot stop you."

We cannot stop you. He rolled the four words around. He hadn't thought about the true meaning of the sentence.

Trying to unravel and name his mother's emotion behind the words, Ben kept his gaze on his toes as he crossed onto the room-temperature hardwood flooring in his room. This new understanding cast a liberating light on his parents and how they'd granted permission for everything he'd gathered the courage to ask for since turning sixteen a couple months ago.

Besides the closing ceremonies, he hadn't asked for much, but it was his desire to visit Crystal the seer, to know if his Samhain Festival winnings were cursed that had sent him to his mom. She had groaned, but granted the request. He'd asked to go to Bauman's Bazaar; she'd grimaced, but allowed it. He wanted to stay the night at Meadows Towing and mustered the courage to ask if he could spend the night a friend's house. She had rolled her eyes hard when he said *friend's house,* but granted him permission.

Understanding turned his lips into a wide smile. *So, that's why I didn't get punished for being away on the night of my sixteenth birthday, and the night I was...* Almost thinking Bastion's name, Ben left a blank and found another way to word the situation he had found himself in. Instead of *abducted* or *captured,* he went with *indisposed.*

The smile turned into a toothy grin full of greed at the endless possibilities and freedom that lay before him. Nodding slightly, he turned his eyes skywards to find the North Star to get Its opinion. But the vibrant clouds had grown dark, blocking the view to *his* star. *Feels like a bad omen.* Mid-nod, Ben began to shake his head.

"You could do it," Tex had been waiting. The robot motioned around the room, again. "We have a roof. The business is bringing in steady funds." His shoulders dropped for a moment before rising for a final point. "If you think about it, it's not like there's any real upkeep here."

Going to the closet, Ben took careful steps as he navigated his counter-thoughts. *Yes, we have a fine roof, but any money this place makes belongs to the orcs and goblins who work it.* About to address the question of upkeep, his stomach growled and he stopped at the work desk. More important to him—right then—Ben's eyes scanned the six spellcard halves he'd saved for the two remaining circuit boards. *They're gone.*

"Good point." As though Ben's gasp had agreed with him, Tex kept on, "You have a staff to cook for you. We have guards."

The clip where he had pinned the half-completed card was empty. He found the board—*this is not the prize-winning design I had been working toward*—finished, and a large, empty sauce pot clamped to the rim. His soldering iron had been strapped to a wooden cooking spoon and suspended from his swivel lamp by six thick, cut-open rubber bands. To the left of the pot were two spent boards with their diodes removed. To the right, another completed board. He eyed the cursory reconfigured extra bits of soldering. *This is one of my designs though...*

Tex said, "The moon is made of cheese."

What the heck is all this extra crap? Ben bumped the desk, making the iron rock. *It's jury-rigged, goblin-style.* He sat and slid a card under the magnifying glass. *This*— analyzing the cross-pointed circuits to boost the cards arcane capacity, Ben rubbed his chin. *This is my Circuitry V final project!*

Tex said, "I swam to China."

I hadn't made a working prototype of this design.

Tex added, "And back."

"I hear you, Tex." Feeling somewhat cheated out of being the first to build his own design, Ben rounded to see Tex imitating a breaststroke in a sea of towels. "Did the goblins do this?"

Tex stopped, stood, and pointed. "The set-up, yes. The boards, no."

Ben scooped up the other completed board to inspect it; the new circuit setup was there, too. "I've thought the design out thoroughly and passed the theoretical ohm tester in the school lab, but I hadn't got around to building it or doing real diagnostics on the design." Having a new respect for this type of work quite literally *blown* into him, Ben's slight jealously at not building the board first turned into concern about destroying Meadows Towing and all inside. He scanned for any burn marks. Ben brought his ramble to a point. "Tex, this configuration hadn't been tested."

Tex replied, "Energy flows. It didn't pop."

"It's great that it works—" Hearing a hanger shift and then the familiar sound of his companion sliding down his coat, Ben turned. Tex had paused his game and left the Anvilsmith behind. "But I haven't done any form of true diagnostics or testing."

The robot pushed over the step-stool the goblins used to access and clean higher parts of the room.

Ben shuddered at the memory of the scraping sound it made. That sound conjured the memory of when he had been helplessly restrained to the bed and the two goblins had checked on him repeatedly. The stool *thunked* against the desk breaking the daze.

"Adept Floyd didn't give your design his *good in theory* ninety-nine percent score, Ben. He gave it a hundred." Tex climbed the step-stool to stand on the desk and looked over the clipped card. "It passed his rigors and—I wouldn't be surprised if you cracked his cards to find your design—your new design works. I tested it."

Tested it? So glad I didn't wake up to an explosion. Ben crossed his arms. "What were the readouts?"

Tex turned to face him, and pointed to the tablet in the closet. His voice modulation took on a confrontational tone. "If it *really* matters, your device has the data."

"Of course it matters." Ben strode across the room, snatched the Anvilsmith down, and swiped away from Tex's game to activate his monitoring program. "There are certain points during the cycles where I need to see the spikes and dips."

Tex's volume raised slightly and his tone modulated to annoyance, "It's all there."

Rotating the tablet to landscape, Ben tapped to the tests and scrolled through the ramp up and steady emerald flow of arcane wattage from the tablet, though the card, and back into the tablet. *Less need. More efficient.* The cyan waste line stayed flat at zero. *Wow!* Well-earned pride pillowed in his chest. *The other cards have loss.* He scanned the readings again. *But not mine.*

"Ben," Tex dropped onto the step-stool. "You know they work. You're always working on the next upgrade." The robot had stopped at the last step from the floor. "I don't understand. Why are you holding back?"

"Well—" Ben drew a sharp breath. He tossed the tablet onto the bed and pressed his fists into his hips. "I don't understand why you're pushing me."

Tex took the final step onto the hardwood floor. "It's called *growing up.*"

What? Ben's brow tightened and his eyes narrowed.

"Sorry," Tex's metal eyebrows rose. "I didn't mean to offend, but you have what many casters your age want. More than they could hope for." The robot motioned with both arms around the room and then brought them back in a wider arc. "This place is yours—and, unlike most who deem themselves World Aware, you will not need your parent's support."

Something about the way Tex moved reminded Ben of himself when he had tried to present the idea of independence to Rembrandt, his first robotic companion.

Ben had tried widening the limits, but Remy's processors couldn't handle the parameters of *do as you will.* Even after hacking the robot's programming to not consider repercussions of decisions, Remy would still freeze up with presented with a choice as simple as whether to plug in for power or run until he was at fifty percent.

Tex isn't the opposite of Remy. His brow loosened. *No, this Golemcast is on an entirely different level. Wait.* His jaw shifted to the right. *Perhaps this is why the school gives certain companions at specific ages…*

At ten, like the rest of the Initiates, Ben had been given the traditional Tech-Toad. Kermit, a simple robotic frog, had been good fun. It hopped where directed and was easy to control. At twelve, they received their first robot. Rembrandt proved to be a plodding machination capable of doing many simple tasks, but was quite basic and—ultimately—very limited.

Ben's frown returned as he began to continue down the line of his companions. He didn't want to go further. *But it might lead to a breakthrough.*

One of the few moments, which made him unique amongst his classmates, was when he had earned the fourteenths gifts a year early as a reward for his rapid progression in Spell Programming. What had been a moment of pure pride turned to ultimate shame when his newest robotic companion, Jimmy, went missing overnight and—having lost one gift—he had to return his untouched Aurora tablet and Ranger bicycle.

Ben's jaw tightened. He coached himself. *Get past the sting, Ben. Keep going.*

"Breakfast is ready!" Nuk U'es yelled from downstairs. "Are you wanting Uk'so Tuk to be bringing it to you?"

Ben opened his mouth and drew a breath to yell back.

Tex made a sound akin to what the robot might sound like if he'd had a throat to clear, and pointed his small hand at a tiny, easily overlooked group of speaker holes above the light switch. "We have intercoms. Just push the switch up."

When Ben did, there was a little play for the upturned switch to move a bit higher. *Probably a second setting to be activated.* Ben said, "I'll be down."

As soon as he lifted his hand, Toad's gruff voice came through the speaker. "Ben, a human calling himself Malcolm has been waiting here at the gates for three hours to speak with you."

"Malcolm?" Ben rocked his head back. *What's he doing here and— more importantly—why would he come here looking for me?* He glanced to Tex. "Has he really been out there that long?"

"Unable to verify." His companion shrugged. "This is the first time they've called. Should I stay behind and record?"

"Yes. Please do." Ben cued the intercom. "What does he want?"

Chapter Nineteen

RETRIBUTIVE PARAMOUNTCY

WITH HIS MOTHER insisting that he wear traditional robes when around the house, and having to dress in his Archon Private Academy uniform when going to school or school-related events. Ben had started to look forward to the night that he'd planned at Meadows Towing as being a nothing but a jeans and t-shirt stay. The short sleeves gave all kinds of freedom and the blue jeans just *felt* comfortable. You could do things in jeans that would rip and ruin slacks. *I'll bet Malcolm's going to ruin this day.*

Nuk's high grumbly voice cut in. "Your plate is ready."

The smell of sausage had begun to battle with bacon for scent superiority. Both made Ben's stomach send out a new round of hunger pangs. About to reply, the intercom cued Toad continued, "He's demanding—"

Malcolm's voice, faint in the background corrected: "*Requesting,* you filthy green skin. *Requesting.*"

Green skin? Ben considered the words. Though he hadn't heard them in combination before, he could easy see them being derogatory. Much in the same way that Orcs often referred to humans as *softies* or used the Servant Giant word for human to slander a fellow orc— whether in jest or in earnest.

"Uh, requesting," Toad paused, "a rematch."

When will he quit? Ben drew a breath and shook his head. "Tell him, 'request denied.' And tell him, 'go home. We'll meet in eleven months.'" Giving up his plan to dress comfortably, Ben began to put on his school uniform in the silence that followed. *Malcom's not going to be turned away so easily. And—if so—that's not Malcolm out there.* He grabbed the rusty nail that he had taken from the Dunn-Blatt last month. *Maybe this'll get him to go away.*

Toad's voice came through eh intercom again, "He says that is unacceptable and now demands a, uh…"

Ben nodded. *Yup, that's Malcolm.*

Malcolm's voice came through loud and clear. "Retributive Paramountcy."

The intercom cut out.

Ben's arm hairs rose as he picked up his Anvilsmith. Ambient emerald, cobalt blue, and amber energies danced between his hairs and floated in ghostly wisps around him. *What's the amber energy?* Putting the question aside for another time, he shrugged on his coat and typed 'Retributive Paramountcy' into his tablet.

Rushing his words, worry colored Toad's stammer, "He demands a Retributive Paramountcy and if you deny…"

Malcolm finished the threat he tried to relay through Toad, "—I'll call a Magistrate Triumvirate to come force the issues."

The definition scrolled on Ben's screen as he rushed back to the intercom and cued it. "No!" *The last thing I want is a Primary at the property, no less three.* "No need for Judges, Malcolm. I accept. Let him in, Toad. I'll be down."

One by one, the three faint wisps of energy dancing on his arm became a visible tether. Each strand, green, blue, and yellow, braided themselves into each other and their tiny hooks coalesced into a single, prismatic hook.

What the heck!

The braided tether drove into Ben's chest. As though punched, the force drove him back a step. Unlike the expanded awareness granted by tethers of what battles of will were going on in the nearby area, a specific knowing of all things Malcolm came to him.

Beside his own, Malcolm possessed ownership over several of his fellow Dunn-Blatt's cars. He owned Clark County Country Kitchens, a small chain of all-hour diners catering to customers with low budgets and late-night cravings. Malcolm also owned a large ranch on the opposite side of town where world-class championship hellhounds —*there are competitions for hellhounds?*—were bred and sold at top dollar. The Dunn-Blatt also had another caster—*can't tell who*— enthralled in a subservient Paramountcy bond.

On a primitive level, Ben understood that similar things about himself—*my secrets are still mine*—were laid bare to Malcolm. The knowledge of each other extend to the physical, too. Each knew, and would know, each other's location.

As though the braided tether wasn't enough. The weight of the challenge began to weigh on Ben conscience. *What in the word did I just agree to?* Reading the definition on his device, he took slow, steady steps across the room.

Paramountcy: Definition (strict) - A three part mystic duel for dominion.

He looked away to put on his tablet holster and spellcard holder.

Retributive Paramountcy: Definition (use) -When a combatant has lost a duel and believes luck played a large part in the defeat, they may call this duel to prove superiority through two more clashes.

Paying more attention to his Anvilsmith than where he was walking, Ben bumped into the doorjamb. He rubbed his shoulder and continued to advance semi-blindly toward the stairs as he read.

The enactor chooses the second duel type and typically plays to their opponent's weakness, though paramountors have been known to play to their own strengths. The paramountee chooses the final combat form. The same strategic thought as above is applied here.

The savory scent of bacon overpowered the sausage as he descended the stairs to the sounds of the goblins' video game characters taking hits. Feeling Malcolm speeding through the scrapyard, Ben scrolled past famous and historic Paramountcies to the note with an asterisk before it at the bottom of the article.

Note[1]: both parties need to exercise sound judgment in calling for or accepting this retributive duel, as the loser is mystically subjected to an irrevocable subservient bond to the victor.

Ben tried to take an extra step down when he came to the living room. He glanced to the gargantuan TV to see abandoned controllers.

They left the game without pausing again. I have to show them how to short cut the wemic stage. He grabbed two strips of bacon from the plate on the dining room table and chomped on one as he returned his eyes to his table to read the double asterisks.

Note[2]: it is common for the loser to choose death versus defeat at the outcome of the final duel.

Ben spoke to himself as he felt Malcolm speeding through the gates and up the main thoroughfare. "Good job, Ben. Win this duel or become the jerk's personal, life-long servant." Though Tex had stayed upstairs, Ben could almost hear his companion add, sarcastically. *Well, don't rule out death. It is an option.*

He adopted Tex's deadpan tone. "Fantastic."

Chapter Twenty

MALCOLM'S MOXIE

STUFFING the other strip of bacon into his mouth, Ben slipped his tablet into its holster and chewed rapidly to finish the bacon before Malcolm made it to the front of the building.

Moving through the kitchen to the garage, he spied three frying pans left out and dirty. *That's unlike Nuk and Uk'so. Wonder what they have going on?* Still looking over his shoulder at the dirty dishes, Ben stopped short of moving out into the garage and a feeling—*something's going on*—stole over him. The sensation intensified as Malcolm drew closer. *But what?*

Wiping the grease from his lips with the back of his hand, Ben moved out into the garage. *Empty as usual, but why are all five bays open?* He wiped at his mouth again and pivoted around the corner into a face full of exhaust. *What made that smell? The only cars present are the wrecks.* Not expecting to see anyone, he stopped short. *Whoa.*

A majority of the Meadow Towing orcs—*only missing Jek and the gate guards*—were present in the hundred-foot span between the garage and the first row of crushed cars. All had longswords and guns strapped to their person. Further out, the orcs who had come on board from Ur-Krurk's Son's traveling vanguard were working in trios as two helped a third into the black studded leather armor they had worn during the battle that ended in them belonging to the property. *Did they feel Malcolm's challenge to me?*

Everyone stopped what they were doing and cheered him as he stepped out into the night. "Ben! Ben! Ben!"

Quiet, motionless, and hunkered down in the shadows, Ben spied the tuzvul. She also belonged to Meadows Towing, but was almost never around. *What brought you out, missy? What are you up to?*

Ben nodded to a couple of the orcs—*Jek's buddies*—as their shouts felt louder *and...* Ben struggled to nail down the growing suspicion. *And...* He eliminated them from the potential problem. Like Jek, the orcs were fairly straightforward. *And, whatever it is, it's not them. Well, not* from *them, but...* At a complete loss, he bit his lip. *But something else.*

The headlights of Malcolm's Transcend grew closer.

And behind the Dunn-Blatt's, the dark silhouette of a tow truck.

Come on, Ben. Think.

Dirt clouds plumed behind the Transcend in the light desert breeze as the car turned, then skidded sideways on the hardpan, coming to a stop sixty feet away.

The orcs, many with swords in hand, rushed to close in on Malcolm's car as Malcolm got out, but the swarm didn't ding the Dunn-Blatt's smug smile.

"Hmph." Ben stifled a longer acknowledgment of Malcolm's moxie. *He's awfully blasé about driving onto hostile ground and being at the center of small army of fully armed, armored, and anxious monsters.*

Obscured by the tall broad-shouldered orc, Ben heard Malcolm call, "Baby Ben. You were lucky in catching me in the middle of a very prosperous Samhain Shenanigans." The orcs parted slightly as Malcolm, in his school's violet jumpsuit, moved around the front of his car.

"Look, I didn't know how important this was to you." Hoping this would placate the jerk, Ben dipped his hand into his pocket and fished out the rusty nail Malcolm had said was a family heirloom. "How about you take your tether back and we call this whole Paramountcy thing off?"

In the middle of sneering brutes, on foreign ground far away from civilization, Malcolm wrapped his arms around his abdomen and threw his head back in laughter.

"So sorry, Benny, but that will no longer be enough." The Dunn-Blatt extended his arms and spun a circle to encompass the scrapyard with a snazzy gesture. "I didn't know you owned all of this! Makes me wonder what favor you were playing to years ago by pretending to be the poorest kid at the APA."

Malcolm shook his head in disbelief and continued, "You're the Might-Fist and you have control over a Node Key?" The Dunn-Blatt's smug smile widened as his voice rose in amazement, joy, and greed. "Oh, this is too good!" He clapped and rubbed his hands together. "I'm glad you're not wearing your Might-Fist belt. When it's mine..." Malcolm pantomimed putting it on. "*When* it's mine, I'm *never* going to take it off."

He knew these things and still chose to continue on instead of backing out. "Malcolm, I didn't come across all these things by luck. Do us both a favor, take your tether and go."

"Shit on that! I want the whole burrito, baby." Malcolm bounced in place and, pointing at Ben, settled into a stance like Bruce Lee. "I choose combat in single conjuration personifications!"

Conjuration. Really? Ben wanted to laugh like Malcolm had moments ago. *I've learned from Gary, the world's best conjurer. I know more about conjuring than probably any student in the Las Vegas Valley.* Fighting a secret smile, which worked hard to turn his lips, Ben dropped the nail into his pocket and motioned for Malcolm to go first. "Let's see your conjuration."

Dark purple magic poured from Malcolm's skin. The radiant Krotosian energy formed an amorphous blob too large for a dusk bison. It rolled and folded upon itself before it solidified in a brief howl into a massive stone bull whose shoulders were level with the nearby orc's brows.

Okay. Ben rubbed his mouth. *He's made a super bull. Programming-wise, it couldn't be more than a four-stone creature, but there's no way my two-stone Orion is going to be able to rip one of those thick horns away and put the bull down like it did with the boars months ago.*

The bull stamped, striking sparks form the dessert hardpan. "Look at your face!" Continuing to point, Malcolm burst out in laughter again. "You thought it was going to be a dusk bison. Admit it, Ben. Admit it."

Okay... Ben felt his breath catch as he modified his initial estimated power level. *Maybe it'd be five stones and, maybe, Gary didn't teach me everything.*

"When you're my servant, I'm to have you lick-shine my shoes before school. Everyday." Malcolm beamed a thrilled smile. "Every single day." As though they were on stage at a talent show, Malcolm extended an opened palm toward Ben. "Okay, baby. Let's see what you got."

Chapter Twenty-One

BEN'S FOLLY

THE SLIGHT BREEZE that had been wafting away Malcolm's dirty clouds died. Without direction, the trailing dirt between the column of wrecked cars began to settle back where it had been disturbed. Without the breeze, the smell of exhaust hung as aimless as the dirt. Ben cut his eyes over to the tuzvul. *Still lurking.* He licked at the bacon flavor on his lips as though he could taste what bothered him about her being out and about.

A loud clack and sparks brought his attention back to the stone bull. *I should—* Ben killed the thought of turning Bastion loose before the beast had a chance to fully form. Since the beast's show of force in the basement, it had become a sleeping dragon. *And there's no way I'm going to go to it for help. This is duel two of three.*

Malcolm prompted, "Any time now."

My parents not allowing me to take the Dueling is coming back to haunt me big time. If I claim World Awareness, I'll be able to take any classes I want at the Academy. Ben nodded. He would take Tex's advice.

For now, though, I should bend to this one and just beat him in another duel. Ben made a face as though someone had served him a heaping serving of sewage soup. *What am I thinking? Give this one a solid go with energy from your tablet. Then, if you do lose this challenge, you'll be at full personal power to stomp him in the third.*

"Alright, Malcolm." Ben laid his hand against his holder, and a finger on his Orion spellcard. "Here we go." Tapping energy from his Anvilsmith, Ben found the energy riding up his arm instead of passing through to the spellcard. Emerald light spouted from his sternum forming an amorphous blob. The energy folded and crackled before shaping into a large, four-armed, green Bastion.

Oh my Gods. Ben's blood went cold. *He's out.*

Malcolm's head reeled back. "A girallon? Perhaps I may have misjudged you…"

Wait. Ben tried to feel for a conjurors bond to the creature and felt a link between the two forms much deeper than anything he'd previously felt. *It feels like they're both my bodies.* Ben shifted his consciousness into—*what Malcolm called*—the girallon. *The tang of fear all over the air. Just under it, anxiety and…* He smacked his lips. *… anticipation.* He balled his four massive green fists and relaxed his hands. *The raw strength… it feels awesome!*

Ben transferred back to his human form. "You have no idea." He extended the nail and offered again. "We can still be civilized and walk away from this."

Malcolm's eyes glassed and closed. Needlessly stamping in place to make sparks fly, the stone bull became more animated.

Ben put the tether away and shifted his sense into the girallon.

The might at my disposal. A grin worked onto his massive mouth. *It's absolutely intoxicating.* He flexed again. His orcs broke out in riotous bellows and cheers.

Malcolm's bull turned toward the orcs.

They scattered.

The bull galloped at breakneck speed away toward the scrapyard entrance.

An instinct to give chase stole over him. Ben fought it back. *Why is he running away all of a sudden? He called this challenge.*

"Get him." Toad urged from his tow-truck, parked behind Malcolm's car. "Make him pay!"

There. That's the trick. Ben leapt, landing before Toad and flexing over the pale green orc.

The shaman bowed deep.

The reek of fear and anxiety oozed from the orc's skin. *What are you up to?* Ben tried asking the words, but all that came from his throat were grunts.

Malcolm's bull continued to move away.

He'll came back eventually. He'll have to if he wants to battle it out. Yet…, Toad's not entirely wrong. Having won Malcolm's rusty nail tether, Ben had considered Malcolm's bully-debt mostly paid off. *Yet…* A small part of him still wanted to hurt the Dunn-Blatt for the physical pain the jerk had inflicted upon him and others not ready to be tethered for the first time. *And in these forms, I can. I can truly fight my former nemesis without doing damage to either of our real bodies.*

Casting one last glance as his and Malcolm's human bodies standing, eyes closed and vacation by the garage, Ben gave into his want.

He pounded his girallon chest and, tromping hard, Ben tore off after Malcolm.

The smell of exhaust faded. Gaining slowly, his nose locked onto the bull's unique earthy scent well before it turned down a row and out of sight.

Expecting a charge when he would turn the corner, Ben leapt. He grabbed a car eight up, and swung high across the free space to the wall of cars on the other side. Under his powerful grip, metal crumpled, cried, and bit at his hands, but failed to pierce his thick green skin.

The bull stood at the far end, facing him. Sparks flew up from the ground as it stamped twice.

It's almost too far to tell, but even his bull has a smug upward turn to its lips.

On thundering hooves, it charged.

With confidence bordering on conceit, Ben dropped to the ground ready to do to the bull what Orion had done to the boar. *Come on, Malcolm. I'll take you head on.*

He hit the ground and crumpled as the bridge to his human form shattered. *What the!* Stuck in the girallon form, Ben hopped back to his feet, and swung back onto the main aisle.

Orcs were piling into white cargo vans.

Glancing his way, the tuzvul loaded Ben's human body into a separate van.

What's that? A scintillating rainbow circlet had been pushed tight down on his forehead and a cloud of pitch black shadows hung over his head.

The galloping clamor behind him ceased.

Ben spun to see the purple stone bull dissipating into smoke. A revving engine—*a Transcend*—snapped his attention back up the aisle.

Middle finger high in the air, Malcolm hopped into his car.

The plain white cargo van's door closed.

My body's in that one!

They all tore away.

No!

Chapter Twenty-Two

CHASING CARS

MOVING parallel with the distant vehicles, Ben's powerful girallon limbs rocketed him down the row. He leapt, gripped metal, his arms pulling him to the top of the crushed cars in three strong heaves. From up here the dust the vans kicked were well behind him, but they were quickly making up the difference.

Not losing any speed, Ben lunged from his current row to the one across the dirt aisle between.

Two white vans flashed by at the end of the column.

There they are. He crunched down on the top of the wrecked cars on the adjacent row. Moving as fast as this body could take him, his feet and fists pounded on collapsed trunks, roofs, and hoods. The crumpled metal beneath his hands and feet *clunked* and *thunked* as he powered on through the stagnant night air.

The dust clouds had pulled past him.

They're way ahead of me now. From habit, his upper left hand swung back to touch his hairy torso where the *Usian* and *Leap* spellcards would've been if he were in his human form. *If I had my magic, I might be able to rival their speed.*

Ben launched across another opening and poured all his strength into getting as close as possible. *I can't catch them, but woe to them if I'm able to capitalize on any miscalculated turn or any other mistake.*

No! The upper bar at the top of the east gates started to roll up the Koffman security shutters he had installed.

Ben leapt across another aisle and continued on.

In the distance, a series of square taillights drove into the darkness, with the thin slits of Malcolm's Transcend punctuating the long procession.

Incapable of words, Ben roared his frustration as his hands gripped a folded fender of the car beneath him. He flipped it from the top. It crashed into the row below with an ear pleasing crunch. *I'd like to crunch those betrayers just. Like. This.* He hopped to where the other car and been, scooped the front of the wreck he had been on and sent it crashing down, too. *And this.* One by one, he dismantled the wrecked wall below his feet. On the ground, he leapt off the last one and slammed all four fists into it. The compacted hinges cried, the sides buckled, and it slid the few inches into the toppled mess he had made.

He stood breathing steady. *This body isn't even winded.* Considering making the gap in the wall wider, he balled and unballed his fists. About to climb to the top, he stopped. *Tearing this place apart won't lead to a solution to my problem. Get productive. Think.*

"Ben?" Tex synthesized voice asked. "Is that you?"

Ben turned. Ready to run, Tex peered at him from the distant corner. A growl, equal parts frustration and disappointment vibrated in his throat as he plopped on a compressed hood with a final *thunk*. *They set a trap for me, and I charged right into it.*

He put a hand on his forehead, ran it down his protruding brow, and down the ramp of his nose and mouth. He held his jaw and dropped his elbow on his leg to support his chin on his knuckles.

Tex had drawn closer. The robot motioned to his bulk. "I can see you're thinking."

Lost in thought, Ben became aware of his body again.

Tex continued, "Except for the extra set of arms, that pose is called *The Thinker*."

He shot Tex a short, angry snort.

"It's true and famous," the robot raised his hands as though he had touched something hot. "I wasn't trying to make a joke."

Quite alright, Tex. I could use a joke right now. Ben tried to smile. The corners of his mouth twitched upwards. *What, I can't even smile?* He tried again and the corners of his mouth quivered up. *Next time.* He set himself to try again.

Abruptly, as though hooked and snatched by a high-strength tension wire, his girallon body—with all its mass—flew sideways from the hood.

What the—

Faster than he could get his feet beneath him, or correct to gallop, the invisible force continued to yank on every fiber of his existence, dragging him across the scrapyard grounds toward the east entrance.

The Meadows Towing building shrank into the distance as his body, scraped deep enough into the dirt, being turned to burger —*I thought it was all desert hardpan*—as it struck long-hidden blacktop, leaving a long streak of blood.

Aware of the damage being done to his body—*it feels like being punched in an arm that's already asleep*—he couldn't help the stray thought. *Wonder if this body will heal as quickly as my real body.*

Then he slammed into the closed Koffman security gate.

At the same time, out in the desert, he felt his human body in the van slam into the van's back doors.

My body, empty, lies out there on a deserted road. He tried to stand. While most of his right side suffered, Ben found several spots of his girallon body had been ground bone deep from the asphalt under the dirt. *What are they doing?*

Distantly, he could feel strong arms wrap around his human torso. They gripped tight, and pulled hard.

"You're at max range!" Tiny in the distance, Tex ran toward him yelling at full volume. "Climb, Ben! Climb right now!"

Ben rolled onto his left flank to get up.

The force pulling on his empty body in the desert thumped him against the buttress. Having experienced it inside his human body, Ben recognized the feel of long tuzvul fingers wrapping around his torso and yank.

The pull translated into his girallon body being slammed against the unyielding Koffman gate. Ben strained up on his good left side and set two hands to climb.

Out in the desert, long, powerful arms—tuzvul arms—gripped his body and yanked, and yanked and yanked, repeatedly slamming his massive body into the gate, causing him to keep losing his grip.

Wait, what's going on with my body now?

The slight awareness he had of his physical body faded as the distant energy source keeping the girallon body together exceeded its maximum range.

His companion continued to close in.

Ben had eye contact with Tex as—*aw, shit*—his girallon body burst into emerald smoke.

Tex covered his face, and yelled, "Nooo—

Chapter Twenty-Three

SMOKE

—ooo!"

WHILE BEN often made observations of the stars and the night sky, he never felt so much a part of them as he did right now. *This is amazing! I can feel myself expanding into... into... The exact name-word escapes me, but this feels great! It's almost like I'm a part of the night and...*

A wide spread of raindrops hung in the air and formed red, green, purple, and black-colored condensation on—*something like a floor*—beneath him.

The view beyond the floor turned into a desolate mix of deep grays except for Tex. His companion had his hands near his bright—*so very lovely and bright*—green orbital sockets, and shook his head repeatedly.

He's upset that my physical being has been taken away. Outside, above, and inside himself, Ben looked at the clear outline of his being. He only had one set of human sized arms. *That's weird, I thought I had two massive sets. Well, it's sort of comforting because that feels right, too.* The momentary certainty that everything was alright slipped when he felt a—*it's some sort of glass*—wall between him and the downward direction he wanted to go.

The green condensation on the window-floor burst into smaller bits before floating out into the great expanse all around him. He smiled at the change as the green—*the same color as those round sockets*—moved away and evaporated.

The colorful raindrops on the glass floor began to burst into smaller drops as they, too, moved further away. Movement beyond the drops on the glass got his attention.

The sad little robot had a name once, but that had long since vanished, just like his own.

Am I a he? Do spirits have a gender?

The small drops moved further away.

The unhappy metallic being was entirely wrong.

The sense of ease that filled the two-armed vessel that made the outline start to fade.

A dark light emanated from the center of the metallic being.

Want. Want into it.

The tempting light called. Perhaps by joining the energy in the metallic lifeform, it could help the metallic being not be sad.

The floor's in the way. The metal thing's crying.

It reached out to comfort the machine, but the clear barrier still lay between them, and now, his formerly faded form had come back coated with... *Droplets?*

Black, red, and purple bled through the outline and floated to the center of his arm, almost as though it were his bone marrow.

Bones. He thought whimsically. *I had bones at one time.* His breath began to fog the window. He wiped at it, making the grey turn into a swirl of muck. The three colors didn't mix to form sludge. Each remained its own in the tightly smeared mess, and began to unsmear into thick drops.

August. Benjamin. Brutus. Jacob. Moil. Baxter.

One of those is my name. No. Two. Three?

He put his hand toward the glass obstruction and the black condensation pooled together to form a letter 'B' before he touched it. *Yes. May name was Ben. Is Ben. Indeed. Benjamin Baxter.*

Ben extended his limbs toward a black raindrop coming toward him. As though rushing home, it flew to him and into his shell. He pointed to a red one. It, too, came rushing back. Each drop that came to him made him feel as though he should have the rest of them, too.

Focusing on bringing back all of the dispersed energy at once, his casing filled and was thrown downward. The glass barrier beneath him shattered into innumerable diamonds of starlight.

Chapter Twenty-Four

SELF-MADE

WHY AM I FALLING? Ben dropped on his knees and got his four arms down to catch himself before he fell face-first to the ground. He wanted to curse, but a weak groaning growl vibrated his throat as it rolled from his mouth. *Why do I feel so weak?*

"Ben?" Tex's voice had a note of worry to it.

I remember, I was slammed against the wall. He looked up to Tex and nodded to his companion as he got back to his feet. He sniffed. *Why is the air so stale?*

Tex took a tentative step away. "What number comes after my current version?"

What's with the quiz? Ben waved a hand to dismiss the question. *Not now, buddy. Things are too hazy.*

Tex took another step away. "The answer?"

Ben gazed up to the stars and a fleeting thought—*I could have joined them*—flickered across his mind. *The sky still full of clouds.* His head tilted to a subtle observation. *Wait. Those are the same cloud formations as when I first woke. They've barely moved.* He sniffed at the stale air again and found faint exhaust. *Yeah, without wind, things would get a bit stale.*

He glanced to Tex. *Okay, there was the original, the robot, and the hybrid. So, the answer is four.*

"I need an answer soon." Tex took another step away. "I'm about done waiting."

Of course he can't hear my telepathy. In retrospect, Ben felt sill for even presuming the robot would be able to. He tried to speak. Only a hoot game out.

Ben sighed and extend his upper arm to present four fingers. His thumb proved slow in following directions. *I can barely bend it.*

Tex turned and ran. "Wrong answer, Bastion!"

Bastion? I should call you a robot name that offends you. Ben went to count version on his digits, but stopped. *My fur's black? What happened to the green?* Ben took a few quick steps before leaping to hoist his body to the top of the row. *Why doesn't my body feel so clumsy?* The more he romped along the wreckage, the better his body began to react. The better his body reacted, the more this style of running with all six appendages began to feel natural.

Ahead of Tex, Ben leapt to the end of the next long row at an angle, purposely falling short so he could grab a rear quarter panel and swing out in front of Tex.

He landed and, trying to signal for his companion to wait when he came around the corner, extend his four arms, palms out.

Then Tex came barreling around the corner and lost his footing, but quickly scrambled back to the edge and looked at him.

Now to figure out a way to explain why my answer was right. Ben went to cross his two sets of arms and found his shoulder's range of motion was worse than when he would put on a school trench coat that he wore two years prior. *Crossing my arms isn't important right now.* Ben eased into a stance just beyond clasping his hands.

Ah, got it! Ben tried snapping his finger at his epiphany, and failed. *Why is my manual dexterity so bad?* He thought back to the well-controlled hand motions Bastion had made to him when they were fighting Ur-Krurk. *How had the Beast been able to sign so well?* Then the memory of It speaking the hiss-gargle language and fluent Ruler-Giant, reminded Ben that he and It were two separate beings. *If that premise is true, then when did Bastion find time to practice?*

Having thought the Beast's name, and It not rising up in his mind, Ben focused inward and sifted through his entire four-armed being for the Nilosian energy the Beast consisted of—instead of just being confined to his head. An elation bloomed in his chest. *Bastion's not here!*

The black nimbus hovering over the rainbow circlet that had been crammed on his head before being loaded into the van… *Was that black cloud the Beast?*

I had thought this entire thing had been perpetuated by Malcolm, but the Dunn-Blatt was just a pawn. Somehow, Bastion—Bastion—had orchestrated all of this to gain control of his body. An angry roar started up Ben's throat, but he stifled it. *Bellowing in primal rage won't return me to my human body.*

Tex turned and ran.

Ben let him go. *I have no way to communicate with him anyway.*

There has to be a way out of this. Trying to improve his range of motion while he tried to think his way out of his situation, Ben stretched his arms, shoulders, and legs as he shuffled, spider-walked, duck-walked, and crab-walked back to the building.

As much as I would like to go to Master Reynolds or any of the other high ranking APA teachers, all of them probably look on black magic the same way Kograkken and the rest of the Starwise Society did. He stopped his motion exercise to wonder. *Why do they fear Nilosian casters so much?* He continued back to the building. *Heck, I could probably only trust Papa Mojo right now and he'll probably just lie to me to get me to do some kind of errand for him.*

Ben smelled the four dead orcs before he saw them, and stopped his weird walks. The tangy odor of anxiety mixed with the musk of fear as both weighed heavy in the air. *The scents make sense. The only ones who probably weren't in on the revolt lay slain at my feet.* Ben looked each of them over and felt a sinking pain. *These were Jek's buddies. The guys who came to Meadows Towing on their own, without having to be subjugated or blood-oathed.*

Wait. Following his nose, Ben sniffed around the area to find a solid pocket of a clean, soapy, rose-water laced with the perfume of joy in the garage, masked well by the smell of old sweat, and hard mechanic work.

Well, hello. And who are you? Trying to further dissect the scent, he noted, *not nervous at all, no sense of worry, in fact, this jerk actually felt pride in doing this.* Ben's fingers curled into fists as he committed the smell to memory. *This is the one who orchestrated the betrayal.* He looked out toward the eastern entrance. *And they're in one of those vans.*

A distant motor droned toward the property. A set of headlights sped up the main aisle.

Please be Malcolm. Please be Malcolm. Still in the garage, Ben peeked out to see who approached. The shape of the vehicle was unmistakable and much too tall and bulky to be the sleek, low-profile of a Transcend. *That's one of our tow trucks.*

Ben stepped out.

The truck slammed on the brakes when the headlights lit his massive form.

Ben charged.

The trucked stopped, kicked into reverse, and gunned it.

Why are you running? With the power of all six of his limbs, Ben leapt through the air at the truck. *Oh, I got you now!*

Chapter Twenty-Five

NOT ALONE

THE DRIVER CRANKED the wheel to dodge.

Too late, buddy! Ben thumped down on the hood. His two upper arms latched onto the cab as his lower right shattered the driver's side window, and hoisted the driver—*orc*—from the seat. The trucked exuded a strong, familiar, salami smell. His other lower arm grabbed the orc's wrist and held it as firmly has Ben would his little brothers. He leapt away with the orc before the tow truck crashed into a row of wrecked cars. He held the orc before him.

Jek spat in his face. "I won't blood oath."

Ben wiped the dribble away. *He's not leaking fear. In fact, there's a whiff of pride clinging to the orc's heady defiance.* Still holding Jek, Ben set him on his feet and projected his thoughts, **I'm not Bastion.**

Jek's stern scowl stayed strong, but some of the hardness in his eyes eased. "Then who are you?"

You can hear me! You can understand me! Ben released Jek and bounded a quick circled to grab the orc by the shoulders. He wanted to hug his elation. Only his understanding of physical contact in orcish culture kept him from doing so. He gave Jek's shoulders a firm, we meet again, shake. **It's me, Ben.**

The familiar greeting made Jek's scowl ease. "If you're really Ben, who was at the carnival when I picked you up to come face Ur-Krurk's son?"

Not realizing he looked like Bastion, Ben didn't get why Tex had questioned him at first. But with what the monster did, it only made sense. About to answer Jek, Ben stopped and inhaled in three punctuated draws. *Jek's scent, shift from defiance to... To...* Ben tried to name the unsullied fragrance. He sniffed near the orc.

Jek leaned away before offering his hand.

Ben sniffed. Beneath the robust smell of salami, relief. He nodded and projected, *There was a Vibrosian Magistrate and Collins.*

"Collins." Jek tapped his right earlobe with both syllables. The orc nodded along with whatever his thoughts were. "What do we do now?"

Ben motioned Jek to come with him as he went to the truck to check the damage to the rear. *They took my body out the east entrance, and drove far out into the desert.*

"So, we need to go out further into the Might-Lands then." Jek shrugged his signature *no big deal* shrug. "Hop on back."

Ben grabbed onto the tow bar, and made sure to step up onto the truck and not on the wench controls.

Jek opened his truck door. "I'll get some real weapons—" He wiped glass from his seat onto the ground. "—summon the men, and we'll head out to get those guys."

Jek. Even though Ben used telepathy to project his thoughts, his throat constricted and his lips tightened to try and keep the bad news locked away. On a deeper level, the painful realization struck at his heart. He had started to think of many of the orcs as friends. It hurt more knowing Toad was out there with whomever was behind this.

When Ben had first seen the four dead orcs, he was—secretly—glad Toad had escaped the sudden betrayal. Now, he wished the orc had been there. He started again. *Jek, everyone who was here either turned or me or was murdered.*

Jek ground gears. The truck lurched forward and the orc had it to top speed before jamming on the brakes to power skid a short distance from the bodies. The orcs salami scent began to ooze a building dread.

He didn't put it in neutral. The truck inched forward. Ben jumped off the back, opened the driver door and tried to get his foot into to hit the clutch, but his massively muscled leg couldn't fit between the steering wheel and seat. *It's going to run up on them in short other.* Worse yet, the length of his leg didn't bend at the right place. Instead of doing what he set out to do, he found his leg stuck.

Nuk climbed through the passenger window, still wearing his red rhinestone jeans. The goblin squeezed past Ben's mass and hair to press the brake and clutch. Another small body came through the window. Uk'so worked the stick shift into neutral and turned the ignition to kill the engine.

The truck stopped a few feet from a seemingly oblivious Jek and the bodies.

"Benja Min'Fist." Nuk pulled on the driver seat lever. "Push seat back."

Ben did and got his leg free, and Nuk and Uk'so both scrambled from the truck to scamper back into the building.

Leaning close to one of the dead, Jek muttered in his native tongue as he took the sheathed knife from the dead orc's belt.

Jek moved to the next body. The orc stroked his left thumb over his heart four time while muttering something that rhymed at every ninth syllable. Solemn, Jek pulled the scabbard, pressed it against the deceased's hands, and brought to his own chest with a *thump*. He replaced the scabbard, continued speaking as he took the knife from the sheath. Jek moved on to kneel over the next body and start the thumb strikes.

Just from the combats since I've been here, there's—easily—one dead orc for each week that I've been the Might-Fist of Meadows Towing. He cast his gaze up to the purple neon star spinning on its six-story tall pillar. *Since my birth, if a death on the property were a coin, how soon will that stack dwarf the sign?* A trailing thought—*how many years until my own coin tower will rival this one*—turned his guts to ice.

Behind him, Jek said, "Might-Fist."

Ben turned from his depressing, imaginary visualization to the heart-twisting reality of Jek with four extra scabbarded blades on his belt. The sorrow emanating from Jek hit Ben's nose. He wanted to say something to help, but his mouth only gave a grunt.

Jek, seeming to understand, nodded. "Once this is done, I would like to bury them."

Of course. Ben nodded as he shifted his gaze to take in their faces again. *Who were they?*

"They were Cracked Skull like me," Jek tensed his body as though he wanted to turn and look, but some rigid code wouldn't allow for it. "Further, they were my first-blood."

Ben tightened his brow and nodded again. *Cracked Skull is probably his clan, but first-blood...* Not certain if it translated directly, Ben connected the term to a similar concept in the Giant's tongue, which meant each one of the four had direct, strong, sentimental and battle-based connections to Jek.

Jek swallowed a visible lump in this throat. "You should rally your allies to aide us in getting your body and extracting vengeance from the oath-breakers."

Allies. Ben pressed his lips together. *I barely have friends.* He shifted his gazed to the empty work bay where Toad and the others orcs had been when he knowingly came into hostile territory to try and save them. Ben laced his fingers together and squeezed down on his growing anger which came out as a deep rumble gurgled in his throat. *I put my neck out for them and this is how they repay me?*

With no small effort, he tossed aside the sense of betrayal to keep his thoughts from going to a much darker place. For a moment he wondered at Jek's phrasing. *How does one 'extract' vengeance? Better yet, what happens to those who break their oath? Is it like lying or are there further repercussions?*

"If you have no worthy allies," Jek prompted, "then call upon your blood."

Ben shook his head. *My mom is barely an Herbalist, and my dad is a mundane.*

"Mundane?"

Uh... He had thought the term was universal. *A human without magic.*

Just when Ben thought he had the meaning in all of Jek's shrugs down, the orc raised a single shoulder. "Have him bring his guns."

A reflexive, mirth-filled hoot escaped Ben's lips at the thought of his father fighting with his always-manicured, Blackjack-dealing hands. Another hoot popped from him.

Jek frowned. "What about other humans?"

Like this? Ben raised his four arms and pulled at his fur. *I could probably explain my being out here, and might be able to get away with being a girallon... However,* Ben found his head shaking rapidly against the idea. *There are not enough words in the world to explain why my body is composed, entirely, of Nilosian energy.*

Jek gave a quick *so?* shrug and offered. "Because you're able to tap into Nilos."

Yeah, about that... Ben clasped his hands in the same patient manner Adept Matton would when explaining a seemingly easily overlooked, but blatantly obvious, modicum of decorum. *While using black magic is acceptable amongst goblinoids, there's a saying amongst the starwise 'Those who used the darkest magic deserve the worst deaths.'* It was a common axiom. He had heard it a few times before Kograkken, the giant in Pepperjacks, had grumbled it at him. However, the Giant speaking it while holding a sword under his chin had left an indelible mark on his memory. Ben rubbed his neck. *They would rather kill me than help me.*

Jek sneered. "That's dumb. Why don't they like Nilosians?"

Ben tried to shrug. *I don't know* And almost pulled it off. To be certain he got his point across, he added, *You got me. And I only know two Nilosians—* About to turn his thoughts inward to recall Collins' inky eye incident, Ben found his thoughts centered on Papa Mojo. In his passing thought, the serpent-eyed psychic stood in the shadows cast by a column of wrecked cars.

Where—Wait, I know that arrangement of cars. It's the same one I had ducked behind with Abe and Oscar before we attacked the building. Recalling what Gary had once told him about his third eye, Ben focused on the formation of cars where Papa Mojo stood in his mind's eye. He turned his conscious gaze to the shadows beyond the first row where Papa Mojo probably stood right now. *There.* Remembering the diviner tricking him, Ben found his fist balled tight. *He's right there.*

Why is he here? Ben's brow tightened to a dangerous knot. His fists cranked tighter, making his knuckles pop. *If he had anything to do with this... I want to speak to him, but know—ultimately—that I can't really trust anything he says. But this time... This time he's come to me!* Ben elbowed Jek and projected his thoughts, *Aim your gun one row out where the yellow car is tacked on the black.*

Without asking why, Jek did.

Now, move your barrel toward where the teal front fender drops down over the yellow.

Jek did. "Done."

Mojo, I know you're there. Just come out.

Nothing, not even the wind, moved.

Mojo and Alice have the same kind of eyes. Could I have misread the vision? I hope so. I mean, presuming she recalls what I did for her and her Sister-Mother as a favor, I could sure use Alice's skill set tonight.

Ben nodded at the lack of action. *Have it your way, Mojo. On three, I'm going to have him pull the trigger. How this plays out is entirely in your freakishly-long fingered hands.*

Still, nothing, and no one, moved.

Okay. Ben shrugged. *You want to play chicken with a bullet, that's your choice. *One... Two...**

Chapter Twenty-Six

A SNAKE IN THE SHADOWS

IN THE SHADOWS, just in front of the battered teal fender bent down over a smashed yelled car, a set of bright golden eyes opened.

High notes of pride exuded from Jek's skin as he kept his arm steady. "Just say three."

No. Ben extended his hand over Jek's to push the orc's arms down to point his gun elsewhere and stopped before touching it. *This body's not meant for subtleties. Doing that could break his arm.* Ben tried to cross his arms. Still a bit short of folding position, his four elbows came closer to his sides.

Ben projected, *I can't be your bag boy like this. So, what do you want from me now, charlatan?*

Papa Mojo's deep, gravelly intonations rolled through the scrapyard so clearly that his southern drawl could've been either audible or telepathic. "I can tell, since you are like this, you did not receive my warning."

Ben glanced to the clouds still suspended in the air and heaved a tired breath. *Do me a favor, okay? Don't try to play me. I'm not in the mood. Tonight's already been a bit of a bear—if you know what I mean. Just tell me what you want.*

Papa Mojo fidgeted a little and moonlight lit his thin fingers as they came up before the shadowed form and folded. "Bluntly, Meadows Towing Might-Fist, I want what you want. I want to live."

Ben rolled his head to the side and blinked rapidly like an enthralled child. *This is where I'm supposed to wonder and ask—with bated breath—'why, whatever could you possible mean, Mr. Papa Mojo, sir?'* He straightened his neck. *However, I'm still waiting for you to cut the crap.*

A soft hiss slithered through the yard and the distant golden eyes narrowed. "The person who is trying to dispose of your body will come for me next."

Ben nodded and unfolded his arms to applaud the most direct sentence the dark diviner had probably said this century. *See? Was that so hard?* As though ready to have a ball thrown to him, Ben extended his arms wide. *You could have answered my next question, too, Mojo, but being forthright is probably hard for you. So I'll give you an easy one. Why does he want us gone? What do we have in common?*

Papa Mojo pulled his steepled fingers back into the shadows. "What's the only possible bond or likeness we can have, brother?"

Ben heaved a sigh. *In case you hadn't noticed, you just went cryptic.*

Another hiss slipped through the area.

Okay, fine. I'll ask then…" Though he didn't have a physical voice, Ben tried to inflect a falsely innocent, mostly naïve tone. "Well, Mr. Mojo, sir. How do I save my life?" He kept the rest of his thought—which will somehow protect yours—to himself.

Papa Mojo stepped forward. He stopped when a slant of light fell across the top of his bald head. Ben couldn't tell the diviner's exact skin tone, but the mystic shone ghostly pale in the moonlight. "Marshal your remaining forces—"

Forces marshaled. Ben motioned to Jek with his two right hands. *There he is. The only one who hadn't betrayed me and has a reason to help.*

Papa Mojo pointed a long accusatory finger. "Don't be dense, boy."

Don't call me boy, trickster.

Jek asked, "Can I shoot him now?"

After the next insult, yes.

A long, barbed hiss slid across the scrapyard and echoed from rows further away. The mystic's voice had a—Fear? Rage?—quiver.

Papa Mojo said, "This is why I had to come. You are not using the greatest resource you have at your disposal. You have goblins, Ben. You have first-blood, Might-Fist."

First-blood? Ben arms folded. Yes! He kept his elation from showing. *That's a goblinoid concept.*

"More than that." Papa Mojo stepped back into the shadows. His eyes finally return to their relaxed, oblong shape. "As I am sure you know, Dwarves have a series of words to pinpoint each aspect of such relationships."

While I know the language, I've never met a single one Ben slid his fist past his arms to tighten his closed expression. *Makes it kind of impossible to make a deal with them, don't you think?*

Somehow, a slat of light shone in a narrow strip over Mojo's mouth to light his short, sharp teeth. Is he smiling? The diviner's slow drawl felt excruciatingly long as he dragged out his next sentence. "The races of Giants draw the same lines."

Bouncing, flippant hoots burst from Ben's throat. Even if I could bypass Pepperjack's formidable protective spells, there's no flippin' way Kograkken is going to come and help me. He projected, *Right. The only giant I know would rather slice me in half!*

"They are often like that," Papa Mojo agreed. He pointed a skeletal finger to the top of the building.

Finally! Ben focused on the seer's digits. They're as black as before, but pale white skin starts at his wrists. Weird.

Mojo continued, "You've taken communion of a giant's son." Papa Mojo stepped back and withdrew his arm. The thin fingers retreated as well and folded again before moving back into the darkness.

Bet as soon as I turn my back, he's going to slink away. Still… Expecting to see the goblins on the roof, Ben turned to see what Papa Mojo had pointed at. He scanned the lip of the building and didn't find anyone standing there, just the 'o' in Meadows Towing, where he'd stashed the Imprisoning Orb with Ur-Krurk in it. I put him up there so he could see what was going on here while locked away. Ben shuddered at the thought of having to watch your own child be devoured. Bastion. Ben found a new level of disdain and disgust for the monster that had inhabited his body. That ritual must've been soul-wrenching for him to watch.

"He closed his eyes," Jek reported. Then asked, "Should I start shooting?"

No. Save your bullets. Ben hustled to where Papa Mojo had been. The diviner was indeed gone, leaving behind a heavy smell of baby oil. Ben sniffed to go deeper. In the oil, he found the mystic's underlying, untrustworthy musk. *There's his scent. Even his skin oozes lies.*

For moment, he imagined Papa Mojo at home with a fictional Mama Mojo. In his fantasy scenario, each was famished and trying to trick the other into picking the restaurant where they wanted to dine.

He felt his cheeks lift. *Wonder if I look happy or mad?*

Having enough of the diviner's scent, Ben blew air out his nose. *I could track you, Mojo. Track you and give you an ultimatum to help me or else.* Ben clenched and unclenched his fists. *However, if I did that, I have a feeling that we'd end up no better off than the turtle and the snake in that fable about the two trying to cross a rising river together.*

Ben bounded back to the building and looked up at the 'o' again. *Jek, tell me about communion.*

"Not much to tell, Might-Fist." Jek heaved his *it is what it is* shrug. "Eat the heart and mind of a fallen foe and gain their first-blood. We orcs don't practice it, but ubbos—who, on the whole, always try to consider themselves giants instead of goblinoids—follow the giants' odious tradition."

Ben put his hands against the side of the dark cinderblock building. His fingertips began to dig into the ledges and crannies to grip. He pulled up. His feet left the ground and started to assist in his ascent. He paused to look down at Jek. *And blam, it's that easy.*

Jek gave a doubtful shrug. "You have to kill one first. Then…" Jek's lips crinkled and turned.

Wow, may wonders never cease. An orc is showing distaste.

"Then, carve out the heart and mind, enact some ancient Nilosian ritual, and eat them." Jek's hands moved over each other in a washing motion before opening to show empty palms. "Then yes—twenty-four hours later, *if* you happen to keep the meal down—you *blam* with the first-blood of the devoured."

Ben continued his climb. *When you put it that way…* Having woken up last month with ogre in his stomach, he knew how hard a gut would work to expel the noxious meal. He had asked Nuk about why they had fed him the onion-based broth and they had only said it was to settle the stomach. When Ben had gotten free, he had unknowingly fought the last of the procedure with antacids. *I should've just puked.*

But by keeping it down, did that mean he now had first-blood? It sure sounded that way.

He reached the two-foot tall purple letters and reached into the hole. His fingers wrapped around orb. *It hardly feels right releasing Ur-Krurk to help me after Bastion ate his son.* About to put the orb back, Ben considered Papa Mojo's words again. *He's right. I'm going to need every single ally I can muster.*

Ben tucked the orb under an armpit and climbed down to the ground. Then, holding it with all four hands, he focused Nilosian energy into the orb to activate it.

Chapter Twenty-Seven

DYNAMICS

THIS IS WRONG. Ben found his gaze fixed upon the orb as tendrils of his black magic sizzled around and through the artifact Elder Komir had giving him to capture the very creature locked away. *This monster beat Penelope and made the orcs battle each other to the death only to have the winner eat the dead one's feet.* The underpinnings of what he knew to be a shame-feast rekindled in his head. Ben shuttered. He was still glad to have swiped the definition on his screen away before it got any worse. *And here I am, releasing him.*

A black-laced howling purple streak of magic arced from the orb and slammed into the ground before him.

Ur-Krurk, the super barrel chested, teal-skinned ogre-magi stood free.

With Ben in his girallon form, they were on the same eye-level. For a moment, the ogre stared hard with his red iris into Ben's.

In primal reaction, Ben's body hair bristled.

Ur-Krurk lowered his eyes and turned his head to spit to the side. He wiped his lips and asked in the strong Ruler-Giant dialect, "What do you want with me, Blood-Son?"

The ogre's breath reeked of jerky. *I left him several cases in case I hadn't been able to return and feed him, but it seems that the ogre prefers it...*

Unless I miscalculated how much he regularly eats and that's what he's down to eating now.

Ben didn't answer. He could only look at the monster that had attempted to kill him on his sixteenth birthday, the monster that had threatened the lives of his family, the creature who had lost a son to the unfeeling parasitic blight on his own soul. And now the creature he often had nightmares of was looking around the space between them and around them. *He fears me and can't meet my eye. Too. Weird.* Ben tried to imagine how the ogre might view the situation. *Our moral codes are so far apart; I don't think I could understand his point of view if he wrote a thousand-page dissertation on it.*

To find the limits, Ben asked, *What can I ask of you?*

The Imprisoning Orb in his hands began to vibrate and spit out the various foods Ben had loaded into it. First out, in rapid succession, were eighteen butcher-paper-wrapped cuts of meat. Then, six white Styrofoam family meals from Caliente Chicken shot out, breaking open when they hit the ground – broiled chicken, wedge potatoes, and half-ears of corn lay where they landed. Ben had gotten those over a month ago, but the food smelled fresh. Two bags of beef jerky flew out.

Ur-Krurk walked over to scoop one up.

Movement at the edge of Ben's vision made him take his eyes off the ogre and the food-spewing Imprisoning Orb for a moment. Jek had opened the door to his truck, and Nuk and Uk'so—each with a small backpack—scurried into the cab.

Crashing splashing retuned Ben's attention to the orb. Gallon jugs of water were lobbed a few short feet from the orb. Some burst open, though most kept their integrity. Last out, cans of tuna, a can opener, and a mounting pile of discarded plastic bags, cardboard boxes, and Styrofoam.

"My Blood-Son, you have treated me well in my defeat and exile. You have taken my title to carry it forward in time so your son or blood-son may honor this ground after your life has been shed, and his son after him." The ogre scratched his crotch as his eyes raise to the sky, searching for a moment before continuing. "You may ask that of me which any blood-son would ask of a blood-father." Ur-Krurk ripped the bag of jerky open and up-ended it into his mouth. Stray pieces fell to the dirt as he chewed and continued to scratch.

While that might help if I understood the blood-family *thing, it doesn't tell* me *anything, really.*

A slight wind stirred and stopped as though the tight grip that kept the air from moving slipped momentarily.

Whoa. Ben thought the ogre would smell foul, but a soapy scent —*pride*—clung to Ur-Krurk's natural musk. *How can he feel pride right now? It has to be a trick. He probably has magic that allows him to control his scent.*

Attempting to get down to the brass tacks, Ben asked, *How long until you turn on me?*

Still chewing, Ur-Krurk tossed the empty bag and scooped the other unopened one. "Here's something your former race may never understand." The ogre swallowed and ran a thumb over his heart. "You can never betray blood." He then drew the same thumb across his throat. "Never."

Ur-Krurk's conviction struck a chord that rung true in Ben. He found himself nodding.

"Load up" Jek pounded on his truck door twice. The engine rumbled to life. "We're burning moonlight."

Guess I'll take the left side and Ur-Krurk can balance out the right. Ben clambered on. The truck groaned and rocked under his mass.

Ur-Krurk's morphed his ten-foot ogre magi body down to a skinny, almost emaciated, five-foot tall orangeish-brown skinned orc. His nose stretched goblinishly long and hooked down and his chin did the same.

Jek called out, "You've got the sniffer, Ben. Rap on the hood when you got something. I'll stop." The engine revved, the truck lurched, and they were off.

Thinking over what Ur-Krurk had said, two of the ogre magi's words echoed an accusation leveled by Alice last month. Alice had asked, *What are you, Ben, really?* And now, the ogre said. *Former race.*

Ben scanned the dark horizon. His brain burned with a horrible wonder. *What have I become?* Then, as they exited through the eastern gate and zoomed into the night, his curiosity soured to dread.

What am I becoming?

Chapter Twenty-Eight

BEYOND THE EASTERN GATE

LIKE A DOG GOING for a car ride, Ben kept his head either off to the side or above the cab. Though the still desert night air had the same stale, uncirculated smell, the effect of feeling wind through his body hair felt good and proved to be rather relaxing. Even better, when he closed his eyes, had discovered a secondary benefit—it helped him focus on scents.

Ben kept his nostrils flared and his mouth open to allow the air to flow in through his nasal cavity. He initially focused on the convoy's heavy exhaust smell until, one by one, the vehicles started to peel away from the main road to the multitude of dirt trails out here.

His group, on the hunt for his body and Jek's vengeance, had left the scrapyard less than half an hour ago and had long since passed the area where his human body had crashed through the back of the van doors and lain in the dark. At that point, smelling the unfamiliar rose-water scent he'd noticed back at the garage, Toad, Malcolm, several orcs, and a bitter reek that could've been the tuzvul, Ben had locked onto Malcolm's trail. If anything, he could count on Malcolm seeing this through long enough to get his family heirloom back.

The Dunn-Blatt's scent had been robust with pride when the train of vehicles had been closer to the scrapyard. Now, as they moved further into the desert, Malcolm's smell started to change. Doubt ate at his pride and worry chased doubt until the three emotions were measured in equal parts before vanishing in an overpowering sting of fear.

Ben pounded on the roof. *Exhaust from the last van and Malcolm's Transcend continue on, but Malcolm's actual scent has gone cold.*

Jek hit the brakes and started to skid.

When they slowed enough, Ben leapt from the tow truck and galloped back down the road to find Malcolm's scent. He closed his mouth as he started to take air in rapid, short sniffs. *Getting close.* A watered-down Malcolm-smell, the vehicles' tailwind disturbed the air and thinned the scent some, filled his nose. *Whoa!* Ben winced and lifted his head away from the ground. The tart, acrid stink of Malcolm's fear burned.

Ben opened his eyes to see he stood over a puddle of piss that smeared out into the desert—*he pissed his pants and they drug him away.* *Here.*

Footprints flanked the piss-mud and a hint of sour, mischievous deception became high notes in both Toad's, and the rose-water scent. The tuzvul's distrustful scent hadn't changed a lick.

In his girallon form, far from the lights of Meadows Towing, Ben found his vision to be in a high contrast greyscale. As though, by giving up trying to distinguish color, he could see even clearer than if he had cast *Elfsight.* Upon hearing Jek's heavy footsteps closing in behind him, Ben used both his eyes and nose to follow the footprints away from the road.

A light, airy voice called, "Stop, Blood-Son."

That's what Ur-Krurk called me, but who's voice is that? Ben turned.

Jek, Nuk, and Uk'so closed in behind him. A little further away, coming from the direction of the truck, a thin human—about as undersized for a man as the orangeish-brown orc had been—spoke, in Ruler-Giant, with the edgy pattern unique to Ur-Krurk. "You're about to breech Blood-Berry Fairy territory."

Why would Ur-Krurk take on a human form? Ben glanced down at his feet and four knuckles on the ground for any indication that he might be crossing a boarder of some sort. Occasional cacti peppered the distance, a few overly-large rocks lay about the dirt. *Just regular desert.*

Holding his ground and not advancing, Ben stood erect. *The scents go further that way.*

"Yes," Ur-Krurk's light-voiced human form pronounced the sharp consonants of his native tongue. "But there are rituals to respect so the fae see us as visitors instead of trespassers." He whispered, "Also, telepathy isn't secret around fae."

Ben nodded.

As the man—*Ur-Krurk*—drew closer, avoiding the footprints, and piss-mud, his ears stretched up to form points level with the top of his forehead. The body that had seemed narrow grew a few inches taller changing the underfed starved look into a slender grace. Ur-Krurk, now in elf form, flipped opened a lighter and struck it against his leg. Color poured back into the nearby world.

Ur-Krurk pointed to one of the round stone and said, in a lilted voice, "Tuk."

Also avoiding the tracks, Uk'so scampered forward. The goblin went to the large, rounded stone and extend his green arm over it. A patchwork of moonlit scars lit the back of thin, sinewy forearm. Uk'so pulled a knife from his inside his jeans waistline and winced slightly as he slid the edge against—and into—his skin. Uk'so then placed the rune-covered blade level on the boulder and pressed his wound on the flat of the steel. He rocked his arm toward the handle to make the blade point rise.

Blood welled, then ran against gravity to pool at the tip of the blade. Little by little, much more slowly than a typical wound would bleed, the droplet swelled until the crimson threatened to break loose and fly up into the sky.

"Elder, Elven Trader Laely is here!"

Who said that? Tracking the light, tinny voice squeaking in the local Elven tongue, Ben scanned the area. He found a diminutive creature— *it can't be more than a foot tall*—with willowy wings and a skinny body that was as non-committed to gender as a small child's doll.

It flittered and landed on Uk'so's shoulder to exclaim, "Two elves in one evening! Amazing! This may prove to be the best night of the season!"

"Or the worst." Part of the rock Uk'so had his arm on shifted. Another skinny body, under a foot tall, moved to stand on the goblin's green arm. When it did, the being's rough stone coloring faded, becoming a translucent crystalline form with gossamer wings and a glass walking stick, before taking on the deep green color of Uk'so's skin. "You say *amazing*, I say inauspicious." Voice as light as the first, this one had a grizzled sound to it. "No offense to our most frequent customer, good Elven Trader Laely, but another elf just came through with a deal which was too good to not regret upon seeing a second elf." It pointed the walking stick, which also had Uk'so's skin color at Ur-Krurk. "You are wise. You know of what I speak."

"Indeed, Deep Root Yilst." Ur-Krurk bowed with enough skill to pass Courtmanship III. *And his Elven would earn top form marks from Adept Y'Favo.* "Your instincts lead you to fact. The last elf did not own, or earn, the contents of his side of the last deal."

"You have an odd-acting abomination." Yilst was pointed the walking stick at Ben. "The upward stance, the slack jaw, the amazed twinkle to its eyes…" The fairy pressed his pole to Uk'so's wound. The green flesh pulled together, puckered, and sealed, adding another moonlit line to the patchwork of scars. "It is also comprised of pure magic!"

That sounds like an accusation.

Yilst's wings fluttered and it turned crystalline during its short flight to Uk'so's head where, upon landing, it turned the same deep green as the goblin's bald head. "What's your game, wily Elven Trader?"

Chapter Twenty-Nine

PLAYING DUMB

I GUESS I'm not supposed to be intelligent. As though chasing a scent, Ben took three short sniffs, closed his mouth, and dropped down to rest his feet and all four sets of knuckles on the desert hardpan. A coyote howled in the distance. Trying to seem uninterested, Ben ranged his gaze along the dark mountains in the distance, set against the last deep purple that remained of an astronomical dusky sky. A good ways out, closer to the horizon, clouds moved in that ever-slow way they have.

Don't look up. Ben fought the urge to see if the local clouds were moving or were still stuck like gum under a desk. *Very few animals look up into the sky, and they always have a reason.* Instead he used his peripheral vision to note what transpired with the Ur-Krurk and Yilst.

Ur-Krurk bowed again. "I would feel more comfortable discussing details of the deal I hope to broker if the Wise and Good Deep Root would first accept out blood-tribute. It would surely be my folly if we were not greeted as guests."

The fairy tapped its staff against Uk'so's head. The goblin blinked at each of the twenty taps. "The foolishness of turning away a true friend would stain my name."

Angling its wings for balance, the young-seeming fairy on Uk'so's shoulder ran up his green arm. A satchel appeared around its body, and it produced a miniscule crystal orb from somewhere previously hidden. It held the orb above the blood. Blue energy—*Uk'so can cast spells?*—flowed into the sphere. "Servant magic, Deep Root."

Thinking back to how charged he had felt while cleaning the basement—*as long as Uk'so sang, I was quite happy scrubbing and didn't feel tired*—Ben nodded with new understanding.

The young fairy considered the power as it filled. "Well bred. Good stock." Once full, the orb was stashed back into the bag as both it, and the fairy, disappeared.

Yilst moved on Uk'so's forehead. "I do so only because of the well-tended and richly soiled garden of our entwined history, good Elven Trader.

"In humility, I appreciate your acceptance." Ur-Krurk bowed again. The thin elven fingers articulated a high-court flair Ben had rarely seen and didn't know.

Wow. He's really good! Ben felt his mouth start to gape again at the ogre's masterful grasp of Elven and etiquette. He closed his mouth.

Yilst became clear again as it flitted from Uk'so and fluttered inches from Ben's face. "Too odd, I say." It pointed the clear staff at him. "I'm getting a feeling, deep down in my vines. This embodiment belongs in the husk brought to us. Does it not?"

"Again, Wise and Good Deep Root, your instincts lead to fact." Ur-Krurk extended his hand towards Ben's face and he stepped forward.

If you think I'm sniffing, or licking, your fingers after that extensive crotch scratch, you are grossly mistaken.

Ur-Krurk stopped so his hand remained under the fluttering fairy. "The mystic girallon before you is the new Meadows Towing Might-Fist."

"A human Might-Fist." Yilst's wings gave out and it dropped, taking on the elven flesh tone of Ur-Krurk's hand. "But what of the ogre magi?

"Please know, Wise and good Deep Root, I speak vaguely because the truth is too deep for a top-soil conversation, but know these facts—the ogre lives, his son is vanquished, and the husk below is now the ogre's Blood-Son."

Sitting for a moment, as though reeling, Yilst lay on its back, eyes cast to the sky.

Ur-Krurk added his other hand to support the fairy's full body across his palms.

Stars which did not shine in the sky above—*and probably never have in this world*—reflected in the glint of the tiny, flesh-colored orbs. Yilst started to stroke the top edge of its wings. The meticulous method of preening made it look as though it would rather be biting its nails, if it had any. *Why is it nervous?* Yilst shifted its eyes to Ur-Krurk. "Human Might-Fist... Human Blood-Son…"

Ur-Krurk nodded. "Dual title. Dual color."

Now they're really talking about me. I feel like a creep sneaking journals away to gain insight into how others perceive him. Ben looked away completely and spied the distant purple dot which was the Meadows Towing neon star on its tower.

"The dragons were black over red this year." Both excitement and worry flicked into Yilst's voice as it whispered, "They say The Black had purple and green."

"Very ominous," in agreement, Ur-Krurk had lowered his voice, as well. "My information is embarrassingly dated. Tri-color then."

Ben looked to Uk'so who kept his arm against the stone. *How long does he have to hold that position?*

Yilst scooted into Ur-Krurk's right palm as though getting closer would elicit more information. It perked its pointed ears. "Laely, between you, me, and the ether, do tell, what were the two colors you knew."

Ur-Krurk brought the fairy closer—*is he going to eat him?*—and whispered. "Nilos over Argos."

"Yes. Makes sense," Yilst began to stroke its wing in that nervous way again. "While gaining Blood-Son, the human gained Krotos; but how would it gain access to the emerald, which belongs to dimension alone?"

Ur-Krurk nodded. "As though tri-color was not bad enough."

Yilst stopped preening. "Do you know the human's third title?"

How do titles play into this?

"Too deep for top soil," Ur-Krurk answered. "But I would guess it would have to do with his school."

"Yes," Yilst stood. "The husk is still quite young." The fairy cleared its throat as it flittered from Ur-Krurk's hand to the stone, and took on its color. Yilst spoke in Servant-Giant to the others, ignoring Ben. "Your eleven guide has set us to trade." The fairy tapped the head of his staff against the stone.

The rock gave out a groan and then the center lifted to arc high into the sky. As it did, a translucent rainbow film rose form the ground to follow the tip as it hit a summit and began to drop to form an archway. Yilst launched from the ground, turning crystalline for a moment before it shimmered with the lights playing behind it. "Now, come. Let us barter for your master's body."

Chapter Thirty

ARCHWAY OF LIGHT

ONE BY ONE, Yilst first, followed by Ur-Krurk, Jek, and then the goblins, everyone entered the lights as the stone archway finished its descent with a *clack* on another round stone. Complete, the film solidified and flashed bright.

Whoa! Recalling—with utter clarity—the prismatic tentacles that had radiated from Alice toward nearby mundanes, Ben hopped back. *That's the Mystique!* Curious enough to forget his dumb act, Ben leaned closed to get a good look at where the sheet of scintillating rainbow light came from the stone. *Too cool.*

Scents radiated form the pane of lights. Yilst's earnestness, Malcolm's fear, the rose-water's joy, the goblins focus, Jek's—Ben sniffed at the lights again to be certain that the self-loathing and guilt coupled with Jek's scent and not anyone else's. *Why?*—his curiosity as to why Jek would possibly feel anything close to those feelings summoned the image of the four dead orcs back at Meadows Towing. Ben's heart went sore panged as guilt mounted his shoulders, too.

Jek called them into service at Meadows Towing and they died because I was too blinded by the opportunity to thrash an old bully to not acknowledge my suspicions.

Ur-Krurk waving his hand brought Ben back to the present. The elf's hand motions indicated that he should come through.

Ben started to walk into the wall of light. His lips pressed against his teeth and his nose smooshed against his face. In that moment, he felt his Nilosian font being to drain away. *Hey.*

He shifted his weight away. *Hey.*

The wall pulled at him.

Hey! He yanked away and leapt back.

The random rolling swirls and flickers froze and formed solid vertical bands of—*white, orange, red, green, blue, purple, black, and a very thin yellow*—light. *I knew of the other seven fonts, but what's yellow?* He sat on his haunches. *Wonder what it's called. Heck, for that matter, what are the green, and blue called?*

Yilst came back. Its crystal form filled with black energy. "Pure Nilosian!" It sounded drunk. "It's magnificent!" A flapping shade against the arc of light, Yilst turned to face Ur-Krurk. "Beckon your beast. Have it use brute force to pass through the Mystique."

So, it is *the Mystique. It's supposed to blanket the entire city. What is it about the stone portal that makes the magic visible?*

Still just on the other side of the bands of light, Ur-Krurk's mouth moved, but no sound came through. The elf planted his feet and leaned forward as though to push with his shoulder.

Shoulder through, huh? Ben drew a breath and caught the smell of the stale desert air settling around. *Well, if I stay here, nothing changes.* Ben lowered his shoulder and—*time to Kool-Aid Man my way in*—charged at the light.

As though slamming into an inertia-sucking gel pack, the force of Ben's charge was sucked away. A myriad of smells came to him—*too many to count or sort. Hey! It's still sucking at my Nilosian chakra!* His Krotosian font swelled to bolster the black. A surge of might rippled within his muscles and—*progress!*—his shoulder pushed into the light which bent with his force like Jell-O.

A reality-ripping tear blasted around him as the light-turned-Jell-O turned to fabric and his shoulder caused a tear.

Getting it! Laying into the fabric, Ben pressed with arms, and legs. His face started to go through.

AHHhhhh!

The tearing slapped in his ears, ripping through his eardrums like a diesel truck through tissue paper.

Ahhh! He tried to pull back.
Ahhh! Stuck! Ahhh!
The web of light had him.

Chapter Thirty-One

BLOOD BERRIES

H<small>IS</small> A<small>RGOSIAN POWER</small> flared and flooded his system. The world flashed red as he channeled his rage against the blood-pounding, reverberating pain in his skull into raw strength and yoked the efforts of his other two energies into moving forward.

Ben's other shoulder and arm pushed through. In his flailing, his hands found the edges of the archway. Getting through, he pulled and pushed, scrabbled and struggled, prayed and cursed.

Finally, as though squeezed through a meat grinder, he fell from the web of light and flopped on his side.

Hopping back to his feet—grasping at his ear—warm fluid flowed through his fingers. No sooner had he stood than his legs and lower arms gave out, and his thousand-pound bulk collapsed onto the sharp stone ground.

Eyes clamped shut against the pain, the world spun as he rolled down hewn-stone stairs, banging his elbows, shoulders, knees, and head on the way.

Clasping his ears, he topped uncontrolled. Though the fall was short, the world kept spinning as he lay sprawled on his side at the foot of the stairs—wishing the pain away.

Something cold tapped his left temple. A soothing wave of energy doused the fire in his left ear. He could hear his hectic bellows as he flopped, but couldn't stop them. Struggling, he managed to get a foot and lower leg against the ground at the same time. Trying to stand, he rocked to the right and, galloping sideway to try and catch his balance, plowed into a rough unworked stone wall.

A humming began near him.

Ben swatted at the annoyance while keeping his right ear cupped. On his second swing, he hit something light in the air. The sound stopped.

Without balance, he pressed against the wall to brace himself, but without equilibrium, the room tilted under his feet before he could recruit his limbs to keep up. He flopped on the floor and rolled along the abrasive ground.

Another cold tap spread relief into the right side of his head.

Agony doused, reason made a rapid return.

An illuminating black, purple, and red glass fairy buzzed away from him to grip a ruddy stalactite. Its wings continued to flutter, making light and shadows dance along the other stalactites that papered the long corridor. One end twisted away and the other ended in stairs—*the stairs that I fell down*—that led up.

Scents, mostly of wild berries filled the air.

The thick uncultivated bouquet would've smelled lovely if not for the blood, pain, and anguish also hanging in the air. Ben sniffed and found the berry aromas were layered with emotions. The delicious scent of blueberry bonded with a loamy sorrow, both entirely inseparable from the other. *Strawberry and pain. Raspberry and anguish. Blackberry and fear.* Traces of pure huckleberry and boysenberry lay untainted beneath.

The light fairy released the stalactite and fluttered in front of him. "Tri-color indeed!" *Yilst.* Ben recognized the voice and the walking stick it held. Yilst continued, "Your master is strong and worthy of his titles."

Ben found additional fragrances in the air as the fairy's flapping wings stirred scents from higher in the cavern. First the tuzvul's fearless musk, then, Malcolm's unbridled, piss-soaked fear. *They're close.* He scanned the area again. The stairs led up to the antechamber at the entrance, then further up and out of sight. Looking to the other end of the corridor—*I'm pretty sure there's an offshoot to the right there, and there*—he spied more corridors curving out from the natural stone pathways than he had seen at first glance.

Ur-Krurk had already navigated halfway down the sharp stone stairs with his hand out.

Yilst fluttered up to him and landed. "It would surely be my folly to possibly impede the forthcoming Black Dragon and the Century of Shadows, but Good and Wise Elven Trader, there is still a matter of entry fees."

Ben rose to his feet and knuckles. With the tuzvul's scent fresh in his mind, he recognized the pain in the laced strawberry as hers—*uh, disgusting*—and it smelled absolutely delicious. His mouth watered at the thought of a sundae made from blackberries, then his throat constricted when the berry's emotion—fear—came combined with a trace of Malcolm's urine.

Both of them come from further down the hall.

"Good and Wise Deep Root, it would be foolish of me not to offer additional in exchange for not presenting sooner. Please understand, concern for the beast delayed my donation. Tuk." Ur-Krurk extended his hand with Yilst up toward the entrance. "I imagine you do not get much *true* servant magic down here."

Uk'so already had the back of his arm cut and three crystalline fairies similar to Yilst, crowded around the wound with glass spheres.

Ben started to venture away.

Yilst turned to eye him.

Act simian. Ben scratched his chest, walked a little further, and plopped down.

Ur-Krurk flourished his hand near his chest, fished out the Imprisoning Orb and, with a pleased smile, brandished it at Ben.

Chapter Thirty-Two

INTO THE HIVE

BEN'S EYES WENT WIDE. His guts quivered. He wanted to bolt. *Now he captures me and leaves me here with these twisted fae. And I never saw it coming.*

"Do not mind the beast, Wise Deep Root." The elf tossed the sphere past Ben. "It just needs a distraction."

Whew! Ben bounded after the sphere and—batting it with his lower arms—knocked it further down the corridor. *That would've been it.*

"He was excited to see it, too," Yilst said. "Simple things for simple minds, right, good Elven Trader?" The fairy continued speaking, but distance and the widening passageway effectively muted the light voice.

Minding his way, so he could find his way back, Ben continuing to act like a simple simian as he batted the sphere further and further down the corridor. After glancing a few times to see if he had been followed, Ben kept this ears keyed for the buzzing hum of fae wings as he scooped the Imprisoning Orb and—*mind the stalactites*—went bipedal to get at the scents at the top of the cavern.

Not able to fully stand up straight, his head pressed against the rough ceiling where the smells of Malcolm and the tuzvul had begun to overpower the smell of berries and the emotions connected to them. *Getting closer.* Ben dodged stalactites, alternating between standing nearly erect and using his lower set of knuckles on the unworked stone floor.

More passageways branched from the twisting main hallway at irregular distances. Occasional small offshoot tunnels rose upward or dropped away. *Malcolm and the tuzvul are too large for those.* The owners of the two scents he followed were too large to fit into those passages; still, if enough fairies got together, they might be able to lift Malcolm. When he thought about fairies grouping up to lift Malcolm, he imagined their small faces contorted with strain.

When the same thought turned to the tuzvul, the image was comical. The thought of them trying to lift the tuzvul conjured a cartoon in his mind of dozens of fairies squealing to get out from beneath her as she sat on the ground thinking, *I'm a dainty princess.*

Keeping the rolling hoots locked away, he grinned at the idea. He amused himself so much that he almost missed when the scents separated.

Whoa... Malcolm's fear drifted from a downward slanted corridor while the tuzvul's undaunted defiance came from up ahead. While the perfume of her scent weighed heavier—*she's probably closer*—he continued forward after Malcolm's waning scent —*have they killed him?*

Two downward winding turns later, the hewn stone passageway leveled out to a hundred-foot circular cavern with a fifty-foot wide pillar in the center. Constant, keening screams and full on flapping sounds—punctuated by an occasional grunt or a groan—rained from the ceiling.

With nothing at eye level, Ben eased forward and cast his gaze upward.

Oh my... The purple top of Malcom's school uniform removed to show a plain black t-shirt, near the top, he clung—*no, he's climbing*—to the wide pillar which rose a good hundred feet into the air and petered out long before the ceilingless, midnight blue night sky high above. Dozens of bats—*wait, are those fairies, too?*—flapped around him. Unlike the thin, delicate pixies at the entrance, these flyers had bulbous bodies, sunken eyes, and screaming mouthfuls of jagged teeth. Most cried a chorus of, "Climb faster!" While a few filled in the lulls in the screams with. "We're going to have to skewer you!"

Rotating as it grew slightly taller, the pillar ground against its stone sleeve in the earth. The handholds and crevices Malcolm used to climb lit bright Krotosian purple, as though a distant, dark light shone to light his path of psychedelic sweat. Other bat-winged fairies pressed glass bubbles—*they're the same items the other fairies use*—against the energy to absorb it away. Entire sections of the stone column, in ten foot rings, rotated widdershins while others remained still or went deosil. New handholds and edges protruded while others—*that's just wicked*—clicked flat.

Malcolm nearly summited.

A higher pitched shrill up near the Dunn-Blatt warned, "Watch out!"

Malcolm pulled his body tight against the column.

The bat-winged fairies released a volley of spears, and cried out, "Down! Down! Down!"

"We gotta go down, human." Ben spied a moonlight crystal fairy bound by the ankle to a length of chain anchored in Malcolm's right ear. Flittering to not yank the cord that bound them, it also dodged spears. "They'll let us rest on the ground."

Most of the spears missed Malcolm, but some sunk into his sides while there were others already in his legs.

They're herding him to extract magic and emotions from him... But they're supposed to be friendly guides to—Ben's jaw started to tighten at the vile act being so against what he had learned about the diminutive protectors in Mythic Monsters—*wait, the crystalline one is trying to help. It's just those bat-winged creatures that are bastards.*

His jaw tightened further. *I'm sure this is more than what Malcolm bargained for.* Cursing his desire to help the very person the still unidentified owner of the rose-water scent had used as bait, Ben slipped back out of sight to work rescue scenarios over in his mind. Anyway he ran it—*they control the column*—each attempt ended poorly. *Only if they didn't control the column.*

Ben turned away. He struggled with a last-ditch thought. *Blitzkrieg in, balls-to-the-wall up to Malcolm first, and figure the rest out on the fly.* He shook his head against it. Perhaps once I have my body, and spells, back.

Heading back the way he came—*where'd these paths come from*—Ben found other paths he had not seen on the way in. *It's like being in a beehive.* He shook his head and corrected. *More like being in a hornets' nest.*

To not get lost, Ben sniffed his way back along Malcolm's weakening trail.

Buzzing sounded ahead.

Ben dropped the orb, batted it, and chased it down the hall toward the tuzvul's growing scent.

Four flyers—two crystalline fairies and two of the bulbous bat creatures—seemed to speak to each other in a language of whistles, clicks, and hums. *The bat creatures and crystal fairies are in this together?* Twinkling laughter came from them as they sipped from each other's bubbles. They all fell silent, and watched him.

Keep drinking. Keep laughing. Ben maintained his charade as he moved through the pungent cloud of blackberry-fear beneath them.

Shortly after he passed, they returned to laughing between their whistles, clicks, and hums.

He bounded on after the orb, and maintained the charade until all trace of their sound was gone. To be sure, he plopped down next to the orb, playing with it between his hands and feet for a few minutes as he scanned up and down the stalactite ceiling and hewn hallway. *Alright.*

Ben stood and pressed his head up against the stalactites and latched onto the tuzvul's heady defiance. *Crap.* Malcolm's scent was also stronger. *Too far.* He kept his eyes peeled for the incline where her smell came from and listened for the four flyer.

If only I had my Silence *spell...*

Inching back, he spied the spot where he'd gone down after Malcolm's scent instead of up. Just short of where the four flyers were, he spied the incline. *I got by them once, but if they see me again... Well, nothing for it. Have to try.*

Instead of chasing the orb, he held it tight in his lower hands, and moved out into the corridor sniffing. *It's only natural for a creature to follow its nose.* Thinking about how dogs looked when on a trail, Ben did his best to look natural following a scent.

He closed in on the where they chirped.

They fell silent.

Act natural... Ben raised his head slightly and began up the incline.

They began to whistle to one another.

He continued up. *Just following a scent, boys. Go back to drinking.*

A buzzing closed in behind him.

Pay it no mind, just keep going.

A series of chirps alternated behind him.

Just keep going. Up ahead, the corridor splayed away like it had to Malcolm's. *This one is closed in.* The fairies didn't tell him to stop—*or at least I don't understand if they did*—and so he kept on.

Their chirps stopped. Their buzzing drew closer—*one on each side*—and continued.

The corridor leveled out to a ledge. Straight ahead, across a forty-foot span, on top of another wide pillar like the one Malcolm had been set to ascend and descend, the tuzvul stood astride his human body.

There I am! And I still have my uniform on. He tried to tell if he had his holster and tablet on. *Can't see inside the coat.* The angle of his body didn't allow for confirmation. Ben found his eyes narrowing at the rainbow circlet which remained squashed down on his forehead and, at one-tenth of its former mass, the black cloud—*Bastion*—hovering over his head.

The buzzing at his flanks went back down the corridor.

Working in unison, both the crystalline fairies and the bulbous ones formed squadrons to swoop at the tuzvul and toss spears at her.

If they got her down here, they have to have a way to take her out in a quick fashion. They seem to be playing—

A squadron of flyers threw spears down on her as another flew up the pillar to release tiny spears to pepper her back.

They're using her as practice.

With her long gangly arms, she swiped like mad, but typically ended up short of contact. On the rare instance she smacked one, it fell buffeting to a group of lower flying fairies whose entire job seemed to be the safety net. They'd catch the falling fae and press it against the wall, where it would stick to recover.

Overall the area was a writhing maelstrom of buzzing, flapping wings, whistles, clicks, and hums. He spied a few fairies who seemed to be the leaders calling shots as the others peppered her body. Her hide—like a pin cushion—had hundreds of tiny spears in it. Her regeneration pushed them from her skin and the weapons fell to join the uncountable others at her feet.

Crap! How do I say 'remove the circlet' in Giant? Trying to find the words, he opted for a different phrase and projected, *Take off the barrier.*

The tuzvul glanced at her hands which were hooked into claws and stood tall, sparing a moment to look down at his body before surveying the area.

Ben waved his arms when her gazed scanned over him.

She nodded, "By your command, Master."

Six squadrons of fairies, their leaders included, swooped to take advance of her new posture.

She ducked them, grabbed the rainbow ring on his forehead, and yanked it from his body.

Yes!

The bridge between his mystic self and physical form reappeared in an instant. *Yes! Yes!*

Just as Ben was about to slide across the connection, the black energy cloud above his human head rained upon his brow and his eyes fluttered.

Trying to curse Bastion, a hearty roar blew though his lips and rocked the cave. Ben belted, *Nooooo!*

Once alive with movement, every being in the cavern froze.

Chapter Thirty-Three

TWO SOULS ONE BODY

BEN FOUND himself on his feet, his fist pounding on his chest as the deafening roar, magnified by the enclosed circular cavern, poured out of him in a long furious breath.

Above the steady buzz and flap of wings, a series of whistles rang out as the hovering swarms searched for the source.

Taking advantage of her distracted attackers, the tuzvul grabbed a bulbous fairy nearby who had been motioning orders. She closed both hands around it and—if it made a noise, it didn't rise above the din of whistles—much like an angry child would do to a doll, twisted its head away with a muted snap. Unlike a toy, dark glimmering blood poured from her first.

She grabbed another leader, a crystalline one.

It gave a single, pleading chirp.

The whistling stopped. The sounds of wings grew silent. All the flyers turned to face the tuzvul, focused upon the fairy she held in her massive, gnarled hands.

She thinks I'm Bastion. If he gains control of my body... Ben jogged back down the hall a ways, planted his feet and used all six of his limbs to get him to top speed and—*gotta make it*—leap from the ledge with every ounce of strength within him.

Shit! The arc of his leap topped out. *I'm not going to make it!*

Elation ripped through doubt—*oomph*—when his upper body flopped against the edge of the pillar. His lower hands and feet dug into the crevices as his upper arms landed flat on the top. To get a grip, he had to release Imprisoning Orb.

It rolled forward as he scrambled to get his body over the shelf.

Ben pointed at the rolling sphere halfway across the plateau. *Get the ball!*

A crisp *snap* played on the air when the tuzvul twisted the crystal fairy's head and tossed it away to catch the artifact before the far edge.

The chamber echoed with an ominous thrum of hundreds of furious hums.

As though she were squeezing a juice bag, bright orange sparkling blood gushed from the top of her hand in long squirts. She plopped the crystal fairy's corpse—which had taken on a pale orange flesh tone—into her mouth and chewed as she went to Ben, hooked her hand under his upper armpit, and helped him up.

Atop the column, Ben scrambled to his human body. He grabbed it by the neck with his lower hands and extended an upper hand back. *Come on, give it to me without prompting.*

The tuzvul didn't.

His husk's eyes fluttered. Darkness on black, similar to Collins' cracked contact lenses played beneath the lids.

Please don't let her have seen that. Ben turned his shell's head away from the tuzvul and blocked her view of his human body with his girallon bulk. *How do I gain her trust?* He shook his hand as he raised his husk to standing and remembered a bit from the video of the horrible Ur-Krurkson feast on his tablet.

Ben projected, *You said your honor is mine.*

"And it always will be." She gave him the orb.

The fairy's hum continued to rise in volume.

Bastion, you've earned this. Leaking Nilosian energy into the sphere to activate it, Ben focused the Imprisoning Orb on the black cloud above his head. The orb began to suck it in. *Yes!*

To his chagrin, the sphere also pulled at the Nilosian magic from within him. His girallon body shimmered to red as his Argosian font took over powering his girallon form and artifact.

More of the black cloud from above his head was sucked into the orb.

His husk's eyes stopped fluttering.

The blackness that was in his human body flew from the top of his head to join the thinning cloud. Thicker, it pushed upward to slowly start floating away from the sphere.

No. Bastion's getting away.

"Liar!" The tuzvul wrapped her powerful arms around his wide girallon torso and squeezed.

The bear hug pushed air from Ben's lungs. He released the sphere and caught it with his foot.

She slid her hold up his body and locked his upper shoulders in a full Nelson.

Too—Ben struggled against her might—*strong.* Ben released his human body.

"Liar!" She yanked his bulk back, and back, and back toward the ledge.

She's going to heave us both from the top.

The last of Bastion left his husk. Amazingly, it also continued to pull think wisps of itself *from* the orb.

No matter, the link between his two forms was perfect and unimpeded. Ben tossed the Imprisoning Orb to his human body, released control of his girallon form, and slid across the link.

Back in his skin—*whoa, this room is dark*—he spied the orb come at him. He caught-trapped it against his body. *Got it!*

Ben slapped a hand to where his spellcards should have been. *Just holder, nothing else.* His girallon form poofed away into swirling motes of black, purple, and red smoke.

On the edge of the pillar, the tuzvul struggled for balance.

Cradling the orb like a football, Ben ran over and kicked out at her torso.

She bent her stomach away from the attack and latched onto his trench coat.

Moving the orb from one hand to the other, Ben spun and slipped out of his jacket.

Clutching his school coat and cursing him in Giant, she fell backward over the ledge.

The throngs of angry fairies went down after her.

As at Meadows Towing, he became keenly aware of Malcom's location and weakening condition. *Sorry, Malcolm, but this is much more important.* Ignoring the knowledge, Ben tossed the sphere into Bastion's escaping—*so hard to see in here*—black cloud. While the mystic prison sucked in what wisps it went through, the majority of the Bastion-cloud—pitch black against a dark background—continued to rise.

Ben caught the orb and sent it up for another smoke-vacuum trip.

A distant *thud* came from below.

Well, that should take care of her. He caught the orb, took a careful step closer to the ledge, and sent it up again. It sucked at more of the cloud. Ben caught it.

The deadly hum of murderous fae started to rise.

Annnd now they're going to 'take care' of me...

Chapter Thirty-Four

DEATH ON TINY WINGS

I HAVE MY BODY BACK, but these senses seem so dull compared to the girallon. Now I only smell berries—in general—and not the emotions entwined with them. My hearing's dulled, but only a person incapable of hearing would miss this deadly buzz.

Bastion-smoke trailed from the Imprisoning Orb to the retreating cloud.

No way am I going to get in that stream. Ben set the Imprisoning Orb down and bent at the waist to be in a perfect folding bow—*sure hope they respect courtmanship*—before they came over the edge.

Uncertain what to do, being bent in the most supplicated courtly position made his mouth move before he really knew what he was saying. "Good fae-folk. I am Benjamin Baxter and I am not your enemy." Avoiding his growing grasp of Giant's tongue, he repeated his introduction in all the core languages he knew: Elven, Gnome, and Dwarven.

The humming continued to build and then closed in from all directions as he started his Dwarven introduction. A tiny prick dug deep into the right side of his neck, making him stutter.

"Ahh!" He stopped Dwarven and retuned to English. "Today's enemy was the tuzvul, and she fell." Ben repeated it in Elven and, when he started to say it in Gnome, another prick dug deep into the left side of his neck.

"Ahh! Her master escapes." A desire to point at where Bastion's cloud had been swelled in him. He stamped it down. *Who know how they'll take the sudden move and, worse, what if Bastion's no longer there?*

Two tiny feet landed on the back of his head, positioned on either side of his spine. A needle's point pierced his skin.

Trying to escape the pain, Ben pulled his chest and head tighter to his knees, but the slow, constant burrowing into his spine continue. *Persevere. Persevere.* Straining to endure it, his teeth ground together and he grunted through his grimace. "Good and Wise Fae, if he escapes, the Century of Shadows is certain."

He remained silent. *If they don't like Elven, that'll be my third strike, and this one will go into my spinal cord, making me a quadriplegic.* Ben struggled for something more to say.

A sharp whistle lit behind him. The digging pinpoint stopped its dig. One tiny voice spoke in English. "Say in Elfish."

Ben did. *It's worth a chance.* He added, "The cloud is known as Bastion. He's wholly Nilosian. Granted, he is more my problem than yours, but soon, he'll be an enemy to all."

A volley of heated whistles and clicks preceded the fine tip being ripped out of his neck at a cruel angle.

"Uhh!" The pain made his knees almost buckle.

A light, musical voice spoke in elegant Elven. "Gather your capturing device, young Baxter, and lock away The Foe of All."

'Foe of All,' have to look that one up. Note for future research in place, Ben put Adept Matton's final lesson before failing him in Courtmanship V into practice. *Respect is in the bow. Grace is in the unfolding.* Controlling his breath to keep from greedily sucking air, his lungs quietly expanded as he stood. "Thank you, Good and Wise Fae." He scooped up the Imprisoning Orb, glanced to find Bastion's dark cloud moving sideways, and began to toss the prison up to gather the smoke.

Inching closer and closer to the ledge until his toes over the edge, Ben kept sending the orb up and catching it. One last time, Ben extended his arm over and tossed the sphere up into the retreating smoke and caught it. He gathered most of Bastion, but he'd need three or four more throws to collect the rest and he could go no further.

Worse, thin wisps of Bastion constantly leaked from the orb to rejoin the mass. If he didn't get all of the Nilosian energy, this who struggle would be for naught.

A whirl of hums surrounded him, and a miniature tornado lifted him from the column. Dozens, if not scores of fairies, both crystalline and bulbous, swarmed around him, waving their fingers in unison, directing him through the air like a balloon on a string.

Unabashed, Ben grinned when he imagined the flight of joy-scented bubbles floating from his skin as he captured the remaining bits of Bastion.

As soon as he completed the task Ben's thoughts turned to somehow saving Malcolm. *But how?*

Chapter Thirty-Five

ON A DARKER ROAD

BEN HAD no idea how hard of a bargain the fairies would drive. Still, leaving from the fae caves with a live Malcom rambling non-stop about how great it was to be rescued was better than leaving him behind. Well, almost.

Jek wasn't pleased in the least, but the orc kept his silence.

In the cab of Jek's truck, the engine droned as they motored away from the fairies' hive with the headlights off. Ben looked past Malcolm between them to Jek's sloped profile against the night sky beyond. Partly feeling the same way, Ben kept his mouth shut, too.

Perhaps, for Malcom's part in the murder of Jek's first-blood, Ben should have left Malcom with the fairies. He had been so against what the fairies were doing that he had forgotten that this night wouldn't have gone the way it had without the Dunn-Blatt assisting the rose-scented person.

Jek's eyes went wider with greater annoyance as Malcolm started in again. "I swear, Baxter, I don't know what I would have done if you hadn't come when you did."

Arm on the window, Ben enjoyed the air running up his coat and shirt sleeve. *Feels great to be above ground, even if I have to put up with the smell of Jek's truck.* He glanced ahead to see the teeny purple neon dot of Meadows Towing sign against the bright lights of distant Las Vegas.

"They were going to kill me." As with the last couple cycles, Malcolm looked up. "I cannot possibly thank you enough."

Ben nodded. "You're not out of the clear yet." Not entirely please with the arrangement—*I feel like that fairy anchored to you, except, instead of giving you a reason to go on, I'm preaching false dread*—he reminded Malcolm of is duty. "You still need to return, monthly, to prove you are worthy of keeping your life."

"I will. You can bet I will." Malcolm went back to looking at his hands. "Twily's life depends on it too."

Ben shook his head as more evidence stacked up against the fairy Malcolm believed was on his side. *Twily, that's almost a perfect anagram of Yilst.* His mind went back to the berry smell of magic and dark emotions. "You know it's probably going to suck."

Malcolm nodded at this hands. "It's better than death."

Cursing in Giant, "Son of a bitch!" Jek punched the roof and pointed forward.

Malcolm slid away from Jek. "What'd he say?"

I don't see anything. Ben scanned out into the dark distance where Jek pointed. He switched to the Giant's tongue. "What is it?"

Malcolm tensed as his eyes shifted to look over Ben's shoulders.

Ur-Krurk's gruff voice came from Ben's right. "Gotta admire the balls on those bastards."

A set of tiny taillights lit far off in the night.

Jek started to slow. "How do you want to play it, Might-Fist?"

"What do you see?" Ben switched back to English. "The only things I see out there is a set of brake lights."

Jek glanced at Malcolm between then and continued speaking in Giant. "A white van is being let into Meadows Towing." The orc reached under his seat and pulled out a large handgun. "If I drop the hammer, we'll make it before the gates close."

"No." *I get that you want revenge, Jek, but us rushing in will benefit them more than us.* "We need to move tactically. We have no way of knowing how many of them are in there."

"Speak Giant, Might-Fist," Jek cut his eyes to Malcolm. "You never know how close your true foe might be."

Ben did. "My Giant is not good enough. No can say—" He switched back to English. "I can't say exactly what I mean quite yet."

"Blood-Son," Ur-Krurk's massive teal face filled half the window. His red irises set against black orbs were fixed on Malcolm. "Do not commit an error. The enemy of your enemy is not your ally."

Ben stole a glance at Malcolm sinking into the seat before replying in Giant. "He has no love for them."

"Nor he for you," Ur-Krurk put his black-nailed thumb to the corner of his eye. "Right now, he's loyal." The ogre pulled down on the flesh to peel his lower eyelid down. "Once he forgets the value of his life, he'll betray you."

"True." Jek agreed and did the same eye-thumbing move. He motioned forward and slight disgust worked into his voice. "Well, the gates are closing. So, what now?"

The complexion of this would be changed greatly if I had access to either my tablet or my spellcards; preferably both. Knowing another gate lay deeper into the scrapyard back lot, but not able to see anything, Ben gestured out into darkness to the left of where the taillights had lit. "We take the entrance closest to the north-east compactor and drive halfway to the building. Ur-Krurk drops me on the roof and I get my Anvilsmith while he surveys the enemies."

"Solid strategy—" The ogre shook his head. "But it won't work. From the looks of things, they were Black Sky orcs."

Ben asked, "Which means?"

Jek answered, *"Which means,* they started ransacking the place and dividing up your possessions the moment they got back on property." He dropped the truck into neutral and let it roll. "And, the longer they have stuff they don't need, the more likely it is to be broken."

"I'm sorry, Ben." They all looked down at Malcolm who had slunk low in the seat. "It's all my fault."

You had no way of knowing this would go so far sideways. Still... Ben opened his mouth to soothe Malcolm's guilt and paused. *Maybe he knows more.* He asked, "How so?"

"I just wanted my hook back." Malcolm gripped his hands, wrung them, and shook them violently before he pulled his hood over his head. At this angle, lavender symbols lit on the inside of the Dunn-Blatt's uniform before darkness filled the hood and obscured his features.

Ur-Krurk's throat rumbled as he spoke English. "Hiding in shame is pure weakness, Boy."

Wow, that almost sounded more like guidance and an insult. Ben turned to see the ogre pull back from the window. A wet snort of snot being summoned rose before Ur-Krurk hawked it into the night.

The pool of shadows around Malcolm's face evaporated as an indignant sneer twisted his lips. Different symbols lit around his sleeve band. Menacing Krotosian energy surrounded the Dunn-Blatt's hand as it sunk into the cuff to form the precursor of a blast around his fist.

Ben had been so focused that he jumped a bit when Ur-Krurk's voice rumbled again in English through the window. "The fairies bled you good, Boy." A hungry smile played on the ogre's black-toothed maw. "Think hard before you start something my Blood-Son wont' be able to pull you from."

Malcolm relaxed his hand, and the power faded.

Hold on a second. Curious, Ben lifted Malcolm's arm to inspect where the symbols had lit mere moments ago.

Malcolm started to withdraw.

Ben grabbed Malcolm's arm. *I just may have spells to cast after all.* He twisted the cuff and pulled from Malcolm to scrutinize the lines of faint needlecraft.

Malcolm sat upright and went with the sleeve. "What are you doing, Ben?"

Ben's eyes narrowed at Malcom the basics of new a plan started to form. "How do Dunn-Blatts cast?"

Chapter Thirty-Six

BACK IN BUSINESS

MALCOLM SQUIRMED in the seat next to Ben, stirring up the pervasive smell of salami ground into the seats. The Dunn-Blatt twisted to yank free and slid his arm free of the sleeve

The cuff remained in Ben's hands. *Wow, this is really soft. Considering how many of Malcom's fellow schoolmates are jerks, I just figured the material would somehow be*—he rubbed it between his thumb and forefinger —*agitating*. Ben ran his fingers over the outermost threads. *Whoa*. Well-crafted knots called for power. About to let a bit of Argosian energy slip, he licked his lips in anticipation. There, Ben rediscovered the taste of bacon… And his hunger.

He tightened his stomach to quiet the rumbling. *All in due time*. Ben let his red magic flow into the sucking knots. A hiss-gargling sentence—

"Malcolm?"

No answer

—flashed through Ben's mind before crimson energy flowed out of the threads. It swam around his fist.

Malcolm gasped.

"Cool." Ben admired the flow for a moment as a Blast spell were his to release. He opened his hand. The spell disbursed and his energy flowed back into his reserve.

Malcolm gasped. "How many sources of magic do you have?"

"Might-Fist," Jek said. "Another set of taillights."

Ben glanced to see the red lights and pulled on the sleeve. "Give me your hoodie."

Malcolm jerked away. "No!"

The ogre's big, teal hand reached in, grabbed Malcolm by the arm, and unceremoniously yanked the former bully out of the window. Malcolm's knee whacked the top of the door.

The soft sleeve slipped from Ben's hands.

Ur-Krurk held Malcolm close to his big, bull-dog like face. "You're in no position to deny anything, Boy."

Malcolm gave his zipper an angry downward yank.

Ur-Krurk snatched the Dunn-Blatt school top from Malcolm before he fully removed it from his body. As requested, the top went to Ben.

Sorry, Malcolm. Ben flipped the cuffs backwards again. The right cuff had seven well-spaced rings across the width. Over half of the left was covered with four similar rings. *There's space for three more.* Ben jumped from the truck. He slipped from his coat. No longer protected from the night's winter chill, a sharp cold began to slip into his skin.

Ben tossed his coat to the Dunn-Blatt.

Malcolm chose to shiver instead of putting it on.

Man, I really hope your school provides a similar comfort knack. He slipped on the violet hoodie and, once he zipped it up, felt the fabric flash warmth into his skin—*ah*—and the mystic threading gave a steady *feed me magic* pull. Ben flipped back the cuff and looked from the fine needlecraft to the shivering, silent Dunn-Blatt. "What spells are these?"

Malcolm crossed his arms, clamped his eyes shut, and turned his face away.

Ur-Krurk tightened one of his large hands into a massive fist. The knuckles popped. "Speak or bleed."

Without opening his eyes, Malcolm pointed to the right and tried to ramble too quickly to be understood. "Burning Grasp, Napalm Arrow, Darkness, Scorching Ray, Fireball, Lighting Bolt, and Firestorm."

Ben ran a finger along each spell thread as Malcolm rattled them off. *Burning Grasp and Napalm arrow must be fire-based versions of Shacking Grasp and Acid Arrow.* Ben slid his thumb along the opposite cuff as Malcolm continue to rattle. "Purple Princesses, Writhing Wreath, Cone of Flames, and you already know how to summon a dusk bison."

I do? Ben thought back to the duel they had last month when he had went to summon one of his conjurations at the same time as Malcolm and discovered he could use his energy to counter the Dunn-Blatt's spell. *Well, I'm not going to correct you.*

"Again." Knuckles popped on the ogre's other hand as it balled into a fist. "This time, say them slower."

"I got 'em." *Well, I have no idea what the Princesses and Wreath spells are, but I know enough.* Ben threw a thumb toward the back of the truck. "Ur-Krurk, hop on." He turned to look at the goblins. "Nuk, Uk'so, watch Malcolm and don't let any harm come to him."

The ogre flew to the back. The goblins hopped down. Nuk held a length of chain and Uk'so Gripped a tire iron.

Ben pointed at Malcolm's feet. "Stay put." He jumped into the cab and shot his hand forward. "Jek, get through the gate."

Jek shifted into first and jumped on the accelerator. Grating rocks spat from under the spinning wheels like a machine gun before the tire caught traction and they launched forward.

I don't know. Those lights look pretty far away. Ben began to doubt Jek's judgment. *Well, if the Black Sky orcs see me, they're going to come after only me.* Ben pulled the hood over his head. The lone stitching along the rim gave that slight, magic-hungry pull as the cuffs. *Sweet, I can activate the face obscuring magic that Malcolm usually uses.* Ben let his Krotosian energy flow into the hoodie to conceal his identity.

A veil of darkness blotted his sight—*shit!*—before, granting him clear vision across the desert, similar to his Elfsight spell. *Instead of stars raining light, everything simply looks slick with the Moon's glow.* Now, unlike last time, he could see the white van around the glow of the tail lights as it pulled past the closing gates. "Slow down. We're not going to make it."

As though it granted the truck more speed, Jek leaned into the steering wheel. "We'll make it."

"Stop!" Ben ordered. "We're not even close."

"So, what, we wait for another one?" The orc jammed on the brakes and punched the dash. "Great, they'll have an army by the time we get in there."

"I doubt it." Noting the lack of movement atop the large brick columns the gates were anchored to, Ben pointed at the scrapyard. "Drive slowly to stay quiet and head in."

They began to inch forward. "The gate is closed."

"I know." Ben rubbed his palms together. "But if these Black Sky orcs scavenge as madly as you two say they do, they wouldn't have set sentries nor would they have taken the time to reconfigure the gate code." He grinned at Jek.

The orc's blank face reminded him that the hood hid his features.

Ben put a small laugh into his voice. "Heck, I'm willing to bet they're even using the remotes from the other tow trucks."

Jek gave a slow *I get it* nod.

Small rocks crunching and dirt shifting were the only signal of their approach. Closing on the scrapyard the ruckus sound of Orcish war-rock—deep drums and chaotic metal striking metal—carried, unimpeded, across the desert.

"Not even Gromsk will be able to help them." Jek flashed Ben a bloodthirsty grin. "You're brilliant. This'll be the perfect ambush."

Chapter Thirty-Seven

FAMILIAR GROUND

AMBUSH... Ben hadn't stopped to consider what they were doing. *Ambush is the right word for it and it's no more insidious than what they did to me...* Still, the word sat wrong on his conscious. *Think about it later.* Ben rubbed the magical stitching, noting the bunches, grooves, and binds in the fine threads. The word began to roll back to the front of Ben's mind before he intercepted it with a different word. *Gromsk.* He asked, "What is Gromsk? Is it a type of weapons?"

"No." Jek's leaned into the steering wheel again and kept this eyes forward, scanning around the ground, up along the buttresses, and the Koffman Security Gate. "He's an Orcish War God."

"Ah." The war-rock had long since swallowed the sounds of the truck rolling forward. *He seems awfully confident for having seen two vans enter the property. I mean, sure, we have Ur-Krurk, but we'll still be greatly outnumbered.*

Ben glanced in the side mirror to glimpse the ogre magi gripping the crane the back. *Still can't figure out why the monster's supporting me. He had two chances to betray me—once with the Imprisoning Orb and he could have just beaten me senseless once we were outside the fairy hive and sold me, and Malcolm, back.* Trying to figure it out still made his head spin. *Well, I'm not going to think of him as a pure ally, let alone a horrid ritual-granted father figure. He's probably waiting for the perfect moment to betray me.*

A *click* brought Ben from his thoughts.

Jek lowered his hand from the remote clipped to the visor to the steering wheel. "Jackpot." The orc grinned as the Koffman gate began to roll up and the double wrought iron gates parted in the center to yawn open.

If not for the war-rock, a keen-eared sentry probably would've heard that. Concern about Ur-Krurk boomeranged back into his thoughts. *Can ogres call for a Retributive Paramountcy? It's so farfetched—Well, Councilor Eastly might have the answer, but then the old bat would demand to know why his valuable time was being squandered on useless twaddle.*

They cruised through rows and rows of wrecked cars.

Ben's mouth dried and his stomach tightened as they had the first time he had come to Meadows Towing. From habit, his fingers went to where his Achilleus spellcard would normally be in his holder. His fingers brushed against his empty holder and slacks.

"Being in the cab makes you an easy target." Ur-Krurk opened the passenger door. "Get on your feet so you can move."

Minding his pace, Ben hopped out and sped-walked alongside the truck. Drawing a breath of steel-laden air, he found courage as his eyes landed on a crumbled aqua sedan under a faded brown station wagon with wood paneling. *This is no longer unfamiliar ground. In two more rows, we'll be on the main path to the building.* "Jek." Ben leaned into the window so he wouldn't have to yell over the frantic clanging metal-music and pointed across the cab. "Turn down this row."

Ur-Krurk had taken to the air and flew just above him. "Since you can multicast, now would be the time to get any defensive spells in action."

The ogre's hot breath wafting over him sent a chill through Ben's spine. *Hope that didn't show.* "I don't have my necklace or tablet, and Malcolm, apparently, doesn't believe in defense."

"Foolish boy. Even the mightiest of offenses cannot be sustain forever." Ur-Krurk drifted from being directly over Ben to hover above the truck's sun baked hood. The ogre raised his voice to be heard over the clamor. "You are going to have to deal with him, Blood-Son."

"Harshly," Jek added.

Ben sighed at the inevitable reality. *They're right. If only I could get Malcolm to act less Malcolmy.*

Light reflected on something small that moved a ways down the row. *Tex?* Ben's hand dropped to his hip to pull his Anvilsmith so he could call his companion. And grabbed air. *Crap!* He shook his empty fist in frustration as the robot moved further away and disappeared around a corner. *We could really use a scout right now.*

Choosing not to compete with the music, Ben projected, *"I'm going to see what kind of numbers we're facing."* Not waiting for their feedback, Ben sped up to a light jog to outpace the truck. The hoodie blew soft, cool air against his torso to help control his body heat. *That's a neat knack.* At the corner, he dropped to a knee and peeked.

The bass-drum of the heavy war-rock thumped across the hundred-foot span to the first row of cars. *Wow, I can feel that on my face. They're going to blow out the speakers in the work bays.* Every light in the place was out, and most of the windows were shattered. *If it weren't for the tools and small fixtures strewn across the clearing, I would've bet the beat broke the windows.* About a dozen motorcycles had been hastily parked around six long, white passenger vans, and Malcolm's Transcend. The two-foot tall *Meadows Towing* letters had been re-worked to read *wooT Mead wings.*

An offended sneer flashed across Ben's face before he hustled back to relay the set up to the other two. Ben thought his question to them, *"About how many orcs per van?"*

Jek answered, "There'll be between six and twelve." He knocked his knuckles together to represent tight seating. "When given a chance, we orcs roll thick."

Ur-Krurk landed and took Ben by the shoulders. The beef jerky reek on his breath had faded and only blackberries pillowed his words. "Blood-Son, draw more blood than you give. I'm taking the orc to a vantage point. We'll wait for your mark." The ogre lifted Jek and flew to the top of the wall of wrecked cars.

Noticing the bulky riffle slung over Jek's shoulder, Ben wondered, *what kind of gun is that long one? It looks one hundred percent pure business.*

Ben ran a finger along the dusk bison stitching in Malcom's hoodie. He opened his Argosian font. The red energy flowed into the hoodie.

His pulse quickened, blood heated, and a tremble washed through him as two long and lean Argosian dusk bison appeared. Almost as tall as him, Ben was about to compare their length to his car—*only two?*—when his thoughts got away from him. *Where'd the rest of my power go?* He tried to pull the remaining two casting's worth of energy from the Dunn-Blatt uniform, but it felt dry. *Crap, I gotta use more energy in this.* Ben gave the uniform a dirty look. *Greedy thing.*

In the moment's distraction, one of the dusk bison—the most feared of school mascot conjurations in the Las Vegas Valley—pulled the long, deadly tendrils on its back tight, plopped on its bottom, tucked its head, kicked a hind leg out and started to preen itself like an idle house dog. The other searched for a scent, prowled it to the corner, and waited to get into action.

Preener and Prowler. Ben shook his head against the names. *No need to become familiar with conjurations I'll never summon again.* Still, he made notes of the names as he grabbed Preener's reins. *Mimic Prowler.*

It did.

Wonder if— He glanced.

With Jek in arms, Ur-Krurk hovered just below the top car.

They're waiting on me. Ben drew a slow, steadying breath as he stalked to the end of the aisle near the readied beasts. He peeked out one more time to survey the building for movement.

Orcs partied upstairs, orcs partied in the kitchen, and, beyond them, orcs partied in the livening room.

Well… Why am I hesitating? Reluctance? Ben let the initial thought peter out. *Fireballs. Two of them.* He rubbed the fifth stich on his soft right sleeve. It sucked at his fingers like a starved calf working an udder for milk. Mentally, he aimed upstairs and at the archway dividing the downstairs rooms. *Alright*—he let his Argosian energy flow into the stitch—*let's do this.*

Chapter Thirty-Eight

RETAKING THE SCRAPYARD

As BEFORE, a hiss-gargle sentence echoed through Ben's mind. *Cool, the hoodie converts—whoa!*

Unlike summoning dusk bison, the magic from the fifth stich came back fast and—*hot potatoes!*—ready for release. Two glowering, crimson beads—*four?*—jumbled restlessly above each of his palms. *If I don't release*—sulfur filled his nose—*they're gonna pop!* He stepped sideways, picked locations near his original points—*twenty feet apart*—and let them fly.

The two roiling orbs from his left hand shot to the kitchen and living room. The two from his right entered separate smashed-out windows on the second floor. There, Orcs, who had been rocking to the raucous music, froze in place. The faint light of his magic reflected in their widening eyes. Colored by the magic, their teeth shone red as their mouths started to move to call out a warning.

Thoom!

All four beads exploded and filled each area to the brim with sudden flame. Framed by the windows, the orcs not instantly incinerated to twitching skeletons, were wreathed in flames, and writhed in pain.

It's like a grotesque shadow puppet show.

One of the burning orcs on the second floor leapt out the window to land flat; unmoving.

Prowler and Preener ached for release.

Go.

They charged across the clearing.

A gunshot barely reported over the noise of the blasting war-rock.

Blood splattered from Prowler's right hindquarters.

The beast turned back.

Go. Ben urged the beast toward the building as he seeped energy in the fifth stitch again. The hiss-gargle sentence—*I can almost make it out*—echoed in his mind as a bead appeared in each of his hands. He sent another to the second floor, and popped around the corner and let the second fly at the shooter.

He barely got a look at the jackal-headed dog-man pointing a gun at his beasts and the two still engrossed in a dice game at their pawed feet—*the orcs weren't the only betrayers*—before the fiery explosion engulfed the gnolls. The three bodies bobbed around as meat burned down to bones in seconds. Their charred skeletons dropped to the ground.

Orcs began to pour out of the building like angry ants.

The lead orc's head kicked back, popping into red mist. The chest of the one behind it burst open form the same round as a *crack*, clearly audible over the music, came from Jek's position.

Purple bolts of magic—*Ur-Krurk*—struck opposition on the roof.

Ben let more red energy flow from his chest chakra into the hoodie and—*something something, Argosana, something*—the hiss-gargle sentence flashed through his head before rewarding him with four more glowing orbs. He strafed them across the front of the cinderblock building.

Most of the orcs that spilled out were swallowed by the flames.

One orc, a massive brute with flames riding his back heaved a greatsword at Preener, chopping it in the gut.

Ben switched to the second stich to blast the orc with Napalm Arrow when something bit into his right flank, lanced pain through his abdomen struck a rib—*I've been shot*—and ricocheted of a rib to exit his back. Another stabbing pain went through his right leg.

He hobbled backward.

Something slammed his ankles together and swept his feet from under him.

"Ooph!" He glanced the direction of the shots.

A lone, wiry orc charged down the second row at him. He had a pistol in one hand and a whirled a bola above his head.

Ben released his Argosian energy into the stitch. In rapid successions, four solid-fire compound bows appeared, twanged a sizzling arrow at the rushing target, and faded.

The orc leapt the first arrow. Let his bola fly as he sidestepped the next. The third hit his leg and the fourth—

Rough twine struck Ben's neck and yanked. The *wizz* of it wrapping tight warned of dread before the tightening registered on his neck and the weights *clacked* together. Against his spine. The force flopped him onto his back.

It's choking me! His hands slapped against the tight ropes. He groped for purchase on the edge of the twine—*too tight*—and found none. *Prowler to me.*

The bitter taste of fear rose in his throat.

Keep cool.

Ben struggled to control the emotion that threatened to suffocate him faster than the bola.

Calm yourself.

He glanced to the orc who threw the weapon and found a lava covered twitching mass.

Burning hands. Opening his chakra, Ben's finger landed on the first stitch. It sucked the raw magic in, hiss-gargled at him, and sizzled the spell into being.

Fiery gloves coated his hands. He gripped the ropes. The smell of his flesh cooking with the ropes, pooled in his nostrils as his flaming fingers dug at the layers of tightly woven cords strangling him. He grimaced against the burning. The choking rope muted his agonized cries into a pissed-off rumbled in his throat.

A gnoll turned the corner with a knife.

Prowler snatched it up with its tendrils and curled in to gore the whining creature.

Ben's fingers gained a millimeter of ground. *A rope broke!* A wisp of air entered his mouth. He sucked at it, and locked it in his stinging lungs as a second rope gave.

More air.

He thought to exhale the old and bring in new, but—*running on automatic*—his lungs continue to expand from the tiny slip of air.

He pulled his knees up to his chest and rocked forward into a kneeling position.

Another gnoll came around the corner. Its black-clawed paw-feet scrabbled and found enough ground to shift its weight and, wild eyes laser focused on Ben's neck, cock a moonlight-sheathed sword back.

Oh shit.

Chapter Thirty-Nine

SITTING DUCK

BEN'S EYES WENT WIDE.

A fine froth broke out at the upward corners of the overjoyed gnoll's furry maw.

Shit! Shit!

It swung.

Ben scrunched down.

A red tendril lashed out. It knocked the gnoll's arms up.

Instead of being beheaded, the blade skimmed the top of Ben's skull. The chop chipped away a fragment of skull, sliced his scalp clean away, and took part of the hoodie.

The pain! Still unable to yell, Ben grasped at the last of the burning ropes around his cooking neck—*the stench!*—and the outer layer fell away. He exhaled and sucked in cool, coal-tasting air. *More.*

The gnoll's paw-feet turned away. Its sword flashed out at the dusk bison gnawing on the first gnoll.

Ben lunge-crawled forward on the dirt covered blacktop. He caught the gnoll's thin ankle and discharged the *Fiery Grasp* spell into it.

The jackal-headed creature yipped and whined as its fur went up in flames and its skin began to boil. It dropped to the ground and began to roll.

Prowler leapt in and clamped its jaws on the gnoll's neck. The dusk bison's fore hooves crashed on the creature's chest as its mouth came away with the majority of a bloody throat.

Engines roared and revved to life and shots rang out over the war-rock.

Ben yanked the last of the rope away with his fiery hand and drank in a true lungful of air. His neck cried against the wide expansion. *So. Much. Pain.*

Vans and motorcycles began to flash past him.

Purple energy—Ur-Krurk—lit from the side of the building.

Surrounded by orcs, Preener crouched defensively in front of the building. Ben touched his fifth stitch. *To me.* Magic flowed in. *Something, blank-cana Argosana, something.*

Enemy orcs cheered and swung at the conjuration as it leapt away, but were soon dumbfounded by the red glowering beads within their midst. Then the spell exploded, engulfing them in fire as they tried to run.

The pain in Ben's gut and leg were all but a memory as he rolled over and eyed a line of motorcycles. Ben touched the sixth-stitch—*chew on a Lightning Bolt, jerks*—switched power reserves to Krotosian magic and let it flow into the hoodie. The purple magic floated around the summoning threads. *I don't want conjurations, darn it. Lightning Bolt!* He directed the truant magic into the stitch which took it happily.

A howling lavender lightning bolt cracked from his hands and down the line of retreating bikers, electrocuting all but the few furthest away in rapid succession.

Ben called both Preener and Prowler near him for cover as, knees to his chest, he worked away the twine of the bola puzzle from his ankles with his remaining flaming hand.

Three bullets rocked into his back. Two passed clear through, but the last exited his stomach and lodged into his upper leg. He flopped over—*there!*— grinding his teeth to bite back yelling. *If my neck hated moving to draw breath, it'll throttle me for shouting.*

He sent Prowler to finish the crispy, gun-toting biker who had survived the stroke of lighting.

Ben scanned around. Other retreating orcs were in range. One by one, *crack* by *crack*, they fell as bits of their skulls, if not the entire head, were blasted away by Jek and his massive gun.

Save your magic. Ben worked the ropes keeping his legs together. *Mind your surroundings.* He kept glancing around. Each time his eyes scanned over burned bodies, charred bodies, and limp bodies missing heads. About to relax and focus on the ropes—*stay alert*—he kept reminding himself to stay mindful of his surroundings as the pain from his bullet wounds began to lessen. *Being shot sucks.*

The slug in his leg pushed back up the hole it had made as muscles mended, finally falling to the ground as the bullet wound healed over. Likewise, the bolts of pain coming from the top of his head eased.

Ur-Krurk landed next to him and cut the rest of the rope away with his black claws. The ogre hauled Ben to his feet to inspect the growing blisters. Something about the way the monster's face twisted in mild disgust shook worry into Ben's core. How bad does it look? Ur-Krurk asked, "Who got close enough to burn you?"

Don't laugh. Ben tried fighting the simper threatening to turn his lips, but lost and winced from the pain both on, and in, his neck.

Ben projected his answer in Giant, *Me.*

Ur-Krurk slapped him hard on the shoulder.

Ouch! So worth it.

Ben finally got to see what mirth looked like on the big, teal, face. The ogre's lips pulled back to show a sneering grin of jagged black teeth. Instead of laughing out, Ur-Krurk sucked air in desperate intake sound as though he were surprised and couldn't get enough breath on one drag.

He rubbed his shoulder—*so worth it*—and pointed to his neck. *Why's this not healing?*

Ur-Krurk recovered quickly. "Fire is the only thing that does lasting damage to us." He lifted Ben from the ground. "Get some ice on that. I'm going to chase down the runners."

Ben fought the urge to rub the searing burns. *Jek?*

"I'll drop him off on a pillar to snipe any who head out toward the goblins." As though waiting to be dismissed, Ur-Krurk gave him a nod.

Ben gave a thumbs up.

The ogre took to the air and scooped up Jek.

Ben gauged his red conjurations' condition. *Boy, you guys are really beat up.* He wanted to thank them aloud, to say their names, but the growing blisters kept him quiet as he wondered about his earlier Liquid Forge detonation in the basement. *How was I able to regenerate from* that *damage?* With an intimate knowledge of what it felt like to have your flesh cooked away, Ben grimaced. *It felt like fire.*

He dismissed the two Argosian dusk bison and remembering the hoodie needed double energy to summon one—*all I should need*—he let a double-casting's worth of Krotosian energy slip into the conjuration stitch. Louder than when he conjured before, and as clear as the *Fireball* spell, a hiss-gargle sentence sounded in his mind. This time, all the words, besides *Krotosiana* where *Argosana* had been, were beyond his understanding.

Two violet flashes energy ushered in purple-black dusk bison. Similar in size to their red versions, these two conjurations had a more healthy-looking muscle mass to them. As before, one prowled forward to stop at the work bays while the other dropped onto its bottom to preen itself.

Motioning for Preener to him, Ben quickened his stride to get up next to Prowler. *The place may have emptied out, but there still may be more hiding inside.*

Moving closer to the booms and clangs of music—*have to turn that music off*—he stepped over charred remains at the entrance to the work bay. *Uhh!* Ben pulled the neckline up to cover his nose and mouth. Too late. He could taste the foul, burnt bodies and entrails on the air. Bile began to rise.

Not having to hold it back or put a strong front around Ur-Krurk or Jek, Ben rushed into the kitchen, leaned over the sink, and let the rising disgust—*I've killed them. I've killed them all*—heave out of him. Two rounds of bile splattered into the basin before he ran dry and continued to heave. Each pulse of his throat inflamed the burns.

Finally, he got his stomach, disgust, and remorse under control. He rinsed out his mouth, washed his hands, and let the water run to carry his mess down the disposal.

Using the hood to mute the smells, Ben held the neckline to his face as moved against the ruckus and entered the work bays to pull the plug on the pounding drums and rhythmless clangs.

The vibrations immediately ceased feeling like they were rubbing along his neck. *Thank goodness.* Ben stifled a sigh when loud grunts and giggles died seconds after the music.

Ben rushed back through the kitchen to the living room.

Clear.

Prowler preceded him up the stairs.

The door to the left had been blasted form its hinges. He scanned the bodies. None stirred. He turned to his bedroom. Prowler moved by his side as he hustled to the door and threw it open.

The conjuration lunged. Preener followed.

Two shots rang out before a high-pitched scream filled the area under the dusk bison's hissing.

Don't kill. He directed. *I'm probably too late.*

"This is not how you issue a Might-Fist challenge!" Toad's voice brimmed with righteous indignation. "This is no way to challenge for the belt."

Son of a... Ben pushed the door open. Blocked mostly by Prowler's length, the body of a slim orc lay beyond the hissing conjuration. A gun lay against the far wall near shattered remains of brown beer bottles. Toad stood on the bare mattress of his bed, wincing as he rubbed his hand. *He's wearing my belt and spare coat.* Noting the pale green orc's total lack of other clothing, Ben switched his gaze to the other being in the room. A short—by orcish standards—pitch-black skinned female orc stood wrapped in blankets, the furs from the bed piled around her, and she held a serrated longsword at the ready.

Like flipping a switch, Toad's tone changed from fear to pleading sympathy. "Malcolm, I swear I didn't know they were going to double-cross you." A nervous laugh bubbled from his throat. "I'm glad you are well." The orc sobered and swallowed hard. "Could you, uh, dismiss your creatures, please?"

Disbelief tilted Ben's head. His wounded neck throbbed. *Does he think Malcolm so dim or easily won over?* Moving at a sloth's pace, Ben raised a hand to the center of the hood and touch the sigil to dismiss the magical darkness concealing his face.

A range of emotions danced on Toad's face as he stuttered, "B-B-Ben..."

"Toad." Fists clenched as hard as his teeth, every wrecked syllable made the boils on Ben's neck blaze. "Who, exactly, did you best to become Might-Fist?"

Chapter Forty

AFTERMATH

TOAD DIDN'T HAVE an answer ready.

The bedroom reeked of beer and feces. Ben's gaze went to what had to be a case of broken bottles smashed against the northern wall. *Can't believe...* The sound of Toad's breathing began to steady. *I trusted...* Ben's eyes went to a pile of shit on the nightstand where he had placed a small oil painting of his family that his father created and given to Ben last December 25th. Under the bottom coil of light brown waste, Ben spied the barest hint of the frame's corner. All of his energy sources began to churn and heat within him at the blatant disrespect. *I should...*

Sensing the coming storm, Toad extended his hands out, palms up to bend in a supplicating bow. "Ben, Might-Fist, please let me explain. I—"

"Get—" Ben reined-in the growing contempt and loathing before they collided into hate. Each word felt like a barbed-wire choker. "—Out." A dim light threw soft shadows from the orcs against the wall. Ben glanced to the heat building around his fist. There, his three energies, black, red and purple, swirled feverishly like electrons around a nucleus. The hoodie sleeve swished out to touch the power which remained just beyond the fabric's reach.

Ben eyed Toad and projected, *Unless, of course, you want to challenge me for the title.*

"No, no," Toad unbuckled the belt. It flopped on the mattress. "I'm not challenging you."

Ben managed to relax his hand. The energies flashed into his fingertips. He pointed to the door. *Then go. Get out of here.*

Toad straightened. "Wonder why I turned on you?"

Don't care. To give the orcs a clear path to the door, Ben motioned Prowler to back into the bathroom and Preener to slide to the left near the closet where it melded with the darkness. He moved around the broken pile of wood that had been his desk and over the body of the slim orc to stand near Prowler.

Ben projected, *If you don't start moving, I'll have them attack.*

Both beast reared their tendrils back and growled as they lowered into a ready-to-charge crouch.

Minding the conjurations, the female kept her sword at the ready for a moment longer before dropping the blade on the bed. She fished black leather clothing from the furs and dressed quickly.

Toad stepped off the bed opposite the woman, closer to the pooped-on painting. He grabbed his jeans and hoisted them on. "You were lucky to retake this place by yourself." Toad zipped his pants and tossed the spare trench coat onto the bed. "Then again, you've always been lucky." He spoke Orcish to the woman.

Continuing to dress, she barked back.

Ben's gaze flicked to the coat to determine if it had waste on it, too.

Pointing to the ground by his side, Toad stabbed the air with his finger.

She shook her head.

Ben projected in Giant, *You do not have to be with him, but you do have to go.*

She nodded, strapped a scabbard to her hip, and soundlessly slid the sword home.

Toad grumbled and scooped up a white Meadows Towing t-shirt.

"No." Ben winced and nearly groaned as his neck tightened to stop any more words from passing through. *Leave the tee, too. You've lost all rights to be anywhere near this place. Ever.*

"You're making a huge mistake, Ben," Toad said, clutching the shirt like a child would his most comforting blanket. "You'll never be able to hold, much less run, this place without me."

Sadly, at one time, I really believed that, Ben pointed toward the door. *However, you've made your choice. Now, out.*

The black-clad woman grabbed a quiver of javelins, hooked it over her shoulder and moved around the bed to bow before Ben. She spoke two sentences in Orcish before leaving.

Speaking pleading-sounding words in their language, Toad followed after her.

With Prowler right behind him where the beast could whap Toad with its tendrils, Ben followed Toad closely.

The orcs argued down the hall and down the stairs.

She never stopped, but Toad froze halfway down and covered his nose.

He pushed Toad to start him moving again. *Every single one of these deaths is due to your betrayal.* As much as was possible, Ben had grown accustomed to the foul stench of burnt flesh sticking to each breath.

Toad continued down. "You've become quite the killer, Ben."

Ben adopted a stoic demeanor. *All on you.*

The orc motioned his head to the sofa. "Some of these orcs were children and had nothing to do with what happened earlier."

You involved them, Ben refused to show any weakness, sympathy, or regret. *It's probably a trick of some sort anyway.* He gave Toad another push when the orc slowed. *Now, you have to explain to their loved ones what happened here.*

Pointing to something beyond the sofa, Toad continued to the door.

Where Toad motioned, a circle of several small, charred bodies remained. *Probably goblins.* Ben couldn't help but notice marbles at the center of the circle. *Oh...* His throat throbbed as it began to constrict with sorrow. He pulled the hood and, wishing he could make the world dark to him instead of his face dark to the world, used Krotosian energy to activate the darkness. His gazed went back to the marbles one last time as they moved from the living room, through the kitchen and out into the work bays. Remorse stung his eyes.

Worried his telepathy might sound as tear-choked as his voice would, Ben didn't correct their course to the main entrance when they started walking east.

Feeling the world close in on him, Ben welcomed the scrapyard's metallic open-air smell as they moved away from the reek of burnt bodies around the building.

As they walked, Ben let the distance between him and the orcs grow, and discontinued feeding energy into the hoodie to keep his face obscured. The magic persisted and would for some minutes. *Papa Mojo had said the assassin would be going after him next and I've already burned through—*

Ben had never known how much magic lay within him and had often wished for a personal awatt-like counter. The Dunn-Blatt hoodie relayed, roughly, how much power he had left.

—I have a quarter of my energy left and will probably need every ounce of it.

Without warning, a sudden breeze from the east grew rapidly into a strong gust. Ben scanned the orcs who trudged on with heads bowed *—they're not doing this—*and beyond them. *What now?*

Chapter Forty-One

JEK'S VENGEANCE

THE WIND GREW STRONGER and stronger. Carrying stinging desert grit, it soon howled through the rows of wrecked cars and whistled through the tiny fissures in the metal.

Out ahead, Toad kneeled to lower his profile.

The shadows filling Ben's hood protected his face and neck from the sandstorm. Though Ben didn't want to concede to the force, he tucked his hands into his armpits and followed the shaman's example.

Arm raised before her face, the black-clad orc leaned into the mighty draft and battled to gain inches.

Ready to release a volley of *Napalm Arrows*, and not in direct danger if the wind carried the magical shots away, Ben thumbed the second stitch and projected, *Is this of your doing?*

"No!" Toad yelled over the wind and looked back at him. "Someone must've cast a spell to hold the wind still and now..." Toad brought an arm in to protect the side of his face from the cutting sand. "Now, nature is trying to catch up with where it should be."

Papa Mojo must've divined the assassination attempt and stopped the wind so I, in the girallon form, could track my human body. A small, ever-hopeful part of him considered an unlikely possibility. *Perhaps I misjudged the diviner?* Not wanting to put the charlatan in a better light,

Ben frowned the thought away. *If he helped me, it's only because he thinks me key in his own continued existence.*

Running his hand along his side to finger a gunshot hole, Ben marveled at the hoodie. *It mended.* He pulled at the side so he could see without turning his neck. *And the bloodstain is shrinking away.* He ran a hand over his head to feel the hole there had been closed over. Ben thought about how he had bought more coats since he turned sixteen than he had during his prior six years at the Academy. *Man, too bad my coats can't do this.*

The near-gale force winds eased to gusts again.

The black orc had advanced several feet against the squall and stumbled forward at the sudden ease.

Toad remained crouched and kept his arm up, protecting his neck and face. "Might-Fist, if you would but give me a second chance."

Ben rose. *One more word to me, and we'll be dueling.*

Silent, the shaman bowed as he stood, then turned on his hells to catch up with the female to rekindle their arguing in Orcish. They went back and forth as they moved through the scrapyard.

Though Toad had the belt on in the room, she seems to be the one in the power position.

"He survives?" Disbelief painted Jek's question.

Ben ranged his eyes up the exit column. Jek had been rubbing his eyes, but swiveled the tripod holding the massive rifle to have the business end directed at Toad.

Crap. I forgot Jek was out this way. Ben grimaced against the pain as he nodded. He projected, *His shame will follow him home.*

"No!" Jek dropped to a knee and pressed his shoulder to the butt of the weapon. "He dies here!"

Toad yelled at Jek in Orcish.

Jek yelled back and switched to English in the middle of his reply, "—which is why I'm going to coat the desert with the cowardice that fills your guts."

Attempting to lower the tension, Ben extended a hand. *Jek—*

The rifle cracked.

Ben tried to look away, but wasn't fast enough to not see Toad's upper chest disintegrate from the high-caliber shot. The remaining body parts thumped and slopped to the ground.

"Might-Fist," Jek's voice carried over the slight ringing in Ben's years. "I won't let you make that mistake."

The woman had started shouting. When Ben turned back, she had one of her javelins cocked back, ready to release at Jek as she continued yelling.

Jek, for his part, stood from the rifle; he had one of his pistol pulled and aimed at her. With his free hand, he ran his thumb over his heart in the opposite direction he had done when speaking over his dead first-blood. With each slow strike, she reduced her volume until she quieted altogether. He stopped midway through the final stroke and rotated the pistol so his hand was palm down while pointed at her. He grunted two Orcish syllables.

Putting the javelin away, she turned her head and spat air at Toad's remains. She then closed the remaining distance between her and the Koffman security gate barring her from exit.

Jek holstered his pistol and dropped his thumb across his heart. Looking at Ben, he pointed to the remaining orc. "She would rather live."

There had to be more exchanged between them than that. Though curious, Ben had no way of being sure. An inner heat began to slowly rise in his neck. Having had a minor burn before, he knew the burning sensation would echo back and would be a long time leaving.

Ben projected, *We cannot open the gates, but you are free to leave.*

She nodded and moved to the column opposite Jek to begin climbing out.

Ben turned away and started back to the building to follow Ur-Krurk's advice and find some ice.

Chapter Forty-Two

NOT YET DONE

SORT OF GETTING into the cold relief the ice granted, Ben winced against the heat building further in his neck. His upper back pressed against the smashed front corner panel of a pink, pre-2000's luxury sedan, he sat a few feet away from where he had lobbed fireball after fireball, holding ice wrapped in a dishtowel to the front and sides of his neck. A second towel-full of ice perched across the back of his neck, and he kept his head bowed slightly so the makeshift icepacks would stay in place.

A gentle breeze from the east kept fresh air coming in, pressing the smell of death and carnage west. From where he sat, he could only see Bola—the body of the orc who had hit him with bolas—if he looked to his left, which he didn't do too often.

A rumbling engine trundled down the main row from the east gate. *Probably Jek with Malcolm and the goblins.* Ben didn't check to see, but thumbed his fifth stitch, in case he was wrong. Glancing toward Meadows Towing would mean looking over the carnage and he felt stuffed to the proverbial gills with seeing shot, blasted, burnt, clawed, and gnawed dead bodies.

It's just like Master Reynolds always says in his annual welcoming speech to the Academy's Initiates. I've finally hit the day when the wonder fades and reality sets in. If only I could've better followed his closing advise to 'hold onto the wonder as long as possible.'

He glanced right, looking down the long row between towers of wrecked cars extending to the eastern wall; then left, to Bola and the long row stretching out to the western wall, and sighed. *The wonder's gone.* Both directions were longer than the school's longest target fields. *Never thought I'd be in a place like this.*

The rolling tires and rumbling engine came to a stop. Doors creaked open. "Benja Min'Fist?" Nuk's raspy, child-like voice called out anxiously, "Benja Min'Fist?"

He answered, *I'm on the first row, to the right.*

"Are you hurt?" Nuk asked as two sets of feet padded over. He turned the corner with Uk'so on his heels before finishing the question.

Hearing the concern, and seeing the two of them made Ben smile.

"No, Benja Min'Fist." Nuk hustled over and hooked his calico hands atop of Ben's wrists. "Ice be making burns worser. Heat no can get out. You keeping the cooking in." The goblin yanked.

The dishtowel came away with bloody burnt skin fused into the fabric. Ben sucked a long hiss of air at the sudden pain. Mildly stunned, the dishtowel fell from his hands and some of the ice fell onto the ground. Warm fluid ran down his neck into his collar.

Nuk tapped Ben on the side of his head, like Ben would've done to his youngest sibling. "You being putting cooked black skin under running water. Then wind dry. Then water."

Is my skin really blackened? Ben hurried up to his feet to get out of the goblin's reach. *I appreciate your advice, and I'd love to, but the person who set all this into action is still out there, and...* Ben bit his lip against the inescapable truth about his debt to Papa Mojo for, more than likely, being the one to still the wind. *And I need to return a favor.*

"Ben?" Tex's synthesized voice came from his right.

Ben turned.

Tex looked him up and down, then crossed his arms. "Why are you wearing a Dunn-Blatt top?"

Inwardly, Ben laughed. *You jerk.* His chest heaved a bit. He'd gotten good at not moving his neck or contracting the muscles. He slowly unzipped the hoodie to reveal his damaged and damp—probably with blood and puss—APA school button on.

"Ee-yuck," Tex turned his head to look away. "Never mind, Mr. Burn Unit. Zip up. Zip up!"

Thought so. Ben kept his slight smile to the corners of his lips and zipped up.

Tex dipped under a car, by the wheel well, and came back out with an Anvilsmith tablet.

Ben projected, *Thanks.* And took it.

"And no 'thank you?' Ingrate." Tex feigned to look around. "Where's the guy who burned you? I want to call him back to give you another lesson."

Forgot, can't mindspeak with him. Ben opened a chat window and typed in, "Thanks, Buddy. Oh, and I'm the one who burned me. I'll be glad to give out another lesson." He set the tablet down and, when his companion looked down to read, channeled Argosian energy to power into *Burning Hands.*

Tex looked up, and jumped back at seeing the fiery gloves. "No. No more lessons needed."

Ben recalled the spell. The ruby energy flashed back into his fingertips.

Tex ducked back into the little wheel well, this time coming out with a checkered washcloth tied up on a stick like an old fashion hobo bag. "I wasn't able to save everything…" He extended the pack. "…but I kept going back until the probability of being able to get back out dropped below ninety percent."

Ben opened the pack to see a handful of goldfish spellcards—*nice, just what I needed*—and the four sets of bonded obdurium steel strips. He gave his companion a thumbs up, plucked three spellcards and returned the bundle to the robot.

Tex blinked at him. "Why only three?"

Ben picked up his tablet, loaded a spellcard, and started the quick reformat of the card. He typed, "That's all I'll have time to reprogram on my way to the bazaar."

Nuk reminded, "Running water…"

Uk'so nodded in agreement, and stepped forward to hand Ben his tablet and spellcard holder.

After I get back, Ben projected.

Nuk said, "Sooner is better."

Ben strapped the case on, slid the tablet home, and turned the corner to head to Malcom's car. *I—*

Ur-Krurk was there. The ogre had a massive teal hand on each of Malcolm's shoulders and held the Dunn-Blatt as though he were a fish trying to wiggle out of his hands. He shook Malcolm. "Tell him."

Malcolm opened his mouth. His gazed dropped to Ben's neck. "Oh my God!" He tried to cringe away.

Ur-Krurk shook him again. "Tell him."

Malcolm clamped his eyes shut, making faces every time Ur-Krurk corrected the direction of his head to face Ben as though he could see the mess of Ben's burns through his closed lids as he explained. "Purple Princesses is Black Tentacles repackaged Dunn-Blatt style, and Writhing Wreath is a four-stone spell of my build that amplifies any other fire-based magic that you cast."

"And…" Ur-Krurk shook him again.

"And…" Malcom added rapidly, "You can shoot a couple of Blasts and Scorching Rays from the wreath, but the spell's real purpose is to augment other fire spells." Malcolm tried to shrug the orc's mighty hands away. "Okay, I told him. Let go."

"You're at my whim, Boy." Ur-Krurk shoved Malcom to the ground. "You might want to keep that in mind *before* you go trying to tell me what to do."

Half the goblin's height, Tex tapped Uk'so's waist and whispered, "Are you hearing Ben because I don't hear him saying anything."

Ben tapped his temple.

Ur-Krurk answered, "Robot, he's using telepathy." The ogre kept eyeing Malcolm as the Dunn-Blatt got to his feet and dusted himself off.

"Great, everyone's hearing voices but me." Tex threw his hands up. "Never knew sanity would suck."

Ben extended his hand to Malcolm. *Ignition code please.*

"What?" Malcolm glanced between Ben and his car. He nearly screamed, "No way."

Ur-Krurk took a step toward the Dunn-Blatt.

"Seven, six, six, nine, zero." Malcolm fumed.

Thanks. Ben focused solely on the black bison-painted, purple Transcend, and made his way to the car. *If anyone is looking for me, it'll *help keep the scent off my trail.* The few blackened or bloody lumps on the Meadows Towing grounds that he had to navigate to get to the car weren't bodies. Ignoring what they were, Ben hadn't classified them as anything else. They just were *not* dead bodies. He opened the car door and slipped into the fine nylon webbing the Dunn-Blatt had for a car seat.

Ur-Krurk gave an attention-getting grunt. He stood behind Malcolm. The ogre pointed down at Malcom's dark hair, then to his own chest. He smiled as he ran his thumb across his throat with a finalizing nod.

What? No! Ben's eyes went round and his neck burned as he adamantly shook his head to deny permission. He switched to Giant. *Do not kill him.*

Malcolm turned to see what was going on behind him.

Unabashed, Ur-Krurk towered over the Dunn-Blatt. "Is there a problem, Boy?"

Malcolm shook his head and moved away.

Ur-Krurk started after him and answered in Giant. "As you wish, Blood-Son."

Ben looked over the standard Kentmoore dashboard set-up and noticed Malcolm had upgraded from the two rows of five buttons numbered zero through nine to the five button, double-number, quick toggles. He touched the seven, rocked it to six, and rocked it to six again. Tapped nine, and rocked it to zero.

The Transcend started up and revved with a dusk bison, growl-like rev.

We have unfinished business, you and I. Ben turned his gaze to Malcom who stared back defiantly. *You'll stay here tonight, and we'll settle it tomorrow at sundown. Understood?*

Malcolm narrowed his eyes and nodded.

Ben eyed Ur-Krurk and asked in Giant, *Understood?*

The ogre nodded and grabbed Malcolm by the neck, leading him to the building. "Time for you to face the carnage you caused."

"How do I strap myself in?" Tex climbed into the passenger seat and looked around the center console.

Wishing he could take his companion along, Ben sighed and suffered the pain to shake his head sadly.

"I know I'm not allowed in the bazaar itself, but I could help you reprogram the cards, or, be ready with the car in case you have to make a hasty retreat." Tex started to climb out. "Or, you know, just hang out in the car."

Ben's chest warmed at his companion's dedication. He lipped, *Sorry*.

"I know," Tex said as he perched on the doorframe. "You'd use me if you could." He dropped out of sight. A light *tink* indicated that he had hit the ground. "Be careful."

An inward cringe shook Ben as he thought about checking his neck in the mirror. *Nope*. He hit the gas.

Chapter Forty-Three

HOW BAZAAR

BEN PULLED INTO THE LARGE, over-stuffed dirt lot surrounding Bauman's Bazaar. Just like every night of the Samhain festival, the cars, carts, and wagons of the starwise filled the area to near capacity. As before, most regular spots were taken and most of the overspill had jammed up the parking lane thoroughfares. Far off, the tents and lights of bazaar played on the not-so dark, distant horizon like a spiced cider-scented mirage. About to head back out to try one of the other entrances, Ben noticed an arrow directing him further in to *Vendors' Parking.*

What in the world could Malcolm possibly have for sale?

Ben followed the arrow deeper into the lot. As he approached a fully-blocked lane, a glowing, forest-green ramp appeared, stretching ahead before curving off to the right. *Okay…* He drove onto the ramp.

The Transcend shut off, the ramp lifted the car to a second-tier track parallel with the ground, and, without turning back on, the car sped down the track like a miniature train.

He passed over people laughing, people arguing, and even some folks conducting transactions between cars, some of whom looked up at him as he went over.

The car crossed into the *Vendor Lot* where it passed over several empty spots and then stopped four rows out from the entrance to lower the Transcend into the closest of the remaining available spots.

If someone is waiting for Malcolm or surveying this… Ben touched the center of the hood and pulsed Krotosian magic into it. As before, it seemed to fill with warm water before activating.

Ben undid the spellcard holder and pulled out the reprogrammed spellcards. He stuffed *Shield* into the hoodie's right pocket—*what's this?*—where he discovered the rough length of a rusty nail. He shrugged at the discovery of Malcolm's hook and placed *Achilleus* in his left pocket. Lastly, he put *Blast* and Malcolm's tether together in his front pants pocket.

Keeping his tablet between his leg and the car door, Ben cued up Eleven Soul Sight and slid the duration to his maximum. *Sixteen awatts for eight hours. That's a huge chunk of the hundred available. It'll be better to cast it hour by hour… But casting from the tablet in there, among the shoppers, would call attention.* Ben pressed the *Cast* button formed from clusters of stars on his tablet.

The Anvilsmith drummed on the door as it vibrated between against the handle and his leg. Starlight started to rain down as the energy settled in his eyes. The spell made the colorful tent city take on an otherworldly sheen.

Ben got out and—can't resist—twisted his torso and leaned back to keep from turning his neck to look to the dark sky above. The North Star shone brightly and had a few friends shining with it through the vault of light over the city.

About to stride across the few rows to one of the pay stations, Ben stopped. His eyes narrowed as he took in the distant auras of the mingling crowds. *What about this made me stop?* He folded his arms and took a moment to analyze what worked at the threshold of comprehension. *Oh…* His eyes widened and his hand went to his chin to keep it from dropping in astonishment.

Most of them only have one type of magic, the blue kind, at their disposal. He held his jaw. *I always thought* everyone *had access to one of the five colors that comprised all traditional casters' mystic energy.* He gawked at the auras that ran the full spectrum of blue from a very faint azure to deep cobalt. The center masses were mostly cerulean and only one out of ten had a font of Vibros, Argos, or Krotos rolling around one of their chakras. *Even fewer have two... I would have never thought...*

Moving through the cars, he made a mental note to question Uk'so about the blue magic the goblins possessed. Closing on the entrance, he steeled his thoughts to obscure them from readers.

Ben stopped at the vacant booth and grabbed one of the small glass orbs. It reminded him of the Blood Berry Fairies' bauble. *It's just a little bigger.* No one ever was inside, but the entrance fee had to be paid or the invisible magical barrier would bar entrance. Keeping his neck stiff, Ben twisted his torso to see if anyone watched him.

Other patrons were infrequent and at other nearly vacant booths on this side of the bazaar.

Alright. Ben took one more look then lowered the orb and placed it against the tablet's microUSB power slot where it ebbed out an arcane watt.

"Keep it." The whisper came from within the booth. A floating feminine face appeared. Her eyes dropped to the Anvilsmith, then rose to wink as they searched for eye contact. The face motioned him to go in. "Don't worry. You're good."

Ben's brow rose in surprise and immediately knitted in suspicion. *Glad my face is hidden.* Bending from his lower back, Ben bowed to show appreciation.

Bodiless, the face lowered a similar distance.

Prior to this, only Toad and his fellow APA students had shown him this much cursory respect. For a moment, Ben considered the deep folding bow Jack—the tattooed thief who had stolen his possessions months ago—performed before him, and quickly discounted it. *The thief used my need for respect to establish, and sustain, his deception.*

Ben placed the glowing emerald bauble into his right front pocket and headed into the Bazaar. Expecting to smack against the invisible field as he had seen anxious kids do before their parents paid the admittance, Ben continued forward as though he knew it wouldn't happen.

The sudden sweet scent of spiced cider signaled that he had passed through the threshold and transitioned into the temporary resident tents on the marketplace's outermost circle. As usual, several of the jovial renters milled around, socializing with one another. Any who noticed the tablet hanging from his hip gave him a deliberate smile and a slight nod.

Further in, unless you were an Archon Private Academy student, merchants at standing stalls on the edge of the bazaar always pressed new arrivals trying to make a quick sell. The crush on him, as a Dunn-Blatt was everything Ben had always seen at a distance. However, instead of hawking their wares, they pressed items upon him without stating a price.

First in his hands was an open backpack from an exotic, scantily veil-clad, dusk-skinned woman. "For your books, a new haversack."

Next, a quill from a tall Asian gentleman in pale robes tailored to be above the knee. "For your papers."

"For your threads." A dark hand rattled a package of needles at him, and Ben's gaze followed it into the backpack. It landed upon a growing pile of items that he had not seen placed into the leather backpack.

What's going on?

The crowd parted, and he stopped before a stocky, eight-foot tall, bald, female merchant in sparkling, full-length orange and red robes. She, with great, purposeful disgust, had looked away from him and any other Academy student who came through. She presented three purple—*it's the same shade of violet as the Dunn-Blatt colors*—velvet-bound vellum volumes.

The hawkers around him gasped appreciatively.

She placed them in the backpack. "May your magic blossom, Bravado, and thrive."

The other vendor's stunned reaction signaled how big a deal this was. Ben bit his lip to prep for the blazing pain before bending his neck in admiration.

Flaring her sparkling robes, she moved to the side and bowed low.

What is going on? Striving to understand, he eased forward. The bazaar proper now lay before him and most of the merchants further in were looking his way to see what was happening. *I wonder if there's a way for them to tell who I'm supposed to be based on the hoodie. If so, what makes Malcolm such a rock star?*

Ben flipped the incredibly light backpack closed, buttoned it, and slid it onto his back. He adjusted the straps to rest on the edge of his shoulders, far away from the burned, sensitive flesh. As he moved deeper into the marketplace, random shoppers patted him gently on the back, and a majority of the merchants took the time to formally bow when he passed.

Trying to scrutinize Malcolm' apparent fame, Ben gritted his teeth. *Alright, he gets preferred parking, free gifts, and general admiration?* He massaged his temples. *Not being able to figure this out is really starting to piss me off. Think, Ben. Think.*

Distracted by his own conundrum, Ben barely managed to stop just in time to keep from bowling into a patron wearing an APA tan trench coat. *Hey a fellow student!* Ben recognized the short, curly-red-haired Dueling Adept instantly. *Adept Love…* Twisting his torso instead of his neck, Ben naturally looked around for others, but, against his own advice, Love shopped alone in the bazaar.

The small man pressed his fist on his hips, narrowed his eyes, and spat anger in his familiar nasal whine, "Bold, Dunn-Blatt." His green eyes appraised Ben in a ruthless way no instructor, Collins included, looked at students. The Adept's lips barely moved when his eyes went form the Anvilsmith on Ben's hip to peer into the dark hood with a deadly, emerald spark in his eyes. "Very. Bold."

Chapter Forty-Four

LARS

BEN'S BREATH abandoned him when he became cognizant of the circle of nonchalant-acting patrons forming around him and the man who taught everyone at his school how to duel.

Love flipped his coat back from his holstered tablet.

Holy.

Shit.

Ben's guts turned to ice and his lungs went cold. His breath refused to return. His knees began to shake. His bladder and bowels quivered with a very real, imminent threat to release their contents.

About to bow deeply to yield, Ben stepped back and bumped into someone inside the circle. He clenched his cheeks. *Don't crap your pants. Don't crap your pants.*

He pivoted to see the Arch-Primary of Las Vegas, Las Lightningpalm. The Chief Magistrate's robes had the same cut as any of his Lesser Judges, but his were a resplendent golden yellow. With the back of his hand, he pushed Ben to a Primary at the side, but still in the circle. The blond man moved his waist-long mane behind him and stood tall without his baton. He set a resolute fist on his hip as Adept Love had.

The hair on Ben's arms stood when he spied the raised gold lightning bolt set in obsidian signet ring.

Both men stared at the other. Neither spoke.

Adept Love didn't bow, but he did turn away.

Lars lowered his fist.

The Adept's red curls bounced as he burst from the circle. Forcing his way through the crowd, he called back over his shoulder, "I'll get a student, then!"

Ben found a breath. And then another. Little by little, his bodily functions began to resume their standard business as usual functions. He unclenched his cheeks.

Lars moved to stand before him.

He clenched up again.

"Relax, Bravado." Lar's breath smelled of dragon fruit and his smooth tenor voice held an intriguing, old-fashioned-radio-announcer quality to it that begged for attention. "I can have Primaries escort you to your car if you are not ready for a duel."

Wide-eyed in being spoken to by the Chief Magistrate as though he were an equal, Ben recovered, blinked, and shook his head—*ahh!*—and grimaced.

"Good." The Arch-Primary nodded to the milling crowd who all turned their backs to walk away. Unlike before, even the nearby merchants abandoned their booths. Lars gathered his hair, wrapping it around him like a shawl as he removed a pin. Released, his hair dangled near the ground.

Wow.

Lars presented the needle for Ben to see.

What are you going to do with that? Ben found his breath leaving again as the Chief Magistrate moved the point closer to his chest. A hand-shaped metal badge appeared around the needlepoints as the tip kinked into a lightning bolt across the palm.

"I can always use folks of your caliber, drive, and dedication to keep magic pure. For tonight, you shall have my shelter from any non-student caster." Lars pointed to a minuscule amber stone inlaid where the end of the bolt met the palm. "Touch this after you kill another. I'll come collect the body, gift you with a seven-stone spell of your choosing, and will have delivered to you, the Ape's weight in obdurium. I expect big things from you, Bravado. Big things."

Stunned, Ben nodded before remembering to bow. *How deep do I go?* He kept bending, moving his head deeper, and then closer to his knees.

The heels of soft leather boots clicked the moment his forehead tapped his shins. "It is I who should bow to you." The Chief Magistrate didn't. He turned to walk away and paused. "Once you have your fill of seven stones, I will up the bounty to eights." Lars strode away and called to the retreating crowd, "One by one!"

The masses pivoted and, instead of repeating what had been said like the night prior, they answered, "Until there are no more!"

Each of the patrons and vendors had returned. Most moved directly toward him to toss small gems, platinum, and gold coins as his feet. They all murmured various forms of sincere appreciation for "the deed that needs doing" or "the task at hand" or "purifying the traditions." Nothing direct like *thanks for killing an technomancer.*

A second wave of passersby lobbed silver on top of the gold as Ben stood rooted to the spot, anchored, completely, by the hatred of the mystical world as it showered him with riches. Even the preteen, who had stolen the white wand, threw a copper on the pile.

"Hold on, Sir," a child, no taller than his waist, in rich orange mink fur smiled up at him.

"Yeah." Another child, this one bald, with a long gazelle-like neck beamed. "We'll get these for you."

A third squat boy with pigtails laid a sack on the ground. "Courtesy of my father." He pointed to the mustachioed merchant who had wanted to buy the platinum sword focus from Ben. The rotund man rubbed his belly before bending as far as his girth allowed. The boy grinned and gushed, "It's a quad-stitched holding bag."

The three worked at a quick, playful pace, each trying to collect more than the other two. The coins and gems were gathered into the sack before they tied it onto the bottom of his backpack. Waving farewells, the three of them went back to their respective parent's tents.

Ben released the breath he'd only just realized he'd been holding.

Blood had withdrawn to his stomach leaving his arms and legs cold. He struggled to grasp what had just happened. *I've just received more respect and adoration than any technocaster in the history of our craft.* The first step away from the spot proved to be the hardest.

They want us all dead.

He took another step.
Every one of us.
And another.
Dead.

Chapter Forty-Five

ONE OF THEM

With the final clue to the riddle of Malcolm's rock star status, the smell of sage-seasoned meat, spiced cider, and various baked good melded into a blur around Ben, punctuated by the frequent murmured affirmations and the endless pats on his back. Everything, even the nodding, smiling crowd parting before him, became vague background observations

The Adepts at the Archon Private Academy made sure to drive home the point about how technomancy was disliked by those outside of the school. The frequency of their warnings increased as they neared major events, and on the week before Samhain festival, each Adept would stress the fact at least twice per class. For students attending the festival, they advised against leaving the fenced fairground and encouraged students to travel in pairs. Having seen other schools' practitioners employ the same tactics, Ben always figured his teachers were spouting, what should've been common sense.

What they failed to mention is how murdering an Academy student—Ben absentmindedly brushed his hand against his tablet—*or appearing to have done so, makes the killer a hero. Lars Lightningplam, the Chief Magistrate himself, offered me nothing short of a true bounty with a promise to keep the slayings secret.*

Recalling the various Initiates and Apprentices who—*faces regularly seen in the halls one week, gone forever the next*—Ben had always figured either failed out or quit the APA, his slow pace began to pick up as his senses returned.

Merchants who spied the device on his hip continued to bow, the crowd murmuring and patting his back.

Ben's posture changed as, behind the hood's darkness, he frowned at the traders and well-wishers. His back rounded as he increased his pace and leaned forward to stalk through the bazaar. Ready to do damage, he hoped *Man, oh man. Please let me be there when the assassin comes for Papa Mojo. I'd love to unleash my Rage from these pompous traditionalists at someone deserving.*

His energies began to roil.

People stopped patting his back. The murmur of congratulations changed to "man on a mission" and "happy hunting" and "put another one down."

Why haven't my parents told me? Do they know? Do any of the other guys or their parents know?

The weight of a hard stare snapped his attention back. *Please be the assassin.* Ben spun.

The small merchant at Goodspice's Goods, the one who had sold Neil a full collection of four and five-stone spells, stood on the stacked barrels outside his solid green tent. The merchant extended his hand and rolled his wrist to point his thumb at the ground. He then crossed his arms over his paunch, and turned his back.

Ben's fist balled tighter. *How dare you thumb me down, you—* As though the realization were a wall, Ben came to a sudden stop. *He's not thumbing me down, he's thumbing me for the very same reason others gave me gifts, currency and adoration.* Ben marveled at the strength of the merchant's character. *And he's doing it publicly.*

"Roasted walnuts, sir?" a short, skinny baker next to Goodspice, who had noticed the thumbing, called. The man waved a peacock-feathered fan. A magical breeze carried several homey scents to Ben's nose.

Ben's stomach growled.

The man switched to fanning loaves of bread. "No one can best my banana. No? Perhaps pumpernickel is more to your liking? No? How about rye?"

Nearly forgotten, a deep hunger gnawed at him. *Right now, I rather starve than eat anywhere I'd be welcomed.*

Amongst the sea of robes and fur coat, a blue jean jacket caught Ben's eye which took in the brown flattop haircut. *Is that that the same guy…?* He recalled the man from a month ago. *Yeah, that's one of the guys who handed mundane cash through the white Legerity's window at the Pinball Hall of Fame and drove one of the neon cars that shot at, and chased, me.* Thinking about breaking off a piece of his rage for this guy put a small smile on Ben's lips. *Blast him, like he did me.*

Ben considered the man's blue aura and the Krotosian energy that floated around his crown chakra. No. Ben let his smile fall. *Perhaps I'll challenge him properly after Mojo is safe. I'd hate to squander power now and come up dry when it matters most.*

On brown flattop's right, as though pulling up next to him in a car —*the other jean jacket guy, the one with red hair*—closed on his compatriot with two tall mugs. Between the two mugs, a familiar red-and-yellow amulet—*Komir's amulet*—bounced on his chest as he bopped and whistled.

Seeing the gift given to him, personally, by Elder Komir on his sixteenth birthday, a symbol that didn't exist on this side of the mystical door deep in Pepperjacks, Ben jammed hands into the hoodie's pockets. Gripping his *Shield* and *Achilleus* spellcards, he channeled Argosian energy into both. The refreshing smell of fresh-cut pineapples filled his nose before Shield's mint scent had a chance to register. His blood started to race as the air before him hardened. *If Red isn't the one who took my body, I'll eat my coat and loafers!* Ben fished the rusty nail from his pants pocket and let Krotosian magic slip into it.

The emerald challenge tether shot form the nail. Arcing around and over the crowd of other casters, it dipped down at the last moment to drive the tiny hook squarely into the whistler's chest, just underneath Komir's pendant.

A myriad of roasting meat, fresh fruit, drink aromas, colognes and perfumes from around the flattop poured into the tether and wafted to Ben.

He fingered the second stitch inside both sleeves—*Writhing Wreath* and *Napalm Arrow*—and fed Argosian energy to both hungry spellstiches. The ground around him lit as two solid-fire compound bows appeared, twanged sizzling arrows at Red, then faded. The arrows left flaming trails as they raced down the line to the target.

The shaft stuck into the air, just short of contact. *Crap, he activated the amulet.*

Azure energy twisted up Red's throat in a waving line.

He's using silence? In a duel? Still, Ben wished he had a way to counter it.

Frantic powder-blue energy caught his attention as it bounced in a star formation in Brown Flattop's chest before a small pyramid shot from his forehead.

What's that spell? Readying for the worst as the spells flew at him, Ben tightened.

Chapter Forty-Six

SPELLBOUND

A STREAM OF AZURE ENERGY, the *Silence* spell anchored on something—the wreath—above Ben's head. The world lost sound as the powder blue pyramid expanded around him, rotated point down, and faded without apparent effect.

Two at once, Ben. Not smart. Keep his left hand on Writhing Wreath, Ben laid a finger across *Napalm Arrow, Fireball,* and *Firestorm. If only I had the other guy tethered, too.*

A yellow-robed arm reached out from his side. The hand with a gold lightning bolt set in obsidian signet ring—*Lightningpalm*—reached out and—*what? How?*—snatched the tether from Ben's chest to take the challenge on for himself. *Why?*

Streams of golden lighting shot down the line.

The whistler's mouth sprang open, twisting in silent agony as the yellow power beat relentlessly at the barrier before his chest.

Brown Flattop turned away, and ran.

Ben reached out to take the tether back.

Mouth moving, as to give order, Lars knocked Ben's hand away before he could steal the challenge back, and pointed after Brown.

Before Ben could project, *To Hell with that guy. This one has my amulet,* a powder-blue pyramid flashed before his eyes and his telepathic sentences came out horribly jumbled, twisted, and warped.

What the heck? Ben's neck flared in pain when he shook his head to dismiss the glyph. He made another play for the tether—

Lars frowned.

—Ben stopped.

Lars pointed. Lars made a fist.

Damn it! Not wanting to, Ben tore off after the guy with the brown flattop. *If Lightningpalm had only tried to give me audible orders, I— Silenced—could've ignored the command, but the hand motions left no questions. He wants me to get this guy and beat him down.*

There was enough distance between him and the runner for the crowd to have parted for the sprinter and come back together after he'd passed.

Even with the extra prowess from Achilleus, there were too many people for Ben to try and navigate. A powder blue pyramid glyph flashed before his eyes again as he tried to project, *Move out of the way!*

Ben ran to the side, jumped onto a merchant's table, and ran across it. The backpack of hate-goods swung and bopped on his back. *Slowing me down.* He shrugged it off, leapt to the next table, and the next.

Further ahead vendors scooped their wares table clear and, their voices muted, cheered him on.

The crowd turned his direction. Chanting, they parted for him. The glyph flashed before he eyes when he tried to read their lips. *What are they saying?*

The runner glanced back, zigzagged, and disappeared down a narrow corridor between red tents.

Holy crap, if this guy's an assassin, too, he's probably head right for Mojo now! Committed to get the guy for his own reasons now, Ben forced his way sideways, bounded off a merchant's table and leapt at the second red pavilion. The tight fabric absorbed his moment and he slid down the mouth of corridor's tight opening.

The few merchants along the narrow way between the shops glanced at the tablet on his waist and pointed to the left side of the intersection ahead.

Ben leaned to take a step in when a hook landed in his shoulder. *Crap!* With a challenge tether hooked into him from behind, he could go no further away. Waiting for Lars to snatch this one, too, Ben turned. *Impossible.* The challenge's arched tether curved high and away into a distance reserved for only the longest-range spell. *No tether could cover half that distance.*

Yet, as the challenge began, nearly the exact same mixture of scents he had sampled when he issued his challenge to Red came to him.

Somewhat amazed, by the incredible distance, and unable to continue his pursuit, Ben watched the bazaar patrons part as the high emerald arch dropped to form a straight light.

Recalling that reasons behind challenges could be felt, the same damn Silence glyph appeared before his eyes when he tried to send the urgent need to postpone the challenge in order to save a life. He tried to swat the tiny pyramid, but it faded and he found expressing his feeling through the tether as difficult as trying to project his thoughts to others. *Well, I have no issue feeling their murderous intent.*

Down the cleared path, some five hundred feet away, three casters in APA tan trench coats stood.

I don't have time for this, guys! Ben bowed to send his surrender down the line.

Surrender denied, their outrage boiled back to him.

As though someone pushed the badge the Chief Magistrate had pinned to his chest, Ben spun. At the edge of patrons forming broken circle—to let the challenger through—Lars stood. The Arch-Primary made a series of motions.

Right. Grab the tether, and... shake it? Dance?

From down the line, the challenger closed at speed beyond perception.

Kevin, looking more like Collins now than when he threatened to duel LeRoy last night, stood fifty feet away—the shortest range for a clean duel.

Closer—*come on, let go*—Ben tried to relent again.

Jaw locked and teeth clenched in the way of Collins, Kevin's lips moved as he gave his head a slight shake.

Well—Ben thumbed the spellstiches—*this sucks.*

Chapter Forty-Seven

DUELING

No one in the crowd around them pretended to mill around. No, these patrons' mouths twisted in yells and chants Ben couldn't hear. Like the throngs who packed the stands at the old WDF Circuit matches, they were animated and most, desiring the duel end either his or Kevin's—preferably Kevin's—death, formed an X with their forearms. The stink of their excitement crowded in and curled Ben's nose. *Monsters. And you think you're civilized.*

Lars pantomimed grabbing the tether, again.

Sensing Kevin about to attack, Ben focused on his aura to read what would be coming—*where's the magic*—and blinked stupidly.

Kevin's aura was a dull, matte gray. *There's life, but not a lick of magic.* Kevin shook as the edge of his aura where the Anvilsmith laid against him started to flash green, pumping emerald energy into the otherwise mystically empty vessel. The power rolled in Kevin's stomach before shooting up to his shoulder.

It's a Blast. Without the spell handy, Ben planned to release a blast from the Writhing Wreath above his head as he grabbed onto the tether—

Ben's awareness expanded. *Three other duels are happening in the bazaar.*

A large battle raged at the base of Sunrise Mountain. A powerful ritual to drive demonic spirits from the last house on Camino Del Norte neared its height.

THE HALO of light around him vanished as the magic in Kevin died and sound returned to the world.

Everyone, shut up! Their yells, chants, and cheers were incomprehensible. Consonants and vowels had no basis and oft warred to topple into each other. *It's as though everyone knows a private dialect of gobbledy-gook.*

One voice rose above the hubbub. Smooth. Confident. Made sense. *Lars.* The words Ben heard didn't match the motions of his mouth. *His voice is coming from the badge.*

Lar projected, **Challenge him with manabarbs. Apes can't keep up.**

Energy from Kevin's Anvilsmith jackhammered into his empty shell. The emerald energy settled in the gray chest before evaporating.

What spell is that? An ice storm broke out around Ben, plunging the temperatures to below zero. His ear and nose froze, becoming frostbitten. Hail rained down. Some of the crowd were in the spell's radius, but the tether assured Ben was the only one to suffer the effects. Ice pellets the size of tennis balls slammed down on him. Two, in rapid succession, cracked on his chest and broke his collarbone.

Ben bit his lip and forced the bellow rising to his throat, down into his chest. His Argosian font swelled. He thumbed the fourth stitch to summon a dusk bison.

Channel raw energy at him. Lar's voice insisted from the badge. **It'll guarantee you the win.**

Ben squeezed the tether. *I don't want to exploit a weakness, but time is on the assassin's side.*

Hailstones pummeled Ben's back. He opened his Krotosian font and channeled it at Kevin.

Violet energy danced down the tether toward the target, just as the yellow had from Lars. *Pure Krotosian energy.* It howled like a banshee at Kevin who flinched away.

Emerald energy shot from Kevin's Anvilsmith meeting Ben's Krotosian energy a few inches before his schoolmate's chest. The device flashed full of green power and, in a painfully sluggish way, began to deplete downward. *It may be a sure win, but it's so freakin' slow.*

Kevin tapped at his device, but it continued to flow in the line to keep the purple from hitting.

Have to make this faster. As though he were casting a second spell, Ben opened his Krotosian font.

Kevin's tablet looked like it had been mystically punctured when energy from the power slot arced out to spill into the tether.

I should open a third... The ice storm ended and Ben's broken bones began to knit.

Kevin shook his Anvilsmith and yelled at it.

Ben empathized with Kevin's frustration. *Wanting to cast spells, but having to watch the awatt meter tick down to nothing is difficult.*

It took thirty seconds for Kevin's Anvilsmith to empty. When it did, Kevin bowed.

The crowd's roar rose to a fever pitch as many of them stroked their arms down through the air signaling for Ben to cut off Kevin's head.

Ben ignored them, his thoughts turning back to chasing the, jean jacket-wearing, brown flat-topped, possible assassin. He began to turn and leave when everything, and everyone, in the bazaar froze in place.

Ben projected, **Hello?**

Chapter Forty-Eight

TO THE VICTOR

EVERYONE'S FROZEN. Ben tried to move again. *Me too.*

Unable to move his eyes, the disgusting bloodthirsty mob around them remained unchanged. Men, women, and children, like a picture, fixated on what they expect to happen.

Kevin stood at the center of his field of vision, his head bowed. Looking at his defeated schoolmate, a vague, revolting understanding —*if I pull on the tether, I'll rip his soul out*—washed over Ben.

No way!

He tried to release the tether—and found his Krotosian energy reluctant to release.

Let go—Wait…

A realization—*Kevin has over fifty arcane abilities, mostly tether-related, and they can all be mine if I pull the tether*—settled on Ben's soul. Gary's lecture during Samhain, about the dangers of dueling and gaining abilities came back to him. Oh man… Over fifty arcane abilities— everything Kevin had worked for—mostly tether-related could be his.

I only have to pull and the Impossible Shot, the Distance, the Near Instant Travel all flow down the tether. All that—plus more—mine.

I only have to pull.

Oh man…

Chapter Forty-Nine

TOP JUNIOR CASTER

No.

As Ben's hand sprang open, movement and sound returned to everyone. Tears forming in his wide eyes, Keven stood upright, looked into the darkness of Ben's hood, and instantly doubled over into a folding bow.

Lightningpalm's face screwed up in confusion as the normally well-composed Arch Primary grabbed his forehead trying to understand why Kevin's soul hadn't been yanked clean.

Kevin's aura remained gray, but his Anvilsmith began to recover energy.

Whoa! Ben's own energy reserves swelled to half full. *Alright!* Ben clacked his heels to acknowledge the deep bow, and took off down the tent corridor. *First left*, he reminded himself, and repeated. *First left.*

A blast slammed into Ben's shoulder as he started to make the turn, turning his world green. He stumbled into the tents and rolled on the ground. *Ah, Kevin, you're just like Malcolm.*

That stupid little pyramid glyph flashed before his eyes, and kept flashing. He glanced back.

Similar to his vision from last night, LeRoy stood at the mouth of the tent corridor, yelling in that same gobbledy-gook that everyone but Ben could understand, motioned for him to get up.

No tether? Ben scanned. *Stupid glyph. No, no tether.* He scrambled to his feet—*Mojo's still at risk*—and took the first left.

LeRoy yelled after him.

"I understand about not publicly executing the ape and forgive you." Lars' voice came to him through the pin, "But you got that one in private. Finish it."

Screw you. Ben stopped at an intersection where, straight ahead, it would lead out into the open bazaar. *Making a left would do the same.* He turned to go right and a second green blast slammed into his nearly-healed shoulder, spinning him like a top into a purple tent.

Crap, which way?

The light blue pyramid glyph continued as he scanned the four directions, spotted LeRoy winding up another spell, and used his schoolmate for bearing.

This way. He got to his feet and ran into a deep dead-end. *Might be some small corridors.*

There weren't.

As he went deeper, he finally spied two dusty black tents at the far end of a row with a rope dangling down. *Just like Diviners' Row at the Samhain festival.*

A third blast slammed into his lower back, sending him flying forward to flop on his face.

Ben spun as he stood.

The colors of the tents, the length of the corridor, the smell of spiced cider, the sound of a pot boiling where and how LeRoy stood…

This was his vision from the other night.

Tablet in hand, LeRoy extended his arms to touching the tents by his side as though to show there was nowhere for Ben to go and no way for him to get out without going through him.

If I turn and run to the rope, he'll blast me and we'll end up dueling. Ben scanned the area as though searching for an alternate escape. *Play worried.*

Play worried? Ben repeated the thought as it occurred to him that he'd just dissed LeRoy.

Before tonight, this exact scenario would've made me break out in cold sweat. I'd hope to be having a nightmare so I could wake up from it. Now… Ben smiled grimly at having complete confidence—*not cocky, not conceit, just confidence*—in his ability to protect himself. ...*I'm just playing worried when I'm not. Not in the least.*

The only "worry" he felt was for Mojo.

LeRoy raised his hands with whatever he was saying and returned his arms to their wide open length as swagger poured into his walk. His mouth kept making arrogant turns and twitches as he spoke his tongue waggling as he kept pace with Ben backing further and further into the dead-end and closer to the ropes dangling between the tents behind him.

The glyph flashed and faded in the middle of LeRoy's boasting. "—go ahead." LeRoy crossed his arms and stopped advancing. He flicked a finger at the rope. "Climb on up, you little bitch. I'll still be here to kick your ass when you come back down."

Ben bumped into the rope. *I don't believe you, LeRoy.* Sensing a trick, Ben slowly put his hand into his front pocket.

"Go ahead, Dumb-Blatt. Tether us. I'll kick your ass and then snuff your ass."

Ben grabbed his Blast spellcard. He made sure not to turn his back as he moved around the rope. Slowly, he extended his other hand to grab the rope.

Energy bounced from LeRoy's gut to his shoulders as he fired two emerald blasts.

Ben channeled Argosian, Krotosian, and Nilosian energy into his card as he returned fire with a triple Blast.

The red and purple diffused LeRoy's greens in midair, and Ben made the third, black, bolt dissipate inches from his schoolmate's chest.

Eyes wide and expecting to be knocked back, LeRoy stumbled backwards from the dissipated black energy.

Ben projected, *You may be able to best your schoolmates, but I'm a whole different matter.* Ben grabbed the ropes with both hands. *It's your choice if you want to be here when I come down.* He pulled on the rope.

Chapter Fifty

TOO LATE

THE TENTS and bazaar fell away to the—*optical illusion*—of infinite darkness. *Papa Mojo's sanctum.* Ben sniffed and then forced air out his nose. *Still reeks of mildew and mothballs.* Recalling his first tip into the diviner's wagons, Ben spun. *Where's the light? Where's the crystal ball?*

Crap. Though it would present him as a target—*if the assassin's in here*—Ben channeled Argosian energy into his *Writing Wreath* spellstich to light the area.

Ben spun again. On the whole, the darkness of Mojo's walls prevailed, but— *There!* He moved toward the diviner who sat still with his skeletal fingers gripping the crystal ball.

Mojo. Ben projected. *Let's get out of—*

As he reached Papa Mojo, he abruptly realized that the diviner had been turned to stone.

Ben tried to yell his rage at not being able to save Papa Mojo in return. His throat burned as his wrecked voice warbled. He balled his fists and looked around, but there was nothing more to Mojo's area than the entryway and the room containing the small table.

To be certain, Ben searched again, but the dimensions of Papa Mojo's stinky sanctum hadn't changed. He sat down across from the diviner and looked into his empty stone gaze.

"Sorry." Pain reawakened, Ben's throat seared as he stood and walked away. As he reached the exit, he looked back once more at the diviner who had saved his life, the scene etching itself in his memory.

Ben sighed. *I really hope LeRoy's not there.*

He turned away from Mojo and left the diviner's tent.

Chapter Fifty-One

JUST IN TIME

THE SMELL of spiced cider swirled back to him as the long corridor where he left LeRoy swam back into being.

LeRoy was there, but his schoolmate stood frozen mid-turn as though he were about to leave. Lars Lightningpalm had just finished cutting a deep line on LeRoy's face with a black blade, and raised the tip to LeRoy's throat.

Hearing distant footsteps, Ben projected, *Their Master's coming!*

Lars glanced to him, then in the direction of the footsteps and touched his ring.

Ben felt as though Lar's hand were on his chest where the pin was as magic flowed through the badge. He caught a glimpse of Kevin at the end of the corridor before the bazaar spun away and he stood alone next to Malcolm's car in the parking lot.

Not knowing what Lars had cut into LeRoy's face, Ben enjoyed the trilled rushed of having stopped the Chief Magistrate from jamming the blade into LeRoy's throat. *That was close.* He thought about Kevin at the corner. *Lars could've had them both.*

"Thank you for the heads up." Lars' voice came to him from the pin. "I still expect big things of you, Bravado. Do not disappoint me."

Ben took the pin off and tossed it in the car. *So very sick of you.*

A hook sunk into his back. Ben sighed.

"I don't' want to duel, Malcolm." It was Neil's voice behind him. The tether confirmed the necromancer's intention to get an item from him. "You went to school with us and I considered Ben a friend. Give me his Anvilsmith so we can bury it in place of his body, or—" Neil's voice took on a fierce edge. "Or perish."

If he could speak, Ben would've been at a loss for words. Holding the hoodie to obscure his burned neck, he turned to face Neil and enjoyed the way his normally indifferent schoolmate's pale eyelids rose in surprise when he pulled the hood back disbursing the shadows that covered his face.

Chapter Fifty-Two

(IN) THE END

Sitting on the back of Neil's Transcend, just outside the property line of the red behemoth that was Pepperjacks, and against the sky threatening to break into dawn at any moment, Ben reached over his schoolmate's dormant Golemcast, and pulled a bottle from the Goodspice Spiced Ale four-pack. As he lifted the bottle out, another rose up from the bottom of the cardboard container to fill the empty slot.

How many bottles does it hold? Ben asked,

Neil sat, staring at Pepperjacks. *Forty-eight.*

Well, Ben began and paused. He kept glancing to Neil's companion and expecting it to move. It remained still. *I'm not sure where to start or how much to share.*

Neil twisted the metal cap form his bottle, tossed it next to the robot, and took a swig. He projected, *Start with how you got Malcolm out of his hoodie and conned him out of his car.*

The Golemcast leaned over to collect the top at half the speed Tex normally used.

The slow movement elicited a smile, and Ben twisted open his own bottle. The cinnamon-apple scent filled his nose. *Okay, I need a believable lie.* Ben took a deep, appreciative whiff before raising the drink to his lips.

Ben pulled it away without a sip. *The bottle's warm.*

Neil spared him a glance. *Goodspice's magical bottles makes their ambrosia act like it was freshly drawn from the tap.* He held his bottle up to the moon.

Ben smiled to himself. *I'd bet he's appreciating the magic more than the contents.*

Neil took a sip. *Quite a hefty deposit.*

Ben raised the bottle and took a pull. *Mmm.* The delectably warm mix of apple, cinnamon, and nutmeg matched, exactly, the beverage he'd had in Goodspice's tent. Moreover, the fluid quieted the pain from his neck. An appreciative sigh escaped him as the goodness dropped into his stomach and spread warmth through his chest.

Got it. Ben smacked his lips. *I'll layer in some truth.* *Took Malcolm's hook during Samhain, and he really wanted it back. Anyway, he called for a rematch.*

Sounds like Malcolm. Neil retuned his attention to Pepperjacks. *What were the stakes?*

Ben tossed his cap further from the robot. It stood, lumbered over to the metal top, picked it up, and retuned to plop where it had started. *He wanted to pit a platinum coin against the hook that he could beat me.* Ben turned his own gaze on Pepperjacks. *It looks ready for business. Why are they keeping it closed?* He continued, *I felt confident and asked that we up the stakes.*

Neil nodded. *Malcolm had always been ambitious, but both car and casting device seems like a really risky wager.* The albino turned his powder pink eyes on Ben. *While I believe he might have gone for it, I really doubt you would have accepted. No matter your level of confidence.*

Looking back into the eyes, Ben steeled his thoughts. *Can't believe I let my guard down.*

Neil looked away. *You do not need to confide in me.* The sides of his face looked as though he were smiling. *I am glad Malcom finally got his proper comeuppance.*

Instead of replying, Ben took a drink.

Neil sipped at his bottle and fell silent, too.

For several minutes, they both sat silently, nodded absently, and enjoyed their drinks.

Neil slid down the side of his car. He placed the empty bottle next to the dormant robot and flipped the seat cushion to pull out a first aid kit. *Changing topics before you lie again.*

Ben smirked.

Neil turned the case over and started to punch in a combination.

Whoa. Ben averted his eyes, staring off at the casinos and the colors their lights—MGM Grand's emerald, Paragon's gold, the Luxor's white—turned the sky above. A bit of Vegas pride swelled in him. *How many other cities paint the night so beautifully?*

An opening click sounded. *Check these out, Ben.* Neil moved away from the kit. Inside were a score of bright green spellcards. *These little guys can hold second tier spells.* Respectful of what he held, Neil presented the case to Ben.

Thanks. Ben grinned. *If only you'd given these to be me before I blew myself up.*

Neil pulled at a Velcro strap and saw, organized in tight elastic slots, twenty unique spellcards.

Ben gawked. *Wow.*

A small smile played on Neil's lips. *Since we're in business together, figured I'd give you all of the four-stones to start working on.* Neil pushed the Velcro back, closed the case, and added, *They bring the quickest return.*

Ben looked up when he heard Neil's car door open.

His albino classmate slid in and started his red school-colored Transcend. Neil angled his rearview mirror instead of turning in his seat. *Once you've filled five with any of the different spells, shoot me a text.*

Ben finished his bottle and set it next to the robot as Neil had. *You can count on it.*

I plan to. Without further ado, Neil drove away.

———

Dawn had made good on its threat, but had yet to blossom into its full radiant glory before Ben made it back to the Meadows Towing.

All the bodies, and body parts are gone. Thank goodness.

Anxious to crack open one of the new spellcards to see if he had been right as to why his goldfish spellcards—*with their single obdurium strip*—would not hold a second tier spell, he rushed into the still-charred kitchen.

Licking barbeque from his fingers, Ur-Krurk stopped in mid-motion when he saw Ben. The ogre large, light-blue face had guilt written across its features like a dog who had been caught digging in the trash.

Ben scanned the blackened kitchen for any indicator of what Ur-Krurk had been up to. His eyes landed on a few naked orc daggers, the kind the dead doubtlessly had carried on their hips. Two of them had blood on them and the other looked licked cleaned.

"Blood-Son," the ogre edged toward the archway to the living room. "You normally only visit weekly."

What did you do? Coming closer, Ben stepped through the archway separating the kitchen and living room. Instantly, he cringed at the sight of Malcolm, in purple underwear, bruised and battered, his hands tied together. The unconscious Dunn-Blatt hung by his bonds from a hook in the center of the room, swaying slightly.

"Blood-Son," Ur-Krurk's voice turned timid as he eased closer. "From day one, you must lay the ground rules so they understand what can happen…"

Memory of the rope-burn rings on Penelope's wrists came rushing back. *Malcolm's not as bloody or beaten as she had been…* But the ogre had done serious damage in the few hours he'd had to work. Ben's gaze followed a thin stream of blood trickling weakly down the length of Malcolm's leg. It dripped from his toes into a deep soup pot beneath him.

"If you don't," Ur-Krurk's tone turned placating as the ogre's warm breath pillowed Ben in the smoky barbeque scent. "They'll begin to think they have equal ownership of the property."

Ben watched another drop fall.

"I didn't do his face." As though Ur-Krurk had made the ultimate concession and Ben knowing would make it better, the ogre added, "He's not dead."

His fingers working *Writhing Wreath* and *Napalm Arrow* spellstitches, Ben rounded on Ur-Krurk who shrank toward the work bays. *Wonder how you'd like to be left hurting with permanent damage?*

Projecting his thoughts, Ben bared his teeth at the ogre, *You will *take him down and place him in the guest quarters.** Ben moved backward to the sink to block Malcolm from his view and pointed to where the Dunn-Blatt hung. *Have the goblins tend to his wounds.**

The monster, which had been the cause of many of Ben's nightmares for the past couple of months cowered and bowed to his commands.

Ben added, *You will not torture—anyone—again unless directed by me. Understood?**

"Understood, Blood-Son."

Ben leaned against the sink for a moment. *I should have never left Malcolm alone with that monster.* Ben crossed his arms, summoned the will to watch, and went back to the archway.

The ogre went into the living room and took the limp body down with care.

Heavy footsteps tromped into the work bay. "Might-Fist..." Jek sounded surprised to see him. "We haven't had a chance to get things all cleaned up."

Ben glanced at the orc entering the kitchen. He pointed into the living room. *Did you know he was doing this?**

Jek moved next to him and watched as Ur-Krurk took out a knife to cut ropes. He gave his usual *doesn't concern me shrug.* "He's an ogre, Ben. Why would you expect anything different?"

I didn't know ogres had a thing for torture. Ben opened his mouth to reply. Instead, he shut his mouth and watched as Ur-Krurk lifted the body and went to the far stairs.

Jek opened the blackened refrigerator and pulled out two bottles of beer. He removed the tops with the knife on his hip, and extended one to Ben.

Ben shook his head. The pain silenced by Goodspice's cider roused slightly.

Jek put away his knife, shrugged, and set the bottle on the counter. "Granted, I don't know humans as I know my own kind, but a part of you must realize that you can never trust that human." Jek took a half-bottle draining guzzle. "Whether you agree with it or not, the kind of treatment Ur-Krurk just doled out will color that man's decisions for as long as he remembers this night."

Ben tried to see it through the orc's eyes. Though Malcolm had played a key role in Toad's plot, the Dunn-Blatt had been doubled-crossed and—*counting what the Blood-Berry Fairies did*—now doubly punished. *He called him a man. Sounds like he had plans for Malcolm.* Ben considered putting the cold beer bottle on his neck for a moment.

As much as Ben didn't want to admit it to himself, Jek had a point. Only time would tell if the coloring would be for betterment or ill.

Ben projected, *He's not much older than me. Why do you call him a man?*

"You own this place. You are a man." Jek picked up the second bottle and moved to the sink to sit on the goblin's work stool. "The Dunn-Blatt came here and challenged for dominance, like a man. And when all this is done, he will reap what he sowed—like a man."

Ben forced his muscles to not shudder when he recalled the way Jek had shot Toad's chest into little more than mist. *Unlike Ur-Krurk, I know you'll disobey any order I give to leave Malcolm alone on a permanent basis.*

Wanting to consider the possibilities for a little longer, Ben prepared for the pain, changed topic, and whispered, "Tell me about the Blood-Son bond."

Jek rubbed his neck, got up to check the living room, and downed the rest of the first bottle. He rubbed his neck a second time and stepped close to Ben. Beer breath haunted his whisper. "I don't know how you came across the knowledge, but the ritual you performed has been the cause for many abrupt changes in allegiances between Giant-kin."

The orc raised the second bottle to his lips, took a long pull, before continuing. "There's a saying amongst the big men which goes, *'Feed your sons the beating heart of your brother, and his strength will be added to your line.'*" Jek took another swig and rocked his free hand from side to side. "Or something like that. The important thing is this." He leaned closer. "Giants believe in the shit and have magic to reinforce it."

Unable to take much more of the beer breath, Ben leaned away.

Still whispering, Jek backed away, "You and the tuzvul ate his son's heart, so, in his eyes—though she's dead—you are both his kin now." As though saying such things left him parched, Jek upended the bottle and guzzled it.

Ben switched back to his Dunn-Blatt problem, and projected, *About Malcom, give me some time to figure it out.*

"Sure thing, Might-Fist," Jek nodded and put both of the bottles in the sink. "I'll make sure he knows—with words alone—the consequences for trying to leave the property."

Ben considered the words. *"Fair enough. Thanks."*

Jek went into the living room.

Planning to go up to his bedroom, Ben followed and froze. Without Malcolm hanging there, his eyes went to where the circle of small charred remains had been. *"Jek?"*

Picking up the pot of blood, the orc turned. "Yeah?"

Ben did his best not to look like he wanted an affirming answer. *"Do goblins like marbles?"*

"More than ogres love to torture," Jek answered without hesitation. He then gave an *I don't get it* shrug. "The little guys can't get enough of 'em."

Conscious eased greatly, Ben went up to his room.

Precisely at sundown, after dinner, Ben, now in his own school uniform, led Malcolm—in his colors—outside for a walk around Meadows Towing.

The neglected metal-and-plastic smell barely hung in the air, and the sky had that nice blue-purple color with several stars shining brightly overhead. They strolled in silence down rows and columns of stacked wrecks until they arrived at the water tower at the center of an almost fairy circle grouping of compactors.

Ben stopped and faced Malcolm. *I brought you out this far because I wanted to assure you clear line of sight to see no one will interrupt our duel.*

Malcolm crossed his arms. His injuries were well hidden by his school uniform. "So?"

Presenting Malcolm's rusty nail, Ben began to back away. He had to focus on Malcolm's wrist to see the rope burn. *When I took your hook, I said you could get it back after a year and a day.*

"You did." Seeing where this was going, Malcolm pulled up his sleeves. The bruises and cuts were quite obvious.

Don't feel sorry for him. Ben told himself. *His situation is all of his own doing.* Ben established eye contact to overlook the wounds, and kept moving backward. *But you didn't wait.*

"No, I didn't." Malcolm's prideful smile kicked up. "I had a shot at getting it back much sooner and when opportunity knocks, I answer."

Which is exactly why the orc who spoke to you last night will blow your head off if I cannot find a way to control you.

"Control me?" Malcolm laughed. "Good luck with that, Benny." He guffawed louder and leaned back to look up at the water tower."

Ben used the rusty nail to hook Malcolm.

"Ah, yes, the Retributive Paramountcy." Malcolm continued to smile and scan the water tower. "Is that orc hiding up there?"

No. Ben had moved fifty feet away to initiate a clean duel. Hoping Malcolm would say something, anything, which could resolve this in another manner, Ben returned to his line of reasoning. *I would let you go, but the orc will kill you, and if the orc fails, the ogre will hunt you down.*

Mention of Ur-Krurk took Malcolm's smile away and turned him feral. "When I beat you! When! I will have you order the orc to murder the filthy goblins, then demand the ogre kill the orc, and command the ogre to sit on a thirty-foot, barbed spike." Sneering Malcom began to roll his shoulders to loosen up. His voice cracked and his eyes moistened. "Then I'll work you like a puppet for the rest of your life." Malcolm's face twisted into a vengeful scowl. "I'll have you working the darkest skin-trade pits catering to those with the worst of desires."

Ben leaned back. *Wow. Where'd all the extra hate come from?* Jek's words about coloring Malcolm's perception rang back. Ben sighed, and projected, *I don't know what I did to you in the past, but I'm sorry it has come to this.*

"I'm not." Malcolm began to dance in place like Bruce Lee. "Come on! Name your duel."

Manabarbs.

Malcolm stiffened. "Come on. We both know you have three magical fonts at your disposal. You'll clobber me. Choose one I have a chance at winning."

Prior to hearing what you have in store for me and mine—by the way, the goblins aren't filthy—I might've. Ben projected. *Have to act now, so he doesn't talk me out of it.* Ben opened his Argosian reserve to send a ruby stream of crackling red energy down the tether. *Now, I know there no question. I have to win.*

Malcolm let out a ruby line of his own.

The energy clashed into a crackling crimson start at the center of the tether.

Malcolm released his howling, violet Krotosian energy.

Ben did the same.

Lavender collided with the violet a few feet from his chest to make a keening purple star.

Sorry, Malcolm. Ben next opened his Nilosian font down the Krotosian line. The vivid purple star darkened and sizzled as it flew down the line, stopping an inch from Malcom's chest. Ben then switched the Nilosian energy to the Argosian line turning the star a deep, sizzle-crackling brown. This star slid down the line, until it also hovered inches from Malcolm.

Ben kept rotating his Nilosian to the Krotosian and Argosian lines to make sure the stars stayed close to Malcolm. Concern wrinkled Ben's brow as his three sources of energy dropped below half. *Malcolm still looks strong.*

Sensing weakness, Malcolm leaned into the tether and grinned like a man possessed.

I have to bring this to an end. Ben opened a third line. Nilosian energy, blacker than the night, sizzled between the others to beat at Malcolm's two.

"You can tri-cast?" Though the struggle was ongoing, Malcolm's determined smirk dropped to a frown. The Dunn-Blatt shook his head. The mad grin returned and he leaned further into the tether trying to dump all of his energy into the line. "To Hell with you, Ben! To Hell with you!"

Shocked, at the stars flying his way, Ben opened up fully and dumped his mana.

Malcolm didn't get a chance to fret as the two stars went out and five lines of scintillating red, purple, and black energy blasted into his chest, throwing the Dunn-Blatt back, unconscious.

The tether between their torsos returned to a wispy emerald line. Ben's end centered in his chest, while Malcom's tether rose up his still body and anchored in his forehead.

A thorough awareness of everything about Malcolm filled him; volumes of information rolling through him.

Malcolm was the youngest of four children, the only one born without the ability to cast in a family of legacy magic-users. Desperate for some form of magic, Malcolm applied for, and was accepted into, the Archon Private Academy which ostracized him from his family. When he turned thirteen, an accident at the school opened him to Mindist energy, enabling him to weave spells like traditional casters.

Mindist! Ben captured the name of the blue energy.

Proving the magic to his parents, they snatched Malcolm away from the APA and enrolled him to the Dunn-Blatt Institute, where he could learn *real* Magic. But he was mocked as an Ape there until he initiated, and won, a Retributive Paramountcy challenge over Allan.

Ben recalled the miserable-looking kid in the back seat of Malcolm's car who had owned a string of twenty-four hour diners and a ranch where hellhounds were bred, which became Malcom's—and were now Ben's.

Malcom groaned and rubbed his temples.

Worked like a puppet, eh? About to command Malcom to stand, the Dunn-Blatt popped up to his feet before Ben could fully form the thought. *Astonishing!* Ben clapped, and made Malcolm clap, and then felt brief shame before amazement pushed it away. *It's almost like he's a conjuration that I control.*

Ben nodded to his next thought, *I want you to make my trench coat mend itself like your hoodie.*

Malcom's eyes became glassy and his voice took on a monotone quality. "It will be done." The Dunn-Blatt blinked and rubbed his temples again. "If you're going to make me do things, at least have the decency to not make me acknowledge it."

I wonder if this link is truly like a conjurers' bond.

Ben cautiously extended his senses into Malcolm. *Whoa!* Sorting whose senses were who's made his knees wobble. *Almost like being in the girallon.* About to swoon, Ben put his, and Malcolm's, arms out for balance. *Whoa.* It helped, but—*whoa!*—Ben pulled back his senses and caught himself before he fell.

Okay. Ben extend his vision. Their points of view wove together. *This is going to take serious practice.*

Ben closed his eyes and viewed the world through Malcolm's sight. *So, that's what it like to be just a little taller.* He opened his eyes and had Malcolm close his. **Can you see anything?**

"No." Malcolm replied, "But if you allow me to, I could."

Ben tried to make it happen.

Malcom fixed his posture and lowered his sleeves. "Damn, I look like Hell."

Ben thought about how he had heard that Malcolm used to make people he beat in Dueling give him a piggy back ride. *I should do the same to him.* Ben dismissed the thought. *That'd just be petty.*

Though he hadn't projected the thought, Malcolm said, "You know, Ben." Malcolm smiled. "You should. You've totally earned it." Malcom bent at the knees.

Tempting, but no. Ben waved off the ride. **Come on, let's get back to the building. We've got some stuff to talk about.** Thrilled at the possibilities that lay before him, Ben smiled all the way back to the building.

EXTRA - NEXUS BAR & GRILL

BY EZEKIEL JAMES BOSTON

Ally

Ally Dazs rolled the heavy silk sleeves of her Census Agency robe back and crossed her arms. She'd never cared for Las Vegas. The casters here were shifty. Not only that, their dealings and allegiances, were tenuous at best. If left up to her, all the branches of her Agency would converge on the city in an unprecedented audit.

She smiled at the thought of the slimiest of the city's creeps crumpling under the weight of all their dark dealings being brought out into the light for the starwise of the world to see. She smirked at the thought of the order that would come from the momentary—in the grand scheme of things—chaos.

But that wasn't why she was here.

The Census Agency had received notice that ownership of the Nexus Bar & Grill had changed hands, and it was her job to figure out who now owned one of the most powerful buildings in the city.

Taking a moment for herself, Ally reveled in the new spring sunshine peaking over Sunrise Mountain and warming her skin. Her smile blossomed wider. The local chapter of her alma mater had a guest house on the mountain. Perhaps, once done here, she'd stop by to visit with the Sisterhood and use their guest dorms to recover from the spell.

Bringing her focus inward, Ally ignored the hum and exhaust from the few mundane cars driving Las Vegas Boulevard, and began to gather her focus to cast Temporas Illum Orchalance. While not the strongest post-cognitive divination spell she knew, it was the most thorough.

Had she been at a lesser structure, she'd be worried about casting even the simplest spell with so many mundanes within easy breach distance, but The Nexus Bar & Grill was one of the city's oldest nodes. Not only that, but there had once been a dueling platform out back; so the Mystique had been laid so thick here that she could almost feel it. The only way a mundane would be able to see or find this place is if they were invited, and—besides being highly illegal—only a true idiot would ever do that.

If in operation, the Nexus Bar & Grill wouldn't be open for another couple hours and, since no one in this city could really be trusted to give her the answer as to who owned the place; it was up to her, and her divination, to ferret it out.

While Temporas Illum Orchalance would reveal everything that transpired during the transfer of ownership, the information would be jumbled and a little loose at first; but she'd get it woven together. Making sense of the independent timelines as they came together was something few could do well, and Ally stood amongst the top in her field.

Transfer of ownership. What a nice and innocuous phrase.

The higher ups at the Agency never dug into the high rates of Paramountcy—the worst kind of legalized theft—that took place in Las Vegas every decade. If North America was on the scale, Las Vegas would rank up there with Cairo, Hong Kong, Paris, and Rio de Janeiro. If anyone really studied the numbers, they'd see that Las Vegas was completely rotten. But, of course, that kind of thing never happened in North America.

Perhaps she'd find a thread, like she had in Montreal, that she could use to make the Agency take notice.

Hoping that would be the case, Ally pushed all thoughts out of her mind so that she could recite the fifteen-minute incantation. She knew the spell well. With so much desire for the information, Ally made sure to take her time and not rush.

She'd know. She just needed to... take... her... time.

The wonderful scen of daisies pillowed the area as her eyes rolled back and the threads of all involved came to her. "Five beings," she whispered. The spell began to weave them together and two slipped out. She nodded. "Three partook." Mist fell from the braid of mindsets as it thickened into a circlet that came to rest on Ally's brow.

She inhaled, and breathed, "Show me."

The Boy

Like stepping into a cross-section of time, Benjamin Baxter pushed through Nexus Bar & Grill's squeaky, rough, old-fashioned saloon doors. Imagining, as he usually had, that he was in a Western, he squinted and growled through gritted teeth. "I'm lookin' for the man who shot my pa'"

No one answered. Could've he beaten all his classmates here?

His favorite part of the diner—the magical ice cream scoopers—floated up from the ice cream bar. Normally at the ready, they hovered in the air to entice any who came in and only went dormant after an hour of non-use. He must've been the first one.

As usual, he rubbed the tall, narrow, jade saber-tooth tiger tiki totem at the end of the entryway. He shuffled across the retro, pink-and-red checkered 1980's tile to toss his school pack into the deep, 1950's-era booth closest to the *21 and older sign* near the rear wall.

His pack deep into the corner he—as though caught by the nose—rose up onto his toes to take in the scent of the eternally-grilling onions. His stomach growled.

Kevin, LeRoy, and Neil would give him crap for ordering without them... But he was ready to eat.

Shrugging off the social pressure, he bounced into the booth. "Should've gotten here faster, guys." He nodded. That's what he'd say to them between bites. They'd probably make a play for his golden steak-cuts fries, and he wouldn't stop them. While delicious, if he ate all of the golden goodies, they'd be nothing but unwanted squatters where ice cream, pie, or cake should go.

Held loosely against the wall by the table's miniature jukebox, Ben pulled one of the plastic-enclosed menus. Only looking to make sure that he had the right side of the menu, he poked *Harkam's Signature Double-Double Bacon Cheeseburger*. He had no idea who Harkam was, but the guy's burger was absolutely stellar.

Sizzling sounds came from the kitchen.

Set to count down from ten minutes, a floating, golden stopwatch appeared before him where the plate would materialize.

Licking his lips, he spun the stop watch and flipped the menu over for the true decision. "What to have for dessert?"

The saloon doors squeaked open.

Though the only one in there, Ben raised his hand to signal his friends to their favorite booth, but they weren't there.

A man in a black suit was looking at his hands as he stepped in. The air pulsed from his head in tight, translucent ripples.

Ben had seen the effect before. The ripples meant that the Mystique was doing its job on concealing the starwise world from the mundane who, somehow, had entered one of the most heavily obscured areas in the whole city.

"Hey," Ben yelled, keeping his eyes on the man, in case he rushed back out. "There's a mundane in here."

To the far left of Ben's peripherals, a flash of green popped over the kitchen counters.

Far more anxious to be the first to verify that there were actual people who worked in the Nexus Bar & Grill, than to point out some random mundane dude who happened to stumble into the place, Ben turned.

Sure enough, someone was there.

But the high, green pointed ears that protruded above a little green bald head indicated that the cook—maybe the dish washer—was a goblin. Whatever the guy's title, he peeked over the kitchen counter at the mundane, who was standing short of the tiki.

While Ben hadn't seen the goblin in full, he saw enough to claim the bounty. But if he did so, he would expose the fact that a goblin was working within city limits. He didn't know what that would mean for the owners, but he knew nothing good would probably befall the goblin if he were to—by default—report it while being the first to claim Nexus's *no visible workers* bounty.

More than the bounty; the status… Like a lot of hard decisions he'd had to make as of late, Ben wrestled the with pros and cons.

The Mundane

"Alright, Wes." Wes Silva spoke to himself as he stamped and dragged his feet across the dust-covered mat outside the saloon-style doors. Dirt came away in voluminous puffs, revealing faded pink rubber letters; *Nexus Bar & Grill.* He answered his early self-talk of *how badly to do you really need the money?* "This is how badly."

He waited for the dust to settle on his black Johnston Murphy dress shoes to obscure the fact that he hadn't had a fresh shine in weeks. Wes stepped back to look through the large windows at the tacky interior. No one was ever in there. He stepped back up to the mat.

Wes placed his palms on the least-worn areas on the old, sun-bleached, wooden doors and carefully pushed them open. They parted with a long, annoyingly loud *squeeeaaak.* While the noise grated, he bit his lip in concentration until the doors were wide enough for him to enter without them banging into him.

He hopped through onto the waxed tile floor and checked his palms. "Ha!" For the first time since he had started coming here over the last six months, they were splinter-free.

Grinning at his un-punctured flesh, he called, "Hello?"

Like always, no one answered and no one was here. And, also, like always, the hairs on his neck registered that someone, somewhere, was watching him. Maybe it was the building itself. While Wes couldn't put his instincts into words, there was always something *off* about the bar & grill, beyond just the horrible hodgepodge of outdated furniture.

In case he was right, and the place was sentient *and* could read his mind; he uttered a soft apology. "Sorry."

The scent of grilled onions fill the air and began to weigh on his tongue as sizzling sounds came from the kitchen. He looked to yell at the cook, again, about holding off on the onions because of his allergies. But, as always—as if magic made the onions start grilling just because he entered—the scent wafted from the kitchen.

It was light for now. Not too bad. But if Abraham didn't get his goofy ass out here, Wes would have to step out and wait for the freak to rush him through to his office.

Music came from behind him.

He spun.

One of the miniature jukeboxes that sat on the tables had powered on all by itself. That kind of shit was always happening here. Part lounge music and part pop chart-topping hit, *Magic is Real* by Jack Bigelow bopped from the jukebox, injecting a bit of fun into the atmosphere.

At least it would have if Wes weren't already weirded out by the jukebox starting on its own in the first place. Then to play *Magic is Real*? Too trippy.

He backed away from the table and bumped into a makeshift wooden stool.

Wes toppled.

As though aimed, the stool followed him; a rusty nail heading right toward his eye.

He flailed, batted it, and yelped.

The damnable thing clattered across the floor back toward the stupid tiki.

"Fuck!" Wes slid his back against the wooden counter and examined the pain on his palm. Three slivers where shoved in. Blood welled from the deepest. He wanted to lick the wound, but didn't to keep the slivers from swelling.

Muttering. "Every Goddamned time." He was able to get the biggest one out, but the two smaller ones would need tweezers.

Composure lost and civility forgotten, Wes yelled for the man he'd come to borrow money from. "Abraham! Are you in here?"

The Man

"Boss." Squek's voice came from his lava lamp. "Wes is here."

The mundane's name alone was enough to make Abraham Lasko pause his sigh of relief from the knot in his shoulder finally being worked free by Hanna. He waved his hand at the door to his private box, and the grill obeyed his will and opened the door.

Across the lounge, in the restaurant section, by the tiki, Wes Silva—sole owner of the failing Silva Saloons—grinned as he looked at his hands. As much as Abraham loathed dealing with mundanes, Wes's three saloons stood on intersecting leylines in the city. Someone in Wes's family had been a pretty crafty mage, but the man down there begging for a lifeline—Abraham exhaled his disgust—was utterly clueless.

Minding the mundane, Abraham rolled his head to the other side so his voice could better travel back to the lava lamp. His breath hitched, and he sighed.

Hanna had started working his other shoulder.

Abraham spoke to the lamp. "Has, he given tribute?"

Squek answered. "No, Boss."

Abraham rolled his eyes at having to give the instructions each and every time. "Make. Him."

"Will do, Boss."

Movement in the restaurant caught his eye. A real customer—a caster—had slipped in.

"Poop." Abraham dislodged himself from the oiled, masterful hands to spring to his feet. He pointed to the jukebox on the table where the caster, a brown-haired boy, had raised up out of his booth to catch a glimpse of Squek.

The jukebox lit. Jack Bigelow's *Magic is Real* also struck up in the lounge.

Wes and the boy both turned to look at it.

Not concerned about the mundane, Abraham closed his right hand. He could feel the boy's complete attention in his full control.

Wes fell from sight and cussed.

Abrahams's hand began to shake.

The boy was shirking him off.

"Your will is mine to control." Clenching his right hand tight, Abraham gripped it with his left and focused on governing the boy. Manipulating the boy.

If the boy saw the goblin, Abraham would have to pay the hundred ounces of gold reward that he'd put in place decades ago to revitalize the joint when he had found the lava lamp-themed nexus node and assumed control of the Nexus Bar & Grill. Worse, the Magistrate would levy fines against him and then toss on sanctions just to be spiteful. But worst of all, would be the bad PR.

His hands popped open. "What?"

The boy's head turned back toward the kitchen.

"It's done, Boss. He's blooded."

Abraham pinched the air to control Wes. "Well done, Squek." He wiped his brow and was confounded at the amount of sweat on his hand. His gaze shifted to the youth in the booth.

He wiped his hand on his towel. "Also, find out who the boy is."

"Will do, Boss."

Hanna had closed on him.

Abraham waved her off. Business first. Massage later.

He went to his closet and thumbed through his various business robes, quickly settling on the burnt goldenrod one with the pointed high-collars. Whipping it on, he made sure the prongs were straight up before adding a pearl to each tip to give them a slight downward pull.

His attention went back to the kid. A young person with that kind of potential was to be brought under his wing. Or—if need be—crushed under his heel.

Ready to impress, Abraham had the robe float him to the doorjamb as he focused on the kitchen door.

The robe set him down at the threshold.

Abraham stepped over it and was transported to the swinging kitchen door. It opened for him and, pinching the air to hold Wes idle, he stepped out and had the swinging door stop.

Though he wanted to focus on the mundane, his gaze drifted over to the boy. There was an absolutely fascinating wild element about him that didn't exist often in today's youth. Also, the Nexus relayed just how much raw potential lay within the teen that, currently, was well beyond his reach.

The boy would be the perfect apprentice.

Ben, The Boy

While Ben planned on calling the goblin out, the jukebox coming on by itself was unusual.

He wanted to check the parking lot to see if his friends were pranking from out there, but he couldn't look away. For some reason, this particular item held his attention like nothing ever had. Like few things ever could.

Scampering sounds came from the kitchen.

Ben tried to turn, but again, the jukebox kept hold of him. It hadn't ever before, and it didn't make sense. *Unless.* Unless someone had cast a spell on him. Ben set his will, and yanked.

The resistance gave.

Ben's hand dropped into his pack and he fished out his Anvilsmith tablet. If it was a friend, he'd chuckle off reacting like he'd been attacked, but he'd been through too much lately to think what had happened was anything else.

The mundane fell, flailed, and cursed. Not a threat.

From muscle memory, Ben's fingers worked the glass faceplate to wake and unlock the tablet.

Awake, it thrummed in his hand.

Ben dropped his thumb and tapped the bottom left corner where Achilles sat. To keep up appearance of magic having to be forced into his being—like it did with all other Technocasters—he shook and worked his jaw as the magic slid smoothly into his center and dispersed; pulsing power through his being.

The fresh-cut-pineapple scent that accompanied his physical prowess spell overpowered the smell of grilled onions as his muscles twitched and begged to be put into action.

The scampering went back into the kitchen.

Hand hovering over his combat spells, Ben turned his head.

The goblin had high-tailed it into the kitchen. The wide-open door swung back and flopped through center to be all the way open, for anyone coming out. Then flopped back all the way the other direction for anyone going in.

Slumped against the oaken bar, the mundane studied his hand, then yelled, "Abraham! Are you in here?"

"Humble sorry, good patron." In the kitchen, a spindly green arm waved a spatula with a white cloth napkin attached.

The door continued its wide flopping. In. Out.

Ben kept his awareness broad. "I'm calling bull crap." Danger played on the air, and his gut registered the apology from the kitchen as the kind that follows a failed attempt. And something larger was going on.

"Truly, good patron." The white flag spatula rose a bit higher and the waving became more pronounced as the goblin stepped out where it could be seen. A dirty white apron with The Nexus Bar and Grill logo lay over long brown sleeves, jeans, and small, dingy tennis shoes. "The mundane was going to lay eyes on me, and we both know we can't have that."

The pineapple smell from Ben's spell began to mix with his saliva. Unable to keep still, his legs began to shake and he bounced in place.

Ready for the real threat, Ben scanned. The parking lot was empty, and only the goblin and the mundane were inside.

The goblin rested the spatula on his shoulder. "You're not surprised to see one of my kind?"

"I've seen goblins before." Ben didn't want to dismiss the little guy, but the attack didn't feel like it had come from him. "Just not within city limits." But it must have. He turned in the booth to face the goblin, and let the words stand on their own. Forget the bounty, using spells on underage casters was a big fat violation and he left the threat of calling the Primaries unspoken.

Skepticism turned the goblins' features. "Like Hell you've seen one of my kind."

"I have." Ben assured him, leveling his gaze. He tried to loosen his shoulders, but his spell kept them tight and ready to spring. "At Meadow's Towing."

"Bullshit. You'd be a blood-spot." The goblin let the spatula drop to the floor with a clatter. He crossed his arms. "Your kind cant' go there."

"Kinda like your kind can't be within city limits." Wound for action, Ben tried to sigh, to ease the internal tension. His spell didn't let it work. He had programmed it well.

Eyes lowered, the goblin stroked his long ears.

Ben smirked at its confusion and, in that moment, he knew he goblin hadn't attacked him. The mundane had gone completely idle. Whoever was doing that was probably the person who had put the jukebox whammy on him, and the one he should report to the Primaries.

"Oh yeah?" The goblin put his fists on his hips like a child giving a dare. "What's your name then, tough guy?"

Ben knew what he was supposed to do. Among golbinoids, introductions were a show of force; meant to intimidate. Having been promptly laughed at when he tried their way, Ben had sworn not to feel that particular type of foolish again. While he ran with them, that aspect of their way wasn't his.

Deadpan, Ben said what his goblins called him, "Benja."

The cook's ears rose a bit, but his face remained unchanged.

That was something Ben hadn't seen before. He had grown accustomed to his name granting instant recognition with local goblinoids. Apparently, this city-goblin hadn't heard of him. Ben tried to dismiss the un-acknowledgment with a shrug, but his magic wouldn't let him relax even that much.

He settled for a slight twist of the neck. "Might want to call a cousin. I hate to toot my own horn, but I'm kind of a big deal."

"Oh, I know who you are." Voice small and quivering, Squek's lips barely moved. In an odd, delayed reaction, the green eyelids went wide to their full range. "My name is Squek Yum-Fire, and it's truly an honor to be meeting you." His small fist thumped against his narrow ribcage. "Benja."

Wes, The Mundane

Finally, one hand raised to shoulder height, the six-four Abraham came from his office in a bed-robe that would've made Liberace jealous. *No matter the color, Men shouldn't wear clothes that sparkle.*

"With all the perfectly fine, tacky-ass chairs that you have in here —" Wes grunted as he used the light green, pillow-topped, vinyl stool next to him to get to his feet. He frowned down the line of chairs that looked like each had been picked from different bars from different decades.

Wes then eyed the sucker that almost blinded him and wished for an axe. "Why do you keep that piece of shit?"

Voice thin as usual, Abraham drolled in his faggy manner. "It, has its uses."

"I presume the tweezers are still in your office?" Wes checked his hand. There was more blood than normal for his mishaps at the Nexus.

"Yes." Abraham nodded absently. "As, is Hanna…"

Wes shook his head against getting a massage, and then unconsciously started to nod as he pictured the hot Swede. Puffing on that lava-lamp-theme hookah that Abraham had, he could chill for an hour or so and let her use that coconut oil to rub away the stress of the day. Man, that oil always took him back to the glory of his honeymoon in Hawaii. The peak of his marriage. The happiest he had been.

Thinking back on his honeymoon, Wes reveled in the memory for a while. Then his ex-wife's face flashed, so young and gorgeous at the time, came into his memory one too many times; reminding him of the biggest mistake he'd ever made—admitting to have cheated on her.

He knew he should've been ashamed of the deed, but most couples they knew had a Hollywood Pass List. And when he slipped up into the greatest opportunity of his life—to bed the gorgeous Angelina Anderson—he wasn't going to let it pass. Since he and Hellen didn't have the list, he shouldn't have, but he did. Still, if he hadn't tried to come clean…

He grinned at his accidental pun.

Shit. What was he doing? It was like he couldn't focus on the moment.

Wes shook his head to get all three women out of his mind.

While he still had a lot of time in the business day to get the money to the bank, he'd already waited until the last day to have come here for a loan. If he didn't stop daydreaming, he'd end up pushing it to the last hour. And—if the Swede got her hands on him—to the very last minute.

While he'd been idle, Abraham had waited.

The bald, robe-wearing freak was looking at an empty booth and smiling when there was obviously nothing there to amuse anyone.

What a weirdo. With hours left in the day, Wes decided to not be anxious about getting a loan. Though desperate, he didn't want to seem like it.

Wes adopted his own bemused smile as he looked outside and

focused on the tourists that formed a haphazard line on the other side of the *Welcome to Las Vegas* sign. Seems like there was always a line of the folks wanting to take their picture with the world-famous landmark.

As long as they brought their green to keep pumping money into Sin City, Wes didn't mind. His bars were focused on serving local. When a tourist came in, he, his works, and his regular patrons called them randoms. But randoms' money spent just as well as locals.

When they no longer interested him, Wes turned back to Abraham.

The same lopsided, toothy grin that Wes had seen every time he had come to get an advance from the gold-slinging loan shark—particularly the first time—was on the guy's face. Though not currently directed at him, the same predatorily menace stalked the corners of the freak's eyes. And he was ready to pounce.

Wes had regretted seeing the smile the first time, and every time since. What was he missing? He scanned the booth again. What could make the weirdo grin like that?

He began to feel a little tingly. The onions were starting to get to him. He knew was coming here. *Why didn't I bring any Benadryl?*

Still, Wes knew the timetable for his breakouts. He had more time. And he still didn't want to be the first one to bring up why he had come. They both knew. He just hated having to admit it. Worse, it seemed as though Abraham loved to make him say it. Which Wes always did, but he sure as Hell wasn't going to be trained like a house dog.

I can do that, too. Wes folded his arms and made an attempt at mimicking Abraham's vacant stare.

It all came back to how desperate Wes was. So desperate that he'd go to an almost always vacant building—one he could only find when he needed money—and break bread with a guy who only wore robes which only got more and more *fabulous* as time went on.

A year ago, he'd already hit up his friends, who were broke. More interested in the land beneath his financially troubled saloons, the banks didn't want to touch them. Lastly, the mob families had treated him as though he was trying to pawn off a plate of steaming shit as fresh sausage. After a week of that, the *We Invest In The Distressed,* flyer that he found jammed under his windshield seemed too impossible to be real.

And, there hadn't been a month that had gone by since that Wes hadn't regretted following the instructions in the trifold. The conditions under which they had to meet, made him feel like he was making a deal with the devil. But, only in South Park, was the devil this gay. Yet, here he was. Again.

Wes found that he was shaking his head. His thoughts formed words and slipped from his mind. *"Desperation's a real motherfucker."*

He smacked his mouth to try and stop the sentence halfway through.

His lips were pressed tight.

They remained sealed as stuff appeared in the booth. Car keys, a cellphone, and a tablet on the table. Then, a red canvas backpack—like the one his boy had—materialized in the corner next to a shimmering form.

Wes gripped his jaw tight and held it closed. Neither it nor his throat moved as his thoughts became audible again. *What in the blue fuck?*

Abraham, The Man

Though Abraham thought about easing his control of Wes as he came through the swinging door, the sight before him made him decide to keep the air pinched to keep the Mundane idle.

Translucent ripples hung around Wes's head, slightly thicker, but still tight, around the temples.

The Mystique would hold.

Better than that was Squek, standing in the booth across from the teen. Somehow, the two of them had really hit it off and were engrossed in a conversation about the tablet.

Squek clapped. "Really?" Almost enamored, he leaned on the table to look directly down on the boy's tablet. "And that's all there is to it?

A faint pineapple scent came when the boy spoke. "Not really. You have to program the spells in first or, like I said, the spellcards. But, after that, yeah, I guess it's pretty much ready to go."

Squek summarized, "The cards just need mana, but you have to press *Cast* on the tablet. Right?"

The teen nodded.

No. Not a technocaster. Please, anything but that. Such potential. Abraham looked past the teen to his backpack. The patch—a red gorilla with a sword and a shield on an orange field—depressed him. An Archon Private Academy student... So much for an apprentice.

Word had spread about technocasters running amok in the city. Officially, Lar Lightningpalm, the Chief Magistrate, would persecute any open attack, but get him the body of a technocaster on the sly and you'd earn the ape's weight in silver.

Abraham would've preferred an apprentice, but the consolation prize made him grin. Picturing the ingots, he rubbed his hands and projected his thoughts. *How much do you weigh?*

The kid turned, opened his mouth to answer, and paused.

It's called telepathy. Abraham gave a mental chuckle after his thought, in case the simpleton proved incapable of registering his disdain. Magic was for the chosen, and magic hadn't chosen this boy, or any of the apes. They'd found a loophole; more to the point, their parents—not potent enough to pass on the gift—had exploited a loophole shown to them by the school's master. *Any monkey can cast with technology, boy. But all traditional casters are raised with both magic and telepathy. It's our birthright. But what would you know about any of that, Ape?*

Using his idiot-mouth, the teen said. "Oh, I know how to mindspeak." He pointed to Abraham's right.

Mindspeak. What a pitiful way to describe the sheer elegance that was telepathy.

The boy gave a quick nod and shifted his eyes to where he pointed. "But it looks like your precious ability is about to cause your friend there to breach."

Desperation's a real motherfucker. Wes slapped his mouth. Rightly, confusion poured from his thoughts. *What in the blue fuck?*

It was still controllable.

Abraham pointed under the table. *Hide!*

Squek dove where commanded.

Like a stupid bobble-head, the boy shook his head.

Not happy and not wearing gloves Abraham would have to actually touch the mundane.

Disgusted, he did.

Abraham rushed around Wes, grabbed him by the shoulders, and pushed. "Quick. To my office."

The translucent ripples gave way to grey and then formed a tendril that started to search its way toward the teen.

Abraham's high-court robe began to cling and stick to him. The arid air became thick with moisture and static. A storm was coming.

At the break in the counter, Wes shrugged Abraham off and turned back.

When the tendril got close to the boy, the Mystique couldn't conceal his prismatic magical aura any longer and, *thoom*, contact.

The storm was coming.

Abraham shoved Wes again.

Wes resisted. "Where'd he come from?"

"So, you can see me?" With a sickening simper, the boy held his phone as an anchor to the mundane world. The little dolt gave a happy, fast wave.

His back almost to the kitchen door, Wes grabbed onto the rear edges of the gap.

Abraham mustered all of his physical might and shoved.

"Who are you?" Wes rocked back, but held his grip. "By your feet!"

"Your buddy there calls me, Ape. And that's a Squek."

Abraham spun.

Wes's grey tendril was now forked. Trying to synchronize with the aura, the part from the fork to the boy scintillated with emerald, crimson, black, and gold energy. Trying to grab on, the thinner piece groped Squek's vibrant azul aura. Though the goblin had dived to hide, the angle made him visible.

Abraham pointed at the boy. "Shut up!" He brought his focus into his center chakra, where his mana bubbled with rage he couldn't rightly express; not with a breach happening *and* in front of the mundane.

Color hadn't hit Wes's head yet. The Mystique would smooth the situation over, but Abraham had to get them out of sight before the mundane fully moored.

Abraham looked around desperately. The he remember Hanna. Hanna and a sack of potatoes in the panty should be near enough mass for the swap.

He fixed his eyes on Squek. "Blood."

"Boss, no!" Lipping curses, Squek fished the needled blood-ring from his pocket.

Centered over his navel, Abraham formed a circle. Thumb to thumb. Forefinger to forefinger. He nodded to Squek.

The goblin babbled apologies, and punched the boy's calf with the needle.

The boy kicked.

Breifly breaking the circle, Abraham flicked his right hand and inverted it to re-form the circle with thumbs touching forefingers. He then put his hand up to obscure Wes's vision.

The boy and Squek were gone.

Hanna and the sack of potatoes had taken their place.

Matte grey, Wes's tendril snapped back, only to slowly stretch toward Hanna.

Crisis averted, Abraham spied the boy's tablet on the table.

"Now's not a good time." Abraham squeezed past Wes. Hanna would do exactly what should be done, and, without the tablet, the boy would be powerless. And he'd soon be receiving the boy's weight in silver.

Abraham didn't know what Lightningpalm did with the apes, and didn't care. Anyone the Chief Magistrate put on his shit list had a way of disappearing, never to be seen again; and, right now, after that little stunt, Abraham looked forward to making the boy beg mightily for his life. Then, once the boy believed that he had sparked a pity that would never kindle, Abraham would call Lars for the exchange.

Elated at the reverse of fortune and promise of incoming wealth, Abraham's frustrated frown gave way to a syrupy sweet pleasantness. He straightened his robes and he focused on the doorjamb to his private box.

"Come back tomorrow." And without a further thought to the mundane, he turned and pushed through the kitchen door.

Wes

Wes's arm hairs stood as Abe pushed him backwards toward the kitchen door. Miniscule streaks of light, like rainbows of energy, danced on the tips. Each time his tongue touched his teeth, it shocked him, like when he used to lick twelve-volt batteries for a kick.

A whiff of pineapple, the stench of an electrical fire. Maybe that's why Abe was in such a hurry to get to his office.

The shimmering form in the booth became a person. And that person was a teenager in a red-and-white private school uniform, that looked just like the one his son wore.

To talk without shock, Wes pressed his tongue to the roof of his mouth, slushing his words. "Where'd he come from."

The teen waved at him. "So, you can see me."

Wes reached out and gripped the counter to stop Abraham from pushing him into his office. The splinters bit deep, but he held firm.

Grimacing, Wes asked, "Who are you?"

Abraham pushed him again. Wes resisted. For a man of Abe's size, he sure was weak.

A shimmering came from under the table. It started to give way to reveal something green and monsterish lurking under there. "By your feet!"

"Your buddy there calls me, Ape." Seemingly fine with the thing under the table, the teen motioned at it. "And that's a Squek."

Abraham pointed at the kid. "Shut up!" He sounded on the verge of tears.

Wes wanted to feel bad for him, but, besides all the weird shit going on, the bald bastard was assuming ownership of his bars; one loan at a time.

Abraham mumbled something that sounded like *blood*. Then flailed at Wes's face.

Refusing to let go, and not wanting to be poked in the eyes, Wes held tight, clamped his eyes shut tight, and leaned away.

The freak didn't touch him.

When Wes opened his eyes, Hanna, the chesty Swedish masseuse waved to him from where the teen had been seated. At least, he thought there had been a teenager there… She shot him a wink.

"Now's not a good time." Abraham said, moving forward again.

Wes braced to keep from being pushed back.

Abraham's sparkly silk robe slid against Wes's hand as the big guy slipped under his arm to get behind him.

No way! Ready to swing, Wes spun.

Instead of trying to grab him from behind, Abe was back near the door. A vicious serenity played at the corner of his mouth as he straightened his robes. "Come back tomorrow." He spun and pushed through the door.

"Come back tomorrow?" Wes repeated. "Tomorrow's no good." He took a deep breath to gather as much of an authoritative tone as the bizarre series of events could allow. "I need the money now!"

He shoved the door.

Instead of flopping open—as usual—to Abraham's plush office, the swinging door opened to a kitchen. Four strips of savory bacon sizzled on the grill next to two thick hamburger patties.

He scratched his neck.

Doubt that Abe's office had ever been through this door began to eat at Wes. He spied a second door toward the back of the kitchen, and that one looked more like it would lead to a manager's office. He'd been so focused on getting a loan that he had forgotten about the trip through the kitchen to Abe's office.

Wes looked back over his shoulder.

Hanna was gone.

Had she been there? Or had he only wanted her to be there? Wes tried to focus through the fog that was clouding his memory. Abe had mentioned her and maybe that was what put the cutie on his mind. Hell, she must've been there at one point, because she'd left her keys, tablet, and red backpack.

No. The backpack and tablet belonged to someone else. Someone… He couldn't remember who, but someone else had been there before her. *No.* Wes felt silly. No one had been there besides Hanna. *Right? … No, that's not right.*

Only one way to tell. Wes went to the booth. The backpack's contents would cement things. Towels and oil would prove that Hanna had been there. He didn't really have to look into the pack though; the booth smelled faintly of her coconut oil with a hint of pineapple.

Still, for his own sanity, Wes slid into the booh to check the bag.

As though against him and trying to force him from the building, that damned grilled onion smell crowded him; made him itch.

He only had a little more time before a full break out. Wes scratched, unzipped the backpack, and pulled the canvas apart. Inside was a book, two thin notebooks, a tablet like the one on the table, and several sheets of—what could only be—money to an unknown board game.

Glints from the corner of the bag caught his eye.

Wes reached in, grabbed one, and reeled it out. He held one of the smooth one-ounce golden pellets that Abraham used as currency.

And more slushed around in there.

For a moment, Wes wondered what—exactly—Hanna did for Abe for him to pay her so well. The idea of prostitution crossed his mind, but Abe looked and acted like the very last person on the planet to ever want to have sex with a woman. Maybe, just maybe, he would, but only if it was to preserve their species. But she had to do something because—Wes ran his hand through the oversized of pellets—damn.

The gold felt like freedom. Wes looked around for cameras. None.

His saloons, built by his father, were at risk. They were a legacy that had been handed down to him, and Wes had plans to eventually give one to each of his kids. If the bank foreclosed on the land beneath them, the plan, the dream, the legacy, would vanish.

Once everything was paid off, he could easily get a loan to pay Hanna back; and he'd rather be indebted to her than to Abe.

Wes spoke to his mounting guilt. "I'll pay back every penny."

Perhaps from shame, the backpack was hard to lift.

He promised again. "Every penny."

The bag came to him. He cradled it under his arm and slid out of the booth.

The oniony smell intensified and chased him out.

The side of his hand lit with splinters from the old saloon doors. Wes winced, but didn't slow to inspect the new wounds, or look back. He had salvation under his arm, and he was headed to the bank before it could be snatched away.

Ben & Abraham

Ben hoped off the cushioned massage table and tried to clue-in to where he'd been sent. Before now, he didn't know it was possible to teleport the unwilling. Apparently, there were loopholes. Recalling a different run-in he'd had with blood magic, he rubbed his leg where he had been pricked.

The red shag carpet that was beneath his feet also upholstered the walls. A pungent, spiced coconut scent hung in the air and a real-life, lava lamp, little burgundy gobs floating in red-tinted gel—what was the foil on top for?—kicked the disco-nightmare room that he found himself in into full gear. Though much more spacious, something about the confines made him think of Papa Mojo's wagon.

"Squek." Ben wanted to curse the goblin, but his temper wouldn't quite rise.

Knowing who he was acting against, the goblin had done as his master commanded, and Ben's experience in dealing with goblinoids for the past few months recognized the merit in the dangerous act. And he'd have to be that guy now.

Ben drew his face into a scowl to take on the demeanor that ruled an army of orcs.

He reached back to his go to spells on his spellcard holder. His fingers brushed against his dress shirt and—not hitting his protruding holder—rubbed against his side. It was gone. It was on the…

Ben's mind went back to Squek. "You little jerk!" He hoped that the goblin could hear him. "Wait until your cousins hear about this."

He moved to the door and recoiled at the flapping bulk coming through.

Giving his mustard robes a grand flourish, Abraham stepped into his booth. "You almost caused a breach in my business, boy." His center chakra warmed as he set his will to prepare another spell. "Are you ready to pay for that?"

The teen brandished his phone like a wand. "Let's do this."

Noting the determination set on the boy's face, Abraham dropped his gaze to the phone. Apes cast spells through technology, but—until now—they'd only used laptop computers and tablets. Instead of being vulnerable, the boy felt more dangerous than before. Just in case, he shifted his mana and brought a shielding spell to mind; on the off chance that he would need to defend.

The boy shook the phone once and it doubled in width. Now, that possibly *could* hold a spell. Abraham asked, "What's that?"

The boy smirked. "It's a phone. Mundanes use them to speak over long distances."

"I know what it *appears* to be." Abraham snapped. He narrowed his eyes and, minding the boys fingers—since the primitives cast by pressing buttons and icons—flowed mana through his body as he stroked his eyebrow, earlobe, and cheek. His Telltale spell would identify all the magical properties the boy's *phone* held. The boy eyed his telltale tentacles. Abraham waggled them.

Fancy ephemeral pink magic sprung from the man's head. Ben felt energy flow through the man, but could do nothing to stop it. The smell of daisies—typical accompaniment to a divination spell— flowered the booth.

Ben began to inch back.

Once one of those tentacles touched his phone, the asshole would see it for the bluff that it was and— Ben didn't want to think about how bad things would get from there. A sudden heat seared his butt.

Expecting Squek with a fiery poker, Ben jumped sideways and stole a glance.

Cubes of coal fell from the tin-foiled top of the lava lamp. The burning embers landed in the deep shag carpet and died there.

Since neither of them had called this a formal duel, Ben had a plan. It wouldn't be elegant, but it could work. He waited for the right moment.

Abraham enjoyed this little game of cat and mouse, but there was nowhere for the boy to really go. Abraham knew his own weaknesses, and he made sure to keep his pride in check as he—and his tentacles— closed in on the boy and his phone.

If the youth had been a real caster, he would've had a bevy of spells at his disposals to mount a true defense, instead of playing for time and praying that whatever spell the small device held would be enough to get the job done.

Abraham's tentacles had reached their full length and he halted his advance to let the spell do the work. Close to a victory, he licked his teeth.

The boy suddenly jumped to the side.

Abraham wanted to laugh. What a pathetic attempt to break a real wizard's concentration.

Then, the boy flicked his phone. The lit thing landed between his feet.

Abraham dove his tentacles in.

As the pink power sank into the phone, and the wizard realized it was just a distraction, Ben grabbed the lava lamp behind him and swung it at the wizards face.

"Savage!" Abraham damned the boy. Against all rules of dueling and civility, the youth had lashed out at him with a physical attack.

An attack that he couldn't dodge.

And attack with the Nexus Node.

The lamp should have shattered against the bridge of the bald wizard's nose. It didn't. Instead, the hookah swung *through* him; turning him into pure crimson, blue, and gold energy.

Not meeting resisting, Ben spun a circle, then set the lava lamp down.

Admitting defeat, Ben bowed his head as he knelt. His gut went cold at the idea, but there was no way he could beat a being made of pure power. And, even at with his personal reserve at full, he had no spells with which to fight. Ben didn't' want to think about all he'd be losing. About the orcs suffering under this guy, the belt transferring, the—

Ben cut of the thoughts. He had amassed a significant amount of holdings since his last birthday. If his surrender was accepted, all ownership would transfer to this jerk, but his life would *probably* be spared.

As he knelt, Ben risked voicing the question on his mind. "Seriously though, what is it with creepy casters and shag carpet?"

Ben dared to look up at the man he knelt to.

The tri-colored man was slowly evaporating.

At the same rate, the building began to go dim.

Knowing he'd be commanded back down to his knee if the other guy claimed victory, Ben stood and once again lifted the lamp.

Like an angry trick of rock-show lighting, the light-man that had been Abraham lashed out at him with impotent rage.

Moving around the flailing arms, Ben moved to the door that Abraham had come in through. A set of carpeted stairs led from the booth down into a cozy lounge. At the far corner of lounge, he spied the 21 *and over* sign. While in the restaurant, he'd always seen a wall, but from this side, everyone—if anyone was there—could see what was going on in the restaurant.

Motes of dust shook from the ceiling as the light dimmed further.

The dust came down in such a way that it settled on objects to look like it, and the objects it covered, hadn't been disturbed in years.

Ben took the stairs two at time. He weaved through the dust-gathering tables and chairs in the lounge and up into the restaurant.

His backpack was gone. "Squek!" He scooped up his tablet and keys from the booth.

The sizzling in the kitchen died and the delicious aroma of grilled onions, turned rotten.

"Oh, no." The light flicked in the restaurant, and then it, too, started to dim. As in the lounge, dust motes stated to fall in the restaurant.

Ben rushed to the tiki—

"No...!" The floating ice cream scoopers oxidized and fell from view. The crystal-clear glass that had shielded the tubs of ice cream grew mold and a crack spidered from the lower right corner; making a fine home for the dust to settle in.

Ben backed through the saloon doors. They squeaked as he pushed out, but flapped close without a sound. Dust chased the shine from the wax floor and pooled on the welcome mat with unearthly speed.

He looked at the lava lamp, the only remnant of his favorite hangout.

Still dumbfounded, Ben moped to his car and put the lava lamp in the back.

Kevin pulled into the lot and screeched to a halt. He then rolled up to Ben while he put down his window. "Man, this place closed again?"

Ben could only muster a faint smile. "Should've gotten here faster."

"Eastly snagged us as we were leaving." Kevin laughed. "I snuck away. The other guys weren't so lucky and got cauldron duty for trying."

Ben shook his head. "I don't even want to know what you guys did."

"It's pretty epic." Kevin grinned. "Anyhow, want to go get burgers from Artic Oasis?"

Ben shrugged. "Sorta wanted a double Hakram."

"Chin up." Kevin tried to cheer him. "This place will be back in action. Either the owner will come back to town or someone will eventually brave the building and blow on the pipe."

Ben asked, "Blow on the pipe?"

"Yeah, this place is a node. Someone's going to be power-hungry to try to claim it. And then, the forever fights start up again because everyone wants to take it over." Kevin kicked a thumb over his shoulder motioning back down the strip. "You know. Like what happened at Pepperjacks back in October."

"Oh yeah." Ben pretended to recall what he couldn't forget. "So," He leaned in. "How would someone hide a node so others don't try to hunt it down?"

"Beats me, but whoever has the node to Pepperjacks knows the trick." Kevin drummed on his steering wheel. "Look. I'm hungry. Are we going to roll or what?"

"No, I'm out." Ben glanced at the lava lamp in his back seat. In the sunlight, he could see that it was a hookah. He looked back to Kevin. "I've got some stuff to take care of."

Kevin shrugged, waved, and tore off.

"Okay, Squek." Ben got into his car and activated his 'find my tablet' app. "Let's see where you took my stuff. Then, we'll have a little talk."

To have total surprise, he retrieved his anti-divination ring from his ashtray and slipped it on.

Ally

Ally blinked at the sudden end of the thread that had grown the thickest. The last thread was flying away from her.

She leapt out and caught it.

Wes

Exiting his bank, Wes loosened his tie, shifted the stolen backpack, and took a deep breath. The first burden-free one that he'd taken in a year. It seemed fitting that his saloons were saved on the first day of spring.

Enjoying the sun, Jack Bigelow's *Magic is Real* came to mind and he bopped along to the song in his head.

And froze.

Abraham's hookah was on the hood of his car.

Wes looked around the parking lot, but no one—particularly not a tall, bald man in silky robes—was paying attention to him.

Cautiously, he eased closer.

A note twisted in the slight breeze.

Wes looked around again before pulling the folded paper on a string. *As a symbol of my not meaning you any ill will, I gift you this: a Nexus Bar & Grill hookah. Please enjoy and clean thoroughly before use.*

It wasn't signed.

Hoping to find Abraham giving him a Chuck Norris-styled thumbs up, Wes scanned again.

No one paid him any mind.

"Thanks." Wes spoke loudly. Whoever delivered this was probably keeping an eye on it, to make sure no one else walked off with it.

He loaded the backpack and hookah into his passenger seat.

When he got behind his wheel, he found a silver ring dangling from his rearview with a smaller note. Inlaid in the amethyst, were two crossed axes. It wasn't his style.

He read the note. *Oh, and one more gift. Take care.*

Wes considered the ring. He didn't like it. It was sort of tacky, but he was getting off scot-free. Whoever had kept an eye on the hookah was probably keeping an eye on the ring, too.

He rolled down his window and said, "Thanks."

Wes held up the ring so whoever was watching could see him put it on.

Ally

Ally nearly fell backward. She'd been shunted twice from the spell and there were no more threads to grab onto to continue the magic. "Crap!" Her shoulders slumped. Knowing what was coming she tried to loosen her body. Tightening up was the wrong thing to do because without a thread—

Her Temporas Illum Orchalance spell arced out and drove into her chest; knocking her from her shoes.

When she came to, Ally lay ten feet from her shoes.

The sun had crossed the sky and begun to set, the building was still closed, and the pong of burnt daisies filled her nose.

Her head and chest felt like they were on fire. They weren't. She knew that, and that the pain from the rebounded spell would fade in a couple of days. It always did.

What hurt more was the loss of the intimate knowledge of what happened.

The spell hadn't left her empty-handed; she recalled the conversations, as though she were a fly on the wall. She knew the teen —Benja—was a technocaster, the wizard—Abraham—was a snatcher, and the mundane—Wes—was a thief.

No, what she lacked were the inside-their-head details. Their inner attitudes. Their opinions.

Abraham wasn't too common of a name. If she ran that, coupled with the fact that he was a snatcher, through the Census Agency, there'd probably only be a few hits. Not that it mattered. Ally was pretty sure that Abraham was now a part of the ether.

No one at the Agency wanted to acknowledge, no less deal with tracking, technocasters; so the teen might as well as been a ghost. And the mundane?

Ally laughed at the idea of trying to track a mundane with only a first name.

The movement made her chest flair.

"Ooh, Ally." She lay there to recover and be with the pain. While she didn't have all the details, she now had a personal project. That teen wasn't *just* a technocaster. He couldn't have been.

He knew to hide from divination, *and* had a way to do it. He could best a snatcher, *and* knew how to hide holdings from officials. And he was willing to use everything available to him; even mundanes and the Mystique.

In total, all the makings of an Agency nightmare.

No one would believe her. They never did. Again, she'd have to do this one on her own.

Planning a couple of career moves and thinking about who owed her favors, Ally set her mind to getting stationed nearby—if not *in*— the Clark/Navaho prefecture. With that teen running around, bad things were going to be coming as he entered into adulthood; and she had to find a way to stop him.

But first, she had to heal. And she would.

EXTRA - BONUS CHAPTERS

BY EZEKIEL JAMES BOSTON

ABOUT THE EXTRA CHAPTERS

Hello, good readers! Ezekiel here. I just wanted to say a little bit about the coming extra chapters.

While creating stories, I tend to write a lot of exploratory scenes to help me understand a particular aspect of the characters—or the world around them—to get a better feel of the whole.

While these may be perfectly fine scenes, if they do not cover enough new ground to merit the space in the story, I remove them.

However, there are times when I revisit one of these scenes and really want it in the book, but since I had previously removed it, it might not slide in quite so easily; but I still consider it to be a part of the whole.

The three chapters presented here are such chapters from Yuletide Yield. They aren't retroactively added continuity to modify the world or undermine the novel. No, they are sections I feel add value, but aren't—in the purest sense—necessary to the book.

If you would like to read the chapters without any preamble, go do so now.

...

..

.

Okay, so, here's my take on the additional chapters.

Clean Up: Originally entitled *About Conjurations*, this was a fun chapter where I took what Ben had done with his original Orion spell in his many detentions and expanded it to fit his increased abilities in his new world. To me, this is Ben subconsciously acknowledging how far he has come.

About Goblins: The goblins in the story have grown to fill a larger role. This chapter was about Ben getting to know the dynamics between Nuk and Uk'so.

Malcolm's Plight: This section was a bridge from Malcolm-being-stuck to Malcolm-being-free. While hosted by the fae, Ben experiences some of their society and discovers an aspect of Malcolm's personality that's worth saving.

Thank you for buying this collection. I sincerely hope you find it, and the bonus content, truly worthwhile.

—Zeek

BOOK 3 - CHAPTER 14.1 - CLEAN UP

LOST IN THOUGHT—*THERE has to be a way to make my body mine again*—Ben hardly noticed the grumbling orcs as they thumped Rubbermaid garbage bins half full of sloshing water up the stairs. While the five green gorillas kept to their task of collecting water, they grunted in unison for pacing. Soon Ben found his foot tapping against the barrel to three separate types of noises—*grunts* from the one emptying a bucket into the large green trashcan, *hoots* from two who splashed water against the wall, and soft *whoops* from the two working brushes on the freshly wetted wall—as they formed a primal chorus.

The junk at the mouth of the stairs had been cleared away and the water level looked to be down around to just above the ankle. Only the fan sitting kitty-corner from the stairs still blew. A new scent—*hmm, steak?*—played under the light burn smell. The hooters and whoopers had cleared the soot from the bottom half of a wall. *Man, only if I'd been this proficient at cleaning the school's cauldrons...* His temporary reprieve from thinking about control of his body started to fade.

Before he slipped back into wondering how Bastion got to be in his body in the first place, Ben noticed Uk'so had come to the stairs with a silver meal tray—large in his small green hands. Ben's stomach grumbled and he perked up a bit. *Man, I'm starving.*

Noticed, the goblin nodded. "Benja Min'Fist, I have food for you to eat."

Though Ben could see the steak and scrambled eggs, he liked the goblins' different way of saying things. He asked, "What's for dinner?"

Uk'so raised the tray. "Cooked cow and not yet chickens."

"Great." Ben's stomach growled and he rubbed it. His finger ran over the bumpy nodule that was the resolidifed scab extending from his body as the wound had healed down to only being a shot glass's diameter. "I'm hungry."

As though called, Uk'so stepped into the water to deliver the tray. The goblin took a long route around the gorillas pouring water into a garbage can.

Watching the small goblin approach, Ben recalled how bad its skin looked a month ago. *Wonder what those pale green splotches had been.* All the loose, lighter skin had ben shed and now the goblin's entire hide was a deep avocado green.

Ben leaned down and accepted the tray with a somewhat greedy inhalation. *It smells delicious.* "Did you make this?"

Rubbing his arm as he looked around the room, Uk'so shook his head. "No, Benja Min'Fist. Food making is the honor of Nuk U'es Uk Tuk."

They always use each other's full names. Wonder if they related. Ben cut into the steak. Heat, fragrance, and juice leaked out. He lifted it to admire the herbal scent before placing the chunk into his mouth. *Mmm.* Before having meals made here, Ben had not been a big meat eater. Conversely, the goblins were horrible at preparing salads. Ben scooped some eggs into his mouth. *They really have a knack for anything needing fire to prepare.* "Are you two somehow related?"

The goblin had found a bucket and—the narrow sinewy arms not trembling from strain—scooped water and hoisted it over his head to dump the contents over the rim of a nearby Rubbermaid. "No, Benja Min'Fist."

Expecting an explanation, Ben had loaded his mouth full of eggs and—*mmm*—found delectable warm bits of crunchy bacon mix in.

Finding the rhythm, Uk'so began to hum.

Ben swallowed. "So, Tuk is a common last name?"

Uk'so stopped scooping momentarily, touched his temple in

thought, and returned to work. "For us who serve, Benja Min'Fist, it is the only one," he said, then dumped another bucket into the big green bin. He touched his temple again and nodded to try to keep the rhythm the gorillas had set. "It is the one way our kind is alike." The goblin's words finally forced him to break sync and he came to a stop. "You are not ogre born-blood, but you are a Fist."

Huh? Ben had been paying close attention as he shoveled, cut, and chewed. Yet, the goblin/ogre analogy lost him. Not sure about phrasing his question to be more specific, Ben asked, "Comparable how?"

Uk'so nodded to the gorilla chorus. "All servants share last name as all rulers share last name." The answer took a while as the goblin's light voice turned melodious as he began to sing his words. "We two Tuk have the honor of being in service to the Benja Min'Fist as slaves."

Eggs, bacon, and steak jumbled in Ben's throat as he nearly choked. He forced a swallow and coughed the rest clear. "You're not slaves! I'm paying you."

Uk'so has stopped singing and, concern painting his face, turned attentive eyes to Ben when he started to cough and sputter. Seemingly sure Ben would continue to breathe, Uk'so agreed, "Yes, Benja Min'Fist. We Tuk are being most grateful. The gray leafy paper makes our beds much more softer."

Gray? Ben put his hand on his forehead and wiped his face in a long downward disbelieving swipe. *Mundane money? Really, Toad? I told you to make sure each goblin received one percent of what this place makes and you pay them with mundane money?* Keeping his calm, Ben gave a slow exhale. "Give me the cash you guys have and I'll get it turned into a proper hard money that you two can spend."

"Would, Benja Min'Fist." Uk'so had returned to working and singing. "But leafy paper gone like leafy not meat on fire."

Confusion tilted Ben's head to the side. "Huh?"

A taxed voice came from the stairs. "It's gone." Ben looked. A muscle-bound orc—*one of Jek's buddies*—set an empty Rubbermaid down. He wiped his sweaty forehead with the back of his thick forearm. "He means it was burned when you made your war-face." Adding a single note to the gorilla chorus, the orc gave a grunt as he lifted a Rubbermaid onto his broad back. "He's saying that the money is gone like salad on a fire." The orc grunted with each step as he hefted the trash can of water up the stairs in time with the established rhythm.

Man, I really don't want to get involved with the finances, but it's probably the only way to make sure the goblins are paid for their work in a form they can understand and appreciate.

Thinking about work—*I'm chilling while they're working to clean up my mess*—Ben hopped off the barrel. His sodden boots splashed into the water. He set the tray of remaining food down, found a bucket, and added his voice to the lone gorilla grunting as it bailed water.

Enthused, Uk'so grinned, bobbed in place like a folk-rock singer and switched tongues to belt out cheerful sounding lyrics in a language full or rolling vowels and soft consonants.

BOOK 3 - CHAPTER 14.2 - ABOUT GOBLINS

STILL HUMMING the last jaunty tune Uk'so sang before the goblin headed up to help Nuk, Ben wrung out the mop—*hopefully for the last time tonight*—he'd been using to sop up the final remaining puddle. The top foot of the wall remained charred black, while not as high as the gorillas could reach, Ben wanted the uneven trimming as another reminder to show above the, once again, matte grey concrete.

A general damp smell hung in the air. Ben chuckled. *Well, at least the room no longer smells like burnt moron.*

Ben propped the mop next to where he had sat, lifted his empty food tray, and glanced at his Anvilsmith. *First time I've run one down to zero awatts.* Though the arcane wattage meter rested on zero, the tablet retained enough energy for mundane tasks.

When did my conjurations vanish? Ben had been so enthralled by Uk'so song that he hadn't noticed the gorillas disappear. Ben shrugged. *Doesn't matter. Job's done now.* He returned to humming as he danced up the bare stairs and frowned when his feet landed on the squishy old carpet and padding. *Yup, time to have this taken up, too. Soon everything will be bare.*

Coming around the hall by the stairs that led to the second floor, Ben opened his mouth to advise the goblins what he wanted done and, hearing the crisp sounds of video game violence, paused. On the beat up couch—*that thing's so dirty I can't tell what color it was originally*—he spied the calico and green tips of the two goblins' ears peeking over the edge. Ben's eyes bounced to the large 100" screen television. *They're playing Dragon Sage 3?* Ben nodded appreciatively. *In co-op, split-screen mode no less. I'm impressed guys. Figured you'd be going head-to-head.*

Almost everything Ben had learned about the many races of creature lumped as goblinoid, put them at constant odds with each other. In each kind, there was an unmistakable tiered hierarchy which was always based upon one form of competition or another.

With orcs, the unspoken ranking is obviously established by pure combat prowess, but—from what I can tell—the goblins' pecking order seems to be all about seniority. To keep the goblins clear in his head, Ben had long since stopped used Nuk U'es Uk Tuk full name. His orcs had bought Nuk the same night Ben he had asked them to clean the building, and Uk'so had been a servant of Ur-Krurk's son. So, that alone, made Nuk the boss goblins on property. *And he sure is bossy.*

Not disturbing them, and using the game's clangs and bellowing incantations to cover his footfalls, Ben crept through the spotless, pine-scented living room and into the pristine, lemony kitchen. Appreciating the cleanliness of the three refrigerators, Ben carefully set his tray into the sink. *Lest the goblins hear it and come running.*

Through several conversations with Nuk, Ben had discovered the orcs hadn't done any cleaning and only lent a hand to move things the goblin could not. The goblin had shared that he was happy when Ben came for his regular Saturday night visits the last couple of months, because the orcs made him hide so it would seem like the orcs were doing the actual clean up. This meant meant he could slip away into the narrow attic and take a nice, long break.

Forgetting his stealth mission, Ben grabbed a room temperature bottle of Erboun Spring Water, looked out into the living room and asked, "You guys want something to drink while I'm here?"

The tips of their ears lowered.

Nuk came around the corner of the sofa in red, rhinestone-encrusted jeans. Uk'so bounded over the back of the sofa, but Ben couldn't take his attention away from Nuk's outlandish pants.

Tired of feeling like he was walking around an unabashed locker room whenever he came to Meadows Towing, Ben had set a rule for everyone to wear bottoms, at the very least. He made is sound as though he had made the rule because of everyone, but he had mainly created it for the goblins as they loathed to wear anything but their black rubber aprons and yellow dish gloves that he had first seen them in.

Uk'so had instantly taken to the jeans and cotton t-shirt look the orcs usually sported, but Nuk resisted for a little while. The calico goblin always turned to face Ben when they were in the same room and walked backwards to exit so as to not have his bare backside show. It took Nuk spilling bleach on Uk'so's jeans for the bossy goblin to get onboard. Nuk became absolutely fascinated by what could be done with the fabric and the goblin had really outdone himself this time —*those jeans are atrocious. Looks like a gang of Bedazzlers jumped his pants.*

Both goblins scampered into the kitchen.

Ben hopped out of the way.

Nuk lagged behind Uk'so who turned the corner tightly, squatted slightly, and placed his hand on his knees. *He's going to trip Nuk, this isn't good.* Nuk cornered into the kitchen and—as though the calico were a circus acrobat—scampered up Uk'so by using the crook of the dark green goblin's bent knee, hip, neck, and leapt from the top of Uk'so head to grab the freezer handle and swing onto the tiled counter.

Using the handles, Uk'so scampered up drawers like a spider monkey.

Hmph. Holding his bottle behind him, Ben took a step further in the kitchen so he could watch both little workers. *Their teamwork is amazing when they work together.*

Nuk opened a small door in the freezer—*there's a sub-freezer?*—to produce a chilled bottle of Erboun Spring. Behind the calico, Uk'so had retrieved a pristine 24-Seven forty-four ounce Big Swig plastic cup by the base and pulled a pair of yellow kitchen gloves from a dispenser by the sink. Nuk pulled out and ice tray, set it on the counter and opened the frosty bottle in his hand. "It is being our honor to serve the Benja Min'Fist."

As Nuk poured, Uk'so extended the gloves to Ben. "Does the Benja Min-Fist want frozen water in his cold water?"

I don't know if I should applaud them or tip them for the show. Ben tucked his bottle the back of his pants. "No frozen water in my water, please."

An agonized screech came from the game.

Ben turned in time to see the Brute character get turned into a pin cushion in an awesome *Death by a Thousand Arrows* animation sequence. "You guys didn't pause?"

Both goblins stood tall. Nuk reported, "We serve before we play."

"But pausing takes less than a second." Ben turned again at a deep bellow from the game. Another Brute character stood tough with a two-foot round ballista bolt shot into its torso, then toppled to complete the special *Death by Flesh Wounds* animation. Indignant, Ben rushed into the living room. "Wait. Both of you were playing Brutes?"

The goblins' bare feet slapped on the kitchen floor and padded behind him. As usual, Nuk did all of the talking. "It is the mightiest."

"Yes." Ben hopped over the back of the sofa to plop down on the resprung base and refilled cushions. *It may look bad, but they made it comfy.* Ben sniffed and smiled. *And it kicks out a pine scent.* He scooped up a controller. "However, the game series is called Dragon *Sage*. The advantage is to use the Sage template."

Nuk took the other controller and subtly tried to trade. "But Sage's head is very bashable. It happens a lot."

Ben kept hold of the player one controller he had picked up. "That's only when playing in co-op mode." Ben restarted from their last save, which had been the last autosave eight levels ago. *And they don't save.* He flicked through the inventory and switched out the chitin platemail. "Rhino hide is the best at this point." His thumb worked. "Why does this character have all five sets of armor?" Without waiting for an answer, he sighed. *Can't believe how much they don't know about the game.* The other character was naked with all Sage and Rouge gear in inventory. *Well, at least I know which character belongs to which goblin.* "If you're both going to be Brutes, you have to share the loot." Ben gave the spider plate to player two.

Nuk let out a long whine.

Ben canceled the trade, switched controllers with Nuk, and looked to the green goblin. "Uk'so, mind if I change your character to a Sage?"

"He does not." Nuk answered. Happy to have his controller back, he jumped on the sofa and had his character don the hairy black chitin.

Ben eyed Uk'so and asked, "Do *you* mind?"

Uk'so shook his head.

Ben clicked class switch. Player Two's experience bobbles drained, and the barrel chested warrior began to shrink. The body shriveled further when the fourteenth-level Brute converted fully into a seventh-level Sage. Ben's fingers danced on the controller. *First, on with the Air Robes and the Cloud Cap.* Full length, light blue robes covered the formerly naked body and a white pointed cap appeared. *Then arm the Whirlwind starter staff and equip the Thunderous Thongs as footwear...* The Sage class title flashed white and light blue text *Air Elementalist* floated over the top. Ben nodded to Nuk. "Let's do this."

While they played, Ben showed them how to distinguish valuable treasure from slot-filling waste. He also showed Uk'so the Sage's different air-based ability and spell combos. He had hit level twenty the same time as Nuk, saved the game, and passed Uk'so the controller. He stayed for a half hour to share the best tactics and to encourage them to split loot by need instead of value.

He slipped from the room at the beginning of the Wicked Wemic's Wide Wave. It was a mean hour-long bonus stage where the characters had to recover gems stolen by gnomes. *I remember how pissed I was when the wemic took all the collected jewels and thanked me with an angel's feather.* He waited long enough to be sure they were going to approach the blind senile lion-man who would claim the quest complete and still award the feather for an empty bag just as he would for one chockful.

Ben smiled to himself as the goblins began to follow the gnome's trail and kept smiling as headed back down to his basement lab. *I can get some work done and make it back in plenty of time to see their reactions. I just hope I can get it done without blowing up again.*

BOOK 3 - CHAPTER 36.1 - MALCOLM'S PLIGHT

WITH THE SMELL of berries all around him and the whistle-click language of fairies behind, Ben stood in one of many secret alcoves away from the battering Ur-Krurk and Yilst. He watched the small crystal fairy anchored to Malcolm's ear. It harried the Dunn-Blatt to his feet from the momentary break he had been allowed upon climbing all the way down. "Quick now, up. Before they slay us for resting too long."

Still inwardly disgusted at what they were doing to Malcolm, to milk magic and emotions from him to infuse into their berries, Ben kept his face indifferent. *Whatever the odds, I'd still bet that shot-calling sprite is in on this.* His arms crossed against the layered deceit. *A little taskmaster of false hope to keep him moving.*

A crystalline fairy flitted neared Ben, carrying a shallow, wide-rimmed frosted platter. A score of plump blackberries lay on a syrupy drizzle at the center.

Ben's gaze picked out patterns in the frosting—*sure hope this isn't some sort of Rorschach test*—faces contorted in pain, fear, shame, agony and other negative emotions. Each twisted expression had a fine line around it in a script of the arcane symbols similar to the ones in the book Elder Komir had gifted Ben on his birthday. The fairy hovered a bit closer and, in its light voice, spoke the gentlest Servant-Giant. "If I am interrupting thoughts of your planned use of the Oslusa, my apologies; however, we would be remiss in our tithing—and it would surely be our folly—if we did not off the rarest of our delicacies to the Meadows Might-Fist. Ur-Krurk Bloodson, please take, ingest, and enjoy."

Wow, it makes the language sounds almost as elegant as elven. I haven't heard 'Oslusa' before. Wonder what it translates to... Ben scanned the clusters and tightened his lips against eating the fear-laced berries.

Still in his elven form, Ur-Krurk drew closer and also spoke gentle Servant-Giant, which remained as unfitting to Ben's ears—used to the ogre only using hard, guttural consonants—as tilting a boiling kettle and getting chilled water. "Meadows Might-Fist, it would be my true pleasure and great delight to partake in your stead."

Shifting his gaze from the fluttering fairy to Malcolm scrabbling up the column, Ben flicked his wrist at the fairy in the *dismissing a servant* way he'd learn in Courtmanship II. He had learned more, so-called 'advanced' ways to dismiss in the latter half of Courtmanship IV, but they always felt either contemptuous or blatantly disrespectful.

A bit of the true Ur-Krurk shone through when he took hold and snatched the entire platter from the fairy instead of just a berry or two.

In a fit of quiet hums, the fairy flitted away.

"They're negotiating extra tough," Ur-Krurk moved next to Ben to also look at the stressed Dunn-Blatt trying to find a path to the top of the pillar. "They don't want to let him go." Ur-Krurk picked a berry, put it into his mouth, and gave a sigh of appreciation. "And I can understand why."

The blackberry smell on Ur-Krurk's breath—*he's relishing Malcolm's taste*—pulled a contemptuous sneer onto Ben's face. *You really are a monster.*

Leaning closer, his berry-scented breath began pressed in to fill the alcove. "A stronger play right now, Might-Fist, would be to let them keep possession of the delectable Oslusa, entitle them to one percent of their harvest and reap the other ninety-nine." Ur-Krurk smeared a berry in the syrup and ate it. He exhaled joy. "This one will bring you wealth beyond comparison."

Ben tensed as the column shifted and the handholds above Malcolm clacked flat against the pillar. Malcolm changed directions to find another way and—*watch out!*—pulled his body close to the pillar to avoid a volley of spears.

"Or we could not sell the berries—" Ur-Krurk smacked his lips. "And just enjoy them ourselves."

Inner warmth filled Ben's chest and rolled up his neck. He rounded on the elf. Teeth clenched, anger throttled his volume down to a deadly hiss. "I am not going to leave him here to be tortured to death."

Ur-Krurk shrank and withdrew.

The warmth flowered into heat as he took a step after Ur-Krurk.

Eyes filled with fear, the elf backpedaled faster.

The room fell silent.

Ben's tight focus broadened as the room brightened slightly and anything capable of moving away from him, did. Still speaking to Ur-Krurk, Ben switched his focus to Yilst. "Either they release him, or I take him."

"Might-Fist Ur-Krurk Bloodson." The farry gave a calm and collected nod. "No need for extremes. We—" The farrie pulled at its wings. "We will come to a mutually beneficial arrangment."

EXTRA - COVERS

EZEKIEL JAMES BOSTON'S

BENJAMIN BAXTER

BIRTHDAY BEDLAM

BOOK ONE OF THE DARKNESS WITHIN TRILOGY

EZEKIEL JAMES BOSTON'S

BENJAMIN BAXTER

SAMHAIN SHENANIGANS

BOOK TWO OF THE DARKNESS WITHIN TRILOGY

EZEKIEL JAMES BOSTON'S
BENJAMIN BAXTER

YULTIDE YIELD

BOOK THREE OF THE DARKNESS WITHIN TRILOGY

EZEKIEL JAMES BOSTON'S
WORLD OF
BENJAMIN
BAXTER

NEXUS BAR & GRILL
A STARWISE NOVELETTE

ABOUT THE AUTHOR

Ezekiel James Boston hales from Las Vegas and currently resides in the Great Northwest. Favoring fantasy, science fiction, and paranormal occult, he's authored over a hundred short stories, a score of short novels, and half a dozen full length novels.

Aside from being an avid writer, Ezekiel enjoys reading and games of all sorts. He chose to give up "active" sports after jamming his fingers and discovering that an author cannot slam their forehead onto the keyboard and have the story appear on the screen.

For exclusive content, please visit:
ezekieljamesboston.com/subscribe-to-ejb/

ALSO BY EZEKIEL JAMES BOSTON

Novels:

Birthday Bedlam: Book One

Samhain Shenanigans: Book Two

Yuletide Yield: Book Three

Novelette:

Nexus Bar & Grill: A World of Benjamin Baxter Starwise Novelette

Short stories:

Gateway Blood, Buck Tales

Soul Survivor, Buck Tales

Jamal & the Skeleton's Heart, Buck Tales

Collections:

Benjamin Baxter — Darkness Within Trilogy

COMING SOON

IMBOLC INSANITY, Book Four

PLEASE NOTE: Word of mouth is crucial for any author to succeed. If you enjoyed this book, please consider rating it or leaving a review where you purchased... Even if it's just a line or two.

Thank you for reading.